PENGUIN CLASSICS

# WILLIAM WORDSWORTH
## SELECTED PROSE

WILLIAM WORDSWORTH was born in Cockermouth, in the Lake District, in 1770, the second of five children. His rural upbringing inspired much of his poetry, and some of his most intense visionary passages, notably in *The Prelude*, stem from childhood and adolescent experience. As a young man, Wordsworth was fired with enthusiasm for the French Revolution. After graduating from Cambridge in 1791 he spent a year in France, where he met and fell in love with Annette Vallon. On his return to England he devoted himself to literature, supporting himself by means of a legacy, and the latter course of the Revolution left him disillusioned with radical politics. He met Coleridge in 1795 and the two men became intimate friends, though they were estranged between 1810 and 1812 on account of a drawn-out quarrel.

In 1799 Wordsworth settled at Dove Cottage, Grasmere in the Lake District with his sister Dorothy, who was a close companion for most of his life and shared his deep love of nature. He married Mary Hutchinson in 1802 and they had five children. His early work was on the whole well received, and, despite some adverse reviews, his reputation grew steadily throughout his career. In 1813 he was appointed Distributor of Stamps for Westmorland, the income enabling him to continue writing. He became Poet Laureate seven years before his death in 1850.

JOHN O. HAYDEN is Professor of English at the University of California, Davis. He has edited the two volumes of *William Wordsworth: The Poems* and *William Wordsworth: Selected Poems* for the Penguin Classics.

# William Wordsworth

## SELECTED PROSE

EDITED, WITH AN
INTRODUCTION AND NOTES BY
JOHN O. HAYDEN

PENGUIN BOOKS

PENGUIN BOOKS

Published by the Penguin Group
Penguin Books Ltd, 27 Wrights Lane, London W8 5TZ, England
Penguin Books USA Inc., 375 Hudson Street, New York, New York 10014, USA
Penguin Books Australia Ltd, Ringwood, Victoria, Australia
Penguin Books Canada Ltd, 10 Alcorn Avenue, Toronto, Ontario, Canada M4V 3B2
Penguin Books (NZ) Ltd, 182–190 Wairau Road, Auckland 10, New Zealand

Penguin Books Ltd, Registered Offices: Harmondsworth, Middlesex, England

This edition first published 1988
3 5 7 9 10 8 6 4

Printed in England by Clays Ltd, St Ives plc
Set in Monotype Bembo

# Contents

꙳ꙮ꙳ꙮ꙳ꙮ꙳

v

# Contents

# *Introduction*

❦❦❦❦❦

This edition contains most of what William Wordsworth wrote in prose and thus makes more easily available the ideas conveyed in prose by one of the greatest poets in English. But this collection provides more than just spin-off from ideas in his poetry as might be inferred, nor does it contain only the repetition of ideas already expressed in verse. Rather, the thought contained in this edition shows Wordsworth to be an original thinker in both literary vehicles.

Wordsworth unfortunately has the contrary reputation of having lived off the crumbs fallen from the tables of various contemporaries, such as David Hartley, William Godwin and, most importantly, Samuel Taylor Coleridge. Yet on closer view these debts seem exaggerated and often appear assumed rather than proven. The reputation as a whole probably derives from the view of Wordsworth as the great poet of feeling, which indeed he was.

For, just as Dr Johnson's obvious intellectuality causes the superficial observer to consider him coldly cerebral despite his volcano-like emotional nature, the strong and pervasive feeling in Wordsworth's early poetry causes his equally strong intellectuality to be overlooked by the casual reader. There are, for example, a high number of paradoxes displayed in *Lyrical Ballads*: the old Cumberland beggar gives far more than he receives; the child in 'Anecdote for Fathers' had naturally to tell a lie; Simon Lee's gratitude was harder to bear than ingratitude. Such intellectually gritty poems should alert us to more in Wordsworth's mind than first meets the eye.

Matthew Arnold, on the other hand, was right of course: William Wordsworth was no philosopher in the sense of a developer or follower of a school or system. But he was a thinker, or, as he enthusiastically described a young contemporary in 1834, 'a *thinking* writer'. Even compared to Coleridge, Wordsworth, I believe, could hold his own in this regard. Henry Crabb Robinson, a contemporary who knew both well, did in fact claim more for Wordsworth than that in a comparison of his *genius* to Coleridge's *talent* (in a journal entry for 8 May 1812):

If genius . . . be creation and original production from the stores of individual mind, and talent show itself in the power of appropriating and assimilating to itself the product of foreign minds, and by so imbibing and adding to its own possessions the attainments of other minds – then I have always given to Wordsworth and Coleridge the respective superiority in genius and talents.

The future may well substantiate this judgement of Wordsworth as the more original and creative thinker who, nevertheless, if not possessing so broad a base in the past was also very well-read, as the notes to this edition demonstrate.

Besides originality, perhaps the most outstanding characteristic of Wordsworth's mind as reflected in his prose was his seriousness, a virtue seldom found in our own age, although its substitute, solemnity, often passes for it. Well grounded in the beliefs and principles that such a virtue requires, Wordsworth describes himself in *Essay upon Epitaphs I* as 'a critic and a moralist speaking seriously upon a serious subject', a description that aptly characterizes most of the pages of this edition. Other terms that help to describe this essential quality are 'earnest' and 'forthright'.

Sometimes the earnestness leads to unpalatable truths to which Wordsworth gravitates by an inexorable rigour of mind: men who do not derive pleasure from nature

are so far from being rare, that they may be said fairly to represent a large majority of mankind. This is a fact, and none but the deceiver and the willingly deceived can be offended by its being stated.

Wordsworth here as always has the courage to be forthright even in the face of that most daunting of threats – the appearance of immodesty or egotism. Anyone who cared about such threats could never have written the *Essay Supplementary* with its long explanation of why his works weren't popular and why they would nonetheless survive.

Yet Wordsworth could soften truth as well, for example, when he proposes that an epitaph should present the character of the deceased 'as a tree through a tender haze or a luminous mist, that spiritualizes and beautifies it'. He then turns to those who might disagree:

Shall we say, then, that this is not truth, not a faithful image; and that, accordingly, the purposes of commemoration cannot be answered? – It is Truth, and of the highest order . . .

Not only that, he concluded, but 'it is truth hallowed by love . . .'

Another characteristic of Wordworth's mind demonstrated by his prose is the variety of his interests: society, literature, politics, natural history, psychology, ethics; just about the only subjects missing are the Transcendental and the Visionary, which are so prominent in *The Prelude* and other of his poems, as well as the focus of so much scholarship. His originality, in any case, is most evident in his literary and political ideas, which we will turn to now.

The importance of Wordsworth's contribution to literary theory can be seen simply in his inclusion in every anthology of criticism. But I have claimed that Wordsworth was not only important but original, and originality in theory often implies a radical divergence from what went before. Indeed, Wordsworth's theory is often seen in just this way; M. H. Abrams saw him as a Romantic expressionist who helped to overturn centuries of mimetic theory; and Wordsworth is often discussed as a Romantic revolutionary.

Such a view is, however, easily refuted, even with the Preface to *Lyrical Ballads* as sole witness: 'Poetry is the image of man and nature,' Wordsworth announced, as if mimesis were a self-evident truth; and, as I point out in the introduction to the Preface, he refers to Aristotle by name while appealing to the principles of the central tradition he began. Traditions by their nature do not proceed in great jolts and jerks but rather evolve organically with principles refined and adapted to new literary situations.

Yet there is ample room for originality as well. Wordsworth made probably the single most important contribution to the central tradition since Aristotle, for he refined the principle of the moral function of literature, changing it from direct teaching by precept and example to a kind of moral indirection – in the terms of the Preface, literature serves to enlighten the understanding and strengthen and purify the affections. This view is reiterated within the Preface and reinforced by remarks in his letters to John Wilson and to Charles James Fox in this edition. Later in the nineteenth century, this view of moral indirection was passed on in turn by Matthew Arnold to anyone since who sees literature as moral – 'in a large sense' of the word (as Arnold insisted).

The Preface to *Lyrical Ballads*, however, is more generally known for presenting Wordsworth's proclamation emancipating diction from the mannerisms that plagued eighteenth-century poets, good and bad alike – circumlocutions, excessive personifications, and compound epithets. In principle, moreover, he made it possible to use less exclusive diction in general by replacing the principle of decorum applied by genre – that an epic requires high diction and a satire low – with a selection of diction appropriate to the feeling elicited by the subject and context of the poem.

But if poets after Wordsworth were to have access to a larger freedom of diction, he was not proposing licence; he himself was very particular about the choice of words in poetry, as can be seen in his close critiques of epitaphs:

'*She bow'd to taste the wave and died.*' The plain truth was, she drank the Bristol waters which failed to restore her, and her death soon followed; but the expression involves a multitude of petty occupations for the fancy – '*She bowed*' – , was there any truth in this? – '*to taste the wave*', the water of a mineral spring which must have been drunk out of a Goblet. Strange application of the word *Wave*! '*and died*'. This would have been a just expression if the water had killed her . . .

The tone here is almost Johnsonian in its rigour and slight note of disdain.

Close scrutiny of a text can also be seen applied to his own verse in the letter to Lady Beaumont and is in fact familiar to anyone who has read much of Wordsworth's correspondence. Wordsworth is again something of a pathfinder, for such scrutiny is not often found in criticism until the New Critical movement of the twentieth century. Wordsworth was a careful craftsman and an unrelenting critic with a clear mind and high expectations.

In his political thinking, Wordsworth's originality also ran in traditional channels; here he refined and expanded upon the theories of Edmund Burke. Even before he fell under Burke's influence, however, his keen interest in political issues was manifested in his 'Letter to the Bishop of Llandaff', which shows how widely he had read in radical political theory, especially the work of Jean-Jacques Rousseau and Thomas Paine. The 'Letter' also demonstrates the fervour of his concern and convictions, but there is considerable question today just how deep his radicalism reached and whether rage against political and social injustice simply covered over for a time a basic conservatism. In any case, by *Lyrical Ballads* (1798) Burkean views of an organic society unreceptive to outside manipulations are clearly prominent in poems like 'The Old Cumberland Beggar' and 'The Brothers', and those views are spelled out in 1802 in the letter to Charles James Fox in this edition.

Wordsworth's conservatism in any event was sufficiently flexible to accommodate contemporary political movements. The new nationalism taking form on the Continent fits into Wordsworth's views as a manifestation of community on a national level (in the *Convention of Cintra* pamphlet). The new humanitarianism is likewise evident in his social concern in *Postscript*, although he was, I believe, well ahead of his time in insisting on the *right* of the unemployed to public maintenance. Wordsworth, contrary to his later reputation as a stolid reactionary, was never simply a *status quo* conservative; he was always thoughtful and well-grounded in principles.

Of Wordsworth's works in prose, only the literary material has appeared in selected editions, all of them now out of print. The gatherings of political material and other items have been largely available only in the three collected editions published since his death, the most recent edited by W. J. B. Owen and J. W. Smyser in 1974 in three volumes, which contain new manuscript items.

No scholarly selected edition of the whole of his prose has been attempted before, possibly because of the problem of bulk. In any event, only five items in the latest definitive edition are completely omitted here. The only early items are some prose fragments from a notebook and his brief report of conversations with Klopstock, the German poet, which is almost stenographic in nature. The other three omitted items are later compositions leaning heavily toward topical concerns: 'Two Addresses to the Freeholders of Westmorland', 'The Speech at Bowness', and 'The Law of Copyright'.

Of the remainder, all but two are given in full. The *Convention of Cintra* pamphlet, the largest of his prose works, is represented by about half of its bulk. Poorly organized and repetitious, it is improved by editing if ever a prose work was. Five passages, containing redundant material and long quotations from Spanish sources, are omitted (as described in brackets). The *Postscript*, the other shortened work, is represented by the first of three sections, each of which addresses a separate issue.

Additional material, on the other hand, not found in the Owen and Smyser edition, is included here. Three important letters, already mentioned, supplement the literary and political ideas presented in more formal pieces. There is also the moving 'Memoir of the Rev. Robert Walker', which was contained in a note to a sonnet. The essay tentatively entitled 'The Sublime and the Beautiful', included in Owen and Smyser, is here presented for the first time in a selected edition as part of the aesthetic theory.

The material is divided into four sections for easier access by the reader. Each item has its own introduction designed to provide the background of the work as well as other information helpful for understanding it. A head-note in brackets, moreover, supplies information on the dates of composition and first publication. Much of this data is taken from Mark Reed's invaluable two volumes of chronology and uses the same code of descending order of likelihood (probably, perhaps, possibly).

As for the works themselves, an accurate text has been the primary concern. All texts taken from sources printed in the poet's lifetime (or prepared for the press by him) represent the latest versions, most often found in the *Poetical Works* of 1849–50. A good deal of material, however, is found only in manuscripts, all of which, even those of the letters, were consulted in preparing this edition. Return to the manuscript of Wordsworth's letter to John Wilson was especially important, since it has never before been correctly transcribed. The Owen and Smyser edition also contains several substantive errors, as well as a number of misreadings of punctuation; these have been silently corrected.

Editing of the texts has been held to a minimum. Spellings have been retained where the modern spelling differs – such words as recal, shew, and burthen. Even aberrant spellings, such as their's and it's (as possessive pronouns), and the abbreviations tho' and thro', were retained. The only change made was from '&' to 'and'. The punctuation in the material published by Wordsworth is likewise untouched except where noted, but it was often necessary to add punctuation to manuscript material, sometimes heavily (as mentioned in the head-notes).

Except for Wordsworth's own notes (always clearly identified), the notes are limited to material that illuminates the meaning of the text or identifies people mentioned, as well as very likely or certain sources. Sources are so often misquoted by Wordsworth (at least three-quarters of the time) that such variations are not mentioned when the source is given in the notes. Although doubtless Wordsworth at times misremembered the originals, more often he is clearly adapting them to fit their new contexts. There is, of course, never a question of the material being misrepresented.

Wordsworth once admitted he was not fond of writing prose. But as one might anticipate from a poetic craftsman, his prose is well-nigh always clear; rarely, for example, is there need to explain the syntax of a sentence. And he is often eloquent as well. To overcome his reluctance to composition in prose, a topical issue of some concern was usually required to rouse him; consequently he was frequently moved to express his ideas with emotion and forthrightness. But it is finally those ideas themselves, original, thought-provoking, well-considered, that make Wordsworth's prose so well worth reading.

My acknowledgements of debts should begin with the most recent edition of Wordsworth's prose, *The Prose Works* (Oxford English Texts, 3 vols., 1974), edited by W. J. B. Owen and Jane Worthington Smyser; the text, introductions and annotations proved invaluable. I wish also to acknowledge the permission of the Dove Cottage Trustees to publish corrected versions of manuscripts under their care. I would also like to acknowledge the welcome assistance of librarians at the Dove Cottage Library, Grasmere; the British Museum; the Victoria and Albert Museum; the Huntington Library; the Pierpont Morgan Library; and especially the Inter-Library Loan Department of Shields Library, University of California, Davis. Gratitude is due also to my indefatigable typist, Diana Dulaney, who was kind and helpful throughout the production of this edition, and to both David Traill and Winfried Schleiner, who were generous with their time in advising me on the classical and foreign translations. I would like to dedicate this volume to the memory of Marvin Mudrick, Professor of English at the University of California, Santa Barbara, who died late in 1986.

# SECTION I

## Nature and the Man

~ue~~ue~~ue~

# Autobiographical Memoranda

※～※～※

[Probably composed between 16 and 31 November 1847. First published 1851.]

*These memoranda were almost certainly the 'family historical notices' dictated by Wordsworth to Susanna, wife of his nephew and biographer, Christopher Wordsworth, for use in his authorized biography of the poet. That Wordsworth believed that 'an Author's — especially a Poet's, works were the only biography the world had any right to call for', probably accounts for the almost strictly factual nature of the memoranda, and the grief at the death of his daughter Dora some four months prior to the dictation probably accounts for the perfunctory treatment of his later life.*

I was born at Cockermouth, in Cumberland, on April 7th, 1770,[1] the second son of John Wordsworth, attorney-at-law, as lawyers of this class were then called, and law-agent to Sir James Lowther, afterwards Earl of Lonsdale. My mother was Anne, only daughter of William Cookson, mercer, of Penrith, and of Dorothy, born Crackanthorp, of the ancient family of that name, who from the times of Edward the Third had lived in Newbiggen Hall, Westmoreland. My grandfather was the first of the name of Wordsworth who came into Westmoreland, where he purchased the small estate of Sockbridge. He was descended from a family who had been settled at Peniston in Yorkshire, near the sources of the Don, probably

3

before the Norman Conquest. Their names appear on different occasions in all the transactions, personal and public, connected with that parish; and I possess, through the kindness of Col. Beaumont,[2] an almery made in 1525, at the expense of a William Wordsworth, as is expressed in a Latin inscription carved upon it, which carries the pedigree of the family back four generations from himself.

The time of my infancy and early boyhood was passed partly at Cockermouth, and partly with my mother's parents at Penrith, where my mother, in the year 1778, died of a decline, brought on by a cold, the consequence of being put, at a friend's house in London, in what used to be called 'a best bedroom.' My father never recovered his usual cheerfulness of mind after this loss, and died when I was in my fourteenth year, a schoolboy, just returned from Hawkshead, whither I had been sent with my elder brother Richard, in my ninth year.

I remember my mother only in some few situations, one of which was her pinning a nosegay to my breast when I was going to say the catechism in the church, as was customary before Easter. I remember also telling her on one week day that I had been at church, for our school stood in the churchyard, and we had frequent opportunities of seeing what was going on there. The occasion was, a woman doing penance in the church in a white sheet. My mother commended my having been present, expressing a hope that I should remember the circumstance for the rest of my life. 'But,' said I, 'Mama, they did not give me a penny, as I had been told they would.' 'Oh,' said she, recanting her praises, 'if that was your motive, you were very properly disappointed.'

My last impression was having a glimpse of her on passing the door of her bedroom during her last illness, when she was reclining in her easy chair. An intimate friend of hers, Miss Hamilton[3] by name, who was used to visit her at Cockermouth, told me that she once said to her, that the only one of her five children about whose future life she was anxious, was William; and he, she said, would be remarkable either for good or for evil. The cause of this was, that I was of a stiff, moody, and violent temper; so much so that I remember going once into the attics of my grandfather's house at Penrith, upon

4

some indignity having been put upon me, with an intention of destroying myself with one of the foils which I knew was kept there. I took the foil in hand, but my heart failed. Upon another occasion, while I was at my grandfather's house at Penrith, along with my eldest brother, Richard, we were whipping tops together in the large drawing-room, on which the carpet was only laid down upon particular occasions. The walls were hung round with family pictures, and I said to my brother, 'Dare you strike your whip through that old lady's petticoat?' He replied, 'No, I won't.' 'Then,' said I, 'here goes;' and I struck my lash through her hooped petticoat, for which no doubt, though I have forgotten it, I was properly punished. But possibly, from some want of judgment in punishments inflicted, I had become perverse and obstinate in defying chastisement, and rather proud of it than otherwise.

Of my earliest days at school I have little to say, but that they were very happy ones, chiefly because I was left at liberty, then and in the vacations, to read whatever books I liked. For example, I read all Fielding's works, Don Quixote, Gil Blas, and any part of Swift that I liked; Gulliver's Travels, and the Tale of the Tub, being both much to my taste. I was very much indebted to one of the ushers of Hawkshead School, by name Shaw,[4] who taught me more of Latin in a fortnight than I had learnt during two preceding years at the school of Cockermouth. Unfortunately for me this excellent master left our school, and went to Stafford, where he taught for many years. It may be perhaps as well to mention, that the first verses which I wrote were a task imposed by my master; the subject, 'The Summer Vacation;' and of my own accord I added others upon 'Return to School.' There was nothing remarkable in either poem; but I was called upon, among other scholars, to write verses upon the completion of the second centenary from the foundation of the school in 1585, by Archbishop Sandys. These verses were much admired, far more than they deserved, for they were but a tame imitation of Pope's versification, and a little in his style. This exercise, however, put it into my head to compose verses from the impulse of my own mind, and I wrote, while yet a schoolboy, a long poem[5] running upon my own adventures, and the scenery of the country in which I was brought up. The only part of that poem which has been preserved is the conclusion of it, which stands at the beginning of my collected Poems.

In the month of October, 1787, I was sent to St John's College, Cambridge, of which my uncle, Dr Cookson,[6] had been a fellow. The master, Dr Chevallier, died very soon after; and, according to the custom of that time, his body, after being placed in the coffin, was removed to the hall of the college, and the pall, spread over the coffin, was stuck over by copies of verses, English or Latin, the composition of the students of St John's. My uncle seemed mortified when upon inquiry he learnt that none of these verses were from my pen, 'because,' said he, 'it would have been a fair opportunity for distinguishing yourself.' I did not, however, regret that I had been silent on this occasion, as I felt no interest in the deceased person, with whom I had had no intercourse, and whom I had never seen but during his walks in the college grounds.

When at school, I, with the other boys of the same standing, was put upon reading the first six books of Euclid, with the exception of the fifth; and also in algebra I learnt simple and quadratic equations; and this was for me unlucky, because I had a full twelve-month's start of the freshmen of my year, and accordingly got into rather an idle way; reading nothing but classic authors according to my fancy, and Italian poetry. My Italian master was named Isola,[7] and had been well acquainted with Gray the poet. As I took to these studies with much interest, he was proud of the progress I made. Under his correction I translated the Vision of Mirza,[8] and two or three other papers of the Spectator, into Italian. In the month of August, 1790, I set off for the Continent, in companionship with Robert Jones,[9] a Welshman, a fellow-collegian. We went staff in hand, without knapsacks, and carrying each his needments tied up in a pocket handkerchief, with about twenty pounds apiece in our pockets. We crossed from Dover and landed at Calais on the eve of the day when the king was to swear fidelity to the new constitution: an event which was solemnised with due pomp at Calais. On the afternoon of that day we started, and slept at Ardres. For what seemed best to me worth recording in this tour, see the Poem of my own Life.

After taking my degree in January, 1791, I went to London, stayed there some time, and then visited my friend Jones, who resided in the Vale of Clwydd, North Wales. Along with him I made a pedestrian tour through North Wales, for which also see the Poem.

In the autumn of 1791 I went to Paris, where I stayed some little time, and then went to Orleans, with a view of being out of the way of my own countrymen, that I might learn to speak the language fluently. At Orleans, and Blois, and Paris, on my return, I passed fifteen or sixteen months. It was a stirring time. The king was dethroned when I was at Blois, and the massacres of September took place when I was at Orleans. But for these matters see also the Poem. I came home before the execution of the king, and passed the subsequent time among my friends in London and elsewhere, till I settled with my only sister at Racedown in Dorsetshire, in the year 1796.

Here we were visited by Mr Coleridge, then residing at Bristol; and for the sake of being near him when he had removed to Nether-Stowey, in Somersetshire, we removed to Alfoxden, three miles from that place. This was a very pleasant and productive time of my life. Coleridge, my sister, and I, set off on a tour to Linton and other places in Devonshire; and in order to defray his part of the expense, Coleridge on the same afternoon commenced his poem of the Ancient Mariner; in which I was to have borne my part, and a few verses were written by me, and some assistance given in planning the poem; but our styles agreed so little, that I withdrew from the concern, and he finished it himself.

In the course of that spring I composed many poems, most of which were printed at Bristol, in one volume,[10] by my friend Joseph Cottle, along with Coleridge's Ancient Mariner, and two or three other of his pieces.

In the autumn of 1798, Mr Coleridge, a friend of his Mr Chester,[11] my sister, and I, crossed from Yarmouth to Hamburgh, where we remained a few days, and saw, several times, Klopstock the poet.[12]

Mr Coleridge and his friend went to Ratzburg, in the north of Germany, and my sister and I preferred going southward; and for the sake of cheapness, and the neighbourhood of the Hartz Mountains, we spent the winter at the old imperial city of Goslar. The winter was perishingly cold – the coldest of this century; and the good people with whom we lodged told me one morning, that they expected to find me frozen to death, my little sleeping room being immediately over an archway. However, neither my sister nor I took any harm.

We returned to England in the following spring, and went to visit our friends the Hutchinsons,[13] at Sockburn-on-Tees, in the county of Durham, with whom we remained till the 19th of December. We then came, on St Thomas's Day, the 21st, to a small cottage at Town-end, Grasmere,[14] which, in the course of a tour some months previously with Mr Coleridge, I had been pleased with, and had hired. This we furnished for about a hundred pounds, which sum had come to my sister by a legacy from her uncle Crackanthorp.

I fell to composition immediately, and published, in 1800, the second volume of the Lyrical Ballads.

In the year 1802 I married Mary Hutchinson, at Brompton, near Scarborough, to which part of the country the family had removed from Sockburn. We had known each other from childhood, and had practised reading and spelling under the same old dame at Penrith, a remarkable personage, who had taught three generations, of the upper classes principally, of the town of Penrith and its neighbourhood.

After our marriage we dwelt, together with our sister, at Town-end, where three of our children were born. In the spring of 1808, the increase of our family caused us to remove to a larger house, then just built, Allan Bank, in the same vale; where our two younger children were born, and who died[15] at the rectory, the house we afterwards occupied for two years. They died in 1812, and in 1813 we came to Rydal Mount, where we have since lived with no further sorrow till 1836, when my sister became a confirmed invalid, and our sister Sarah Hutchinson died. She lived alternately with her brother and with us.

# Description of the Scenery of the Lakes

*≈≈≈≈≈≈*

[*As the anonymous introduction to Joseph Wilkinson's* Select Views of Cumberland, Westmoreland, and Lancashire, *composed probably between mid-June and early November (by 17 November), 1809. First published 1810. The text printed here is that found in Wordsworth's own* A Guide through the District of the Lakes, *fifth edition (1835), which contains changes made in the various versions published in* Topographical Description of the Country of the Lakes in the North of England *(1820) and* A Description of the Scenery of the Lakes in the North of England *(1822, 1823).*]

*This work, which eventually became the main body of Wordsworth's* A Guide through the District of the Lakes, *began as an introduction to, and comment upon, a collection of engravings,* Select Views of Cumberland, Westmoreland, and Lancashire, *by Joseph Wilkinson, a friend of the Lake poets and at one time a resident of the Lake District. Even before completion of this introduction, and apparently as early as 1807, Wordsworth had conceived of writing a guide for travellers to the District, already long a tourist attraction. Each of the versions of this guide (1820, 1822, 1823), which essentially follow the text of the original* Select Views, *received consecutively larger printings, and the final* Guide *(1835) is still sold as a guidebook in the area. The remaining parts of the* Guide, *which are more strictly directional, are contained in Appendix A.*

9

SECTION FIRST
*View of the country as formed by Nature*

At Lucerne, in Switzerland, is shewn a Model of the Alpine country which encompasses the Lake of the four Cantons. The Spectator ascends a little platform, and sees mountains, lakes, glaciers, rivers, woods, waterfalls, and vallies, with their cottages, and every other object contained in them, lying at his feet; all things being represented in their appropriate colours. It may be easily conceived that this exhibition affords an exquisite delight to the imagination, tempting it to wander at will from valley to valley, from mountain to mountain, through the deepest recesses of the Alps. But it supplies also a more substantial pleasure: for the sublime and beautiful region, with all its hidden treasures, and their bearings and relations to each other, is thereby comprehended and understood at once.

Something of this kind, without touching upon minute details and individualities which would only confuse and embarrass, will here be attempted, in respect to the Lakes in the north of England, and the vales and mountains enclosing and surrounding them. The delineation, if tolerably executed, will, in some instances, communicate to the traveller, who has already seen the objects, new information; and will assist in giving to his recollections a more orderly arrangement than his own opportunities of observing may have permitted him to make; while it will be still more useful to the future traveller, by directing his attention at once to distinctions in things which, without such previous aid, a length of time only could enable him to discover. It is hoped, also, that this Essay may become generally serviceable, by leading to habits of more exact and considerate observation than, as far as the writer knows, have hitherto been applied to local scenery.

To begin, then, with the main outlines of the country; – I know not how to give the reader a distinct image of these more readily, than by requesting him to place himself with me, in imagination, upon some given point; let it be the top of either of the mountains, Great Gavel, or Scawfell; or, rather, let us suppose our station to be a cloud hanging midway between those two mountains, at not more than half a mile's distance from the summit of each, and not many yards above their highest elevation; we shall then see stretched at our feet a number of vallies, not fewer than eight, diverging from the point, on which we are supposed to stand, like spokes from the nave of a wheel. First, we note, lying to the south-east, the vale of Langdale,[1] which will conduct the eye to the long lake of Winandermere, stretched nearly to the sea; or rather to the sands of the vast bay of Morcamb, serving here for the rim of this imaginary wheel; — let us trace it in a direction from the south-east towards the south, and we shall next fix our eyes upon the vale of Coniston, running up likewise from the sea, but not (as all the other vallies do) to the nave of the wheel, and therefore it may be not inaptly represented as a broken spoke sticking in the rim. Looking forth again, with an inclination towards the west, we see immediately at our feet the vale of Duddon, in which is no lake, but a copious stream winding among fields, rocks, and mountains, and terminating its course in the sands of Duddon. The fourth vale, next to be observed, viz. that of the Esk, is of the same general character as the last, yet beautifully discriminated from it by peculiar features. Its stream passes under the woody steep upon which stands Muncaster Castle, the ancient seat of the Penningtons, and after forming a short and narrow aestuary enters the sea below the small town of Ravenglass. Next, almost due west, look down into, and along the deep valley of Wastdale, with its little chapel and half a dozen neat dwellings scattered upon a plain of meadow and corn-ground intersected with stone walls apparently innumerable, like a large piece of lawless patch-work, or an array of mathematical figures, such as in the ancient schools of geometry might have been sportively and fantastically traced out upon sand. Beyond this little fertile plain lies, within a bed of steep mountains, the long, narrow, stern, and desolate lake of Wastdale; and, beyond this, a dusky tract of level ground conducts the eye to the Irish Sea. The stream that issues from Wast-water is named the Irt, and falls into the aestuary of the river Esk. Next comes in view Ennerdale, with its lake of bold and somewhat savage shores. Its stream, the

Ehen or Enna, flowing through a soft and fertile country, passes the town of Egremont, and the ruins of the castle, – then, seeming, like the other rivers, to break through the barrier of sand thrown up by the winds on this tempestuous coast, enters the Irish Sea. The vale of Buttermere, with the lake and village of that name, and Crummock-water, beyond, next present themselves. We will follow the main stream, the Coker, through the fertile and beautiful vale of Lorton, till it is lost in the Derwent, below the noble ruins of Cockermouth Castle. Lastly, Borrowdale, of which the vale of Keswick is only a continuation, stretching due north, brings us to a point nearly opposite to the vale of Winandermere with which we began. From this it will appear, that the image of a wheel, thus far exact, is little more than one half complete; but the deficiency on the eastern side may be supplied by the vales of Wytheburn, Ulswater, Hawswater, and the vale of Grasmere and Rydal; none of these, however, run up to the central point between Great Gavel and Scawfell. From this, hitherto our central point, take a flight of not more than four or five miles eastward to the ridge of Helvellyn, and you will look down upon Wytheburn and St John's Vale, which are a branch of the vale of Keswick; upon Ulswater, stretching due east: – and not far beyond to the south-east (though from this point not visible) lie the vale and lake of Hawswater; and lastly, the vale of Grasmere, Rydal, and Ambleside, brings you back to Winander-mere, thus completing, though on the eastern side in a somewhat irregular manner, the representative figure of the wheel.

Such, concisely given, is the general topographical view of the country of the Lakes in the north of England; and it may be observed, that, from the circumference to the centre, that is, from the sea or plain country to the mountain stations specified, there is – in the several ridges that enclose these vales, and divide them from each other, I mean in the forms and surfaces, first of the swelling grounds, next of the hills and rocks, and lastly of the mountains – an ascent of almost regular gradation, from elegance and richness, to their highest point of grandeur and sublimity. It follows therefore from this, first, that these rocks, hills, and mountains, must present themselves to view in stages rising above each other, the mountains clustering together towards the central point; and next, that an observer familiar with the several vales, must, from their various position in relation to the sun, have had before his eyes every possible embellishment of beauty, dignity, and splendour, which light and shadow can bestow upon objects so diversified. For example, in the vale of Winandermere, if the spectator looks for gentle and lovely scenes, his eye is turned towards the south; if for the grand, towards the north: in the vale of Keswick, which (as hath been said) lies almost due north of this, it is directly the reverse. Hence, when the sun is setting in summer far to the north-west, it is seen, by the spectator from the shores or breast of Winandermere, resting among the summits of the loftiest mountains, some of which will perhaps be half or wholly hidden by clouds, or by the blaze of light which the orb diffuses around it; and the surface of the lake will reflect before the eye correspondent colours through every variety of beauty, and through all degrees of splendour. In the vale of Keswick, at the same period, the sun sets over the humbler regions of the landscape, and showers down upon *them* the radiance which at once veils and glorifies, – sending forth, meanwhile, broad streams of rosy, crimson, purple, or golden light, towards the grand mountains in the south and south-east, which, thus illuminated, with all their projections and cavities, and with an intermixture of solemn shadows, are seen distinctly through a cool and clear atmosphere. Of course, there is as marked a difference between the *noontide* appearance of these two opposite vales. The bedimming haze that overspreads the south, and the clear atmosphere and determined shadows of the clouds in the north, at the same time of the day, are each seen in these several vales, with a contrast as striking. The reader will easily conceive in what degree the intermediate vales partake of a kindred variety.

I do not indeed know any tract of country in which, within so narrow a compass, may be found an equal variety in the influences of light and shadow upon the sublime or beautiful features of landscape; and it is owing to the combined circumstances to which the reader's attention has been directed. From a point between Great

13

Gavel and Scawfell, a shepherd would not require more than an hour to descend into any one of eight of the principal vales by which he would be surrounded; and all the others lie (with the exception of Hawswater) at but a small distance. Yet, though clustered together, every valley has its distinct and separate character: in some instances, as if they had been formed in studied contrast to each other, and in others with the united pleasing differences and resemblances of a sisterly rivalship. This concentration of interest gives to the country a decided superiority over the most attractive districts of Scotland and Wales, especially for the pedestrian traveller. In Scotland and Wales are found, undoubtedly, individual scenes, which, in their several kinds, cannot be excelled. But, in Scotland, particularly, what long tracts of desolate country intervene! so that the traveller, when he reaches a spot deservedly of great celebrity, would find it difficult to determine how much of his pleasure is owing to excellence inherent in the landscape itself; and how much to an instantaneous recovery from an oppression left upon his spirits by the barrenness and desolation through which he has passed.

But to proceed with our survey; – and, first, of the MOUNTAINS. Their *forms* are endlessly diversified, sweeping easily or boldly in simple majesty, abrupt and precipitous, or soft and elegant. In magnitude and grandeur they are individually inferior to the most celebrated of those in some other parts of this island; but, in the combinations which they make, towering above each other, or lifting themselves in ridges like the waves of a tumultuous sea, and in the beauty and variety of their surfaces and colours, they are surpassed by none.

The general *surface* of the mountains is turf, rendered rich and green by the moisture of the climate. Sometimes the turf, as in the neighbourhood of Newlands, is little broken, the whole covering being soft and downy pasturage. In other places rocks predominate; the soil is laid bare by torrents and burstings of water from the sides of the mountains in heavy rains; and not unfrequently their perpendicular sides are seamed by ravines (formed also by rains and

14

torrents) which, meeting in angular points, entrench and scar the surface with numerous figures like the letters W. and Y.

In the ridge that divides Eskdale from Wasdale, granite is found; but the MOUNTAINS are for the most part composed of the stone by mineralogists termed schist, which, as you approach the plain country, gives place to lime-stone and free-stone; but schist being the substance of the mountains, the predominant *colour* of their *rocky* parts is bluish, or hoary grey – the general tint of the lichens with which the bare stone is encrusted. With this blue or grey colour is frequently intermixed a red tinge, proceeding from the iron that interveins the stone, and impregnates the soil. The iron is the principle of decomposition in these rocks; and hence, when they become pulverized, the elementary particles crumbling down, overspread in many places the steep and almost precipitous sides of the mountains with an intermixture of colours, like the compound hues of a dove's neck. When in the heat of advancing summer, the fresh green tint of the herbage has somewhat faded, it is again revived by the appearance of the fern profusely spread over the same ground: and, upon this plant, more than upon any thing else, do the changes which the seasons make in the colouring of the mountains depend. About the first week in October, the rich green, which prevailed through the whole summer, is usually passed away. The brilliant and various colours of the fern are then in harmony with the autumnal woods; bright yellow or lemon colour, at the base of the mountains, melting gradually, through orange, to a dark russet brown towards the summits, where the plant, being more exposed to the weather, is in a more advanced state of decay. Neither heath nor furze are *generally* found upon the *sides* of these mountains, though in many places they are adorned by those plants, so beautiful when in flower. We may add, that the mountains are of height sufficient to have the surface towards the summit softened by distance, and to imbibe the finest aërial hues. In common also with other mountains, their apparent forms and colours are perpetually changed by the clouds and vapours which float round them: the effect indeed of mist or haze, in a country of this character, is like that of magic. I have seen six or seven ridges rising above each other, all created in a moment, by the vapours upon the side of a mountain, which, in its ordinary appearance, shewed not a projecting point to furnish even a hint for such an operation.

I will take this opportunity of observing, that they who have studied the appearances of nature feel that the superiority, in point of visual interest, of mountainous over other countries – is more strikingly displayed in winter than in summer. This, as must be obvious, is partly owing to the *forms* of the mountains, which, of course, are not affected by the seasons; but also, in no small degree, to the greater variety that exists in their winter than their summer *colouring*. This variety is such, and so harmoniously preserved, that it leaves little cause of regret when the splendour of autumn is passed away. The oak-coppices, upon the sides of the mountains, retain russet leaves; the birch stands conspicuous with its silver stem and puce-coloured twigs; the hollies, with green leaves and scarlet berries, have come forth to view from among the deciduous trees, whose summer foliage had concealed them: the ivy is now plentifully apparent upon the stems and boughs of the trees, and upon the steep rocks. In place of the deep summer-green of the herbage and fern, many rich colours play into each other over the surface of the mountains; turf (the tints of which are interchangeably tawny-green, olive, and brown,) beds of withered fern, and grey rocks, being harmoniously blended together. The mosses and lichens are never so fresh and flourishing as in winter, if it be not a season of frost; and their minute beauties prodigally adorn the foreground. Wherever we turn, we find these productions of nature, to which winter is rather favourable than unkindly, scattered over the walls, banks of earth, rocks, and stones, and upon the trunks of trees, with the intermixture of several species of small fern, now green and fresh; and, to the observing passenger, their forms and colours are a source of inexhaustible admiration. Add to this the hoar-frost and snow, with all the varieties they create, and which volumes would not be sufficient to describe. I will content myself with one instance of the colouring produced by snow, which may not be uninteresting to painters. It is extracted from the memorandum-book of a friend;[2] and for its accuracy I can speak, having been an eye-witness of the appearance. 'I observed,' says he, 'the beautiful effect of the drifted snow upon the mountains, and the perfect *tone* of colour. From the top of the mountains downwards a rich olive was produced by the powdery snow and the grass, which olive was warmed with a little brown, and in this way harmoniously combined, by insensible gradations, with the white. The drifting took away the monotony of snow; and the whole vale of Grasmere, seen from the terrace walk in Easedale, was as varied, perhaps more so, than even in the pomp of autumn. In the distance was Loughrigg-Fell, the basin-wall of the lake: this, from the summit downward, was a rich orange-olive; then the lake of a bright olive-green, nearly the same tint as the snow-powdered mountain tops and high slopes in Easedale; and lastly, the church, with its firs, forming the centre of the view. Next to the church came nine distinguishable hills, six of them with woody sides turned towards us, all of them oak-copses with their bright red leaves and snow-powdered twigs; these hills – so variously situated in relation to each other, and to the view in general, so variously powdered, some only enough to give the herbage a rich brown tint, one intensely white and lighting up all the others – were yet so placed, as in the most inobtrusive manner to harmonise by contrast with a perfect naked, snowless bleak summit in the far distance.'

Having spoken of the forms, surface, and colour of the mountains, let us descend into the VALES. Though these have been represented under the general image of the spokes of a wheel, they are, for the most part, winding; the windings of many being abrupt and intricate. And, it may be observed, that, in one circumstance, the general shape of them all has been determined by that primitive conformation through which so many became receptacles of lakes. For they are not formed, as are most of the celebrated Welsh vallies, by an approximation of the sloping bases of the opposite mountains towards each other, leaving little more between than a channel for the passage of a hasty river; but the bottom of these vallies is mostly a spacious and gently declining area, apparently level as the floor of a temple, or the surface of a lake, and broken in many cases, by rocks and hills, which rise up like islands from the plain. In such of the vallies as make many windings, these level areas open upon the traveller in succession, divided from each other sometimes by a mutual approximation of the hills, leaving only passage for a river, sometimes by correspondent windings, without such approximation; and sometimes by a bold advance of one mountain towards that which is opposite it. It may here be observed with propriety that the several rocks and hills, which have been described as rising up like islands from the level area of the vale, have regulated the choice of the inhabitants in the situation of their dwellings. Where none of these are found, and the inclination of the ground is not sufficiently rapid easily to carry off the waters, (as in the higher part of Langdale, for instance,) the houses are not sprinkled over the middle of the vales, but confined to their sides, being placed merely so far up the mountain as to be protected from the floods. But where these rocks and hills have been scattered over the plain of the vale, (as in Grasmere, Donnerdale, Eskdale, &c.) the beauty which they give to the scene is much heightened by a single cottage, or cluster of cottages, that will be almost always found under them, or upon their sides; dryness and shelter having tempted the Dalesmen to fix their habitations there.

I shall now speak of the LAKES of this country. The form of the lake is most perfect when, like Derwent-water, and some of the smaller lakes, it least resembles that of a river; – I mean, when being looked at from any given point where the whole may be seen at once, the width of it bears such proportion to the length, that, however the outline may be diversified by far-receding bays, it never assumes the shape of a river, and is contemplated with that placid and quiet feeling which belongs peculiarly to the lake – as a body of still water under the influence of no current; reflecting therefore the clouds, the light, and all the imagery of the sky and surrounding hills; expressing also and making visible the changes of the atmosphere, and motions of the lightest breeze, and subject to agitation only from the winds –

> – The visible scene
> Would enter unawares into his mind
> With all its solemn imagery, its rocks,
> Its woods, and that uncertain heaven received
> Into the bosom of the *steady* lake! [3]

It must be noticed, as a favourable characteristic of the lakes of this country, that, though several of the largest, such as Winandermere, Ulswater, Hawswater, do, when the whole length of them is commanded from an elevated point, lose somewhat of the peculiar form of the lake, and assume the resemblance of a magnificent river; yet, as their shape is winding, (particularly that of Ulswater and Hawswater) when the view of the whole is obstructed by those barriers which determine the windings, and the spectator is confined to one reach, the appropriate feeling is revived; and one lake may thus in succession present to the eye the essential characteristic of many. But, though the forms of the large lakes have this advantage, it is nevertheless favourable to the beauty of the country that the largest of them are comparatively small; and that the same vale generally furnishes a succession of lakes, instead of being filled with one. The vales in North Wales, as hath been observed, are not formed for the reception of lakes; those of Switzerland, Scotland, and this part of the North of England, *are* so formed; but, in Switzerland and Scotland, the proportion of diffused water is often too great, as at the lake of Geneva for instance, and in most of the Scotch lakes. No doubt it sounds magnificent and flatters the imagination, to hear at a distance of expanses of water so many leagues in length and miles in width; and such ample room may be delightful to the fresh-water sailor, scudding with a lively breeze amid the rapidly-shifting scenery. But, who ever travelled along the banks of Loch-Lomond, variegated as the lower part is by islands, without feeling that a speedier termination of the long vista of blank water would be acceptable; and without wishing for an interposition of green meadows, trees, and cottages, and a sparkling stream to run by his side? In fact, a notion of grandeur, as connected with magnitude, has seduced persons of taste into a general mistake upon this subject. It is much more desirable, for the purposes of pleasure, that lakes should be numerous, and small or middle-sized, than large, not only for communication by walks and rides, but for variety, and for recurrence of similar appearances. To illustrate this by one instance: – how pleasing is it to have a ready and frequent opportunity of watching, at the outlet of a lake, the stream pushing its way among the rocks in lively contrast with the stillness from which it has escaped; and how amusing to compare its noisy and turbulent motions with the gentle playfulness of the breezes, that may be starting up or wandering here and there over the faintly-rippled surface of the broad water! I may add, as a general remark, that, in lakes of great width, the shores cannot be distinctly seen at the same time, and therefore contribute little to mutual illustration and ornament; and, if the opposite shores are out of sight of each other, like those of the American and Asiatic lakes, then unfortunately the traveller is reminded of a nobler object; he has the blankness of a sea-prospect without the grandeur and accompanying sense of power.

As the comparatively small size of the lakes in the North of England is favourable to the production of variegated landscape, their *boundary-line* also is for the most part gracefully or boldly indented. That uniformity which prevails in the primitive frame of the lower grounds among all chains or clusters of mountains where large bodies of still water are bedded, is broken by the *secondary* agents of nature, ever at work to supply the deficiences of the mould in which things were originally cast. Using the word *deficiences*, I do not speak with reference to those stronger emotions which a region of mountains is peculiarly fitted to excite. The bases of those huge barriers may run for a long space in straight lines, and these parallel to each other; the opposite sides of a profound vale may ascend as exact counterparts, or in mutual reflection, like the billows of a troubled sea; and the impression be, from its very simplicity, more awful and sublime. Sublimity is the result of Nature's first great dealings with the superficies of the earth; but the general tendency of her subsequent operations is towards the production of beauty, by a multiplicity of symmetrical parts uniting in a consistent whole. This is every where exemplified along the margins of these lakes. Masses of rock, that have been precipitated from the heights into the area of waters, lie in some places like stranded ships; or have acquired the compact structure of jutting piers; or project in little peninsulas crested with native wood. The smallest rivulet — one whose silent influx is scarcely noticeable in a season of dry weather — so faint is the dimple made by it on the surface of the smooth lake — will be found to have been not useless in shaping, by its deposits of gravel and soil in time of flood, a curve that would not otherwise have existed. But the more powerful brooks, encroaching upon the level of the lake, have, in course of time, given birth to ample promontories of sweeping outline that contrasts boldly with the longitudinal base of the steeps on the opposite shore; while their flat or gently-sloping surfaces never fail to introduce, into the midst of desolation and barrenness, the elements of fertility, even where the habitations of men may not have been raised. These alluvial promontories, however, threaten, in some places, to bisect the waters which they have long adorned; and, in course of ages, they will cause some of the lakes to dwindle into numerous and insignificant pools; which, in their turn, will finally be filled up. But, checking these intrusive calculations, let us rather be content with appearances as they are, and pursue in imagination the meandering shores, whether rugged steeps, admitting of no cultivation, descend into the water; or gently-sloping lawns and woods, or flat and fertile meadows stretch between the margin of the lake and the mountains. Among minuter recommendations will be noticed, especially along bays exposed to the setting-in of strong winds, the curved rim of fine blue gravel, thrown up in course of time by the waves, half of it perhaps gleaming from under the water, and the corresponding half of a lighter hue; and in other parts bordering the lake, groves, if I may so call them, of reeds and bulrushes; or plots of water-lilies lifting up their large target-shaped leaves to the breeze, while the white flower is heaving upon the wave.

To these may naturally be added the birds that enliven the waters. Wild-ducks in spring-time hatch their young in the islands, and upon reedy shores; — the sand-piper, flitting along the stony margins, by its restless note attracts the eye to motions as restless: – upon some jutting rock, or at the edge of a smooth meadow, the stately heron may be descried with folded wings, that might seem to have caught their delicate hue from the blue waters, by the side of which she watches for her sustenance. In winter, the lakes are sometimes resorted to by wild swans; and in that season habitually by widgeons, goldings, and other aquatic fowl of the smaller species. Let me be allowed the aid of verse to describe the evolutions which these visitants sometimes perform, on a fine day towards the close of winter.

[Here Wordsworth quotes his 'Water Fowl'.]

The ISLANDS, dispersed among these lakes, are neither so numerous nor so beautiful as might be expected from the account that has been given of the manner in which the level areas of the vales are so frequently diversified by rocks, hills, and hillocks, scattered over them; nor are they ornamented (as are several of the lakes in Scotland and Ireland) by the remains of castles or other places of defence; nor with the still more interesting ruins of religious edifices. Every one must regret that scarcely a vestige is left of the Oratory, consecrated to the Virgin, which stood upon Chapel-Holm in Windermere, and that the Chauntry has disappeared, where mass used to be sung, upon St Herbert's Island, Derwent-water. The islands of the last-mentioned lake are neither fortunately placed nor of pleasing shape; but if the wood upon them were managed with more taste, they might become interesting features in the landscape. There is a beautiful cluster on Winandermere; a pair pleasingly contrasted upon Rydal; nor must the solitary green island of Grasmere be forgotten. In the bosom of each of the lakes of Ennerdale and Devockwater is a single rock, which, owing to its neighbourhood to the sea, is –

'The haunt of cormorants and sea-mews' clang,'[4]

a music well suited to the stern and wild character of the several scenes! It may be worth while here to mention (not as an object of beauty, but of curiosity) that there occasionally appears above the surface of Derwent-water, and always in the same place, a considerable tract of spongy ground covered with aquatic plants, which is called the Floating, but with more propriety might be named the Buoyant, Island; and, on one of the pools near the lake of Esthwaite, may sometimes be seen a mossy Islet, with trees upon it, shifting about before the wind, a lusus naturae [5] frequent on the great rivers of America, and not unknown in other parts of the world.

> − 'fas habeas invisere Tiburis arva,
> Albuneaeque lacum, atque umbras terrasque natantes.' [6]

This part of the subject may be concluded with observing − that, from the multitude of brooks and torrents that fall into these lakes, and of internal springs by which they are fed, and which circulate through them like veins, they are truly living lakes, '*vivi lacus*'; [7] and are thus discriminated from the stagnant and sullen pools frequent among mountains that have been formed by volcanoes, and from the shallow meres found in flat and fenny countries. The water is also of crystalline purity; so that, if it were not for the reflections of the incumbent mountains by which it is darkened, a delusion might be felt, by a person resting quietly in a boat on the bosom of Winandermere or Derwent-water, similar to that which Carver so beautifully describes when he was floating alone in the middle of lake Erie or Ontario, and could almost have imagined that his boat was suspended in an element as pure as air, or rather that the air and water were one. [8]

Having spoken of Lakes I must not omit to mention, as a kindred feature of this country, those bodies of still water called TARNS. In the economy of nature these are useful, as auxiliars to Lakes; for if the whole quantity of water which falls upon the mountains in time of storm were poured down upon the plains without intervention, in some quarters, of such receptacles, the habitable grounds would be much more subject than they are to inundation. But, as some of the collateral brooks spend their fury, finding a free course toward and also down the channel of the main stream of the vale before those that have to pass through the higher tarns and lakes have filled their several basins, a gradual distribution is effected; and the waters thus reserved, instead of uniting, to spread ravage and deformity, with those which meet with no such detention, contribute to support, for a length of time, the vigour of many streams without a fresh fall of rain. Tarns are found in some of the vales, and are numerous upon the mountains. A Tarn, in a *Vale*, implies, for the most part, that the bed of the vale is not happily formed; that the water of the brooks can neither wholly escape, nor diffuse itself over a large area. Accordingly, in such situations, Tarns are often surrounded by an unsightly tract of boggy ground; but this is not always the case, and in the cultivated parts of the country, when the shores of the Tarn are determined, it differs only from the Lake in being smaller, and in belonging mostly to a smaller valley, or circular recess. Of this class of miniature lakes, Loughrigg Tarn, near Grasmere, is the most beautiful example. It has a margin of green firm meadows, of rocks, and rocky woods, a few reeds here, a little company of water-lilies there, with beds of gravel or stone beyond; a tiny stream issuing neither briskly nor sluggishly out of it; but its feeding rills, from the shortness of their course, so small as to be scarcely visible. Five or six cottages are reflected in its peaceful bosom; rocky and barren steeps rise up above the hanging enclosures; and the solemn pikes of Lang-dale overlook, from a distance, the low cultivated ridge of land that forms the northern boundary of this small, quiet, and fertile domain. The *mountain* Tarns can only be recommended to the notice of the inquisitive traveller who has time to spare. They are difficult of access and naked; yet some of them are, in their permanent forms, very grand; and there are accidents of things which would make the meanest of them interesting. At all events, one of these pools is an acceptable sight to the mountain wanderer; not merely as an incident that diversifies the prospect, but as forming in his mind a centre or conspicuous point to which objects, otherwise disconnected or in-subordinated, may be referred. Some few have a varied outline, with bold heath-clad promontories; and, as they mostly lie at the foot of a steep precipice, the water where the sun is not shining upon it, appears black and sullen; and, round the margin, huge stones and masses of rock are scattered; some defying conjecture as to the means by which they came thither; and others obviously fallen from on high – the contribution of ages! A not unpleasing sadness is induced by this perplexity, and these images of decay; while the prospect of a body of pure water unattended with groves and other cheerful rural images by which fresh water is usually accompanied, and unable to give furtherance to the meagre vegetation around it – excites a sense of some repulsive power strongly put forth, and thus deepens the melancholy natural to such scenes. Nor is the feeling of solitude often more forcibly or more solemnly impressed than by the side of one of these mountain pools: though desolate and forbidding, it seems a distinct place to repair to; yet where the visitants must be rare, and there can be no disturbance. Water-fowl flock hither; and the lonely Angler may here be seen; but the imagination, not content with this scanty allowance of society, is tempted to attribute a voluntary power to every change which takes place in such a spot, whether it be the breeze that wanders over the surface of the water, or the splendid lights of evening resting upon it in the midst of awful precipices.

> 'There, sometimes does a leaping fish
> Send through the tarn a lonely cheer;
> The crags repeat the raven's croak
> In symphony austere:
> Thither the rainbow comes, the cloud,
> And mists that spread the flying shroud,
> And sunbeams, and the sounding blast.'[9]

It will be observed that this country is bounded on the south and west by the sea, which combines beautifully, from many elevated points, with the inland scenery; and, from the bay of Morcamb, the sloping shores and back-ground of distant mountains are seen, composing pictures equally distinguished for amenity and grandeur. But the aestuaries on this coast are in a great measure bare at low water;[10] and there is no instance of the sea running far up among the mountains, and mingling with the Lakes, which are such in the strict and usual sense of the word, being of fresh water. Nor have the streams, from the shortness of their course, time to acquire that body of water necessary to confer upon them much majesty. In fact, the most considerable, while they continue in the mountain and lake-country, are rather large brooks than rivers. The water is perfectly pellucid, through which in many places are seen, to a great depth, their beds of rock, or of blue gravel, which give to the water itself an exquisitely cerulean colour: this is particularly striking in the rivers Derwent and Duddon, which may be compared, such and so various are their beauties, to any two rivers of equal length of course in any country. The number of the torrents and smaller brooks is infinite, with their water-falls and water-breaks; and they need not here be described. I will only observe that, as many, even of the smallest rills, have either found, or made for themselves, recesses in the sides of the mountains or in the vales, they have tempted the primitive inhabitants to settle near them for shelter; and hence, cottages so placed, by seeming to withdraw from the eye, are the more endeared to the feelings.

The W o o d s consist chiefly of oak, ash, and birch, and here and there Wych-elm, with underwood of hazle, the white and black thorn, and hollies; in moist places alders and willows abound; and yews among the rocks. Formerly the whole country must have been covered with wood to a great height up the mountains; where native Scotch firs[11] must have grown in great profusion, as they do in the northern part of Scotland to this day. But not one of these old inhabitants has existed, perhaps, for some hundreds of years; the beautiful traces, however, of the universal sylvan[12] appearance the country formerly had, yet survive in the native coppice-woods that have been protected by inclosures, and also in the forest-trees and hollies, which, though disappearing fast, are yet scattered both over the inclosed and uninclosed parts of the mountains. The same is expressed by the beauty and intricacy with which the fields and coppice-woods are often intermingled: the plough of the first settlers having followed naturally the veins of richer, dryer, or less stony soil; and thus it has shaped out an intermixture of wood and lawn, with a grace and wildness which it would have been impossible for the hand of studied art to produce. Other trees have been introduced within these last fifty years, such as beeches, larches, limes, &c. and plantations of firs, seldom with advantage, and often with great injury to the appearance of the country; but the sycamore (which I believe was brought into this island from Germany, not more than two hundred years ago) has long been the favourite of the cottagers; and, with the fir, has been chosen to screen their dwellings; and is sometimes found in the fields whither the winds or the waters may have carried its seeds.

The want most felt, however, is that of timber trees. There are few *magnificent* ones to be found near any of the lakes; and unless greater care be taken, there will, in a short time, scarcely be left an ancient oak that would repay the cost of felling. The neighbourhood of Rydal, notwithstanding the havoc which has been made, is yet nobly distinguished. In the woods of Lowther, also, is found an almost matchless store of ancient trees, and the majesty and wildness of the native forest.

Among the smaller vegetable ornaments must be reckoned the bilberry, a ground plant, never so beautiful as in early spring, when it is seen under bare or budding trees, that imperfectly intercept the sun-shine, covering the rocky knolls with a pure mantle of fresh verdure, more lively than the herbage of the open fields; – the broom that spreads luxuriantly along rough pastures, and in the month of June interveins the steep copses with its golden blossoms; – and the juniper, a rich evergreen, that thrives in spite of cattle, upon the uninclosed parts of the mountains: – the Dutch myrtle diffuses fragrance in moist places; and there is an endless variety of brilliant flowers in the fields and meadows, which, if the agriculture of the country were more carefully attended to, would disappear. Nor can I omit again to notice the lichens and mosses: their profusion, beauty, and variety, exceed those of any other country I have seen.

It may now be proper to say a few words respecting climate, and 'skiey influences,' [13] in which this region, as far as the character of its landscapes is affected by them, may, upon the whole, be considered fortunate. The country is, indeed, subject to much bad weather, and it has been ascertained that twice as much rain falls here as in many parts of the island; but the number of black drizzling days, that blot out the face of things, is by no means *proportionally* great. Nor is a continuance of thick, flagging, damp air, so common as in the West of England and Ireland. The rain here comes down heartily, and is frequently succeeded by clear, bright weather, when every brook is vocal, and every torrent sonorous; brooks and torrents, which are never muddy, even in the heaviest floods, except, after a drought, they happen to be defiled for a short time by waters that have swept along dusty roads, or have broken out into ploughed fields. Days of unsettled weather, with partial showers, are very frequent; but the showers, darkening, or brightening, as they fly from hill to hill, are not less grateful[14] to the eye than finely interwoven passages of gay and sad music are touching to the ear. Vapours exhaling from the lakes and meadows after sun-rise, in a hot season, or, in moist weather, brooding upon the heights, or descending towards the valleys with inaudible motion, give a visionary character to everything around them; and are in themselves so beautiful, as to dispose us to enter into the feelings of those simple nations (such as the Laplanders of this day) by whom they are taken for guardian deities of the mountains; or to sympathise with others who have fancied these delicate apparitions to be the spirits of their departed ancestors. Akin to these are fleecy clouds resting upon the hill-tops; they are not easily managed in picture, with their accompaniments of blue sky; but how glorious are they in nature! how pregnant with imagination for the poet! and the height of the Cumbrian mountains is sufficient to exhibit daily and hourly instances of those mysterious attachments. Such clouds, cleaving to their stations, or lifting up suddenly their glittering heads from behind rocky barriers, or hurrying out of sight with speed of the sharpest edge – will often tempt an inhabitant to congratulate himself on belonging to a country of mists and clouds and storms, and make him think of the blank sky of Egypt, and of the cerulean vacancy of Italy, as an unanimated and even a sad spectacle. The atmosphere, however, as in every country subject to much rain, is frequently unfavourable to landscape, especially when keen winds succeed the rain which are apt to produce coldness, spottiness, and an unmeaning or repulsive detail in the distance; – a sunless frost, under a canopy of leaden and shapeless clouds, is, as far as it allows things to be seen, equally disagreeable.

It has been said that in human life there are moments worth ages. In a more subdued tone of sympathy may we affirm, that in the climate of England there are, for the lover of nature, days which are worth whole months, – I might say – even years. One of these favoured days sometimes occurs in spring-time, when that soft air is breathing over the blossoms and new-born verdure, which inspired Buchanan with his beautiful Ode to the first of May; the air, which, in the luxuriance of his fancy, he likens to that of the golden age, – to that which gives motion to the funereal cypresses on the banks of Lethe; – to the air which is to salute beatified spirits when expiatory fires shall have consumed the earth with all her habitations.[15] But it is in autumn that days of such affecting influence most frequently intervene; – the atmosphere seems refined, and the sky rendered more crystalline, as the vivifying heat of the year abates; the lights and shadows are more delicate; the coloring is richer and more finely harmonized; and, in this season of stillness, the ear being unoccupied, or only gently excited, the sense of vision becomes more susceptible of its appropriate enjoyments. A resident in a country like this which we are treating of, will agree with me, that the presence of a lake is indispensable to exhibit in perfection the beauty of one of these days; and he must have experienced, while looking on the unruffled waters, that the imagination, by their aid, is carried into recesses of feeling otherwise impenetrable. The reason of this is, that the heavens are not only brought down into the bosom of the earth, but that the earth is mainly looked at, and thought of, through the medium of a purer element. The happiest time is when the equinoxial gales are departed; but their fury may probably be called to mind by the sight of a few shattered boughs, whose leaves do not differ in colour from the faded foliage of the stately oaks from which these relics of the storm depend: all else speaks of tranquillity; – not a breath of air, no restlessness of insects, and not a moving object perceptible – except the clouds gliding in the depths of the lake, or the traveller passing along, an inverted image, whose motion seems governed by the quiet of a time, to which its archetype, the living person, is, perhaps, insensible: – or it may happen, that the figure of one of the larger birds, a raven or a heron, is crossing silently among the reflected clouds, while the voice of the real bird, from the element aloft, gently awakens in the spectator the recollection of appetites and instincts, pursuits and occupations, that deform and agitate the world, – yet have no power to prevent nature from putting on an aspect capable of satisfying the most intense cravings for the tranquil, the lovely, and the perfect, to which man, the noblest of her creatures, is subject.

Thus far, of climate, as influencing the feelings through its effect on the objects of sense. We may add, that whatever has been said upon the advantages derived to these scenes from a changeable atmosphere, would apply, perhaps still more forcibly, to their appearance under the varied solemnities of night. Milton, it will be remembered, has given a *clouded* moon to Paradise itself.[16] In the night-season also, the narrowness of the vales, and comparative smallness of the lakes, are especially adapted to bring surrounding objects home to the eye and to the heart. The stars, taking their stations above the hill-tops, are contemplated from a spot like the Abyssinian recess of Rasselas,[17] with much more touching interest than they are likely to excite when looked at from an open country with ordinary undulations: and it must be obvious, that it is the *bays* only of large lakes that can present such contrasts of light and shadow as those of smaller dimensions display from every quarter. A deep contracted valley, with diffused waters, such a valley and plains level and wide as those of Chaldea, are the two extremes in which the beauty of the heavens and their connexion with the earth are most sensibly felt. Nor do the advantages I have been speaking of imply here an exclusion of the aerial effects of distance. These are insured by the height of the mountains, and are found, even in the narrowest vales, where they lengthen in perspective, or act (if the expression may be used) as telescopes for the open country.

The subject would bear to be enlarged upon: but I will conclude this section with a night-scene suggested by the Vale of Keswick. The Fragment is well known; but it gratifies me to insert it, as the Writer was one of the first who led the way to a worthy admiration of this country.

> 'Now sunk the sun, now twilight sunk, and night
> Rode in her zenith; not a passing breeze
> Sigh'd to the grove, which in the midnight air
> Stood motionless, and in the peaceful floods
> Inverted hung: for now the billows slept
> Along the shore, nor heav'd the deep; but spread
> A shining mirror to the moon's pale orb,
> Which, dim and waning, o'er the shadowy cliffs,
> The solemn woods, and spiry mountain tops,
> Her glimmering faintness threw: now every eye,
> Oppress'd with toil, was drown'd in deep repose,
> Save that the unseen Shepherd in his watch,
> Propp'd on his crook, stood listening by the fold,
> And gaz'd the starry vault, and pendant moon;
> Nor voice, nor sound, broke on the deep serene;
> But the soft murmur of swift-gushing rills,
> Forth issuing from the mountain's distant steep,
> (Unheard till now, and now scarce heard) proclaim'd
> All things at rest, and imag'd the still voice
> Of quiet, whispering in the ear of night.'[18]

## SECTION SECOND
*Aspects of the Country, as Affected by its Inhabitants*

Hitherto I have chiefly spoken of the features by which nature has discriminated this country from others. I will now describe, in general terms, in what manner it is indebted to the hand of man. What I have to notice on this subject will emanate most easily and perspicuously from a description of the ancient and present inhabitants, their occupations, their condition of life, the distribution of landed property among them, and the tenure by which it is holden.

The reader will suffer me here to recall to his mind the shapes of the vallies, and their position with respect to each other, and the forms and substance of the intervening mountains. He will people the vallies with lakes and rivers: the coves and sides of the mountains with pools and torrents; and will bound half of the circle which we have contemplated by the sands of the sea, or by the sea itself. He will conceive that, from the point upon which he stood, he looks down upon this scene before the country had been penetrated by any inhabitants: – to vary his sensations, and to break in upon their stillness, he will form to himself an image of the tides visiting and revisiting the friths, the main sea dashing against the bolder shore, the rivers pursuing their course to be lost in the mighty mass of waters. He may see or hear in fancy the winds sweeping over the lakes, or piping with a loud voice among the mountain peaks; and, lastly, may think of the primeval woods shedding and renewing their leaves with no human eye to notice, or human heart to regret or welcome the change. 'When the first settlers entered this region (says an animated writer) they found it overspread with wood; forest trees, the fir, the oak, the ash, and the birch had skirted the fells, tufted the hills, and shaded the vallies, through centuries of silent solitude; the birds and beasts of prey reigned over the meeker species; and the *bellum inter omnia* maintained the balance of nature in the empire of beasts.'[19]

Such was the state and appearance of this region when the aboriginal colonists of the Celtic tribes were first driven or drawn towards it, and became joint tenants with the wolf, the boar, the wild bull, the red deer, and the leigh, a gigantic species of deer which has been long extinct; while the inaccessible crags were occupied by the falcon, the raven, and the eagle. The inner parts were too secluded, and of too little value, to participate much of the benefit of Roman manners; and though these conquerors encouraged the Britons to the improvement of their lands in the plain country of Furness and Cumberland, they seem to have had little connexion with the mountains, except for military purposes, or in subservience to the profit they drew from the mines.

When the Romans retired from Great Britain, it is well known that these mountain-fastnesses furnished a protection to some unsubdued Britons, long after the more accessible and more fertile districts had been seized by the Saxon or Danish invader. A few, though distinct, traces of Roman forts or camps, as at Ambleside, and upon Dunmallet, and a few circles of rude stones attributed to the Druids,[20] are the only vestiges that remain upon the surface of the country, of these ancient occupants; and, as the Saxons and Danes, who succeeded to the possession of the villages and hamlets which had been established by the Britons, seem at first to have confined themselves to the open country, — we may descend at once to times long posterior to the conquest by the Normans, when their feudal polity was regularly established. We may easily conceive that these narrow dales and mountain sides, choaked up as they must have been with wood, lying out of the way of communication with other parts of the Island, and upon the edge of a hostile kingdom, could have little attraction for the high-born and powerful; especially as the more open parts of the country furnished positions for castles and houses of defence, sufficient to repel any of those sudden attacks, which, in the then rude state of military knowledge, could be made upon them. Accordingly, the more retired regions (and to such I am now confining myself) must have been neglected or shunned even by the persons whose baronial or signorial rights extended over them, and left, doubtless, partly as a place of refuge for outlaws and robbers, and partly granted out for the more settled habitation of a few vassals following the employment of shepherds or woodlanders. Hence these lakes and inner vallies are unadorned by any remains of ancient grandeur, castles, or monastic edifices, which are only found upon the skirts of the country, as Furness Abbey, Calder Abbey, the Priory of Lannercost, Gleaston Castle, — long ago a residence of the Flemings, — and the numerous ancient castles of the Cliffords, the Lucys, and the Dacres. On the southern side of these mountains, (especially in that part known by the name of Furness Fells, which is more remote from the borders,) the state of society would necessarily be more settled; though it also was fashioned, not a little, by its neighbourhood to a hostile kingdom. We will, therefore, give a sketch of the economy of the Abbots in the distribution of lands among their tenants, as similar plans were doubtless adopted by other Lords, and as the consequences have affected the face of the country materially to the present day, being, in fact, one of the principal causes which give it such a striking superiority, in beauty and interest, over all other parts of the island.

'When the Abbots of Furness,' says an author before cited, 'enfranchised their villains, and raised them to the dignity of customary tenants, the lands, which they had cultivated for their lord, were divided into whole tenements; each of which, besides the customary annual rent, was charged with the obligation of having in readiness a man completely armed for the king's service on the borders, or elsewhere; each of these whole tenements was again subdivided into four equal parts; each villain had one; and the party tenant contributed his share to the support of the man of arms, and of other burdens. These divisions were not properly distinguished; the land remained mixed; each tenant had a share through all the arable and meadowland, and common of pasture over all the wastes. These subtenements were judged sufficient for the support of so many families; and no further division was permitted. These divisions and subdivisions were convenient at the time for which they were calculated: the land, so parcelled out, was of necessity more attended to, and the industry greater, when more persons were to be supported by the produce of it. The frontier of the kingdom, within which Furness was considered, was in a constant state of attack and defence; more hands, therefore, were necessary to guard the coast, to repel an invasion from Scotland, or make reprisals on the hostile neighbour. The dividing the lands in such manner as has been shown, increased the number of inhabitants, and kept them at home till called for: and, the land being mixed, and the several tenants united in equipping the plough, the absence of the fourth man was no prejudice to the cultivation of his land, which was committed to the care of three.

'While the villains of Low Furness were thus distributed over the land, and employed in agriculture; those of High Furness were charged with the care of flocks and herds, to protect them from the wolves which lurked in the thickets, and in winter to browze them with the tender sprouts of hollies and ash. This custom was not till lately discontinued in High Furness; and holly-trees were carefully preserved for that purpose when all other wood was cleared off; large tracts of common being so covered with these trees, as to have the appearance of a forest of hollies. At the Shepherd's call, the flocks surrounded the holly-bush, and received the croppings at his hand, which they greedily nibbled up, bleating for more. The Abbots of Furness enfranchised these pastoral vassals, and permitted them to enclose *quillets* to their houses, for which they paid encroachment rent.' – West's *Antiquities of Furness*.[21]

However desirable, for the purposes of defence, a numerous population might be, it was not possible to make at once the same numerous allotments among the untilled vallies, and upon the sides of the mountains, as had been made in the cultivated plains. The enfranchised shepherd, or woodlander, having chosen there his place of residence, builds it of sods, or of the mountain-stone, and, with the permission of his lord, encloses, like Robinson Crusoe,[22] a small croft or two immediately at his door for such animals as he wishes to protect. Others are happy to imitate his example, and avail themselves of the same privileges: and thus a population, mainly of Danish or Norse origin, as the dialect indicates, crept on towards the more secluded parts of the vallies. Chapels, daughters of some distant mother church, are first erected in the more open and fertile vales, as those of Bowness and Grasmere, offsets of Kendal: which again, after a period, as the settled population increases, become mother-churches to smaller edifices, planted, at length, in almost every dale throughout the country. The inclosures, formed by the tenantry, are for a long time confined to the home-steads; and the arable and meadow land of the vales is possessed in common field; the several portions being marked out by stones, bushes, or trees: which portions, where the custom has survived, to this day are called *dales*, from the word *deylen*, to distribute; but, while the valley was thus lying open, enclosures seem to have taken place upon the sides of the mountains;

because the land there was not intermixed, and was of little comparative value; and, therefore, small opposition would be made to its
being appropriated by those to whose habitations it was contiguous.
Hence the singular appearance which the sides of many of these
mountains exhibit, intersected, as they are, almost to the summit,
with stone walls. When first erected, these stone fences must have
little disfigured the face of the country; as part of the lines would
every where be hidden by the quantity of native wood then remaining; and the lines would also be broken (as they still are) by the rocks
which interrupt and vary their course. In the meadows, and in those
parts of the lower grounds where the soil has not been sufficiently
drained, and could not afford a stable foundation, there, when the
increasing value of land, and the inconvenience suffered from intermixed plots of ground in common field, had induced each inhabitant
to enclose his own, they were compelled to make the fences of
alders, willows, and other trees. These, where the native wood had
disappeared, have frequently enriched the vallies with a sylvan appearance; while the intricate intermixture of property has given to
the fences a graceful irregularity, which, where large properties are
prevalent, and large capitals employed in agriculture, is unknown.
This sylvan appearance is heightened by the number of ash-trees
planted in rows along the quick fences, and along the walls, for the
purpose of browzing the cattle at the approach of winter. The
branches are lopped off and strewn upon the pastures; and when the
cattle have stripped them of the leaves, they are used for repairing
the hedges or for fuel.

We have thus seen a numerous body of Dalesmen creeping into
the possession of their home-steads, their little crofts, their mountain-
enclosures; and, finally, the whole vale is visibly divided; except,
perhaps, here and there some marshy ground, which, till fully
drained, would not repay the trouble of enclosing. But these last
partitions do not seem to have been general, till long after the paci-
fication of the Borders, by the union of the two crowns:[23] when the
cause, which had first determined the distribution of land into such
small parcels, had not only ceased, – but likewise a general im-

provement had taken place in the country, with a correspondent rise in the value of its produce. From the time of the union, it is certain that this species of feudal population must rapidly have diminished. That it was formerly much more numerous than it is at present, is evident from the multitude of tenements (I do not mean houses, but small divisions of land) which belonged formerly each to a several proprietor, and for which separate fines are paid to the man-orial lord at this day. These are often in the proportion of four to one of the present occupants. 'Sir Launcelot Threlkeld, who lived in the reign of Henry VII., was wont to say, he had three noble houses, one for pleasure, Crosby, in Westmoreland, where he had a park full of deer; one for profit and warmth, wherein to reside in winter, namely, Yanwith, nigh Penrith; and the third, Threlkeld, (on the edge of the vale of Keswick), well stocked with tenants to go with him to the wars.'[24] But, as I have said, from the union of the two crowns, this numerous vassalage (their services not being wanted) would rapidly diminish; various tenements would be united in one possessor; and the aboriginal houses, probably little better than hovels, like the kraels of savages, or the huts of the Highlanders of Scotland, would fall into decay, and the places of many be supplied by substantial and comfort-able buildings, a majority of which remain to this day scattered over the vallies, and are often the only dwellings found in them.

From the time of the erection of these houses, till within the last sixty years, the state of society, though no doubt slowly and gradually improving, underwent no material change. Corn was grown in these vales (through which no carriage-road had yet been made) sufficient upon each estate to furnish bread for each family, and no more: notwithstanding the union of several tenements, the possessions of each inhabitant still being small, in the same field was seen an intermixture of different crops; and the plough was interrupted by little rocks, mostly overgrown with wood, or by spongy places, which the tillers of the soil had neither leisure nor capital to convert into firm land. The storms and moisture of the climate induced them to sprinkle their upland property with outhouses of native stone, as places of shelter for their sheep, where, in tempestuous weather, food was distributed to them. Every family spun from its own flock the wool with which it was clothed; a weaver was here and there found among them; and the rest of their wants was supplied by the produce of the yarn, which they carded and spun in their own houses, and carried to market, either under their arms, or more frequently on pack-horses, a small train taking their way weekly down the valley or over the mountains to the most commodious town. They had, as I have said, their rural chapel, and of course their minister, in clothing or in manner of life, in no respect differing from themselves, except on the Sabbath-day; this was the sole distinguished individual among them; every thing else, person and possession, exhibited a perfect equality, a community of shepherds and agriculturists, proprietors, for the most part, of the lands which they occupied and cultivated.

While the process above detailed was going on, the native forest must have been every where receding; but trees were planted for the sustenance of the flocks in winter, – such was then the rude state of agriculture; and, for the same cause, it was necessary that care should be taken of some part of the growth of the native woods. Accordingly, in Queen Elizabeth's time, this was so strongly felt, that a petition was made to the Crown, praying, 'that the Blomaries in High Furness might be abolished, on account of the quantity of wood which was consumed in them for the use of the mines, to the great detriment of the cattle.' But this same cause, about a hundred years after, produced effects directly contrary to those which had been deprecated. The re-establishment, at that period, of furnaces upon a large scale, made it the interest of the people to convert the steeper and more stony of the enclosures, sprinkled over with remains of the native forest, into close woods, which, when cattle and sheep were excluded, rapidly sowed and thickened themselves. The reader's attention has been directed to the cause by which tufts of wood, pasturage, meadow, and arable land, with its various produce, are intricately intermingled in the same field; and he will now see, in like manner, how enclosures entirely of wood, and those of cultivated ground, are blended all over the country under a law of similar wildness.

An historic detail has thus been given of the manner in which the hand of man has acted upon the surface of the inner regions of this mountainous country, as incorporated with and subservient to the powers and processes of nature. We will now take a view of the same agency – acting, within narrower bounds, for the production of the few works of art and accommodations of life which, in so simple a state of society, could be necessary. These are merely habitations of man and coverts for beasts, roads and bridges, and places of worship.

And to begin with the COTTAGES. They are scattered over the vallies, and under the hill sides, and on the rocks; and, even to this day, in the more retired dales, without any intrusion of more assuming buildings;

> Cluster'd like stars some few, but single most,
> And lurking dimly in their shy retreats,
> Or glancing on each other cheerful looks,
> Like separated stars with clouds between.

MS.[25]

The dwelling-houses, and contiguous outhouses, are, in many instances, of the colour of the native rock, out of which they have been built; but, frequently the Dwelling or Fire-house, as it is ordinarily called, has been distinguished from the barn or byer by rough-cast and white wash, which, as the inhabitants are not hasty in renewing it, in a few years acquires, by the influence of weather, a tint at once sober and variegated. As these houses have been, from father to son, inhabited by persons engaged in the same occupations, yet necessarily with changes in their circumstances, they have received without incongruity additions and accommodations adapted to the needs of each successive occupant, who, being for the most part proprietor, was at liberty to follow his own fancy: so that these humble dwellings remind the contemplative spectator of a production of nature, and may (using a strong expression) rather be said to have grown than to have been erected; – to have risen, by an instinct of their own, out of the native rock – so little is there in them of formality, such is their wildness and beauty. Among the numerous recesses and projections

39

in the walls and in the different stages of their roofs, are seen bold and harmonious effects of contrasted sunshine and shadow. It is a favourable circumstance, that the strong winds, which sweep down the vallies, induced the inhabitants, at a time when the materials for building were easily procured, to furnish many of these dwellings with substantial porches; and such as have not this defence, are seldom unprovided with a projection of two large slates over their thresholds. Nor will the singular beauty of the chimneys escape the eye of the attentive traveller. Sometimes a low chimney, almost upon a level with the roof, is overlaid with a slate, supported upon four slender pillars, to prevent the wind from driving the smoke down the chimney. Others are of a quadrangular shape, rising one or two feet above the roof; which low square is often surmounted by a tall cylinder, giving to the cottage chimney the most beautiful shape in which it is ever seen. Nor will it be too fanciful or refined to remark, that there is a pleasing harmony between a tall chimney of this circular form, and the living column of smoke, ascending from it through the still air. These dwellings, mostly built, as has been said, of rough unhewn stone, are roofed with slates, which were rudely taken from the quarry before the present art of splitting them was understood, and are, therefore, rough and uneven in their surface, so that both the coverings and sides of the houses have furnished places of rest for the seeds of lichens, mosses, ferns, and flowers. Hence buildings, which in their very form call to mind the processes of nature, do thus, clothed in part with a vegetable garb, appear to be received into the bosom of the living principle of things, as it acts and exists among the woods and fields; and, by their colour and their shape, affectingly direct the thoughts to that tranquil course of nature and simplicity, along which the humble-minded inhabitants have, through so many generations, been led. Add the little garden with its shed for bee-hives, its small bed of pot-herbs, and its borders and patches of flowers for Sunday posies, with sometimes a choice few too much prized to be plucked; an orchard of proportioned size; a cheese-press, often supported by some tree near the door; a cluster of embowering sycamores for summer shade; with a tall fir, through which the winds sing when other trees are leafless; the little rill or household spout murmuring in all seasons; – combine these incidents and images together, and you have the representative idea of a mountain-cottage in this country so beautifully formed in itself, and so richly adorned by the hand of nature.

Till within the last sixty years there was no communication between any of these vales by carriage-roads; all bulky articles were transported on pack-horses. Owing, however, to the population not being concentrated in villages, but scattered, the vallies themselves were intersected as now by innumerable lanes and path-ways leading from house to house and from field to field. These lanes, where they are fenced by stone walls, are mostly bordered with ashes, hazels, wild roses, and beds of tall fern, at their base; while the walls themselves, if old, are overspread with mosses, small ferns, wild strawberries, the geranium, and lichens: and, if the wall happen to rest against a bank of earth, it is sometimes almost wholly concealed by a rich facing of stone-fern. It is a great advantage to a traveller or resident, that these numerous lanes and paths, if he be a zealous admirer of nature, will lead him on into all the recesses of the country, so that the hidden treasures of its landscapes may, by an ever-ready guide, be laid open to his eyes.

Likewise to the smallness of the several properties is owing the great number of bridges over the brooks and torrents, and the daring and graceful neglect of danger or accommodation with which so many of them are constructed, the rudeness of the forms of some, and their endless variety. But, when I speak of this rudeness, I must at the same time add, that many of these structures are in themselves models of elegance, as if they had been formed upon principles of the most thoughtful architecture. It is to be regretted that these monuments of the skill of our ancestors, and of that happy instinct by which consummate beauty was produced, are disappearing fast; but sufficient specimens remain [26] to give a high gratification to the man of genuine taste. Travellers who may not have been accustomed to pay attention to things so inobtrusive, will excuse me if I point out the proportion between the span and elevation of the arch, the lightness of the parapet, and the graceful manner in which its curve follows faithfully that of the arch.

Upon this subject I have nothing further to notice, except the PLACES OF WORSHIP, which have mostly a little school-house adjoining.[27] The architecture of these churches and chapels, where they have not been recently rebuilt or modernised, is of a style not less appropriate and admirable than that of the dwelling-houses and other structures. How sacred the spirit by which our forefathers were directed! The *religio loci*[28] is no where violated by these unstinted, yet unpretending, works of human hands. They exhibit generally a well-proportioned oblong, with a suitable porch, in some instances a steeple tower, and in others nothing more than a small belfry, in which one or two bells hang visibly. But these objects, though pleasing in their forms, must necessarily, more than others in rural scenery, derive their interest from the sentiments of piety and reverence for the modest virtues and simple manners of humble life with which they may be contemplated. A man must be very insensible who would not be touched with pleasure at the sight of the chapel of Buttermere, so strikingly expressing, by its diminutive size, how small must be the congregation there assembled, as it were, like one family; and proclaiming at the same time to the passenger, in connection with the surrounding mountains, the depth of that seclusion in which the people live, that has rendered necessary the building of a separate place of worship for so few. A patriot, calling to mind the images of the stately fabrics of Canterbury, York, or Westminster, will find a heart-felt satisfaction in presence of this lowly pile, as a monument of the wise institutions of our country, and as evidence of the all-pervading and paternal care of that venerable Establishment, of which it is, perhaps, the humblest daughter. The edifice is scarcely larger than many of the single stones or fragments of rock which are scattered near it.

We have thus far confined our observations on this division of the subject, to that part of these Dales which runs up far into the mountains.

As we descend towards the open country, we meet with halls and mansions, many of which have been places of defence against the incursions of the Scottish borderers; and they not unfrequently retain their towers and battlements. To these houses, parks are sometimes attached, and to their successive proprietors we chiefly owe whatever ornament is still left to the country of majestic timber. Through the open parts of the vales are scattered, also, houses of a middle rank between the pastoral cottage and the old hall residence of the knight or esquire. Such houses differ much from the rugged cottages before described, and are generally graced with a little court or garden in front, where may yet be seen specimens of those fantastic and quaint figures which our ancestors were fond of shaping out in yew-tree, holly, or box-wood. The passenger will sometimes smile at such elaborate display of petty art, while the house does not deign to look upon the natural beauty or the sublimity which its situation almost unavoidably commands.

Thus has been given a faithful description, the minuteness of which the reader will pardon, of the face of this country as it was, and had been through centuries, till within the last sixty years. Towards the head of these Dales was found a perfect Republic of Shepherds and Agriculturists, among whom the plough of each man was confined to the maintenance of his own family, or to the occasional accommodation of his neighbour.[29] Two or three cows furnished each family with milk and cheese. The chapel was the only edifice that presided over these dwellings, the supreme head of this pure Commonwealth; the members of which existed in the midst of a powerful empire, like an ideal society or an organized community, whose constitution had been imposed and regulated by the mountains which protected it. Neither high-born nobleman, knight, nor esquire, was here; but many of these humble sons of the hills had a consciousness that the land, which they walked over and tilled, had for more than five hundred years been possessed by men of their name and blood; and venerable was the transition, when a curious traveller, descending from the heart of the mountains, had come to some ancient manorial residence in the more open parts of the Vales, which, through the rights attached to its proprietor, connected the almost visionary mountain republic he had been contemplating with the substantial frame of society as existing in the laws and constitution of a mighty empire.

## SECTION THIRD
*Changes, and Rules of Taste for Preventing Their Bad Effects*

Such, as hath been said, was the appearance of things till within the last sixty years. A practice, denominated Ornamental Gardening, was at that time becoming prevalent over England. In union with an admiration of this art, and in some instances in opposition to it, had been generated a relish for select parts of natural scenery: and Travellers, instead of confining their observations to Towns, Manufactories, or Mines, began (a thing till then unheard of) to wander over the island in search of sequestered spots, distinguished as they might accidently have learned, for the sublimity or beauty of the forms of Nature there to be seen. – Dr Brown, the celebrated Author of the Estimate of the Manners and Principles of the Times, published a letter to a friend, in which the attractions of the Vale of Keswick were delineated with a powerful pencil, and the feeling of a genuine Enthusiast.[30] Gray, the Poet, followed: he died soon after his forlorn and melancholy pilgrimage to the Vale of Keswick, and the record left behind him of what he had seen and felt in this journey, excited that pensive interest with which the human mind is ever disposed to listen to the farewell words of a man of genius. The journal of Gray feelingly showed how the gloom of ill health and low spirits had been irradiated by objects, which the Author's powers of mind enabled him to describe with distinctness and unaffected simplicity. Every reader of this journal must have been impressed with the words which conclude his notice of the Vale of Grasmere: – 'Not a single red tile, no flaring gentleman's house or garden-wall, breaks in upon the repose of this little unsuspected paradise; but all is peace, rusticity, and happy poverty, in its neatest and most becoming attire.'[31]

What is here so justly said of Grasmere applied almost equally to all its sister Vales. It was well for the undisturbed pleasure of the Poet that he had no forebodings of the change which was soon to take place; and it might have been hoped that these words, indicating how much the charm of what *was*, depended upon what was *not*, would of themselves have preserved the ancient franchises of this and other kindred mountain retirements from trespass; or (shall I dare to say?) would have secured scenes so consecrated from profanation. The lakes had now become celebrated; visitors flocked hither from all parts of England; the fancies of some were smitten so deeply, that they became settlers; and the Islands of Derwentwater and Winandermere, as they offered the strongest temptation, were the first places seized upon, and were instantly defaced by the intrusion.

The venerable wood that had grown for centuries round the small house called St Herbert's Hermitage, had indeed some years before been felled by its native proprietor, and the whole island planted anew with Scotch firs, left to spindle up by each other's side – a melancholy phalanx, defying the power of the winds, and disregarding the regret of the spectator, who might otherwise have cheated himself into a belief, that some of the decayed remains of those oaks, the place of which was in this manner usurped, had been planted by the Hermit's own hand. This sainted spot, however, suffered comparatively little injury. At the bidding of an alien improver, the Hind's Cottage, upon Vicar's island, in the same lake, with its embowering sycamores and cattle-shed, disappeared from the corner where they stood; and right in the middle, and upon the precise point of the island's highest elevation, rose a tall square habitation, with four sides exposed, like an astronomer's observatory, or a warren-house reared upon an eminence for the detection of depredators, or, like the temple of Oeolus, where all the winds pay him obeisance. Round this novel structure, but at a respectful distance, platoons of firs were stationed, as if to protect their commander when weather and time should somewhat have shattered his strength. Within the narrow limits of this island were typified also the state and strength of a kingdom, and its religion as it had been, and was, – for neither was the druidical circle uncreated, nor the church of the present establishment; nor the stately pier, emblem of commerce and navigation; nor the fort to deal out thunder upon the approaching invader. The taste of a succeeding proprietor rectified the mistakes as far as was practicable, and has ridded the spot of its puerilities. The church, after having been docked of its steeple, is applied, both ostensibly and really, to the purpose for which the body of the pile was actually erected, namely, a boat-house; the fort is demolished; and, without indignation on the part of the spirits of the ancient Druids who officiated at the circle upon the opposite hill, the mimic arrangement of stones, with its *sanctum sanctorum*, has been swept away.

The present instance has been singled out, extravagant as it is, because, unquestionably, this beautiful country has, in numerous other places, suffered from the same spirit, though not clothed exactly in the same form, nor active in an equal degree. It will be sufficient here to utter a regret for the changes that have been made upon the principal Island at Winandermere, and in its neighbourhood. What could be more unfortunate than the taste that suggested the paring of the shores, and surrounding with an embankment this spot of ground, the natural shape of which was so beautiful! An artificial appearance has thus been given to the whole, while infinite varieties of minute beauty have been destroyed. Could not the margin of this noble island be given back to nature? Winds and waves work with a careless and graceful hand: and, should they in some places carry away a portion of the soil, the trifling loss would be amply compensated by the additional spirit, dignity, and loveliness, which these agents and the other powers of nature would soon communicate to what was left behind. As to the larch-plantations upon the main shore, – they who remember the original appearance of the rocky steeps, scattered over with native hollies and ash-trees, will be prepared to agree with what I shall have to say hereafter upon plantations [32] in general.

But, in truth, no one can now travel through the more frequented tracts, without being offended, at almost every turn, by an introduction of discordant objects, disturbing that peaceful harmony of form and colour, which had been through a long lapse of ages most happily preserved.

All gross transgressions of this kind originate, doubtless, in a feeling natural and honourable to the human mind, viz. the pleasure which it receives from distinct ideas, and from the perception of order, regularity, and contrivance. Now, unpractised minds receive these impressions only from objects that are divided from each other by strong lines of demarcation; hence the delight with which such minds are smitten by formality and harsh contrast. But I would beg of those who are eager to create the means of such gratification, first carefully to study what already exists; and they will find, in a country so lavishly gifted by nature, an abundant variety of forms marked out with a precision that will satisfy their desires. Moreover, a new habit of pleasure will be formed opposite to this, arising out of the perception of the fine gradations by which in nature one thing passes away into another, and the boundaries that constitute individuality disappear in one instance only to be revived elsewhere under a more alluring form. The hill of Dunmallet, at the foot of Ulswater, was once divided into different portions, by avenues of fir-trees, with a green and almost perpendicular lane descending down the steep hill through each avenue; – contrast this quaint appearance with the image of the same hill overgrown with self-planted wood, – each tree springing up in the situation best suited to its kind, and with that shape which the situation constrained or suffered it to take. What endless melting and playing into each other of forms and colours does the one offer to a mind at once attentive and active; and how insipid and lifeless, compared with it, appear those parts of the former exhibition with which a child, a peasant perhaps, or a citizen unfamiliar with natural imagery, would have been most delighted!

The disfigurement which this country has undergone, has not, however, proceeded wholly from the common feelings of human nature which have been referred to as the primary sources of bad taste in rural imagery; another cause must be added, that has chiefly shown itself in its effect upon buildings. I mean a warping of the natural mind occasioned by a consciousness that, this country being an object of general admiration, every new house would be looked at and commented upon either for approbation or censure. Hence all the deformity and ungracefulness that ever pursue the steps of constraint or affectation. Persons, who in Leicestershire or Northamptonshire would probably have built a modest dwelling like those of their sensible neighbours, have been turned out of their course; and, acting a part, no wonder if, having had little experience, they act it ill. The craving for prospect, also, which is immoderate, particularly in new settlers, has rendered it impossible that buildings, whatever might have been their architecture, should in most instances be ornamental to the landscape; rising as they do from the summits of naked hills in staring contrast to the snugness and privacy of the ancient houses.

No man is to be condemned for a desire to decorate his residence and possessions; feeling a disposition to applaud such an endeavour, I would show how the end may be best attained. The rule is simple; with respect to grounds – work, where you can, in the spirit of nature, with an invisible hand of art. Planting, and a removal of wood, may thus, and thus only, be carried on with good effect; and the like may be said of building, if Antiquity, who may be styled the co-partner and sister of Nature, be not denied the respect to which she is entitled. I have already spoken of the beautiful forms of the ancient mansions of this country, and of the happy manner in which they harmonise with the forms of nature. Why cannot such be taken as a model, and modern internal convenience be confined within their external grace and dignity. Expense to be avoided, or difficulties to be overcome, may prevent a close adherence to this model; still, however, it might be followed to a certain degree in the style of architecture and in the choice of situation, if the thirst for prospect were mitigated by those considerations of comfort, shelter, and convenience, which used to be chiefly sought after. But should an aversion to old fashions unfortunately exist, accompanied with a desire to transplant into the cold and stormy North, the elegancies of a villa formed upon a model taken from countries with a milder climate, I will adduce a passage from an English poet, the divine Spenser, which will show in what manner such a plan may be realised without injury to the native beauty of these scenes.

> 'Into that forest farre they thence him led,
> Where was their dwelling in a pleasant glade
> With MOUNTAINS round about environed,
> And MIGHTY WOODS which did the valley shade,

> And like a stately theatre it made,
> Spreading itself into a spacious plaine;
> And in the midst a little river plaide
> Emongst the pumy stones which seem'd to 'plaine
> With gentle murmure that his course they did restraine.
>
> Beside the same a dainty place there lay,
> Planted with mirtle trees and laurels green,
> In which the birds sang many a lovely lay
> Of God's high praise, and of their sweet loves teene,
> As it an earthly paradise had beene;
> In whose *enclosed shadow* there was pight
> A fair pavilion, *scarcely to be seen,*
> The which was all within most richly dight,
> That greatest princes living it mote well delight.' [33]

Houses or mansions suited to a mountainous region, should be 'not obvious, not obtrusive, but retired;' [34] and the reasons for this rule, though they have been little adverted to, are evident. Mountainous countries, more frequently and forcibly than others, remind us of the power of the elements, as manifested in winds, snows, and torrents, and accordingly make the notion of exposure very unpleasing; while shelter and comfort are in proportion necessary and acceptable. Far-winding vallies difficult of access, and the feelings of simplicity habitually connected with mountain retirements, prompt us to turn from ostentation as a thing there eminently unnatural and out of place. A mansion, amid such scenes, can never have sufficient dignity or interest to become principal in the landscape, and to render the mountains, lakes, or torrents, by which it may be surrounded, a subordinate part of the view. It is, I grant, easy to conceive, that an ancient castellated building, hanging over a precipice or raised upon an island, or the peninsula of a lake, like that of Kilchurn Castle, upon Loch Awe, may not want, whether deserted or inhabited, sufficient majesty to preside for a moment in the spectator's thoughts over the high mountains among which it is embosomed; but its titles are from antiquity – a power readily submitted to upon occasion as the viceregent of Nature: it is respected, as having owed its existence to the necessities of things, as a monument of security in times of disturbance and danger long passed away, – as a record of the pomp and violence of passion, and a symbol of the wisdom of law; – it bears a countenance of authority, which is not impaired by decay.

> 'Child of loud-throated war, the mountain-stream
> Roars in thy hearing; but thy hour of rest
> Is come, and thou art silent in thy age!' [35]

To such honours a modern edifice can lay no claim; and the puny efforts of elegance appear contemptible, when, in such situations, they are obtruded in rivalship with the sublimities of Nature. But, towards the verge of a district like this of which we are treating, where the mountains subside into hills of moderate elevation, or in an undulating or flat country, a gentleman's mansion may, with propriety, become a principal feature in the landscape; and, itself being a work of art, works and traces of artificial ornament may, without censure, be extended around it, as they will be referred to the common centre, the house; the right of which to impress within certain limits a character of obvious ornament will not be denied, where no commanding forms of nature dispute it, or set it aside. Now, to a want of the perception of this difference, and to the causes before assigned, may chiefly be attributed the disfigurement which the Country of the Lakes has undergone, from persons who have built, demolished, and planted, with full confidence, that every change and addition was or would become an improvement.

The principle that ought to determine the position, apparent size, and architecture of a house, viz. that it should be so constructed, and (if large) so much of it hidden, as to admit of its being gently incorporated into the scenery of nature – should also determine its colour. Sir Joshua Reynolds used to say, 'If you would fix upon the best colour for your house, turn up a stone, or pluck up a handful of grass by the roots, and see what is the colour of the soil where the house is to stand, and let that be your choice.' [36] Of course, this precept given in conversation, could not have been meant to be taken literally. For example, in Low Furness, where the soil, from its strong impregnation with iron, is universally of a deep red, if this rule were strictly followed, the house also must be of a glaring red; in other places it must be of a sullen black; which would only be adding annoyance to annoyance. The rule, however, as a general guide, is good; and, in agricultural districts, where large tracts of soil are laid bare by the plough, particularly if (the face of the country being undulating) they are held up to view, this rule, though not to be implicitly adhered to, should never be lost sight of; – the colour of the house ought, if possible, to have a cast or shade of the colour of the soil. The principle is, that the house must harmonise with the surrounding landscape: accordingly, in mountainous countries, with still more confidence may it be said, 'look at the rocks and those parts of the mountains where the soil is visible, and they will furnish a safe direction.' Nevertheless, it will often happen that the rocks may bear so large a proportion to the rest of the landscape, and may be of such a tone of colour, that the rule may not admit, even here, of being implicitly followed. For instance, the chief defect in the colouring of the Country of the Lakes (which is most strongly felt in the summer season) is an over-prevalence of a bluish tint, which the green of the herbage, the fern, and the woods, does not sufficiently counteract. If a house, therefore, should stand where this defect prevails, I have no hesitation in saying, that the colour of the neighbouring rocks would not be the best that could be chosen. A tint ought to be introduced approaching nearer to those which, in the technical language of painters, are called *warm*: this, if happily selected, would not disturb, but would animate the landscape. How often do we see this exemplified upon a small scale by the native cottages, in cases where the glare of white-wash has been subdued by time and enriched by weather-stains! No harshness is then seen; but one of these cottages, thus coloured, will often form a central point to a landscape by which the whole shall be connected, and an influence of pleasure diffused over all the objects that compose the picture. But where the cold blue tint of the rocks is enriched by the iron tinge, the colour cannot be too closely imitated; and it will be produced of itself by the stones hewn from the adjoining quarry, and by the mortar, which may be tempered with the most gravelly part of the soil. The pure blue gravel, from the bed of the river, is, however, more suitable to the mason's purpose, who will probably insist also that the house must be covered with rough-cast, otherwise it cannot be kept dry; if this advice be taken, the builder of taste will set about contriving such means as may enable him to come the nearest to the effect aimed at.

The supposed necessity of rough-cast to keep out rain in houses not built of hewn stone or brick, has tended greatly to injure English landscape, and the neighbourhood of these Lakes especially, by furnishing such apt occasion for whitening buildings. That white should be a favorite colour for rural residences is natural for many reasons. The mere aspect of cleanliness and neatness thus given, not only to an individual house, but, where the practice is general, to the whole face of the country, produces moral associations so powerful, that, in many minds, they take place of all others. But what has already been said upon the subject of cottages, must have convinced men of feeling and imagination, that a human dwelling of the humblest class may be rendered more deeply interesting to the affections, and far more pleasing to the eye, by other influences, than a sprightly tone of colour spread over its outside. I do not, however, mean to deny, that a small white building, embowered in trees, may, in some situations, be a delightful and animating object – in no way injurious to the landscape; but this only where it sparkles from the midst of a thick shade, and in rare and solitary instances; especially if the country be itself rich and pleasing, and abound with grand forms. On the sides of bleak and desolate moors, we are indeed thankful for the sight of white cottages and white houses plentifully scattered, where, without these, perhaps every thing would be cheerless: this is said, however, with hesitation, and with a wilful sacrifice of some higher enjoyments. But I have certainly seen such buildings glittering at sunrise, and in wandering lights, with no common pleasure. The continental traveller also will remember, that the convents hanging from the rocks of the Rhine, the Rhone, the Danube, or among the Appenines, or the mountains of Spain, are not looked at with less complacency when, as is often the case, they happen to be of a brilliant white. But this is perhaps owing, in no small degree, to the contrast of that lively colour with the gloom of monastic life, and to the general want of rural residences of smiling and attractive appearance, in those countries.

The objections to white, as a colour, in large spots or masses in landscape, especially in a mountainous country, are insurmountable. In nature, pure white is scarcely ever found but in small objects, such as flowers; or in those which are transitory, as the clouds, foam of rivers, and snow. Mr Gilpin, who notices this, has also recorded the just remark of Mr Locke, of N—, that white destroys the *gradations* of distance; and, therefore, an object of pure white can scarcely ever be managed with good effect in landscape-painting.[37] Five or six white houses, scattered over a valley, by their obtrusiveness, dot the surface, and divide it into triangles, or other mathematical figures, haunting the eye, and disturbing that repose which might otherwise be perfect. I have seen a single white house materially impair the majesty of a mountain; cutting away, by a harsh separation, the whole of its base, below the point on which the house stood. Thus was the apparent size of the mountain reduced, not by the interposition of another object in a manner to call forth the imagination, which will give more than the eye loses; but what had been abstracted in this case was left visible; and the mountain appeared to take its beginning, or to rise, from the line of the house, instead of its own natural base. But, if I may express my own individual feeling, it is after sunset, at the coming on of twilight, that white objects are most to be complained of. The solemnity and quietness of nature at that time are always marred, and often destroyed by them. When the ground is covered with snow, they are of course inoffensive; and in moonshine they are always pleasing – it is a tone of light with which they accord: and the dimness of the scene is enlivened by an object at once conspicuous and cheerful. I will conclude this subject with noticing, that the cold, slaty colour, which many persons, who have heard the white condemned, have adopted in its stead, must be disapproved of for the reason already given. The flaring yellow runs into the opposite extreme, and is still more censurable. Upon the whole, the safest colour, for general use, is something between a cream and a dust-colour, commonly called stone colour; – there are, among the Lakes, examples of this that need not be pointed out.[38]

The principle taken as our guide, viz. that the house should be so formed, and of such apparent size and colour, as to admit of its being gently incorporated with the works of nature, should also be applied to the management of the grounds and plantations, and is here more urgently needed; for it is from abuses in this department, far more even than from the introduction of exotics in architecture (if the phrase may be used), that this country has suffered. Larch and fir plantations have been spread, not merely with a view to profit, but in many instances for the sake of ornament. To those who plant for profit, and are thrusting every other tree out of the way, to make room for their favourite, the larch, I would utter first a regret, that they should have selected these lovely vales for their vegetable manufactory, when there is so much barren and irreclaimable land in the neighbouring moors, and in other parts of the island, which might have been had for this purpose at a far cheaper rate. And I will also beg leave to represent to them, that they ought not to be carried away by flattering promises from the speedy growth of this tree; because in rich soils and sheltered situations, the wood, though it thrives fast, is full of sap, and of little value; and is, likewise, very subject to ravage from the attacks of insects, and from blight. Accordingly, in Scotland, where planting is much better understood, and carried on upon an incomparably larger scale than among us, good soil and sheltered situations are appropriated to the oak, the ash, and other deciduous trees; and the larch is now generally confined to barren and exposed ground. There the plant, which is a hardy one, is of slower growth; much less liable to injury; and the timber is of better quality. But the circumstances of many permit, and their taste leads them, to plant with little regard to profit; and there are others, less wealthy, who have such a lively feeling of the native beauty of these scenes, that they are laudably not unwilling to make some sacrifices to heighten it. Both these classes of persons, I would entreat to enquire of themselves wherein that beauty which they admire consists. They would then see that, after the feeling has been gratified that prompts us to gather round our dwelling a few flowers and shrubs, which from the circumstance of their not being native, may, by their very looks, remind us that they owe their existence to our hands, and their prosperity to our care; they will see that, after this natural desire has been provided for, the course of all beyond has been predetermined by the spirit of the place. Before I proceed, I will remind those who are not satisfied with the restraint thus laid upon them, that they are liable to a charge of inconsistency, when they are so eager to change the face of that country, whose native attractions, by the act of erecting their habitations in it, they have so emphatically acknowledged. And surely there is not a single spot that would not have, if well managed, sufficient dignity to support itself, unaided by the productions of other climates, or by elaborate decorations which might be becoming elsewhere.

Having adverted to the feelings that justify the introduction of a few exotic plants, provided they be confined almost to the doors of the house, we may add, that a transition should be contrived, without abruptness, from these foreigners to the rest of the shrubs, which ought to be of the kinds scattered by Nature, through the woods – holly, broom, wild-rose, elder, dogberry, white and black thorn, &c. – either these only, or such as are carefully selected in consequence of their being united in form, and harmonising in colour with them, especially with respect to colour, when the tints are most diversified, as in autumn and spring. The various sorts of fruit-and-blossom-bearing trees usually found in orchards, to which may be added those of the woods, – namely, the wilding, black cherry tree, and wild cluster-cherry (here called heck-berry) – may be happily admitted as an intermediate link between the shrubs and the forest trees; which last ought almost entirely to be such as are natives of the country. Of the birch, one of the most beautiful of the native trees, it may be noticed, that, in dry and rocky situations, it outstrips even the larch, which many persons are tempted to plant merely on account of the speed of its growth. The Scotch fir is less attractive during its youth than any other plant; but, when full-grown, if it has had room to spread out its arms, it becomes a noble tree; and, by those who are disinterested enough to plant for posterity, it may be placed along with the sycamore near the house; for, from their massiveness, both these trees unite well with buildings, and in some situations with rocks also; having, in their forms and apparent substances, the effect of something intermediate betwixt the immoveableness and solidity of stone, and the spray and foliage of the lighter trees. If these general rules be just, what shall we say to whole acres of artificial shrubbery and exotic trees among rocks and dashing torrents, with their own wild wood in sight – where we have the whole contents of the nursery-man's catalogue jumbled together – colour at war with colour, and form with form? – among the most peaceful subjects of Nature's kingdom, everywhere discord, distraction, and bewilderment! But this deformity, bad as it is, is not so obtrusive as the small patches and large tracts of larch-plantations that are over-running the hill sides. To justify our condemnation of these, let us again recur to Nature. The process, by which she forms woods and forests, is as follows. Seeds are scattered indiscriminately by winds, brought by waters, and dropped by birds. They perish, or produce, according as the soil and situation upon which they fall are suited to them: and under the same dependence, the seedling or the sucker, if not cropped by animals, (which Nature is often careful to prevent by fencing it about with brambles or other prickly shrubs) thrives, and the tree grows, sometimes single, taking its own shape without constraint, but for the most part compelled to conform itself to some law imposed upon it by its neighbours. From low and sheltered places, vegetation travels upwards to the more exposed; and the young plants are protected, and to a certain degree fashioned, by those that have preceded them. The continuous mass of foliage which would be thus produced, is broken by rocks, or by glades or open places, where the browzing of animals has prevented the growth of wood. As vegetation ascends, the winds begin also to bear their part in moulding the forms of the trees; but, thus mutually protected, trees, though not of the hardiest kind, are enabled to climb high up the mountains. Gradually, however, by the quality of the ground, and by increasing exposure, a stop is put to their ascent; the hardy trees only are left: those also, by little and little, give way – and a wild and irregular boundary is established, graceful in its outline, and never contemplated without some feeling, more or less distinct, of the powers of Nature by which it is imposed.

Contrast the liberty that encourages, and the law that limits, this joint work of nature and time, with the disheartening necessities, restrictions, and disadvantages, under which the artificial planter must proceed, even he whom long observation and fine feeling have best qualified for his task. In the first place his trees, however well chosen and adapted to their several situations, must generally start all at the same time; and this necessity would of itself prevent that fine connection of parts, that sympathy and organization, if I may so express myself, which pervades the whole of a natural wood, and appears to the eye in its single trees, its masses of foliage, and their various colours, when they are held up to view on the side of a mountain; or when, spread over a valley, they are looked down upon from an eminence. It is therefore impossible, under any circumstances, for the artificial planter to rival the beauty of nature. But a moment's thought will show that, if ten thousand of this spiky tree, the larch, are stuck in at once upon the side of a hill, they can grow up into nothing but deformity; that, while they are suffered to stand, we shall look in vain for any of those appearances which are the chief sources of beauty in a natural wood.

It must be acknowledged that the larch, till it has outgrown the size of a shrub, shows, when looked at singly, some elegance in form and appearance, especially in spring, decorated, as it then is, by the pink tassels of its blossoms; but, as a tree, it is less than any other pleasing: its branches (for *boughs* it has none) have no variety in the youth of the tree, and little dignity, even when it attains its full growth; *leaves* it cannot be said to have, consequently neither affords shade nor shelter. In spring the larch becomes green long before the native trees; and its green is so peculiar and vivid, that, finding nothing to harmonize with it, wherever it comes forth, a disagreeable speck is produced. In summer, when all other trees are in their pride, it is of a dingy lifeless hue; in autumn of a spiritless unvaried yellow, and in winter it is still more lamentably distinguished from every other deciduous tree of the forest, for they seem only to sleep, but the larch appears absolutely dead. If an attempt be made to mingle thickets, or a certain proportion of other forest-trees, with the larch, its horizontal branches intolerantly cut them down as with a scythe, or force them to spindle up to keep pace with it. The terminating spike renders it impossible that the several trees, where planted in numbers, should ever blend together so as to form a mass or masses of wood. Add thousands to tens of thousands, and the appearance is still the same – a collection of separate individual trees, obstinately presenting themselves as such; and which, from whatever point they are looked at, if but seen, may be counted upon the fingers. Sunshine, or shadow, has little power to adorn the surface of such a wood; and the trees not carrying up their heads, the wind raises among them no majestic undulations. It is indeed true, that, in countries where the larch is a native, and where, without interruption, it may sweep from valley to valley, and from hill to hill, a sublime image may be produced by such a forest, in the same manner as by one composed of any other single tree, to the spreading of which no limits can be assigned. For sublimity will never be wanting, where the sense of innumerable multitude is lost in, and alternates with, that of intense unity; and to the ready perception of this effect, similarity and almost identity of individual form and monotony of colour contribute. But this feeling is confined to the native immeasurable forest; no artificial plantation can give it.

The foregoing observations will, I hope, (as nothing has been condemned or recommended without a substantial reason) have some influence upon those who plant for ornament merely. To such as plant for profit, I have already spoken. Let me then entreat that the native deciduous trees may be left in complete possession of the lower ground; and that plantations of larch, if introduced at all, may be confined to the highest and most barren tracts. Interposition of rocks would there break the dreary uniformity of which we have been complaining; and the winds would take hold of the trees, and imprint upon their shapes a wildness congenial to their situation.

Having determined what kinds of trees must be wholly rejected, or at least very sparingly used, by those who are unwilling to disfigure the country; and having shown what kinds ought to be chosen; I should have given, if my limits had not already been overstepped, a few practical rules for the manner in which trees ought to be disposed in planting. But to this subject I should attach little importance, if I could succeed in banishing such trees as introduce deformity, and could prevail upon the proprietor to confine himself, either to those found in the native woods, or to such as accord with them. This is, indeed, the main point; for, much as these scenes have been injured by what has been taken from them – buildings, trees, and woods, either through negligence, necessity, avarice, or caprice – it is not the removals, but the harsh *additions* that have been made, which are the worst grievance – a standing and unavoidable annoyance. Often have I felt this distinction, with mingled satisfaction and regret; for, if no positive deformity or discordance be substituted or superinduced, such is the benignity of Nature, that, take away from her beauty after beauty, and ornament after ornament, her appearance cannot be marred – the scars, if any be left, will gradually disappear before a healing spirit; and what remains will still be soothing and pleasing. –

> 'Many hearts deplored
> The fate of those old trees; and oft with pain
> The traveller at this day will stop and gaze
> On wrongs which nature scarcely seems to heed:
> For sheltered places, bosoms, nooks, and bays,
> And the pure mountains, and the gentle Tweed,
> And the green silent pastures, yet remain.'[39]

There are few ancient woods left in this part of England upon which such indiscriminate ravage as is here 'deplored', could now be committed. But, out of the numerous copses, fine woods might in time be raised, probably without sacrifice of profit, by leaving, at the periodical fellings, a due proportion of the healthiest trees to grow up into timber. – This plan has fortunately, in many instances, been adopted; and they, who have set the example, are entitled to

the thanks of all persons of taste. As to the management of planting with reasonable attention to ornament, let the images of nature
be your guide, and the whole secret lurks in a few words; thickets or
underwoods — single trees — trees clustered or in groups — groves —
unbroken woods, but with varied masses of foliage — glades — invisible
or winding boundaries — in rocky districts, a seemly proportion of
rock left wholly bare, and other parts half hidden — disagreeable
objects concealed, and formal lines broken — trees climbing up to the
horizon, and, in some places, ascending from its sharp edge, in which
they are rooted, with the whole body of the tree appearing to stand
in the clear sky — in other parts, woods surmounted by rocks utterly
bare and naked, which add the sense of height, as if vegetation could
not thither be carried, and impress a feeling of duration, power of
resistance, and security from change!

The author has been induced to speak thus at length, by a wish to
preserve the native beauty of this delightful district, because still
further changes in its appearance must inevitably follow, from the
change of inhabitants and owners which is rapidly taking place. —
About the same time that strangers began to be attracted to the
country, and to feel a desire to settle in it, the difficulty, that would
have stood in the way of their procuring situations, was lessened by
an unfortunate alteration in the circumstances of the native peasantry,
proceeding from a cause which then began to operate, and is now
felt in every house. The family of each man, whether *estatesman* or
farmer, formerly had a twofold support; first, the produce of his
lands and flocks; and, secondly, the profit drawn from the employment of the women and children, as manufacturers; spinning their
own wool in their own houses (work chiefly done in the winter
season), and carrying it to market for sale. Hence, however numerous
the children, the income of the family kept pace with its increase.
But, by the invention and universal application of machinery, this
second resource has been cut off; the gains being so far reduced, as
not to be sought after but by a few aged persons disabled from other
employment. Doubtless, the invention of machinery has not been to
these people a pure loss; for the profits arising from home-manufac-

tures operated as a strong temptation to choose that mode of labour in neglect of husbandry. They also participate in the general benefit which the island has derived from the increased value of the produce of land, brought about by the establishment of manufactories, and in the consequent quickening of agricultural industry. But this is far from making them amends; and now that home-manufactures are nearly done away, though the women and children might, at many seasons of the year, employ themselves with advantage in the fields beyond what they are accustomed to do, yet still all possible exertion in this way cannot be rationally expected from persons whose agricultural knowledge is so confined, and, above all, where there must necessarily be so small a capital. The consequence, then, is – that proprietors and farmers being no longer able to maintain themselves upon small farms, several are united in one, and the buildings go to decay, or are destroyed; and that the lands of the *estatesmen* being mortgaged, and the owners constrained to part with them, they fall into the hands of wealthy purchasers, who in like manner unite and consolidate; and, if they wish to become residents, erect new mansions out of the ruins of the ancient cottages, whose little enclosures, with all the wild graces that grew out of them, disappear. The feudal tenure under which the estates are held has indeed done something towards checking this influx of new settlers; but so strong is the inclination, that these galling restraints are endured; and it is probable, that in a few years the country on the margin of the Lakes will fall almost entirely into the possession of gentry, either strangers or natives. It is then much to be wished, that a better taste should prevail among these new proprietors; and, as they cannot be expected to leave things to themselves, that skill and knowledge should prevent unnecessary deviations from that path of simplicity and beauty along which, without design and unconsciously, their humble predecessors have moved. In this wish the author will be joined by persons of pure taste throughout the whole island, who, by their visits (often repeated) to the Lakes in the North of England, testify that they deem the district a sort of national property, in which every man has a right and interest who has an eye to perceive and a heart to enjoy.

## MISCELLANEOUS OBSERVATIONS

Mr West, in his well-known Guide to the Lakes, recommends, as the best season for visiting this country, the interval from the beginning of June to the end of August;[40] and, the two latter months being a time of vacation and leisure, it is almost exclusively in these that strangers resort hither. But that season is by no means the best; the colouring of the mountains and woods, unless where they are diversified by rocks, is of too unvaried a green; and, as a large portion of the vallies is allotted to hay-grass, some want of variety is found there also. The meadows, however, are sufficiently enlivened after hay-making begins, which is much later than in the southern part of the island. A stronger objection is rainy weather, setting in sometimes at this period with a vigour, and continuing with a perseverance, that may remind the disappointed and dejected traveller of those deluges of rain which fall among the Abyssinian mountains, for the annual supply of the Nile. The months of September and October (particularly October) are generally attended with much finer weather; and the scenery is then, beyond comparison, more diversified, more splendid, and beautiful; but, on the other hand, short days prevent long excursions, and sharp and chill gales are unfavourable to parties of pleasure out of doors. Nevertheless, to the sincere admirer of nature, who is in good health and spirits, and at liberty to make a choice, the six weeks following the 1st of September may be recommended in preference to July and August. For there is no inconvenience arising from the season which, to such a person, would not be amply compensated by the *autumnal* appearance of any of the more retired vallies, into which discordant plantations and unsuitable buildings have not yet found entrance. – In such spots, at this season, there is an admirable compass and proportion of natural harmony in colour, through the whole scale of objects; in the tender green of the after-grass upon the meadows, interspersed with islands of grey or mossy rock, crowned by shrubs and trees; in the irregular inclosures of standing corn, or stubble-fields, in like manner broken; in the mountain-sides glowing with fern of divers colours; in the calm blue lakes and river-pools; and in the foliage of the trees, through all the tints of autumn, – from the pale and brilliant yellow of the birch and ash, to the deep greens of the unfaded oak and alder, and of the ivy upon the rocks, upon the trees, and the cottages. Yet, as most travellers are either stinted, or stint themselves, for time, the space between the middle or last week in May, and the middle or last week of June, may be pointed out as affording the best combination of long days, fine weather, and variety of impressions. Few of the native trees are then in full leaf; but, for whatever may be wanting in depth of shade, more than an equivalent will be found in the diversity of foliage, in the blossoms of the fruit-and-berry-bearing trees which abound in the woods, and in the golden flowers of the broom and other shrubs, with which many of the copses are interveined. In those woods, also, and on these mountain-sides which have a northern aspect, and in the deep dells, many of the spring-flowers still linger; while the open and sunny places are stocked with the flowers of the approaching summer. And, besides, is not an exquisite pleasure still untasted by him who has not heard the choir of linnets and thrushes chaunting their love-songs in the copses, woods, and hedge-rows of a mountainous country; safe from the birds of prey, which build in the inaccessible crags, and are at all hours seen or heard wheeling about in the air? The number of these formidable creatures is probably the cause, why, in the *narrow* vallies, there are no skylarks; as the destroyer would be enabled to dart upon them from the near and surrounding crags, before they could descend to their ground-nests for protection. It is not often that the nightingale resorts to these vales; but almost all the other tribes of our English warblers are numerous; and their notes, when listened to by the side of broad still waters, or when heard in unison with the murmuring of mountain-brooks, have the compass of their power enlarged accordingly. There is also an imaginative influence in the voice of the cuckoo, when that voice has taken possession of a deep mountain valley, very different from any thing which can be excited by the same sound in a flat country. Nor must a circumstance be omitted, which here renders the close of spring especially interesting; I mean the practice of bringing down the ewes from the mountains to yean [41] in the vallies and enclosed grounds. The herbage being thus cropped as it springs, *that* first tender emerald green of the season, which would otherwise have lasted little more than a fortnight, is prolonged in the pastures and meadows for many weeks: while they are farther enlivened by the multitude of lambs bleating and skipping about. These sportive creatures, as they gather strength, are turned out upon the open mountains, and with their slender limbs, their snow-white colour, and their wild and light motions, beautifully accord or contrast with the rocks and lawns, upon which they must now begin to seek their food. And last, but not least, at this time the traveller will be sure of room and comfortable accommodation, even in the smaller inns. I am aware that few of those who may be inclined to profit by this recommendation will be able to do so, as the time and manner of an excursion of this kind are mostly regulated by circumstances which prevent an entire freedom of choice. It will therefore be more pleasant to observe, that, though the months of July and August are liable to many objections, yet it often happens that the weather, at this time, is not more wet and stormy than they, who are really capable of enjoying the sublime forms of nature in their utmost sublimity, would desire. For no traveller, provided he be in good health, and with any command of time, would have a just privilege to visit such scenes, if he could grudge the price of a little confinement among them, or interruption in his journey, for the sight or sound of a storm coming on or clearing away. Insensible must he be who would not congratulate himself upon the bold bursts of sunshine, the descending vapours, wandering lights and shadows, and the invigorated torrents and water-falls, with which broken weather, in a mountainous region, is accompanied. At such a time there is no cause to complain, either of the monotony of mid-summer colouring, or the glaring atmosphere of long, cloudless, and hot days.

Thus far concerning the respective advantages and disadvantages of the different seasons for visiting this country. As to the order in which objects are best seen – a lake being composed of water flowing from higher grounds, and expanding itself till its receptacle is filled to the brim, – it follows, that it will appear to most advantage when approached from its outlet, especially if the lake be in a mountainous country; for, by this way of approach, the traveller faces the grander features of the scene, and is gradually conducted into its most sublime recesses. Now, every one knows, that from amenity and beauty the transition to sublimity is easy and favourable; but the reverse is not so; for, after the faculties have been elevated, they are indisposed to humbler excitement.[42]

It is not likely that a mountain will be ascended without disappointment, if a wide range of prospect be the object, unless either the summit be reached before sun-rise, or the visitant remain there until the time of sun-set, and afterwards. The precipitous sides of the mountain, and the neighbouring summits, may be seen with effect under any atmosphere which allows them to be seen at all; but *he* is the most fortunate adventurer, who chances to be involved in vapours which open and let in an extent of country partially, or, dispersing suddenly, reveal the whole region from centre to circumference.

A stranger to a mountainous country may not be aware that his walk in the early morning ought to be taken on the eastern side of the vale, otherwise he will lose the morning light, first touching the tops and thence creeping down the sides of the opposite hills, as the sun ascends, or he may go to some central eminence, commanding both the shadows from the eastern, and the lights upon the western mountains. But, if the horizon line in the east be low, the western side may be taken for the sake of the reflections, upon the water, of light from the rising sun. In the evening, for like reasons, the contrary course should be taken.

After all, it is upon the *mind* which a traveller brings along with him that his acquisitions, whether of pleasure or profit, must principally depend. – May I be allowed a few words on this subject?

Nothing is more injurious to genuine feeling than the practice of hastily and ungraciously depreciating the face of one country by comparing it with that of another. True it is Qui *bene* distinguit bene *docet*;[43] yet fastidiousness is a wretched travelling companion; and the best guide to which, in matters of taste we can entrust ourselves, is a disposition to be pleased. For example, if a traveller be among the Alps, let him surrender up his mind to the fury of the gigantic torrents, and take delight in the contemplation of their almost irresistible violence, without complaining of the monotony of their foaming course, or being disgusted with the muddiness of the water – apparent even where it is violently agitated. In Cumberland and Westmorland, let not the comparative weakness of the streams prevent him from sympathising with such impetuosity as they possess; and, making the most of the present objects, let him, as he justly may do, observe with admiration the unrivalled brilliancy of the water, and that variety of motion, mood, and character, that arises out of the want of those resources by which the power of the streams in the Alps is supported. – Again, with respect to the mountains; though these are comparatively of diminutive size, though there is little of perpetual snow, and no voice of summer-avalanches is heard among them; and though traces left by the ravage of the elements are here comparatively rare and unimpressive, yet out of this very deficiency proceeds a sense of stability and permanence that is, to many minds, more grateful –

> 'While the coarse rushes to the sweeping breeze
> Sigh forth their ancient melodies.' [44]

Among the Alps are few places that do not preclude this feeling of tranquil sublimity. Havoc, and ruin, and desolation, and encroachment, are everywhere more or less obtruded; and it is difficult, notwithstanding the naked loftiness of the *pikes*, and the snow-capped summits of the *mounts*, to escape from the depressing sensation, that the whole are in a rapid process of dissolution; and, were it not that the destructive agency must abate as the heights diminished, would, in time to come, be levelled with the plains. Nevertheless, I would relish to the utmost the demonstrations of every species of power at work to effect such changes.

From these general views let us descend a moment to detail. A stranger to mountain imagery naturally on his first arrival looks out for sublimity in every object that admits of it; and is almost always disappointed. For this disappointment there exists, I believe, no general preventive; nor is it desirable that there should. But with regard to one class of objects, there is a point in which injurious expectations may be easily corrected. It is generally supposed that waterfalls are scarcely worth being looked at except after much rain, and that, the more swoln the stream, the more fortunate the spectator; but this however is true only of large cataracts with sublime accompaniments; and not even of these without some drawbacks. In other instances, what becomes, at such a time, of that sense of refreshing coolness which can only be felt in dry and sunny weather, when the rocks, herbs, and flowers glisten with moisture diffused by the breath of the precipitous water? But, considering these things as objects of sight only, it may be observed that the principal charm of the smaller waterfalls or cascades consists in certain proportions of form and affinities of colour, among the component parts of the scene; and in the contrast maintained between the falling water and that which is apparently at rest, or rather settling gradually into quiet in the pool below. The beauty of such a scene, where there is naturally so much agitation, is also heightened, in a peculiar manner, by the *glimmering*, and, towards the verge of the pool, by the *steady*, reflection of the surrounding images. Now, all those delicate distinctions are destroyed by heavy floods, and the whole stream rushes along in foam and tumultuous confusion. A happy proportion of component parts is indeed noticeable among the landscapes of the North of England; and, in this characteristic essential to a perfect picture, they surpass the scenes of Scotland, and, in a still greater degree, those of Switzerland.

As a resident among the Lakes, I frequently hear the scenery of this country compared with that of the Alps; and therefore a few words shall be added to what has been incidentally said upon that subject.

If we could recall, to this region of lakes, the native pine-forests, with which many hundred years ago a large portion of the heights was covered, then, during spring and autumn, it might frequently, with much propriety, be compared to Switzerland, – the elements of the landscape would be the same – one country representing the other in miniature. Towns, villages, churches, rural seats, bridges and roads: green meadows and arable grounds, with their various produce, and deciduous woods of diversified foliage which occupy the vales and lower regions of the mountains, would, as in Switzerland, be divided by dark forests from ridges and round-topped heights covered with snow, and from pikes and sharp declivities imperfectly arrayed in the same glittering mantle: and the resemblance would be still more perfect on those days when vapours, resting upon, and floating around the summits, leave the elevation of the mountains less dependent upon the eye than on the imagination. But the pine-forests have wholly disappeared; and only during late spring and early autumn is realized here that assemblage of the imagery of different seasons, which is exhibited through the whole summer among the Alps, – winter in the distance, – and warmth, leafy woods, verdure and fertility at hand, and widely diffused.

Striking, then, from among the permanent materials of the landscape, that stage of vegetation which is occupied by pine-forests, and, above that, the perennial snows, we have mountains, the highest of which little exceed 3,000 feet, while some of the Alps do not fall short of 14,000 or 15,000, and 8,000 or 10,000 is not an uncommon elevation. Our tracts of wood and water are almost as diminutive in comparison; therefore, as far as sublimity is dependent upon absolute bulk and height, and atmospherical influences in connection with these, it is obvious, that there can be no rivalship. But a short residence among the British Mountains will furnish abundant proof, that, after a certain point of elevation, viz. that which allows of compact and fleecy clouds settling upon, or sweeping over, the summits, the sense of sublimity depends more upon form and relation of objects to each other than upon their actual magnitude; and, that an elevation of 3,000 feet is sufficient to call forth in a most impressive degree the creative, and magnifying, and softening powers of the atmosphere. Hence, on the score even of sublimity, the superiority of the Alps is by no means so great as might hastily be inferred; – and, as to the *beauty* of the lower regions of the Swiss Mountains, it is noticeable – that, as they are all regularly mown, their surface has nothing of that mellow tone and variety of hues by which mountain turf, that is never touched by the scythe, is distinguished. On the smooth and steep slopes of the Swiss hills, these plots of verdure do indeed agreeably unite their colour with that of the deciduous trees, or make a lively contrast with the dark green pine-groves that define them, and among which they run in endless variety of shapes – but this is most pleasing *at first sight*; the permanent gratification of the eye requires finer gradations of tone, and a more delicate blending of hues into each other. Besides, it is only in spring and late autumn that cattle animate by their presence the Swiss lawns; and, though the pastures of the higher regions where they feed during the summer are left in their natural state of flowery herbage, those pastures are so remote, that their texture and colour are of no consequence in the composition of any picture in which a lake of the Vales is a feature. Yet in those lofty regions, how vegetation is invigorated by the genial climate of that country! Among the luxuriant flowers there met with, groves, or forests, if I may so call them, of Monks-hood are frequently seen; the plant of deep, rich blue, and as tall as in our gardens; and this at an elevation where, in Cumberland, Icelandic moss would only be found, or the stony summits be utterly bare.

We have, then, for the colouring of Switzerland, *principally* a vivid green herbage, black woods, and dazzling snows, presented in masses with a grandeur to which no one can be insensible; but not often graduated by Nature into soothing harmony, and so ill suited to the pencil, that though abundance of good subjects may be there found, they are not such as can be deemed *characteristic* of the country; nor is this unfitness confined to colour: the forms of the mountains, though many of them in some points of view the noblest that can be conceived, are apt to run into spikes and needles, and present a jagged outline which has a mean effect, transferred to canvass. This must have been felt by the ancient masters; for, if I am not mistaken, they have not left a single landscape, the materials of which are taken from the *peculiar* features of the Alps; yet Titian passed his life almost in their neighbourhood; the Poussins and Claude must have been well acquainted with their aspects; and several admirable painters, as Tibaldi and Luino, were born among the Italian Alps.[45] A few experiments have lately been made by Englishmen, but they only prove that courage, skill, and judgment, may surmount any obstacles; and it may be safely affirmed, that they who have done best in this bold adventure, will be the least likely to repeat the attempt. But, though our scenes are better suited to painting than those of the Alps, I should be sorry to contemplate either country in reference to that art, further than as its fitness or unfitness for the pencil renders it more or less pleasing to the eye of the spectator, who has learned to observe and feel, chiefly from Nature herself.

Deeming the points in which Alpine imagery is superior to British too obvious to be insisted upon, I will observe that the deciduous woods, though in many places unapproachable by the axe, and triumphing in the pomp and prodigality of Nature, have, in general,[46] neither the variety nor beauty which would exist in those of the mountains of Britain, if left to themselves. Magnificent walnut-trees grow upon the plains of Switzerland; and fine trees, of that species, are found scattered over the hill-sides: birches also grow here and there in luxuriant beauty; but neither these, nor oaks, are ever a prevailing tree, nor can even be said to be common; and the oaks, as far as I had an opportunity of observing, are greatly inferior to those of Britain. Among the interior vallies the proportion of beeches and pines is so great that other trees are scarcely noticeable; and surely such woods are at all seasons much less agreeable than that rich and harmonious distribution of oak, ash, elm, birch, and alder, that formerly clothed the sides of Snowdon and Helvellyn; and of which no mean remains still survive at the head of Ulswater. On the Italian side of the Alps, chesnut and walnut-trees grow at a considerable height on the mountains; but, even there, the foliage is not equal in beauty to the 'natural product' of this climate. In fact the sunshine of the South of Europe, so envied when heard of at a distance, is in many respects injurious to rural beauty, particularly as it incites to the cultivation of spots of ground which in colder climates would be left in the hands of nature, favouring at the same time the culture of plants that are more valuable on account of the fruit they produce to gratify the palate, than for affording pleasure to the eye, as materials of landscape. Take, for instance, the Promontory of Bellagio, so fortunate in its command of the three branches of the Lake of Como, yet the ridge of the Promontory itself, being for the most part covered with vines interspersed with olive trees, accords but ill with the vastness of the green unappropriated mountains, and derogates not a little from the sublimity of those finely contrasted pictures to which it is a fore-ground. The vine, when cultivated upon a large scale, notwithstanding all that may be said of it in poetry,[47] makes but a dull formal appearance in landscape; and the olive-tree (though one is loth to say so) is not more grateful to the eye than our common willow, which it much resembles; but the hoariness of hue, common to both, has in the aquatic plant an appropriate delicacy, harmonising with the situation in which it most delights. The same may no doubt be said of the olive among the dry rocks of Attica, but I am speaking of it as found in gardens and vineyards in the North of Italy. At Bellagio, what Englishman can resist the temptation of substituting, in his fancy, for these formal treasures of cultivation, the natural variety of one of our parks – its pastured lawns, coverts of hawthorn, of wild-rose, and honeysuckle, and the majesty of forest trees? – such wild graces as the banks of Derwent-water shewed in the time of the Ratcliffes; and Gowbarrow Park, Lowther, and Rydal do at this day.

As my object is to reconcile a Briton to the scenery of his own country, though not at the expense of truth, I am not afraid of asserting that in many points of view our LAKES, also, are much more interesting than those of the Alps; first, as is implied above, from being more happily proportioned to the other features of the landscape; and next, both as being infinitely more pellucid, and less subject to agitation from the winds.[48] Como, (which may perhaps be styled the King of Lakes, as Lugano is certainly the Queen) is disturbed by a periodical wind blowing *from* the head in the morning, and *towards* it in the afternoon. The magnificent Lake of the four Cantons, especially its noblest division, called the Lake of Uri, is not only much agitated by winds, but in the night time is disturbed from the bottom, as I was told, and indeed, as I witnessed, without any apparent commotion in the air; and when at rest, the water is not pure to the eye, but of a heavy green hue — as is that of all the other lakes, apparently according to the degree in which they are fed by melted snows. If the Lake of Geneva furnish an exception, this is probably owing to its vast extent, which allows the water to deposit its impurities. The water of the English lakes, on the contrary, being of a crystalline clearness, the reflections of the surrounding hills are frequently so lively, that it is scarcely possible to distinguish the point where the real object terminates, and its unsubstantial duplicate begins. The lower part of the Lake of Geneva, from its narrowness, must be much less subject to agitation than the higher divisions, and, as the water is clearer than that of the other Swiss Lakes, it will frequently exhibit this appearance, though it is scarcely possible in an equal degree. During two comprehensive tours among the Alps,[49] I did not observe, except on one of the smaller lakes, between Lugano and Ponte Tresa, a single instance of those beautiful repetitions of surrounding objects on the bosom of the water, which are so frequently seen here: not to speak of the fine dazzling trembling network, breezy motions, and streaks and circles of intermingled smooth and rippled water, which make the surface of our lakes a field of endless variety. But among the Alps, where every thing tends to the grand and the sublime, in surfaces as well as in forms, if the lakes do not court the placid reflections of land objects, those of first-rate magnitude make compensation, in some degree, by exhibiting those ever-changing fields of green, blue, and purple shadows or lights, (one scarcely knows which to name them) that call to mind a sea-prospect contemplated from a lofty cliff.

The subject of torrents and water-falls has already been touched upon; but it may be added that in Switzerland, the perpetual accompaniment of snow upon the higher regions takes much from the effect of foaming white streams; while, from their frequency, they obstruct each other's influence upon the mind of the spectator; and, in all cases, the effect of an individual cataract, excepting the great Fall of the Rhine at Schaffhausen, is diminished by the general fury of the stream of which it is a part.

Recurring to the reflections from still water, I will describe a singular phenomenon of this kind of which I was an eye-witness.

Walking by the side of Ulswater upon a calm September morning,[50] I saw, deep within the bosom of the lake, a magnificent Castle, with towers and battlements, nothing could be more distinct than the whole edifice; – after gazing with delight upon it for some time, as upon a work of enchantment, I could not but regret that my previous knowledge of the place enabled me to account for the appearance. It was in fact the reflection of a pleasure-house called Lyulph's Tower – the towers and battlements magnified and so much changed in shape as not to be immediately recognized. In the meanwhile, the pleasure-house itself was altogether hidden from my view by a body of vapour stretching over it and along the hill-side on which it stands, but not so as to have intercepted its communication with the lake; and hence this novel and most impressive object, which, if I had been a stranger to the spot, would, from its being inexplicable, have long detained the mind in a state of pleasing astonishment.

Appearances of this kind, acting upon the credulity of early ages, may have given birth to, and favoured the belief in, stories of subaqueous palaces, gardens, and pleasure-grounds – the brilliant ornaments of Romance.

With this *inverted* scene I will couple a much more extraordinary phenomenon, which will shew how other elegant fancies may have had their origin, less in invention than in the actual processes of nature.

About eleven o'clock on the forenoon of a winter's day, coming suddenly, in company of a friend, into view of the Lake of Grasmere, we were alarmed by the sight of a newly-created Island; the transitory thought of the moment was, that it had been produced by an earthquake or some other convulsion of nature. Recovering from the alarm, which was greater than the reader can possibly sympathize with, but which was shared to its full extent by my companion, we proceeded to examine the object before us. The elevation of this new island exceeded considerably that of the old one, its neighbour; it was likewise larger in circumference, comprehending a space of about five acres; its surface rocky, speckled with snow, and sprinkled over with birch trees; it was divided towards the south from the other island by a narrow frith, and in like manner from the northern shore of the lake; on the east and west it was separated from the shore by a much larger space of smooth water.

Marvellous was the illusion! Comparing the new with the old Island, the surface of which is soft, green, and unvaried, I do not scruple to say that, as an object of sight, it was much the more distinct. 'How little faith,' we exclaimed, 'is due to one sense, unless its evidence be confirmed by some of its fellows! What Stranger could possibly be persuaded that this, which we know to be an unsubstantial mockery, is *really* so; and that there exists only a single Island on this beautiful Lake?' At length the appearance underwent a gradual transmutation; it lost its prominence and passed into a glimmering and dim *inversion*, and then totally disappeared; – leaving behind it a clear open area of ice of the same dimensions. We now perceived that this bed of ice, which was thinly suffused with water, had produced the illusion, by reflecting and refracting (as persons skilled in optics would no doubt easily explain) a rocky and woody section of the opposite mountain named Silver-how.

Having dwelt so much upon the beauty of pure and still water, and pointed out the advantage which the Lakes of the North of England have in this particular over those of the Alps, it would be injustice not to advert to the sublimity that must often be given to Alpine scenes, by the agitations to which those vast bodies of diffused water are there subject. I have witnessed many tremendous thunder-storms among the Alps, and the most glorious effects of light and shadow; but I never happened to be present when any Lake was agitated by those hurricanes which I imagine must often torment them. If the commotions be at all proportionable to the expanse and depth of the waters, and the height of the surrounding mountains, then, if I may judge from what is frequently seen here, the exhibition must be awful and astonishing. – On this day, March 30, 1822, the winds have been acting upon the small Lake of Rydal, as if they had received command to carry its waters from their bed into the sky;

the white billows in different quarters disappeared under clouds, or rather drifts, of spray, that were whirled along, and up into the air by scouring winds, charging each other in squadrons in every direction, upon the Lake. The spray, having been hurried aloft till it lost its consistency and whiteness, was driven along the mountain tops like flying showers that vanish in the distance. Frequently an eddying wind scooped the waters out of the basin, and forced them upwards in the very shape of an Icelandic Geyser, or boiling fountain, to the height of several hundred feet.

This small Mere of Rydal, from its position, is subject in a peculiar degree to these commotions. The present season, however, is unusually stormy; – great numbers of fish, two of them not less than 12 pounds weight, were a few days ago cast on the shores of Derwentwater by the force of the waves.

Lest, in the foregoing comparative estimate, I should be suspected of partiality to my native mountains, I will support my general opinion by the authority of Mr West, whose Guide to the Lakes has been eminently serviceable to the Tourist for nearly 50 years. The Author, a Roman Catholic Clergyman, had passed much time abroad, and was well acquainted with the scenery of the Continent. He thus expresses himself: 'They who intend to make the continental tour should begin here; as it will give, in miniature, an idea of what they are to meet with there, in traversing the Alps and Appenines; to which our northern mountains are not inferior in beauty of line, or variety of summit, number of lakes, and transparency of water; not in colouring of rock, or softness of turf; but in height and extent only. The mountains here are all accessible to the summit, and furnish prospects no less surprising, and with more variety, than the Alps themselves. The tops of the highest Alps are inaccessible, being covered with everlasting snow, which commencing at regular heights above the cultivated tracts, or wooded and verdant sides, form indeed the highest contrast in nature. For there may be seen all the variety of climate in one view. To this, however, we oppose the sight of the ocean, from the summits of all the higher mountains, as it appears intersected with promontories, decorated with islands, and animated with navigation.' – West's *Guide*.[51]

# Kendal and Windermere Railway

~*~ ~*~ ~*~

[*The first letter was probably composed early December (by 8 December)*
*1844, and was first published 11 December 1844 in the* Morning Post. *The*
*second letter was composed between 8 and 17 December 1844 and was first*
*published 20 December 1844 in the* Morning Post. *Both letters were revised*
*in early January (especially January 6–8) 1845 and were published together*
*as a pamphlet 23 January 1845 – the text followed here.*]

   *In the summer of 1844, a new company was formed to bring a railway*
*line from Kendal to Windermere in the Lake District. Wordsworth immedi-*
*ately opposed this invasion of the District; his efforts brought resentment*
*against him and were finally ineffectual: the line opened in the spring of*
*1847.*
   *As prefatory material, Wordsworth printed his sonnet 'On the Projected*
*Kendal and Windermere Railway', and the following letter:*

RYDAL MOUNT,
October 12th, 1844.
   The degree and kind of attachment which many of the yeo-
manry feel to their small inheritances can scarcely be over-rated.
Near the house of one of them stands a magnificent tree, which a
neighbour of the owner [Mr Birkett] advised him to fell for profit's
sake. 'Fell it,' exclaimed the yeoman, 'I had rather fall on my knees

and worship it.' It happens, I believe, that the intended railway would pass through this little property, and I hope that an apology for the answer will not be thought necessary by one who enters into the strength of the feeling.

W.W.

## NO. I
### TO THE EDITOR OF THE MORNING POST

Sir – Some little time ago you did me the favour of inserting a sonnet expressive of the regret and indignation which, in common with others all over these Islands, I felt at the proposal of a railway to extend from Kendal to Low Wood, near the head of Windermere. The project was so offensive to a large majority of the proprietors through whose lands the line, after it came in view of the Lake, was to pass, that, for this reason, and the avowed one of the heavy expense without which the difficulties in the way could not be overcome, it has been partially abandoned, and the terminus is now announced to be at a spot within a mile of Bowness. But as no guarantee can be given that the project will not hereafter be revived, and an attempt made to carry the line forward through the vales of Ambleside and Grasmere, and as in one main particular the case remains essentially the same, allow me to address you upon certain points which merit more consideration than the favourers of the scheme have yet given them. The matter, though seemingly local, is really one in which all persons of taste must be interested, and, therefore, I hope to be excused if I venture to treat it at some length.

I shall barely touch upon the statistics of the question, leaving these to the two adverse parties, who will lay their several statements before the Board of Trade, which may possibly be induced to refer the matter to the House of Commons; and, contemplating that possibility, I hope that the observations I have to make may not be altogether without influence upon the public, and upon individuals whose duty it may be to decide in their place whether the proposed measure shall be referred to a Committee of the House. Were the case before us an ordinary one, I should reject such an attempt as presumptuous and futile; but it is not only different from all others, but, in truth, peculiar.

In this district the manufactures are trifling; mines it has none, and its quarries are either wrought out or superseded; the soil is light, and the cultivateable parts of the country are very limited; so that it has little to send out, and little has it also to receive. Summer TOURISTS,[1] (and the very word precludes the notion of a railway) it has in abundance; but the inhabitants are so few and their intercourse with other places so infrequent, that one daily coach, which could not be kept going but through its connection with the Post-office, suffices for three-fourths of the year along the line of country as far as Keswick. The staple of the district is, in fact, its beauty and its character of seclusion and retirement; and to these topics and to others connected with them my remarks shall be confined.

The projectors have induced many to favour their schemes by declaring that one of their main objects is to place the beauties of the Lake district within easier reach of those who cannot afford to pay for ordinary conveyances. Look at the facts. Railways are completed, which, joined with others in rapid progress, will bring travellers who prefer approaching by Ullswater to within four miles of that lake. The Lancaster and Carlisle Railway will approach the town of Kendal, about eight or nine miles from eminences that command the whole vale of Windermere. The Lakes are therefore at present of very easy access for *all* persons; but if they be not made still more so, the poor it is said, will be wronged. Before this be admitted let the question be fairly looked into, and its different bearings examined. No one can assert that, if this intended mode of approach be not effected, anything will be taken away that is actually possessed. The wrong, if any, must lie in the unwarrantable obstruction of an attainable benefit. First, then, let us consider the probable amount of that benefit.[2]

Elaborate gardens, with topiary works, were in high request, even among our remote ancestors, but the relish for choice and picturesque natural *scenery* (a poor and mean word which requires an apology, but will be generally understood),[3] is quite of recent origin. Our earlier travellers — Ray, the naturalist,[4] one of the first men of his age — Bishop Burnet, and others who had crossed the Alps, or lived some time in Switzerland, are silent upon the sublimity and beauty of those regions; and Burnet even uses these words, speaking of the Grisons — 'When they have made up estates elsewhere they are glad to leave Italy and the best parts of Germany, and to come and live among those mountains of which the very sight is enough to fill a man with horror.'[5] The accomplished Evelyn, giving an account of his journey from Italy through the Alps, dilates upon the terrible, the melancholy, and the uncomfortable; but, till he comes to the fruitful country in the neighbourhood of Geneva, not a syllable of delight or praise.[6] In the Sacra Telluris Theoria of the other Burnet there is a passage — omitted, however, in his own English translation of the work — in which he gives utterance to his sensations, when, from a particular spot he beheld a tract of the Alps rising before him on the one hand, and on the other the Mediterranean Sea spread beneath him. Nothing can be worthier of the magnificent appearances he describes than his language.[7] In a noble strain also does the Poet Gray address, in a Latin Ode,[8] the *Religio loci* at the Grande Chartruise. But before his time, with the exception of the passage from Thomas Burnet just alluded to, there is not, I believe, a single English traveller whose published writings would disprove the assertion, that, where precipitous rocks and mountains are mentioned at all, they are spoken of as objects of dislike and fear, and not of admiration. Even Gray himself, describing, in his Journal, the steeps at the entrance of Borrowdale, expresses his terror in the language of Dante: — 'Let us not speak of them, but look and pass on.'[9] In my youth, I lived some time in the vale of Keswick, under the roof of a shrewd and sensible woman, who more than once exclaimed in my hearing, 'Bless me! folk are always talking about prospects: when I was young there was never sic a thing neamed.' In fact, our ancestors, as every where appears, in choosing the site of their houses, looked only at shelter and convenience, especially of water, and often would place a barn or any other out-house directly in front of their habitations, however beautiful the landscape which their windows might otherwise have commanded. The first house that was built in the Lake district for the sake of the beauty of the country was the work of a Mr English, who had travelled in Italy, and chose for his site, some eighty years ago, the great island of Windermere; but it was sold before his building was finished, and he showed how little he was capable of appreciating the character of the situation by setting up a length of high garden-wall, as exclusive as it was ugly, almost close to the house. The nuisance was swept away when the late Mr Curwen [10] became the owner of this favoured spot. Mr English was followed by Mr Pocklington, a native of Nottinghamshire, who played strange pranks by his buildings and plantations upon Vicar's Island, in Derwentwater, which his admiration, such as it was, of the country, and probably a wish to be a leader in a new fashion, had tempted him to purchase. But what has all this to do with the subject? – Why, to show that a vivid perception of romantic scenery is neither inherent in mankind, nor a necessary consequence of even a comprehensive education. It is benignly ordained that green fields, clear blue skies, running streams of pure water, rich groves and woods, orchards, and all the ordinary varieties of rural nature, should find an easy way to the affections of all men, and more or less so from early childhood till the senses are impaired by old age and the sources of mere earthly enjoyment have in a great measure failed. But a taste beyond this, however desirable it may be that every one should possess it, is not to be implanted at once; it must be gradually developed both in nations and individuals. Rocks and mountains, torrents and wide-spread waters, and all those features of nature which go to the composition of such scenes as this part of England is distinguished for, cannot, in their finer relations to the human mind, be comprehended, or even very imperfectly conceived, without processes of culture or opportunities of observation in some degree habitual. In the eye of thousands and tens of thousands, a rich meadow, with fat cattle grazing upon it, or the sight of what they would call a heavy crop of corn, is worth all that the Alps and Pyrenees in their utmost grandeur and beauty could show to them; and, notwithstanding the grateful influence, as we have observed, of ordinary nature and the productions of the fields, it is noticeable what trifling conventional prepossessions will, in common minds, not only preclude pleasure from the sight of natural beauty, but will even turn it into an object of disgust. 'If I had to do with this garden,' said a respectable person, one of my neighbours, 'I would sweep away all the black and dirty stuff from that wall.' The wall was backed by a bank of earth, and was exquisitely decorated with ivy, flowers, moss, and ferns, such as grow of themselves in like places; but the mere notion of fitness associated with a trim garden-wall prevented, in this instance, all sense of the spontaneous bounty and delicate care of nature. In the midst of a small pleasure-ground, immediately below my house, rises a detached rock, equally remarkable for the beauty of its form, the ancient oaks that grow out of it, and the flowers and shrubs which adorn it. 'What a nice place would this be,' said a Manchester tradesman, pointing to the rock, 'if that ugly lump were but out of the way.' Men as little advanced in the pleasure which such objects give to others are so far from being rare, that they may be said fairly to represent a large majority of mankind. This is a fact, and none but the deceiver and the willingly deceived can be offended by its being stated. But as a more susceptible taste is undoubtedly a great acquisition, and has been spreading among us for some years, the question is, what means are most likely to be beneficial in extending its operation? Surely that good is not to be obtained by transferring at once uneducated persons in large bodies to particular spots, where the combinations of natural objects are such as would afford the greatest pleasure to those who have been in the habit of observing and studying the peculiar character of such scenes, and how they differ one from another. Instead of tempting artisans and labourers, and the humbler classes of shopkeepers, to ramble to a distance, let us rather look with lively sympathy upon persons in that condition, when, upon a holiday, or on the Sunday, after having attended divine worship, they make little excursions with their wives and children among neighbouring fields, whither the whole of each family might stroll, or be conveyed at much less cost than would be required to take a single individual of the number to the shores of Windermere by the cheapest conveyance. It is in some such way as this only, that persons who must labour daily with their hands for bread in large towns, or are subject to confinement through the week, can be trained to a profitable intercourse with nature where she is the most distinguished by the majesty and sublimity of her forms.

For further illustration of the subject, turn to what we know of a man of extraordinary genius, who was bred to hard labour in agricultural employments, Burns, the poet. When he had become distinguished by the publication of a volume of verses, and was enabled to travel by the profit his poems brought him, he made a tour, in the course of which, as his companion, Dr Adair, tells us, he visited scenes inferior to none in Scotland in beauty, sublimity, and romantic interest; and the Doctor having noticed, with other companions, that he seemed little moved upon one occasion by the sight of such a scene, says – 'I doubt if he had much taste for the picturesque.'[11] The personal testimony, however, upon this point is conflicting; but when Dr Currie refers to certain local poems as decisive proofs that Burns' fellow-traveller was mistaken, the biographer is surely unfortunate.[12] How vague and tame are the poet's expressions in those few local poems, compared with his language when he is describing objects with which his position in life allowed him to be familiar! It appears, both from what his works contain, and from what is not to be found in them, that, sensitive as they abundantly prove his mind to have been in its intercourse with common rural images, and with the general powers of nature exhibited in storm and in stillness, in light or darkness, and in the various aspects of the seasons, he was little affected by the sight of one spot in preference to another, unless where it derived an interest from history, tradition, or local associations. He lived many years in Nithsdale, where he was in daily sight of Skiddaw, yet he never crossed the Solway for a better acquaintance with that mountain; and I am persuaded that, if he had been induced to ramble among our Lakes, by that time sufficiently celebrated, he would have seldom been more excited than by some ordinary

Scottish stream or hill with a tradition attached to it, or which had been the scene of a favourite ballad or love song. If all this be truly said of such a man, and the like cannot be denied of the eminent individuals before named, who to great natural talents added the accomplishments of scholarship or science, then what ground is there for maintaining that the poor are treated with disrespect, or wrong done to them or any class of visitants, if we be reluctant to introduce a railway into this country for the sake of lessening, by eight or nine miles only, the fatigue or expense of their journey to Windermere? – And wherever any one among the labouring classes has made even an approach to the sensibility which drew a lamentation from Burns when he had uprooted a daisy with his plough,[13] and caused him to turn the 'weeder-clips aside' from the thistle, and spare 'the symbol dear'[14] of his country, then surely such a one, could he afford by any means to travel as far as Kendal, would not grudge a two hours' walk across the skirts of the beautiful country that he was desirous of visiting.

The wide-spread waters of these regions are in their nature peaceful; so are the steep mountains and the rocky glens; nor can they be profitably enjoyed but by a mind disposed to peace. Go to a pantomime, a farce, or a puppet-show, if you want noisy pleasure – the crowd of spectators who partake your enjoyment will, by their presence and acclamations, enhance it; but may those who have given proof that they prefer other gratifications continue to be safe from the molestation of cheap trains pouring out their hundreds at a time along the margin of Windermere; nor let any one be liable to the charge of being selfishly disregardful of the poor, and their innocent and salutary enjoyments, if he does not congratulate himself upon the especial benefit which would thus be conferred on such a concourse.

> 'O, Nature, a' thy shows an' forms,
> To feeling pensive hearts hae charms!'[15]

So exclaimed the Ayrshire ploughman, speaking of ordinary rural nature under the varying influences of the seasons, and the sentiment has found an echo in the bosoms of thousands in as humble a condition as he himself was when he gave vent to it. But then they were feeling, pensive hearts; men who would be among the first to lament the facility with which they had approached this region, by a sacrifice of so much of its quiet and beauty, as, from the intrusion of a railway, would be inseparable. What can, in truth, be more absurd, than that either rich or poor should be spared the trouble of travelling by the high roads over so short a space, according to their respective means, if the unavoidable consequence must be a great disturbance of the retirement, and in many places a destruction of the beauty of the country, which the parties are come in search of? Would not this be pretty much like the child's cutting up his drum to learn where the sound came from?

Having, I trust, given sufficient reason for the belief that the imperfectly educated classes are not likely to draw much good from rare visits to the Lakes performed in this way, and surely on their own account it is not desirable that the visits should be frequent, let us glance at the mischief which such facilities would certainly produce. The directors of railway companies are always ready to devise or encourage entertainments for tempting the humbler classes to leave their homes. Accordingly, for the profit of the shareholders and that of the lower class of innkeepers, we should have wrestling matches, horse and boat races without number, and pot-houses and beer-shops would keep pace with these excitements and recreations, most of which might too easily be had elsewhere. The injury which would thus be done to morals, both among this influx of strangers and the lower class of inhabitants, is obvious; and, supposing such extraordinary temptations not to be held out, there cannot be a doubt that the Sabbath day in the towns of Bowness and Ambleside, and other parts of the district, would be subject to much additional desecration.

Whatever comes of the scheme which we have endeavoured to discountenance, the charge against its opponents of being selfishly regardless of the poor, ought to cease. The cry has been raised and kept up by three classes of persons – they who wish to bring into

84

discredit all such as stand in the way of their gains or gambling speculations; they who are dazzled by the application of physical science to the useful arts, and indiscriminately applaud what they call the spirit of the age as manifested in this way; and, lastly, those persons who are ever ready to step forward in what appears to them to be the cause of the poor, but not always with becoming attention to particulars. I am well aware that upon the first class what has been said will be of no avail, but upon the two latter some impression will, I trust, be made.

To conclude. The railway power, we know well, will not admit of being materially counteracted by sentiment; and who would wish it where large towns are connected, and the interests of trade and agriculture are substantially promoted, by such mode of inter-communication? But be it remembered, that this case is, as has been said before, a peculiar one, and that the staple of the country is its beauty and its character of retirement. Let then the beauty be undisfigured and the retirement unviolated, unless there be reason for believing that rights and interests of a higher kind and more apparent than those which have been urged in behalf of the projected intrusion will compensate the sacrifice. Thanking you for the judicious observations that have appeared in your paper upon the subject of railways, I remain, Sir, your obliged,

WM. WORDSWORTH.

Rydal Mount, Dec. 9, 1844.

Note. — To the instances named in this letter of the indifference even of men of genius to the sublime forms of nature in mountainous districts, the author of the interesting Essays, in the Morning Post,[16] entitled Table Talk has justly added Goldsmith, and I give the passage in his own words.

'The simple and gentle-hearted Goldsmith, who had an exquisite sense of rural beauty in the familiar forms of hill and dale, and meadows with their hawthorn-scented hedges, does not seem to have dreamt of any such thing as beauty in the Swiss Alps, though he traversed them on foot, and had therefore the best opportunities of observing them. In his poem "The Traveller," he describes the Swiss as loving their mountain homes, not by reason of the romantic beauty of the situation, but in spite of the miserable character of the soil, and the stormy horrors of their mountain steeps —

> "Turn we to survey
> Where rougher climes a nobler race display,
> Where the bleak Swiss their stormy mansion tread,
> And force a churlish soil for scanty bread.
> No produce here the barren hills afford,
> But man and steel, the soldier and his sword:
> No vernal blooms their torpid rocks array,
> But winter lingering chills the lap of May;
> No Zephyr fondly sues the mountain's breast,
> But meteors glare and stormy glooms invest.
> Yet still, *even here*, content can spread a charm,
> Redress the clime, and all its rage disarm." [17]

In the same Essay, (December 18th, 1844,) are many observations judiciously bearing upon the true character of this and similar projects.

### NO. II
#### TO THE EDITOR OF THE MORNING POST

Sir — As you obligingly found space in your journal for observations of mine upon the intended Kendal and Windermere Railway, I venture to send you some further remarks upon the same subject. The scope of the main argument, it will be recollected, was to prove that the perception of what has acquired the name of picturesque and romantic scenery is so far from being intuitive, that it can be produced only by a slow and gradual process of culture; and to show, as a consequence, that the humbler ranks of society are not, and cannot be, in a state to gain material benefit from a more speedy access than they now have to this beautiful region. Some of our opponents dissent from this latter proposition, though the most judicious of them readily admit the former; but then, overlooking not only positive assertions, but reasons carefully given, they say, 'As you allow that a more comprehensive taste is desirable, you ought to side with us;' and they illustrate their position, by reference to the British Museum and National Picture Gallery. 'There,' they add, 'thanks to the easy entrance now granted, numbers are seen, indicating by their dress and appearance their humble condition, who, when admitted for the first time, stare vacantly around them, so that one is inclined to ask what brought them hither? But an impression is made, something gained which may induce them to repeat the visit until light breaks in upon them, and they take an intelligent interest in what they behold.' Persons who talk thus forget that, to produce such an improvement, frequent access at small cost of time and labour is indispensable. Manchester lies, perhaps, within eight hours' railway distance of London; but surely no one would advise that Manchester operatives should contract a habit of running to and fro between that town and London, for the sake of forming an intimacy with the British Museum and National Gallery? No, no; little would all but a very few gain from the opportunities which, consistently with common sense, could be afforded them for such expeditions. Nor would it fare better with them in respect of trips to the lake district; an assertion, the truth of which no one can doubt, who has learned by experience how many men of the same or higher rank, living from their birth in this very region, are indifferent to those objects around them in which a cultivated taste takes so much pleasure. I should not have detained the reader so long upon this point, had I not heard (glad tidings for the directors and traffickers in shares!) that among the affluent and benevolent manufacturers of Yorkshire and Lancashire are some who already entertain the thought of sending, at their own expense, large bodies of their workmen, by railway, to the banks of Windermere. Surely those gentlemen will think a little more before they put such a scheme into practice. The rich man cannot benefit the poor, nor the superior the inferior, by anything that degrades him. Packing off men after this fashion, for holiday entertainment, is, in fact, treating them like children. They go at the will of their master, and must return at the same, or they will be dealt with as transgressors.

A poor man, speaking of his son, whose time of service in the army was expired, once said to me, (the reader will be startled at the expression, and I, indeed, was greatly shocked by it), 'I am glad he has done with that *mean* way of life.' But I soon gathered what was at the bottom of the feeling. The father overlooked all the glory that attaches to the character of a British soldier, in the consciousness that his son's will must have been in so great a degree subject to that of others. The poor man felt where the true dignity of his species lay, namely, in a just proportion between actions governed by a man's own inclinations and those of other men; but, according to the father's notion, that proportion did not exist in the course of life from which his son had been released. Had the old man known from experience the degree of liberty allowed to the common soldier, and the moral effect of the obedience required, he would have thought differently, and had he been capable of extending his views, he would have felt how much of the best and noblest part of our civic spirit is owing to our military and naval institutions, and that perhaps our very existence as a free people has by them been maintained. This extreme instance has been adduced to show how deeply seated in the minds of Englishmen is their sense of personal independence. Master-manufacturers ought never to lose sight of this truth. Let them consent to a Ten Hours' Bill, with little or, if possible, no diminution of wages, and the necessaries of life being more easily procured, the mind would develope itself accordingly, and each individual would be more at liberty to make at his own cost excursions in any direction which might be most inviting to him. There would then be no need for their masters sending them in droves scores of miles from their homes and families to the borders of Windermere, or anywhere else. Consider also the state of the lake district; and look, in the first place, at the little town of Bowness, in the event of such railway inundations. What would become of it in this, not the Retreat, but the Advance, of the Ten Thousand?[18] Leeds, I am told, has sent as many at once to Scarborough. We should have the whole of Lancashire, and no small part of Yorkshire, pouring in upon us to meet the men of Durham, and the borderers from Cumberland and Northumberland. Alas, alas, if the lakes are to pay this penalty for their own attractions!

> '– Vane could tell what ills from beauty spring,
> And Sedley cursed the form that pleased a king.' [19]

The fear of adding to the length of my last long letter prevented me from entering into details upon private and personal feelings among the residents, who have cause to lament the threatened intrusion. These are not matters to be brought before a Board of Trade, though I trust there will always be of that board members who know well that as we do 'not live by bread alone,' [20] so neither do we live by political economy alone. Of the present board I would gladly believe there is not one who, if his duty allowed it, would not be influenced by considerations of what may be felt by a gallant officer [21] now serving on the coast of South America, when he shall learn that the nuisance, though not intended actually to enter his property, will send its omnibuses, as fast as they can drive, within a few yards of his modest abode, which he built upon a small domain purchased at a price greatly enhanced by the privacy and beauty of the situation. Professor Wilson [22] (him I take the liberty to name), though a native of Scotland, and familiar with the grandeur of his own country, could not resist the temptation of settling long ago among our mountains. The place which his public duties have compelled him to quit as a residence, and may compel him to part with, is probably dearer to him than any spot upon earth. The reader should be informed with what respect he has been treated. Engineer agents, to his astonishment, came and intruded with their measuring instruments, upon his garden. He saw them; and who will not admire the patience that kept his hands from their shoulders? I must stop.

But with the fear before me of the line being carried, at a day not distant, through the whole breadth of the district, I could dwell, with much concern for other residents, upon the condition which they would be in if that outrage should be committed; nor ought it to be deemed impertinent were I to recommend this point to the especial regard of Members of Parliament who may have to decide upon the question. The two Houses of Legislature have frequently shown themselves not unmindful of private feeling in these matters. They have, in some cases, been induced to spare parks and pleasure grounds. But along the great railway lines these are of rare occurrence. They are but a part, and a small part; here it is far otherwise. Among the ancient inheritances of the yeomen, surely worthy of high respect, are interspersed through the entire district villas, most of them with such small domains attached that the occupants would be hardly less annoyed by a railway passing through their neighbour's ground than through their own. And it would be unpardonable not to advert to the effect of this measure on the interests of the very poor in this locality. With the town of Bowness I have no *minute* acquaintance; but of Ambleside, Grasmere, and the neighbourhood, I can testify from long experience, that they have been favoured by the residence of a gentry whose love of retirement has been a blessing to these vales; for their families have ministered, and still minister, to the temporal and spiritual necessities of the poor, and have personally superintended the education of the children in a degree which does those benefactors the highest honour, and which is, I trust, gratefully acknowledged in the hearts of all whom they have relieved, employed, and taught. Many of those friends of our poor would quit this country if the apprehended change were realised, and would be succeeded by strangers not linked to the neighbourhood, but flitting to and fro between their fancy-villas and the homes where their wealth was accumulated and accumulating by trade and manufactures. It is obvious that persons, so unsettled, whatever might be their good wishes and readiness to part with money for charitable purposes, would ill supply the loss of the inhabitants who had been driven away.

It will be felt by those who think with me upon this occasion that I have been writing on behalf of a social condition which no one who is competent to judge of it would be willing to subvert, and that

I have been endeavouring to support moral sentiments and intellectual pleasures of a high order against an enmity which seems growing more and more formidable every day; I mean 'Utilitarianism,' serving as a mask for cupidity and gambling speculations. My business with this evil lies in its reckless mode of action by Railways, now its favourite instruments. Upon good authority I have been told that there was lately an intention of driving one of these pests, as they are likely too often to prove, through a part of the magnificent ruins of Furness Abbey – an outrage which was prevented by some one pointing out how easily a deviation might be made; and the hint produced its due effect upon the engineer.

Sacred as that relic of the devotion of our ancestors deserves to be kept, there are temples of Nature, temples built by the Almighty, which have a still higher claim to be left unviolated. Almost every reach of the winding vales in this district might once have presented itself to a man of imagination and feeling under that aspect, or, as the Vale of Grasmere appeared to the Poet Gray more than seventy years ago. 'No flaring gentleman's-house' says he, 'nor garden-walls break in upon the repose of this little unsuspected *paradise*, but all is peace,' [23] &c., &c. Were the Poet now living, how would he have lamented the probable intrusion of a railway with its scarifications, its intersections, its noisy machinery, its smoke, and swarms of pleasure-hunters, most of them thinking that they do not fly fast enough through the country which they have come to see. Even a broad highway may in some places greatly impair the characteristic beauty of the country, as will be readily acknowledged by those who remember what the Lake of Grasmere was before the new road that runs along its eastern margin had been constructed.

> Quanto praestantias esset
> Numen aquae viridi si margine clauderet undas
> Herba – [24]

As it once was, and fringed with wood, instead of the breastwork of bare wall that now confines it. In the same manner has the beauty, and still more the sublimity of many Passes in the Alps been injuriously affected. Will the reader excuse a quotation from a MS. poem in which I attempted to describe the impression made upon my mind by the descent towards Italy along the Simplon before the new military road had taken place of the old muleteer track with its primitive simplicities?

> Brook and road
> Were fellow-travellers in this gloomy pass,
> And with them did we journey several hours
> At a slow step. The immeasurable height
> Of woods decaying, never to be decayed,
> The stationary blasts of waterfalls,
> And in the narrow rent, at every turn,
> Winds thwarting winds bewildered and forlorn,
> The torrent shooting from the clear blue sky,
> The rocks that muttered close upon our ears,
> Black drizzling crags that spake by the way-side
> As if a voice were in them, the sick sight
> And giddy prospect of the raving stream,
> The unfettered clouds and region of the heavens,
> Tumult and peace, the darkness and the light,
> Were all like workings of one mind, the features
> Of the same face, blossoms upon one tree,
> Characters of the great Apocalypse,
> The types and symbols of Eternity,
> Of first, and last, and midst, and without end.
>                                                        1799 [25]

Thirty years afterwards I crossed the Alps by the same Pass:[26] and what had become of the forms and powers to which I had been indebted for those emotions? Many of them remained of course undestroyed and indestructible. But, though the road and torrent continued to run parallel to each other, their fellowship was put an end to. The stream had dwindled into comparative insignificance, so much had Art interfered with and taken the lead of Nature; and although the utility of the new work, as facilitating the intercourse of great nations, was readily acquiesced in, and the workmanship, in some places, could not but excite admiration, it was impossible to suppress regret for what had vanished for ever. The oratories heretofore not unfrequently met with, on a road still somewhat perilous, were gone; the simple and rude bridges swept away; and instead of travellers proceeding, with leisure to observe and feel, were pilgrims of fashion hurried along in their carriages, not a few of them perhaps discussing the merits of 'the last new Novel,' or poring over their Guide-books, or fast asleep. Similar remarks might be applied to the mountainous country of Wales; but there too, the plea of utility, especially as expediting the communications between England and Ireland, more than justifies the labours of the Engineer. Not so would it be with the Lake District. A railroad is already planned along the sea coast, and another from Lancaster to Carlisle is in great forwardness: an intermediate one is therefore, to say the least of it, superfluous. Once for all let me declare that it is not against Railways but against the abuse of them that I am contending.

How far I am from undervaluing the benefit to be expected from railways in their legitimate application will appear from the following lines published in 1837, and composed some years earlier.[27]

### Steamboats and Railways

Motions and Means, on sea and land at war
With old poetic feeling, not for this
Shall ye, by poets even, be judged amiss!
Nor shall your presence, howsoe'er it mar
The loveliness of nature, prove a bar
To the mind's gaining that prophetic sense
Of future good, that point of vision, whence
May be discovered what in soul ye are.
In spite of all that Beauty must disown
In your harsh features, Nature doth embrace
Her lawful offspring in man's Art; and Time,
Pleased with your triumphs o'er his brother Space,
Accepts from your bold hands the proffered crown
Of hope, and welcomes you with cheer sublime.

I have now done with the subject. The time of life at which I have arrived may, I trust, if nothing else will, guard me from the imputation of having written from any selfish interests, or from fear of disturbance which a railway might cause to myself. If gratitude for what repose and quiet in a district hitherto, for the most part, not disfigured but beautified by human hands, have done for me through the course of a long life, and hope that others might hereafter be benefited in the same manner and in the same country, *be* selfishness, then, indeed, but not otherwise, I plead guilty to the charge. Nor have I opposed this undertaking on account of the inhabitants of the district *merely*, but, as hath been intimated, for the sake of every one, however humble his condition, who coming hither shall bring with him an eye to perceive, and a heart to feel and worthily enjoy. And as for holiday pastimes, if a scene is to be chosen suitable to them for persons thronging from a distance, it may be found elsewhere at less cost of every kind. But, in fact, we have too much hurrying about in these islands; much for idle pleasure, and more from over activity in the pursuit of wealth, without regard to the good or happiness of others.

[At the end, Wordsworth printed his sonnet, 'Proud Were Ye, Mountains' – omitted here.]

# SECTION II

## *Morals*

# *Preface to* The Borderers

※— —※— —※—

[*Composed between the latter half (probably late) 1796 and late February 1797. First published 1940.*]

*This unusual prose analysis by a playwright of a dramatic character of his own creation was almost certainly written because of adverse criticism; Covent Garden reportedly rejected* The Borderers *in 1797 due to the 'metaphysical obscurity' of Oswald, the villain and the central character of Wordsworth's play. The revised play was finally published over forty years later in 1842 with a brief note substituted for this essay. By that time the name 'Rivers' mentioned in this essay had been changed to 'Oswald'.*

Let us suppose a young Man of great intellectual powers, yet without any solid principles of genuine benevolence.[1] His master passions are pride and the love of distinction – He has deeply imbibed a spirit of enterprize in a tumultuous age. He goes into the world and is betrayed into a great crime. – That influence on which all his happiness is built immediately deserts him. His talents are robbed of their weight – his exertions are unavailing, and he quits the world in disgust, with strong misanthropic feelings. In his retirement, he is impelled to examine the reasonableness of established opinions, and the force of his mind exhausts itself in constant efforts to separate the elements of virtue and vice. It is his pleasure and his consolation to hunt out whatever is bad in actions usually esteemed virtuous and to detect the

97

good in actions which the universal sense of mankind teaches us to reprobate. While the general exertion of his intellect seduces him from the remembrance of his own crime, the particular conclusions to which he is led have a tendency to reconcile him to himself. His feelings are interested in making him a moral sceptic and as his scepticism encreases, he is raised in his own esteem. After this process has been continued some time his natural energy and restlessness impel him again into the world. In this state, pressed by the recollection of his guilt, he seeks relief from two sources, action and meditation. Of actions those are most attractive which best exhibit his own powers, partly from the original pride of his character and still more because the loss of authority and influence which followed upon his crime was the first circumstance which impressed him with the magnitude of that crime and brought along with it those tormenting sensations by which he is assailed. The recovery of his original importance and the exhibition of his own powers are therefore in his mind almost identified with the extinction of those painful feelings which attend the recollection of his guilt. Perhaps there is no cause which has greater weight in preventing the return of bad men to virtue than that good actions being for the most part in their nature silent and regularly progressive, they do not present those sudden results which can afford a sufficient stimulus to a troubled mind. In processes of vice the effects are more frequently immediate, palpable, and extensive. Power is much more easily manifested in destroying than in creating. A child, Rousseau has observed,[2] will tear in pieces fifty toys before he will think of making one. From these causes, assisted by disgust and misanthropic feeling, the character we are now contemplating will have a strong tendency to vice. His energies are most impressively manifested in works of devastation. He is the Orlando of Ariosto,[3] the Cardenio of Cervantes,[4] who lays waste the groves that should shelter him. He has rebelled against the world and the laws of the world and he regards them as tyrannical masters, convinced that he is right in some of his conclusions, he nourishes a contempt for mankind the more dangerous because he has been led to it by reflexion. Being in the habit of considering the world as a body which is in some sort at war with him, he has a feeling borrowed from that habit which gives an additional zest to his hatred of those members of society whom he hates and to his contempt of those whom he despises. Add to this, that a mind fond of nourishing sentiments of contempt will be prone to the admission of those feelings which are considered under any uncommon bond of relation (as must be the case with a man who has quarrelled with the world); the feelings will mutually strengthen each other. In this morbid state of mind he cannot exist without occupation, he requires constant provocatives, all his pleasures are prospective, he is perpetually ch[u]sing [5] a phantom, he commits new crimes to drive away the memory of the past. But the lenitives of his pain are twofold: meditation as well as action. Accordingly his reason is almost exclusively employed in justifying his past enormities and in enabling him to commit new ones. He is perpetually imposing upon himself; he has a sophism for every crime. The *mild* effusions of thought, the milk of human reason, [6] are unknown to him. His imagination is powerful, being strengthened by the habit of picturing possible forms of society where his crimes would be no longer crimes, and he would enjoy that estimation to which from his intellectual attainments he deems himself entitled. The nicer shades of manners he disregards, but whenever, upon looking back upon past ages, or in surveying the practices of different countries in the age in which he lives he finds such contrarieties as seem to affect the principles of *morals*, he exults over his discovery and applies it to his heart as the dearest of his consolations. Such a mind cannot but discover some truths, but he is unable to profit by them and in his hands they become instruments of evil.

He presses truth and falsehood into the same service. He looks at society through an optical glass of a peculiar tint; something of the forms of objects he takes from objects, but their colour is exclusively what he gives them; it is one, and it is his own. Having indulged a habit, dangerous in a man who has fallen, of dallying with moral calculations, he becomes an empiric, [7] and a daring and unfeeling empiric. He disguises from himself his own malignity by assuming the character of a speculator in morals, and one who has the hardihood to realize his speculations.

It will easily be perceived that to such a mind those enterprizes which are the most extraordinary will in time appear the most inviting. His appetite from being exhausted becomes unnatural. Accordingly, he will struggle [      ]⁸ to characterize and to exalt actions little and contemptible in themselves, by a forced greatness of *manner*, and will chequer and degrade enterprizes great in their atrocity by grotesque littleness of manner and fantastic obliquities. He is like a worn-out voluptuary — he finds his temptation in strangeness — he is unable to suppress a low hankering after the *double entendre* in vice; yet his thirst after the extraordinary buoys him up, and supported by a habit of constant reflexion he frequently breaks out into what has the appearance of greatness; and in sudden emergencies, when he is called upon by surprize and thrown out of the path of his regular habits, or when dormant associations are awakened tracing the revolutions through which his character has passed, in painting his former self he really *is* great.

Benefits conferred on a man like this will be the seeds of a worse feeling than ingratitude. They will give birth to positive hatred. Let him be deprived of power, though by means which he despises, and he will never forgive. It will scarcely be denied that such a mind, by very slight external motives may be led to the commission of the greatest enormities. Let its malignant feelings be fixed on a particular object and the rest follows of itself.

Having shaken off the obligations of religion and morality in a dark and tempestuous age, it is probable that such a character will be infected with a tinge of superstition. The period in which he lives teems with great events which he feels he cannot controul. That influence which his pride makes him unwilling to allow to his fellowmen he has no reluctance to ascribe to invisible agents: his pride impels him to superstition and shapes out the nature of his belief: his creed is his own: it is made and not adopted.

A character like this, or some of its features at least, I have attempted to delineate in the following drama. I have introduced him deliberately prosecuting the destruction of an amiable young man by the most atrocious means and with a pertinacity, as it should seem, not to be accounted for but on the supposition of the most malignant injuries. No such injuries, however, appear to have been sustained. What are then his motives? First, it must be observed that to make the non-existence of a common motive itself a motive to action is a practice which we are never so prone to attribute exclusively to madmen as when we forget ourselves. Our love of the marvellous is not confined to external things. There is no object on which it settles with more delight than on our own minds. This habit is in the very essence of the habit which we are delineating.

But there are particles of that poisonous mineral of which Iago speaks [9] gnawing his inwards; his malevolent feelings are excited, and he hates the more deeply because he feels he ought not to hate.

We all know that the dissatisfaction accompanying the first impulses towards a criminal action, where the mind is familiar with guilt, acts as a stimulus to proceed in that action. Uneasiness must be driven away by fresh uneasiness; obstinacy, waywardness, and wilful blindness are alternatives resorted to, till there is an universal insurrection of every depraved feeling of the heart.

Besides, in a course of criminal conduct every fresh step that we make appears a justification of the one that preceded it, it seems to bring back again the moment of liberty and choice; it banishes the idea of repentance and seems to set remorse at defiance. Every time we plan a fresh accumulation of our guilt we have restored to us something like that original state of mind, that perturbed pleasure, which first made the crime attractive.

If, after these general remarks, [I am asked] [10] what are Rivers's motives to the atrocity detailed in the drama? I answer they are founded chiefly in the very constitution of his character; in his pride which borders even upon madness, in his restless disposition, in his disturbed mind, in his superstition, in irresistible propensities to embody in practical experiments his worst and most extravagant speculations, in his thoughts and in his feelings, in his general habits and his particular impulses, in his perverted reason justifying his perverted instincts. The general moral intended to be impressed by the delineation of such a character is obvious: it is to shew the dangerous use which may be made of reason when a man has committed a great crime.

There is a kind of superstition [11] which makes us shudder when we find moral sentiments to which we attach a sacred importance applied to vicious purposes. In real life this is done every day and we do not feel the disgust. The difference is here. In works of imagination we see the motive and the end. In real life we rarely see either the one or the other, and when the distress comes it prevents us from attending to the cause. This superstition of which I have spoken is not without its use; yet it appears to be one great source of our vices; it is our constant engine in seducing each other. We are lulled asleep by its agency and betrayed before we know that an attempt is made to betray us.

I have endeavoured to shake this prejudice, persuaded that in so doing I was well employed. It has been a further object with me to shew that from abuses interwoven with the texture of society a bad man may be furnished with sophisms in support of his crimes which it would be difficult to answer.

One word more upon the subject of motives. In private life what is more common than when we hear of law-suits prosecuted to the utter ruin of the parties, and the most deadly feuds in families, to find them attributed to trifling and apparently inadequate sources? But when our malignant passions operate, the original causes which called them forth are soon supplanted, yet when we account for the effect we forget the immediate impulse, and the whole is attributed to the force from which the first motion was received. The vessel keeps sailing on, and we attribute her progress in the voyage to the ropes which first towed her out of harbour.

To this must be added that we are too apt to apply our own moral sentiments as a measure of the conduct of others. We insensibly suppose that a criminal action assumes the same form to the agent as to ourselves. We forget that his feelings and his reason are equally busy in contracting its dimensions and pleading for its necessity.

## *Preface to* The Borderers

*a Tragedy*

On human actions reason though you can,
It may be reason, but it is not man;
His principle of action once explore,
That instant 'tis his principle no more.
Pope.[12]

# [Essay on Morals]

[*Probably composed between 26 September 1798 and 23 February 1799. First published in 1961. Most of the punctuation has been added.*]

*Manuscript evidence suggests that this fragment of an essay was probably not continued by Wordsworth much beyond the point where it ends in the text here.*

I think publications in which we formally and systematically lay down rules for the actions of Men cannot be too long delayed. I shall scarcely express myself too strongly when I say that I consider such books as Mr Godwyn's, Mr Paley's,[1] and those of the whole tribe of authors of that class as impotent to all their intended good purposes; to which I wish I could add that they were equally impotent to all bad ones. This sentence will, I am afraid, be unintelligible. You will at least have a glimpse of my meaning when I observe that our attention ought principally to be fixed upon that part of our conduct and actions which is the result of our habits. In a strict sense all our actions are the result of our habits – but I mean here to exclude those accidental and indefinite actions, which do not regularly and in common flow from this or that particular habit. As, for example, a tale of distress is related in *a mixed company*, relief for the sufferers proposed. The vain man, the proud man, the avaricious man etc., all contribute, but from very different feelings. Now in all the cases

[Essay on Morals]

except in that of the affectionate and benevolent man, I would call the act of giving more or less accidental – I return to our habits – Now, I know no book or system of moral philosophy written with sufficient power to melt into our affections, to incorporate itself with the blood and vital juices of our minds, and thence to have any influence worth our notice in forming those habits of which I am speaking. Perhaps by the plan which these authors pursue this effect is rendered unattainable. Can it be imagined by any man who has deeply examined his own heart that an old habit will be foregone, or a new one formed, by a series of propositions, which, presenting no image to the mind, can convey no feeling which has any connection with the supposed archetype or fountain of the proposition existing in human life? These moralists attempt to strip the mind of all its old clothing when their object ought to be to furnish it with new. All this is the consequence of an undue value set upon that faculty which we call reason. The whole secret of this juggler's trick lies (not in fitting words to things (which would be a noble employment) but) in fitting things to words – I have said that these bald and naked reasonings are impotent over our habits; they cannot form them; from the same cause they are equally powerless in regulating our judgments concerning the value of men and things. They contain no picture of human life; they *describe* nothing. They in no respect enable us to be practically useful by informing us how men placed in such or such situations will necessarily act, and thence enabling us to apply ourselves to the means of turning them into a more beneficial course, if necessary, or of giving them new ardour and new knowledge when they are proceeding as they ought.

We do not *argue* in defence of our *good* actions; we feel internally their beneficent effect; we are satisfied with this delicious sensation; and, even when we are called upon to justify our conduct, we perform the task with languor and indifference. Not so when we have been unworthily employed; then it is that we are all activity and keenness; then it is that we repair to systems of morality for arguments in defence of ourselves; and sure enough are we to find them. In this state of our mind, lifeless words, and abstract propositions, will not

105

be destitute of power to lay asleep the spirit of self-accusation and exclude the uneasiness of repentance. Thus confirmed and comforted, we are prepared immediately to transgress anew, and, following up this process, we shall find that I have erred when I said that

# Reply to Mathetes

~~~~~~~~~~~~~~~~~~~~~~~~~

[Probably composed from early November to early December (by 11 December) 1809. First published in The Friend 14 December 1809 and 4 January 1810. The text followed here is the manuscript version, except at the point at which the two parts of the letter are joined, where the text of The Friend (1818) is followed.]

*A letter concerning the moral difficulties of adolescence was contributed to Samuel Taylor Coleridge's weekly periodical The Friend by two young Scots, John Wilson and Alexander Blair, under the joint pseudonym 'Mathetes' (Greek for* pupil*). Coleridge thereupon asked Wordsworth to provide a reply to the letter and printed both in separate issues of The Friend. Wordsworth does not address many of 'Mathetes'' specific points but rather the general issues raised.*

The Friend might rest satisfied that his exertions thus far have not been wholly unprofitable, if no other proof had been given of their influence, than that of having called forth the foregoing Letter, with which he has been so much interested, that he could not deny himself the pleasure of communicating it to his Readers. – In answer to his Correspondent, it need scarcely here be repeated, that one of the main purposes of his work is to weigh, honestly and thoughtfully, the moral worth and intellectual power of the Age in which we live; to ascertain our gain and our loss; to determine what we are in ourselves positively, and what we are compared with our Ancestors; and thus, and by every other means within his power, to discover what may be hoped for future times, what and how lamentable are the evils to be feared, and how far there is cause for fear. If this attempt should not be made wholly in vain, my ingenuous Correspondent, and all who are in a state of mind resembling that of which he gives so lively a picture, will be enabled more readily and surely to distinguish false from legitimate objects of admiration: and thus may the personal errors which he would guard against, be more effectually prevented or removed, by the development of general truth for a general purpose, than by instructions specifically adapted to himself or to the Class of which he is the able Representative. There is a life and spirit in knowledge which we extract from truths scattered for the benefit of all, and which the mind, by its own activity, has appropriated to itself – a life and a spirit, which is seldom found in knowledge communicated by formal and direct precepts, even when they are exalted and endeared by reverence and love for the Teacher.

Nevertheless, though I trust that the assistance which my Correspondent has done me the honour to request, will in course of time flow naturally from my labours, in a manner that will best serve him, I cannot resist the inclination to connect, at present, with his Letter a few remarks of direct application to the subject of it – *remarks*, I say, for to such I shall confine myself, independent of the main point out of which his complaint and request both proceed, I mean the assumed inferiority of the present Age in moral dignity and intellectual power, to those which have preceded it. For if the fact were true, that we had even surpassed our Ancestors in the best of what is good, the main part of the dangers and impediments which my Correspondent has feelingly pourtrayed, could not cease to exist for minds like his, nor indeed would they be much diminished; as they arise out of the Constitution of things, from the nature of Youth, from the laws that govern the growth of the Faculties, and from the necessary condition of the great body of Mankind. Let us throw ourselves back to the age of Elizabeth, and call up to mind the

Heroes, the Warriors, the Statesmen, the Poets, the Divines, and the Moral Philosophers, with which the reign of the Virgin Queen was illustrated.[1] Or if we be more strongly attracted by the moral purity and greatness, and that sanctity of civil and religious duty, with which the Tyranny of Charles the first was struggled against, let us cast our eyes, in the hurry of admiration, round that circle of glorious Patriots – but do not let us be persuaded, that each of these, in his course of discipline, was uniformly helped forward by those with whom he associated, or by those whose care it was to direct him. Then as now existed objects, to which the wisest attached undue importance; then as now judgment was misled by factions and parties – time wasted in controversies fruitless, except as far as they quickened the faculties; then as now Minds were venerated or idolized, which owed their influence to the weakness of their Contemporaries rather than to their own power. Then, though great Actions were wrought, and great works in literature and science produced, yet the general taste was capricious, fantastical, or grovelling: and in this point as in all others, was Youth subject to delusion, frequent in proportion to the liveliness of the sensibility, and strong as the strength of the imagination. Every Age hath abounded in instances of Parents, Kindred, and Friends, who, by indirect influence of example, or by positive injunction and exhortation have diverted or discouraged the Youth, who, in the simplicity and purity of Nature, had determined to follow his intellectual genius through good and through evil, and had devoted himself to knowledge, to the practice of Virtue and the preservation of integrity, in slight of temporal rewards. Above all, have not the common duties and cares of common life, at all times exposed Men to injury, from causes whose action is the more fatal from being silent and unremitting, and which, wherever it was not jealously watched and steadily opposed, must have pressed upon and consumed the diviner spirit?

There are two errors, into which we easily slip when thinking of past times. One lies in forgetting, in the excellence of what remains, the large overbalance of worthlessness that has been swept away. Ranging over the wide tracts of Antiquity, the situation of the Mind may be likened to that of a Traveller[2] in some unpeopled part of America, who is attracted to the burial place of one of the primitive Inhabitants. It is conspicuous upon an eminence, 'a mount upon a mount!'[3] He digs into it, and finds that it contains the bones of a Man of mighty stature: and he is tempted to give way to a belief, that as there were Giants in those days,[4] so that all Men were Giants. But a second and wiser thought may suggest to him, that this Tomb would never have forced itself upon his notice, if it had not contained a Body that was distinguished from others, that of a Man who had been selected as a Chieftain or Ruler for the very reason that he surpassed the rest of his Tribe in stature, and who now lies thus conspicuously inhumed upon the mountain-top, while the bones of his Followers are laid unobtrusively together in their burrows upon the Plain below. The second habitual error is, that in this compari-son of Ages we divide time merely into past and present, and place these in the balance to be weighed against each other, not consider-ing that the present is in our estimation not more than a period of thirty years, or half a century at most, and that the past is a mighty accumulation of many such periods, perhaps the whole of recorded time, or at least the whole of that portion of it in which our own Country has been distinguished. We may illustrate this by a familiar use of the words Ancient and Modern,[5] when applied to Poetry – what can be more inconsiderate or unjust than to compare a few existing Writers with the whole succession of their Progenitors? The delusion, from the moment that our thoughts are directed to it, seems too gross to deserve mention; yet Men will talk for hours upon Poetry, balancing against each other the words Ancient and Modern, and be unconscious that they have fallen into it.

These observations are not made as implying a dissent from the belief of my Correspondent, that the moral spirit and intellectual powers of this Country are declining; but to guard against *unqualified* admiration, even in cases where admiration has been rightly fixed, and to prevent that depression, which must necessarily follow, where the notion of the peculiar unfavourableness of the present times to dignity of mind, has been carried too far. For in proportion as we imagine obstacles to exist out of ourselves to retard our progress, will, in fact, our progress be retarded, – Deeming then, that in all ages an ardent mind will be baffled and led astray in the manner under contemplation, though in various degrees, I shall at present content myself with a few practical and desultory comments upon some of those general causes, to which my Correspondent justly attributes the errors in opinion, and the lowering or deadening of sentiment, to which ingenuous and aspiring Youth is exposed. And first, for the heart-cheering belief in the perpetual progress of the Species towards a point of unattainable perfection. If the present Age do indeed transcend the past in what is most beneficial and honorable, he that perceives this, being in no error, has no cause for complaint; but if it be not so, a Youth of genius might, it should seem, be preserved from any wrong influence of this faith, by an insight into a simple truth, namely, that it is not necessary, in order to satisfy the desires of our Nature, or to reconcile us to the economy of Providence, that there should be at all times a continuous advance in what is of highest worth. In fact it is not, as a Writer of the present day has admirably observed, in the power of fiction, to pourtray in words, or of the imagination to conceive in spirit, Actions or Characters of more exalted virtue, than those which thousands of years ago have existed upon earth, as we know from the records of authentic history. Such is the inherent dignity of human nature, that there belong to it sublimities of virtue which all men may attain, and which no man can transcend: And, though this be not true in an equal degree, of intellectual power, yet in the persons of Plato, Demosthenes, and Homer, – and in those of Shakespeare, Milton, and lord Bacon, – were enshrined as much of the divinity of intellect as the inhabitants of this planet can hope will ever take up its abode among them. But the question is not of the power or worth of individual Minds, but of the general moral or intellectual merits of an Age – or a People, or of the human Race. Be it so – let us allow and believe that there is a progress in the Species towards unattainable perfection, or whether this be so or not, that it is a necessity of a good and greatly-gifted

Nature to believe it – surely it does not follow, that this progress should be constant in those virtues, and intellectual qualities, and in those departments of knowledge, which in themselves absolutely considered are of most value – things independant and in their degree indispensible. The progress of the Species neither is nor can be like that of a Roman road in a right line. It may be more justly compared to that of a River, which both in its smaller reaches and larger turnings, is frequently forced back towards its fountains, by objects which cannot otherwise be eluded or overcome; yet with an accompanying impulse that will ensure its advancement hereafter, it is either gaining strength every hour, or conquering in secret some difficulty, by a labour that contributes as effectually to further it in its course, as when it moves forward uninterrupted in a line, direct as that of the Roman road with which we began the comparison.[6]

It suffices to content the mind, though there may be an apparent stagnation, or a retrograde movement in the Species, that something is doing which is necessary to be done, and the effects of which, will in due time appear; – that something is unremittingly gaining, either in secret preparation or in open and triumphant progress. But in fact here, as every where, we are deceived by creations which the mind is compelled to make for itself: we speak of the Species not as an aggregate, but as endued with the form and separate life of an Individual. But human kind, what is it else than myriads of rational beings in various degrees obedient to their Reason; some torpid, some aspiring, some in eager chace to the right hand, some to the left; these wasting down their moral nature, and those feeding it for immortality? A whole generation may appear even to sleep, or may be exasperated with rage – they that compose it, tearing each other to pieces with more than brutal fury. It is enough for complacency and hope, that scattered and solitary minds are always labouring some-where in the service of truth and virtue; and that by the sleep of the multitude, the energy of the multitude may be prepared; and that by the fury of the people, the chains of the people may be broken. Happy moment was it for England when her Chaucer, who has rightly been called the morning star of her literature, appeared above the horizon – when her Wickliff, like the Sun, 'shot orient beams' [7] through the night of Romish superstition! – Yet may the darkness and the desolating hurricane which immediately followed in the wars of York and Lancaster, be deemed in their turn a blessing, with which the Land has been visited.

May I return to the thought of progress, of accumulation, of increasing light or of any other image, by which it may please us to represent the improvement of the Species? The hundred years that followed the Usurpation of Henry the fourth, were a hurling-back of the mind of the Country, a delapidation, an extinction; yet institutions, laws, customs and habits, were then broken down, which would not have been so readily, nor perhaps so thoroughly destroyed by the gradual influence of increasing knowledge; and under the oppression of which, if they had continued to exist, the Virtue and intellectual Prowess of the succeeding Century could not have appeared at all, much less could they have displayed themselves with that eager haste and with those beneficent triumphs which will to the end of time be looked back upon with admiration and gratitude.

If the foregoing obvious distinctions be once clearly perceived, and steadily kept in view, – I do not see why a belief in the progress of human Nature towards perfection should dispose a youthful Mind, however enthusiastic, to an undue admiration of his own Age, and thus tend to degrade that mind.

But let me strike at once at the root of the evil complained of in my Correspondent's Letter. – Protection from any fatal effect of seductions and hindrances which opinion may throw in the way of pure and high-minded Youth can only be obtained with certainty at the same price by which every thing great and good is obtained, namely, steady dependence upon voluntary and self-originating effort, and upon the practice of self-examination sincerely aimed at and rigourously enforced. But how is this to be expected from Youth? Is it not to demand the fruit when the blossom is barely put forth and is hourly at the mercy of the frosts and winds? To expect from Youth these virtues and habits in that degree of excellence to which in mature years they *may* be carried would indeed be preposterous.

Yet has Youth many helps and aptitudes, for the discharge of these difficult duties, which are withdrawn for the most part from the more advanced stages of Life. For Youth has its own wealth and independence; it is rich in health of Body and animal Spirits, in its sensibility to the impressions of the natural Universe, in the conscious growth of Knowledge, in lively sympathy and familiar communion with the generous actions recorded in History and with the high passions of Poetry; and, above all, Youth is rich in the possession of Time, and the accompanying consciousness of Freedom and Power. The Young Man feels that he stands at a distance from the Season when his harvest is to be reaped, – that he had Leisure and may look around – may defer both the choice and the execution of his purposes. If he makes an attempt and shall fail, new hopes immediately rush in and new promises. Hence, in the happy confidence of his feelings and in the elasticity of his Spirit, neither worldly ambition, nor the love of praise nor dread of censure, nor the necessity of worldly maintenance, nor any of those causes which tempt or compel the mind habitually to look out of itself for support; neither these, nor the passions of envy, fear, hatred, despondency, and the rankling of disappointed hopes (all which in after life give birth to and regulate the efforts of Men and determine their opinions) – have power to preside over the choice of the Young, if the disposition be not naturally bad, or the circumstances have not been in an uncommon degree unfavourable.

In contemplation, then, of this disinterested and free condition of the Youthful mind, I deem it in many points peculiarly capable of searching into itself, and of profiting by a few simple questions – such as these that follow. Am I chiefly gratified by the exertion of my power from the pure pleasure of intellectual activity, and from the knowledge thereby acquired? In other words, to what degree do I value my faculties and my attainments for their own sakes? or are they chiefly prized by me on account of the distinction which they confer, or the superiority which they give me over others? Am I aware that immediate influence and a general acknowledgment of merit are no necessary adjuncts of a successful adherence to study and meditation, in those departments of knowledge which are of most value to mankind? – that a recompence of honours and emoluments is far less to be expected – in fact, that there is little natural connection between them? Have I perceived this truth? – and, perceiving it, does the countenance of philosophy continue to appear as bright and beautiful in my eyes? – has no haze bedimmed it? has no cloud passed over and hidden from me that look which was before so encouraging? Knowing that it is my duty, and feeling that it is my inclination, to mingle as a social Being with my fellow Men; prepared also to submit chearfully to the necessity that will probably exist of re-linquishing, for the purpose of gaining a livelihood, the greatest portion of my time to employments where I shall have little or no choice how or when I am to act; have I, at this moment when I stand as it were upon the threshold of the busy world, a clear intuition of that preeminence in which virtue and truth (involving in this latter word the sanctities of religion) sit enthroned above all dominations and dignities which, in various degrees of exaltation, rule over the desires of Men? – Do I feel that, if their solemn Mandates shall be forgotten, or disregarded, or denied the obedience due to them when opposed to others, I shall not only have lived for no good purpose, but that I shall have sacrificed my birth-right as a Rational being; and that every other acquisition will be a bane and a disgrace to me? This is not spoken with reference to such sacrifices as present them-selves to the Youthful imagination in the shape of crimes, acts by which the conscience is violated; such a thought, I know, would be recoiled from at once not without indignation; but I write in the Spirit of the ancient fable of Prodicus,[8] representing the choice of Hercules. – Here is the WORLD, a female figure approaching at the head of a train of willing or giddy followers: – her air and deportment are at once careless, remiss, self-satisfied, and haughty: – and there is INTELLECTUAL PROWESS, with a pale cheek and severe brow, leading in chains Truth, her beautiful and modest Captive. The One makes her salutation with a discourse of ease, pleasure, freedom, and domestic tranquillity; or, if she invite to labour, it is labour in the busy and beaten track, with assurance of the complacent regards of Parents, Friends, and of those with whom we associate. The promise also may be upon her lip of the huzzas of the multitude, of the smile of Kings, and the munificent rewards of senates. The Other does not venture to hold forth any of these allurements; she does not conceal from him whom she addresses the impediments, the disappointments, the ignorance and prejudice which her Follower will have to encounter, if devoted when duty calls, to active life; and if to contemplative, she lays nakedly before him a scheme of solitary and unremitting labour, a life of entire neglect perhaps, or assuredly a life exposed to scorn, insult, persecution, and hatred; but cheared by encouragement from a grateful few, by applauding Conscience, and by a prophetic anticipation, perhaps, of fame – a late though lasting consequence. Of these two, each in this manner soliciting you to become her Adherent, you doubt not which to prefer; – but oh! the thought of moment is not preference, but the *degree* of preference; – the passionate and pure choice, the inward sense of absolute and unchangeable devotion.

I spoke of a few simple questions – the question involved in this deliberation *is* simple; but at the same time it is high and awful: and I would gladly know whether an answer can be returned satisfactory to the mind. – We will for a moment suppose that it can not; that there is a startling and a hesitation. – Are we then to despond? to retire from all contest? and to reconcile ourselves at once to cares without generous hope, and to efforts in which there is no more Moral life than that which is found in the business and labours of the unfavoured and unaspiring Many? No – but, if the enquiry have not been on just ground satisfactorily answered, we may refer confidently our Youth to that Nature of which he deems himself an enthusiastic follower, and one who wishes to continue no less faithful and enthusiastic. – We would tell him that there are paths which he has not trodden; recesses which he has not penetrated; that there is a beauty which he has not seen – a pathos which he has not felt – a sublimity to which he hath not been raised. If he has trembled, because there has occasionally taken place in him a lapse of which he is conscious; if he foresee open or secret attacks which he has had intimations that he will neither be strong enough to resist nor watchful enough to elude, let him not hastily ascribe this weakness, this deficiency, and the painful apprehensions accompanying them, in any degree to the virtues or noble qualities with which Youth by Nature is furnished; but let him first be assured, before he looks about for the means of attaining the insight, the discriminating powers, and the confirmed wisdom of Manhood, that his soul has more to demand of the appropriate excellences of Youth than Youth has yet supplied to it; — that the evil under which he labours is not a superabundance of the instincts and the animating spirit of that age, but a falling short, or a failure. — But what can he gain from this admonition? he cannot recall past time; he cannot begin his journey afresh; he cannot untwist the links by which, in no undelightful harmony, images and sentiments are wedded in his mind. Granted that the sacred light of Childhood is and must be for him no more than a remembrance. He may, notwithstanding, be remanded to Nature; and with trust-worthy hopes; founded less upon his sentient than upon his intel-lectual Being — to Nature, not as leading on insensibly to the society of Reason; but to Reason and Will, as leading back to the wisdom of Nature. A re-union, in this order accomplished, will bring reforma-tion and timely support; and the two powers of Reason and Nature, thus reciprocally teacher and taught, may advance together in a track to which there is no limit.

We have been discoursing (by implication at least) of Infancy, Childhood, Boyhood, and Youth — of pleasures lying upon the un-folding Intellect plenteously as morning dew-drops — of Knowledge inhaled insensibly like a fragrance — of dispositions stealing into the Spirit like Music from unknown quarters — of images uncalled for and rising up like exhalations — of hopes plucked like beautiful wild flowers from the ruined tombs that border the high-ways of Anti-quity to make a garland for a living forehead; — in a word, we have been treating of Nature as a Teacher of Truth through joy and through gladness, and as a Creatress of the faculties by a process of smoothness and delight. We have made no mention of fear, shame, sorrow, nor of ungovernable and vexing thoughts; because, although these have been and have done mighty service, they are overlooked in that stage of life when Youth is passing into Manhood, – overlooked, or forgotten. We now apply for succour, which we need, to a faculty that works after a different course: that faculty is Reason: she gives much spontaneously but she seeks for more; she works by thought, through feeling; yet in thought she begins and ends.

A familiar incident may elucidate this contrast in the operations of Nature, may render plain the manner in which a process of intellectual improvement, the reverse of that which Nature pursues is by Reason introduced. – There never perhaps existed a School-boy who, having when he retired to rest carelessly blown out his candle, and having chanced to notice as he lay upon his bed in the ensuing darkness the sullen light which had survived the extinguished flame, did not, at some time or other, watch that light as if his mind were bound to it by a spell. It fades and revives – gathers to a point – seems as if it would go out in a moment – again recovers its strength, nay becomes brighter than before: it continues to shine with an endurance which in its apparent weakness is a mystery – it protracts its existence so long, clinging to the power which supports it, that the Observer, who had lain down in his bed so easy-minded, becomes sad and melancholy: his sympathies are touched – it is to him an intimation and an image of departing human life; – the thought comes nearer to him – it is the life of a venerated Parent, of a beloved Brother or Sister, or of an aged Domestic; who are gone to the grave, or whose destiny it soon may be thus to linger, thus to stand upon the last point of mortal existence, thus finally to depart and be seen no more – This is Nature teaching seriously and sweetly through the affections – melting the heart, and through that instinct of tenderness, developing the understanding. – In this instance the object of solicitude is the bodily life of another. Let us accompany this same Boy to that period between Youth and Manhood when a solicitude may be awakened for the moral life of himself. – Are there any powers by which, beginning with a sense of inward decay that affects not however the natural life, he could call up to mind the same image and hang over it with an equal interest as a visible type of his own perishing Spirit? – Oh! surely, if the being of the individual be under his own care – if it be his first care – if duty begin from the point of accountableness to our Conscience, and, through that, to God and human Nature; – if without such primary sense of duty all secondary care of Teacher, of Friend, or Parent, must be baseless and fruitless; if, lastly, the motions of the Soul transcend in worth those of the animal functions, nay give to them their sole value; then truly are there such powers: and the image of the dying taper may be recalled and contemplated, though with no sadness in the nerves, no disposition to tears, no unconquerable sighs, yet with a melancholy in the soul, a sinking inward into ourselves from thought to thought, a steady remonstrance, and a high resolve. – Let then the Youth go back, as occasion will permit, to Nature and to Solitude, thus admonished by Reason, and relying upon this newly-acquired support. A world of fresh sensations will gradually open upon him as his mind puts off its infirmities, and as, instead of being propelled restlessly towards others in admiration or too hasty love, he makes it his prime business to understand himself. New sensations, I affirm, will be opened out – pure, and sanctioned by that reason which is their original Author: and precious feelings of disinterested, that is self-disregarding, joy and love may be regenerated and restored: – and, in this sense, he may be said to measure back the track of life which he has trod.

In such disposition of mind let the Youth return to the visible Universe; and to conversation with ancient Books; and to those, if such there be, which in the present day breathe the ancient spirit: and let him feed upon that beauty which unfolds itself, not to his eye as it sees carelessly the things which cannot possibly go unseen and are remembered or not as accident shall decide, but to the thinking mind; which searches, discovers, and treasures up, – infusing by meditation into the objects with which it converses an intellectual life; whereby they remain planted in the memory, now, and for ever. Hitherto the Youth, I suppose, has been content, for the most part, to look at his own mind after the manner in which he ranges along the Stars in the firmament with naked unaided sight: Let him now apply the telescope of Art – to call the invisible Stars out of their hiding-places; and let him endeavour to look through the system of his Being with the organ of Reason; summoned to penetrate, as far as it has power, in discovery of the impelling forces and the governing laws.

These expectations are not immoderate: they demand nothing more than the perception of a few plain truths; namely that Knowledge efficacious for the production of virtue, is the ultimate end of all effort, the sole dispenser of complacency and repose. A perception also is implied of the inherent superiority of Contemplation to Action. The FRIEND does not in this contradict his own words where he had said heretofore, that 'doubtless it is nobler to Act than to Think.' [9] In those words, it was his purpose to censure that barren Contemplation which rests satisfied with itself in cases where the thoughts are of such quality that they may be, and ought to be, embodied in Action. But he speaks now of the general superiority of thought to action; – as preceeding and governing all action that moves to salutary purposes: and, secondly, as leading to elevation, the absolute possession of the individual mind, and to a consistency or harmony of the Being within itself which no outward agency can reach, to disturb, or to impair: – and lastly, as producing works of pure science, or of the combined faculties of imagination, feeling, and reason; – works which, both from their independence in their origin upon accident, their nature, their duration, and the wide spread of their influence, are entitled rightly to take place of [10] the noblest and most beneficent deeds of Heroes, Statesmen, Legislators, or Warriors.

Yet, beginning from the perception of this established superiority, we do not suppose that the Youth, whom we wish to guide and encourage, is to be insensible to those influences of Wealth, or Rank, or Station, by which the bulk of Mankind are swayed. Our eyes have not been fixed upon virtue which lies apart from human Nature, or transcends it. In fact there is no such Virtue. We neither suppose nor wish him to undervalue or slight these distinctions as modes of power, things that may enable him to be more useful to his Contemporaries; nor as gratifications that may confer dignity upon his living person; and, through him, upon those who love him; nor as they may connect his name, through a Family to be founded by his success, in a closer chain of gratitude with some portion of posterity; who shall speak of him, as among their Ancestry, with a more tender interest than the mere general bond of patriotism or humanity would supply. We suppose no indifference to, much less a contempt of, these rewards; but let them have their due place; let it be ascertained, when the Soul is searched into, that they are only an auxiliary motive to exertion, never the principal or originating force. If this be too much to expect from a Youth who, I take for granted, possesses no ordinary endowments, and whom circumstances with respect to the more dangerous passions have favoured, then, indeed, must the noble Spirit of the Country be wasted away: then would our Institutions be deplorable; and the Education prevalent among us utterly vile and debasing.

But the Correspondent, who drew forth these thoughts, has said rightly that the character of the age may not without injustice be thus branded: he will not deny that, without speaking of other Countries, there is in these Islands, in the departments of Natural philosophy, of mechanic ingenuity, in the general activities of the country, and in the particular excellence of individual Minds in high Stations civil or military, enough to excite admiration and love in the sober-minded, and more than enough to intoxicate the Youthful and inexperienced. – I will compare, then, an aspiring Youth, leaving the Schools in which he has been disciplined, and preparing to bear a part in the concerns of the World, I will compare him in this season of eager admiration, to a newly-invested Knight appearing with his blank unsignalized Shield, upon some day of solemn tournament, at the Court of the Fairy Queen, as that Sovereignty was conceived to exist by the moral and imaginative genius of our divine Spenser. He does not himself immediately enter the lists as a Combatant, but he looks round him with a beating heart; dazzled by the gorgeous pageantry, the banners, the impresses, the Ladies of overcoming beauty, the Persons of the Knights – now first seen by him, the fame of whose actions is carried by the Traveller, like Merchandize, through the World; and resounded upon the harp of the Minstrel. – But I am not at liberty to make this comparison. If a Youth were to begin his career in such an Assemblage, with such examples to guide and to animate, it will be pleaded, there would be no cause for apprehension: he could not falter, he could not be misled. But ours is, notwithstanding its manifold excellences, a degenerate Age: and recreant Knights are among us, far outnumbering the true. A false Gloriana in these days imposes worthless services, which they who perform them, in their blindness, know not to be such; and which are recompenced by rewards as worthless – yet eagerly grasped at, as if they were the immortal guerdon of Virtue.

I have in this declaration insensibly overstepped the limits which I had determined not to pass: – let me be forgiven; for it is hope which hath carried me forward. In such a mixed assemblage as our age presents with its genuine merit and its large overbalance of alloy, I may boldly ask into what errors, either with respect to Person or Thing, could a young Man fall, who has sincerely entered upon the course of moral discipline which has been recommended, and to which the condition of youth, it has been proved, is favourable? His opinions could no where deceive him beyond the point to which, after a season, he would find that it was salutary for him to have been deceived. For, as that Man cannot set a right value upon health who has never known sickness, nor feel the blessing of ease who has been through his life a stranger to pain, so can there be no confirmed and passionate love of truth for him who has not experienced the hollowness of error. We may safely affirm that, in relation to subjects which could in any stage of life admit of a doubt, to points which can fairly be called matter of speculation or opinion, there is nothing whereupon the Mind reposes with a confidence equal to that with which it rests on those conclusions, by which truths have been established the direct opposite of errours once rapturously cherished and which have been passed through and are rejected for ever.[11] – Range against each other as Advocates, oppose as Combatants, two several

Intellects, each strenuously asserting doctrines which he sincerely believes; but the one contending for the worth and beauty of that garment which the other had outgrown and cast away. Mark the superiority, the ease, the dignity, on the side of the more advanced Mind; how he overlooks [12] his Subject, commands it from centre to circumference; and hath the same thorough knowledge of the tenets which his Adversary, with impetuous zeal, but in confusion also and thrown off his guard at every turn of the argument, is labouring to maintain! If it be a question of the fine Arts (Poetry for instance) the riper mind not only sees that his Opponent is deceived; but, what is of far more importance, sees *how* he is deceived. The imagination stands before him with all its imperfections laid open; as duped by shews, enslaved by words, corrupted by mistaken delicacy and false refinement, – as not having even attended with care to the reports of the senses, and therefore deficient grossly in the rudiments of her own power. He has noted how, as a supposed necessary condition, the Understanding sleeps in order that the Fancy may dream. Studied in the history of Society, and versed in the secret laws of thought, he can pass regularly through all the gradations, can pierce infallibly all the windings, which false taste through ages has pursued, – from the very time when first, through inexperience, heedlessness, or affectation, she took her departure from the side of Truth, her original parent. – Can a disputant thus accoutred be withstood? – to whom, further, every movement in the thoughts of his Antagonist is revealed by the light of his own experience; who, therefore, sympathises with weakness gently, and wins his way by forbearance; and hath, when needful, an irresistible power of onset, – arising from gratitude to the truth which he vindicates, not merely as a positive good for Mankind, but as his own especial rescue and redemption.

I might here conclude: but my Correspondent toward the close of his letter, has written so feelingly upon the advantages to be derived, in his estimation, from a living Instructor, that I must not leave this part of the Subject without a word of direct notice. The FRIEND cited some time ago a passage [13] from the prose works of Milton, eloquently describing the manner in which good and evil grow up together in the field of the World almost inseparably; and insisting, consequently, upon the knowledge and survey of vice as necessary to the constituting of human virtue, and the scanning of Error to the confirmation of Truth. If this be so, and I have been reasoning to the same effect in the preceeding paragraph, the fact, and the thoughts which it may suggest, will, if rightly applied, tend to moderate an anxiety for the guidance of a more experienced or superior Mind. The advantage, where it is possessed, is far from being an absolute good: nay, such a preceptor, ever at hand, might prove an oppression not to be thrown off, and a fatal hindrance. Grant that in the general tenor of his intercourse with his Pupil he is forbearing and circumspect, inasmuch as he is rich in that Knowledge (above all other necessary for a teacher) which cannot exist without a liveliness of memory, preserving for him an unbroken image of the winding, excursive, and often retrograde course along which his own intellect has passed. Grant that, furnished with these distinct remembrances, he wishes that the mind of his pupil should be free to luxuriate in the enjoyments, loves, and admirations appropriate to its age; that he is not in haste to kill what he knows will in due time die of itself; or be transmuted, and put on a nobler form and higher faculties, otherwise unattainable. In a word, that the Teacher is governed habitually by the wisdom of Patience, waiting with pleasure. Yet, perceiving how much the outward help of Art can facilitate the progress of Nature, he may be betrayed into many unnecessary or pernicious mistakes where he deems his interference warranted by substantial experience. And, in spite of all his caution, remarks may drop insensibly from him which shall wither in the mind of his pupil a generous sympathy, destroy a sentiment of approbation or dislike not merely innocent but salutary; and, for the inexperienced Disciple how many pleasures may be thus cut off, what joy, what admiration, and what love! While in their stead are introduced into the ingenuous mind misgivings, a mistrust of its own evidence, dispositions to affect to feel where there can be no real feeling, indecisive judgments, a superstructure of opinions that has no base to support it, and words uttered by rote with the impertinence of a Parrot or a Mocking-bird, yet which may not be listened to with the same indifference, as they cannot be heard without some feeling of moral disapprobation.

These results, I contend, whatever may be the benefit to be derived from such an enlightened Teacher, are in their degree inevitable. And, by this process, humility and docile dispositions may exist towards the Master, endued as he is with the power which personal presence confers; but at the same time they will be liable to overstep their due bounds, and to degenerate into passiveness and prostration of mind. This towards him; while, with respect to other living Men, nay even to the mighty Spirits of past times, there may be associated with such weakness a want of modesty and humility. Insensibly may steal in presumption and a habit of sitting in judgment in cases where no sentiment ought to have existed but diffidence or veneration. Such virtues are the sacred attributes of Youth: its appropriate calling is not to distinguish in the fear of being deceived or degraded, not to analyze with scrupulous minuteness, but to accumulate in genial confidence; its instinct, its safety, its benefit, its glory, is to love, to admire, to feel, and to labour. Nature has irrevocably decreed that our prime dependence in all stages of life after Infancy and Childhood have been passed through (nor do I know that this latter ought to be excepted) must be upon our own minds; and that the way to know-ledge shall be long, difficult, winding, and often-times returning upon itself.

What has been said is a mere sketch; and that only of a part of the interesting Country into which we have been led; but my Correspondent will be able to enter the paths that have been pointed out. Should he do this and advance steadily for a while, he needs not fear any deviations from the truth which will be finally injurious to him. He will not long have his admiration fixed upon unworthy objects; he will neither be clogged nor drawn aside by the love of friends or kindred, betraying his understanding through his affections; he will neither be bowed down by conventional arrangements of manners producing too often a lifeless decency; nor will the rock of his Spirit wear away in the endless beating of the waves of the World: neither will that portion of his own time, which he must surrender to labours by which his livelihood is to be earned or his social duties performed, be unprofitable to himself indirectly, while it is directly useful to others: for that time has been primarily surrendered through an act of obedience to a moral law established by himself, and therefore he moves then also along the orbit of perfect liberty.

Let it be remembered that the advice requested does not relate to the government of the more dangerous passions, or to the fundamental principles of right and wrong as acknowledged by the universal Conscience of Mankind. I may therefore assure my Youthful Correspondent, if he will endeavour to look into himself in the manner which I have exhorted him to do, that in him the wish will be realized, to him in due time the prayer granted, which was uttered by that living Teacher [14] of whom he speaks with gratitude as of a Benefactor when, in his character of Philosophical Poet, having thought of Morality as implying in its essence voluntary obedience, and producing the effect of order, he transfers, in the transport of imagination, the law of Moral to physical Natures, and, having contemplated, through the medium of that order, all modes of existence as subservient to one spirit, concludes his address to the power of Duty in the following words: [15]

> To humbler functions, awful Power!
> I call thee: I myself commend
> Unto thy guidance from this hour;
> Oh, let my weakness have an end!
> Give unto me, made lowly wise,
> The spirit of self-sacrifice;
> *The confidence of reason give;*
> *And in the light of truth thy Bondman let me live!*

M. M. [16]

# Memoir of the Rev. Robert Walker

— ✳ — ✳ — ✳ —

[Probably composed between 6 September 1811 and September 1812 and 1820. First published 1820.]

This memoir was part of a note to Sonnet XVIII of The River Duddon series. The subject was the vicar of Seathwaite Chapel in the Duddon Valley, whom Wordsworth may have met, for Rev. Robert Walker died at ninety-three years of age in June 1802. He was also the subject of a panegyric in The Excursion (VII, 315–60). Several passages of extracts from other sources are omitted below as indicated.

In the year 1709, Robert Walker was born at Under-crag, in Seathwaite; he was the youngest of twelve children. His eldest brother, who inherited the small family estate, died at Under-crag, aged ninety-four, being twenty-four years older than the subject of this Memoir, who was born of the same mother. Robert was a sickly infant; and, through his boyhood and youth, continuing to be of delicate frame and tender health, it was deemed best, according to the country phrase, to breed him a scholar; for it was not likely that he would be able to earn a livelihood by bodily labour. At that period few of these dales were furnished with school-houses; the children being taught to read and write in the chapel; and in the same consecrated building, where he officiated for so many years both as preacher and schoolmaster, he himself received the rudiments of his education. In his youth he became schoolmaster at Loweswater; not being called upon, probably, in that situation to teach more than reading, writing, and arithmetic. But, by the assistance of a 'Gentleman' in the neighbourhood, he acquired, at leisure hours, a knowledge of the classics, and became qualified for taking holy orders. Upon his ordination, he had the offer of two curacies: the one, Torver, in the vale of Coniston, – the other, Seathwaite, in his native vale. The value of each was the same, *viz.* five pounds *per annum*: but the cure of Seathwaite having a cottage attached to it, as he wished to marry, he chose it in preference. The young person on whom his affections were fixed, though in the condition of a domestic servant, had given promise, by her serious and modest deportment, and by her virtuous dispositions, that she was worthy to become the helpmate of a man entering upon a plan of life such as he had marked out for himself. By her frugality she had stored up a small sum of money, with which they began housekeeping. In 1735 or 1736, he entered upon his curacy . . .

[Various letters by Walker and others are omitted here.]

The same man, who was thus liberal in the education of his numerous family, was even munificent in hospitality as parish priest. Every Sunday, were served, upon the long table, at which he has been described [1] sitting with a child upon his knee, messes of broth, for the refreshment of those of his congregation who came from a distance, and usually took their seats as parts of his own household. It seems scarcely possible that this custom could have commenced before the augmentation of his cure; and what would to many have been a high price of self-denial, was paid, by the pastor and his family, for this gratification; as the treat could only be provided by dressing at one time the whole, perhaps, of their weekly allowance of fresh animal food; consequently, for a succession of days, the table was covered with cold victuals only. His generosity in old age may be still further illustrated by a little circumstance relating to an orphan grandson, then ten years of age, which I find in a copy of a letter to one of his sons; he requests that half a guinea may be left for 'little Robert's pocket money,' who was then at school: intrusting it to the care of a lady, who, as he says, 'may sometimes frustrate his squandering it away foolishly,' and promising to send him an equal allowance annually for the same purpose. The conclusion of the same letter is so characteristic, that I cannot forbear to transcribe it. 'We,' meaning his wife and himself, 'are in our wonted state of health, allowing for the hasty strides of old age knocking daily at our door, and threateningly telling us, we are not only mortal, but must expect ere long to take our leave of our ancient cottage, and lie down in our last dormitory. Pray pardon my neglect to answer yours: let us hear sooner from you, to augment the mirth of the Christmas holidays. Wishing you all the pleasures of the approaching season, I am, dear Son, with lasting sincerity, yours affectionately,

Robert Walker.'

He loved old customs and old usages, and in some instances stuck to them to his own loss; for, having had a sum of money lodged in the hands of a neighbouring tradesman, when long course of time had raised the rate of interest, and more was offered, he refused to accept it; an act not difficult to one, who, while he was drawing seventeen pounds a year from his curacy, declined, as we have seen, to add the profits of another small benefice to his own, lest he should be suspected of cupidity. – From this vice he was utterly free; he made no charge for teaching school; such as could afford to pay, gave him what they pleased. When very young, having kept a diary of his expenses, however trifling, the large amount at the end of the year surprised him; and from that time the rule of his life was to be economical, not avaricious. At his decease he left behind him no less a sum than £2,000; and such a sense of his various excellencies was prevalent in the country, that the epithet of WONDERFUL is to this day attached to his name.

There is in the above sketch something so extraordinary as to require further *explanatory* details. – And to begin with his industry: eight hours in each day, during five days in the week, and half of Saturday, except when the labours of husbandry were urgent, he was occupied in teaching. His seat was within the rails of the altar; the communion table was his desk; and, like Shenstone's schoolmistress,[2] the master employed himself at the spinning-wheel, while the children were repeating their lessons by his side. Every evening, after school hours, if not more profitably engaged, he continued the same kind of labour, exchanging, for the benefit of exercise, the small wheel at which he had sate, for the large one on which wool is spun, the spinner stepping to and fro. Thus, was the wheel constantly in readiness to prevent the waste of a moment's time. Nor was his industry with the pen, when occasion called for it, less eager. Intrusted with extensive management of public and private affairs, he acted, in his rustic neighbourhood, as scrivener, writing out petitions, deeds of conveyance, wills, covenants, &c., with pecuniary gain to himself, and to the great benefit of his employers. These labours (at all times considerable) at one period of the year, viz. between Christmas and Candlemas, when money transactions are settled in this country, were often so intense, that he passed great part of the night, and sometimes whole nights, at his desk. His garden also was tilled by his own hand; he had a right of pasturage upon the mountains for a few sheep and a couple of cows, which required his attendance; with this pastoral occupation he joined the labours of husbandry upon a small scale, renting two or three acres in addition to his own less than one acre of glebe; and the humblest drudgery which the cultivation of these fields required was performed by himself.

He also assisted his neighbours in haymaking and shearing their flocks, and in the performance of this latter service he was eminently dexterous. They, in their turn, complimented him with the present of a haycock, or a fleece; less as a recompense for this particular service than as a general acknowledgment. The Sabbath was in a strict sense kept holy; the Sunday evenings being devoted to reading the Scripture and family prayer. The principal festivals appointed by the Church were also duly observed; but through every other day in the week, through every week in the year he was incessantly occupied in work of hand or mind; not allowing a moment for recreation, except upon a Saturday afternoon, when he indulged himself with a

Newspaper, or sometimes with a Magazine. The frugality and temperance established in his house were as admirable as the industry. Nothing to which the name of luxury could be given was there known; in the latter part of his life, indeed, when tea had been brought into almost general use, it was provided for visitors, and for such of his own family as returned occasionally to his roof, and had been accustomed to this refreshment elsewhere; but neither he nor his wife ever partook of it. The raiment worn by his family was comely and decent, but as simple as their diet; the homespun materials were made up into apparel by their own hands. At the time of the decease of this thrifty pair, their cottage contained a large store of webs of woollen and linen cloth, woven from thread of their own spinning. And it is remarkable that the pew in the chapel in which the family used to sit, remains neatly lined with woollen cloth spun by the pastor's own hands. It is the only pew in the chapel so distinguished; and I know of no other instance of his conformity to the delicate accommodations of modern times. The fuel of the house, like that of their neighbors, consisted of peat, procured from the mosses by their own labour. The lights by which, in the winter evenings, their work was performed, were of their own manufacture, such as still continue to be used in these cottages; they are made of the pith of rushes dipped in any unctuous substance that the house affords. *White* candles, as tallow candles are here called, were reserved to honour the Christmas festivals, and were perhaps produced upon no other occasions. Once a month, during the proper season, a sheep was drawn from their small mountain flock and killed for the use of the family; and a cow, towards the close of the year, was salted and dried for winter provision: the hide was tanned to furnish them with shoes. – By these various resources, this venerable clergyman reared a numerous family, not only preserving them, as he affectingly says, 'from wanting the necessaries of life'; but affording them an unstinted education, and the means of raising themselves in society. In this they were eminently assisted by the effects of their father's example, his precepts, and injunctions: he was aware that truth-speaking, as a moral virtue, is best secured by inculcating attention to accuracy of report even on trivial occasions; and so rigid were the rules of honesty by which he endeavoured to bring up his family, that if one of them had chanced to find in the lanes or fields anything of the least use or value without being able to ascertain to whom it belonged, he always insisted upon the child's carrying it back to the place from which it had been brought.

No one it might be thought could, as has been described, convert his body into a machine, as it were, of industry for the humblest uses, and keep his thoughts so frequently bent upon secular concerns, without grievous injury to the more precious parts of his nature. How could the powers of intellect thrive, or its graces be displayed, in the midst of circumstances apparently so unfavourable, and where, to the direct cultivation of the mind, so small a portion of time was allotted? But, in this extraordinary man, things in their nature adverse were reconciled. His conversation was remarkable, not only for being chaste and pure, but for the degree in which it was fervent and eloquent; his written style was correct, simple, and animated. Nor did his *affections* suffer more than his intellect; he was tenderly alive to all the duties of his pastoral office: the poor and needy 'he never sent empty away,'[3] – the stranger was fed and refreshed in passing that unfrequented vale – the sick were visited; and the feelings of humanity found further exercise among the distresses and embarrassments in the worldly estate of his neighbours, with which his talents for business made him acquainted; and the disinterestedness, impartiality, and uprightness which he maintained in the management of all affairs confided to him, were virtues seldom separated in his own conscience from religious obligation. Nor could such conduct fail to remind those who witnessed it of a spirit nobler than law or custom: they felt convictions which, but for such intercourse, could not have been afforded, that, as in the practice of their pastor, there was no guile, so in his faith there was nothing hollow; and we are warranted in believing, that upon these occasions, selfishness, obstinacy, and discord would often give way before the breathings of his good-will and saintly integrity. It may be presumed also – while his humble congregation were listening to the moral precepts which he delivered from the pulpit, and to the Christian exhortations that they should love their neighbours as themselves, and do as they would be done unto — that peculiar efficacy was given to the preacher's labours by recollections in the minds of his congregation, that they were called upon to do no more than his own actions were daily setting before their eyes.

The afternoon service in the chapel was less numerously attended than that of the morning, but by a more serious auditory; the lesson from the New Testament, on those occasions, was accompanied by Burkitt's Commentaries. These lessons he read with impassioned emphasis, frequently drawing tears from his hearers, and leaving a lasting impression upon their minds. His devotional feelings and the powers of his own mind were further exercised, along with those of his family, in perusing the Scriptures: not only on the Sunday evenings, but on every other evening, while the rest of the household were at work, some one of the children, and in her turn the servant, for the sake of practice in reading, or for instruction, read the Bible aloud; and in this manner the whole was repeatedly gone through. That no common importance was attached to the observance of religious ordinances by his family, appears from the following memorandum by one of his descendants, which I am tempted to insert at length, as it is characteristic, and somewhat curious. 'There is a small chapel in the county palatine of Lancaster, where a certain clergyman has regularly officiated above sixty years, and a few months ago administered the sacrament of the Lord's Supper in the same, to a decent number of devout communicants. After the clergyman had received himself, the first company out of the assembly who approached the altar, and kneeled down to be partakers of the sacred elements, consisted of the parson's wife; to whom he had been married upwards of sixty years; one son and his wife; four daughters, each with her husband; whose ages, all added together, amount to above 714 years. The several and respective distances from the place of each of their abodes, to the chapel where they all communicated, will measure more than 1,000 English miles. Though the narration will appear surprising, it is without doubt a fact that the same persons, exactly four years before, met at the same place, and all joined in performance of the same venerable duty.'

He was indeed most zealously attached to the doctrine and frame of the Established Church. We have seen him congratulating himself that he had no dissenters in his cure of any denomination. Some allowance must be made for the state of opinion when his first religious impressions were received, before the reader will acquit him of bigotry, when I mention, that at the time of the augmentation of the cure, he refused to invest part of the money in the purchase of an estate offered to him upon advantageous terms, because the proprietor was a Quaker; – whether from scrupulous apprehension that a blessing would not attend a contract framed for the benefit of the church between persons not in religious sympathy with each other; or, as a seeker of peace, he was afraid of the uncomplying disposition which at one time was too frequently conspicuous in that sect. Of this an instance had fallen under his own notice; for, while he taught school at Loweswater, certain persons of that denomination had refused to pay annual interest due under the title of Church-stock;[4] a great hardship upon the incumbent, for the curacy of Loweswater was then scarcely less poor than that of Seathwaite. To what degree this prejudice of his was blameable need not be determined; – certain it is, that he was not only desirous, as he himself says, to live in peace, but in love, with all men. He was placable, and charitable in his judgments; and, however correct in conduct and rigorous to himself, he was ever ready to forgive the trespasses of others, and to soften the censure that was cast upon their frailties. – It would be unpardonable to omit that, in the maintenance of his virtues, he received due support from the partner of his long life. She was equally strict, in attending to her share of their joint cares, nor less diligent in her appropriate occupations. A person who had been some time their servant in the latter part of their lives, concluded the panegyric of her mistress by saying to me, 'She was no less excellent than her husband; she was good to the poor; she was good to everything!' He survived for a short time this virtuous companion. When she died, he ordered that her body should be borne to the grave by three of her daughters and one grand-daughter; and, when the corpse was lifted from the threshold, he insisted upon lending his aid, and feeling about, for he was then almost blind, took hold of a napkin fixed to the coffin; and, as a bearer of the body, entered the chapel, a few steps from the lowly parsonage.

What a contrast does the life of this obscurely-seated, and, in point of worldly wealth, poorly-repaid Churchman, present to that of a Cardinal Wolsey!

> 'O 'tis a burthen, Cromwell, 'tis a burthen
> Too heavy for a man who hopes for heaven!' [5]

We have been dwelling upon images of peace in the moral world, that have brought us again to the quiet enclosure of consecrated ground, in which this venerable pair lie interred. The sounding brook, that rolls close by the churchyard, without disturbing feeling or meditation, is now unfortunately laid bare; but not long ago it participated, with the chapel, the shade of some stately ash-trees, which will not spring again. While the spectator from this spot is looking round upon the girdle of stony mountains that encompasses the vale, – masses of rock, out of which monuments for all men that ever existed might have been hewn – it would surprise him to be told, as with truth he might be, that the plain blue slab dedicated to the memory of this aged pair is a production of a quarry in North Wales. It was sent as a mark of respect by one of their descendants from the vale of Festiniog, a region almost as beautiful as that in which it now lies!

Upon the Seathwaite Brook, at a small distance from the parsonage, has been erected a mill for spinning yarn; it is a mean and disagreeable object, though not unimportant to the spectator, as calling to mind the momentous changes wrought by such inventions in the frame of society – changes which have proved especially unfavourable to these mountain solitudes. So much had been effected by those new powers, before the subject of the preceding biographical sketch closed his life, that their operation could not escape his notice, and doubtless excited touching reflections upon the comparatively insignificant results of his own manual industry. But Robert Walker was not a man of times and circumstances: had he lived at a later period, the principle of duty would have produced application as unremitting; the same energy of character would have been displayed, though in many instances with widely-different effects.

[Extracts from an article on Walker by his great-grandson are omitted.]

# SECTION III

## *Politics*

# A Letter to the Bishop of Llandaff

~~~~~~~~~~~~

[*Probably composed in February or March 1793. First published in 1876. The full title reads: 'A Letter to the Bishop of Llandaff on the extraordinary avowal of his Political Principles contained in the Appendix to [his] late Sermon by a Republican.' Much of the punctuation has been added.*]

*As the full title given above indicates, this unfinished letter was written by Wordsworth when he was an ardent republican and supporter of the French Revolution. It was a response to a published protest of a well-known liberal of the time, Bishop Richard Watson, for whom the execution of Louis XVI on 21 January 1793 was the occasion of a political reversal. Much of Wordsworth's fervour and ideas probably came from his own recent experiences in Revolutionary France and from familiarity with political writers such as Jean-Jacques Rousseau and Thomas Paine. As the recent editors of Wordsworth's prose have argued (W. J. B. Owen and Jane W. Smyser, eds.,* Prose Works, *I, 24–5), the Letter was most likely not published by Wordsworth because of the repressive atmosphere of the time and the changing political scene in France itself that was quickly making some of his points obsolete.*

My Lord,
Reputation may not improperly be termed the moral life of man. Alluding to our natural existence, Addison, in a sublime allegory [1] well known to your Lordship, has represented us as crossing an

immense bridge, from whose surface from a variety of causes we disappear one after another, and are seen no more. Every one, who enters upon public life, has such a bridge to pass, some slip through at the very commencement of their career from thoughtlessness, others pursue their course a little longer till, misled by the phantoms of avarice and ambition, they fall victims to their delusion. Your Lordship was either seen, or supposed to be seen, continuing your way for a long time, unseduced and undismayed; but those, who now look for you, will look in vain, and it is feared you have at last fallen, through one of the numerous trap-doors, into the tide of contempt to be swept down to the ocean of oblivion.

It is not my intention to be illiberal; these latter expressions have been forced from me by indignation. Your Lordship had given a proof that even religious controversy may be conducted without asperity;[2] I hope I shall profit by your example. At the same time with a spirit which you may not approve, for it is a republican spirit, I shall not preclude myself from any truths, however severe, which I may think beneficial to the cause which I have undertaken to defend. You will not then be surprized when I inform you that it is only the name of its author which has induced me to notice an Appendix to a sermon,[3] which you have lately given to the world, with a hope that it may have some effect in calming a perturbation which you say has been *excited* in the minds of the lower orders of the community.[4] While, with a servility which has prejudiced many people against religion itself, the ministers of the church of England have appeared as writers upon public measures only to be the advocates of slavery civil and religious, your Lordship stood almost alone as the defender of truth and political charity. The names of levelling prelate, bishop of the dissenters, which were intended as a dishonour to your character were looked upon by your friends, perhaps by yourself, as an acknowledgment of your possessing an enlarged and philosophical mind; and like the generals in a neighbouring country, if it had been equally becoming your profession, you might have adopted, as an honourable title, a denomination intended as a stigma.

On opening your Appendix, your admirers will naturally expect to find an impartial statement of the grievances which harass this nation, and a sagacious enquiry into the proper modes of redress. They will be disappointed. Sensible how large a portion of mankind receive opinions upon authority, I am apprehensive lest the doctrines which they will there find should derive a weight from your name to which they are by no means intrinsically intitled. I will therefore examine what you have advanced from a hope of being able to do away any impression left on the minds of such as may be liable to confound with argument a strong prepossession for your Lordship's talents, experience, and virtues.

Before I take notice of what you appear to have laid down as principles, it may not be improper to advert to some incidental opinions found at the commencement of your political confession of faith. At a period big with the fate of the human race, I am sorry that you attach so much importance to the personal sufferings of the late royal martyr [5] and that an anxiety for the issue of the present convulsions should not have prevented you from joining in the idle cry of modish lamentation which has resounded from the court to the cottage. You wish it to be supposed you are one of those who are unpersuaded of the guilt of Louis XVI. If you had attended to the history of the French revolution as minutely as its importance demands, so far from stopping to bewail his death, you would rather have regretted that the blind fondness of his people had placed a human being in that monstrous situation which rendered him unaccountable before a human tribunal. A bishop,[6] a man of philosophy and humanity as distinguished as your Lordship, declared at the opening of the national convention, and twenty-five millions of men were convinced of the truth of the assertion, that there was not a citizen on the tenth of August who, if he could have dragged before the eyes of Louis the corse of one of his murdered brothers, might not have exclaimed to him, 'Tyran, voila ton ouvrage.'[7] Think of this and you will not want consolation under any depression your spirits may feel at the contrast exhibited by Louis on the most splendid throne of the universe, and Louis alone in the tower of the Temple or on the scaffold. But there is a class of men who received the news of the late execution with much more heart-felt sorrow than that which you among such a multitude so officiously express. The passion of pity is one of which, above all others, a Christian teacher should be cautious of cherishing the abuse; when under the influence of reason, it is regulated by the disproportion of the pain suffered to the guilt incurred. It is from the passion thus directed that the men of whom I have just spoken are afflicted by the catastrophe of the fallen monarch. They are sorry that the prejudice and weakness of mankind have made it necessary to force an individual into an unnatural situation, which requires more than human talents and human virtues, and at the same time precludes him from attaining even a moderate knowledge of common life and from feeling a particular share in the interests of mankind. But, above all, these men lament that any combination of circumstances should have rendered it necessary or advisable to veil for a moment the statutes of the laws and that by such emergency the cause of twenty-five millions of people, I may say of the whole human race, should have been so materially injured. Any other sorrow for the death of Louis is irrational and weak. In France royalty is no more; the person of the last anointed is no more also, and I flatter myself I am not alone, even in this *kingdom*, when I wish that it may please the almighty neither by the hands of his priests nor his nobles (I allude to a striking passage of Racine) to raise his posterity to the rank of his ancestors and reillume the torch of extinguished David.[8]

You say, 'I fly with terror and abhorrence even from the altar of liberty when I see it stained with the blood of the aged, of the innocent, of the defenceless sex, of the ministers of religion, and of the faithful adherents of a fallen monarch.' What! have you so little knowledge of the nature of man as to be ignorant, that a time of revolution is not the season of true Liberty? Alas! the obstinacy and perversion of men is such that she is too often obliged to borrow the very arms of despotism to overthrow him, and in order to reign in peace must establish herself by violence. She deplores such stern necessity, but the safety of the people, her supreme law, is her consolation. This apparent contradiction between the principles of liberty and the march of revolutions, this spirit of jealousy, of severity, of disquietude, of vexation, indispensable from a state of war between the oppressors and oppressed, must of necessity confuse the ideas of morality and contract the benign exertion of the best affections of the human heart. Political virtues are developed at the expence of moral ones; and the sweet emotions of compassion, evidently dangerous where traitors are to be punished, are too often altogether smothered. But is this a sufficient reason to reprobate a convulsion from which is to spring a fairer order of things? It is the province of education to rectify the erroneous notions which a habit of oppression, and even of resistance, may have created, and to soften this ferocity of character proceeding from a necessary suspension of the mild and social virtues; it belongs to her to create a race of men who, truly free, will look upon their fathers as only enfranchised.

I proceed to the sorrow you express for the fate of the French priesthood. The measure by which that body was immediately stripped of part of its possessions, and a more equal distribution enjoined of the rest, does not meet with your Lordship's approbation. You do not question the right of the nation over ecclesiastical wealth; you have voluntarily abandoned a ground which you were conscious was altogether untenable. Having allowed this right, can you question the propriety of exerting it at that particular period? The urgencies of the state were such as required the immediate application of a remedy. Even the clergy were conscious of such necessity; and, aware from the immunities they had long enjoyed that the people would insist upon their bearing some share of the burden, offered of themselves a considerable portion of their superfluities. The assembly were true to justice and refused to compromise the interests of the nation by accepting as a satisfaction the insidious offerings of compulsive charity. They enforced their right: they took from the clergy a considerable portion of their wealth, and applied it to the alleviation of the national misery. Experience shews daily the wise employment of the ample provision which yet remains to them. While you reflect on the vast diminution which some men's fortunes must have undergone, your sorrow for these individuals will be diminished by recollecting the unworthy motives which induced the bulk of them to undertake the office, and the scandalous arts which enabled so many to attain the rank and enormous wealth, which it has seemed necessary to annex to the charge of a christian pastor. You will rather look upon it as a signal act of justice that they should thus unexpectedly be stripped of the rewards of their vices and their crimes. If you should lament the sad reverse by which the hero of the necklace⁹ has been divested of about 1,300,000 livres of annual revenue, you may find some consolation that a part of this prodigious mass of riches is gone to preserve from famine some thousands of curés who were pining in villages unobserved by courts.

I now proceed to principles. Your lordship very properly asserts that 'the liberty of man in a state of society consists in his being subject to no law but the law enacted by general will of the society to which he belongs'. You approved of the object which the French had in view when in the infancy of the revolution they were attempting to destroy arbitrary power and to erect a temple to liberty on its ruins. It is with surprize then that I find you afterwards presuming to dictate to the world a servile adopt[ion] of the British constitution. It is with indignation I perceive you 'reprobate' a people for having imagined happiness and liberty more likely to flourish in the open field of a republic than under the shade of monarchy. You are therefore guilty of a most glaring contradiction. Twenty-five millions of Frenchmen have felt that they could have no security for their liberties under any modification of monarchical power. They have in consequence unanimously chosen a republic. You cannot but observe that they have only exercised that right in which by your own confession liberty essentially resides.

As to your arguments by which you pretend to justify your anathemas of a republic, if arguments they may be called, they are so concise, that I cannot but transcribe them. 'I dislike a republic for this reason, because of all forms of government, scarcely excepting the most despotic, I think a republic the most oppressive to the bulk of the people: they are deceived in it with a shew of liberty; but they live in it, under the most odious of all tyrannies, the tyranny of their equals.'

This passage is a singular proof of that fatality by which the advocates of error furnish weapons for their own destruction; while it is merely *assertion* in respect to a justification of your aversion to Republicanism, a strong *argument* may be drawn from it in its favour. Mr Burke, in a philosophic lamentation over the extinction of Chivalry, told us that in those times vice lost half its evil, by losing all its grossness; infatuated moralist! [10] Your Lordship excites compassion as labouring under the same delusion. Slavery is a bitter and a poisonous draught; we have but one consolation under it – that a nation may dash the cup to the ground when she pleases; do not imagine that by taking from its bitterness you weaken its deadly quality; no, by rendering it more palatable you contribute to its power of destruction. We submit without repining to the chastisements of providence, aware that we are creatures, that opposition is vain and remonstrance impossible. But when redress is in our own power and resistance is rational, we suffer with the same humility from beings like ourselves, because we are taught from infancy that we were born in a state of inferiority to our oppressors, that they were sent into the world to scourge and we to be scourged. Accordingly we see the bulk of mankind actuated by these fatal prejudices, even more ready to lay themselves under the feet of *the great*, than the great are to trample upon them. Now taking for granted that in republics men live under the tyranny of what you call their equals, the circumstance of this being the most odious of all tyrannies is what a republican would boast of; as soon as tyranny becomes odious, the principal step is made towards its destruction. Reflecting on the degraded state of the mass of mankind, a philosopher will lament that oppression is not odious to them, that the iron, while it eats the soul, is not felt to enter into it. [11] 'Tout homme né dans l'esclavage naît pour l'esclavage: rien n'est plus certain: les esclaves perdent tout dans leurs fers, jusqu'au désir d'en sortir; ils aiment leur servitude, comme les compagnons d'Ulysse aimaient leur abrutissement.' [12]

I return to the quotation in which you reprobate republicanism.

Relying upon the temper of the times, you have surely thought little argument necessary to combat what few will be hardy enough to support: the strongest of auxiliaries, imprisonment and the pillory, have left your arm little to perform. But the happiness of mankind is so closely connected with this subject that I cannot suffer such considerations to deter me from throwing out a few hints which may lead to a conclusion that a republic legitimately constructed contains less of an oppressive principle than any other form of government.

Your Lordship will scarcely question that much of human misery, that the great evils which desolate states, proceed from the governors' having an interest distinct from that of the governed. It should seem a natural deduction that whatever has a tendency to identify the two must also in the same degree promote the general welfare. As the magnitude of almost all states prevents the possibility of their enjoying a pure democracy, philosophers, from a wish, as far as is in their power, to make the governors and the governed one, will turn their thoughts to the system of universal representation, and will annex an equal importance to the suffrage of every individual. Jealous of giving up no more of the authority of the people than is necessary, they will be solicitous of finding out some method by which the office of their delegates may be confined as much as is practicable to the proposing and deliberating upon laws, rather than to enacting them; reserving to the people the power of finally inscribing them in the national code. Unless this is attended to, – as soon as a people has chosen representatives it no longer has a political existence except as it is understood to retain the privilege of annihilating the trust when it shall think proper and of resuming its original power. Sensible that at the moment of election an interest distinct from that of the general body is created, an enlightened legislator will endeavour by every possible method to diminish the operation of such interest. The first and most natural mode that presents itself is that of shortening the regular duration of this trust, in order that the man who has betrayed it may soon be superseded by a more worthy successor. But this is not enough: aware of the possibility of imposition and of the natural tendency of power to corrupt the heart of man, a sensible republican will think it essential that the office of legislator be not intrusted to the same man for a succession of years. He will also be induced to this wise restraint by the grand principle of identification: he will be more sure of the virtue of the legislator by knowing that in the capacity of private citizen tomorrow he must either smart under the oppression or bless the justice of the law which he has enacted today.

Perhaps in the very outset of this inquiry the principle on which I proceed will be questioned and I shall be told that the people are not the proper judges of their own welfare. But, because under every government of modern times till the foundation of the American republic, the bulk of mankind have appeared incapable of discerning their true interests, no conclusion can be drawn against my principle. At this moment have we not daily the strongest proofs of the success with which, in what you call the best of all monarchical governments, the popular mind may be debauched? Left to the quiet exercise of their own judgment do you think that the people would have thought it necessary to set fire to the house of the philosophic Priestley [13] and to hunt down his life like that of a traitor or a parricide; — that, deprived almost of the necessaries of existence by the burden of their taxes, they would cry out as with one voice for a war from which not a single ray of consolation can visit them to compensate for the additional keenness with which they are about to smart under the scourge of labour, of cold, and of hunger?

Appearing as I do the advocate of republicanism, let me not be misunderstood. I am well aware from the abuse of the executive power in states that there is not a single European nation but what affords a melancholy proof that if at this moment the original authority of the people should be restored, all that could be expected from such restoration would in the beginning be but a change of tyranny. Considering the nature of a republic in reference to the present condition of Europe, your Lordship stops here: but a philosopher will extend his views much farther; having dried up the source from which flows the corruption of the public opinion, he will be sensible that the stream will go on gradually refining itself. I must add also that the coercive power is of necessity so strong in all the old governments that a people could not but at first make an abuse of that liberty which a legitimate republic supposes. The animal just released from its stall will exhaust the overflow of its spirits in a round of wanton vagaries, but it will soon return to itself and enjoy its freedom in moderate and regular delight.

But, to resume the subject of universal representation, I ought to have mentioned before that in the choice of its representatives a people will not immorally hold out wealth as a criterion of integrity, nor lay down as a fundamental rule that to be qualified for the trying duties of legislation a citizen should be possessed of a certain fixed property. Virtues, talents, and acquirements are all that it will look for.

Having destroyed every external object of delusion, let us now see what makes the supposition necessary that the people will mislead themselves. Your Lordship respects 'peasants and mechanics when they intrude not themselves into concerns for which their education has not fitted them'. Setting aside the idea of a peasant or mechanic being a legislator, what vast education is requisite to enable him to judge amongst his neighbours which is most qualified by his industry and integrity to be intrusted with the care of the interests of himself and of his fellow citizens? But leaving this ground, as governments formed on such a plan proceed in a plain and open manner, their administration would require much less of what is usually called talents and experience, that is of disciplined treachery and hoary machiavelism; and, at the same time, as it would no longer be their interest to keep the mass of the nation in ignorance, a moderate portion of useful knowledge would be universally disseminated. If your lordship has travelled in the democratic cantons of Switzerland you must have seen the herdsman with the staff in one hand and the book in the other. In the constituent assembly of France was found a peasant whose sagacity was as distinguished as his integrity, whose blunt honesty overawed and baffled the refinements of hypocritical patriots. The people of Paris followed him with acclamations, and the name of Père Gérard [14] will long be mentioned with admiration and respect through the eighty-three departments.

From these hints, if pursued further, might be demonstrated the expediency of the whole people 'intruding themselves' on the office of legislation, and the wisdom of putting into force what they may claim as a right. But government is divided into two parts, the legislative and executive. The executive power you would lodge in the hands of an individual. Before we inquire into the propriety of this measure, it will be necessary to state the proper objects of the executive power in governments where the principle of universal representation is admitted. With regard to that portion of this power which is exerted in the application of the laws, it may be observed that much of it would be superseded. As laws, being but the expression of the general will,[15] would be enacted only from an almost universal conviction of their utility, any resistance to such laws, any desire of eluding them, must proceed from a few refractory individuals. As far then as relates to the internal administration of the country, a republic has a manifest advantage over a monarchy, inasmuch as less force is requisite to compel obedience to its laws. From the judicial tribunals of our own country, though we labour under a variety of partial and oppressive laws, we have an evident proof of the nullity of regal interference; as the king's name is confessedly a mere fiction, and justice is known to be most equitably administered when the judges are least dependent on the crown. I have spoken of laws partial and oppressive; our penal code is so crowded with disproportioned penalties and indiscriminate severity that a conscientious man would sacrifice in many instances his respect for the laws to the common feelings of humanity; and there must be a strange vice in that legislation from which can proceed laws in whose execution a man cannot be instrumental without forfeiting his self-esteem and incurring the contempt of his fellow citizens. But to return from this digression; with regard to the other branches of the executive government, which relate rather to original measures than to administering the law, it may be observed, that the power exercised in conducting them is distinguished by almost imperceptible shades from the legislative, and that all such as admit of open discussion, and of the delay attendant on public deliberations, are properly the province of the representative assembly. If this observation be duly attended to, it will appear that this part of executive power will be extremely circumscribed, will be stripped almost entirely of a deliberative capacity, and will be reduced to a mere hand or instrument. As a republican government would leave this power to a select body destitute of the means of corruption, and whom the people, continually controuling, could at all times bring to account, or dismiss, will it not necessarily ensue that a body, so selected and supported, would perform their simple functions with greater efficacy and fidelity, than the complicated concerns of royalty can be expected to meet with in the councils of princes; composed as they usually are of favourites; of men who, from their wealth and interest, have forced themselves into trust; and of statesmen, whose constant object is to exalt themselves by laying pitfalls for their colleagues and for their country?

I shall pursue this subject no further; but, adopting your Lordship's method of argument, instead of continuing to demonstrate the superiority of a republican executive government, I will repeat some of the objections, which have been often made to monarchy, and have never been answered. My first objection to regal government is its instability, proceeding from a variety of causes. Where monarchy is found in its greatest intensity, as in Morocco and Turkey, this observation is illustrated in a very pointed manner; and, indeed, is more or less striking, as governments are more or less despotic. The reason is obvious: as the monarch is the chooser of his ministers, and as his own passions and caprice are, in general, the sole guides of his conduct, these ministers, instead of pursuing directly the one grand object of national welfare, will make it their sole study to vary their measures according to his humours. But a minister *may* be refractory; his successor will naturally run headlong into plans totally the reverse of the former system: for, if he treads in the same path, he is well aware that a similar fate will attend him. This observation will apply to each succession of kings, who, from vanity and a desire of distinction, will, in general, studiously avoid any step, which may lead to a suspicion that they are so spiritless as to imitate their predecessor.

That a similar instability is not incident to republics is evident from their very constitution.

As, from the nature of monarchy, particularly of hereditary monarchy, there must always be a vast disproportion, between the duties to be performed, and the powers that are to perform them, and as the measures of government, far from gaining additional vigour, are on the contrary enfeebled by being entrusted to one hand, what arguments can be used for allowing to the will of a single being a weight which, as history shews, will subvert that of the whole body politic? And this brings me to my grand objection to monarchy, which is drawn from the eternal nature of man. The office of king is a trial to which human virtue is not equal. Pure and universal representation, by which alone liberty can be secured, cannot, I think, exist together with monarchy. It seems madness to expect a manifestation of the *general* will, at the same time that we allow to a *particular* will that weight, which it must obtain in all governments, that can, with any propriety, be called monarchical. They must war with each other, till one of them is extinguished. It was so in France, and ★★★ I shall not pursue this topic further, but, as you are a teacher of purity of morals, I cannot but remind you of that atmosphere of corruption, without which it should seem that courts cannot exist.

You seem anxious to explain what ought to be understood by the equality of men in a state of civil society, but your Lordship's success has not answered your trouble. If you had looked in the articles of the rights of man you would have found your efforts superseded. Equality, without which liberty cannot exist, is to be met with in perfection in that state in which no distinctions are admitted but such as have evidently for their object the general good. The end of government cannot be attained without authorising some members of the society to command, and, of course, without imposing on the rest the necessity of obedience. Here then is an inevitable inequality which may be denominated that of power. In order to render this as small as possible, a legislator will be careful not to give greater force to such authority than is essential to its due execution. Government is, at best, but a necessary evil:[16] compelled to place themselves in a state of subordination, men will obviously endeavour to prevent the abuse of that superiority to which they submit: accordingly they will cautiously avoid whatever may lead those in whom it is acknowledged to suppose they hold it as a right. Nothing will more effectually contribute to this than that the person in whom authority has been lodged should occasionally descend to the level of private citizen; he will learn from it a wholesome lesson, and the people will be less liable to confound the person with the power. On this principle, hereditary authority will be proscribed; and on another also, – that on such a system as that of hereditary authority no security can be had for talents adequate to the discharge of the office, and consequently the people can only feel the mortification of having humbled without having protected themselves.

Another distinction will arise amongst mankind, which, though it may be easily modified by government, exists independent of it; I mean the distinction of wealth which always will attend superior talents and industry. It cannot be denied that the security of individual property is one of the strongest and most natural motives to induce men to bow their necks to the yoke of civil government. In order to attain this end of security to property, a legislator will proceed with impartiality. He should not suppose that, when he has ensured to their proprietors the possession of lands and moveables against the depredation of the necessitous, nothing remains to be done. The history of all ages has demonstrated that wealth not only can secure itself but includes even an oppressive principle. Aware of this, and that the extremes of poverty and riches have a necessary tendency to corrupt the human heart, he will banish from his code all laws such as the unnatural monster of primogeniture, such as encourage associations against labour in the form of corporate bodies, and indeed all that monopolising system of legislation whose baleful influence is shewn in the depopulation of the country and in the necessity which reduces the sad relicks to owe their very existence to the ostentatious bounty of their oppressors. If it is true in common life, it is still more true in governments that we should be just before we are generous:

but our legislators seem to have forgotten or despised this homely maxim. They have unjustly left unprotected that most important part of property, not less real because it has no material existence, that which ought to enable the labourer to provide food for himself and his family. I appeal to innumerable statutes whose constant and professed object it is to lower the price of labour, to compel the workman to be *content* with arbitrary wages, evidently too small from the necessity of legal enforcement of the acceptance of them. Even from the astonishing amount of the sums raised for the support of one description of the poor may be concluded the extent and greatness of that oppression, whose effects have rendered it possible for the few to afford so much, and have shewn us that such a multitude of our brothers exist in even helpless indigence. Your lordship tells us that the science of civil government has received all the perfection of which it is capable. For my part, I am more enthusiastic: the sorrow I feel from the contemplation of this melancholy picture is not unconsoled by a comfortable hope that the class of wretches called mendicants will not much longer shock the feelings of humanity; that the miseries entailed upon the marriage of those who are not rich will no longer tempt the bulk of mankind to fly to that promiscuous intercourse to which they are impelled by the instincts of nature, and the dreadful satisfaction of escaping the prospect of infants, sad fruit of such intercourse, whom they are unable to support. If these flattering prospects be ever realised, it must be owing to some wise and salutary regulations counteracting that inequality among mankind which proceeds from the present *forced* disproportion of their possessions.

I am not an advocate for the agrarian law, nor for sumptuary regulations, but I contend that the people amongst whom the law of primogeniture exists, and among whom corporate bodies are encouraged and immense salaries annexed to useless and indeed hereditary offices, is oppressed by an inequality in the distribution of wealth which does not necessarily attend men in a state of civil society.

Thus far we have considered inequalities inseparable from civil society. But other arbitrary distinctions exist among mankind, either from choice or usurpation. I allude to titles, to stars, ribbands, and garters, and other badges of fictitious superiority. Your lordship will not question the grand principle on which this enquiry set out; I look upon it, then, as my duty to try the propriety of these distinctions by that criterion, and think it will be no difficult task to prove that these separations among mankind are absurd, impolitic, and immoral. Considering hereditary nobility as a reward for services rendered to the state, and it is to my charity that you owe the permission of taking up the question on this ground, what services can a man render to the state adequate to such a compensation that the making of laws, upon which the happiness of millions is to depend, shall be lodged in him and his posterity, however depraved may be their principles, however contemptible their understandings? But here I may be accused of sophistry; I ought to subtract every idea of power from such distinction though from the weakness of mankind it is impossible to disconnect them: what services then can a man render to society to compensate for the outrage done to the dignity of our nature when we bind ourselves to address him and his posterity with humiliating circumlocutions, calling him most noble, most honourable, most high, most august, serene, excellent, eminent and so forth: when it is more than probable that such unnatural flattery will but generate vices which ought to consign him to neglect and solitude, or make him the perpetual object of the finger of scorn. And does not experience justify the observation that, where titles, a thing very rare, have been conferred as the rewards of merit, those to whom they have descended, far from being thereby animated to imitate their ancestor, have presumed upon that lustre which they supposed thrown round them, and prodigally relying on such resources lavished what alone was their own, their personal reputation.

It would be happy if this delusion were confined to themselves; but, alas! the world is weak enough to grant the indulgence which they assume. Vice which is forgiven in one character will soon cease to meet with sternness of rebuke when found in others. Even at first she will intreat pardon with confidence, assured that ere long she will be charitably supposed to stand in no need of it.

But let me ask you seriously, from the mode in which these distinctions are originally conferred, is it not almost necessary that, far from being the rewards of services rendered to the state, they should usually be the recompense of an industrious sacrifice of the general welfare to the particular aggrandizement of that power by which they are bestowed? Let us even alter their source, and consider them as proceeding from the nation itself, and deprived of their hereditary quality: even here I should proscribe them and for this most evident reason; that a man's past services are no sufficient security for his future character: he who today merits the civic wreath may tomorrow deserve the Tarpeian rock.[17] Besides where respect is not perverted, where the world is not taught to reverence men without regarding their conduct, the esteem of mankind will have a very different value, and, when a proper independence is secured, will be regarded as a sufficient recompense for services however important, and will be a much surer guarantee of the continuance of such virtues as may deserve it.

I have another strong objection to nobility which is that it has a necessary tendency to dishonour labour, a prejudice which extends far beyond its own circle; that it binds down whole ranks of men to idleness while it gives the enjoyment of a reward which exceeds the hopes of the most active exertions of human industry. The languid tedium of this noble repose must be dissipated; and gaming with the tricking manoeuvres of the horse-race, afford occupation to hours, which it would be happy for mankind had they been totally unemployed. Reflecting on the corruption of the public manners, does your lordship shudder at the prostitution which miserably deluges our streets? You may find the cause in our aristocratical prejudices. Are you disgusted with the hypocrisy and sycophancy of our intercourse in private life? You may find the cause in the necessity of dissimulation which we have established by regulations which oblige us to address as our superiors, indeed as our masters, men whom we cannot but internally despise. Do you lament that such large portions of mankind should stoop to occupations unworthy of the dignity of their nature? You may find in the pride and luxury thought necessary to nobility how such servile arts are encouraged. Besides where the most honourable of the land do not blush to accept such offices as groom of the bedchamber, master of the hounds, lords in waiting, captain of the honourable band of gentlemen pensioners, is it astonishing that the bulk of the people should not ask of an occupation, what is it? but what may be gained by it? If the long equestrian train of equipage should make your lordship sigh for the poor who are pining in hunger, you will find that little is thought of snatching the bread from their mouths to eke out the '*necessary* splendour'[18] of nobility.

I have not time to pursue this subject farther, but am so strongly impressed with the baleful influence of aristocracy and nobility upon human happiness and virtue that if, as I am persuaded, monarchy cannot exist without such supporters, I think that reason sufficient for the preference I have given to the republican system.

It is with reluctance that I quit the subjects I have just touched upon; but the nature of this address does not permit me to continue the discussion. I proceed to what more immediately relates to this kingdom, at the present crisis. You ask with triumphant confidence, to what other law are the people of England subject than to the general will of the society to which they belong? Is your lordship to be told that acquiescence is not choice, and that obedience is not freedom? If there is a single man in Great Britain, who has no suffrage in the election of a representative, the will of the society of which he is a member is not generally expressed; he is a helot in that society. You answer the question, so confidently put, in this singular manner. 'The King, we are all justly persuaded, has not the inclination; and we all know that, if he had the inclination, he has not the power, to substitute his will in the place of law. The house of lords has no such power. The house of commons has no such power.' This passage, so artfully and unconstitutionally framed to agree with the delusions of the moment, cannot deceive a thinking reader. The expression of your full persuasion of the upright intentions of the king can only be the language of flattery. You are not to be told that it is constitutionally a maxim not to attribute to the person of the king the measures and misconduct of government. Had you chosen to speak, as you ought to have done, openly and explicitly, you must have expressed your just persuasion and implicit confidence in the integrity, moderation, and wisdom of his majesty's ministers. Have you forgot the avowed ministerial maxims of Sir Robert Walpole? [19] are you ignorant of the overwhelming corruption of the present day?

You seem unconscious of the absurdity of separating what is inseparable even in imagination. Would it have been any consolation to the miserable Romans under the second triumvirate to have been asked insultingly, is it Octavius, is it Anthony, or is it Lepidus that has caused this bitterness of affliction? and when the answer could not be returned with certainty, to have been reproached that their sufferings were imaginary? The fact is that the king *and* lords *and* commons, by what is termed the omnipotence of parliament, have constitutionally the right of enacting whatever laws they please, in defiance of the petitions or remonstrances of the nation; they have the power of doubling our enormous debt of 240 millions, and *may* pursue measures, which could never be supposed the emanation of the general will, without concluding the people stripped of reason, of sentiment, and even of that first instinct, which prompts them to preserve their own existence.

I congratulate your lordship upon your enthusiastic fondness for the judicial proceedings of this country. I am happy to find you have passed through life without having your fleece torn from your back in the thorny labyrinth of litigation. But you have not lived always in colleges, and must have passed by some victims whom it cannot be supposed, without a reflection on your heart, that you have forgotten. Here I am reminded of what I have said on the subject of representation; to be qualified for the office of legislation you should have felt like the bulk of mankind; their sorrows should be familiar to you, of which if you are ignorant how can you redress them? As a member of the assembly which, from a confidence in its experience, sagacity, and wisdom, the constitution has invested with the supreme appellant jurisdiction to determine the most doubtful points of an intricate jurisprudence, your lordship cannot, I presume, be ignorant of the consuming expense of our never-ending process, the verbosity of unintelligible statutes, and the perpetual contrariety in our judicial decisions.

'The greatest freedom that can be enjoyed by man in a state of civil society; the greatest security that can be given him with respect to the protection of his character, property, personal liberty, limb, and life is afforded to every individual by our present constitution.'

'Let it never be forgotten by ourselves and let us impress the observation upon the hearts of our children that we are in possession of both (liberty and equality), of as much of both, as can be consistent with the end for which civil society was introduced among mankind.'

Many of my readers will hardly believe me when I inform them that these passages are copied verbatim from your appendix. Mr Burke rouzed the indignation of all ranks of men, when by a refinement in cruelty superiour to that which in the East yokes the living to the dead he strove to persuade us that we and our posterity to the end of time were riveted to a constitution by the indissoluble compact of a dead parchment, and were bound to cherish a corse at the bosom, when reason might call aloud that it should be entombed. Your lordship aims at the same detestable object by means more criminal because more dangerous and insidious. Attempting to lull the people of England into a belief that any enquiries directed towards the nature of liberty and equality can in no other way lead to their happiness than by convincing them that they have already arrived at perfection in the science of government, what is your object but to exclude them for ever from the most fruitful field of human knowledge? Besides, it is another cause to execrate this doctrine that the consequence of such fatal delusion would be that they must entirely draw off their attention not only from the government but from their governors; that the stream of public vigilance, far from chearing and enriching the prospect of society, would by its stagnation consign it to barrenness and by its putrefaction infect it with death. You have aimed an arrow at liberty and philosophy, the eyes of the human race: — why, like the inveterate enemy of Philip, in putting your name to the shaft,[20] did you not declare openly its destination?

As a teacher of religion your lordship cannot be ignorant of a class of breaches of duty which may be denominated faults of omission. You profess to give your opinions upon the present turbulent crisis, expressing a wish that they may have some effect in tranquillizing the minds of the people. From your silence respecting the general call for a parliamentary reform, supported by your assertion that we at present enjoy as great a portion of liberty and equality as is consistent with civil society, what can be supposed but that you are a determined enemy to the redress of what the people of England call and feel to be grievances?

From your omitting to speak upon the war, and your general disapprobation of French measures and French principles expressed particularly at this moment, we are necessarily led also to conclude that you have no wish to dispel an infatuation which is now giving up to the sword so large a portion of the poor and consigning the rest to the more slow and more painful consumption of want. I could excuse your silence on this point as it would ill become an English bishop at the close of the eighteenth century to make the pulpit the vehicle of exhortations which would have disgraced the incendiary of the crusades, the hermit Peter.[21] But you have deprived yourself of the plea of decorum by giving no opinion on the reform of the legislature: as undoubtedly, you have some secret reason for the reservation of your sentiments on this latter head, I cannot but apply the same reason to the former. Upon what principle is your conduct to be explained? In some parts of England it is quaintly said, when a drunken man is seen reeling towards his home, that he has business on both sides of the road. Observing your lordship's tortuous path, the spectators will be far from insinuating that you have partaken of Mr Burke's intoxicating bowl; they will content themselves, shaking their heads as you stagger along, with remarking that you have business on both sides of the road.

The friends of liberty congratulate themselves upon the odium under which they are at present labouring; as the causes which have produced it have obliged so many of her false adherents to disclaim with officious earnestness any desire to promote her interest; nor are they disheartened by the diminution which their body is supposed already to have sustained. Conscious that an enemy lurking in our ranks is ten times more formidable than when drawn out against us, that the unblushing aristocracy of a Maury or a Cazalès is far less dangerous than the insidious mask of patriotism assumed by a La Fayette or a Mirabeau,[22] we thank you for your desertion. Political convulsions have been said particularly to call forth concealed abilities; but it has been seldom observed how vast is their consumption of them. Reflecting upon the fate of the greatest portion of the members of the constituent and legislative assemblies, we must necessarily be struck with a prodigious annihilation of human talents. – Aware that this necessity is attached to a struggle for Liberty, we are the less sorry that we can expect no advantage from the mental endowments of your Lordship. Besides the names which I

# [Letter to Charles James Fox (1801)]

✤᳁᳁᳁✤᳁᳁᳁✤

[Dated 14 January 1801. First published 1851. The text printed here follows the manuscript of the letter.]

This letter to Charles James Fox, the liberal Whig politician, was one of about six sent to 'persons of eminence' along with presentation copies of Lyrical Ballads (1800) on the urging of Samuel Taylor Coleridge. Fox answered the letter on 25 May 1801, stating that he preferred '"Harry Gill", "We are Seven", "The Mad Mother" and "The Idiot"' to 'Michael' and 'The Brothers', which he felt too simple in subject to warrant the use of blank verse. He and Wordsworth met in 1806, several months before Fox's death.

It is not without much difficulty, that I have summoned the courage to request your acceptance of these Volumes. Should I express my real feelings, I am sure that I should seem to make a parade of diffidence and humility.

Several of the poems contained in these Volumes are written upon subjects, which are the common property of all Poets, and which, at some period of your life, must have been interesting to a man of your sensibility, and perhaps may still continue to be so. It would be highly gratifying to me to suppose that even in a single instance the manner in which I have treated these general topics should afford you any pleasure; but such a hope does not influence me upon the present occasion; in truth I do not feel it. Besides, I am convinced that there must be many things in this collection, which may impress you with an unfavorable idea of my intellectual powers. I do not say this with a wish to degrade myself; but I am sensible that this must be the case, from the different circles in which we have moved, and the different objects with which we have been conversant.

Being utterly unknown to you as I am, I am well aware, that if I am justified in writing to you at all, it is necessary, my letter should be short; but I have feelings within me which I hope will so far shew themselves in this letter, as to excuse the trespass which I am afraid I shall make. In common with the whole of the English people I have observed in your public character a constant predominance of sensibility of heart. Necessitated as you have been from your public situation to have much to do with men in bodies, and in classes, and accordingly to contemplate them in that relation, it has been your praise that you have not thereby been prevented from looking upon them as individuals, and that you have habitually left your heart open to be influenced by them in that capacity. This habit cannot but have made you dear to Poets; and I am sure that, if since your first entrance into public life there has been a single true poet living in England, he must have loved you.

But were I assured that I myself had a just claim to the title of a Poet, all the dignity being attached to the word which belongs to it, I do not think that I should have ventured for that reason to offer these volumes to you: at present it is solely on account of two poems in the second volume, the one entitled 'The Brothers,' and the other 'Michael,' that I have been emboldened to take this liberty.

It appears to me that the most calamitous effect, which has followed the measures which have lately been pursued in this country, is a rapid decay of the domestic affections among the lower orders of society. This effect the present Rulers of this country are not conscious of, or they disregard it. For many years past, the tendency of society amongst almost all the nations of Europe has been to produce it. But recently by the spreading of manufactures through every part of the country, by the heavy taxes upon postage, by workhouses, Houses of Industry, and the invention of Soup-shops &c. &c. super-added to the encreasing disproportion between the price of labour and that of the necessaries of life, the bonds of domestic feeling among the poor, as far as the influence of these things has extended, have been weakened, and in innumerable instances entirely destroyed. The evil would be the less to be regretted, if these institutions were regarded only as palliatives to a disease; but the vanity and pride of their promoters are so subtly interwoven with them, that they are deemed great discoveries and blessings to humanity. In the mean time parents are separated from their children, and children from their parents; the wife no longer prepares with her own hands a meal for her husband, the produce of his labour; there is little doing in his house in which his affections can be interested, and but little left in it which he can love. I have two neighbours, a man and his wife, both upwards of eighty years of age; they live alone; the husband has been confined to his bed many months and has never had, nor till within these few weeks has ever needed, any body to attend to him but his wife. She has recently been seized with a lameness which has often prevented her from being able to carry him his food to his bed; the neighbours fetch water for her from the well, and do other kind offices for them both, but her infirmities encrease. She told my Servant two days ago that she was afraid they must both be boarded out among some other Poor of the parish (they have long been supported by the parish) but she said, it was hard, having kept house together so long, to come to this, and she was sure that 'it would burst her heart'. I mention this fact to shew how deeply the spirit of independence is, even yet, rooted in some parts of the country. These people could not express themselves in this way without an almost sublime conviction of the blessings of independent domestic life. If it is true, as I believe, that this spirit is rapidly disappearing, no greater curse can befal a land.

I earnestly entreat your pardon for having detained you so long. In the two Poems, 'The Brothers' and 'Michael' I have attempted to draw a picture of the domestic affections as I know they exist amongst a class of men who are now almost confined to the North of England. They are small independent *proprietors* of land here called statesmen, men of respectable education who daily labour on their own little properties. The domestic affections will always be strong amongst men who live in a country not crowded with population, if these men are placed above poverty. But if they are proprietors of small estates which have descended to them from their ancestors, the power which these affections will acquire amongst such men is inconceivable by those who have only had an opportunity of observing hired labourers, farmers, and the manufacturing Poor. Their little tract of land serves as a kind of permanent rallying point for their domestic feelings, as a tablet upon which they are written which makes them objects of memory in a thousand instances when they would otherwise be forgotten. It is a fountain fitted to the nature of social man from which supplies of affection, as pure as his heart was intended for, are daily drawn. This class of men is rapidly disappearing. You, Sir, have a consciousness, upon which every good man will congratulate you, that the whole of your public conduct has in one way or other been directed to the preservation of this class of men, and those who hold similar situations. You have felt that the most sacred of all property is the property of the Poor. The two poems which I have mentioned were written with a view to shew that men who do not wear fine cloaths can feel deeply. 'Pectus enim est quod disertos facit, et vis mentis. Ideoque imperitis quoque, si modo sint aliquo affectu concitati, verba non desunt.'[1] The poems are faithful copies from nature; and I hope, whatever effect they may have upon you, you will at least be able to perceive that they may excite profitable sympathies in many kind and good hearts, and may in some small degree enlarge our feelings of reverence for our species, and our knowledge of human nature, by shewing that our best qualities are possessed by men whom we are too apt to consider, not with reference to the points in which they resemble us, but to those in which they manifestly differ from us. I thought, at a time when these feelings are sapped in so many ways that the two poems might co-operate, however feebly, with the illustrious efforts which you have made to stem this and other evils with which the country is labouring, and it is on this account alone that I have taken the liberty of thus addressing you.[2]

# From *The Convention of Cintra*

~~~~~~~~~

[*Probably composed between about mid-November (after 6 November) 1808
and 26 March 1809 (with minor revisions till 10 May 1809). Approximately
the first tenth was first published as two instalments in the* Courier, *27
December 1808 and 13 January 1809. The whole work was first published
as a pamphlet 27 May 1809 with the following title: 'Concerning the
Relations of Great Britain, Spain, and Portugal, to Each Other, and to
the Common Enemy, at This Crisis; and Specifically as Affected by the*
CONVENTION OF CINTRA: *The whole brought to the test
of those Principles, by which alone the Independence and Freedom of
Nations can be Preserved or Recovered.' The text printed below follows
this first complete version, supervised through the press by Thomas De
Quincey (who provided much of the punctuation), with corrections made
from several errata but with deletion of five passages (described below)
constituting about half the work.*]

In the Peninsular War, the French, faced with revolt in Spain and badly
beaten in battle in Portugal by the British on 21 August 1808, sued for a
convention, and armistice, with the British. The Convention of Cintra was
negotiated 23–30 August 1808, was reported in English newspapers 16
September and, beginning 14 November, was investigated by a board of
inquiry, an event that reflected widespread public antagonism. Wordsworth's
pamphlet did not appear for another six months and did not sell even the
original printing of 500 copies probably because of the tardy publication as
well as the rapidly changing situation at home and abroad.

*This pamphlet, Wordsworth's longest work in prose, suffers from poor organization and prolixity and consequently gains from editing. Rather than constantly deleting material, leaving behind annoying tracks of ellipses marks, I have deleted five passages (four of them quite long), always beginning and ending at paragraph breaks. The deleted material is described in brackets in the text and consists of long quotations from Spanish sources, redundant descriptions of the English reaction to the Convention, details of the terms of the Convention, accounts of the Spanish resistance to the French, and advice on future conduct of the war. Relieved of this extraneous material, the remaining half presents more clearly the general political, moral and psychological backgrounds to the Convention, the righteous indignation directed by Wordsworth at the British generals, at Parliament, and at the ministers involved, and his eloquent appeals for moral regeneration.*

*The title page carried a Latin quotation from Horace's* Ars Poetica *(lines 312, 314–5), which in English reads:*

> *He who has learned what he owes his country . . .*
> *What is the obligation of a senator and of a judge,*
> *What the duty of a commander sent into battle . . .*

*There was also a motto on the reverse from Lord Bacon's* An Advertisement Touching the Controversies of the Church of England *(1641) [Works (1740), IV, 460]: 'Bitter and earnest writing must not hastily be condemned; for men cannot contend coldly, and without affection, about things which they hold dear and precious. A politic man may write from his brain, without touch and sense of his heart; as in a speculation that appertaineth not unto him; – but a feeling Christian will express, in his words, a character of hate or love.'*

*Wordsworth's own emotional involvement can be seen in the manuscript of the Fenwick notes (on a separate page within the notes on the 'Poems Dedicated to National Independence and Liberty') where Wordsworth commented, apparently at random:*

It would not be easy to conceive with what a depth of feeling I entered into the struggle carried on by the Spaniards for their deliverance from the usurped power of the French. Many times have I gone from Allan Bank in Grasmere Vale, where we

*were then residing, to the top of the Raise-Gap, as it is called, so late as two o'clock*
*in the morning to meet the carrier bringing the newspaper from Keswick. Imperfect*
*traces of the state of mind in which I then was may be found in my tract on the*
*Convention of Cintra as well as in these Sonnets.*

### ADVERTISEMENT

The following pages originated in the opposition which was made
by his Majesty's ministers to the expression, in public meetings and
otherwise, of the opinions and feelings of the people concerning the
Convention of Cintra. For the sake of immediate and general circulation, I determined (when I had made a considerable progress in
the manuscript) to print it in different portions in one of the daily
newspapers. Accordingly two portions of it (extending to page [185])
were printed, in the months of December and January, in the Courier,
– as being one of the most impartial and extensively circulated
journals of the time. The reader is requested to bear in mind this
previous publication: otherwise he will be at a loss to account for the
arrangement of the matter in one instance in the earlier part of the
work. An accidental loss of several sheets of the manuscript delayed
the continuance of the publication in that manner, till the close of the
Christmas holidays; and – the pressure of public business rendering it
then improbable that room could be found, in the columns of the
paper, regularly to insert matter extending to such a length – this
plan of publication was given up.

It may be proper to state that, in the extracts which have been
made from the Spanish Proclamations, I have been obliged to content
myself with the translations which appeared in the public journals;
having only in one instance had access to the original. This is, in
some cases, to be regretted – where the language falls below the
dignity of the matter: but in general it is not so; and the feeling has
suggested correspondent expressions to the translators; hastily as, no
doubt, they must have performed their work.

I must entreat the reader to bear in mind that I began to write
upon this subject in November last; and have continued without

bringing my work earlier to a conclusion, partly from accident, and partly from a wish to possess additional documents and facts. Passing occurrences have made changes in the situation of certain objects spoken of; but I have not thought it necessary to accommodate what I had previously written to these changes: the whole stands without alteration; except where additions have been made, or errors corrected.

As I have spoken without reserve of things (and of persons as far as it was necessary to illustrate things, but no further); and as this has been uniformly done according to the light of my conscience; I have deemed it right to prefix my name to these pages, in order that this last testimony of a sincere mind might not be wanting.

May 20th, 1809.

## CONCERNING THE CONVENTION OF CINTRA

The Convention, recently concluded by the Generals at the head of the British army in Portugal, is one of the most important events of our time. It would be deemed so in France, if the Ruler[1] of that country could dare to make it public with those merely of its known bearings and dependences with which the English people are acquainted; it has been deemed so in Spain and Portugal as far as the people of those countries have been permitted to gain, or have gained, a knowledge of it; and what this nation has felt and still feels upon the subject is sufficiently manifest. Wherever the tidings were communicated, they carried agitation along with them – a conflict of sensations in which, though sorrow was predominant, yet, through force of scorn, impatience, hope, and indignation, and through the universal participation in passions so complex, and the sense of power which this necessarily included – the whole partook of the energy and activity of congratulation and joy. Not a street, not a public room, not a fire-side in the island which was not disturbed as by a local or private trouble; men of all estates, conditions, and tempers were affected apparently in equal degrees. Yet was the event by none received as an open and measurable affliction: it had indeed features bold and intelligible to every one; but there was an under-expression which was strange, dark, and mysterious – and, accordingly as different notions prevailed, or the object was looked at in different points of view, we were astonished like men who are overwhelmed without forewarning – fearful like men who feel themselves to be helpless, and indignant and angry like men who are betrayed. In a word, it would not be too much to say that the tidings of this event did not spread with the commotion of a storm which sweeps visibly over our heads, but like an earthquake which rocks the ground under our feet.

How was it possible that it could be otherwise? For that army had been sent upon a service which appealed so strongly to all that was human in the heart of this nation – that there was scarcely a gallant father of a family who had not his moments of regret that he was not a soldier by profession, which might have made it his duty to accompany it; every high-minded youth grieved that his first impulses, which would have sent him upon the same errand, were not to be yielded to, and that after-thought did not sanction and confirm the instantaneous dictates or the reiterated persuasions of an heroic spirit. The army took its departure with prayers and blessings which were as widely spread as they were fervent and intense. For it was not doubted that, on this occasion, every person of which it was composed, from the General to the private soldier, would carry both into his conflicts with the enemy in the field, and into his relations of peaceful intercourse with the inhabitants, not only the virtues which might be expected from him as a soldier, but the antipathies and sympathies, the loves and hatreds of a citizen – of a human being – acting, in a manner hitherto unprecedented under the obligation of his human and social nature. If the conduct of the rapacious and merciless adversary rendered it neither easy nor wise – made it, I might say, impossible to give way to that unqualified admiration of courage and skill, made it impossible in relation to him to be exalted by those triumphs of the courteous affections, and to be purified by those refinements of civility which do, more than any thing, reconcile a man of thoughtful mind and humane dispositions to the horrors of

# From *The Convention of Cintra*

ordinary war; it was felt that for such loss the benign and accomplished soldier would upon this mission be abundantly recompensed by the enthusiasm of fraternal love with which his Ally, the oppressed people whom he was going to aid in rescuing themselves, would receive him; and that this, and the virtues which he would witness in them, would furnish his heart with never-failing and far nobler objects of complacency and admiration. The discipline of the army was well known; and as a machine, or a vital organized body, the Nation was assured that it could not but be formidable; but thus to the standing excellence of mechanic or organic power seemed to be superadded, at this time, and for this service, the force of *inspiration*: could any thing therefore be looked for, but a glorious result? The army proved its prowess in the field; and what has been the result is attested, and long will be attested, by the downcast looks — the silence — the passionate exclamations — the sighs and shame of every man who is worthy to breathe the air or to look upon the green-fields of Liberty in this blessed and highly-favoured Island which we inhabit.

If I were speaking of things however weighty, that were long past and dwindled in the memory, I should scarcely venture to use this language; but the feelings are of yesterday — they are of to-day; the flower, a melancholy flower it is! is still in blow, nor will, I trust, its leaves be shed through months that are to come: for I repeat that the heart of the nation is in this struggle. This just and necessary war, as we have been accustomed to hear it styled from the beginning of the contest in the year 1793, had, some time before the Treaty of Amiens,[2] viz. after the subjugation of Switzerland, and not till then, begun to be regarded by the body of the people, as indeed both just and necessary; and this justice and necessity were by none more clearly perceived, or more feelingly bewailed, than by those who had most eagerly opposed the war in its commencement, and who continued most bitterly to regret that this nation had ever borne a part in it. Their conduct was herein consistent: they proved that they kept their eyes steadily fixed upon principles; for, though there was a shifting or transfer of hostility in their minds as far as regarded persons, they only combated the same enemy opposed to them under a different shape; and that enemy was the spirit of selfish tyranny and lawless ambition. This spirit, the class of persons of whom I have been speaking, (and I would now be understood, as associating them with an immense majority of the people of Great Britain, whose affections, notwithstanding all the delusions which had been practised upon them, were, in the former part of the contest, for a long time on the side of their nominal enemies,) this spirit, when it became undeniably embodied in the French government, they wished, in spite of all dangers, should be opposed by war; because peace was not to be procured without submission, which could not but be followed by a communion, of which the word of greeting would be, on the one part, insult, – and, on the other, degradation. The people now wished for war, as their rulers had done before, because open war between nations is a defined and effectual partition, and the sword, in the hands of the good and the virtuous, is the most intelligible symbol of abhorrence. It was in order to be preserved from spirit-breaking submissions – from the guilt of seeming to approve that which they had not the power to prevent, and out of a consciousness of the danger that such guilt would otherwise actually steal upon them, and that thus, by evil communications[3] and participations, would be weakened and finally destroyed, those moral sensibilities and energies, by virtue of which alone, their liberties, and even their lives, could be preserved, – that the people of Great Britain determined to encounter all perils which could follow in the train of open resistance. – There were some, and those deservedly of high character in the country, who exerted their utmost influence to counteract this resolution; nor did they give to it so gentle a name as want of prudence, but they boldly termed it blindness and obstinacy. Let them be judged with charity! But there are promptings of wisdom from the penetralia of human nature, which a people can hear, though the wisest of their practical Statesmen be deaf towards them. This authentic voice, the people of England had heard and obeyed: and, in opposition to French tyranny growing daily more insatiate and implacable, they ranged themselves zealously under their

Government; though they neither forgot nor forgave its transgressions, in having first involved them in a war with a people then struggling for its own liberties under a twofold affliction – confounded by inbred faction, and beleaguered by a cruel and imperious external foe. But these remembrances did not vent themselves in reproaches, nor hinder us from being reconciled to our Rulers, when a change or rather a revolution in circumstances had imposed new duties: and, in defiance of local and personal clamour, it may be safely said, that the nation united heart and hand with the Government in its resolve to meet the worst, rather than stoop its head to receive that which, it was felt, would not be the garland but the yoke of peace. Yet it was an afflicting alternative; and it is not to be denied, that the effort, if it had the determination, wanted the cheerfulness of duty. Our condition savoured too much of a grinding constraint – too much of the vassalage of necessity; – it had too much of fear, and therefore of selfishness, not to be contemplated in the main with rueful emotion. We desponded though we did not despair. In fact a deliberate and preparatory fortitude – a sedate and stern melancholy, which had no sunshine and was exhilarated only by the lightnings of indignation – this was the highest and best state of moral feeling to which the most noble-minded among us could attain.

But, from the moment of the rising of the people of the Pyrenean peninsula,[4] there was a mighty change; we were instantaneously animated; and, from that moment, the contest assumed the dignity, which it is not in the power of any thing but hope to bestow: and, if I may dare to transfer language, prompted by a revelation of a state of being that admits not of decay or change, to the concerns and interests of our transitory planet, from that moment 'this corruptible put on incorruption, and this mortal put on immortality.'[5] This sudden elevation was on no account more welcome – was by nothing more endeared, than by the returning sense which accompanied it of inward liberty and choice, which gratified our moral yearnings, inasmuch as it would give henceforward to our actions as a people, an origination and direction unquestionably moral – as it was free – as it was manifestly in sympathy with the species – as it admitted therefore of fluctuations of generous feeling – of approbation and of complacency. We were intellectualized also in proportion; we looked backward upon the records of the human race with pride, and, instead of being afraid, we delighted to look forward into futurity. It was imagined that this new-born spirit of resistance, rising from the most sacred feelings of the human heart, would diffuse itself through many countries; and not merely for the distant future, but for the present, hopes were entertained as bold as they were disinterested and generous.

Never, indeed, was the fellowship of our sentient nature more intimately felt – never was the irresistible power of justice more gloriously displayed than when the British and Spanish Nations, with an impulse like that of two ancient heroes throwing down their weapons and reconciled in the field, cast off at once their aversions and enmities, and mutually embraced each other [6] – to solemnize this conversion of love, not by the festivities of peace, but by combating side by side through danger and under affliction in the devotedness of perfect brotherhood. This was a conjunction which excited hope as fervent as it was rational. On the one side was a nation which brought with it sanction and authority, inasmuch as it had tried and approved the blessings for which the other had risen to contend: the one was a people which, by the help of the surrounding ocean and its own virtues, had preserved to itself through ages its liberty, pure and inviolated by a foreign invader; the other a high-minded nation, which a tyrant, presuming on its decrepitude, had, through the real decrepitude of its Government, perfidiously enslaved. What could be more delightful than to think of an intercourse beginning in this manner? On the part of the Spaniards their love towards us was enthusiasm and adoration; the faults of our national character were hidden from them by a veil of splendour; they saw nothing around us but glory and light; and, on our side, we estimated *their* character with partial and indulgent fondness; – thinking on their past greatness, not as the undermined foundation of a magnificent building, but as the root of a majestic tree recovered from a long disease, and beginning again to flourish with promise of wider branches and a deeper shade than it had boasted in the fulness of its strength. If in the sensations with which the Spaniards prostrated themselves before the religion of their country we did not keep pace with them — if even their loyalty was such as, from our mixed constitution of government and from other causes, we could not thoroughly sympathize with, — and if, lastly, their devotion to the person of their Sovereign appeared to us to have too much of the alloy of delusion, — in all these things we judged them gently: and, taught by the reverses of the French revolution, we looked upon these dispositions as more human — more social — and therefore as wiser, and of better omen, than if they had stood forth the zealots of abstract principles, drawn out of the laboratory of unfeeling philosophists. Finally, in this reverence for the past and present, we found an earnest that they were prepared to contend to the death for as much liberty as their habits and their knowledge enabled them to receive. To assist them and their neighbours the Portuguese in the attainment of this end, we sent to them in love and in friendship a powerful army to aid — to invigorate —and to chastise: — they landed; and the first proof they afforded of their being worthy to be sent on such a service — the first pledge of amity given by them was the victory of Vimiera;[7] the second pledge (and this was from the hand of their Generals,) was the Convention of Cintra.

The reader will by this time have perceived, what thoughts were uppermost in my mind, when I began with asserting, that this Convention is among the most important events of our times: — an assertion, which was made deliberately, and after due allowance for that infirmity which inclines us to magnify things present and passing, at the expence of those which are past. It is my aim to prove, wherein the real importance of this event lies: and, as a necessary preparative for forming a right judgment upon it, I have already given a representation of the sentiments, with which the people of Great Britain and those of Spain looked upon each other. I have indeed spoken rather of the Spaniards than of the Portuguese; but what has been said, will be understood as applying in the main to the whole Peninsula. The wrongs of the two nations have been equal, and their cause is the same: they must stand or fall together. What their wrongs have been, in what degree they considered themselves united, and what their hopes and resolutions were, we have learned from public Papers issued by themselves and by their enemies. These were read by the people of this Country, at the time when they were severally published, with due impression. – Pity, that those impressions could not have been as faithfully retained as they were at first received deeply! Doubtless, there is not a man in these Islands, who is not convinced that the cause of Spain is the most righteous cause in which, since the opposition of the Greek Republics to the Persian Invader at Thermopylae and Marathon,[8] sword ever was drawn! But this is not enough. We are actors in the struggle; and, in order that we may have steady PRINCIPLES to controul and direct us, (without which we may do much harm, and can do no good,) we ought to make it a duty to revive in the memory those words and facts, which first carried the conviction to our hearts: that, as far as it is possible, we may see as we then saw, and feel as we then felt. Let me therefore entreat the Reader seriously to peruse once more such parts of those Declarations as I shall extract from them. I feel indeed with sorrow, that events are hurrying us forward, as down the Rapid of an American river, and that there is too much danger *before*, to permit the mind easily to turn back upon the course which is past. It is indeed difficult. – But I need not say, that to yield to the difficulty, would be degrading to rational beings. Besides, if from the retrospect, we can either gain strength by which we can overcome, or learn prudence by which we may avoid, such submission is not only degrading, but pernicious. I address these words to those who have feeling, but whose judgment is overpowered by their feelings: – such as have not, and who are mere slaves of curiosity, calling perpetually for something new, and being able to create nothing new for themselves out of old materials, may be left to wander about under the yoke of their own unprofitable appetite. – Yet not so! Even these I would include in my request: and conjure them, as they are men, not to be impatient, while I place before their eyes, a composition made out of fragments of those Declarations from various parts of the Peninsula, which, disposed as it were in a tesselated pavement, shall set forth a story which may be easily understood; which will move and teach, and be consolatory to him who looks upon it. I say, consolatory: and let not the Reader shrink from the word. I am well aware of the burthen which is to be supported, of the discountenance from recent calamity under which every thing, which speaks of hope for the Spanish people, and through *them* for mankind, will be received. But this, far from deterring, ought to be an encouragement; it makes the duty more imperious. Nevertheless, whatever confidence any individual of meditative mind may have in these representations of the principles and feelings of the people of Spain, both as to their sanctity and truth, and as to their competence in ordinary circumstances to make these acknowledged, it would be unjust to recall them to the public mind, stricken as it is by present disaster,[9] without attempting to mitigate the bewildering terror which accompanies these events, and which is caused as much by their nearness to the eye, as by any thing in their own nature. I shall, however, at present confine myself to suggest a few considerations, some of which will be developed hereafter, when I resume the subject.

It appears then, that the Spanish armies have sustained great defeats, and have been compelled to abandon their positions, and that these reverses have been effected by an army greatly superior to the Spanish forces in number, and far excelling them in the art and practice of war. This is the sum of those tidings, which it was natural we should receive with sorrow, but which too many have received with dismay and despair, though surely no events could be more in the course of rational expectation. And what is the amount of the evil? – It is manifest that, though a great army may easily defeat or disperse another *army*, less or greater, yet it is not in a like degree formidable to a determined *people*, nor efficient in a like degree to subdue them, or to keep them in subjugation – much less if this people, like those of Spain in the present instance, be numerous, and, like them, inhabit a territory extensive and strong by nature. For a great army, and even several great armies, cannot accomplish this by marching about the country, unbroken, but each must split itself into many portions, and the several detachments become weak accordingly, not merely as they are small in size, but because the soldiery, acting thus, necessarily relinquish much of that part of their superiority, which lies in what may be called the enginery of war; and far more, because they lose, in proportion as they are broken, the power of profiting by the military skill of the Commanders, or by their own military habits. The experienced soldier is thus brought down nearer to the plain ground of the inexperienced, man to the level of man: and it is then, that the truly brave man rises, the man of good hopes and purposes; and superiority in moral brings with it superiority in physical power. Hence, if the Spanish armies have been defeated, or even dispersed, it not only argues a want of magnanimity, but of sense, to conclude that the cause *therefore* is lost. Supposing that the spirit of the people is not crushed, the war is now brought back to that plan of conducting it, which was recommended by the Junta of Seville in that inestimable paper entitled 'PRECAUTIONS', which plan ought never to have been departed from, except by compulsion, or with a moral certainty of success; and which the Spaniards will now be constrained to re-adopt, with the advantage, that the lesson, which has been received, will preclude the possibility of their ever committing the same error. In this paper it is said, 'let the first object be 'to avoid all general actions, and to convince ourselves of the very 'great hazards without any advantage or the hope of it, to which 'they would expose us.' The paper then gives directions, how the war ought to be conducted as a war of partizans, and shews the peculiar fitness of the country for it. Yet, though relying solely on this unambitious mode of warfare, the framers of the paper, which is in every part of it distinguished by wisdom, speak with confident thoughts of success. To this mode of warfare, then, after experience of calamity from not having trusted in it; to this, and to the people in whom the contest originated, and who are its proper depository, that contest is now referred.

Secondly, if the spirits of the Spaniards be not broken by defeat, which is impossible, if the sentiments that have been publicly expressed be fairly characteristic of the nation, and do not belong only to particular spots or to a few individuals of superior mind, – a doubt, which the internal evidence of these publications, sanctioned by the resistance already made, and corroborated by the universal consent with which certain qualities have been attributed to the Spaniards in all ages, encourages us to repel; – then are there mighty resources in the country which have not yet been called forth. For all has hitherto been done by the spontaneous efforts of the people, acting under little or no compulsion of the Government, but with its advice and exhortation. It is an error to suppose, that, in proportion as a people are strong, and act largely for themselves, the Government must therefore be weak. This is not a necessary consequence even in the heat of Revolution, but only when the people are lawless from want of a steady and noble object among themselves for their love, or in the presence of a foreign enemy for their hatred. In the early part of the French Revolution, indeed as long as it was evident that the end was the common safety, the National Assembly had the power to turn the people into any course, to constrain them to any task, while their voluntary efforts, as far as these could be exercised, were not abated in consequence. That which the National Assembly did for France, the Spanish Sovereign's authority acting through those whom the people themselves have deputed to represent him, would, in their present enthusiasm of loyalty, and condition of their general feelings, render practicable and easy for Spain. The Spaniards, it is true, with a thoughtfulness most hopeful for the cause which they have undertaken, have been loth to depart from established laws, forms, and practices. This dignified feeling of self-restraint they would do well to cherish so far as never to depart from it without some reluctance; – but, when old and familiar means are not equal to the exigency, new ones must, without timidity, be resorted to, though by many they may be found harsh and ungracious. Nothing but good would result from such conduct. The well-disposed would rely more confidently upon a Government which thus proved that it had confidence in itself. Men, less zealous, and of less comprehensive minds, would soon be reconciled to measures from which at first they had revolted; the remiss and selfish might be made servants of their country, through the influence of the same passions which had prepared them to become slaves of the Invader; or, should this not be possible, they would appear in their true character, and the main danger to be feared from them would be prevented. The course which ought to be pursued is plain. Either the cause has lost the people's love, or it has not. If it has, let the struggle be abandoned. If it has not, let the Government, in whatever shape it may exist, and however great may be the calamities under which it may labour, act up to the full stretch of its rights, nor doubt that the people will support it to the full extent of their power. If, therefore, the Chiefs of the Spanish Nation be men of wise and strong minds, they will bring both the forces, those of the Government and of the people, into their utmost action; tempering them in such a manner that neither shall impair or obstruct the other, but rather that they shall strengthen and direct each other for all salutary purposes.

Thirdly, it was never dreamt by any thinking man, that the Spaniards were to succeed by their army; if by their *army* be meant any thing but the people. The whole people is their army, and their true army is the people, and nothing else. Five hundred men, who in the early part of the struggle had been taken prisoners, – I think it was at the battle of Rio Seco – were returned by the French General under the title of Galician Peasants, a title, which the Spanish General, Blake, rejected and maintained in his answer that they were genuine soldiers, meaning regular troops. The conduct of the Frenchman was politic, and that of the Spaniard would have been more in the spirit of his cause and of his own noble character, if, waiving on this occasion the plea of any subordinate and formal commission which these men might have, he had rested their claim to the title of Soldiers on its true ground, and affirmed that this was no other than the rights of the cause which they maintained, by which rights every Spaniard was a soldier who could appear in arms, and was authorized to take that place, in which it was probable, to those under whom he acted, and on many occasions to himself, that he could most annoy the enemy. But these patriots of Galicia were not clothed alike, nor perhaps armed alike, nor had the outward appearance of those bodies, which are called regular troops; and the Frenchman availed himself of this pretext, to apply to them that insolent language, which might, I think, have been more nobly repelled on a more comprehensive principle. For thus are men of the gravest minds imposed upon by the presumptuous; and through these influences it comes, that the strength of a tyrant is in opinion [10] – not merely in the opinion of those who support him, but alas! even of those who willingly resist, and who would resist effectually, if it were not that their own understandings betray them, being already half enslaved by shews and forms. The whole Spanish nation ought to be encouraged to deem themselves an army, embodied under the authority of their country and of human nature. A military spirit should be there, and a military action, not confined like an ordinary river in one channel, but spreading like the Nile over the whole face of the land. Is this possible? I believe it is: if there be minds among them worthy to lead, and if those leading minds cherish a *civic* spirit by all warrantable aids and appliances, and, above all other means, by combining a reverential memory of their elder ancestors with distinct hopes of solid advantage, from the privileges of freedom, for themselves and their posterity – to which the history and the past state of Spain furnish such enviable facilities; and if they provide for the sustenance of this spirit, by organizing it in its primary sources, not timidly jealous of a people, whose toils and sacrifices have approved them worthy of all love and confidence, and whose failing of excess, if such there exist, is assuredly on the side of loyalty to their Sovereign, and predilection for all established institutions. We affirm, then, that a universal military spirit may be produced; and not only this, but that a much more rare and more admirable phenomenon may be realized – the civic and military spirit united in one people, and in enduring harmony with each other. The people of Spain, with arms in their hands, are already in an elevated mood, to which they have been raised by the indignant passions, and the keen sense of insupportable wrong and insult from the enemy, and its infamous instruments. But they must be taught, not to trust too exclusively to the violent passions, which have already done much of their peculiar task and service. They must seek additional aid from affections, which less imperiously exclude all individual interests, while at the same time they consecrate them to the public good. – But the enemy is in the heart of their land! We have not forgotten this. We would encourage their military zeal, and all qualities especially military, by all rewards of honourable ambition, and by rank and dignity conferred on the truly worthy, whatever may be their birth or condition, the elevating influence of which would extend from the individual possessor to the class from which he may have sprung. For the necessity of thus raising and upholding the military spirit, we plead: but yet the *professional* excellencies of the soldier must be contemplated according to their due place and relation. Nothing is done, or worse than nothing, unless something higher be taught, *as* higher, something more fundamental, *as* more fundamental. In the moral virtues and qualities of passion which belong to a people, must the ultimate salvation of a people be sought for. Moral qualities of a high order, and vehement passions, and virtuous as vehement, the Spaniards have already displayed; nor is it to be anticipated, that the conduct of their enemies will suffer the heat and glow to remit and languish. These may be trusted to themselves, and to the provocations of the merciless Invader. They must now be taught, that their strength *chiefly* lies in moral qualities, more silent in their operation, more permanent in their nature; in the virtues of perseverance, constancy, fortitude, and watchfulness, in a long memory and a quick feeling, to rise upon a favourable summons, a texture of life which, though cut through (as hath been feigned of the bodies of the Angels) unites again [11] – these are the virtues and qualities on which the Spanish People must be taught *mainly* to depend. These it is not in the power of their Chiefs to create; but they may preserve and procure to them opportunities of unfolding themselves, by guarding the Nation against an intemperate reliance on other qualities and other modes of exertion, to which it could never have resorted in the degree in which it appears to have resorted to them without having been in contradiction to itself, paying at the same time an indirect homage to its enemy. Yet, in hazarding this conditional censure, we are still inclined to believe, that, in spite of our deductions on the score of exaggeration, we have still given too easy credit to the accounts furnished by the enemy, of the rashness with which the Spaniards engaged in pitched battles, and of their dismay after defeat. For the Spaniards have repeatedly proclaimed, and they have inwardly felt, that their strength was from their cause – of course, that it was moral. Why then should they abandon this, and endeavour to prevail by means in which their opponents are confessedly so much superior? Moral strength is their's; but physical power for the purposes of immediate or rapid destruction is on the side of their enemies. This is to them no disgrace, but, as soon as they understand themselves, they will see that they are disgraced by mistrusting their appropriate stay, and throwing themselves upon a power which for them must be weak. Nor will it then appear to them a sufficient excuse, that they were seduced into this by the splendid qualities of courage and enthusiasm, which, being the frequent companions, and, in given circumstances, the necessary agents of virtue, are too often themselves hailed as virtues by their own title. But courage and enthusiasm have equally characterised the best and the worst beings, a Satan, equally with an ABDIEL – a BONAPARTE equally with a LEONIDAS.[12] They are indeed indispensible to the Spanish soldiery, in order that, man to man, they may not be inferior to their enemies in the field of battle. But inferior they are and long must be in warlike skill and coolness; inferior in assembled numbers, and in blind mobility to the preconceived purposes of their leader. If therefore the Spaniards are not superior in some superior quality, their fall may be predicted with the certainty of a mathematical calculation. Nay, it is right to acknowledge, however depressing to false hope the thought may be, that from a people prone and disposed to war, as the French are, through the very absence of those excellencies which give a contra-distinguishing dignity to the Spanish character; that, from an army of men presumptuous by nature, to whose presumption the experience of constant success has given the confidence and stubborn strength of reason, and who balance against the devotion of patriotism the superstition so naturally attached by the sensual and disordinate to the strange fortunes and

continual felicity of their Emperor; that, from the armies of such a
people a more manageable enthusiasm, a courage less under the
influence of accidents, may be expected in the confusion of immediate
conflict, than from forces like the Spaniards, united indeed by devotion to a common cause, but not equally united by an equal
confidence in each other, resulting from long fellowship and brotherhood in all conceivable incidents of war and battle. Therefore, I
do not hesitate to affirm, that even the occasional flight of the Spanish
levies, from sudden panic under untried circumstances, would not be
so injurious to the Spanish cause; no, nor so dishonourable to the
Spanish character, nor so ominous of ultimate failure, as a paramount
reliance on superior valour, instead of a principled reposal on superior
constancy and immutable resolve. Rather let them have fled once
and again, than direct their prime admiration to the blaze and ex-
plosion of animal courage, in slight of the vital and sustaining warmth
of fortitude; in slight of that moral contempt of death and privation,
which does not need the stir and shout of battle to call it forth or
support it, which can smile in patience over the stiff and cold wound,
as well as rush forward regardless, because half senseless of the fresh
and bleeding one. Why did we give our hearts to the present cause of
Spain with a fervour and elevation unknown to us in the commencement of the late Austrian or Prussian resistance to France?
Because we attributed to the former an heroic temperament which
would render their transfer to such domination an evil to human
nature itself, and an affrightening perplexity in the dispensations of
Providence. But if in oblivion of the prophetic wisdom of their own
first leaders in the cause, they are surprised beyond the power of
rallying, utterly cast down and manacled by fearful thoughts from
the first thunder-storm of defeat in the field, wherein do they differ
from the Prussians and Austrians? Wherein are they a PEOPLE, and
not a mere army or set of armies? If this be indeed so, what have we
to mourn over but our own honourable impetuosity, in hoping
where no just ground of hope existed? A nation, without the virtues
necessary for the attainment of independence, have failed to attain it.
This is all. For little has that man understood the majesty of true

national freedom, who believes that a population, like that of Spain, in a country like that of Spain, may want the qualities needful to fight out their independence, and yet possess the excellencies which render men susceptible of true liberty. The Dutch, the Americans, did possess the former; but it is, I fear, more than doubtful whether the one ever did, or the other ever will, evince the nobler morality indispensible to the latter.

[Nine paragraphs containing mostly extracts of documents from the British government, the French, and especially the Spanish, are here omitted. What follows concerns Spain and Portugal]

I will now beg of my reader to pause a moment, and to review in his own mind the whole of what has been laid before him. He has seen of what kind, and how great have been the injuries endured by these two nations; what they have suffered, and what they have to fear; he has seen that they have felt with that unanimity which nothing but the light of truth spread over the inmost concerns of human nature can create; with that simultaneousness which has led Philosophers upon like occasions to assert, that the voice of the people is the voice of God. He has seen that they have submitted as far as human nature could bear; and that at last these millions of suffering people have risen almost like one man, with one hope; for whether they look to triumph or defeat, to victory or death, they are full of hope – despair comes not near them – they will die, they say – each individual knows the danger, and, strong in the magnitude of it, grasps eagerly at the thought that he himself is to perish; and more eagerly, and with higher confidence, does he lay to his heart the faith that the nation will survive and be victorious; – or, at the worst, let the contest terminate how it may as to superiority of outward strength, that the fortitude and the martyrdom, the justice and the blessing, are their's and cannot be relinquished. And not only are they moved by these exalted sentiments of universal morality, and of direct and universal concern to mankind, which have impelled them to resist evil and to endeavour to punish the evil-doer, but also they descend (for even this, great as in itself it is, may be here considered as a descent) to express a rational hope of reforming domestic abuses, and of re-constructing, out of the materials of their ancient institutions, customs, and laws, a better frame of civil government, the same in the great outlines of its architecture, but exhibiting the knowledge, and genius, and the needs of the present race, harmoniously blended with those of their forefathers. Woe, then, to the unworthy who intrude with their help to maintain this most sacred cause! It calls aloud for the aid of intellect, knowledge, and love, and rejects every other. It is in vain to send forth armies if these do not inspire and direct them. The stream is as pure as it is mighty, fed by ten thousand springs in the bounty of untainted nature; any augmentation from the kennels and sewers of guilt and baseness may clog, but cannot strengthen it. — It is not from any thought that I am communicating new information, that I have dwelt thus long upon this subject, but to recall to the reader his own knowledge, and to re-infuse into that knowledge a breath and life of appropriate feeling; because the bare sense of wisdom is nothing without its powers, and it is only in these feelings that the powers of wisdom exist. If then we do not forget that the Spanish and Portugueze Nations stand upon the loftiest ground of principle and passion, and do not suffer on our part those sympathies to languish which a few months since were so strong, and do not negligently or timidly descend from those heights of magnanimity to which as a nation we were raised, when they first represented to us their wrongs and entreated our assistance, and we devoted ourselves sincerely and earnestly to their service, making with them a common cause under a common hope; if we are true in all this to them and to ourselves, we shall not be at a loss to conceive what actions are entitled to our commendation as being in the spirit of a friendship so nobly begun, and tending assuredly to promote the common welfare; and what are abject, treacherous, and pernicious, and therefore to be condemned and abhorred. Is then, I may now ask, the Convention of Cintra an act of this latter kind? Have the Generals, who signed and ratified that agreement, thereby proved themselves unworthy associates in such a cause? And has the Ministry, by whose appointment these men were enabled to act in this manner, and which sanctioned the Convention by permitting them to carry it into execution, thereby taken to itself a weight of guilt, in which the Nation must feel that it participates, until the transaction shall be solemnly reprobated by the Government, and the remote and immediate authors of it brought to merited punishment? An answer to each of these questions will be implied in the proof which will be given that the condemnation, which the People did with one voice pronounce upon this Convention when it first became known, was just; that the nature of the offence of those who signed it was such, and established by evidence of such a kind, making so imperious an exception to the ordinary course of action, that there was no need to wait here for the decision of a Court of Judicature, but that the People were compelled by a necessity involved in the very constitution of man as a moral Being to pass sentence upon them. And this I shall prove by trying this act of their's by principles of justice which are of universal obligation, and by a reference to those moral sentiments which rise out of that retrospect of things which has been given.

[Four paragraphs on the generally depressing effects of the Convention are here omitted.]

As soon as men had recovered from the shock, and could bear to look somewhat steadily at these documents, it was found that the gross body of the transaction, considered as a military transaction, was this; that the Russian fleet, of nine sail of the line, which had been so long watched, and could not have escaped, was to be delivered up to us; the ships to be detained till six months after the end of the war, and the sailors sent home by us, and to be by us protected in their voyage through the Swedish fleet, and to be at liberty to fight immediately against our ally, the king of Sweden. Secondly, that a French army of more than twenty thousand men, already beaten, and no longer able to appear in the field, cut off from all possibility of receiving reinforcements or supplies, and in the midst of a hostile country loathing and abhorring it, was to be transported with its arms, ammunition, and plunder, at the expence of Great Britain, in British vessels, and landed within a few days march of the Spanish frontier, – there to be at liberty to commence hostilities immediately!

Omitting every characteristic which distinguishes the present contest from others, and looking at this issue merely as an affair between two armies, what stupidity of mind to provoke the accusation of not merely shrinking from future toils and dangers, but of basely shifting the burthen to the shoulders of an ally, already overpressed! – What infatuation, to convey the imprisoned foe to the very spot, whither, if he had had wings, he would have flown! This last was an absurdity as glaring as if, the French having landed on our own island, we had taken them from Yorkshire to be set on shore in Sussex; but ten thousand times worse! from a place where without our interference they had been virtually blockaded, where they were cut off, hopeless, useless, and disgraced, to become an efficient part of a mighty host, carrying the strength of their numbers, and alas! the strength of their glory, (not to mention the sight of their plunder) to animate that host; while the British army, more numerous in the proportion of three to two, with all the population and resources of the peninsula to aid it, within ten days sail of it's own country, and the sea covered with friendly shipping at it's back, was to make a long march to encounter this same enemy, (the British forfeiting instead of gaining by the treaty as to superiority of numbers, for that this would be the case was clearly foreseen) to encounter, in a new condition of strength and pride, those whom, by its deliberate act, it had exalted, – having taken from itself, meanwhile, all which it had conferred, and bearing into the presence of its noble ally an infection of despondency and disgrace. The motive assigned for all this, was the great importance of gaining time; fear of an open beach and of equinoctial gales for the shipping; fear that reinforcements could not be landed; fear of famine; – fear of every thing but dishonour! [13]

The nation had expected that the French would surrender immediately at discretion; and, supposing that Sir Arthur Wellesley had told them the whole truth, they had a right to form this expectation. It has since appeared, from the evidence given before the Board of Inquiry, that Sir Arthur Wellesley earnestly exhorted his successor in command (Sir Harry Burrard) to pursue the defeated enemy at the battle of Vimiera; and that, if this had been done, the affair, in Sir Arthur Wellesley's opinion, would have had a much more satisfactory termination. But, waiving any considerations of this advice, or of the fault which might be committed in not following it; and taking up the matter from the time when Sir Hew Dalrymple entered upon the command, and when the two adverse armies were in that condition, relatively to each other, that none of the Generals has pleaded any difference of opinion as to their ability to advance against the enemy, I will ask what confirmation has appeared before the Board of Inquiry, of the reasonableness of the causes, assigned by Sir Hew Dalrymple in his letter, for deeming a Convention adviseable. A want of cavalry, (for which they who occasioned it are heavily censurable,) has indeed been proved; and certain failures of duty in the Commissariat department with respect to horses, &c; but these deficiencies, though furnishing reasons against advancing upon the enemy in the open field, had ceased to be of moment, when the business was to expel him from the forts to which he might have the power of retreating. It is proved, that, though there are difficulties in landing upon that coast, (and what military or marine operation can be carried on without difficulty?) there was not the slightest reason to apprehend that the army, which was then abundantly supplied, would suffer hereafter from want of provisions; proved also that heavy ordnance, for the purpose of attacking the forts, was ready on ship-board, to be landed when and where it might be needed. Therefore, so far from being exculpated by the facts which have been laid before the Board of Inquiry, Sir Hew Dalrymple and the other Generals, who deemed *any* Convention necessary or expedient upon the grounds stated in his letter, are more deeply criminated. But grant, (for the sake of looking at a different part of the subject,) grant a case infinitely stronger than Sir Hew Dalrymple has even hinted at; – why was not the taste of some of those evils, in apprehension so terrible, actually tried? It would not have been the first time that Britons had faced hunger and tempests, had endured the worst of such enmity, and upon a call, under an obligation, how faint and feeble, compared with that which the brave men of that army must have felt upon the present occasion! In the proclamation quoted before, addressed to the Portugueze, and signed Charles Cotton and Arthur Wellesley, they were told, that the objects, for which they contended, 'could only be attained by distinguished examples of fortitude and constancy'. Where were the fortitude and constancy of the teachers? When Sir Hew Dalrymple had been so busy in taking the measure of his own weakness, and feeding his own fears, how came it to escape him, that General Junot must also have had *his* weaknesses and *his* fears? Was it nothing to have been defeated in the open field, where he himself had been the assailant? Was it nothing that so proud a man, the servant of so proud a man, had stooped to send a General Officer to treat concerning the evacuation of the country? Was the hatred and abhorrence of the Portugueze and Spanish Nations nothing? the people of a large metropolis under his eye – detesting him, and stung almost to madness, nothing? The composition of his own army made up of men of different nations and languages, and forced into the service, – was there no cause of mistrust in this? And, finally, among the many unsound places which, had his mind been as active in this sort of inquiry as Sir Hew Dalrymple's was, he must have found in his constitution, could a bad cause have been missed – a worse cause than ever confounded the mind of a soldier when boldly pressed upon, or gave courage and animation to a righteous assailant? But alas! in Sir Hew Dalrymple and his brethren, we had Generals who had a power of sight only for the strength of their enemies and their own weakness.[14]

Let me not be misunderstood. While I am thus forced to repeat things, which were uttered or thought of these men in reference to their military conduct, as heads of that army, it is needless to add, that their personal courage is in no wise implicated in the charge brought against them. But, in the name of my countrymen, I do repeat these accusations, and tax them with an utter want of *intellectual* courage – of that higher quality, which is never found without one or other of the three accompaniments, talents, genius, or principle; – talents matured by experience, without which it cannot exist at all; or the rapid insight of peculiar genius, by which the fitness of an act may be instantly determined, and which will supply higher motives than mere talents can furnish for encountering difficulty and danger, and will suggest better resources for diminishing or overcoming them. Thus, through the power of genius, this quality of intellectual courage may exist in an eminent degree, though the moral character be greatly perverted; as in those personages, who are so conspicuous in history, conquerors and usurpers, the Alexanders, the Caesars, and Cromwells; and in that other class still more perverted, remorseless and energetic minds, the Catilines and Borgias, whom poets have denominated 'bold, bad men'. [15] But, though a course of depravity will neither preclude nor destroy this quality, nay, in certain circumstances will give it a peculiar promptness and hardihood of decision, it is not on this account the less true, that, to *consummate* this species of courage, and to render it equal to all occasions, (especially when a man is not acting for himself, but has an additional claim on his resolution from the circumstance of responsibility to a superior) *Principle* is indispensibly requisite. I mean that fixed and habitual principle, which implies the absence of all selfish anticipations, whether of hope or fear, and the inward disavowal of any tribunal higher and more dreaded than the mind's own judgment upon its own act. The existence of such principle cannot but elevate the most commanding genius, add rapidity to the quickest glance, a wider range to the most ample comprehension; but, without this principle, the man of ordinary powers must, in the trying hour, be found utterly wanting. Neither, without it, can the man of excelling powers be trustworthy, or have at all times a calm and confident repose in himself. But he, in whom talents, genius, and principle are united, will have a firm mind, in whatever embarrassment he may be placed; will look steadily at the most undefined shapes of difficulty and danger, of possible mistake or mischance; nor will they appear to him more formidable than they really are. For HIS attention is not distracted – he has but one business, and that is with the object before him. Neither in general conduct nor in particular emergencies, are HIS plans subservient to considerations of rewards, estate, or title: these are not to have precedence in his thoughts, to govern his actions, but to follow in the train of his duty. Such men, in ancient times, were Phocion, Epaminondas, and Philopoemen;[16] and such a man was Sir Philip Sidney, of whom it has been said, that he first taught this country *the majesty of honest dealing.*[17] With these may be named, the honour of our own age, Washington, the deliverer of the American Continent; with these, though in many things unlike, Lord Nelson, whom we have lately lost. Lord Peterborough,[18] who fought in Spain a hundred years ago, had the same excellence; with a sense of exalted honour, and a tinge of romantic enthusiasm, well suited to the country which was the scene of his exploits. Would that we had a man, like Peterborough or Nelson, at the head of our army in Spain at this moment! I utter this wish with more earnestness, because it is rumoured, that some of those, who have already called forth such severe reprehension from their countrymen, are to resume a command, which must entrust to them a portion of those sacred hopes in which, not only we, and the people of Spain and Portugal, but the whole human race are so deeply interested.[19]

I maintain then that, merely from want of this intellectual courage, of courage as generals or chiefs, (for I will not speak at present of the want of other qualities equally needful upon this service,) grievous errors were committed by Sir Hew Dalrymple and his colleagues in estimating the relative state of the two armies. A precious moment, it is most probable, had been lost after the battle of Vimiera; yet still the inferiority of the enemy had been proved; they themselves had admitted it – not merely by withdrawing from the field, but by proposing terms: – monstrous terms! and how ought they to have been received? Repelled undoubtedly with scorn, as an insult. If our Generals had been men capable of taking the measure of their real strength, either as existing in their own army, or in those principles of liberty and justice which they were commissioned to defend, they must of necessity have acted in this manner; – if they had been men of common sagacity for business, they must have acted in this manner; – nay, if they had been upon a level with an ordinary bargain-maker in a fair or a market, they could not have acted otherwise. – Strange that they should so far forget the nature of their calling! They were soldiers, and their business was to fight. Sir Arthur Wellesley had fought, and gallantly; it was not becoming his high situation, or that of his successors, to treat, that is, to beat down, to chaffer, or on their part to propose: it does not become any general at the head of a victorious army so to do.[20] They were to *accept*, – and, if the terms offered were flagrantly presumptuous, our commanders ought to have rejected them with dignified scorn, and to have referred the proposer to the sword for a lesson of decorum and humility. This is the general rule of all high-minded men upon such occasions; and meaner minds copy them, doing in prudence what they do from principle. But it has been urged, before the Board of Inquiry, that the conduct of the French armies upon like occasions, and their known character, rendered it probable that a determined resistance would in the present instance be maintained. We need not fear to say that this conclusion, from reasons which have been adverted to, was erroneous. But, in the mind of him who had admitted it upon whatever ground, whether false or true, surely the first thought which followed, ought to have been, not that we should bend to the enemy, but that, if they were resolute in defence, we should learn from that example to be courageous in attack. The tender feelings, however, are pleaded against this determination; and it is said, that one of the motives for the cessation of hostilities was to prevent the further effusion of human blood. – When, or how? The enemy was delivered over to us; it was not to be hoped that, cut off from all assistance as they were, these, or an equal number of men, could ever be reduced to such straits as would ensure their destruction as an enemy, with so small a sacrifice of life on their part, or on ours. What then was to be gained by this tenderness? The shedding of a few drops of blood is not to be risked in Portugal to-day, and streams of blood must shortly flow from the same veins in the fields of Spain! And, even if this had not been the assured consequence, let not the consideration, though it be one which no humane man can ever lose sight of, have more than its due weight. For national independence and liberty, and *that* honour by which these and other blessings are to be preserved, honour – which is no other than the most elevated and pure conception of justice which can be formed, these are more precious than life: else why have we already lost so many brave men in this struggle? – Why not submit at once, and let the Tyrant mount upon his throne of universal dominion, while the world lies prostrate at his feet in indifference and apathy, which he will proclaim to it is peace and happiness? But peace and happiness can exist only by knowledge and virtue; slavery has no enduring connection with tranquillity or security – she cannot frame a league with any thing which is desirable – she has no charter even for her own ignoble ease and darling sloth.[21] Yet to this abject condition, mankind, betrayed by an ill-judging tenderness, would surely be led; and in the face of an inevitable contradiction! For neither in this state of things would the shedding of blood be prevented, nor would warfare cease. The only difference would be, that, instead of wars like those which prevail at this moment, presenting a spectacle of such character that, upon one side at least, a superior Being might look down with favour and blessing, there would follow endless commotions and quarrels without the presence of justice any where, – in which the alternations of success would not excite a wish or regret; in which a prayer could not be uttered for a decision either this way or that; – wars from no impulse in either of the combatants, but rival instigations of demoniacal passion. If, therefore, by the faculty of reason we can prophecy concerning the shapes which the future may put on, – if we are under any bond of duty to succeeding generations, there is high cause to guard against a specious sensibility, which may encourage the hoarding up of life for its own sake, seducing us from those considerations by which we might learn when it ought to be resigned. Moreover disregarding future ages, and confining ourselves to the present state of mankind, it may be safely affirmed that he, who is the most watchful of the honour of his country, most determined to preserve her fair name at all hazards, will be found, in any view of things which looks beyond the passing hour, the best steward of the *lives* of his countrymen. For, by proving that she is of a firm temper, that she will only submit or yield [22] to a point of her own fixing, and that all beyond is immutable resolution, he will save her from being wantonly attacked; and, if attacked, will awe the aggressor into a speedier abandonment of an unjust and hopeless attempt. Thus will he preserve not only that which gives life its value, but life itself; and not for his own country merely, but for that of his enemies, to whom he will have offered an example of magnanimity, which will ensure to them like benefits; an example, the re-action of which will be felt by his own countrymen, and will prevent them from becoming assailants unjustly or rashly. Nations will thus be taught to respect each other, and mutually to abstain from injuries. And hence, by a benign ordinance of our nature, genuine honour is the hand-maid of humanity; the attendant and sustainer — both of the sterner qualities which constitute the appropriate excellence of the male character, and of the gentle and tender virtues which belong more especially to motherliness and womanhood. These general laws, by which mankind is purified and exalted, and by which Nations are preserved, suggest likewise the best rules for the preservation of individual armies, and for the accomplishment of all equitable service upon which they can be sent.

Not therefore rashly and unfeelingly, but from the dictates of thoughtful humanity, did I say that it was the business of our Generals to fight, and to persevere in fighting; and that they did not bear this duty sufficiently in mind; this, almost the sole duty which professional soldiers, till our time, (happily for mankind) used to think of. But the victories of the French have been attended every where by the subversion of Governments; and their generals have accordingly united *political* with military functions; and with what success this has been done by them, the present state of Europe affords melancholy proof. But have they, on this account, ever neglected to calculate upon the advantages which might fairly be anticipated from future warfare? Or, in a treaty of to-day, have they ever forgotten a victory of yesterday? Eager to grasp at the double honour of captain and negociator, have they ever sacrificed the one to the other; or, in the blind effort, lost both? Above all, in their readiness to flourish with the pen, have they ever overlooked the sword, the symbol of their power, and the appropriate instrument of their success and glory? I notice this assumption of a double character on the part of the French, not to lament over it and its consequences, but to render somewhat more intelligible the conduct of our own Generals; and to explain how far men, whom we have no reason to believe other than brave, have, through the influence of such example, lost sight of their primary duties, apeing instead of imitating, and following only to be misled.

It is indeed deplorable, that our Generals, from this infirmity, or from any other cause, did not assume that lofty deportment which the character and relative strength of the two armies authorized them, and the nature of the service upon which they were sent, enjoined them to assume; — that they were in such haste to treat — that, with such an enemy (let me say at once,) and in such circumstances, they should have treated at all. Is it possible that they could ever have asked themselves who that enemy was, how he came into that country, and what he had done there? From the manifesto of the Portugueze government, issued at Rio Janeiro, and from other official papers, they might have learned, what was notorious to all Europe, that this body of men commissioned by Bonaparte, in the time of profound peace, without a declaration of war, had invaded Portugal under the command of Junot, who had perfidiously entered the country, as the General of a friendly and allied Power, assuring the people, as he advanced, that he came to protect their Sovereign against an invasion of the English; and that, when in this manner he had entered a peaceable kingdom, which offered no resistance, and had expelled its lawful Sovereign, he wrung from it unheard-of-contributions, ravaged it, cursed it with domestic pillage and open sacrilege; and that, when this unoffending people, unable to endure any longer, rose up against the tyrant, he had given their towns and villages to the flames, and put the whole country, thus resisting, under military execution. — Setting aside all natural sympathy with the Portugueze and Spanish nations, and all prudential considerations of regard or respect for *their feelings* towards these men, and for *their expectations* concerning the manner in which they ought to be dealt with, it is plain that the French had forfeited by their crimes all right to those privileges, or to those modes of intercourse, which one army may demand from another according to the laws of war. They were not soldiers in any thing but the power of soldiers, and the outward frame of any army. During their occupation of Portugal, the laws and customs of war had never been referred to by them, but as a plea for some enormity, to the aggravated oppression of that unhappy country! Pillage, sacrilege, and murder – sweeping murder and individual assassination, had been proved against them by voices from every quarter. They had outlawed themselves by their offences from membership in the community of war, and from every species of community acknowledged by reason. But even, should any one be so insensible as to question this, he will not at all events deny, that the French ought to have been dealt with as having put on a double character. For surely they never considered themselves merely as an army. They had dissolved the established authorities of Portugal, and had usurped the civil power of the goverment; and it was in this compound capacity, under this two-fold monstrous shape, that they had exercised, over the religion and property of the country, the most grievous oppressions. What then remained to protect them but their power? – Right they had none, – and power! it is a mortifying consideration, but I will ask if Bonaparte, (nor do I mean in the question to imply any thing to his honour,) had been in the place of Sir Hew Dalrymple, what would he have thought of their power? – Yet before this shadow the solid substance of *justice* melted away.

And this leads me from the contemplation of their errors in the estimate and application of means, to the contemplation of their heavier errors and worse blindness in regard to ends. The British Generals acted as if they had no purpose but that the enemy should be removed from the country in which they were, upon *any* terms. Now the evacuation of Portugal was not the prime object, but the manner in which that event was to be brought about; this ought to have been deemed first both in order and importance; – the French were to be subdued, their ferocious warfare and heinous policy to be confounded; and in this way, and no other, was the deliverance of that country to be accomplished. It was not for the soil, or for the cities and forts, that Portugal was valued, but for the human feeling which was there; for the rights of human nature which might be there conspicuously asserted; for a triumph over injustice and oppression there to be achieved, which could neither be concealed nor disguised, and which should penetrate the darkest corner of the dark Continent of Europe by its splendour. We combated for victory in the empire of reason, for strong-holds in the imagination. Lisbon and Portugal, as city and soil, were chiefly prized by us as a *language*; but our Generals mistook the counters of the game for the stake played for. The nation required that the French should surrender at discretion; – grant that the victory of Vimiera had excited some unreasonable impatience – we were not so overweening as to demand that the enemy should surrender within a given time, but that they should surrender. Every thing, short of this, was felt to be below the duties of the occasion; not only no service, but a grievous injury. Only as far as there was a prospect of forcing the enemy to an unconditional submission, did the British nation deem that they had a right to interfere; – if that prospect failed, they expected that their army would know that it became it to retire, and take care of itself. But our Generals have told us, that the Convention would not have been admitted, if they had not judged it right to effect, even upon these terms, the evacuation of Portugal – as ministerial to their future services in Spain. If this had been a common war between two established governments measuring with each other their regular resources, there might have been some appearance of force in this plea. But who does not cry out at once, that the affections and opinions, that is, the souls of the people of Spain and Portugal, must be the inspiration and the power, if this labour is to be brought to a happy end? Therefore it was worse than folly to think of supporting Spain by physical strength, at the expence of moral. Besides, she was strong in men; she never earnestly solicited troops from us; some of the Provinces had even refused them when offered, – and all had been lukewarm in the acceptance of them. The Spaniards could not *ultimately* be benefited but by allies acting under the same impulses of honour, rouzed by a sense of their wrongs, and sharing their loves and hatreds – above all, their *passion* for justice. They had themselves given an example, at Baylen,[23] proclaiming to all the world what ought to be aimed at by those who would uphold their cause, and be associated in arms with them. And was the law of justice, which Spaniards, Spanish peasantry, I might almost say, would not relax in favour of Dupont, to be relaxed by a British army in favour of Junot? Had the French commander at Lisbon, or his army, proved themselves less perfidious, less cruel, or less rapacious than the other? Nay, did not the pride and crimes of Junot call for humiliation and punishment far more importunately, inasmuch as his power to do harm, and therefore his will, keeping pace with it, had been greater? Yet, in the noble letter of the Governor of Cadiz to Dupont, he expressly tells him, that his conduct, and that of his army, had been such, that they owed their lives only to that honour which forbad the Spanish army to become executioners. The Portugueze also, as appears from various letters produced before the Board of Inquiry, have shewn to our Generals, as boldly as their respect for the British nation would permit them to do, what *they* expected. A Portugueze General, who was also a member of the regency appointed by the Prince Regent, says, in a protest addressed to Sir Hew Dalrymple, that he had been able to drive the French out of the provinces of Algarve and Alentejo; and therefore he could not be convinced, that such a Convention was necessary.[24] What was this but implying that it was dishonourable, and that it would frustrate the efforts which his country was making, and destroy the hopes which it had built upon its own power? Another letter from a magistrate inveighs against the Convention, as leaving the crimes of the French in Portugal unpunished; as giving no indemnification for all the murders, robberies, and atrocities, which had been committed by them. But I feel that I shall be wanting in respect to my countrymen, if I pursue this argument further. I blush that it should be necessary to speak upon the subject at all. And these are men and things, which we have been reproved for condemning, because evidence was wanting both as to fact and person! If there ever was a case, which could not, in any rational sense of the word, be prejudged, this is one. As to the fact – it appears, and sheds from its own body, like the sun in heaven, the light by which it is seen; as to the person – each has written down with his own hand, *I am the man*. Condemnation of actions and men like these is not, in the minds of a people, (thanks to the divine Being and to human nature!) a matter of choice; it is like a physical necessity, as the hand must be burned which is thrust into the furnace – the body chilled which stands naked in the freezing north-wind. I am entitled to make this assertion here, when the *moral* depravity of the Convention, of which I shall have to speak hereafter, has not even been touched upon. Nor let it be blamed in any man, though his station be in private life, that upon this occasion he speaks publickly, and gives a decisive opinion concerning that part of this public event, and those measures, which are more especially military. All have a right to speak, and to make their voices heard, as far as they have power. For these are times, in which the conduct of military men concerns us, perhaps, more intimately than that of any other class; when the business of arms comes unhappily too near to the fire side; when the character and duties of a soldier ought to be understood by every one who values his liberty, and bears in mind how soon he may have to fight for it. Men will and ought to speak upon things in which they are so deeply interested; how else are right notions to spread, or is error to be destroyed? These are times also in which, if we may judge from the proceedings and results of the Court of Inquiry, the heads of the army, more than at any other period, stand in need of being taught wisdom by the voice of the people. It is their own interest, both as men and as soldiers, that the people should speak fervently and fearlessly of their actions: – from no other quarter can they be so powerfully reminded of the duties which they owe to themselves, to their country, and to human nature. Let any one read the evidence given before that Court, and he will there see, how much the intellectual and moral constitution of many of our military officers, has suffered by a profession, which, if not counteracted by admonitions willingly listened to, and by habits of meditation, does, more than any other, denaturalize – and therefore degrade the human being; – he will note with sorrow, how faint are their sympathies with the best feelings, and how dim their apprehension of some of the most awful truths, relating to the happiness and dignity of man in society. But on this I do not mean to insist at present; it is too weighty a subject to be treated incidentally: and my purpose is – not to invalidate the authority of military men, *positively* considered, upon a military question, but *comparatively*; – to maintain that there are military transactions upon which the people have a right to be heard, and upon which their authority is entitled to far more respect than any man or number of men can lay claim to, who speak merely with the ordinary professional views of soldiership; – that there are such military transactions; – and that *this* is one of them.

The condemnation, which the people of these islands pronounced upon the Convention of Cintra considered as to its main *military* results, that is, as a treaty by which it was established that the Russian fleet should be surrendered on the terms specified; and by which, not only the obligation of forcing the French army to an unconditional surrender was abandoned, but its restoration in freedom and triumph to its own country was secured; – the condemnation, pronounced by the people upon a treaty, by virtue of which these things were to be done, I have recorded – accounted for – and thereby justified. – I will now proceed to another division of the subject, on which I feel a still more earnest wish to speak; because, though in itself of the highest importance, it has been comparatively neglected; – I mean the political injustice and moral depravity which are stamped upon the front of this agreement, and pervade every regulation which it contains. I shall shew that our Generals (and with them our Ministers, as far as they might have either given directions to this effect, or have countenanced what has been done) – when it was their paramount duty to maintain at all hazards the noblest principles in unsuspected integrity; because, upon the summons of these, and in defence of them, their Allies had risen, and by these alone could stand – not only did not perform this duty, but descended as far below the level of ordinary principles as they ought to have mounted above it; – imitating not the majesty of the oak with which it lifts its branches towards the heavens, but the vigour with which, in the language of the poet, it strikes its roots downwards towards hell: –

Radice in Tartara tendit.[25]

The Armistice is the basis of the Convention; and in the first article we find it agreed, 'That there shall be a suspension of hostilities between the forces of his Britannic Majesty, and those of his Imperial and Royal Majesty, Napoleon I.' I will ask if it be the practice of military officers, in instruments of this kind, to acknowledge, in the person of the head of the government with which they are at war, titles which their own government – for which they are acting – has not acknowledged. If this be the practice, which I will not stop to determine, it is grossly improper; and ought to be abolished. Our Generals, however, had entered Portugal as allies of a Government by which this title had been acknowledged; and they might have pleaded this circumstance in mitigation of their offence; but surely not in an instrument, where we not only look in vain for the name of the Portugueze Sovereign, or of the Government which he appointed, or of any heads or representatives of the Portugueze armies or people as a party in the contract, – but where it is stipulated (in the 4th article) that the British General shall engage to include the Portugueze armies in this Convention. What an outrage! – We enter the Portugueze territory as allies; and, without their consent – or even consulting them, we proceed to form the basis of an agreement, relating – not to the safety or interests of our own army – but to Portugueze territory, Portugueze persons, liberties, and rights, – and engage, out of our own will and power, to include the Portugueze army, they or their Government willing or not, within the obligation of this agreement. I place these things in contrast, viz. the acknowledgement of Bonaparte as emperor and king, and the utter neglect of the Portugueze Sovereign and Portugueze authorities, to shew in what spirit and temper these agreements were entered upon. I will not here insist upon what was our duty, on this occasion, to the Portugueze – as dictated by those sublime precepts of justice which it has been proved that they and the Spaniards had risen to defend, – and without feeling the force and sanctity of which, they neither could have risen, nor can oppose to their enemy resistance which has any hope in it; but I will ask, of any man who is not dead to the common feelings of his social nature – and besotted in understanding, if this be not a cruel mockery, and which must have been felt, unless it were repelled with hatred and scorn, as a heart-breaking insult. Moreover, this conduct acknowledges, by implication, that principle which by his actions the enemy has for a long time covertly maintained, and now openly and insolently avows in his words – that power is the measure of right; – and it is in a steady adherence to this abominable doctrine that his strength mainly lies. I do maintain then that, as far as the conduct of our Generals in framing these instruments tends to reconcile men to this course of action, and to sanction this principle, they are virtually his Allies: their weapons may be against him, but he will laugh at their weapons, – for he knows, though they themselves do not, that their souls are for him. Look at the preamble to the Armistice! In what is omitted and what is inserted, the French Ruler could not have fashioned it more for his own purpose if he had traced it with his own hand. We have then trampled upon a fundamental principle of justice, and countenanced a prime maxim of iniquity; thus adding, in an unexampled degree, the foolishness of impolicy to the heinousness of guilt. A conduct thus grossly unjust and impolitic, without having the hatred which it inspires neutralised by the contempt, is made contemptible by utterly wanting that colour of right which authority and power, put forth in defence of our Allies – in asserting their just claims and avenging their injuries, might have given. But we, instead of triumphantly displaying our power towards our enemies, have ostentatiously exercised it upon our friends; reversing here, as every where, the practice of sense and reason; – conciliatory even to abject submission where we ought to have been haughty and commanding, – and repulsive and tyrannical where we ought to have been gracious and kind. Even a common law of good breeding would have served us here, had we known how to apply it. We ought to have endeavoured to raise the Portugueze in their own estimation by concealing our power in comparison with theirs; dealing with them in the spirit of those mild and humane delusions, which spread such a genial grace over the intercourse, and add so much to the influence of love in the concerns of private life. It is a common saying, presume that a man is dishonest, and that is the readiest way to make him so: in like manner it may be said, presume that a nation is weak, and that is the surest course to bring it to weakness, — if it be not rouzed to prove its strength by applying it to the humiliation of your pride. The Portugueze had been weak; and, in connection with their allies the Spaniards, they were prepared to become strong. It was, therefore, doubly incumbent upon us to foster and encourage them — to look favourably upon their efforts — generously to give them credit upon their promises — to hope with them and for them; and, thus anticipating and foreseeing, we should, by a natural operation of love, have contributed to create the merits which were anticipated and foreseen. I apply these rules, taken from the intercourse between individuals, to the conduct of large bodies of men, or of nations towards each other, because these are nothing but aggregates of individuals; and because the maxims of all just law, and the measures of all sane practice, are only an enlarged or modified application of those dispositions of love and those principles of reason, by which the welfare of individuals, in their connection with each other, is promoted. There was also here a still more urgent call for these courteous and humane principles as guides of conduct; because, in exact proportion to the physical weakness of Governments, and to the distraction and confusion which cannot but prevail, when a people is struggling for independence and liberty, are the well-intentioned and the wise among them remitted for their support to those benign elementary feelings of society, for the preservation and cherishing of which, among other important objects, government was from the beginning ordained.

Therefore, by the strongest obligations, we were bound to be studious of a delicate and respectful bearing towards those ill-fated

nations, our allies: and consequently, if the government of the Portugueze, though weak in power, possessed their affections, and was
strong in right, it was incumbent upon us to turn our first thoughts
to that government – to look for it if it were hidden – to call it forth,
– and, by our power combined with that of the people, to assert its
rights. Or, if the government were dissolved and had no existence, it
was our duty, in such an emergency, to have resorted to the nation,
expressing its will through the most respectable and conspicuous
authority, through that which seemed to have the best right to stand
forth as its representative. In whatever circumstances Portugal had
been placed, the paramount right of the Portugueze nation, or
government, to appear not merely as a party but a principal, ought
to have been established as a primary position, without the admission
of which, all proposals to treat would be peremptorily rejected. But
the Portugueze *had* a government; they had a lawful prince in Brazil;
and a regency, appointed by him, at home; and generals, at the head
of considerable bodies of troops, appointed also by the regency or the
prince. Well then might one of those generals[26] enter a formal
protest against the treaty, on account of its being 'totally void of that
deference due to the prince regent, or the government that represents
him; as being hostile to the sovereign authority and independence of
that government; and as being against the honour, safety, and independence of the nation.' I have already reminded the reader, of the
benign and happy influences which might have attended upon a
different conduct; how much good we might have added to that
already in existence; how far we might have assisted in strengthening,
among our allies, those powers, and in developing those virtues,
which were producing themselves by a natural process, and to which
these breathings of insult must have been a deadly check and interruption. Nor would the evil be merely negative; for the interference
of professed friends, acting in this manner, must have superinduced
dispositions and passions, which were alien to the condition of the
Portugueze; – scattered weeds which could not have been found
upon the soil, if our ignorant hands had not sown them. Of this I will
not now speak, for I have already detained the reader too long at the

threshold; – but I have put the master-key into his possession; and every chamber which he opens will be found loathsome as the one which he last quitted. Let us then proceed.

By the first article of the Convention it is covenanted, that all the places and forts in the kingdom of Portugal, occupied by the French troops, shall be delivered to the British army. Articles IV. and XII. are to the same effect – determining the surrender of Portugueze fortified places, stores, and ships, to the English forces; but not a word of their being to be holden in trust for the prince regent, or his government, to whom they belonged! The same neglect or contempt of justice and decency is shewn here, as in the preamble to these instruments. It was further shewn afterwards, by the act of hoisting the British flag instead of the Portugueze upon these forts, when they were first taken possession of by the British forces. It is no excuse to say that this was not intended. Such inattentions are among the most grievous faults which can be committed; and are *impossible*, when the affections and understandings of men are of that quality, and in that state, which are required for a service in which there is any thing noble or virtuous. Again, suppose that it was the purpose of the generals, who signed and ratified a Convention containing the articles in question, that the forts and ships, &c. should be delivered immediately to the Portugueze government, – would the delivering up of them wipe away the affront? Would it not rather appear, after the omission to recognize the right, that we had ostentatiously taken upon us to bestow – as a boon – that which they felt to be their own?

Passing by, as already deliberated and decided upon, those conditions, (Articles II. and III.) by which it is stipulated, that the French army shall not be considered as prisoners of war, shall be conveyed with arms, &c. to some port between Rochefort and L'Orient, and be at liberty to serve, I come to that memorable condition, (Article V.) 'that the French army shall carry with it all its equipments, that is to say, its military chests and carriages, attached to the field commissariat and field hospitals, or shall be allowed to dispose of such part, as the Commander in Chief may judge it unnecessary to embark. In like manner all individuals of the army shall be at liberty to dispose of *their private property* of *every* description, with full security hereafter for the purchasers.' This is expressed still more pointedly in the Armistice, – though the meaning, implied in the two articles, is precisely the same. For, in the fifth article of the Armistice, it is agreed provisionally, 'that all those, of whom the French army consists, shall be conveyed to France with arms and baggage, *and* all their private property of every description, no part of which shall be wrested from them.' In the Convention it is only expressed, that they shall be at liberty to depart, (Article II.) with arms and baggage, and (Article V.) to dispose of their private property of every description. But, if they had a right to dispose of it, *this* would include a right to carry it away – which was undoubtedly understood by the French general. And in the Armistice it is expressly said, that their private property of every description shall be conveyed to France along with their persons. What then are we to understand by the words, *their private property of every description*? Equipments of the army in general, and baggage of individuals, had been stipulated for before: now we all know that the lawful professional gains and earnings of a soldier must be small; that he is not in the habit of carrying about him, during actual warfare, any accumulation of these or other property; and that the ordinary private property, which he can be supposed to have a *just* title to, is included under the name of his *baggage*; – therefore this was something more; and what it was – is apparent. No part of their property, says the Armistice, shall be *wrested from them*. Who does not see in these words the consciousness of guilt, an indirect self-betraying admission that they had in their hands treasures which might be lawfully taken from them, and an anxiety to prevent that act of justice by a positive stipulation? Who does not see, on what sort of property the Frenchman had his eye; that it was not property by right, but their *possessions* – their plunder – every thing, by what means soever acquired, that the French army, or any individual in it, was possessed of? But it has been urged, that the monstrousness of such a supposition precludes this interpretation, renders it impossible that it could either be intended by the one party, or so understood by the other. What right they who signed, and he who ratified this Convention, have to shelter themselves under this plea – will appear from the 16th and 17th articles. In these it is stipulated, 'that all subjects of France, or of Powers in alliance with France, domiciliated in Portugal, or accidentally in the country, shall have their property of every kind – moveable and immoveable – guaranteed to them, with liberty of retaining or disposing of it, and passing the produce into France': the same is stipulated, (Article XVII.) for such natives of Portugal as have sided with the French, or occupied situations under *the French government*. Here then is a direct avowal, still more monstrous, that every Frenchman, or native of a country in alliance with France, however obnoxious his crimes may have made him, and every traitorous Portugueze, shall have his property guaranteed to him (both previously to and after the re-instatement of the Portugueze government) by the British army! Now let us ask, what sense the word property must have had fastened to it in *these* cases. Must it not necessarily have included all the rewards which the Frenchman had received for his iniquity, and the traitorous Portugueze for his treason? (for no man would bear a part in such oppressions, or would be a traitor for nothing; and, moreover, all the rewards, which the French could bestow, must have been taken from the Portugueze, extorted from the honest and loyal, to be given to the wicked and disloyal.) These rewards of iniquity must necessarily have been included; for, on our side, no attempt is made at a distinction; and, on the side of the French, the word *immoveable* is manifestly intended to preclude such a distinction, where alone it could have been effectual. Property, then, here means – possessions thus infamously acquired; and, in the instance of the Portugueze, the fundamental notion of the word is subverted; for a traitor can have no property, till the government of his own country has remitted the punishment due to his crimes. And these wages of guilt, which the master by such exactions was enabled to pay, and which the servant thus earned, are to be guaranteed to him by a British *army*! Where does there exist a power on earth that could confer this right? If the Portugueze government itself had acted in this manner, it would have been guilty of wilful suicide; and the nation, if it had acted so, of high treason against itself. Let it not, then, be said, that the monstrousness of covenanting to convey, along with the persons of the French, their plunder, secures the article from the interpretation which the people of Great Britain gave, and which, I have now proved, they were bound to give to it. – But, conceding for a moment, that it was not intended that the words should bear this sense, and that, neither in a fair grammatical construction, nor as illustrated by other passages or by the general tenour of the document, they actually did bear it, had not unquestionable voices proclaimed the cruelty and rapacity – the acts of sacrilege, assassination, and robbery, by which these treasures had been amassed? Was not the perfidy of the French army, and its contempt of moral obligation, both as a body and as to the individuals which composed it, infamous through Europe? – Therefore, the concession would signify nothing: for our Generals, by allowing an army of this character to depart with its equipments, waggons, military chest, and baggage, had provided abundant means to enable it to carry off whatsoever it desired, and thus to elude and frustrate any stipulations which might have been made for compelling it to restore that which had been so iniquitously seized. And here are we brought back to the fountainhead of all this baseness; to that apathy and deadness to the principle of justice, through influence of which, this army, outlawed by its crimes, was suffered to depart from the land, over which it had so long tyrannized – other than as a band of disarmed prisoners. – I maintain, therefore, that permission to carry off the booty was distinctly expressed; and, if it had not been so, that the principle of justice could not here be preserved; as a violation of it must necessarily have followed from other conditions of the treaty. Sir Hew Dalrymple himself, before the Court of Inquiry, has told us, in two letters (to Generals Beresford and Friere), that 'such part of the plunder as was in money, it would be difficult, if not impossible, to identify'; and, consequently, the French could not be prevented from carrying it away with them. From the same letters we learn, that 'the French were intending to carry off a considerable part of their plunder, by calling it public money, and saying that it belonged to the military chest; and that their evasions of the article were most shameful, and evinced a want of probity and honour, which was most disgraceful to them.' If the French had given no other proofs of their want of such virtues, than those furnished by this occasion, neither the Portugueze, nor Spanish, nor British nations would condemn them, nor hate them as they now do; nor would this article of the Convention have excited such indignation. For the French, by so acting, could not deem themselves breaking an engagement; no doubt they looked upon themselves as injured, – that the failure in good faith was on the part of the British; and that it was in the lawlessness of power, and by a mere quibble, that this construction was afterwards put upon the article in question.

[Fourteen paragraphs containing more objections to the Convention, especially the handling of booty and the poor treatment of the Portuguese, are omitted here.]

But, – whether these suspicions were reasonable or not, whatever motives produced a determination that the Convention should be acted upon, – there can be no doubt of the manner in which the ministry wished that the people should appreciate it; when the same persons, who had ordered that it should at first be received with rejoicing, availed themselves of his Majesty's high authority to give a harsh reproof to the City of London for having prayed 'that an enquiry might be instituted into this dishonourable and unprecedented transaction.' In their petition they styled it also 'an afflicting event – humiliating and degrading to the country, and injurious to his Majesty's Allies.' And for this, to the astonishment and grief of all sound minds, the petitioners were severely reprimanded; and told, among other admonitions, 'that it was inconsistent with the principles of British jurisprudence to pronounce judgement without previous investigation.'

Upon this charge, as re-echoed in its general import by persons who have been over-awed or deceived, and by others who have been wilful deceivers, I have already incidentally animadverted; and repelled it, I trust, with becoming indignation. I shall now meet the charge for the last time formally and directly; on account of considerations applicable to all times; and because the whole course of domestic proceedings relating to the Convention of Cintra, combined with menaces which have been recently thrown out in the lower House of Parliament, renders it too probable that a league has been framed for the purpose of laying further restraints upon freedom of speech and of the press; and that the reprimand to the City of London was devised by ministers as a preparatory overt act of this scheme; to the great abuse of the Sovereign's Authority, and in contempt of the rights of the nation. In meeting this charge, I shall shew to what desperate issues men are brought, and in what woeful labyrinths they are entangled, when, under the pretext of defending instituted law, they violate the laws of reason and nature for their own unhallowed purposes.

If the persons, who signed this petition, acted inconsistently with the principles of British jurisprudence; the offence must have been committed by giving an answer, before adequate and lawful evidence had entitled them so to do, to one or other of these questions: – 'What is the act? and who is the agent?' – or to both conjointly. Now the petition gives no opinion upon the agent; it pronounces only upon the act, and that some one must be guilty; but *who* – it does not take upon itself to say. It condemns the act; and calls for punishment upon the authors, whosoever they may be found to be; and does no more. After the analysis which has been made of the Convention, I may ask if there be any thing in this which deserves reproof; and reproof from an authority which ought to be most enlightened and most dispassionate, – as it is, next to the legislative, the most solemn authority in the land.

It is known to every one that the privilege of complaint and petition, in cases where the nation feels itself aggrieved, *itself* being the judge, (and who else ought to be, or can be?) – a privilege, the exercise of which implies condemnation of something complained of, followed by a prayer for its removal or correction – not only is established by the most grave and authentic charters of Englishmen, who have been taught by their wisest statesmen and legislators to be jealous over its preservation, and to call it into practice upon every reasonable occasion; but also that this privilege is an indispensable condition of all civil liberty. Nay, of such paramount interest is it to mankind, existing under any frame of Government whatsoever; that, either by law or custom, it has universally prevailed under all governments – from the Grecian and Swiss Democracies to the Despotisms of Imperial Rome, of Turkey, and of France under her present ruler. It must then be a high principle which could exact obeisance from governments at the two extremes of polity, and from all modes of government inclusively; from the best and from the worst; from magistrates acting under obedience to the stedfast law which expresses the general will; and from depraved and licentious tyrants, whose habit it is – to express, and to act upon, their own individual will. Tyrants have seemed to feel that, if this principle were acknowledged, the subject ought to be reconciled to any thing; that, by permitting the free exercise of this right alone, an adequate price was paid down for all abuses; that a standing pardon was included in it for the past, and a daily renewed indulgence for every future enormity. It is then melancholy to think that the time is come when an attempt has been made to tear, out of the venerable crown of the Sovereign of Great Britain, a gem which is in the very front of the turban of the Emperor of Morocco.[27]

To enter upon this argument is indeed both astounding and humiliating: for the adversary in the present case is bound to contend that we cannot pronounce upon evil or good, either in the actions of our own or in past times, unless the decision of a Court of Judicature has empowered us so to do. Why then have historians written? and why do we yield to the impulses of our nature, hating or loving – approving or condemning according to the appearances which their records present to our eyes? But the doctrine is as nefarious as it is absurd. For those public events in which men are most interested, namely, the crimes of rulers and of persons in high authority, for the most part are such as either have never been brought before tribunals at all, or before unjust ones: for, though offenders may be in hostility with each other, yet the kingdom of guilt is not wholly divided against itself; its subjects are united by a general interest to elude or overcome that law which would bring them to condign punishment. Therefore to make a verdict of a Court of Judicature a necessary condition for enabling men to determine the quality of an act, when the 'head and front'[28] — the life and soul of the offence may have been, that it eludes or rises above the reach of all judicature, is a contradiction which would be too gross to merit notice, were it not that men willingly suffer their understandings to stagnate. And hence this rotten bog, rotten and unstable as the crude consistence[29] of Milton's Chaos, 'smitten' (for I will continue to use the language of the poet) 'by the petrific mace — and bound with Gorgonian rigour by the look'[30] — of despotism, is transmuted; and becomes a highway of adamant for the sorrowful steps of generation after generation.

Again: in cases where judicial inquiries can be and are instituted, and are equitably conducted, this suspension of judgment, with respect to act or agent, is only supposed necessarily to exist in the court itself; not in the witnesses, the plaintiffs or accusers, or in the minds even of the people who may be present. If the contrary supposition were realized, how could the arraigned person ever have been brought into court? What would become of the indignation, the hope, the sorrow, or the sense of justice, by which the prosecutors, or the people of the country who pursued or apprehended the presumed criminal, or they who appear in evidence against him, are actuated? If then this suspension of judgment, by a law of human nature and a requisite of society, is not supposed *necessarily* to exist — except in the minds of the court; if this be undeniable in cases where the eye and ear-witnesses are few; — how much more so in a case like the present; where all, that constitutes the essence of the act, is avowed by the agents themselves, and lies bare to the notice of the whole world? — Now it was in the character of complainants and denunciators, that the petitioners of the City of London appeared before his Majesty's throne; and they have been reproached by his Majesty's ministers under the cover of a sophism, which, if our anxiety to interpret favourably words sanctioned by the First Magistrate — makes us unwilling to think it a deliberate artifice meant for the delusion of the people, must however (on the most charitable comment) be pronounced an evidence of no little heedlessness and self-delusion on the part of those who framed it.[31]

To sum up the matter — the right of petition (which, we have shewn as a general proposition, supposes a right to condemn, and is in itself an act of qualified condemnation) may in too many instances take the ground of absolute condemnation, both with respect to the crime and the criminal. It was confined, in this case, to the crime; but, if the City of London had proceeded farther, they would have been justifiable; because the delinquents had set their hands to their own delinquency. The petitioners, then, are not only clear of all blame; but are entitled to high praise: and we have seen whither the doctrines lead, upon which they were condemned. — And now, mark the discord which will ever be found in the actions of men, where there is no inward harmony of reason or virtue to regulate the outward conduct.

Those ministers, who advised their Sovereign to reprove the City of London for uttering prematurely, upon a measure, an opinion in which they were supported by the unanimous voice of the nation, had themselves before publickly prejudged the question by ordering that the tidings should be communicated with rejoicings. One of their body has since attempted to wipe away this stigma by repre- senting that these orders were given out of a just tenderness for the reputation of the generals, who would otherwise have appeared to be condemned without trial. But did these rejoicings leave the matter indifferent? Was not the *positive* fact of thus expressing an opinion (above all in a case like this, in which surely no man could ever dream that there were any features of splendour) far stronger lan- guage of approbation, than the *negative* fact could be of disapproba- tion? For these same ministers who had called upon the people of Great Britain to rejoice over the Armistice and Convention, and who reproved and discountenanced and suppressed to the utmost of their power every attempt at petitioning for redress of the injury caused by those treaties, have now made publick a document from which it appears that, 'when the instruments were first laid before his Majesty, the king felt himself compelled *at once*' (i.e. previously to all investigation) 'to express his disapprobation of those articles, in which stipulations were made directly affecting the interests or feelings of the Spanish and Portugueze nations.'

And was it possible that a Sovereign of a free country could be otherwise affected? It is indeed to be regretted that his Majesty's censure was not, upon this occasion, radical — and pronounced in a sterner tone; that a council was not in existence sufficiently intelligent and virtuous to advise the king to give full expression to the sentiments of his own mind; which, we may reasonably conclude, were in sympathy with those of a brave and loyal people. Never surely was there a public event more fitted to reduce men, in all ranks of society, under the supremacy of their common nature; to impress upon them one belief; to infuse into them one spirit. For it was not done in a remote corner by persons of obscure rank; but in the eyes of Europe and of all mankind; by the leading authorities, military and civil, of a mighty empire. It did not relate to a petty immunity, or a local and insulated privilege — but to the highest feelings of honour to which a nation may either be calmly and gradually raised by a long course of independence, liberty, and glory; or to the level of which it may be lifted up at once, from a fallen state, by a sudden and extreme pressure of violence and tyranny. It not only related to these high feelings of honour; but to the fundamental principles of justice, by which life and property, that is the means of living, are secured.

A people, whose government had been dissolved by foreign tyranny, and which had been left to work out its salvation by its own virtues, prayed for our help. And whence were we to learn how that help could be most effectually given, how they were even to be preserved from receiving injuries instead of benefits at our hands, — whence were we to learn this but from their language and from our own hearts? They had spoken of unrelenting and inhuman wrongs; of patience wearied out; of the agonizing yoke cast off; of the blessed

215

service of freedom chosen; of heroic aspirations; of constancy, and fortitude, and perseverance; of resolution even to the death; of gladness in the embrace of death; of weeping over the graves of the slain, by those who had not been so happy as to die; of resignation under the worst final doom; of glory, and triumph, and punishment. This was the language which we heard – this was the devout hymn that was chaunted; and the responses, with which our country bore a part in the solemn service, were from her soul and from the depths of her soul.

O sorrow! O misery for England, the land of liberty and courage and peace; the land trustworthy and long approved; the home of lofty example and benign precept; the central orb to which, as to a fountain, the nations of the earth 'ought to repair, and in their golden urns draw light'; [32] – O sorrow and shame for our country; for the grass which is upon her fields, and the dust which is in her graves; – for her good men who now look upon the day; – and her long train of deliverers and defenders, her Alfred, her Sidneys, and her Milton;[33] whose voice yet speaketh for our reproach; and whose actions survive in memory to confound us, or to redeem!

For what hath been done? look at it: we have looked at it: we have handled it: we have pondered it steadily: we have tried it by the principles of absolute and eternal justice; by the sentiments of high-minded honour, both with reference to their general nature, and to their especial exaltation under present circumstances; by the rules of expedience; by the maxims of prudence, civil and military: we have weighed it in the balance of all these, and found it wanting; in that, which is most excellent, most wanting.[34]

Our country placed herself by the side of Spain, and her fellow nation; she sent an honourable portion of her sons to aid a suffering people to subjugate or destroy an army – but I degrade the word – a banded multitude of perfidious oppressors, of robbers and assassins, who had outlawed themselves from society in the wantonness of power; who were abominable for their own crimes, and on account of the crimes of him whom they served – to subjugate or destroy these; not exacting that it should be done within a limited time;

admitting even that they might effect their purpose or not; she could have borne either issue, she was prepared for either; but she was not prepared for such a deliverance as hath been accomplished; not a deliverance of Portugal from French oppression, but of the oppressor from the anger and power (at least from the animating efforts) of the Peninsula: she was not prepared to stand between her allies, and their worthiest hopes: that, when chastisement could not be inflicted, honour – as much as bad men could receive – should be conferred: that them, whom her own hands had humbled, the same hands and no other should exalt: that finally the sovereign of this horde of devastators, himself the destroyer of the hopes of good men, should have to say, through the mouth of his minister,[35] and for the hearing of all Europe, that his army of Portugal had 'DICTATED THE TERMS OF ITS GLORIOUS RETREAT'.

I have to defend my countrymen: and, if their feelings deserve reverence, if there be any stirrings of wisdom in the motions of their souls, my task is accomplished. For here were no factions to blind; no dissolution of established authorities to confound; no ferments to distemper; no narrow selfish interests to delude. The object was at a distance; and it rebounded upon us, as with force collected from a mighty distance; we were calm till the very moment of transition; and all the people were moved – and felt as with one heart, and spake as with one voice. Every human being in these islands was unsettled; the most slavish broke loose as from fetters; and there was not an individual – it need not be said of heroic virtue, but of ingenuous life and sound discretion – who, if his father, his son, or his brother, or if the flower of his house had been in that army, would not rather that they had perished, and the whole body of their countrymen, their companions in arms, had perished to a man, than that a treaty should have been submitted to upon such conditions. This was the feeling of the people; an awful feeling: and it is from these oracles that rulers are to learn wisdom.

For, when the people speaks loudly, it is from being strongly possessed either by the Godhead or the Demon,[36] and he, who cannot discover the true spirit from the false, hath no ear for profitable communion. But in all that regarded the destinies of Spain, and her own as connected with them, the voice of Britain had the unquestionable sound of inspiration. If the gentle passions of pity, love, and gratitude, be porches of the temple; if the sentiments of admiration and rivalry be pillars upon which the structure is sustained; if, lastly, hatred, and anger, and vengeance, be steps which, by a mystery of nature, lead to the House of Sanctity; – than was it manifest to what power the edifice was consecrated; and that the voice within was of Holiness and Truth.

[Twenty-five paragraphs dealing with the Spanish, especially their motives, successes and disappointment by England, are omitted here.]

After the view of things which has been taken, – we may confidently affirm that nothing, but a knowledge of human nature directing the operations of our government, can give it a right to an intimate association with a cause which is that of human nature. I say, an intimate association founded on the right of thorough knowledge; – to contradistinguish this best mode of exertion from another which might found *its* right upon a vast and commanding military power put forth with manifestation of sincere intentions to benefit our allies – from a conviction merely of policy that their liberty, independence, and honour, are our genuine gain; – to distinguish the pure brotherly connection from this other (in its appearance at least more magisterial) which such a power, guided by such intention uniformly displayed, might authorize. But of the former connection (which supposes the main military effort to be made, even at present, by the people of the Peninsula on whom the moral interest more closely presses), and of the knowledge which it demands, I have hitherto spoken – and have further to speak.

It is plain *à priori* that the minds of Statesmen and Courtiers are unfavourable to the growth of this knowledge. For they are in a situation exclusive and artificial; which has the further disadvantage, that it does not separate men from men by collateral partitions which

# From *The Convention of Cintra*

leave, along with difference, a sense of equality – that they, who are divided, are yet upon the same level; but by a degree of superiority which can scarcely fail to be accompanied with more or less of pride. This situation therefore must be eminently unfavourable for the reception and establishment of that knowledge which is founded not upon things but upon sensations; – sensations which are general, and under general influences (and this it is which makes them what they are, and gives them their importance); – not upon things which may be *brought*; but upon sensations which must be *met*. Passing by the kindred and usually accompanying influence of birth in a certain rank – and, where education has been pre-defined from childhood for the express purpose of future political power, the tendency of such education to warp (and therefore weaken) the intellect; – we may join at once, with the privation which I have been noticing, a delusion equally common. It is this: that practical Statesmen assume too much credit to themselves for their ability to see into the motives and manage the selfish passions of their immediate agents and de-pendants; and for the skill with which they baffle or resist the aims of their opponents. A promptness in looking through the most super-ficial part of the characters of those men – who, by the very circum-stance of their contending ambitiously for the rewards and honours of government, are separated from the mass of the society to which they belong – is mistaken for a knowledge of human kind. Hence, where higher knowledge is a prime requisite, they not only are unfurnished; but, being unconscious that they are so, they look down contemptuously upon those who endeavour to supply (in some degree) their want. – The instincts of natural and social man; the deeper emotions; the simpler feelings; the spacious range of the dis-interested imagination; the pride in country for country's sake, when to serve has not been a formal profession – and the mind is therefore left in a state of dignity only to be surpassed by having served nobly and generously; the instantaneous accomplishment in which they start up who, upon a searching call, stir for the land which they love – not from personal motives, but for a reward which is undefined and cannot be missed; the solemn fraternity which a great nation

composes – gathered together, in a stormy season, under the shade of
ancestral feeling; the delicacy of moral honour which pervades the
minds of a people, when despair has been suddenly thrown off and
expectations are lofty; the apprehensiveness to a touch unkindly or
irreverent, where sympathy is at once exacted as a tribute and welcomed as a gift; the power of injustice and inordinate calamity to
transmute, to invigorate, and to govern – to sweep away the barriers
of opinion – to reduce under submission passions purely evil – to exalt
the nature of indifferent qualities, and to render them fit companions
for the absolute virtues with which they are summoned to associate –
to consecrate passions which, if not bad in themselves, are of such
temper that, in the calm of ordinary life, they are rightly deemed so –
to correct and embody these passions – and, without weakening them
(nay, with tenfold addition to their strength), to make them worthy of
taking their place as the advanced guard of hope, when a sublime
movement of deliverance is to be originated; – these arrangements and
resources of nature, these ways and means of society, have so little
connection with those others upon which a ruling minister of a
long-established government is accustomed to depend; these – elements as it were of a universe, functions of a living body – are so
opposite, in their mode of action, to the formal machine which it has
been his pride to manage; – that he has but a faint perception of their
immediate efficacy; knows not the facility with which they assimilate
with other powers; nor the property by which such of them – as, from
necessity of nature, must change or pass away – will, under wise and
fearless management, surely generate lawful successors to fill their
place when their appropriate work is performed. Nay, of the majority
of men, who are usually found in high stations under old governments,
it may without injustice be said; that, when they look about them in
times (alas! too rare) which present the glorious product of such
agency to their eyes, they have not a right to say – with a dejected man
in the midst of the woods, the rivers, the mountains, the sunshine, and
shadows of some transcendant landscape –

'I see, not feel, how beautiful they are:'[37]

These spectators neither see nor feel. And it is from the blindness and insensibility of these, and the train whom they draw along with them that the throes of nations have been so ill recompensed by the births which have followed; and that revolutions, after passing from crime to crime and from sorrow to sorrow, have often ended in throwing back such heavy reproaches of delusiveness upon their first promises.

I am satisfied that no enlightened Patriot will impute to me a wish to disparage the characters of men high in authority, or to detract from the estimation which is fairly due to them. My purpose is to guard against unreasonable expectations. That specific knowledge, – the paramount importance of which, in the present condition of Europe, I am insisting upon, – they, who usually fill places of high trust in old governments, neither do – nor, for the most part, can – possess: nor is it necessary, for the administration of affairs in ordinary circumstances, that they should. – The progress of their own country, and of the other nations of the world, in civilization, in true refinement, in science, in religion, in morals, and in all the real wealth of humanity, might indeed be quicker, and might correspond more happily with the wishes of the benevolent, – if Governors better understood the rudiments of nature as studied in the walks of common life; if they were men who had themselves felt every strong emotion 'inspired by nature and by fortune taught'; [38] and could calculate upon the force of the grander passions. Yet, at the same time, there is temptation in this. To know may seduce; and to have been agitated may compel. Arduous cares are attractive for their own sakes. Great talents are naturally driven towards hazard and difficulty; as it is there that they are most sure to find their exercise, and their evidence, and joy in anticipated triumph – the liveliest of all sensations. Moreover; magnificent desires, when least under the bias of personal feeling, dispose the mind – more than itself is conscious of – to regard commotion with complacency, and to watch the aggravations of distress with welcoming; from an immoderate confidence that, when the appointed day shall come, it will be in the power of intellect to relieve. There is danger in being a zealot in any cause – not excepting that of humanity. Nor is it to be forgotten that the incapacity and ignorance of the regular agents of long-established governments do not prevent some progress in the dearest concerns of men; and that society may owe to these very deficiencies, and to the tame and unenterprizing course which they necessitate, much security and tranquil enjoyment.

Nor, on the other hand, (for reasons which may be added to those already given) is it so desirable as might at first sight be imagined, much less is it desirable as an absolute good, that men of comprehensive sensibility and tutored genius – either for the interests of mankind or for their own – should, in ordinary times, have vested in them political power. The Empire, which they hold, is more independent: its constituent parts are sustained by a stricter connection: the dominion is purer and of higher origin; as mind is more excellent than body – the search of truth an employment more inherently dignified than the application of force – the determinations of nature more venerable than the accidents of human institution. Chance and disorder, vexation and disappointment, malignity and perverseness within or without the mind, are a sad exchange for the steady and genial processes of reason. Moreover; worldly distinctions and offices of command do not lie in the path – nor are they any part of the appropriate retinue – of Philosophy and Virtue. Nothing, but a strong spirit of love, can counteract the consciousness of pre-eminence which ever attends pre-eminent intellectual power with correspondent attainments: and this spirit of love is best encouraged by humility and simplicity in mind, manners, and conduct of life; virtues, to which wisdom leads. But, – though these be virtues in a Man, a Citizen, or a Sage, – they cannot be recommended to the especial culture of the Political or Military Functionary; and still less of the Civil Magistrate. Him, in the exercise of his functions, it will often become to carry himself highly and with state; in order that evil may be suppressed, and authority respected by those who have not understanding. The power also of office, whether the duties be discharged well or ill, will ensure a never-failing supply of flattery and praise: and of these – a man (becoming at once double-dealer

From *The Convention of Cintra*

and dupe) may, without impeachment of his modesty, receive as much as his weakness inclines him to; under the shew that the homage is not offered up to himself, but to that portion of the public dignity which is lodged in his person. But, whatever may be the cause, the fact is certain – that there is an unconquerable tendency in all power, save that of knowledge acting by and through knowledge, to injure the mind of him who exercises that power; so much so, that best natures cannot escape the evil of such alliance. Nor is it less certain that things of soundest quality, issuing through a medium to which they have only an arbitrary relation, are vitiated: and it is inevitable that there should be a reäscent of unkindly influence to the heart of him from whom the gift, thus unfairly dealt with, proceeded. – In illustration of these remarks, as connected with the management of States, we need only refer to the Empire of China – where superior endowments of mind and acquisitions of learning are the sole acknowledged title to offices of great trust; and yet in no country is the government more bigotted or intolerant, or society less progressive.

To prevent misconception; and to silence (at least to throw discredit upon) the clamours of ignorance; – I have thought proper thus, in some sort, to strike a balance between the claims of men of routine – and men of original and accomplished minds – to the management of State affairs in ordinary circumstances. But ours is not an age of this character: and, – after having seen such a long series of misconduct, so many unjustifiable attempts made and sometimes carried into effect, good endeavours frustrated, disinterested wishes thwarted, and benevolent hopes disappointed, – it is reasonable that we should endeavour to ascertain to what cause these evils are to be ascribed. I have directed the attention of the Reader to one primary cause: and can he doubt of its existence, and of the operation which I have attributed to it?

In the course of the last thirty years we have seen two wars waged against Liberty – the American war, and the war against the French People in the early stages of their Revolution. In the latter instance the Emigrants and the Continental Powers and the British did, in all their expectations and in every movement of their efforts, manifest a common ignorance – originating in the same source. And, for what more especially belongs to ourselves at this time, we may affirm – that the same presumptuous irreverence of the principles of justice, and blank insensibility to the affections of human nature, which determined the conduct of our government in those two wars *against* liberty, have continued to accompany its exertions in the present struggle *for* liberty, – and have rendered them fruitless. The British government deems (no doubt), on its own part, that its intentions are good. It must not deceive itself: nor must we deceive ourselves. Intentions – thoroughly good – could not mingle with the unblessed actions which we have witnessed. A disinterested and pure intention is a light that guides as well as cheers, and renders desperate lapses impossible.

Our duty is – our aim ought to be – to employ the true means of liberty and virtue for the ends of liberty and virtue. In such policy, thoroughly understood, there is fitness and concord and rational subordination; it deserves a higher name – organization, health, and grandeur. Contrast, in a single instance, the two processes; and the qualifications which they require. The ministers of that period found it an easy task to hire a band of Hessians, and to send it across the Atlantic, that they might assist *in bringing the Americans* (according to the phrase then prevalent) *to reason*. The force, with which these troops would attack, was gross – tangible, – and might be calculated; but the spirit of resistance, which their presence would create, was subtle – ethereal – mighty – and incalculable. Accordingly, from the moment when these foreigners landed – men who had no interest, no business, in the quarrel, but what the wages of their master bound him to, and he imposed upon his miserable slaves; – nay, from the first rumour of their destination, the success of the British was (as hath since been affirmed by judicious Americans) impossible.

The British government of the present day have been seduced, as we have seen, by the same common-place facilities on the one side; and have been equally blind on the other. A physical auxiliar force of thirty-five thousand men is to be added to the army of Spain: but the

moral energy, which thereby *might* be taken away from the principal,
is overlooked or slighted; the material being too fine for their calculation. What does it avail to graft a bough upon a tree; if this be
done so ignorantly and rashly that the trunk, which can alone supply
the sap by which the whole must flourish, receives a deadly wound?
Palpable effects of the Convention of Cintra, and self-contradicting
consequences even in the matter especially aimed at, may be seen in
the necessity which it entailed of leaving 8,000 British troops to
protect Portuguese traitors from punishment by the laws of their
country. A still more serious and fatal contradiction lies in this – that
the English army was made an instrument of injustice, and was
dishonoured, in order that it might be hurried forward to uphold a
cause which could have no life but by justice and honour. The nation
knows how that army languished in the heart of Spain: that it
accomplished nothing except its retreat, is sure: what great service it
might have performed, if it had moved from a different impulse, we
have shewn.

It surely then behoves those who are in authority – to look to the
state of their own minds. There is indeed an inherent impossibility
that they should be equal to the arduous duties which have devolved
upon them: but it is not unreasonable to hope that something higher
might be aimed at; and that the People might see, upon great occasions, – in the practice of its Rulers – a more adequate reflection of its
own wisdom and virtue. Our Rulers, I repeat, must begin with their
own minds. This is a precept of immediate urgency; and, if attended
to, might be productive of immediate good. I will follow it with
further conclusions directly referring to future conduct.

[Eighteen paragraphs, offering advice for conducting the war and
describing the necessary resistance of the Spanish and their eventual
defeat of the French, are here omitted.]

This cannot be accomplished (scarcely can it be aimed at) without
an accompanying and an inseparable resolution, in the souls of the
Spaniards, to be and remain their own masters; that is, to preserve

themselves in the rank of Men; and not become as the Brute that is driven to the pasture, and cares not who owns him. It is a common saying among those who profess to be lovers of civil liberty, and give themselves some credit for understanding it, – that, if a Nation be not free, it is mere dust in the balance whether the slavery be bred at home, or comes from abroad; be of their own suffering, or of a stranger's imposing. They see little of the under-ground part of the tree of liberty, and know less of the nature of man, who can think thus. Where indeed there is an indisputable and immeasurable superiority in one nation over another; to be conquered may, in course of time, be a benefit to the inferior nation: and, upon this principle, some of the conquests of the Greeks and Romans may be justified. But in what of really useful or honourable are the French superior to their Neighbours? Never far advanced, and, now barbarizing apace, they may carry – amongst the sober and dignified Nations which surround them – much to be avoided, but little to be imitated.

There is yet another case in which a People may be benefited by resignation or forfeiture of their rights as a separate independent State; I mean, where – of two contiguous or neighbouring countries, both included by nature under one conspicuously defined limit – the weaker is united with, or absorbed into, the more powerful; and one and the same Government is extended over both. This, with due patience and foresight, may (for the most part) be amicably effected, without the intervention of conquest; but – even should a violent course have been resorted to, and have proved successful – the result will be matter of congratulation rather than of regret, if the countries have been incorporated with an equitable participation of natural advantages and civil privileges. Who does not rejoice that former partitions have disappeared, – and that England, Scotland, and Wales, are under one legislative and executive authority; and that Ireland (would that she had been more justly dealt with!) follows the same destiny? The large and numerous Fiefs, which interfered injuriously with the grand demarcation assigned by nature to France, have long since been united and consolidated. The several independent Sovereignties of Italy (a country, the boundary of which is still more expressly traced out by nature; and which has no less the further definition and cement of country which Language prepares) have yet this good to aim at: and it will be a happy day for Europe, when the natives of Italy and the natives of Germany (whose duty is, in like manner, indicated to them) shall each dissolve the pernicious barriers which divide them, and form themselves into a mighty People. But Spain, excepting a free union with Portugal, has no benefit of this kind to look for: she has long since attained it. The Pyrenees on the one side, and the Sea on every other; the vast extent and great resources of the territory; a population numerous enough to defend itself against the whole world, and capable of great increase; language; and long duration of independence; – point out and command that the two nations of the Peninsula should be united in friendship and strict alliance; and, as soon as it may be effected without injustice, form one independent and indissoluble sovereignty. The Peninsula cannot be protected but by itself: it is too large a tree to be framed by nature for a station among underwoods; it must have power to toss its branches in the wind, and lift a bold forehead to the sun.

Allowing that the 'regni novitas' [39] should either compel or tempt the Usurper to do away some ancient abuses, and to accord certain insignificant privileges to the People upon the purlieus of the forest of Freedom (for assuredly he will never suffer them to enter the body of it); allowing this, and much more; that the mass of the Population would be placed in a condition outwardly more thriving – would be *better off* (as the phrase in conversation is); it is still true that – in the act and consciousness of submission to an imposed lord and master, to a will not growing out of themselves, to the edicts of another People their triumphant enemy – there would be the loss of a sensation within for which nothing external, even though it should come close to the garden and the field – to the door and the fire-side, can make amends. The Artisan and the Merchant (men of classes perhaps least attached to their native soil) would not be insensible to this loss; and the Mariner, in his thoughtful mood, would sadden under it upon the wide ocean. The central or cardinal feeling of these thoughts may, at a future time, furnish fit matter for the genius of some patriotic Spaniard to express in his own noble language – as an inscription for the Sword of Francis the First; if that Sword, which was so ingloriously and perfidiously surrendered,[40] should ever, by the energies of Liberty, be recovered, and deposited in its ancient habitation in the Escurial. The Patriot will recollect that, – if the memorial, then given up by the hand of the Government, had also been abandoned by the heart of the People, and that indignity patiently subscribed to, – his country would have been lost for ever.

There are multitudes by whom, I know, these sentiments will not be languidly received at this day; and sure I am – that, a hundred and fifty years ago, they would have been ardently welcomed by all. But, in many parts of Europe (and especially in our own country), men have been pressing forward, for some time, in a path which has betrayed by its fruitfulness; furnishing them constant employment for picking up things about their feet, when thoughts were perishing in their minds. While Mechanic Arts, Manufactures, Agriculture, Commerce, and all those products of knowledge which are confined to gross – definite – and tangible objects, have, with the aid of Experimental Philosophy, been every day putting on more brilliant colours; the splendour of the Imagination has been fading: Sensibility, which was formerly a generous nursling of rude Nature, has been chased from its ancient range in the wide domain of patriotism and religion with the weapons of derision by a shadow calling itself Good Sense: calculations of presumptuous Expediency – groping its way among partial and temporary consequences – have been substituted for the dictates of paramount and infallible Conscience, the supreme embracer of consequences: lifeless and circumspect Decencies have banished the graceful negligence and unsuspicious dignity of Virtue.

The progress of these arts also, by furnishing such attractive stores of outward accommodation, has misled the higher orders of society in their more disinterested exertions for the service of the lower. Animal comforts have been rejoiced over, as if they were the end of being. A neater and more fertile garden; a greener field; implements and utensils more apt; a dwelling more commodious and better furnished; – let these be attained, say the actively benevolent, and we are sure not only of being in the right road, but of having successfully terminated our journey. Now a country may advance, for some time, in this course with apparent profit: these accommodations, by zealous encouragement, may be attained: and still the Peasant or Artisan, their master, be a slave in mind; a slave rendered even more abject by the very tenure under which these possessions are held: and – if they veil from us this fact, or reconcile us to it – they are worse than worthless. The springs of emotion may be relaxed or destroyed within him; he may have little thought of the past, and less interest in the future. – The great end and difficulty of life for men of all classes, and especially difficult for those who live by manual labour, is a union of peace with innocent and laudable animation. Not by bread alone is the life of Man sustained;[41] not by raiment alone is he warmed; – but by the genial and vernal inmate of the breast, which at once pushes forth and cherishes; by self-support and self-sufficing endeavours; by anticipations, apprehensions, and active remembrances; by elasticity under insult, and firm resistance to injury; by joy, and by love; by pride which his imagination gathers in from afar; by patience, because life wants not promises; by admiration; by gratitude which – debasing him not when his fellow-being is its object – habitually expands itself, for his elevation, in complacency towards his Creator.

Now, to the existence of these blessings, national independence is indispensible; and many of them it will itself produce and maintain. For it is some consolation to those who look back upon the history of the world to know – that, even without civil liberty, society may possess – diffused through its inner recesses in the minds even of its humblest members – something of dignified enjoyment. But, without national independence, this is impossible. The difference, between inbred oppression and that which is from without, is *essential*; inasmuch as the former does not exclude, from the minds of a people, the feeling of being self-governed; does not imply (as the latter does, when patiently submitted to) an abandonment of the first duty imposed by the faculty of reason. In reality: where this feeling has no place, a people are not a society, but a herd; man being indeed distinguished among them from the brute; but only to his disgrace. I am aware that there are too many who think that, to the bulk of the community, this independence is of no value; that it is a refinement with which they feel they have no concern; inasmuch as, under the best frame of Government, there is an inevitable dependence of the poor upon the rich – of the many upon the few – so unrelenting and imperious as to reduce this other, by comparison, into a force which has small influence, and is entitled to no regard. Superadd civil liberty to national independence; and this position is overthrown at once: for there is no more certain mark of a sound frame of polity than this; that, in all individual instances (and it is upon these generalized that this position is laid down), the dependence is in reality far more strict on the side of the wealthy; and the labouring man leans less upon others than any man in the community. – But the case before us is of a country not internally free, yet supposed capable of repelling an external enemy who attempts its subjugation. If a country have put on chains of its own forging; in the name of virtue, let it be conscious that to itself it is accountable: let it not have cause to look beyond its own limits for reproof: and, – in the name of humanity, – if it be self-depressed, let it have its pride and some hope within itself. The poorest Peasant, in an unsubdued land, feels this pride. I do not appeal to the example of Britain or of Switzerland, for the one is free, and the other lately was free (and, I trust, will ere long be so again): but talk with the Swede; and you will see the joy he finds in these sensations. With him animal courage (the substitute for many and the friend of all the manly virtues) has space to move in; and is at once elevated by his imagination, and softened by his affections: it is invigorated also; for the whole courage of his Country is in his breast.

In fact: the Peasant, and he who lives by the fair reward of his manual labour, has ordinarily a larger proportion of his gratifications dependent upon these thoughts – than, for the most part, men in other classes have. For he is in his person attached, by stronger roots, to the soil of which he is the growth: his intellectual notices are generally confined within narrower bounds: in him no partial or antipatriotic interests counteract the force of those nobler sympathies and antipathies which he has in right of his Country;[42] and lastly the belt or girdle of his mind has never been stretched to utter relaxation by false philosophy, under a conceit of making it sit more easily and gracefully. These sensations are a social inheritance to him; more important, as he is precluded from luxurious – and those which are usually called refined – enjoyments.

Love and admiration must push themselves out towards some quarter: otherwise the moral man is killed. Collaterally they advance with great vigour to a certain extent – and they are checked: in that direction, limits hard to pass are perpetually encountered: but upwards and downwards, to ancestry and to posterity, they meet with gladsome help and no obstacles; the tract is interminable. – Perdition to the Tyrant who would wantonly cut off an independent Nation from its inheritance in past ages; turning the tombs and burial-places of the Forefathers into dreaded objects of sorrow, or of shame and reproach, for the Children! Look upon Scotland and Wales: though, by the union of these with England under the same Government (which was effected without conquest in one instance), ferocious and desolating wars, and more injurious intrigues, and sapping and disgraceful corruptions, have been prevented; and tranquillity, security, and prosperity, and a thousand interchanges of amity, not otherwise attainable, have followed; – yet the flashing eye, and the agitated voice, and all the tender recollections, with which the names of Prince Llewellin and William Wallace[43] are to this day pronounced by the fire-side and on the public road, attest that these substantial blessings have not been purchased without the relinquishment of something most salutary to the moral nature of Man: else the remembrances would not cleave so faithfully to their abiding-place in the human heart. But, if these affections be of general interest, they are of especial interest to Spain; whose history, written and traditional, is pre-eminently stored with the sustaining food of such affections: and in no country are they more justly and generally prized, or more feelingly cherished.

In the conduct of this argument I am not speaking *to* the humbler ranks of society: it is unnecessary: *they* trust in nature, and are safe. The People of Madrid, and Corunna, and Ferrol, resisted to the last;

from an impulse which, in their hearts, was its own justification. The failure was with those who stood higher in the scale. In fact; the universal rising of the Peninsula, under the pressure and in the face of the most tremendous military power which ever existed, is evidence which cannot be too much insisted upon; and is decisive upon this subject, as involving a question of virtue and moral sentiment. All ranks were penetrated with one feeling: instantaneous and universal was the acknowledgement. If there have been since individual fallings-off; those have been caused by that kind of after-thoughts which are the bastard offspring of selfishness. The matter was brought home to Spain; and no Spaniard has offended herein with a still conscience. – It is to the worldlings of our own country, and to those who think without carrying their thoughts far enough, that I address myself. Let them know, there is no true wisdom without imagination; no genuine sense; – that the man, who in this age feels no regret for the ruined honour of other Nations, must be poor in sympathy for the honour of his own Country; and that, if he be wanting here towards that which circumscribes the whole, he neither has – nor can have – a social regard for the lesser communities which Country includes. Contract the circle, and bring him to his family; such a man cannot protect *that* with dignified love. Reduce his thoughts to his own person; he may defend himself, – what *he* deems his honour; but it is the *action* of a brave man from the impulse of the brute, or the motive of a coward.

But it is time to recollect that this vindication of human feeling began from an *hypothesis*, – that the *outward* state of the mass of the Spanish people would be improved by the French usurpation. To this I now give an unqualified denial. Let me also observe to those men, for whose infirmity this hypothesis was tolerated, – that the true point of comparison does not lie between what the Spaniards have been under a government of their own, and what they may become under French domination; but between what the Spaniards may do (and, in all likelihood, will do) for themselves, and what Frenchmen would do for them. But, – waiving this, – the sweeping away of the most splendid monuments of art, and rifling of the public treasuries in the conquered countries, are an apt prologue to the tragedy which is to ensue. Strange that there are men who can be so besotted as to see, in the decrees of the Usurper concerning feudal tenures and a worn-out inquisition,[44] any other evidence than that of insidiousness and of a constrained acknowledgement of the strength which he felt he had to overcome. What avail the lessons of history, if men can be duped thus? Boons and promises of this kind rank, in trustworthiness, many degrees lower than amnesties after expelled kings have recovered their thrones. The fate of subjugated Spain may be expressed in these words, – pillage – depression – and helotism – for the supposed aggrandizement of the imaginary freeman its master. There would indeed be attempts at encouragement, that there might be a supply of something to pillage: studied depression there would be, that there might arise no power of resistance: and lastly helotism; – but of what kind? that a vain and impious Nation might have slaves, worthier than itself, for work which its own hands would reject with scorn.

What good can the present arbitrary power confer upon France itself? Let that point be first settled by those who are inclined to look farther. The earlier proceedings of the French Revolution no doubt infused health into the country; something of which survives to this day: but let not the now-existing Tyranny have the credit of it. France neither owes, nor can owe, to this any rational obligation. She has seen decrees without end for the increase of commerce and manufactures; pompous stories without number of harbours, canals, warehouses, and bridges: but there is no worse sign in the management of affairs than when that, which ought to follow as an effect, goes before under a vain notion that it will be a cause. – Let us attend to the springs of action, and we shall not be deceived. The works of peace cannot flourish in a country governed by an intoxicated Despot; the motions of whose distorted benevolence must be still more pernicious than those of his cruelty. '*I have bestowed; I have created; I have regenerated; I have been pleased to organize;*' – this is the language perpetually upon his lips, when his ill-fated activities turn that way. Now commerce, manufactures, agriculture, and all the peaceful arts, are of the nature of virtues or intellectual powers: they cannot be given; they cannot be stuck in here and there; they must spring up; they must grow of themselves: they may be encouraged; they thrive better with encouragement, and delight in it; but the obligation must have bounds nicely defined; for they are delicate, proud, and independent. But a Tyrant has no joy in any thing which is endued with such excellence: he sickens at the sight of it: he turns away from it, as an insult to his own attributes. We have seen the present ruler of France publicly addressed as a Providence upon earth; styled, among innumerable other blasphemies, the supreme Ruler of things; and heard him say, in his answers, that he approved of the language of those who thus saluted him.[45] – Oh folly to think that plans of reason can prosper under such countenance! If this be the doom of France, what a monster would be the double-headed tyranny of Spain!

It is immutably ordained that power, taken and exercised in contempt of right, never can bring forth good. Wicked actions indeed have oftentimes happy issues: the benevolent oeconomy of nature counter-working and diverting evil; and educing finally benefits from injuries, and turning curses to blessings. But I am speaking of good in a direct course. All good in this order – all moral good – begins and ends in reverence of right. The whole Spanish People are to be treated not as a mighty multitude with feeling, will, and judgment; not as rational creatures; – but as objects without reason; in the language of human law, insuperably laid down not as Persons but as Things. Can good come from this beginning; which, in matter of civil government, is the fountain-head and the main feeder of all the pure evil upon earth? Look at the past history of our sister Island for the quality of foreign oppression: turn where you will, it is miserable at best; but, in the case of Spain! – it might be said, engraven upon the rocks of her own Pyrenees,

> Per me si va nella città dolente;
> Per me si va nell' eterno dolore;
> Per me si va tra la perduta gente.[46]

## From *The Convention of Cintra*

So much I have thought it necessary to speak upon this subject;
with a desire to enlarge the views of the short-sighted, to chear the
desponding, and stimulate the remiss. I have been treating of duties
which the People of Spain feel to be solemn and imperious; and have
referred to springs of action (in the sensations of love and hatred, of
hope and fear), – for promoting the fulfilment of these duties, –
which cannot fail. The People of Spain, thus animated, will move
now; and will be prepared to move, upon a favourable summons, for
ages. And it is consolatory to think that, – even if many of the
leading persons of that country, in their resistance to France, should
not look beyond the two first objects (viz. riddance of the enemy,
and security of national independence); – it is, I say, consolatory to
think that the conduct, which can alone secure either of these ends,
leads directly to a free internal Government. We have therefore both
the passions and the reason of these men on our side in two stages of
the common journey: and, when this is the case, surely we are
justified in expecting some further companionship and support from
their reason – acting independent of their partial interests, or in
opposition to them. It is obvious that, to the narrow policy of this
class (men loyal to the Nation and to the King, yet jealous of the
People), the most dangerous failures, which have hitherto taken place,
are to be attributed: for, though from acts of open treason Spain may
suffer and has suffered much, these (as I have proved) can never
affect the vitals of the cause. But the march of Liberty has begun;
and they, who will not lead, may be borne along. – At all events,
the road is plain. Let members for the Cortes be assembled from
those Provinces which are not in the possession of the Invader: or at
least (if circumstances render this impossible at present) let it be
announced that such is the intention, to be realized the first moment
when it shall become possible. In the mean while speak boldly to
the People: and let the People write and speak boldly. Let the expectation be familiar to them of open and manly institutions of law
and liberty according to knowledge. Let them be universally trained
to military exercises, and accustomed to military discipline: let them
be drawn together in civic and religious assemblies; and a general

communication of those assemblies with each other be established through the country: so that there may be one zeal and one life in every part of it.

With great profit might the Chiefs of the Spanish Nation look back upon the earlier part of the French Revolution. Much, in the outward manner, might there be found worthy of qualified imitation: and, where there is a difference in the inner spirit (and there is a mighty difference!), the advantage is wholly on the side of the Spaniards. – Why should the People of Spain be dreaded by their leaders? I do not mean the profligate and flagitious leaders; but those who are well-intentioned, yet timid. That there are numbers of this class who have excellent intentions, and are willing to make large personal sacrifices, is clear; for they have put every thing to risk – all their privileges, their honours, and possessions – by their resistance to the Invader. Why then should they have fears from a quarter – whence their safety must come, if it come at all? – Spain has nothing to dread from Jacobinism. Manufactures and Commerce have there in far less degree than elsewhere – by unnaturally clustering the people together – enfeebled their bodies, inflamed their passions by intemperance, vitiated from childhood their moral affections, and destroyed their imaginations. Madrid is no enormous city, like Paris; overgrown, and disproportionate; sickening and bowing down, by its corrupt humours, the frame of the body politic. Nor has the pestilential philosophism of France made any progress in Spain. No flight of infidel harpies has alighted upon their ground. A Spanish understanding is a hold too strong to give way to the meagre tactics of the 'Système de la Nature'; [47] or to the pellets of logic which Condillac has cast in the foundry of national vanity, and tosses about at haphazard – self-persuaded that he is proceeding according to art. The Spaniards are a people with imagination: and the paradoxical reveries of Rousseau, and the flippancies of Voltaire, are plants which will not naturalise in the country of Calderon and Cervantes. Though bigotry among the Spaniards leaves much to be lamented; I have proved that the religious habits of the nation must, in a contest of this kind, be of inestimable service.

Yet further: contrasting the present condition of Spain with that of France at the commencement of her revolution, we must not overlook one characteristic; the Spaniards have no division among themselves by and through themselves; no numerous Priesthood – no Nobility – no large body of powerful Burghers – from passion, interest, and conscience – opposing the end which is known and felt to be the duty and only honest and true interest of all. Hostility, wherever it is found, must proceed from the seductions of the Invader: and these depend solely upon his power: let that be shattered; and they vanish.

And this once again leads us directly to that immense military force which the Spaniards have to combat; and which, many think, more than counterbalances every internal advantage. It is indeed formidable: as of revolutionary appetites and energies must needs be; when, among a people numerous as the people of France, they have ceased to spend themselves in conflicting factions within the country for objects perpetually changing shape; and are carried out of it under the strong controul of an absolute despotism, as opportunity invites, for a definite object – plunder and conquest. It is, I allow, a frightful spectacle – to see the prime of a vast nation propelled out of their territory with the rapid sweep of a horde of Tartars; moving from the impulse of like savage instincts; and furnished, at the same time, with those implements of physical destruction which have been produced by science and civilization. Such are the motions of the French armies; unchecked by any thought which philosophy and the spirit of society, progressively humanizing, have called forth – to determine or regulate the application of the murderous and desolating apparatus with which by philosophy and science they have been provided. With a like perversion of things, and the same mischievous reconcilement of forces in their nature adverse, these revolutionary impulses and these appetites of barbarous (nay, what is far worse, of barbarized) men are embodied in a new frame of polity; which possesses the consistency of an ancient Government, without its embarrassments and weaknesses. And at the head of all is the mind of one man who acts avowedly upon the principle that every thing, which can be done safely by the supreme power of a state, may be done;[48] and who has, at his command, the greatest part of the continent of Europe – to fulfil what yet remains unaccomplished of his nefarious purposes.

Now it must be obvious to a reflecting mind that every thing which is desperately immoral, being in its constitution monstrous, is of itself perishable: decay it cannot escape; and, further, it is liable to sudden dissolution: time would evince this in the instance before us; though not, perhaps, until infinite and irreparable harm had been done. But, even at present, each of the sources of this preternatural strength (as far as it is formidable to Europe) has its corresponding seat of weakness; which, were it fairly touched, would manifest itself immediately. – The power is indeed a Colossus: but, if the trunk be of molten-brass, the members are of clay;[49] and would fall to pieces upon a shock which need not be violent. Great Britain, if her energies were properly called forth and directed, might (as we have already maintained) give this shock. 'Magna parvis obscurantur'[50] was the appropriate motto (the device a Sun Eclipsed) when Lord Peterborough, with a handful of men opposed to fortified cities and large armies, brought a great part of Spain to acknowledge a sovereign of the House of Austria. We have *now* a vast military force; and, – even without a Peterborough or a Marlborough, – at this precious opportunity (when, as is daily more probable, a large portion of the French force must march northwards to combat Austria) we might easily, by expelling the French from the Peninsula, secure an immediate footing there for liberty; and the Pyrenees would then be shut against them for ever. The disciplined troops of Great Britain might overthrow the enemy in the field; while the Patriots of Spain, under wise management, would be able to consume him slowly but surely.

For present annoyance his power is, no doubt, mighty: but liberty – in which it originated, and of which it is a depravation – is far mightier; and the good in human nature is stronger than the evil. The events of our age indeed have brought this truth into doubt with some persons: and scrupulous observers have been astonished and have repined at the sight of enthusiasm, courage, perseverance, and fidelity, put forth seemingly to their height, – and all engaged in the furtherance of wrong. But the minds of man are not always devoted to this bad service as strenuously as they appear to be. I have personal knowledge that, when the attack was made which ended in the subjugation of Switzerland, the injustice of the undertaking was grievously oppressive to many officers of the French army; and damped their exertions. Besides, were it otherwise, there is no just cause for despondency in the perverted alliance of these qualities with oppression. The intrinsic superiority of virtue and liberty, even for politic ends, is not affected by it. If the tide of success were, by any effort, fairly turned; – not only a general desertion, as we have the best reason to believe, would follow among the troops of the enslaved nations; but a moral change would also take place in the minds of the native French soldiery. Occasion would be given for the discontented to break out; and, above all, for the triumph of human nature, it would *then* be seen whether men fighting in a bad cause, – men without magnanimity, honour, or justice, – could recover; and stand up against champions who by these virtues were carried forward in good fortune, as by these virtues in adversity they had been sustained. As long as guilty actions thrive, guilt is strong: it has a giddiness and transport of its own; a hardihood not without superstition, as if Providence were a party to its success. But there is no independent spring at the heart of the machine which can be relied upon for a support of these motions in a change of circumstances. Disaster opens the eyes of conscience; and, in the minds of men who have been employed in bad actions, defeat and a feeling of punishment are inseparable.

On the other hand; the power of an unblemished heart and a brave spirit is shewn, in the events of war, not only among unpractised citizens and peasants; but among troops in the most perfect discipline. Large bodies of the British army have been several times broken – that is, technically vanquished – in Egypt, and elsewhere. Yet they, who were conquered as formal soldiers, stood their ground and became conquerors as men. This paramount efficacy of moral causes is not willingly admitted by persons high in the profession of arms; because it seems to diminish their value in society – by taking from the importance of their art: but the truth is indisputable: and those Generals are as blind to their own interests as to the interests of their country, who, by submitting to inglorious treaties or by other misconduct, hazard the breaking down of those personal virtues in the men under their command – to which they themselves, as leaders, are mainly indebted for the fame which they acquire.

Combine, with this moral superiority inherent in the cause of Freedom, the endless resources open to a nation which shews constancy in defensive war; resources which, after a lapse of time, leave the strongest invading army comparatively helpless. Before six cities, resisting as Saragossa hath resisted during her two sieges, the whole of the military power of the adversary would melt away. Without any advantages of natural situation; without fortifications; without even a ditch to protect them; with nothing better than a mud wall; with not more than two hundred regular troops; with a slender stock of arms and ammunition; with a leader inexperienced in war; – the Citizens of Saragossa began the contest. Enough of what was needful – was produced and created; and – by courage, fortitude, and skill, rapidly matured – they baffled for sixty days, and finally repulsed, a large French army with all its equipments. In the first siege the natural and moral victory were both on their side; nor less so virtually (though the termination was different) in the second. For, after another resistance of nearly three months, they have given the enemy cause feelingly to say, with Pyrrhus of old, – 'A little more of such conquest, and I am destroyed.'[51]

If evidence were wanting of the efficacy of the principles which throughout this Treatise have been maintained, – it has been furnished in overflowing measure. A private individual, I had written; and knew not in what manner tens of thousands were enacting, day after day, the truths which, in the solitude of a peaceful vale, I was meditating. Most gloriously have the Citizens of Saragossa proved that the true army of Spain, in a contest of this nature, is the whole people. The same city has also exemplified a melancholy – yea a dismal truth; yet consolatory, and full of joy; that, — when a people are called suddenly to fight for their liberty, and are sorely pressed upon, — their best field of battle is the floors upon which their children have played; the chambers where the family of each man has slept (his own or his neighbours'); upon or under the roofs by which they have been sheltered; in the gardens of their recreation; in the street, or in the market-place; before the Altars of their Temples; and among their congregated dwellings — blazing, or up-rooted.

The Government of Spain must never forget Saragossa for a moment. Nothing is wanting, to produce the same effects every where, but a leading mind such as that city was blessed with. In the latter contest this has been proved; for Saragossa contained, at that time, bodies of men from almost all parts of Spain. The narrative of those two sieges should be the manual of every Spaniard: he may add to it the ancient stories of Numantia and Saguntum:[52] let him sleep upon the book as a pillow; and, if he be a devout adherent to the religion of his country, let him wear it in his bosom for his crucifix to rest upon.

Beginning from these invincible feelings, and the principles of justice which are involved in them; let nothing be neglected, which policy and prudence dictate, for rendering subservient to the same end those qualities in human nature which are indifferent or even morally bad; and for making the selfish propensities contribute to the support of wise arrangements, civil and military. — Perhaps there never appeared in the field more steady soldiers — troops which it would have been more difficult to conquer with such knowledge of the art of war as then existed — than those commanded by Fairfax and Cromwell: let us see from what root these armies grew. 'Cromwell,' says Sir Philip Warwick, 'made use of the zeal and credulity of these persons' (that is — such of the people as had, in the author's language, the fanatic humour); 'teaching them (as they too readily taught themselves) that they engaged for God, when he led them against his vicegerent the King. And, where this opinion met with a natural courage, it made them bolder — and too often crueller;

and, where natural courage wanted, zeal supplied its place. And at first they chose rather to die than flee; and custom removed fear of danger: and afterwards — finding the sweet of good pay, and of opulent plunder, and of preferment suitable to activity and merit — the lucrative part made gain seem to them a natural member of godliness. And I cannot here omit' (continues the author) 'a character of this army which General Fairfax gave unto myself; when, complimenting him with the regularity and temperance of his army, he told me, The best common soldiers he had — came out of our army and from the garrisons he had taken in. So (says he) I found you had made them good soldiers; and I have made them good men. But, upon this whole matter, it may appear' (concludes the author) 'that the spirit of discipline of warr may beget that spirit of discipline which even Solomon describes as the spirit of wisdom and obedience.'[53] Apply this process to the growth and maturity of an armed force in Spain. In making a comparison of the two cases; to the sense of the insults and injuries which, as Spaniards and as human Beings, they have received and have to dread, — and to the sanctity which an honourable resistance has already conferred upon their misfortunes, — add the devotion of that people to their religion as Catholics; — and it will not be doubted that the superiority of the radical feeling is, on their side, immeasurable. There is (I cannot refrain from observing) in the Catholic religion, and in the character of its Priesthood especially, a source of animation and fortitude in desperate struggles — which may be relied upon as one of the best hopes of the cause. The narrative of the first siege of Zaragoza, lately published in this country, and which I earnestly recommend to the reader's perusal, informs us that, — 'In every part of the town where the danger was most imminent, and the French the most numerous, — was Padre St Iago Sass, curate of a parish in Zaragoza. As General Palafox made his rounds through the city, he often beheld Sass alternately playing the part of a Priest and a Soldier; sometimes administering the sacrament to the dying; and, at others, fighting in the most determined manner against the enemies of his country. — He was found so serviceable in inspiring the people with religious sentiments, and in leading them on to danger, that the General has placed him in a situation where both his piety and courage may continue to be as useful as before; and he is now both Captain in the army, and Chaplain to the commander-in-chief.' [54]

The reader will have been reminded, by the passage above cited from Sir Philip Warwick's memoirs, of the details given, in the earlier part of this tract, concerning the course which (as it appeared to me) might with advantage be pursued in Spain: I must request him to combine those details with such others as have since been given: the whole would have been further illustrated, if I could sooner have returned to the subject; but it was first necessary to examine the grounds of hope in the grand and disinterested passions, and in the laws of universal morality. My attention has therefore been chiefly directed to these laws and passions; in order to elevate, in some degree, the conceptions of my readers; and with a wish to rectify and fix, in this fundamental point, their judgements. The truth of the general reasoning will, I have no doubt, be acknowledged by men of uncorrupted natures and practised understandings; and the conclusion, which I have repeatedly drawn, will be acceded to; namely, that no resistance can be prosperous which does not look, for its chief support, to these principles and feelings. If, however, there should be men who still fear (as I have been speaking of things under combinations which are transitory) that the action of these powers cannot be sustained; to such I answer that, – if there be a necessity that it should be sustained at the point to which it first ascended, or should recover that height if there have been a fall, – nature will provide for that necessity. The cause is in Tyranny: and that will again call forth the effect out of its holy retirements. Oppression, its own blind and predestined enemy, has poured this of blessedness upon Spain, – that the enormity of the outrages, of which she has been the victim, has created an object of love and of hatred – of apprehensions and of wishes – adequate (if that be possible) to the utmost demands of the human spirit. The heart that serves in this cause, if it languish, must languish from its own constitutional weakness; and not through want of nourishment from without. But it is a belief propagated in books, and which passes currently among talking men as part of their familiar wisdom, that the hearts of the many *are* constitutionally weak; that they *do* languish; and are slow to answer to the requisitions of things. I entreat those, who are in this delusion, to look behind them and about them for the evidence of experience. Now this, rightly understood, not only gives no support to any such belief; but proves that the truth is in direct opposition to it. The history of all ages; tumults after tumults; wars, foreign or civil, with short or with no breathing-spaces, from generation to generation; wars – why and wherefore? yet with courage, with perseverance, with self-sacrifice, with enthusiasm – with cruelty driving forward the cruel man from its own terrible nakedness, and attracting the more benign by the accompaniment of some shadow which seems to sanctify it; the senseless weaving and interweaving of factions – vanishing and reviving and piercing each other like the Northern Lights; public commotions, and those in the bosom of the individual; the long calenture of fancy to which the Lover is subject; the blast, like the blast of the desart, which sweeps perennially through a frightful solitude of its own making in the mind of the Gamester; the slowly quickening but ever quickening descent of appetite down which the Miser is propelled; the agony and cleaving oppression of grief; the ghost-like hauntings of shame; the incubus of revenge; the life-distemper of ambition; – these inward existences, and the visible and familiar occurrences of daily life in every town and village; the patient curiosity and contagious acclamations of the multitude in the streets of the city and within the walls of the theatre; a procession, or a rural dance; a hunting, or a horse-race; a flood, or a fire; rejoicing and ringing of bells for an unexpected gift of good fortune, or the coming of a foolish heir to his estate; – these demonstrate incontestibly that the passions of men (I mean, the soul of sensibility in the heart of man) – in all quarrels, in all contests, in all quests, in all delights, in all employments which are either sought by men or thrust upon them – do immeasurably transcend their objects. The true sorrow of humanity consists in this; – not that the mind of man fails; but that the course and demands of action and of life so rarely correspond with the dignity and intensity of human desires: and hence that, which is slow to languish, is too easily turned aside and abused. But – with the remembrance of what has been done, and in the face of the interminable evils which are threatened – a Spaniard can never have cause to complain of this, while a follower of the Tyrant remains in arms upon the Peninsula.

Here then they, with whom I *hope*, take their stand. There is a spiritual community binding together the living and the dead; the good, the brave, and the wise, of all ages. We would not be rejected from this community; and therefore do we hope. We look forward with erect mind, thinking and feeling: it is an obligation of duty: take away the sense of it, and the moral being would die within us. – Among the most illustrious of that fraternity, whose encouragement we participate, is an Englishman who sacrificed his life in devotion to a cause bearing a stronger likeness to this than any recorded in history. It is the elder Sidney – a deliverer and defender, whose name I have before uttered with reverence; who, treating of the war in the Netherlands against Philip the Second, thus writes: 'If her Majesty,' says he, 'were the fountain; I wold fear, considering what I daily find, that we shold wax dry. But she is but a means whom God useth. And I know not whether I am deceaved; but I am fully persuaded, that, if she shold withdraw herself, other springs wold rise to help this action. For, methinks, I see the great work indeed in hand against the abusers of the world; wherein it is no greater fault to have confidence in man's power, than it is too hastily to despair of God's work.' [55]

The pen, which I am guiding, has stopped in my hand; and I have scarcely power to proceed. – I will lay down one principle; and then shall contentedly withdraw from the sanctuary.

When wickedness acknowledges no limit but the extent of her power, and advances with aggravated impatience like a devouring fire; the only worthy or adequate opposition is – that of virtue submitting to no circumscription of her endeavours save that of her rights, and aspiring from the impulse of her own ethereal zeal. The Christian exhortation for the individual is here the precept for nations

– 'Be ye therefore perfect; even as your Father, which is in Heaven, is perfect.'[56]

Upon a future occasion (if what has been now said meets with attention) I shall point out the steps by which the practice of life may be lifted up towards these high precepts. I shall have to speak of the child as well as the man; for with the child, or the youth, may we begin with more hope: but I am not in despair even for the man; and chiefly from the inordinate evils of our time. There are (as I shall attempt to shew) tender and subtile ties by which these principles, that love to soar in the pure region, are connected with the ground-nest in which they were fostered and from which they take their flight.

The outermost and all-embracing circle of benevolence has inward concentric circles which, like those of the spider's web, are bound together by links, and rest upon each other; making one frame, and capable of one tremor; circles narrower and narrower, closer and closer, as they lie more near to the centre of self from which they proceeded, and which sustains the whole. The order of life does not require that the sublime and disinterested feelings should have to trust long to their own unassisted power. Nor would the attempt consist either with their dignity or their humility. They condescend, and they adopt: they know the time of their repose; and the qualities which are worthy of being admitted into their service – of being their inmates, their companions, or their substitutes. I shall strive to shew that these principles and movements of wisdom – so far from towering above the support of prudence, or rejecting the rules of experience, for the better conduct of those multifarious actions which are alike necessary to the attainment of ends good or bad – do instinctively prompt the sole prudence which cannot fail. The higher mode of being does not exclude, but necessarily includes, the lower; the intellectual does not exclude, but necessarily includes, the sentient; the sentient, the animal; and the animal, the vital – to its lowest degrees. Wisdom is the hidden root which thrusts forth the stalk of prudence; and these uniting feed and uphold 'the bright consummate flower'[57] – National Happiness – the end, the conspicuous crown, and ornament of the whole.

# From *The Convention of Cintra*

I have announced the feelings of those who hope: yet one word more to those who despond. And first; *he* stands upon a hideous precipice (and it will be the same with all who may succeed to him and his iron sceptre) – he who has outlawed himself from society by proclaiming, with word and act, that he acknowledges no mastery but power. This truth must be evident to all who breathe – from the dawn of childhood, till the last gleam of twilight is lost in the darkness of dotage. But take the tyrant as he is, in the plenitude of his supposed strength. The vast country of Germany, in spite of the rusty but too strong fetters of corrupt princedoms and degenerate nobility, – Germany – with its citizens, its peasants, and its philosophers – will not lie quiet under the weight of injuries which has been heaped upon it. There is a sleep, but no death, among the mountains of Switzerland. Florence, and Venice, and Genoa, and Rome, – have their own poignant recollections, and a majestic train of glory in past ages. The stir of emancipation may again be felt at the mouths as well as at the sources of the Rhine. Poland perhaps will not be insensible; Kosciusko [58] and his compeers may not have bled in vain. Nor is Hungarian loyalty to be overlooked. And, for Spain itself, the territory is wide: let it be overrun: the torrent will weaken as the water spreads. And, should all resistance disappear, be not daunted: extremes meet: and how often do hope and despair almost touch each other – though unconscious of their neighbourhood, because their faces are turned different ways! yet, in a moment, the one shall vanish; and the other begin a career in the fulness of her joy.

But we may turn from these thoughts: for the present juncture is most auspicious. Upon liberty, and upon liberty alone, can there be permanent dependence; but a temporary relief will be given by the share which Austria is about to take in the war. Now is the time for a great and decisive effort; and, if Britain does not avail herself of it, her disgrace will be indelible, and the loss infinite. If there be ground of hope in the crimes and errors of the enemy, he has furnished enough of both: but imbecility in his opponents (above all, the imbecility of the British) has hitherto preserved him from the natural consequences of his ignorance, his meanness of mind, his transports of infirm fancy, and his guilt. Let us hasten to redeem ourselves. The field is open for a commanding British military force to clear the Peninsula of the enemy, while the better half of his power is occupied with Austria. For the South of Spain, where the first effort of regeneration was made, is yet free. Saragossa (which, by a truly efficient British army, might have been relieved) has indeed fallen; but leaves little to regret; for consummate have been her fortitude and valour. The citizens and soldiers of Saragossa are to be envied: for they have completed the circle of their duty; they have done all that could be wished – all that could be prayed for. And, though the cowardly malice of the enemy gives too much reason to fear that their leader Palafox [59] (with the fate of Toussaint) will soon be among the dead, it is the high privilege of men who have performed what he has performed – that they cannot be missed; and, in moments of weakness only, can they be lamented: their actions represent them every where and for ever. Palafox has taken his place as parent and ancestor of innumerable heroes.

Oh! that the surviving chiefs of the Spanish people may prove worthy of their situation! With such materials, – their labour would be pleasant, and their success certain. But – though heads of a nation venerable for antiquity, and having good cause to preserve with reverence the institutions of their elder forefathers – they must not be indiscriminately afraid of new things. It is their duty to restore the good which has fallen into disuse; and also to create, and to adopt. Young scions of polity must be engrafted on the time-worn trunk: a new fortress must be reared upon the ancient and living rock of justice. Then would it be seen, while the superstructure stands inwardly immoveable, in how short a space of time the ivy and wild plant would climb up from the base, and clasp the naked walls; the storms, which could not shake, would weather-stain; and the edifice, in the day of its youth, would appear to be one with the rock upon which it was planted, and to grow out of it.

But let us look to ourselves. Our offences are unexpiated: and, wanting light, we want strength. With reference to this guilt and to this deficiency, and to my own humble efforts towards removing both, I shall conclude with the words of a man of disciplined spirit, who withdrew from the too busy world – not out of indifference to its welfare, or to forget its concerns – but retired for wider compass of eye-sight, that he might comprehend and see in just proportions and relations; knowing above all that he, who hath not first made himself master of the horizon of his own mind, must look beyond it only to be deceived. It is Petrarch who thus writes: 'Haec dicerem, et quicquid in rem praesentem et indignatio dolorque dictarent; nisi obtorpuisse animos, actumque de rebus nostris, crederem. Nempe, qui aliis iter rectum ostendere solebamus, nunc (quod exitio proximum est) coeci coecis ducibus per abrupta rapimur; alienoque circumvolvimur exemplo; quid velimus, nescii. Nam (ut coeptum exequar) totum hoc malum, seu nostrum proprium seu potius omnium gentium commune, IGNORATIO FINIS facit. Nesciunt inconsulti homines quid agant: ideo quicquid agunt, mox ut coeperint, vergit in nauseam. Hinc ille discursus sine termino; hinc, medio calle, discordiae; et, ante exitum, DAMNATA PRINCIPIA; et expleti nihil.' [60]

As an act of respect to the English reader – I shall add, to the same purpose, the words of our own Milton; who, contemplating our ancestors in his day, thus speaks of them and their errors: – 'Valiant, indeed, and prosperous to win a field; but, to know the end and reason of winning, injudicious and unwise. Hence did their victories prove as fruitless, as their losses dangerous; and left them still languishing under the same grievances that men suffer conquered. Which was indeed unlikely to go otherwise; unless men more than vulgar bred up in the knowledge of ancient and illustrious deeds, invincible against many and vain titles, impartial to friendships and relations, had conducted their affairs.' [61]

# Postscript (1835), Part I

[*Probably composed between 3 and 27 March 1835. First published 1835 in* Yarrow Revisited and Other Poems. *The version of the first section printed here is that in* Poetical Works *(1850), V, 215–63.*]

*The first section of the* Postscript *addresses the Poor Law Amendment Act of 1834, about which Wordsworth felt grave concern. This repressive Act attracted opposition from many other quarters; but it is good in any case to be reminded of the humanitarian side of Wordsworth's conservatism. Two sections are omitted here: the brief second section that favoured the ability of the working classes to invest savings in the industries in which they worked, and the final section, about the same length as the first, that dealt with the Government Commission on Church reform.*

In the present volume,[1] as in those that have preceded it, the reader will have found occasionally opinions expressed upon the course of public affairs, and feelings given vent to as national interests excited them. Since nothing, I trust, has been uttered but in the spirit of reflective patriotism, those notices are left to produce their own effect; but, among the many objects of general concern, and the changes going forward, which I have glanced at in verse, are some especially affecting the lower orders of society: in reference to these, I wish here to add a few words in plain prose.

Were I conscious of being able to do justice to those important topics, I might avail myself of the periodical press for offering anonymously my thoughts, such as they are, to the world; but I feel that, in procuring attention, they may derive some advantage, however small, from my name, in addition to that of being presented in a less fugitive shape. It is also not impossible that the state of mind which some of the foregoing poems[2] may have produced in the reader, will dispose him to receive more readily the impression which I desire to make, and to admit the conclusions I would establish.

I. The first thing that presses upon my attention is the Poor-Law Amendment Act. I am aware of the magnitude and complexity of the subject, and the unwearied attention which it has received from men of far wider experience than my own; yet I cannot forbear touching upon one point of it, and to this I will confine myself, though not insensible to the objection which may reasonably be brought against treating a portion of this, or any other, great scheme of civil polity separately from the whole. The point to which I wish to draw the reader's attention is, that *all* persons who cannot find employment, or procure wages sufficient to support the body in health and strength, are entitled to a maintenance by law.[3]

This dictate of humanity is acknowledged in the Report of the Commissioners: but is there not room for apprehension that some of the regulations of the new act have a tendency to render the principle nugatory by difficulties thrown in the way of applying it? If this be so, persons will not be wanting to show it, by examining the provisions of the act in detail, – an attempt which would be quite out of place here; but it will not, therefore, be deemed unbecoming in one who fears that the prudence of the head may, in framing some of those provisions, have supplanted the wisdom of the heart, to enforce a principle which cannot be violated without infringing upon one of the most precious rights of the English people, and opposing one of the most sacred claims of civilised humanity.

There can be no greater error, in this department of legislation, than the belief that this principle does by necessity operate for the degradation of those who claim, or are so circumstanced as to make it likely they may claim, through laws founded upon it, relief or assistance. The direct contrary is the truth: it may be unanswerably maintained that its tendency is to raise, not to depress; by stamping a value upon life, which can belong to it only where the laws have placed men who are willing to work, and yet cannot find employment, above the necessity of looking for protection against hunger and other natural evils, either to individual and casual charity, to despair and death, or to the breach of law by theft or violence.

And here, as in the Report of the Commissioners, the fundamental principle has been recognised, I am not at issue with them any farther than I am compelled to believe that their 'remedial measures'[4] obstruct the application of it more than the interests of society require.

And, calling to mind the doctrines of political economy which are now prevalent, I cannot forbear to enforce the justice of the principle, and to insist upon its salutary operation.

And first for its justice: If self-preservation be the first law of our nature, would not every one in a state of nature be morally justified in taking to himself that which is indispensable to such preservation, where, by so doing, he would not rob another of that which might be equally indispensable to *his* preservation? And if the value of life be regarded in a right point of view, may it not be questioned whether this right of preserving life, at any expense short of endangering the life of another, does not survive man's entering into the social state; whether this right can be surrendered or forfeited, except when it opposes the divine law, upon any supposition of a social compact, or of any convention for the protection of mere rights of property?

But, if it be not safe to touch the abstract question of man's right in a social state to help himself even in the last extremity, may we not still contend for the duty of a christian government, standing *in loco parentis*[5] towards all its subjects, to make such effectual provision, that no one shall be in danger of perishing either through the neglect or harshness of its legislation? Or, waiving this, is it not indisputable that the claim of the state to the allegiance, involves the protection, of the subject? And, as all rights in one party impose a correlative duty upon another, it follows that the right of the state to require the services of its members, even to the jeoparding of their lives in the common defence, establishes a right in the people (not to be gainsaid by utilitarians and economists) to public support when, from any cause, they may be unable to support themselves.

Let us now consider the salutary and benign operation of this principle. Here we must have recourse to elementary feelings of human nature, and to truths which from their very obviousness are apt to be slighted, till they are forced upon our notice by our own sufferings or those of others. In the Paradise Lost, Milton represents Adam, after the Fall, as exclaiming, in the anguish of his soul –

> 'Did I request Thee, Maker, from my clay
> To mould me man; did I solicit Thee
> From darkness to promote me?
> .     .     .     .     .     .     My will
> Concurred not to my being.' [6]

Under how many various pressures of misery have men been driven thus, in a strain touching upon impiety, to expostulate with the Creator! and under few so afflictive as when the source and origin of earthly existence have been brought back to the mind by its impending close in the pangs of destitution. But as long as, in our legislation, due weight shall be given to this principle, no man will be forced to bewail the gift of life in hopeless want of the necessaries of life.

Englishmen have, therefore, by the progress of civilisation among them, been placed in circumstances more favourable to piety and resignation to the divine will, than the inhabitants of other countries, where a like provision has not been established. And as Providence, in this care of our countrymen, acts through a human medium, the objects of that care must, in like manner, be more inclined towards a grateful love of their fellow-men. Thus, also, do stronger ties attach the people to their country, whether while they tread its soil, or, at a distance, think of their native land as an indulgent parent, to whose arms, even they who have been imprudent and undeserving may, like the prodigal son,[7] betake themselves, without fear of being rejected.

Such is the view of the case that would first present itself to a reflective mind; and it is in vain to show, by appeals to experience, in contrast with this view, that provisions founded upon the principle have promoted profaneness of life, and dispositions the reverse of philanthropic, by spreading idleness, selfishness, and rapacity: for these evils have arisen, not as an inevitable consequence of the principle, but for want of judgment in framing laws based upon it; and, above all, from faults in the mode of administering the law. The mischief that has grown to such a height from granting relief in cases where proper vigilance would have shown that it was not required, or in bestowing it in undue measure, will be urged by no truly enlightened statesman, as a sufficient reason for banishing the principle itself from legislation.

Let us recur to the miserable states of consciousness that it precludes.

There is a story told, by a traveller in Spain, of a female who, by a sudden shock of domestic calamity, was driven out of her senses, and ever after looked up incessantly to the sky, feeling that her fellow-creatures could do nothing for her relief. Can there be Englishmen who, with a good end in view, would, upon system, expose their brother Englishmen to a like necessity of looking upwards only; or downwards to the earth, after it shall contain no spot where the destitute can demand, by civil right, what by right of nature they are entitled to?

Suppose the objects of our sympathy not sunk into this blank despair, but wandering about as strangers in streets and ways, with the hope of succour from casual charity; what have we gained by such a change of scene? Woful is the condition of the famished Northern Indian, dependent, among winter snows, upon the chance-passage of a herd of deer, from which one, if brought down by his rifle-gun, may be made the means of keeping him and his companions alive.[8] As miserable is that of some savage Islander, who, when the land has ceased to afford him sustenance, watches for food which the waves may cast up, or in vain endeavours to extract it from the inexplorable deep. But neither of these is in a state of wretchedness comparable to that, which is so often endured in civilised society: multitudes, in all ages, have known it, of whom may be said: –

> 'Homeless, near a thousand homes they stood,
> And near a thousand tables pined, and wanted food.'[9]

Justly might I be accused of wasting time in an uncalled-for attempt to excite the feelings of the reader, if systems of political economy, widely spread, did not impugn the principle, and if the safeguards against such extremities were left unimpaired. It is broadly asserted by many, that every man who endeavours to find work, *may* find it: were this assertion capable of being verified, there still would remain a question, what kind of work, and how far may the labourer be fit for it? For if sedentary work is to be exchanged for standing; and some light and nice exercise of the fingers, to which an artisan has been accustomed all his life, for severe labour of the arms; the best efforts would turn to little account, and occasion would be given for the unthinking and the unfeeling unwarrantably to reproach those who are put upon such employment, as idle, froward, and unworthy of relief, either by law or in any other way! Were this statement correct, there would indeed be an end of the argument, the principle here maintained would be superseded. But, alas! it is far otherwise. That principle, applicable to the benefit of all countries, is indispensable for England, upon whose coast families are perpetually deprived of their support by shipwreck, and where large masses of men are so liable to be thrown out of their ordinary means of gaining bread, by changes in commercial intercourse, subject mainly or solely to the will of foreign powers; by new discoveries in arts and manufactures; and by reckless laws, in conformity with theories of political economy, which, whether right or wrong in the abstract, have proved a scourge to tens of thousands, by the abruptness with which they have been carried into practice.

But it is urged, – refuse altogether compulsory relief to the able-bodied, and the number of those who stand in need of relief will steadily diminish through a conviction of an absolute necessity for greater forethought, and more prudent care of a man's earnings. Undoubtedly it would, but so also would it, and in a much greater degree, if the legislative provisions were retained, and parochial relief administered under the care of the upper classes, as it ought to be. For it has been invariably found, that wherever the funds have been raised and applied under the superintendence of gentlemen and substantial proprietors, acting in vestries, and as overseers, pauperism has diminished accordingly. Proper care in that quarter would effectually check what is felt in some districts to be one of the worst evils in the poor law system, viz. the readiness of small and needy proprietors to join in imposing rates that seemingly subject them to great hardships, while, in fact, this is done with a mutual understanding, that the relief each is ready to bestow upon his still poorer neighbours will be granted to himself, or his relatives, should it hereafter be applied for.

But let us look to inner sentiments of a nobler quality, in order to know what we have to build upon. Affecting proofs occur in every one's experience, who is acquainted with the unfortunate and the indigent, of their unwillingness to derive their subsistence from aught but their own funds or labour, or to be indebted to parochial assistance for the attainment of any object, however dear to them. A case was reported, the other day, from a coroner's inquest, of a pair [10] who, through the space of four years, had carried about their dead infant from house to house, and from lodging to lodging, as their necessities drove them, rather than ask the parish to bear the expense of its interment: – the poor creatures lived in the hope of one day being able to bury their child at their own cost. It must have been heart-rending to see and hear the mother, who had been called upon to account for the state in which the body was found, make this deposition. By some, judging coldly, if not harshly, this conduct might be imputed to an unwarrantable pride, as she and her husband had, it is true, been once in prosperity. But examples, where the spirit of independence works with equal strength, though not with like miserable accompaniments, are frequently to be found even yet among the humblest peasantry and mechanics. There is not, then, sufficient cause for doubting that a like sense of honour may be revived among the people, and their ancient habits of independence restored, wihout resorting to those severities which the new Poor Law Act has introduced.

But even if the surfaces of things only are to be examined, we have a right to expect that lawgivers should take into account the various tempers and dispositions of mankind: while some are led, by the existence of a legislative provision, into idleness and extravagance, the economical virtues might be cherished in others by the knowledge that, if all their efforts fail, they have in the Poor Laws a 'refuge from the storm and a shadow from the heat'. [11] Despondency and distraction are no friends to prudence: the springs of industry will relax, if cheerfulness be destroyed by anxiety; without hope men become reckless, and have a sullen pride in adding to the heap of their own wretchedness. He who feels that he is abandoned by his fellow-men will be almost irresistibly driven to care little for himself; will lose his self-respect accordingly, and with that loss what remains to him of virtue?

With all due deference to the particular experience, and general intelligence of the individuals who framed the Act, and of those who in and out of parliament have approved of and supported it; it may be said, that it proceeds too much upon the presumption that it is a labouring man's own fault if he be not, as the phrase is, beforehand with the world. [12] But the most prudent are liable to be thrown back by sickness, cutting them off from labour, and causing to them expense: and who but has observed how distress creeps upon multitudes without misconduct of their own; and merely from a gradual fall in the price of labour, without a correspondent one in the price of provisions; so that men who may have ventured upon the marriage state with a fair prospect of maintaining their families in comfort and happiness, see them reduced to a pittance which no effort of theirs can increase? Let it be remembered, also, that there are thousands with whom vicious habits of expense are not the cause why they do not store up their gains; but they are generous and kind-hearted, and ready to help their kindred and friends; moreover, they have a faith in Providence that those who have been prompt to assist others, will not be left destitute, should they themselves come to need. By acting from these blended feelings, numbers have rendered themselves incapable of standing up against a sudden reverse. Nevertheless, these men, in common with all who have the misfortune to be in want, if many theorists had their wish, would be thrown upon one or other of those three sharp points of condition before adverted to, from which the intervention of law has hitherto saved them.

All that has been said tends to show how the principle contended for makes the gift of life more valuable, and has, it may be hoped, led to the conclusion that its legitimate operation is to make men worthier of that gift: in other words, not to degrade but to exalt human nature. But the subject must not be dismissed without adverting to the indirect influence of the same principle upon the moral sentiments of a people among whom it is embodied in law. In our criminal jurisprudence there is a maxim, deservedly eulogised, that it is better that ten guilty persons should escape, than that one innocent man should suffer;[13] so, also, might it be maintained, with regard to the Poor Laws, that it is better for the interests of humanity among the people at large, that ten undeserving should partake of the funds provided, than that one morally good man, through want of relief, should either have his principles corrupted, or his energies destroyed; than that such a one should either be driven to do wrong, or be cast to the earth in utter hopelessness. In France, the English maxim of criminal jurisprudence is reversed; there, it is deemed better that ten innocent men should suffer, than one guilty escape: in France, there is no universal provision for the poor; and we may judge of the small value set upon human life in the metropolis of that country, by merely noticing the disrespect with which, after death, the body is treated, not by the thoughtless vulgar, but in schools of anatomy, presided over by men allowed to be, in their own art and in physical science, among the most enlightened in the world. In the East, where countries are overrun with population as with a weed, infinitely more respect is shown to the remains of the deceased; and what a bitter mockery is it, that this insensibility should be found where civil polity is so busy in minor regulations, and ostentatiously careful to gratify the luxurious propensities, whether social or intellectual, of the multitude! Irreligion is, no doubt, much concerned with this offensive disrespect, shown to the bodies of the dead in France; but it is mainly attributable to the state in which so many of the living are left by the absence of compulsory provision for the indigent so humanely established by the law of England.

Sights of abject misery, perpetually recurring, harden the heart of the community. In the perusal of history, and of works of fiction, we are not, indeed, unwilling to have our commiseration excited by such objects of distress as they present to us; but, in the concerns of real life, men know that such emotions are not given to be indulged for their own sakes: there, the conscience declares to them that sympathy must be followed by action; and if there exist a previous conviction that the power to relieve is utterly inadequate to the demand, the eye shrinks from communication with wretchedness, and pity and compassion languish, like any other qualities that are deprived of their natural aliment. Let these considerations be duly weighed by those who trust to the hope that an increase of private charity, with all its advantages of superior discrimination, would more than compensate for the abandonment of those principles, the wisdom of which has been here insisted upon. How discouraging, also, would be the sense of injustice, which could not fail to arise in the minds of the well-disposed, if the burden of supporting the poor, a burden of which the selfish have hitherto by compulsion borne a share, should now, or hereafter, be thrown exclusively upon the benevolent.

By having put an end to the Slave Trade and Slavery,[14] the British people are exalted in the scale of humanity; and they cannot but feel so, if they look into themselves, and duly consider their relation to God and their fellow-creatures. That was a noble advance; but a retrograde movement will assuredly be made, if ever the principle, which has been here defended, should be either avowedly abandoned or but ostensibly retained.

But after all, there may be little reason to apprehend permanent injury from any experiment that may be tried. On the one side will be human nature rising up in her own defence, and on the other prudential selfishness acting to the same purpose, from a conviction that, without a compulsory provision for the exigencies of the labouring multitude, that degree of ability to regulate the price of labour, which is indispensable for the reasonable interest of arts and manufactures, cannot, in Great Britain, be upheld.

# SECTION IV

## *Literature*

# [The Sublime and the Beautiful]

⭑~⭑~⭑

[*Probably composed between September 1811 and late November 1812 (probably close to the later date). First published 1974. Most of the punctuation has been added.*]

*This fragment was most likely originally intended as part of what eventually became* A Guide Through the District of the Lakes (1835) – *printed above as* Description of the Scenery of the Lakes – *although this essay presents a wider philosophical reference than the* Guide. *It is not known how much of the beginning is missing, but it is thought to be little. There is also a lacuna, thought to have been a quarto sheet filled on both sides, about three-quarters of the way through (see note 6).*

. . . amongst them. It is not likely that a person so situated, provided his imagination be exercised by other intercourse, as it ought to be, will become, by any continuance of familiarity, insensible to sublime impressions from the scenes around him. Nay, it is certain that his conceptions of the sublime, far from being dulled or narrowed by commonness or frequency, will be rendered more lively and comprehensive by more accurate observation and by encreasing knowledge. Yet, tho' this effect will take place with respect to grandeur, it will be much more strikingly felt in the influences of beauty. Neither the immediate nor final cause of this need here be examined; yet we may observe that, though it is impossible that a mind can be in a healthy state that is not frequently and strongly moved both by sublimity and beauty, it is more dependent for its daily well-being upon the love and gentleness which accompany the one, than upon the exaltation or awe which are created by the other. – Hence, as we advance in life, we can escape upon the invitation of our more placid and gentle nature from those obtrusive qualities in an object sublime in its general character; which qualities, at an earlier age, precluded imperiously the perception of beauty which that object if contemplated under another relation would have been capable of imparting. I need not observe to persons at all conversant in these speculations that I take for granted that the same object may be both sublime and beautiful; or, speaking more accurately, that it may have the power of affecting us both with the sense of beauty and the sense of sublimity; tho' (as for such Readers I need not add) the mind cannot be affected by both these sensations at the same time, for they are not only different from, but opposite to, each other. Now a Person unfamiliar with the appearances of a Mountainous Country is, with respect to its more conspicuous sublime features, in a [?situation] resembling that of a Man of mature years when he looked upon such objects with the eye of childhood or youth. There appears to be something ungracious in this observation; yet it is nevertheless true, and the fact is mentioned both for its connection with the present work and for the importance of the general truth. Sensations of beauty and sublimity impress us very early in life; nor is it easy to determine which have precedence in point of time, and to which the sensibility of the mind in its natural constitution is more alive. But it may be confidently affirmed that, where the beautiful and the sublime co-exist in the same object, if that object be new to us, the sublime always precedes the beautiful in making us conscious of its presence – but all this may be both tedious and uninstructive to the Reader, as I have not explained what I mean by either of the words sublime or beautiful; nor is this the place to enter into a general disquisition upon the subject, or to attempt to clear away the errors by which it has been clouded. – But as I am persuaded that it is of infinite importance to the noblest feelings of the Mind and to its very highest powers that the forms of Nature should be accurately contemplated, and, if described, described in language that shall prove that we understand the several grand constitutional laws under which it has been ordained that these objects should everlastingly affect the mind, I shall deem myself justified in calling the Reader, upon the present humble occasion, to attend to a few words which shall be said upon two of these principal laws: the law of sublimity and that of beauty. These shall be considered so far at least as they may be collected from the objects amongst which we are about to enter, viz., those of a mountainous region – and to begin with the sublime as it exists in such landscape.

Let me then invite the Reader to turn his eyes with me towards that cluster of Mountains at the Head of Windermere; it is probable that they will settle ere long upon the Pikes of Langdale and the black precipice contiguous to them. – If these objects be so distant that, while we look at them, they are only thought of as the crown of a comprehensive Landscape; if our minds be not perverted by false theories, unless those mountains be seen under some accidents of nature, we shall receive from them a grand impression, and nothing more. But if they be looked at from a point which has brought us so near that the mountain is almost the sole object before our eyes, yet not so near but that the whole of it is visible, we shall be impressed with a sensation of sublimity. – And if this is analyzed, the body of this sensation would be found to resolve itself into three component parts: a sense of individual form or forms; a sense of duration; and a sense of power. The whole complex impression is made up of these elementary parts, and the effect depends upon their co-existence. For, if any one of them were abstracted, the others would be deprived of their power to affect.

I first enumerated individuality of form; this individual form was then invested with qualities and powers, ending with duration. Duration is evidently an element of the sublime; but think of it without reference to individual form, and we shall perceive that it has no power to affect the mind. Cast your eye, for example, upon any commonplace ridge or eminence that cannot be separated, without some effort of the mind, from the general mass of the planet; you may be persuaded, nay, convinced, that it has borne that shape as long as or longer than Cader Idris, or Snowdon, or the Pikes of Langdale that are before us; and the mind is wholly unmoved by the thought; and the only way in which such an object can affect us, contemplated under the notion of duration, is when the faint sense which we have of its individuality is lost in the general sense of duration belonging to the Earth itself. Prominent individual form must, therefore, be conjoined with duration, in order that Objects of this kind may impress a sense of sublimity; and, in the works of Man, this conjunction is, for obvious reasons, of itself sufficient for the purpose. But in works of Nature it is not so: with these must be combined impressions of power, to a sympathy with and a participation of which the mind must be elevated — or to a dread and awe of which, as existing out of itself, it must be subdued. A mountain being a stationary object is enabled to effect this in connection with duration and individual form, by the sense of motion which in the mind accompanies the lines by which the Mountain itself is shaped out. These lines may either be abrupt and precipitous, by which danger and sudden change is expressed; or they may flow into each other like the waves of the sea, and, by involving in such image a feeling of self-propagation infinitely continuous and without cognizable beginning, these lines may thus convey to the Mind sensations not less sublime than those which were excited by their opposites, the abrupt and the precipitous. And, to compleat this sense of power expressed by these permanent objects, add the torrents which take their rise within its bosom, and roll foaming down its sides; the clouds which it attracts; the stature with which it appears to reach the sky; [1] the storms with which it arms itself; the triumphant ostentation with which its snows defy the sun, &c.

Thus has been given an analysis of the attributes or qualities the co-existence of which gives to a Mountain the power of affecting the mind with a sensation of sublimity. The capability of perceiving these qualities, and the degree in which they are perceived, will of course depend upon the state or condition of the mind, with respect to habits, knowledge, and powers, which is brought within the reach of their influence. It is to be remembered that I have been speaking of a visible object; and it might seem that when I required duration to be combined with individual form, more was required than was necessary; for a native of a mountainous country, looking back upon his childhood, will remember how frequently he has been impressed by a sensation of sublimity from a precipice, in which awe or personal apprehension were the predominant feelings of his mind and from which the milder influence of duration seemed to be excluded. And it is true that the relative proportions in which we are affected by the qualities of these objects are different at different periods of our lives; yet there cannot be a doubt that upon all ages they act conjointly. The precipitous form of an individual cloud which a Child has been taught by tales and pictures to think of as sufficiently solid to support a substantial body and upon which he finds it easy to conceive himself as seated in imagination, and thus to invest it with some portion of the terror which belongs to the precipice, would affect him very languidly, and surely much more from the knowledge which he has of its evanescence than from the less degree in which it excites in him feelings of dread. Familiarity with these objects tends very much to mitigate and to destroy the power which they have to produce the sensation of sublimity as dependent upon personal fear or upon wonder; a comprehensive awe takes the place of the one, and a religious admiration of the other, and the condition of the mind is exalted accordingly. – Yet it cannot be doubted that a Child or an unpracticed person whose mind is possessed by the sight of a lofty precipice, with its attire of hanging rocks and starting trees, &c., has been visited by a sense of sublimity, if personal fear and surprize or wonder have not been carried beyond certain bounds. For whatever suspends the comparing power of the mind and possesses it with a feeling or image of intense unity, without a conscious contemplation of parts, has produced that state of the mind which is the consummation of the sublime. – But if personal fear be strained beyond a certain point, this sensation is destroyed, for there are two ideas that divide and distract the attention of the Spectator with an accompanying repulsion or a wish in the soul [that] they should be divided: the object exciting the fear and the subject in which it is excited. And this leads me to a remark which will remove the main difficulties of this investigation. Power awakens the sublime either when it rouses us to a sympathetic energy and calls upon the mind to grasp at something towards which it can make approaches but which it is incapable of attaining – yet so that it participates the force which is acting upon it; or, 2dly, by producing a humiliation or prostration of the mind before some external agency which it presumes not to make an effort to participate, but is absorbed in the contemplation of the might in the external power, and, as far as it has any consciousness of itself, its grandeur subsists in the naked fact of being conscious of external Power at once awful and immeasurable; so that in both cases the head and the front [2] of the sensation is intense unity. But if that Power which is exalted above our sympathy impresses the mind with personal fear, so as the sensation becomes more lively than the impression or thought of the exciting cause, then self-consideration and all its accompanying littleness takes place of [3] the sublime, and wholly excludes it. Or if the object contemplated be of a spiritual nature, as that of the Supreme Being, for instance (though few minds, I will hope, are so far degraded that with reference to the Deity they can be affected by sensations of personal fear, such as a precipice, a conflagration, a torrent, or a shipwreck might excite), yet it may be confidently affirmed that no sublimity can be raised by the contemplation of such power when it presses upon us with pain and individual fear to a degree which takes precedence in our thoughts [over] the power itself. For connect with such sensations the notion of infinity, or any other ideas of a sublime nature which different religious sects have connected with it: the feeling of self being still predominant, the condition of the mind would be mean and abject. – Accordingly Belial, the most sensual spirit of the fallen Angels, tho' speaking of himself and his Companions as full of pain, yet adds:

Who would lose those thoughts
Which wander thro' Eternity? [4]

The thoughts are not chained down by anguish, but they are free and tolerate neither limit nor circumscription. Though by the opinions of many religious sects, not less than by many other examples, it is lamentably shewn how industrious Man is in perverting and degrading his mind, yet such is its inherent dignity that, like that of the fallen Spirit as exhibited by the Philosophic and religious Poet, he is perpetually thwarted and baffled and rescued in his own despite.

But to return: Whence comes it then that that external power, to a union or communion with which we feel that we can make no approximation while it produces humiliation and submission, reverence or adoration, and all those sensations which may be denominated passive, does nevertheless place the mind in a state that is truly sublime? As I have said before, this is done by the notion or image of intense unity, with which the Soul is occupied or possessed. – But how is this produced or supported, and, when it remits, and the mind is distinctly conscious of his own being and existence, whence comes it that it willingly and naturally relapses into the same state? The cause of this is either that our physical nature has only to a certain degree been endangered, or that our moral Nature has not in the least degree been violated. – The point beyond which apprehensions for our physical nature consistent with sublimity may be carried, has been ascertained; and, with respect to power acting upon our moral or spiritual nature, by awakening energy either that would resist or that hopes to participate, the sublime is called forth. But if the Power contemplated be of that kind which neither admits of the notion of resistance or participation, then it may be confidently said that, unless the apprehensions which it excites terminate in repose, there can be no sublimity, and that this sense of repose is the result of reason and the moral law. Could this be abstracted and the reliance upon it taken away, no species of Power that was absolute over the mind could beget a sublime sensation; but, on the contrary, it could never be thought of without fear and degradation.

I have been seduced to treat the subject more generally than I had at first proposed; if I have been so fortunate as to make myself understood, what has been said will be forgiven. Let us now contract the speculation, and confine it to the sublime as it exists in a mountainous Country, and to the manner in which it makes itself felt. I enumerated the qualities which must be perceived in a Mountain before a sense of sublimity can be received from it. Individuality of form is the primary requisite; and the form must be of that character that deeply impresses the sense of power. And power produces the sublime either as it is thought of as a thing to be dreaded, to be resisted, or that can be participated. To what degree consistent with sublimity power may be dreaded has been ascertained; but as power, contemplated as something to be opposed or resisted, implies a twofold agency of which the mind is conscious, this state seems to be irreconcilable to what has been said concerning the consummation of sublimity, which, as has been determined, exists in the extinction of the comparing power of the mind, and in intense unity. But the fact is, there is no sublimity excited by the contemplation of power thought of as a thing to be resisted and which the moral law enjoins us to resist, saving only as far as the mind, either by glances or continuously, conceives that that power may be overcome or rendered evanescent, and as far as it feels itself tending towards the unity that exists in security or absolute triumph. – (When power is thought of under a mode which we can and do participate, the sublime sensation consists in a manifest approximation towards absolute unity.) If the resistance contemplated be of a passive nature (such, for example, as the Rock in the middle of the fall of the Rhine at Chafhausen, [5] as opposed for countless ages to that mighty mass of Waters), there are undoubtedly here before us two distinct images and thoughts; and there is a most complex instrumentality acting upon the senses, such as the roar of the Water, the fury of the foam, &c.; and an instrumentality still more comprehensive, furnished by the imagination, and drawn from the length of the River's course, the Mountains from which it rises, the various countries thro' which it flows, and the distant Seas in which its waters are lost. These images and thoughts will, in such a place, be present to the mind, either personally or by representative abstractions more or less vivid. – Yet to return to the rock and the Waterfall: these objects will be found to have exalted the mind to the highest state of sublimity when they are thought of in that state of opposition and yet reconcilement, analogous to parallel lines in mathematics, which, being infinitely prolonged, can never come nearer to each other; and hence, tho' the images and feelings above enumerated have exerted a preparative influence upon the mind, the absolute crown of the impression is infinity, which is a modification of unity.

Having had the image of a mighty River before us, I cannot but, in connection with it, observe that the main source of all the difficulties and errors which have attended these disquisitions is that the attention of those who have been engaged in them has been primarily and chiefly fixed upon external objects and their powers, qualities, and properties, and not upon the mind itself, and the laws by which it is acted upon. Hence the endless disputes about the characters of objects, and the absolute denial on the part of many that sublimity or beauty exists. To talk of an object as being sublime or beautiful in itself, without references to some subject by whom that sublimity or beauty is perceived, is absurd; nor is it of the slightest importance to mankind whether there be any object with which their minds are conversant that Men would universally agree (after having ascertained that the words were used in the same sense) to denominate sublime or beautiful. It is enough that there are, both in moral qualities and in the forms of the external universe, such qualities and powers as have affected Men, in different states of civilization and without communication with each other, with similar sensations either of the sublime or beautiful. The true province of the philosopher is not to grope about in the external world and, when he has perceived or detected in an object such or such a quality or power, to set himself to the task of persuading the world that such is a sublime or beautiful object, but to look into his own mind and determine the law by which he is affected. – He will then find that the same object has power to affect him in various manners at different times; so that, ludicrous as it . . .⁶ to power as governed some where by the intelligence of law and reason, and lastly to the transcendent sympathies which have been vouchsafed to her with the calmness of eternity.

Thus, then, is apparent how various are the *means* by which we are conducted to the same end – the elevation of our being; and the practical influences [7] to be drawn from this are most important, but I shall consider them only with reference to the forms of nature which have occasioned this disquisition.

I have already given a faint sketch of the manner in which a familiarity with these objects acts upon the minds of men of cultivated imagination. I will now suppose a person of mature age to be introduced amongst them for the first time. I will not imagine him to be a man particularly conversant with pictures, nor an enthusiast in poetry; but he shall be modest and unpresumptuous, one who has not been insensible to impressions of grandeur from the universal or less local appearance and forms of nature (such as the sky, the clouds, the heavenly bodies, rivers, trees, and perhaps the Ocean), and coming hither desirous to have his knowledge increased and the means of exalting himself in thought and feeling multiplied and extended. I can easily conceive that such a man, in his first intercourse with these objects, might be grievously disappointed, and, if that intercourse should be short, might depart without being raised from that depression which such disappointment might reasonably cause. Such would have been the condition of the most eminent of our English Painters if his visits to the sublime pictures in the Vatican and The Cistine Chapel had not been repeated till the sense of strangeness had worn off, till the twilight of novelty began to dispel, and he was made conscious of the mighty difference between seeing and perceiving. I have heard of a Lady, a native of the Orcades (which naked solitudes from her birth she had never quitted), whose imagination, endeavouring to compleat whatever had been left imperfect in pictures and books, had feasted in representing to itself the forms of trees. With delight did she look forward to the day when it would be permitted to her to behold the reality, and to learn by experience how far its grandeur or beauty surpassed the conceptions which she had formed – but sad and heavy was her disappointment when this wish was satisfied. A journey to a fertile Vale in the South of Scotland gave her an opportunity of seeing some of the finest trees in the

Island; but she beheld them without pleasure or emotion, and complained that, compared with the grandeur of the living and ever-varying ocean in all the changes and appearances and powers of which she was thoroughly versed – that a tree or a wood were objects insipid and lifeless. [8] – Something of a like disappointment, or perhaps a kind of blank and stupid wonder (one of the most oppressive of sensations), might be felt by one who had passed his life in the plains of Lincolnshire and should be suddenly transported to the recesses of Borrowdale or Glencoe. And if this feeling should not burthen his mind, innumerable are the impressions which may exclude him from a communication with the sublime in the midst of objects eminently capable of exciting that feeling: he may be depressed by the image of barrenness; or the chaotic appearance of crags heaped together, or seemingly ready to fall upon each other, may excite in him sensations as uncomfortable as those with which he would look upon an edifice that the Builder had left unfinished; and many of the forms before his eyes, by associations of outward likeness, merely may recal to his mind mean or undignified works of art; and every where might he be haunted or disturbed by a sense of incongruity, either light and trivial or resembling in kind that intermixture of the terrible and the ludicrous which dramatists who understand the constitution of the human mind have not unfrequently represented when they introduce a character disturbed by an agency supernatural or horrible to a degree beyond what the mind is prepared to expect from the ordinary course of human calamities or afflictions. So that it appears that even those impressions that do most easily make their way to the human mind, such as I deem those of the sublime to be, cannot be received from an object however eminently qualified to impart them, without a preparatory intercourse with that object or with others of the same kind.

But impediments arising merely from novelty or inexperience in a well disposed mind disappear gradually and assuredly. Yet, though it will not be long before the Stranger will become conscious of the sublime where the power to raise it eminently exists, yet, if I may judge from my own experience, it is only very slowly that the mind is opened out to a perception of images of Beauty co-existing in the same object with those of sublimity. As I have explained at large what I mean by the word sublimity, I might with propriety here proceed to treat of beauty, and to explain in what manner I conceive the mind to be affected when it has a sense of the beautiful. But I cannot pass from the sublime without guarding the ingenuous reader against those caprices of vanity and presumption derived from false teachers in the philosophy of the fine arts and of taste, which Painters, connoiseurs, and amateurs are perpetually interposing between the light of nature and their own minds. Powerful indeed must be the spells by which such an eclipse is to be removed; but nothing is wanting, save humility, modesty, diffidence, and an habitual, kindly, and confident communion with Nature, to prevent such a darkness from ever being superinduced. 'Oh,' says one of these tutored spectators, 'what a scene should we have before us here upon the shores of Windermere, if we could but strike out those pikes of Langdale by which it is terminated; they are so intensely *picturesque* that their presence excludes from the mind all sense of the sublime.'[9] Extravagant as such an ejaculation is, it has been heard from the mouths of Persons who pass for intelligent men of cultivated mind.

# Advertisement to Lyrical Ballads (1798)

~~~~~~~~~~

[*Composed 30 April – 13 September 1798. First published 1798.*]

*Much of this simple introduction to the first edition of* Lyrical Ballads
*(1798) was used in the composition of the more famous Preface that followed
in the edition of 1800.*

It is the honourable characteristic of Poetry that its materials are to be
found in every subject which can interest the human mind. The
evidence of this fact is to be sought, not in the writings of Critics, but
in those of Poets themselves.

The majority of the following poems are to be considered as
experiments. They were written chiefly with a view to ascertain
how far the language of conversation in the middle and lower classes
of society is adapted to the purposes of poetic pleasure. Readers
accustomed to the gaudiness and inane phraseology of many modern
writers, if they persist in reading this book to its conclusion, will
perhaps frequently have to struggle with feelings of strangeness and
aukwardness: they will look round for poetry, and will be induced to
enquire by what species of courtesy these attempts can be permitted
to assume that title. It is desirable that such readers, for their own
sakes, should not suffer the solitary word Poetry, a word of very
disputed meaning, to stand in the way of their gratification; but that,
while they are perusing this book, they should ask themselves if it

contains a natural delineation of human passions, human characters, and human incidents; and if the answer be favorable to the author's wishes, that they should consent to be pleased in spite of that most dreadful enemy to our pleasures, our own pre-established codes of decision.

Readers of superior judgment may disapprove of the style in which many of these pieces are executed; it must be expected that many lines and phrases will not exactly suit their taste. It will perhaps appear to them, that wishing to avoid the prevalent fault of the day, the author has sometimes descended too low, and that many of his expressions are too familiar, and not of sufficient dignity. It is apprehended, that the more conversant the reader is with our elder writers, and with those in modern times who have been the most successful in painting manners and passions, the fewer complaints of this kind will he have to make.

An accurate taste in poetry, and in all the other arts, Sir Joshua Reynolds has observed, is an acquired talent, which can only be produced by severe thought, and a long continued intercourse with the best models of composition.[1] This is mentioned not with so ridiculous a purpose as to prevent the most inexperienced reader from judging for himself; but merely to temper the rashness of decision, and to suggest that if poetry be a subject on which much time has not been bestowed, the judgment may be erroneous, and that in many cases it necessarily will be so.

The tale of Goody Blake and Harry Gill is founded on a well-authenticated fact[2] which happened in Warwickshire. Of the other poems in the collection, it may be proper to say that they are either absolute inventions of the author, or facts which took place within his personal observation or that of his friends. The poem of the Thorn, as the reader will soon discover, is not supposed to be spoken in the author's own person: the character of the loquacious narrator will sufficiently shew itself in the course of the story. The Rime of the Ancyent Marinere[3] was professedly written in imitation of the *style*, as well as of the spirit of the elder poets; but with a few exceptions, the Author believes that the language adopted in it has been equally intelligible for these three last centuries. The lines entitled Expostulation and Reply, and those which follow, arose out of conversation with a friend [4] who was somewhat unreasonably attached to modern books of moral philosophy.

# Preface to Lyrical Ballads and Appendix (1850)

꙳꙳꙳

[*Preface (1800) composed between 29 June and 27 September 1800; first published 1800. In 1802 additions to the text and a new appendix increased the length of the 1800 version by more than half; they were composed perhaps early 1802 (by 6 April 1802) and were first published 1802. Substantial modifications were made by Wordsworth in 1836. The version printed below appeared in* The Poetical Works *(1850), V, 157–95.*]

*This preface and its appendix are the best-known of Wordworth's prose writings and together constitute a major document in the history of literary theory. Wordsworth clearly considers himself to be operating in the central tradition, subscribing by name to Aristotle's mimetic belief that poetry's 'object is truth, not individual and local, but general, and operative'. Wordsworth's more particular debts are not so easily determined, for there are few ideas, even those sometimes ascribed to David Hartley, that were not generally current in the eighteenth century. Wordsworth's major original contribution to literary theory was his view that the morality inherent in literature worked subtly and indirectly, not through precept and example as taught by the central tradition. His creative theory — 'the spontaneous overflow' exposition — was likewise original as derived from the psychology of his own practice. And poetic practice itself received a revolutionary jolt when he both broke from the eighteenth-century rule of decorum by opening up serious poetry to what would previously have been considered 'undignified' subjects (leech-gatherers, beggars and the like) and also from the exclusive kind of poetical diction in which serious poetry was written in the*

278

eighteenth century. *Poetry and literary theory would never be quite the same
again.*

## *Appendix, Prefaces,*
### *etc. etc.*

Much the greatest part of the foregoing Poems has been so long
before the Public that no prefatory matter, explanatory of any portion of them, or of the arrangement which has been adopted, appears
to be required; and had it not been for the observations contained in
those Prefaces upon the principles of Poetry in general they would
not have been reprinted even as an Appendix in this Edition.[1]

### PREFACE

*to the second edition of several of the foregoing poems, published, with an
additional volume, under the title of 'Lyrical Ballads'.*[2]

(Note.—In succeeding Editions, when the Collection was much
enlarged and diversified, this Preface was transferred to the end of
the Volumes as having little of a special application to their contents.[3])

The first Volume of these Poems has already been submitted to
general perusal. It was published, as an experiment, which, I hoped,
might be of some use to ascertain, how far, by fitting to metrical
arrangement a selection of the real language of men in a state of vivid
sensation, that sort of pleasure and that quantity of pleasure may be
imparted, which a Poet may rationally endeavour to impart.
  I had formed no very inaccurate estimate of the probable effect
of those Poems: I flattered myself that they who should be pleased

with them would read them with more than common pleasure: and, on the other hand, I was well aware, that by those who should dislike them, they would be read with more than common dislike. The result has differed from my expectation in this only, that a greater number have been pleased than I ventured to hope I should please.[4]

\*     \*     \*

Several of my Friends are anxious for the success of these Poems, from a belief, that, if the views with which they were composed were indeed realised, a class of Poetry would be produced, well adapted to interest mankind permanently, and not unimportant in the quality, and in the multiplicity of its moral relations: and on this account they have advised me[5] to prefix a systematic defence of the theory upon which the Poems were written. But I was unwilling to undertake the task, knowing that on this occasion the Reader would look coldly upon my arguments, since I might be suspected of having been principally influenced by the selfish and foolish hope of *reasoning* him into an approbation of these particular Poems: and I was still more unwilling to undertake the task, because, adequately to display the opinions, and fully to enforce the arguments, would require a space wholly disproportionate to a preface. For, to treat the subject with the clearness and coherence of which it is susceptible, it would be necessary to give a full account of the present state of the public taste in this country, and to determine how far this taste is healthy or depraved; which, again, could not be determined, without pointing out in what manner language and the human mind act and re-act on each other, and without retracing the revolutions, not of literature alone, but likewise of society itself. I have therefore altogether declined to enter regularly upon this defence; yet I am sensible, that there would be something like impropriety in abruptly obtruding upon the Public, without a few words of introduction, Poems so materially different from those upon which general approbation is at present bestowed.

It is supposed, that by the act of writing in verse an Author makes a formal engagement that he will gratify certain known habits of association; that he not only thus apprises the Reader that certain classes of ideas and expressions will be found in his book, but that others will be carefully excluded. This exponent or symbol held forth by metrical language must in different eras of literature have excited very different expectations: for example, in the age of Catullus, Terence, and Lucretius, and that of Statius or Claudian; [6] and in our own country, in the age of Shakspeare and Beaumont and Fletcher, and that of Donne and Cowley, or Dryden, or Pope. [7] I will not take upon me to determine the exact import of the promise which, by the act of writing in verse, an Author, in the present day makes to his reader: but it will undoubtedly appear to many persons that I have not fulfilled the terms of an engagement thus voluntarily contracted. They who have been accustomed to the gaudiness and inane phraseology of many modern writers, if they persist in reading this book to its conclusion, will, no doubt, frequently have to struggle with feelings of strangeness and awkwardness: they will look round for poetry, and will be induced to inquire by what species of courtesy these attempts can be permitted to assume that title. I hope therefore the reader will not censure me for attempting to state what I have proposed to myself to perform; and also (as far as the limits of a preface will permit) to explain some of the chief reasons which have determined me in the choice of my purpose: that at least he may be spared any unpleasant feeling of disappointment, and that I myself may be protected from one of the most dishonourable accusations which can be brought against an Author; namely, that of an indolence which prevents him from endeavouring to ascertain what is his duty, or, when his duty is ascertained, prevents him from performing it.

The principal object, then, proposed in these Poems was to choose incidents and situations from common life, and to relate or describe them, throughout, as far as was possible in a selection of language really used by men, and, at the same time, to throw over them a certain colouring of imagination, whereby ordinary things should be presented to the mind in an unusual aspect; and, further, and above all, to make these incidents and situations interesting by tracing in them, truly though not ostentatiously, the primary laws of our

nature: chiefly, as far as regards the manner in which we associate
ideas in a state of excitement. Humble and rustic life was generally
chosen, because, in that condition, the essential passions of the heart
find a better soil in which they can attain their maturity, are less
under restraint, and speak a plainer and more emphatic language;
because in that condition of life our elementary feelings co-exist in a
state of greater simplicity, and, consequently, may be more accurately
contemplated, and more forcibly communicated; because the
manners of rural life germinate from those elementary feelings, and,
from the necessary character of rural occupations, are more easily
comprehended, and are more durable; and, lastly, because in that
condition the passions of men are incorporated with the beautiful
and permanent forms of nature. The language, too, of these men has
been adopted (purified indeed from what appear to be its real defects,
from all lasting and rational causes of dislike or disgust) because such
men hourly communicate with the best objects from which the best
part of language is originally derived; and because, from their rank in
society and the sameness and narrow circle of their intercourse, being
less under the influence of social vanity, they convey their feelings
and notions in simple and unelaborated expressions. Accordingly, such
a language, arising out of repeated experience and regular feelings, is
a more permanent, and a far more philosophical language, than that
which is frequently substituted for it by Poets, who think that they
are conferring honour upon themselves and their art, in proportion
as they separate themselves from the sympathies of men, and indulge
in arbitrary and capricious habits of expression, in order to furnish
food for fickle tastes, and fickle appetites, of their own creation.[8]

I cannot, however, be insensible to the present outcry against the
triviality and meanness, both of thought and language, which some
of my contemporaries have occasionally introduced into their metrical compositions; and I acknowledge that this defect, where it exists, is
more dishonourable to the Writer's own character than false refinement or arbitrary innovation, though I should contend at the same
time, that it is far less pernicious in the sum of its consequences. From
such verses the Poems in these volumes will be found distinguished at

least by one mark of difference, that each of them has a worthy *purpose*. Not that I always began to write with a distinct purpose formally conceived; but habits of meditation have, I trust, so prompted and regulated my feelings, that my descriptions of such objects as strongly excite those feelings, will be found to carry along with them a *purpose*. If this opinion be erroneous, I can have little right to the name of a Poet. For all good poetry is the spontaneous overflow of powerful feelings: and though this be true, Poems to which any value can be attached were never produced on any variety of subjects but by a man who, being possessed of more than usual organic sensibility, had also thought long and deeply. For our continued influxes of feeling are modified and directed by our thoughts, which are indeed the representatives of all our past feelings; and, as by contemplating the relation of these general representatives to each other, we discover what is really important to men, so, by the repetition and continuance of this act, our feelings will be connected with important subjects, till at length, if we be originally possessed of much sensibility, such habits of mind will be produced, that, by obeying blindly and mechanically the impulses of those habits, we shall describe objects, and utter sentiments, of such a nature, and in such connection with each other, that the understanding of the Reader must necessarily be in some degree enlightened, and his affections strengthened and purified.[9]

It has been said that each of these poems has a purpose. Another circumstance must be mentioned which distinguishes these Poems from the popular Poetry of the day; it is this, that the feeling therein developed gives importance to the action and situation, and not the action and situation to the feeling.

A sense of false modesty shall not prevent me from asserting, that the Reader's attention is pointed to this mark of distinction, far less for the sake of these particular Poems than from the general importance of the subject. The subject is indeed important! For the human mind is capable of being excited without the application of gross and violent stimulants; and he must have a very faint perception of its beauty and dignity who does not know this, and who does not further know, that one being is elevated above another, in proportion as he possesses this capability. It has therefore appeared to me, that to endeavour to produce or enlarge this capability is one of the best services in which, at any period, a Writer can be engaged; but this service, excellent at all times, is especially so at the present day. For a multitude of causes, unknown to former times, are now acting with a combined force to blunt the discriminating powers of the mind, and, unfitting it for all voluntary exertion, to reduce it to a state of almost savage torpor. The most effective of these causes are the great national events [10] which are daily taking place, and the increasing accumulation of men in cities, where the uniformity of their occupations produces a craving for extraordinary incident, which the rapid communication [11] of intelligence hourly gratifies. To this tendency of life and manners the literature and theatrical exhibitions of the country have conformed themselves. The invaluable works of our elder writers, I had almost said the works of Shakspeare and Milton, are driven into neglect by frantic novels, sickly and stupid German Tragedies, [12] and deluges of idle and extravagant stories in verse. — When I think upon this degrading thirst after outrageous stimulation, I am almost ashamed to have spoken of the feeble endeavour made in these volumes to counteract it; and, reflecting upon the magnitude of the general evil, I should be oppressed with no dishonourable melancholy, had I not a deep impression of certain inherent and indestructible qualities of the human mind, and likewise of certain powers in the great and permanent objects that act upon it, which are equally inherent and indestructible; and were there not added to this impression a belief, that the time is approaching when the evil will be systematically opposed, by men of greater powers, and with far more distinguished success.

Having dwelt thus long on the subjects and aim of these Poems, I shall request the Reader's permission to apprise him of a few circumstances relating to their *style*, in order, among other reasons, that he may not censure me for not having performed what I never attempted. The Reader will find that personifications of abstract ideas rarely occur in these volumes; and are utterly rejected, as an ordinary device to elevate the style, and raise it above prose. My purpose was to imitate, and, as far as is possible, to adopt the very language of men; and assuredly such personifications do not make any natural or regular part of that language. They are, indeed, a figure of speech occasionally prompted by passion, and I have made use of them as such; but have endeavoured utterly to reject them as a mechanical device of style, or as a family language which Writers in metre seem to lay claim to by prescription. I have wished to keep the Reader in the company of flesh and blood, persuaded that by so doing I shall interest him. Others who pursue a different track will interest him likewise; I do not interfere with their claim, but wish to prefer a claim of my own. There will also be found in these volumes little of what is usually called poetic diction; as much pains has been taken to avoid it as is ordinarily taken to produce it; this has been done for the reason already alleged, to bring my language near to the language of men; and further, because the pleasure which I have proposed to myself to impart, is of a kind very different from that which is supposed by many persons to be the proper object of poetry. Without being culpably particular, I do not know how to give my Reader a more exact notion of the style in which it was my wish and intention to write, than by informing him that I have at all times endeavoured to look steadily at my subject; consequently, there is I hope in these Poems little falsehood of description, and my ideas are expressed in language fitted to their respective importance. Something must have been gained by this practice, as it is friendly to one property of all good poetry, namely, good sense: but it has necessarily cut me off from a large portion of phrases and figures of speech which from father to son have long been regarded as the common inheritance of Poets. I have also thought it expedient to restrict myself still further, having abstained from the use of many expressions, in themselves proper and beautiful, but which have been foolishly repeated by bad Poets, till such feelings of disgust are connected with them as it is scarcely possible by any art of association to overpower.

If in a poem there should be found a series of lines, or even a single line, in which the language, though naturally arranged, and according to the strict laws of metre, does not differ from that of prose, there is a numerous class of critics, who, when they stumble upon these prosaisms, as they call them, imagine that they have made a notable discovery, and exult over the Poet as over a man ignorant of his own profession. Now these men would establish a canon of criticism which the Reader will conclude he must utterly reject, if he wishes to be pleased with these volumes. And it would be a most easy task to prove to him, that not only the language of a large portion of every good poem, even of the most elevated character, must necessarily, except with reference to the metre, in no respect differ from that of good prose, but likewise that some of the most interesting parts of the best poems will be found to be strictly the language of prose when prose is well written.[13] The truth of this assertion might be demonstrated by innumerable passages from almost all the poetical writings, even of Milton himself. To illustrate the subject in a general manner, I will here adduce a short composition of Gray, who was at the head of those who, by their reasonings, have attempted to widen the space of separation betwixt Prose and Metrical composition,[14] and was more than any other man curiously elaborate in the structure of his own poetic diction.

> 'In vain to me the smiling mornings shine,
> And reddening Phoebus lifts his golden fire:
> The birds in vain their amorous descant join,
> Or cheerful fields resume their green attire.
> These ears, alas! for other notes repine;
> *A different object do these eyes require;*
> *My lonely anguish melts no heart but mine;*
> *And in my breast the imperfect joys expire;*
> Yet morning smiles the busy race to cheer,
> And new-born pleasure brings to happier men;
> The fields to all their wonted tribute bear;
> To warm their little loves the birds complain.
> *I fruitless mourn to him that cannot hear,*
> *And weep the more because I weep in vain.'*[15]

It will easily be perceived, that the only part of this Sonnet which is of any value is the lines printed in Italics; it is equally obvious, that, except in the rhyme, and in the use of the single word 'fruitless' for fruitlessly, which is so far a defect, the language of these lines does in no respect differ from that of prose.

By the foregoing quotation it has been shown that the language of Prose may yet be well adapted to Poetry; and it was previously asserted, that a large portion of the language of every good poem can in no respect differ from that of good Prose. We will go further. It may be safely affirmed, that there neither is, nor can be, any *essential* difference between the language of prose and metrical composition. We are fond of tracing the resemblance between Poetry and Painting, and, accordingly, we call them Sisters: but where shall we find bonds of connection sufficiently strict to typify the affinity betwixt metrical and prose composition? They both speak by and to the same organs; the bodies in which both of them are clothed may be said to be of the same substance, their affections are kindred, and almost identical, not necessarily differing even in degree; Poetry [16] sheds no tears 'such as Angels weep,' [17] but natural and human tears; she can boast of no celestial ichor that distinguishes her vital juices from those of prose; the same human blood circulates through the veins of them both.

If it be affirmed that rhyme and metrical arrangement of themselves constitute a distinction which overturns what has just been said on the strict affinity of metrical language with that of prose, and paves the way for other artificial distinctions which the mind voluntarily admits, I answer that the language of such Poetry as is here recommended is, as far as is possible, a selection of the language really spoken by men; that this selection, wherever it is made with true taste and feeling, will of itself form a distinction far greater than would at first be imagined, and will entirely separate the composition from the vulgarity and meanness of ordinary life; and, if metre be superadded thereto, I believe that a dissimilitude will be produced altogether sufficient for the gratification of a rational mind. What other distinction would we have? Whence is it to come? And where is it to exist? Not, surely, where the Poet speaks through the mouths of his characters: it cannot be necessary here, either for elevation of style, or any of its supposed ornaments: for, if the Poet's subject be judiciously chosen, it will naturally, and upon fit occasion, lead him to passions the language of which, if selected truly and judiciously, must necessarily be dignified and variegated, and alive with metaphors and figures. I forbear to speak of an incongruity which would shock the intelligent Reader, should the Poet interweave any foreign splendour of his own with that which the passion naturally suggests: it is sufficient to say that such addition is unnecessary. And, surely, it is more probable that those passages, which with propriety abound with metaphors and figures, will have their due effect, if, upon other occasions where the passions are of a milder character, the style also be subdued and temperate.

But, as the pleasure which I hope to give by the Poems now presented to the Reader must depend entirely on just notions upon this subject, and, as it is in itself of high importance to our taste and moral feelings, I cannot content myself with these detached remarks. And if, in what I am about to say, it shall appear to some that my labour is unnecessary, and that I am like a man fighting a battle without enemies, such persons may be reminded, that, whatever be the language outwardly holden by men, a practical faith in the opinions which I am wishing to establish is almost unknown. If my conclusions are admitted, and carried as far as they must be carried if admitted at all, our judgments concerning the works of the greatest Poets both ancient and modern will be far different from what they are at present, both when we praise, and when we censure: and our moral feelings influencing and influenced by these judgments will, I believe, be corrected and purified.

Taking up the subject, then, upon general grounds, let me ask, what is meant by the word Poet? What is a Poet? To whom does he address himself? And what language is to be expected from him? — He is a man speaking to men: a man, it is true, endowed with more lively sensibility, more enthusiasm and tenderness, who has a greater knowledge of human nature, and a more comprehensive soul,[18] than are supposed to be common among mankind; a man pleased with his own passions and volitions, and who rejoices more than other men in the spirit of life that is in him; delighting to contemplate similar volitions and passions as manifested in the goings-on of the Universe, and habitually impelled to create them where he does not find them. To these qualities he has added a disposition to be affected more than other men by absent things as if they were present;[19] an ability of conjuring up in himself passions, which are indeed far from being the same as those produced by real events, yet (especially in those parts of the general sympathy which are pleasing and delightful) do more nearly resemble the passions produced by real events, than anything which, from the motions of their own minds merely, other men are accustomed to feel in themselves: — whence, and from practice, he has acquired a greater readiness and power in expressing what he thinks and feels, and especially those thoughts and feelings which, by his own choice, or from the structure of his own mind, arise in him without immediate external excitement.

But whatever portion of this faculty we may suppose even the greatest Poet to possess, there cannot be a doubt that the language which it will suggest to him, must often, in liveliness and truth, fall short of that which is uttered by men in real life, under the actual pressure of those passions, certain shadows of which the Poet thus produces, or feels to be produced, in himself.[20]

However exalted a notion we would wish to cherish of the character of a Poet, it is obvious, that while he describes and imitates passions, his employment is in some degree mechanical, compared with the freedom and power of real and substantial action and suffering. So that it will be the wish of the Poet to bring his feelings near to those of the persons whose feelings he describes, nay, for short spaces of time, perhaps, to let himself slip into an entire delusion, and even confound and identify his own feelings with theirs;[21] modifying only the language which is thus suggested to him by a consideration that he describes for a particular purpose, that of giving pleasure. Here, then, he will apply the principle of selection which has been already insisted upon. He will depend upon this for removing what would otherwise be painful or disgusting in the passion; he will feel that there is no necessity to trick out or to elevate nature: and, the more industriously he applies this principle, the deeper will be his faith that no words, which *his* fancy or imagination can suggest, will be to be compared with those which are the emanations of reality and truth.

But it may be said by those who do not object to the general spirit of these remarks, that, as it is impossible for the Poet to produce upon all occasions language as exquisitely fitted for the passion as that which the real passion itself suggests, it is proper that he should consider himself as in the situation of a translator, who does not scruple to substitute excellencies of another kind for those which are unattainable by him; and endeavours occasionally to surpass his original, in order to make some amends for the general inferiority to which he feels that he must submit. But this would be to encourage idleness and unmanly despair. Further, it is the language of men who speak of what they do not understand; who talk of Poetry as of a matter of amusement and idle pleasure; who will converse with us as gravely about a *taste* for Poetry, as they express it, as if it were a thing as indifferent as a taste for rope-dancing, or Frontiniac or Sherry. Aristotle, I have been told, has said, that Poetry is the most philosophic of all writing: it is so: its object is truth, not individual and local, but general, and operative; [22] not standing upon external testimony, but carried alive into the heart by passion; truth which is its own testimony, which gives competence and confidence to the tribunal to which it appeals, and receives them from the same tribunal. Poetry is the image of man and nature. The obstacles which stand in the way of the fidelity of the Biographer and Historian, and of their consequent utility, are incalculably greater than those which are to be encountered by the Poet who comprehends the dignity of his art. The Poet writes under one restriction only, namely, the necessity of giving immediate pleasure to a human Being possessed of that information which may be expected from him, not as a lawyer, a physician, a mariner, an astronomer, or a natural philosopher, but as a Man. Except this one restriction, there is no object standing between the Poet and the image of things; between this, and the Biographer and Historian, there are a thousand.

Nor let this necessity of producing immediate pleasure be considered as a degradation of the Poet's art. It is far otherwise. It is an acknowledgment of the beauty of the universe, an acknowledgment the more sincere, because not formal, but indirect; it is a task light and easy to him who looks at the world in the spirit of love: further, it is a homage paid to the native and naked dignity of man, to the grand elementary principle of pleasure, by which he knows, and feels, and lives, and moves. We have no sympathy but what is propagated by pleasure: I would not be misunderstood; but wherever we sympathise with pain, it will be found that the sympathy is produced and carried on by subtle combinations with pleasure. We have no knowledge, that is, no general principles drawn from the contemplation of particular facts, but what has been built up by pleasure, and exists in us by pleasure alone. The Man of science, the Chemist and Mathematician, whatever difficulties and disgusts they may have had to struggle with, know and feel this. However painful may be the objects with which the Anatomist's knowledge is connected, he feels that his knowledge is pleasure; and where he has no pleasure he has no knowledge. What then does the Poet? He considers man and the objects that surround him as acting and re-acting upon each other, so as to produce an infinite complexity of pain and pleasure; he considers man in his own nature and in his ordinary life as contemplating this with a certain quantity of immediate knowledge, with certain convictions, intuitions, and deductions, which from habit acquire the quality of intuitions; he considers him as looking upon this complex scene of ideas and sensations, and finding every where objects that immediately excite in him sympathies which, from the necessities of his nature, are accompanied by an overbalance of enjoyment.

To this knowledge which all men carry about with them, and to these sympathies in which, without any other discipline than that of our daily life, we are fitted to take delight, the Poet principally directs his attention. He considers man and nature as essentially adapted to each other, and the mind of man as naturally the mirror of the fairest and most interesting properties of nature. And thus the Poet, prompted by this feeling of pleasure, which accompanies him through the whole course of his studies, converses with general nature, with affections akin to those, which, through labour and length of time, the Man of science has raised up in himself, by conversing with those particular parts of nature which are the objects of his studies. The knowledge both of the Poet and the Man of science is pleasure; but the knowledge of the one cleaves to us as a necessary part of our existence, our natural and unalienable inheritance; the other is a personal and individual acquisition, slow to come to us, and by no habitual and direct sympathy connecting us with our fellow-beings. The Man of science seeks truth as a remote and unknown benefactor; he cherishes and loves it in his solitude: the Poet, singing a song in which all human beings join with him, rejoices in the presence of truth as our visible friend and hourly companion. Poetry is the breath and finer spirit of all knowledge; it is the impassioned expression which is in the countenance of all Science. Emphatically may it be said of the Poet, as Shakspeare hath said of man, 'that he looks before and after.' [23] He is the rock of defence for human nature; an upholder and preserver, carrying everywhere with him relationship and love. In spite of difference of soil and climate, of language and manners, of laws and customs: in spite of things silently gone out of mind, and things violently destroyed; the Poet binds together by passion and knowledge the vast empire of human society, as it is spread over the whole earth, and over all time. The objects of the Poet's thoughts are every where; though the eyes and senses of man are, it is true, his favourite guides, yet he will follow wheresoever he can find an atmosphere of sensation in which to move his wings. Poetry is the first and last of all knowledge – it is as immortal as the heart of man. If the labours of Men of science should ever create any material revolution, direct or indirect, in our condition, and in the impressions which we habitually receive, the Poet will sleep then no more than at present; he will be ready to follow the steps of the Man of science, not only in those general indirect effects, but he will be at his side, carrying sensation into the midst of the objects of the science itself. The remotest discoveries of the Chemist, the Botanist, or Mineralogist, will be as proper objects of the Poet's art as any upon which it can be employed, if the time should ever come when these things shall be familiar to us, and the relations under which they are contemplated by the followers of these respective sciences shall be manifestly and palpably material to us as enjoying and suffering beings. If the time should ever come when what is now called science, thus familiarised to men, shall be ready to put on, as it were, a form of flesh and blood, the Poet will lend his divine spirit to aid the transfiguration, and will welcome the Being thus produced, as a dear and genuine inmate of the household of man. – It is not, then, to be supposed that any one, who holds that sublime notion of Poetry which I have attempted to convey, will break in upon the sanctity and truth of his pictures by transitory and accidental ornaments, and endeavour to excite admiration of himself by arts, the necessity of which must manifestly depend upon the assumed meanness of his subject.

What has been thus far said applies to Poetry in general; but especially to those parts of composition where the Poet speaks through the mouths of his characters; and upon this point it appears to authorise the conclusion that there are few persons of good sense, who would not allow that the dramatic parts of composition are defective, in proportion as they deviate from the real language of nature, and are coloured by a diction of the Poet's own, either peculiar to him as an individual Poet or belonging simply to Poets in general; to a body of men who, from the circumstance of their compositions being in metre, it is expected will employ a particular language.

It is not, then, in the dramatic parts of composition that we look for this distinction of language; but still it may be proper and necessary where the Poet speaks to us in his own person and character. To this I answer by referring the Reader to the description before given of a Poet. Among the qualities there enumerated as principally conducing to form a Poet, is implied nothing differing in kind from other men, but only in degree. The sum of what was said is, that the Poet is chiefly distinguished from other men by a greater promptness to think and feel without immediate external excitement, and a greater power in expressing such thoughts and feelings as are produced in him in that manner. But these passions and thoughts and feelings are the general passions and thoughts and feelings of men. And with what are they connected? Undoubtedly with our moral sentiments and animal sensations, and with the causes which excite these; with the operations of the elements, and the appearances of the visible universe; with storm and sunshine, with the revolutions of the seasons, with cold and heat, with loss of friends and kindred, with injuries and resentments, gratitude and hope, with fear and sorrow. These, and the like, are the sensations and objects which the Poet describes, as they are the sensations of other men, and the objects which interest them. The Poet thinks and feels in the spirit of human passions. How, then, can his language differ in any material degree from that of all other men who feel vividly and see clearly? It might be *proved* that it is impossible. But supposing that this were not the case, the Poet might then be allowed to use a peculiar language when expressing his feelings for his own gratification, or that of men like himself. But Poets do not write for Poets alone, but for men. Unless therefore we are advocates for that admiration which subsists upon ignorance, and that pleasure which arises from hearing what we do not understand, the Poet must descend from this supposed height; and, in order to excite rational sympathy, he must express himself as other men express themselves. To this it may be added, that while he is only selecting from the real language of men, or, which amounts to the same thing, composing accurately in the spirit of such selection, he is treading upon safe ground, and we know what we are to expect from him. Our feelings are the same with respect to metre; for, as it may be proper to remind the Reader, the distinction of metre is regular and uniform, and not, like that which is produced by what is usually called POETIC DICTION, arbitrary, and subject to infinite caprices upon which no calculation whatever can be made. In the one case, the Reader is utterly at the mercy of the Poet, respecting what imagery or diction he may choose to connect with the passion; whereas, in the other, the metre obeys certain laws, to which the Poet and Reader both willingly submit because they are certain, and because no interference is made by them with the passion, but such as the concurring testimony of ages has shown to heighten and improve the pleasure which co-exists with it.

It will now be proper to answer an obvious question, namely, Why, professing these opinions, have I written in verse? To this, in addition to such answer as is included in what has been already said, I reply, in the first place, Because, however I may have restricted myself, there is still left open to me what confessedly constitutes the most valuable object of all writing, whether in prose or verse; the great and universal passions of men, the most general and interesting of their occupations, and the entire world of nature before me – to supply endless combinations of forms and imagery. Now, supposing for a moment that whatever is interesting in these objects may be as vividly described in prose, why should I be condemned for attempting to superadd to such description, the charm which, by the consent of all nations, is acknowledged to exist in metrical language? To this, by such as are yet unconvinced, it may be answered that a very small part of the pleasure given by Poetry depends upon the metre, and that it is injudicious to write in metre, unless it be accompanied with the other artificial distinctions of style with which metre is usually accompanied, and that, by such deviation, more will be lost from the shock which will thereby be given to the Reader's associations than will be counterbalanced by any pleasure which he can derive from the general power of numbers. In answer to those who still contend for the necessity of accompanying metre with certain appropriate colours of style in order to the accomplishment of its appropriate end, and who also, in my opinion, greatly underrate the power of metre in itself, it might, perhaps, as far as relates to these Volumes, have been almost sufficient to observe, that poems are extant,[24] written upon more humble subjects, and in a still more naked and simple style, which have continued to give pleasure from generation to generation. Now, if nakedness and simplicity be a defect, the fact here mentioned affords a strong presumption that poems somewhat less naked and simple are capable of affording pleasure at the present day; and, what I wished *chiefly* to attempt, at present, was to justify myself for having written under the impression of this belief.

But various causes might be pointed out why, when the style is manly, and the subject of some importance, words metrically arranged will long continue to impart such a pleasure to mankind as he who proves the extent of that pleasure will be desirous to impart. The end of Poetry is to produce excitement in co-existence with an overbalance of pleasure; but, by the supposition, excitement is an unusual and irregular state of the mind; ideas and feelings do not, in that state, succeed each other in accustomed order. If the words, however, by which this excitement is produced be in themselves powerful, or the images and feelings have an undue proportion of pain connected with them, there is some danger that the excitement may be carried beyond its proper bounds. Now the co-presence of something regular, something to which the mind has been accustomed in various moods and in a less excited state, cannot but have great efficacy in tempering and restraining the passion by an intertexture of ordinary feeling, and of feeling not strictly and necessarily connected with the passion. This is unquestionably true; and hence, though the opinion will at first appear paradoxical, from the tendency of metre to divest language, in a certain degree, of its reality, and thus to throw a sort of half-consciousness of unsubstantial existence over the whole composition, there can be little doubt but that more pathetic situations and sentiments, that is, those which have a greater proportion of pain connected with them, may be endured in metrical composition, especially in rhyme, than in prose. The metre of the old ballads is very artless; yet they contain many passages which would illustrate this opinion; and, I hope, if the following Poems be attentively perused, similar instances will be found in them. This opinion may be further illustrated by appealing to the Reader's own experience of the reluctance with which he comes to the re-perusal of the distressful parts of Clarissa Harlowe, or the Gamester; [25] while Shakspeare's writings, in the most pathetic scenes, never act upon us, as pathetic, beyond the bounds of pleasure – an effect which, in a much greater degree than might at first be imagined, is to be ascribed to small, but continual and regular impulses of pleasurable surprise from the metrical arrangement. – On the other hand (what it must be allowed will much more frequently happen) if the Poet's words should be incommensurate with the passion, and inadequate to raise the Reader to a height of desirable excitement, then, (unless the Poet's choice of his metre has been grossly injudicious) in the feelings of pleasure which the Reader has been accustomed to connect with metre in general, and in the feeling, whether cheerful or melancholy, which he has been accustomed to connect with that particular movement of metre, there will be found something which will greatly contribute to impart passion to the words, and to effect the complex end which the Poet proposes to himself.

If I had undertaken a SYSTEMATIC defence of the theory here maintained, it would have been my duty to develope the various causes upon which the pleasure received from metrical language depends. Among the chief of these causes is to be reckoned a principle which must be well known to those who have made any of the Arts the object of accurate reflection; namely, the pleasure which the mind derives from the perception of similitude in dissimilitude. This principle is the great spring of the activity of our minds, and their chief feeder. From this principle the direction of the sexual appetite, and all the passions connected with it, take their origin: it is the life of our ordinary conversation; and upon the accuracy with which similitude in dissimilitude, and dissimilitude in similitude are perceived, depend our taste and our moral feelings. It would not be a useless employment to apply this principle to the consideration of metre, and to show that metre is hence enabled to afford much pleasure, and to point out in what manner that pleasure is produced. But my limits will not permit me to enter upon this subject, and I must content myself with a general summary.

I have said that poetry is the spontaneous overflow of powerful feelings: it takes its origin from emotion recollected in tranquillity: the emotion is contemplated till, by a species of re-action, the tranquillity gradually disappears, and an emotion, kindred to that which was before the subject of contemplation, is gradually produced, and does itself actually exist in the mind. In this mood successful composition generally begins, and in a mood similar to this it is carried on; but the emotion, of whatever kind, and in whatever degree, from various causes, is qualified by various pleasures, so that in describing any passions whatsoever, which are voluntarily described, the mind will, upon the whole, be in a state of enjoyment. If Nature be thus cautious to preserve in a state of enjoyment a being so employed, the Poet ought to profit by the lesson held forth to him, and ought especially to take care, that, whatever passions he communicates to his Reader, those passions, if his Reader's mind be sound and vigorous, should always be accompanied with an overbalance of pleasure. Now the music of harmonious metrical language, the sense of difficulty overcome, and the blind association of pleasure which has been previously received from works of rhyme or metre of the same or similar construction, an indistinct perception perpetually renewed of language closely resembling that of real life, and yet, in the circumstance of metre, differing from it so widely – all these imperceptibly make up a complex feeling of delight, which is of the most important use in tempering the painful feeling always found intermingled with powerful descriptions of the deeper passions. This effect is always produced in pathetic and impassioned poetry; while, in lighter compositions, the ease and gracefulness with which the Poet manages his numbers are themselves confessedly a principal source of the gratification of the Reader. All that it is *necessary* to say, however, upon this subject, may be effected by affirming, what few persons will deny, that, of two descriptions, either of passions, manners, or characters, each of them equally well executed, the one in prose and the other in verse, the verse will be read a hundred times where the prose is read once.

Having thus explained a few of my reasons for writing in verse, and why I have chosen subjects from common life, and endeavoured to bring my language near to the real language of men, if I have been too minute in pleading my own cause, I have at the same time been treating a subject of general interest; and for this reason a few words shall be added with reference solely to these particular poems, and to some defects which will probably be found in them. I am sensible that my associations must have sometimes been particular instead of general, and that, consequently, giving to things a false importance, I may have sometimes written upon unworthy subjects; but I am less apprehensive on this account, than that my language may frequently have suffered from those arbitrary connections of feelings and ideas with particular words and phrases, from which no man can altogether protect himself. Hence I have no doubt, that, in some instances, feelings, even of the ludicrous, may be given to my Readers by expressions which appeared to me tender and pathetic. Such faulty expressions, were I convinced they were faulty at present, and that they must necessarily continue to be so, I would willingly take all reasonable pains to correct. But it is dangerous to make these alterations on the simple authority of a few individuals, or even of certain classes of men; for where the understanding of an Author is not convinced, or his feelings altered, this cannot be done without great injury to himself: for his own feelings are his stay and support; and, if he set them aside in one instance, he may be induced to repeat this act till his mind shall lose all confidence in itself, and become utterly debilitated. To this it may be added, that the critic ought never to forget that he is himself exposed to the same errors as the Poet, and, perhaps, in a much greater degree: for there can be no presumption in saying of most readers, that it is not probable they will be so well acquainted with the various stages of meaning through which words have passed, or with the fickleness or stability of the relations of particular ideas to each other; and, above all, since they are so much less interested in the subject, they may decide lightly and carelessly.

Long as the Reader has been detained, I hope he will permit me to caution him against a mode of false criticism which has been applied to Poetry, in which the language closely resembles that of life and nature. Such verses have been triumphed over in parodies, of which Dr Johnson's stanza is a fair specimen: —

> 'I put my hat upon my head
> And walked into the Strand,
> And there I met another man
> Whose hat was in his hand.'[26]

Immediately under these lines let us place one of the most justly-admired stanzas of the '*Babes in the Wood*'.

> 'These pretty Babes with hand in hand
> Went wandering up and down;
> But never more they saw the Man
> Approaching from the Town.'[27]

In both these stanzas the words, and the order of the words, in no respect differ from the most unimpassioned conversation. There are words in both, for example, 'the Strand', and 'the Town', connected with none but the most familiar ideas; yet the one stanza we admit as admirable, and the other as a fair example of the superlatively contemptible. Whence arises this difference? Not from the metre, not from the language, not from the order of the words; but the *matter* expressed in Dr Johnson's stanza is contemptible. The proper method of treating trivial and simple verses, to which Dr Johnson's stanza would be a fair parallelism, is not to say, this is a bad kind of poetry, or, this is not poetry; but, this wants sense; it is neither interesting in itself, nor can *lead* to any thing interesting; the images neither originate in that sane state of feeling which arises out of thought, nor can excite thought or feeling in the Reader. This is the only sensible manner of dealing with such verses. Why trouble yourself about the species till you have previously decided upon the genus? Why take pains to prove that an ape is not a Newton, when it is self-evident that he is not a man?

One request I must make of my reader, which is, that in judging these Poems he would decide by his own feelings genuinely, and not by reflection upon what will probably be the judgment of others. How common is it to hear a person say, I myself do not object to this style of composition, or this or that expression, but, to such and such classes of people it will appear mean or ludicrous! This mode of criticism, so destructive of all sound unadulterated judgment, is almost universal: let the Reader then abide, independently, by his own feelings, and, if he finds himself affected, let him not suffer such conjectures to interfere with his pleasure.

If an Author, by any single composition, has impressed us with respect for his talents, it is useful to consider this as affording a presumption, that on other occasions where we have been displeased, he, nevertheless, may not have written ill or absurdly; and further, to give him so much credit for this one composition as may induce us to review what has displeased us, with more care than we should otherwise have bestowed upon it. This is not only an act of justice, but, in our decisions upon poetry especially, may conduce, in a high degree, to the improvement of our own taste; for an *accurate* taste in poetry, and in all the other arts, as Sir Joshua Reynolds has observed, is an *acquired* talent, which can only be produced by thought and a long-continued intercourse with the best models of composition.[28] This is mentioned, not with so ridiculous a purpose as to prevent the most inexperienced Reader from judging for himself, (I have already said that I wish him to judge for himself;) but merely to temper the rashness of decision, and to suggest, that, if Poetry be a subject on which much time has not been bestowed, the judgment may be erroneous; and that, in many cases, it necessarily will be so.

Nothing would, I know, have so effectually contributed to further the end which I have in view, as to have shown of what kind the pleasure is, and how that pleasure is produced, which is confessedly produced by metrical composition essentially different from that which I have here endeavoured to recommend: for the Reader will say that he has been pleased by such composition; and what more can be done for him? The power of any art is limited; and he will suspect, that, if it be proposed to furnish him with new friends, that can be only upon condition of his abandoning his old friends. Besides, as I have said, the Reader is himself conscious of the pleasure which he has received from such composition, composition to which he has peculiarly attached the endearing name of Poetry; and all men feel an habitual gratitude, and something of an honourable bigotry, for the objects which have long continued to please them: we not only wish to be pleased, but to be pleased in that particular way in which we have been accustomed to be pleased. There is in these feelings enough to resist a host of arguments; and I should be the less able to combat them successfully, as I am willing to allow, that, in order entirely to enjoy the Poetry which I am recommending, it would be necessary to give up much of what is ordinarily enjoyed. But, would my limits have permitted me to point out how this pleasure is produced, many obstacles might have been removed, and the Reader assisted in perceiving that the powers of language are not so limited as he may suppose; and that it is possible for poetry to give other enjoyments, of a purer, more lasting, and more exquisite nature. This part of the subject has not been altogether neglected, but it has not been so much my present aim to prove, that the interest excited by some other kinds of poetry is less vivid, and less worthy of the nobler powers of the mind, as to offer reasons for presuming, that if my purpose were fulfilled, a species of poetry would be produced, which is genuine poetry; in its nature well adapted to interest mankind permanently, and likewise important in the multiplicity and quality of its moral relations.[29]

From what has been said, and from a perusal of the Poems, the Reader will be able clearly to perceive the object which I had in view: he will determine how far it has been attained; and, what is a much more important question, whether it be worth attaining: and upon the decision of these two questions will rest my claim to the approbation of the Public.

## APPENDIX [30]

Perhaps, as I have no right to expect that attentive perusal, without which, confined, as I have been, to the narrow limits of a preface, my meaning cannot be thoroughly understood, I am anxious to give an exact notion of the sense in which the phrase poetic diction has been used; and for this purpose, a few words shall here be added, concerning the origin and characteristics of the phraseology, which I have condemned under that name.

The earliest poets of all nations generally wrote from passion excited by real events; they wrote naturally, and as men: feeling powerfully as they did, their language was daring, and figurative.[31]

In succeeding times, Poets, and Men ambitious of the fame of Poets, perceiving the influence of such language, and desirous of producing the same effect without being animated by the same passion, set themselves to a mechanical adoption of these figures of speech, and made use of them, sometimes with propriety, but much more frequently applied them to feelings and thoughts with which they had no natural connection whatsoever. A language was thus insensibly produced, differing materially from the real language of men in *any situation*. The Reader or Hearer of this distorted language found himself in a perturbed and unusual state of mind: when affected by the genuine language of passion he had been in a perturbed and unusual state of mind also: in both cases he was willing that his common judgment and understanding should be laid asleep, and he had no instinctive and infallible perception of the true to make him reject the false; the one served as a passport for the other. The emotion was in both cases delightful, and no wonder if he confounded the one with the other, and believed them both to be produced by the same, or similar causes. Besides, the Poet spake to him in the character of a man to be looked up to, a man of genius and authority. Thus, and from a variety of other causes, this distorted language was received with admiration; and Poets, it is probable, who had before contented themselves for the most part with misapplying only expressions which at first had been dictated by real passion, carried the abuse still further, and introduced phrases composed apparently in the spirit of the original figurative language of passion, yet altogether of their own invention, and characterised by various degrees of wanton deviation from good sense and nature.

It is indeed true, that the language of the earliest Poets was felt to differ materially from ordinary language, because it was the language of extraordinary occasions; but it was really spoken by men, language which the Poet himself had uttered when he had been affected by the events which he described, or which he had heard uttered by those around him. To this language it is probable that metre of some sort or other was early superadded. This separated the genuine language of Poetry still further from common life, so that whoever read or heard the poems of these earliest Poets felt himself moved in a way in which he had not been accustomed to be moved in real life, and by causes manifestly different from those which acted upon him in real life. This was the great temptation to all the corruptions which have followed: under the protection of this feeling succeeding Poets constructed a phraseology which had one thing, it is true, in common with the genuine language of poetry, namely, that it was not heard in ordinary conversation; that it was unusual. But the first Poets, as I have said, spake a language which, though unusual, was still the language of men. This circumstance, however, was disregarded by their successors; they found that they could please by easier means: they became proud of modes of expression which they themselves had invented, and which were uttered only by themselves. In process of time metre became a symbol or promise of this unusual language, and whoever took upon him to write in metre, according as he possessed more or less of true poetic genius, introduced less or more of this adulterated phraseology into his compositions, and the true and the false were inseparably interwoven until, the taste of men becoming gradually perverted, this language was received as a natural language: and at length, by the influence of books upon men, did to a certain degree really become so. Abuses of this kind were imported from one nation to another, and with the progress of refinement this diction became daily more and more corrupt, thrusting out of sight the plain humanities of nature by a motley masquerade of tricks, quaintnesses, hieroglyphics, and enigmas.

It would not be uninteresting to point out the causes of the pleasure given by this extravagant and absurd diction. It depends upon a great variety of causes, but upon none, perhaps, more than its influence in impressing a notion of the peculiarity and exaltation of the Poet's character, and in flattering the Reader's self-love by bringing him nearer to a sympathy with that character; an effect which is accomplished by unsettling ordinary habits of thinking, and thus assisting the Reader to approach to that perturbed and dizzy state of mind in which if he does not find himself, he imagines that he is *balked* of a peculiar enjoyment which poetry can and ought to bestow.

The sonnet quoted from Gray, in the Preface, except the lines printed in Italics, consists of little else but this diction, though not of the worst kind; and indeed, if one may be permitted to say so, it is far too common in the best writers both ancient and modern. Perhaps in no way, by positive example, could more easily be given a notion of what I mean by the phrase *poetic diction* than by referring to a comparison between the metrical paraphrases which we have of passages in the Old and New Testament, and those passages as they exist in our common Translation. See Pope's 'Messiah' throughout; Prior's 'Did sweeter sounds adorn my flowing tongue,' &c. &c. 'Though I speak with the tongues of men and of angels,' &c. &c. 1st Corinthians, chap. xiii.[32] By way of immediate example, take the following of Dr Johnson:

> 'Turn on the prudent Ant thy heedless eyes,
> Observe her labours, Sluggard, and be wise;
> No stern command, no monitory voice,
> Prescribes her duties, or directs her choice;
> Yet, timely provident, she hastes away
> To snatch the blessings of a plenteous day;
> When fruitful Summer loads the teeming plain,
> She crops the harvest, and she stores the grain.
> How long shall sloth usurp thy useless hours,
> Unnerve thy vigour, and enchain thy powers?
> While artful shades thy downy couch enclose,
> And soft solicitation courts repose,
> Amidst the drowsy charms of dull delight,
> Year chases year with unremitted flight,
> Till Want now following, fraudulent and slow,
> Shall spring to seize thee, like an ambush'd foe.'[33]

From this hubbub of words pass to the original. 'Go to the Ant, thou Sluggard, consider her ways, and be wise: which having no guide, overseer, or ruler, provideth her meat in the summer, and gathereth her food in the harvest. How long wilt thou sleep, O Sluggard? when wilt thou arise out of thy sleep? Yet a little sleep, a little slumber, a little folding of the hands to sleep. So shall thy

poverty come as one that travelleth, and thy want as an armed man.'
Proverbs, chap. vi.[34]

One more quotation, and I have done. It is from Cowper's Verses
supposed to be written by Alexander Selkirk: –

> 'Religion! what treasure untold
> Resides in that heavenly word!
> More precious than silver and gold,
> Or all that this earth can afford.
> But the sound of the church-going bell
> These valleys and rocks never heard,
> Ne'er sighed at the sound of a knell,
> Or smiled when a sabbath appeared.
>
> Ye winds, that have made me your sport
> Convey to this desolate shore
> Some cordial endearing report
> Of a land I must visit no more.
> My Friends, do they now and then send
> A wish or a thought after me?
> O tell me I yet have a friend,
> Though a friend I am never to see.' [35]

This passage is quoted as an instance of three different styles of
composition. The first four lines are poorly expressed; some Critics
would call the language prosaic; the fact is, it would be bad prose, so
bad, that it is scarcely worse in metre. The epithet 'church-going' [36]
applied to a bell, and that by so chaste a writer as Cowper, is an
instance of the strange abuses which Poets have introduced into their
language, till they and their Readers take them as matters of course,
if they do not single them out expressly as objects of admiration. The
two lines 'Ne'er sighed at the sound,' &c., are, in my opinion, an
instance of the language of passion wrested from its proper use, and,
from the mere circumstance of the composition being in metre,
applied upon an occasion that does not justify such violent expressions; and I should condemn the passage, though perhaps few Readers
will agree with me, as vicious [37] poetic diction. The last stanza is

throughout admirably expressed: it would be equally good whether in prose or verse, except that the Reader has an exquisite pleasure in seeing such natural language so naturally connected with metre. The beauty of this stanza tempts me to conclude with a principle which ought never to be lost sight of, and which has been my chief guide in all I have said, — namely, that in works *of imagination and sentiment*, for of these only have I been treating, in proportion as ideas and feelings are valuable, whether the composition be in prose or in verse, they require and exact one and the same language.[38] Metre is but adventitious to composition, and the phraseology for which that passport is necessary, even where it may be graceful at all, will be little valued by the judicious.

# [Letter to John Wilson (1802)]

꧁꧂

[Composed between 5 and 7 June 1802. First published 1851. Dated 7 June 1802. The draft of the letter, which provides our only copy, has sections torn out of the margins of all four pages; hence the many conjectures. All previously printed versions of this letter contain substantive errors; this printing follows the manuscript. Because the letter has never been accurately transcribed, added punctuation is placed in brackets.]

John Wilson, who was later to become the 'Christopher North' of Blackwood's Magazine and a neighbour of Wordsworth, at the age of eighteen wrote him a very enthusiastic and flattering letter containing large questions about nature and poetry. Wordsworth directs his main attention to Wilson's questions about 'The Idiot Boy' and in the process conveys his ideas about the moral effect of poetry. A brief conventional ending has been omitted here.

Had it not been for a very amiable modesty you could not have imagined that your letter could give me any offence. It was on many accounts highly grateful [1] to me. I was pleas'd to find that I had given so much pleasure to an ingenuous and able mind and I further considered the enjoyment which you had had from my poems as an earnest that others might be delighted with them in the same or a like manner. It is plain from your letter that the pleasure which I have given you has not been blind or unthinking[;] you have studied the poems and prove that you have entered into the spirit of them.

They have not given you a cheap or vulgar pleasure[;] therefore I feel that you are entitled to my kindest thanks for having done some violence to your natural diffidence in the communication which you have made to me.

There is scarcely any part of your letter that does not deserve particular notice, but partly from a weakness in my stomach and digestion and partly from certain habits of mind I do not write any letters unless upon business, not ev[en] to my dearest Friends. Except during absence from my own family I ha[ve] not written five letters of friendship during the last five years. I have mentioned this in order that I may retain your good opinion should my le[tter] be less minute than you are entitled to expect.

You seem to be desirous [of] my opinion on the influence of natural objects in forming the character of nati[ons.] This cannot be understood without first considering their influence upon men in [general,] first with reference to such objects as are common to all countries: and [then] such as belong exclusively to any particular country or in a greater d[egree] to it than to another. Now it is manifest that no human being can be so besotted and debased by oppression, penury or any other evil which unhum[anizes] man as to be utterly insensible to the colours, forms, or smell of flowers[,] the [sounds] and motions of birds and beasts, the appearances of the sky and heavenly bodie[s,] the general warmth of a fine day, the terror and uncomfortableness of a storm, &c &[c.] How dead soever many full[-]grown men may outwardly seem to these thi[ngs] they all are more or less affected by them, and in childhood, in the first practice and exe[rcise] of their senses they must have bee[n] not the nourish[-ers] merely, but often the fathers of their passions. There cannot be a doubt that in tracts of country where images of danger, melancholy, grandeur, or loveliness[,] softness, and ease prevail that they will make themselves felt powerfully in forming the characters of the people, so as to produce an uniformity or national character, where the nation is small and is not made up of men who[,] inhabiting different soils, climates, &c by their civil usages, and relations materially interfere with each other.

It was so formerly, no doubt, in the Highlands of Scotland but we cannot perhaps observe much of it in our own island at the present day, because, even in the most sequestered places, by manufactures, traffic, religion, Law, interchange of inhabitants &c distinctions are done away which would otherwise have been strong and obvious. This complex state of society does not, however, prevent the characters of individuals from frequently receiving a strong bias not merely from the impressions of general nature, but also from local objects and images. But it seems that to produce these effects in the degree in which we frequently find them to be produced there must be a peculiar sensibility of original organization combining with moral accidents, as is exhibited in THE BROTHERS and in RUTH – I mean to produce this in a marked degree, not that I believe that any man was ever brought up in the country without loving it, especially in his better moments, or in a district of particular grandeur or beauty without feeling some stronger attachment to it on that account than he would otherwise have felt. I include, you will observe, in these considerations the influence of climate, changes in the atmosphere and elements and the labours and occupations which particular districts require.

You begin what you say upon the Idiot Boy with this observation, that nothing is a fit subject for poetry which does not please. But here follows a question, Does not please whom? Some have little knowledge of natural imagery of any kind, and, of course, little relish for it, some are disgusted with the very mention of the words pastoral poetry, sheep or shepherds,[2] some cannot tolerate a poem with a ghost or any supernatural agency in it, others would shrink from an animated description of the pleasures of love, as from a thing carnal and libidinous[,] some cannot bear to see delicate and refined feelings ascribed to men in low conditions in society, because their vanity and self-love tell them that these belong only to themselves, and men like themselves in dress[,] station, and way of life: others are disgusted with the naked language of some of the most interesting passions of men, because either it is indelicate, or gross, or vu[lgar]. As many fine ladies could not bear certain expressions in

The [Mad] Mother[3] and the Thorn, and, as in the instance of Adam Smith, who, we [are] told could not endure the Ballad of Clym of the Clough, because the [au]thor had not written like a gentleman;[4] then there are professional [, loca]l, and national prejudices for evermore[;] some take no interest in the [descri]ption of a particular passion or quality, as love of solitariness, we will say, [geni]al activity of fancy, love of nature, religion and so forth because they have [little] or nothing of it in themselves, and so on without end. I return then to [the] question, please whom? or what? I answer, human nature as it has been, [and eve]r will be. But, where are we to find the best measure of this? I answer [, with]in by stripping our own hearts naked and by looking out of ourselves to [me]n who lead the simplest lives and most according to nature[,] men who [ha]ve never known false refinements, wayward and artificial desires, false criti[-ci]sms, effeminate habits of thinking and feeling, or who, having known these [t]hings[,] have outgrown them. This latter class is the most to be depended upon, but it is very small in number. People in our rank of life are perpetually falling into one sad mistake, namely, that of supposing that human nature and the persons they associate with are one and the same thing. Whom do we generally associate with? Gentlemen, persons of fortune, professional men, ladies[,] persons who can afford to buy or can easily procure books of half a guinea price, hot-pressed, and printed upon superfine paper. These persons are, it is true, a part of human nature but we err lamentably if we suppose them to be fair representatives of the vast mass of human existence. And yet few ever consider books but with reference to their power of pleasing these persons and men of a higher rank[;] few descend lower among cottages and fields and among children. A man must have done this habitually before his judgment upon the Idiot Boy would be in any way decisive with me. I *know* I have done this myself habitually; I wrote the poem with exceeding delight and pleasure, and whenever I read it I read it with pleasure. You have given me prais[e] for having reflected faithfully in my poems the feelings of human nature[;] I would fain hope that I have done so. But a great Poet ought to do more than this[;] he ought to a certain degree to rectify men's feelings, to give them new compositions of feeling, to render their feelings more sane[,] pure and permanent, in short, more consonant to nature, that is, to eternal nature and the great moving spirit of things. He ought to travel before men occasionally as well as at their sides[.] I may illustrate this by a reference to natural objects. What false notions have prevailed from generation to generation of the true character of the nightingale. As far as my Friend's Poem,[5] in the Lyrical Ballads, is read it will contribute greatly to rectify these. You will recollect a passage in Cowper where, speaking of rural sounds, he says —

> 'and *even* the boding Owl
> That hails the rising moon has charms for me.'[6]

Cowper was passionately fond of natural objects yet you see he mentions it as a marvellous thing that he could connect pleasure with the cry of the owl. In the same poem he speaks in the same manner of that beautiful plant, the gorse; making in some degree an amiable boast, of his loving it '*unsightly* and unsmooth['][7] as it is. There are many aversions of this kind, which, though they have some foundation in nature, have yet so slight a one, that though they may have prevailed hundreds of years a philosopher will look upon them as a[cc]idents. So with respect to many moral feelings either of [lo]ve or dislike[;] what excessive admiration was payed in former times to personal prowess and military success — it is so with [the] latter even at the present day but surely not nearly so much as hereto[fore.] So with regard to birth, and innumerable other modes of sentiment, civil and religious. But you will be inclined to ask by this time how all this applies to the Idiot Boy. To this I can only say that the loathing and disgust which many peo[ple] have at the sight of an Idiot, is a feeling which, though having som[e] foundation in human nature is not necessarily attached to it in any vi[tal] degree, but is owing, in a great measure to a false delicacy, and, if I [may] say it without rudeness, a certain want of comprehensiveness of think[ing] and feeling. Persons in the lower classes of society have little or nothing [of] this: if an Idiot is born in a poor man's house it must be taken car[e of] and cannot be boarded out, as it would be by gentle-folks, or sent to [a] public or private receptacle for such unfortunate be[in]gs. Po[or people] seeing frequently among their neighbours such objects easily [dismiss what]ever there is of natural disgust about them, and have t[herefore] a sane state, so that without pain or suffering they [perform] their duties towards them. I could with pleasure pursue this subj[ject, but] I must now strictly adopt the plan which I proposed [to my]self when I began to write this letter, namely that of setting down [a] few hints or memorandums which you will think of for my sake.

I have often applied to Idiots, in my own mind, that sublime expression of scripture that, '*their life is hidden with God.*'⁸ They are worshipped, probably from a feeling of this sort, in several parts of the East. Among the Alps where they are numerous, they are con-sidered I believe, as a blessing to the family to which they belong[;] I have indeed often looked upon the conduct of fathers and mothers of the lower classes of society towards Idiots as the great triumph of the human heart. It is there that we see the strength, disinterestedness, and grandeur of love, nor have I ever been able to contemplate an object that calls out so many excellent and virtuous sentiments with-out finding it hallowed thereby and having something in me which bears down before it, like a deluge, every feeble sensation of disgust and aversion.

There are in my opinion, several important mistakes in the latter part of your letter which I could have wished to notice; but I find myself much fatigued. These refer both to the Boy and the Mother. I must content myself simply with observing that it is probable that the principal cause of your dislike to this particular poem lies in the *word* Idiot. If there had been any such word in our language, *to which we had attached passion*, as lack-wit, half-wit, witless &c I should have certainly employed it in preference but there is no such word. Observe, (this is entirely in reference to this particular poem) my Idiot is not one of those who cannot articulate and such as are usually disgusting in their persons [–] 'Whether in cunning or in joy' 'And then his words were not a few' &c [–]⁹ and the last speech at the end

313

of the poem. The Boy whom I had in my mind was, by no means disgusting in his appearance[,] quite the contrary[,] and I have known several with imperfect faculties who are handsome in their persons and features. There is one, at present, within a mile of my own house remarkably so, though there is something of a stare and vacancy in his countenance. A Friend [of] mine, knowing that some persons had a dislike to the poem such as you have expressed advised me to add a stanza describing the person of the Boy [so a]s entirely to separate him in the imaginations of my Readers from [tha]t class of idiots who are disgusting in their persons, but the narration [of] the poem is so rapid and impassioned that I could not find a place [in] which to insert the stanza without checking the progress of it, and [so lea]ving a deadness upon the feeling. This poem has, I know, frequently produced [the s]ame effect as it did upon you and your Friends but there are many [peo]ple also to whom it affords exquisite delight, and who indeed, prefer [it] to any other of my Poems. This proves that the feelings there delineated [are] such as all men *may* sympathize with. This is enough for my purpose. [It] is not enough for me as a poet, to delineate merely such feelings as all men *do* sympathise [with] but it is also highly desirable to add to these other, such as all men *may* sympathize with and such as there is reason to believe they would be better and more moral beings if they did sympathize with.

# [Letter to Lady Beaumont (1807)]

*[Dated 21 May 1807. First published 1851. Some punctuation and paragraphing have been added here, although less than in the last definitive edition. Several substantive errors also found in that edition have been silently corrected.]*

*Lady Beaumont, wife of Sir George Beaumont, the painter, and along with him a close friend of the Wordsworths, had written the poet of her concern about the recently published* Poems in Two Volumes. *Wordsworth here responds by sketching the sort of reader his poetry requires and by analysing the very subtle psychology of one of his recent sonnets. A brief conventional ending and personal postscript are omitted from the letter below.*

Though I am to see you so soon I cannot but write a word or two, to thank you for the interest you take in my Poems [1] as evinced by your solicitude about their immediate reception. I write partly to thank you for this and to express the pleasure it has given me, and partly to remove any uneasiness from your mind which the disappointments you sometimes meet [with] in this labour of love may occasion. I see that you have many battles to fight for me; more than in the ardour and confidence of your pure and elevated mind you had ever thought of being summoned to; but be assured that this opposition is nothing more than what I distinctly foresaw that you and my other Friends

315

would have to enounter. I say this, not to give myself credit for an eye of prophecy, but to allay any vexatious thoughts on my account which this opposition may have produced in you. It is impossible that any expectations can be lower than mine concerning the immediate effect of this little work upon what is called the Public. I do not here take into consideration the envy and malevolence, and all the bad passions which always stand in the way of a work of any merit from a living Poet; but merely think of the pure, absolute, honest ignorance, in which all worldlings of every rank and situation must be enveloped, with respect to the thoughts, feelings, and images, on which the life of my Poems depends. The things which I have taken, whether from within or without, – what have they to do with routs, dinners, morning calls, hurry from door to door, from street to street, on foot or in Carriage; with Mr Pitt or Mr Fox,[2] Mr Paul or Sir Francis Burdett, the Westminster Election[3] or the Borough of Honiton;[4] in a word, for I cannot stop to make my way through the hurry of images that present themselves to me, what have they to do with endless talking about things nobody cares any thing for except as far as their own vanity is concerned, and this with persons they care nothing for but as their vanity or *selfishness* is concerned; what have they to do (to say all at once) with a life without love? – in such a life there can be no thought; for we have no thought (save thoughts of pain) but as far as we have love and admiration.[5] It is an awful truth, that there neither is, nor can be, any genuine enjoyment of Poetry among nineteen out of twenty of those persons who live or wish to live in the broad light of the world – among those who either are, or are striving to make themselves, people of consideration in society. This is a truth and an awful one because to be incapable of a feeling of Poetry in my sense of the word is to be without love of human nature and reverence for God.

Upon this I shall insist elsewhere; at present let me confine myself to my object, which is to make you, my dear Friend, as easy-hearted as myself with respect to these Poems. Trouble not yourself upon their present reception; of what moment is that compared with what I trust is their destiny, to console the afflicted, to add sunshine to daylight by making the happy happier, to teach the young and the gracious of every age, to see, to think and feel, and therefore to become more actively and securely virtuous; this is their office, which I trust they will faithfully perform long after we (that is, all that is mortal of us) are mouldered in our graves. I am well aware how far it would seem to many I overrate my own exertions when I speak in this way, in direct connection with the Volumes I have just made public.

I am not, however, afraid of such censure, insignificant as probably the majority of those poems would appear to very respectable persons; I do not mean London Wits and Witlings, for these have too many bad passions about them to be respectable even if they had more intellect than the benign laws of providence will allow to such a heartless existence as theirs is; but grave, kindly natured, worthy persons, who would be pleased if they could. I hope that these Volumes are not without some recommendations, even for Readers of this class, but their imagination has slept; and the voice which is the voice of my Poetry without Imagination cannot be heard. –

Leaving these, I was going to say a word to such Readers as Mr Rogers.[6] Such! how would he be offended if he knew I considered him only as a representative of a class, and not as unique! 'Pity,' says Mr R., 'that so many trifling things should be admitted to obstruct the view of those that have merit'; now, let this candid judge take, by way of example, the sonnets, which probably with the exception of two or three other Poems for which I will not contend appear to him the most trifling, as they are the shortest, I would say to him, omitting things of higher consideration, there is one thing which must strike you at once if you will only read these poems, – that those to Liberty, at least, have a connection with, or a bearing upon, each other, and therefore, if individually they want weight, perhaps, as a Body, they may not be so deficient; at least this ought to induce you to suspend your judgment, and qualify it so far as to allow that the writer aims at least at comprehensiveness. But dropping this, I would boldly say at once, that these Sonnets, while they each fix the attention upon some important sentiment separately considered, do at the same time collectively make a Poem on the subject of civil Liberty and national independence, which, either for simplicity of style or grandeur of moral sentiment, is, alas! likely to have few parallels in the Poetry of the present day. Again, turn to the 'Moods of my own Mind'. There is scarcely a Poem here of above thirty Lines, and very trifling these poems will appear to many; but, omitting to speak of them individually, do they not, taken collectively, fix the attention upon a subject eminently poetical, viz., the interest which objects in nature derive from the predominance of certain affections more or less permanent, more or less capable of salutary renewal in the mind of the being contemplating these objects? – This is poetic, and essentially poetic, and why? because it is creative. But I am wasting words, for it is nothing more than you know, and if said to those for whom it is intended, it would not be understood.

I see by your last Letter that Mrs Fermor[7] has entered into the spirit of these 'Moods of my own Mind'. Your transcript from her Letter gave me the greatest pleasure; but I must say that even she has something yet to receive from me. I say this with confidence, from her thinking that I have fallen below myself in the Sonnet beginning – 'With ships the sea was sprinkled far and nigh.' As to the other[8] which she objects to, I will only observe that there is a misprint in the last line but two, 'And *though* this wilderness' for 'And *through* this wilderness' – that makes it unintelligible. This latter Sonnet for many reasons (though I do not abandon it) I will not now speak of; but upon the other, I could say something important in conversation, and will attempt now to illustrate it by a comment which I feel will be very inadequate to convey my meaning. There is scarcely one of my Poems which does not aim to direct the attention to some moral sentiment, or to some general principle, or law of thought, or of our intellectual constitution. For instance in the present case, who is there that has not felt that the mind can have no rest among a multitude of objects, of which it either cannot make one whole, or from which it cannot single out one individual, whereupon may be concentrated the attention divided among or distracted by a multitude? After a

certain time we must either select one image or object, which must
put out of view the rest wholly, or must subordinate them to itself
while it stands forth as a Head:

> Now glowed the firmament
> With living sapphires! Hesperus, that *led*
> The starry host, rode brightest; till the Moon,
> Rising in clouded majesty, at length,
> Apparent *Queen*, unveiled *her peerless* light,
> And o'er the dark her silver mantle threw.[9]

Having laid this down as a general principle, take the case before
us. I am represented in the Sonnet [10] as casting my eyes over the sea,
sprinkled with a multitude of Ships, like the heavens with stars, my
mind may be supposed to float up and down among them in a kind
of dreamy indifference with respect either to this or that one, only in
a pleasurable state of feeling with respect to the whole prospect.
'Joyously it showed,' this continues till that feeling may be supposed
to have passed away, and a kind of comparative listlessness or apathy
to have succeeded, as at this line, 'Some veering up and down, one
knew not why.' All at once, while I am in this state, comes forth an
object, an individual; and my mind, sleepy and unfixed, is awakened
and fastened in a moment. 'Hesperus, that *led* The starry host,' is a
poetical object, because the glory of his own Nature gives him the
pre-eminence the moment he appears; he calls forth the poetic faculty,
receiving its exertions as a tribute; but this Ship in the Sonnet may, in
a manner still more appropriate, be said to come upon a mission of
the poetic Spirit, because in its own appearance and attributes it is
barely sufficiently distinguish[ed] to rouse the creative faculty of the
human mind; to exertions at all times welcome, but doubly so when
they come upon us when in a state of remissness. The mind being
once fixed and rouzed, all the rest comes from itself; it is merely a
lordly Ship, nothing more:

> This ship was nought to me, nor I to her,
> Yet I pursued her with a lover's look.

My mind wantons with grateful joy in the exercise of its own powers, and, loving its own creation,

> This ship to all the rest I did prefer,

making her a sovereign or a regent, and thus giving body and life to all the rest; mingling up this idea with fondness and praise –

> Where she comes the winds must stir;

and concluding the whole with

> On went She, and due north her journey took.

Thus taking up again the Reader with whom I began, letting him know how long I must have watched this favourite Vessel, and inviting him to rest his mind as mine is resting.

Having said so much upon a mere 14 lines, which Mrs Fermor did not approve of, I cannot but add a word or two upon my satisfaction in finding that my mind has so much in common with hers, and that we participate so many of each other's pleasures. I collect this from her having singled out the two little Poems, the Daffodils, and the Rock crowned with snowdrops.[11] I am sure that whoever is much pleased with either of these quiet and tender delineations must be fitted to walk through the recesses of my poetry with delight, and will there recognise, at every turn, something or other in which, and over which, it has that property and right which knowledge and love confer. The line, 'Come, blessed barrier, etc.,' in the sonnet upon Sleep,[12] which Mrs F. points out, had before been mentioned to me by Coleridge, and indeed by almost everybody who had heard it, as eminently beautiful. My letter (as this 2nd sheet, which I am obliged to take, admonishes me) is growing to an enormous length; and yet, saving that I have expressed my calm confidence that these Poems will live, I have said nothing which has a particular application to the object of it, which was to remove all disquiet from your mind on account of the condemnation they may at present incur from that portion of my contemporaries who are called the Public. I am sure, my dear Lady Beaumont, if you attach any importance [to it] it can only be from an apprehension that it may affect me, upon which I have already set you at ease, or from a fear that this present blame is ominous of their future or final destiny. If this be the case, your tenderness for me betrays you; be assured that the decision of these persons has nothing to do with the Question; they are altogether incompetent judges. These people in the senseless hurry of their idle lives do not *read* books, they merely snatch a glance at them that they may talk about them. And even if this were not so, never forget what I believe was observed to you by Coleridge, that every great and original writer, in proportion as he is great or original, must himself create the taste by which he is to be relished; [13] he must teach the art by which he is to be seen; this, in a certain degree, even to all persons, however wise and pure may be their lives, and however unvitiated their taste; but for those who dip into books in order to give an opinion of them, or talk about them to take up an opinion – for this multitude of unhappy, and misguided, and misguiding beings, an entire regeneration must be produced; and if this be possible, it must be a work of *time*. To conclude, my ears are stone-dead to this idle buzz, and my flesh as insensible as iron to these petty stings; and after what I have said I am sure yours will be the same. I doubt not that you will share with me an invincible confidence that my [wri]tings (and among them these little Poems) will cooperate with [the ben]ign tendencies in human nature and society wherever found; and that they will, in their degree, be efficacious in making men wiser, better, and happier.

# Essays upon Epitaphs

~ꝗ~ ~ꝗ~ ~ꝗ~

[*Probably composed between about December 1809 and (Essay I) 22 February 1810, (Essays II and III) 28 February 1810. Essay I was first published 22 February 1810 in Samuel Taylor Coleridge's* The Friend, *and Essays II and III were first published in 1876. The text for Essay I given below is taken from* Poetical Works *(1850), VI, 287–300; the text for Essays II and III is from manuscripts in the Dove Cottage Library.*]

*The first essay was not only printed in* The Friend *but also appeared as a note to* The Excursion, *Books Five, Six, and Seven of which were written at about the same time and share thoughts and even occasional phrasing with the essay. The second and third essays were also meant to appear in* The Friend, *but for some reason did not; in any case they are not as polished as the first essay and contain mistakes and other signs of haste.*

It need scarcely be said, that an Epitaph presupposes a Monument, upon which it is to be engraven. Almost all Nations have wished that certain external signs should point out the places where their dead are interred. Among savage tribes unacquainted with letters this has mostly been done either by rude stones placed near the graves, or by mounds of earth raised over them. This custom proceeded obviously from a twofold desire; first, to guard the remains of the deceased from irreverent approach or from savage violation: and, secondly, to preserve their memory. 'Never any,' says Camden, 'neglected burial but some savage nations; as the Bactrians, which cast their dead to the dogs; some varlet philosophers, as Diogenes, who desired to be devoured of fishes; some dissolute courtiers, as Maecenas, who was wont to say, Non tumulum curo; sepelit natura relictos.

I'm careless of a grave: – Nature her dead will save.'[1]

As soon as nations had learned the use of letters, epitaphs were inscribed upon these monuments; in order that their intention might be more surely and adequately fulfilled. I have derived monuments and epitaphs from two sources of feeling: but these do in fact resolve themselves into one. The invention of epitaphs, Weever, in his Discourse of Funeral Monuments, says rightly, 'proceeded from the presage or fore-feeling of immortality, implanted in all men naturally, and is referred to the scholars of Linus the Theban poet, who flourished about the year of the world two thousand seven hundred; who first bewailed this Linus their Master, when he was slain, in doleful verses, then called of him Oelina, afterwards Epitaphia, for that they were first sung at burials, after engraved upon the sepulchres.'[2]

And, verily, without the consciousness of a principle of immortality in the human soul, Man could never have had awakened in him the desire to live in the remembrance of his fellows: mere love, or the yearning of kind towards kind, could not have produced it. The dog or horse perishes in the field, or in the stall, by the side of his companions, and is incapable of anticipating the sorrow with which his surrounding associates shall bemoan his death, or pine for his loss; he cannot preconceive this regret, he can form no thought of it; and therefore cannot possibly have a desire to leave such regret or remembrance behind him. Add to the principle of love which exists in the inferior animals, the faculty of reason which exists in Man alone; will the conjunction of these account for the desire? Doubtless it is a necessary consequence of this conjunction; yet not I think as a direct result, but only to be come at through an intermediate thought, viz. that of an intimation or assurance within us, that some part of our nature is imperishable. At least the precedence, in order of birth, of one feeling to the other, is unquestionable. If we look back upon the days of childhood, we shall find that the time is not in remembrance when, with respect to our own individual Being, the mind was without this assurance;[3] whereas, the wish to be remembered by our friends or kindred after death, or even in absence, is, as we shall discover, a sensation that does not form itself till the *social* feelings have been developed, and the Reason has connected itself with a wide range of objects. Forlorn, and cut off from communication with the best part of his nature, must that man be, who should derive the sense of immortality, as it exists in the mind of a child, from the same unthinking gaiety or liveliness of animal spirits with which the lamb in the meadow, or any other irrational creature is endowed; who should ascribe it, in short, to blank ignorance in the child; to an inability arising from the imperfect state of his faculties to come, in any point of his being, into contact with a notion of death; or to an unreflecting acquiescence in what had been instilled into him! Has such an unfolder of the mysteries of nature, though he may have forgotten his former self, ever noticed the early, obstinate, and unappeasable inquisitiveness of children upon the subject of origination? This single fact proves outwardly the monstrousness of those suppositions: for, if we had no direct external testimony that the minds of very young children meditate feelingly upon death and immortality, these inquiries, which we all know they are perpetually making concerning the *whence*, do necessarily include correspondent habits of interrogation concerning the *whither*. Origin and tendency are notions inseparably co-relative. Never did a child stand by the side of a running stream, pondering within himself what power was the feeder of the perpetual current, from what never-wearied sources the body of water was supplied, but he must have been inevitably propelled to follow this question by another: 'Towards what abyss is it in progress? what receptacle can contain the mighty influx?' And the spirit of the answer must have been, though the word might be sea or ocean, accompanied perhaps with an image gathered from a map, or from the real object in nature – these might have been the *letter*, but the *spirit* of the answer must have been *as* inevitably, – a receptacle without bounds or dimensions; – nothing less than infinity. We may, then, be justified in asserting, that the sense of immortality, if not a co-existent and twin birth with Reason, is among the earliest of her offspring: and we may further assert, that from these conjoined, and under their countenance, the human affections are gradually formed and opened out. This is not the place to enter into the recesses of these investigations; but the subject requires me here to make a plain avowal, that, for my own part, it is to me inconceivable, that the sympathies of love towards each other, which grow with our growth, could ever attain any new strength, or even preserve the old, after we had received from the outward senses the impression of death, and were in the habit of having that impression daily renewed and its accompanying feeling brought home to ourselves, and to those we love; if the same were not counteracted by those communications with our internal Being, which are anterior to all these experiences, and with which revelation coincides, and has through that coincidence alone (for otherwise it could not possess it) a power to affect us. I confess, with me the conviction is absolute, that, if the impression and sense of death were not thus counterbalanced, such a hollowness would pervade the whole system of things, such a want of correspondence and consistency, a disproportion so astounding betwixt means and ends, that there could be no repose, no joy. Were we to grow up unfostered by this genial warmth, a frost would chill the spirit, so penetrating and powerful, that there could be no motions of the life of love; and infinitely less could we have any wish to be remembered after we had passed away from a world in which each man had moved about like a shadow. – If, then, in a creature endowed with the faculties of foresight and reason, the social affections could not have unfolded themselves uncountenanced by the faith that Man is an immortal being; and if, consequently, neither could the individual dying have had a desire to survive in the remembrance of his fellows, nor on their side could they have felt a wish to preserve for future times vestiges of the departed; it follows, as a final inference, that without the belief in immortality, wherein these several desires originate, neither monuments nor epitaphs, in affectionate or laudatory commemoration of the deceased, could have existed in the world.

Simonides,[4] it is related, upon landing in a strange country, found the corse of an unknown person lying by the sea-side; he buried it, and was honoured throughout Greece for the piety of that act. Another ancient Philosopher,[5] chancing to fix his eyes upon a dead body, regarded the same with slight, if not with contempt; saying, 'See the shell of the flown bird!' But it is not to be supposed that the moral and tender-hearted Simonides was incapable of the lofty movements of thought, to which that other Sage gave way at the moment while his soul was intent only upon the indestructible being; nor, on the other hand, that he, in whose sight a lifeless human body was of no more value than the worthless shell from which the living fowl had departed, would not, in a different mood of mind, have been affected by those earthly considerations which had incited the philosophic Poet to the performance of that pious duty. And with regard to this latter we may be assured that, if he had been destitute of the capability of communing with the more exalted thoughts that appertain to human nature, he would have cared no more for the corse of the stranger than for the dead body of a seal or porpoise which might have been cast up by the waves. We respect the corporeal frame of Man, not merely because it is the habitation of a rational, but of an immortal Soul. Each of these Sages was in sympathy with the best feelings of our nature; feelings which, though they seem opposite to each other, have another and a finer connection than that of contrast. – It is a connection formed through the subtle progress by which, both in the natural and the moral world, qualities pass insensibly into their contraries, and things revolve upon each other. As, in sailing upon the orb of this planet, a voyage towards the regions where the sun sets, conducts gradually to the quarter where we have been accustomed to behold it come forth at its rising; and, in like manner, a voyage towards the east, the birth-place in our imagination of the morning, leads finally to the quarter where the sun is last seen when he departs from our eyes; so the contemplative

Soul, travelling in the direction of mortality, advances to the country of everlasting life; and, in like manner, may she continue to explore those cheerful tracts, till she is brought back, for her advantage and benefit, to the land of transitory things – of sorrow and of tears.

On a midway point, therefore, which commands the thoughts and feelings of the two Sages whom we have represented in contrast, does the Author of that species of composition, the laws of which it is our present purpose to explain, take his stand. Accordingly, recurring to the twofold desire of guarding the remains of the deceased and preserving their memory, it may be said that a sepulchral monument is a tribute to a man as a human being; and that an epitaph (in the ordinary meaning attached to the word) includes this general feeling and something more; and is a record to preserve the memory of the dead, as a tribute due to his individual worth, for a satisfaction to the sorrowing hearts of the survivors, and for the common benefit of the living: which record is to be accomplished, not in a general manner, but, where it can, in *close connection with the bodily remains of the deceased:* and these, it may be added, among the modern nations of Europe, are deposited within, or contiguous to, their places of worship. In ancient times, as is well known, it was the custom to bury the dead beyond the walls of towns and cities; and among the Greeks and Romans they were frequently interred by the way-sides.

I could here pause with pleasure, and invite the Reader to indulge with me in contemplation of the advantages which must have attended such a practice. We might ruminate upon the beauty which the monuments, thus placed, must have borrowed from the surrounding images of nature – from the trees, the wild flowers, from a stream running perhaps within sight or hearing, from the beaten road stretching its weary length hard by. Many tender similitudes must these objects have presented to the mind of the traveller leaning upon one of the tombs, or reposing in the coolness of its shade, whether he had halted from weariness or in compliance with the invitation, 'Pause, Traveller!' so often found upon the monuments. And to its epitaph also must have been supplied strong appeals to visible appearances or immediate impressions, lively and affecting analogies of life as a journey – death as a sleep overcoming the tired wayfarer – of misfortune as a storm that falls suddenly upon him – of beauty as a flower that passeth away, or of innocent pleasure as one that may be gathered – of virtue that standeth firm as a rock against the beating waves; – of hope 'undermined insensibly like the poplar by the side of the river that has fed it,'[6] or blasted in a moment like a pine-tree by the stroke of lightning upon the mountain-top – of admonitions and heart-stirring remembrances, like a refreshing breeze that comes without warning, or the taste of the waters of an unexpected fountain. These, and similar suggestions, must have given, formerly, to the language of the senseless stone a voice enforced and endeared by the benignity of that nature with which it was in unison. – We, in modern times, have lost much of these advantages; and they are but in a small degree counterbalanced to the inhabitants of large towns and cities, by the custom of depositing the dead within, or contiguous to, their places of worship; however splendid or imposing may be the appearance of those edifices, or however interesting or salutary the recollections associated with them. Even were it not true that tombs lose their monitory virtue when thus obtruded upon the notice of men occupied with the cares of the world, and too often sullied and defiled by those cares, yet still, when death is in our thoughts, nothing can make amends for the want of the soothing influences of nature, and for the absence of those types of renovation and decay, which the fields and woods offer to the notice of the serious and contemplative mind. To feel the force of this sentiment, let a man only compare in imagination the unsightly manner in which our monuments are crowded together in the busy, noisy, unclean, and almost grassless church-yard of a large town, with the still seclusion of a Turkish cemetery, in some remote place; and yet further sanctified by the grove of cypress in which it is embosomed. Thoughts in the same temper as these have already been expressed with true sensibility by an ingenuous Poet of the present day. The subject of his poem is 'All Saints Church, Derby': he has been deploring the forbidding and unseemly appear-

ance of its burial-ground, and uttering a wish, that in past times the
practice had been adopted of interring the inhabitants of large towns
in the country: —

> 'Then in some rural, calm, sequestered spot,
> Where healing Nature her benignant look
> Ne'er changes, save at that lorn season, when,
> With tresses drooping o'er her sable stole,
> She yearly mourns the mortal doom of man,
> Her noblest work, (so Israel's virgins erst,
> With annual moan upon the mountains wept
> Their fairest gone,) there in that rural scene,
> So placid, so congenial to the wish
> The Christian feels, of peaceful rest within
> The silent grave, I would have stray'd.
>
>     \*     \*     \*     \*
>
> — wandered forth, where the cold dew of heaven
> Lay on the humbler graves around, what time
> The pale moon gazed upon the turfy mounds,
> Pensive, as though like me, in lonely muse,
> 'Twere brooding on the dead inhumed beneath.
> There while with him, the holy man of Uz,
> O'er human destiny I sympathised,
> Counting the long, long periods prophecy
> Decrees to roll, ere the great day arrives
> Of resurrection, oft the blue-eyed Spring
> Had met me with her blossoms, as the Dove,
> Of old, returned with olive leaf, to cheer
> The Patriarch mourning o'er a world destroyed:
> And I would bless her visit; for to me
> 'Tis sweet to trace the consonance that links
> As one, the works of Nature and the word
> Of God.' —

John Edwards[7]

A village church-yard, lying as it does in the lap of nature, may
indeed be most favourably contrasted with that of a town of crowded

population; and sepulture therein combines many of the best tendencies which belong to the mode practised by the Ancients, with others peculiar to itself. The sensations of pious cheerfulness, which attend the celebration of the sabbath-day in rural places, are profitably chastised by the sight of the graves of kindred and friends, gathered together in that general home towards which the thoughtful yet happy spectators themselves are journeying. Hence a parish-church, in the stillness of the country, is a visible centre of a community of the living and the dead; a point to which are habitually referred the nearest concerns of both.

As, then, both in cities and in villages, the dead are deposited in close connection with our places of worship, with us the composition of an epitaph naturally turns, still more than among the nations of antiquity, upon the most serious and solemn affections of the human mind; upon departed worth – upon personal or social sorrow and admiration – upon religion, individual and social – upon time, and upon eternity. Accordingly, it suffices, in ordinary cases, to secure a composition of this kind from censure, that it contain nothing that shall shock or be inconsistent with this spirit. But, to entitle an epitaph to praise, more than this is necessary. It ought to contain some thought or feeling belonging to the mortal or immortal part of our nature touchingly expressed; and if that be done, however general or even trite the sentiment may be, every man of pure mind will read the words with pleasure and gratitude. A husband bewails a wife; a parent breathes a sigh of disappointed hope over a lost child; a son utters a sentiment of filial reverence for a departed father or mother; a friend perhaps inscribes an encomium recording the companionable qualities, or the solid virtues, of the tenant of the grave, whose departure has left a sadness upon his memory. This and a pious admonition to the living, and a humble expression of Christian confidence in immortality, is the language of a thousand churchyards; and it does not often happen that anything, in a greater degree discriminate or appropriate to the dead or to the living, is to be found in them. This want of discrimination has been ascribed by Dr Johnson, in his Essay upon the epitaphs of Pope, to two causes; first, the scantiness of the objects of human praise; and, secondly, the want of variety in the characters of men; or, to use his own words, 'to the fact, that the greater part of mankind have no character at all.' [8] Such language may be holden without blame among the generalities of common conversation; but does not become a critic and a moralist speaking seriously upon a serious subject. The objects of admiration in human-nature are not scanty, but abundant: and every man has a character of his own, to the eye that has skill to perceive it. The real cause of the acknowledged want of discrimination in sepulchral memorials is this: That to analyse the characters of others, especially of those whom we love, is not a common or natural employment of men at any time. We are not anxious unerringly to understand the constitution of the minds of those who have soothed, who have cheered, who have supported us: with whom we have been long and daily pleased or delighted. The affections are their own justification. The light of love in our hearts is a satisfactory evidence that there is a body of worth in the minds of our friends or kindred, whence that light has proceeded. We shrink from the thought of placing their merits and defects to be weighed against each other in the nice balance of pure intellect; nor do we find much temptation to detect the shades by which a good quality or virtue is discriminated in them from an excellence known by the same general name as it exists in the mind of another; and, least of all, do we incline to these re-finements when under the pressure of sorrow, admiration, or regret, or when actuated by any of those feelings which incite men to prolong the memory of their friends and kindred, by records placed in the bosom of the all-uniting and equalising receptacle of the dead.

The first requisite, then, in an Epitaph is, that it should speak, in a tone which shall sink into the heart, the general language of humanity as connected with the subject of death – the source from which an epitaph proceeds – of death, and of life. To be born and to die are the two points in which all men feel themselves to be in absolute coincidence. This general language may be uttered so strikingly as to entitle an epitaph to high praise; yet it cannot lay claim to the highest unless other excellencies be superadded. Passing through all intermediate steps, we will attempt to determine at once what these excellencies are, and wherein consists the perfection of this species of composition. – It will be found to lie in a due proportion of the common or universal feeling of humanity to sensations excited by a distinct and clear conception, conveyed to the reader's mind, of the individual, whose death is deplored and whose memory is to be preserved; at least of his character as, after death, it appeared to those who loved him and lament his loss. The general sympathy ought to be quickened, provoked, and diversified, by particular thoughts, actions, images, – circumstances of age, occupation, manner of life, prosperity which the deceased had known, or adversity to which he had been subject; and these ought to be bound together and solemnised into one harmony by the general sympathy. The two powers should temper, restrain, and exalt each other. The reader ought to know who and what the man was whom he is called upon to think of with interest. A distinct conception should be given (implicitly where it can, rather than explicitly) of the individual lamented. – But the writer of an epitaph is not an anatomist, who dissects the internal frame of the mind; he is not even a painter, who executes a portrait at leisure and in entire tranquillity: his delineation, we must remember, is performed by the side of the grave; and, what is more, the grave of one whom he loves and admires. What purity and brightness is that virtue clothed in, the image of which must no longer bless our living eyes! The character of a deceased friend or beloved kinsman is not seen, no – nor ought to be seen, otherwise than as a tree through a tender haze or a luminous mist, that spiritualises and beautifies it; that takes away, indeed, but only to the end that the parts which are not abstracted may appear more dignified and lovely; may impress and affect the more. Shall we say, then, that this is not truth, not a faithful image; and that, accordingly, the purposes of commemoration cannot be answered? – It *is* truth, and of the highest order; for, though doubtless things are not apparent which did exist; yet, the object being looked at through this medium, parts and proportions are brought into distinct view which before had been only imperfectly or unconsciously seen: it is truth hallowed by love – the joint offspring of the worth of the dead and the affections of the living! This may easily be brought to the test. Let one, whose eyes have been sharpened by personal hostility to discover what was amiss in the character of a good man, hear the tidings of his death, and what a change is wrought in a moment! Enmity melts away; and, as it disappears, unsightliness, disproportion, and deformity, vanish; and, through the influence of commiseration, a harmony of love and beauty succeeds. Bring such a man to the tombstone on which shall be inscribed an epitaph on his adversary, composed in the spirit which we have recommended. Would he turn from it as from an idle tale? No; – the thoughtful look, the sigh, and perhaps the involuntary tear, would testify that it had a sane, a generous, and good meaning; and that on the writer's mind had remained an impression which was a true abstract of the character of the deceased; that his gifts and graces were remembered in the simplicity in which they ought to be remembered. The composition and quality of the mind of a virtuous man, contemplated by the side of the grave where his body is mouldering, ought to appear, and be felt as something midway between what he was on earth walking about with his living frailties, and what he may be presumed to be as a Spirit in heaven.

It suffices, therefore, that the trunk and the main branches of the worth of the deceased be boldly and unaffectedly represented. Any further detail, minutely and scrupulously pursued, especially if this be done with laborious and antithetic discriminations, must inevitably frustrate its own purpose; forcing the passing Spectator to this conclusion, – either that the dead did not possess the merits ascribed to him, or that they who have raised a monument to his memory, and must therefore be supposed to have been closely connected with him, were incapable of perceiving those merits; or at least during the act of composition had lost sight of them; for, the understanding having been so busy in its petty occupation, how could the heart of the mourner be other than cold? and in either of these cases, whether the fault be on the part of the buried person or the survivors, the memorial is unaffecting and profitless.

Much better is it to fall short in discrimination than to pursue it too far, or to labour it unfeelingly. For in no place are we so much disposed to dwell upon those points, of nature and condition, wherein all men resemble each other, as in the temple where the universal Father is worshipped, or by the side of the grave which gathers all human Beings to itself, and 'equalises the lofty and the low.'[9] We suffer and we weep with the same heart; we love and are anxious for one another in one spirit; our hopes look to the same quarter; and the virtues by which we are all to be furthered and supported, as patience, meekness, good-will, justice, temperance, and temperate desires, are in an equal degree the concern of us all. Let an Epitaph, then, contain at least these acknowledgments to our common nature; nor let the sense of their importance be sacrificed to a balance of opposite quali-ties or minute distinctions in individual character; which if they do not, (as will for the most part be the case,) when examined, resolve themselves into a trick of words, will, even when they are true and just, for the most part be grievously out of place; for, as it is probable that few only have explored these intricacies of human nature, so can the tracing of them be interesting only to a few. But an epitaph is not a proud writing shut up for the studious: it is exposed to all – to the wise and the most ignorant; it is condescending, perspicuous, and lovingly solicits regard; its story and admonitions are brief, that the thoughtless, the busy, and indolent, may not be deterred, nor the impatient tired: the stooping old man cons the engraven record like a second horn-book; – the child is proud that he can read it; – and the stranger is introduced through its mediation to the company of a friend: it is concerning all, and for all: – in the church-yard it is open to the day; the sun looks down upon the stone, and the rains of heaven beat against it.

Yet, though the writer who would excite sympathy is bound in this case, more than in any other, to give proof that he himself has been moved, it is to be remembered, that to raise a monument is a sober and a reflective act; that the inscription which it bears is intended to be permanent, and for universal perusal; and that, for this reason, the thoughts and feelings expressed should be permanent also

– liberated from that weakness and anguish of sorrow which is in nature transitory, and which with instinctive decency retires from notice. The passions should be subdued, the emotions controlled; strong, indeed, but nothing ungovernable or wholly involuntary. Seemliness requires this, and truth requires it also: for how can the narrator otherwise be trusted? Moreover, a grave is a tranquillising object: resignation in course of time springs up from it as naturally as the wild flowers, besprinkling the turf with which it may be covered, or gathering round the monument by which it is defended. The very form and substance of the monument which has received the inscription, and the appearance of the letters, testifying with what a slow and laborious hand they must have been engraven, might seem to reproach the author who had given way upon this occasion to transports of mind, or to quick turns of conflicting passion; though the same might constitute the life and beauty of a funeral oration or elegiac poem.

These sensations and judgments, acted upon perhaps unconsciously, have been one of the main causes why epitaphs so often personate the deceased, and represent him as speaking from his own tomb-stone. The departed Mortal is introduced telling you himself that his pains are gone; that a state of rest is come; and he conjures you to weep for him no longer. He admonishes with the voice of one experienced in the vanity of those affections which are confined to earthly objects, and gives a verdict like a superior Being, performing the office of a judge, who has no temptations to mislead him, and whose decision cannot but be dispassionate. Thus is death disarmed of its sting, and affliction unsubstantialised. By this tender fiction, the survivors bind themselves to a sedater sorrow, and employ the intervention of the imagination in order that the reason may speak her own language earlier than she would otherwise have been enabled to do. This shadowy interposition also harmoniously unites the two worlds of the living and the dead by their appropriate affections. And it may be observed, that here we have an additional proof of the propriety with which sepulchral inscriptions were referred to the consciousness of immortality as their primal source.

I do not speak with a wish to recommend that an epitaph should be cast in this mould preferably to the still more common one, in which what is said comes from the survivors directly; but rather to point out how natural those feelings are which have induced men, in all states and ranks of society, so frequently to adopt this mode. And this I have done chiefly in order that the laws, which ought to govern the composition of the other, may be better understood. This latter mode, namely, that in which the survivors speak in their own persons, seems to me upon the whole greatly preferable: as it admits a wider range of notices; and, above all, because, excluding the fiction which is the groundwork of the other, it rests upon a more solid basis.

Enough has been said to convey our notion of a perfect epitaph; but it must be borne in mind that one is meant which will best answer the *general* ends of that species of composition. According to the course pointed out, the worth of private life, through all varieties of situation and character, will be most honourably and profitably preserved in memory. Nor would the model recommended less suit public men, in all instances save of those persons who by the greatness of their services in the employments of peace or war, or by the surpassing excellence of their works in art, literature, or science, have made themselves not only universally known, but have filled the heart of their country with everlasting gratitude. Yet I must here pause to correct myself. In describing the general tenour of thought which epitaphs ought to hold, I have omitted to say, that if it be the *actions* of a man, or even some *one* conspicuous or beneficial act of local or general utility, which have distinguished him, and excited a desire that he should be remembered, then, of course, ought the attention to be directed chiefly to those actions or that act: and such sentiments dwelt upon as naturally arise out of them or it. Having made this necessary distinction, I proceed. – The mighty benefactors of mankind, as they are not only known by the immediate survivors, but will continue to be known familiarly to latest posterity, do not stand in need of biographic sketches, in such a place; nor of delineations of character to individualise them. This is already done by their Works, in the memories of men. Their naked names, and a grand comprehensive sentiment of civic gratitude, patriotic love, or human admiration – or the utterance of some elementary principle most essential in the constitution of true virtue; – or a declaration touching that pious humility and self-abasement, which are ever most profound as minds are most susceptible of genuine exaltation – or an intuition, communicated in adequate words, of the sublimity of intellectual power; – these are the only tribute which can here be paid – the only offering that upon such an altar would not be unworthy.

[The first ten lines of Milton's sonnet 'On Shakespeare' are omitted here.]

### ESSAY UPON EPITAPHS, II

> Yet even these bones from insult to protect
> Some frail memorial still erected nigh,
> With uncouth rhymes and shapeless sculpture deck'd,
> Implores the passing tribute of a sigh.
>
> Their name, their years, spelt by the unletter'd Muse,
> The place of fame and elegy supply,
> And many a holy text around she strews,
> That teach the rustic moralist to die. [10]

When a Stranger has walked round a Country Church-yard and glanced his eye over so many brief Chronicles,[11] as the tomb-stones usually contain, of faithful Wives, tender Husbands, dutiful Children, and good Men of all classes; he will be tempted to exclaim, in the language of one of the Characters of a modern Tale in a similar situation, 'Where are all the *bad* people buried?' [12] He may smile to himself an answer to this question, and may regret that it has intruded upon him so soon. For my own part such has been my lot. And, indeed, a Man, who is in the habit of suffering his mind to be carried passively towards truth as well as of going with conscious effort in search of it, may be forgiven, if he has sometimes insensibly yielded to the delusion of those flattering recitals, and found a pleasure in believing that the prospect of real life had been as fair as it was in that picture represented. And such a transitory oversight will without difficulty be forgiven by those who have observed a trivial fact in daily life, namely, how apt, in a series of calm weather, we are to forget that rain and storms have been, and will return, to interrupt any scheme of business or pleasure which our minds are occupied in arranging. Amid the quiet of a Church-yard thus decorated as it seemed by the hand of Memory, and shining, if I may so say, in the light of love, I have been affected by sensations akin to those which have risen in my mind while I have been standing by the side of a smooth Sea, on a Summer's day. It is such a happiness to have, in an unkind World, one Enclosure where the voice of detraction is not heard; where the traces of evil inclinations are unknown; where contentment prevails, and there is no jarring tone in the peaceful Concert of amity and gratitude.[13] I have been rouzed from this reverie by a consciousness, suddenly flashing upon me, of the anxieties, the perturbations, and, in many instances, the vices and rancorous dispositions, by which the hearts of those who lie under so smooth a surface and so fair an outside must have been agitated. The image of an unruffled Sea has still remained; but my fancy has penetrated into the depths of that Sea – with accompanying thoughts of Shipwreck, of the destruction of the Mariner's hopes, the bones of drowned Men heaped together, monsters of the deep,[14] and all the hideous and confused sights which Clarence saw in his Dream![15]

Nevertheless, I have been able to return, (and who may not?) to a steady contemplation of the benign influence of such a favourable Register lying open to the eyes of all. Without being so far lulled as to imagine I saw in a Village Church-yard the eye or central point of a rural Arcadia, I have felt that with all the vague and general expressions of love, gratitude, and praise with which it is usually crowded, it is a far more faithful representation of homely life as existing among a Community in which circumstances have not been untoward, than any report which might be made by a rigorous

338

observer deficient in that spirit of forbearance and those kindly prepossessions, without which human life can in no condition be profitably looked at or described. For we must remember that it is the nature of Vice to force itself upon notice, both in the act and by its consequences. Drunkenness, cruelty, brutal manners, sensuality, impiety, thoughtless prodigality, and idleness, are obstreperous while they are in the height and heyday of their enjoyment; and, when that is passed away, long and obtrusive is the train of misery which they draw after them! But, on the contrary, the virtues, especially those of humble life, are retired; and many of the highest must be sought for or they will be overlooked. Industry, oeconomy, temperance, and cleanliness, are indeed made obvious by flourishing fields, rosy complexions, and smiling countenances; but how few know anything of the trials to which Men in a lowly condition are subject, or of the steady and triumphant manner in which those trials are often sustained, but they themselves? The afflictions which Peasants and rural Artizans have to struggle with are for the most part secret; the tears which they wipe away, and the sighs which they stifle, – this is all a labour of privacy. In fact their victories are to themselves known only imperfectly: for it is inseparable from virtue, in the pure sense of the word, to be unconscious of the might of her own prowess. This is true of minds the most enlightened by reflection; who have forecast what they may have to endure, and prepared themselves accordingly. It is true even of these, when they are called into action, that they necessarily lose sight of their own accomplishments, and support their conflicts in self-forgetfulness and humility. That species of happy ignorance, which is the consequence of these noble qualities, must exist still more frequently, and in a greater degree, in those persons to whom duty has never been matter of laborious speculation, and who have no intimations of the power to act and to resist which is in them, till they are summoned to put it forth. I could illustrate this by many examples, which are now before my eyes; but it would detain me too long from my principal subject which was to suggest reasons for believing that the encomiastic language of rural Tombstones does not so far exceed reality as might lightly be supposed.

Doubtless, an inattentive or ill-disposed Observer, who should apply to the surrounding Cottages the knowledge which he may possess of any rural neighbourhood, would upon the first impulse confidently report that there was little in their living Inhabitants which reflected the concord and the virtue there dwelt upon so fondly. Much has been said, in a former paper tending to correct this disposition; and which will naturally combine with the present considerations. Besides, to slight the uniform language of these memorials as on that account not trustworthy would obviously be unjustifiable. Enter a Church-yard by the Sea-coast, and you will be almost sure to find the Tomb-stones crowded with metaphors taken from the Sea and a Sea-faring life. These are uniformly in the same strain; but surely we ought not thence to infer that the words are used of course without any heart-felt sense of their propriety. Would not the contrary conclusion be right? But I will adduce a fact which more than a hundred analogical arguments will carry to the mind a conviction of the strength and sanctity of these feelings which persons in humble stations of society connect with their departed Friends and Kindred. We learn from the Statistical account of Scotland[16] that, in some districts, a general transfer of Inhabitants has taken place; and that a great majority of those who live, and labour, and attend public worship in one part of the Country, are buried in another. Strong and inconquerable still continues to be the desire of all, that their bones should rest by the side of their forefathers, and very poor Persons provide that their bodies should be conveyed if necessary to a great distance to obtain that last satisfaction. Nor can I refrain from saying that this natural interchange by which the living Inhabitants of a Parish have small knowledge of the dead who are buried in their Church-yards is grievously to be lamented wheresoever it exists. For it cannot fail to preclude not merely much but the best part of the wholesome influence of that communion between living and dead which the conjunction in rural districts of the place of burial and place of worship tends so effectually to promote. Finally let us remember that if it be the nature of Man to be insensible to vexations and afflictions when they have passed away he is equally insensible to the height and depth of his blessings till they are removed from him.

An experienced and well-regulated mind will not, therefore, be insensible to this monotonous language of sorrow and affectionate admiration; but will find under that veil a substance of individual truth. Yet, upon all Men, and upon such a mind in particular, an Epitaph must strike with a gleam of pleasure, when the expression is of that kind which carried conviction to the heart at once that the Author was a sincere mourner, and that the Inhabitant of the Grave deserved to be so lamented. This may be done sometimes by a naked ejaculation; as in an instance which a friend of mine met with in a Church-yard in Germany; thus literally translated. 'Ah! they have laid in the Grave a brave Man – he was to me more than many!'

> Ach! sie haben
> Einen Braven
> Mann begraben –
> Mir war er mehr als *viele*.[17]

An effect as pleasing is often produced by the recital of an affliction endured with fortitude, or of a privation submitted to with contentment; or by a grateful display of the temporal blessings with which Providence had favoured the Deceased, and the happy course of life through which he had passed. And where these individualities are untouched upon it may still happen that the estate of man in his helplessness, in his dependence upon his Maker or some other inherent [          ][18] of his nature shall be movingly and profitably expressed. Every Reader will be able to supply from his own observation instances of all these kinds, and it will be more pleasing for him to refer to his memory than to have the page crowded with unnecessary Quotations. I will, however, give one or two from an old Book cited before. The following, of general application, was a great favourite with our Forefathers.

> Farwel my Frendys, the tyd abidyth no man,
> I am departed hens, and so sal ye,

> But in this passage the best song I can
> Is *Requiem Eternam*, now Jesu grant it me.
> When I have ended all myn adversity
> Grant me in Paradys to have a mansion
> That shedst thy bloud for my redemption.[19]

This Epitaph might seem to be of the age of Chaucer, for it has the very tone and manner of his Prioress's Tale.

The next opens with a thought somewhat interrupting that complacency and gracious repose which the language and imagery of a Church-yard tend to diffuse; but the truth is weighty, and will not be less acceptable for the rudeness of the expression.

> When the bells be merrely roung
> And the Masse devoutly soung
> And the meate merrely eaten
> Then sall Robert Trappis his Wyffs and his Chyldren
> be forgotten.
>
> Wherfor Jesu that of Mary sproung
> Set their soulys thy Saynts among
> Though it be undeservyd on their syde
> Yet good Lord let them evermor thy mercy abyde![20]

It is well known how fond our Ancestors were of a play upon the Name of the deceased when it admitted of a double sense. The following is an instance of this propensity not idly indulged. It brings home a general truth to the individual by the medium of a Pun, which will be readily pardoned, for the sake of the image suggested by it, for the happy mood of mind in which the Epitaph is composed, for the beauty of the language, and for the sweetness of the versification, which indeed, the date considered, is not a little curious – it is upon a man whose name was Palmer. I have modernized the spelling in order that its uncouthness may not interrupt the Reader's gratification.

> Palmers all our Fathers were
> I a *Palmer* lived here

And travelled still till worn with age
I ended this world's pilgrimage,
On the blest Ascension-day
In the chearful month of May;
One thousand with four hundred seven,
And took my journey hence to heaven.[21]

With this join the following, which was formerly to be seen upon a fair marble under the Portraiture of one of the Abbots of St Albans.

Hic quidem terra tegitur
Peccati solvens debitum
Cujus nomen non impositum
In libro vitae sit inscriptum.[22]

The spirit of it may be thus given. 'Here lies, covered by the Earth, and paying his debt to sin, one whose Name is not set forth; may it be inscribed in the book of Life!'

But these instances, of the humility, the pious faith, and simplicity of our Forefathers have led me from the scene of our contemplations – a Country Church-yard! and from the memorials at this day commonly found in it. I began with noticing such as might be wholly uninteresting from the uniformity of the language which they exhibit; because, without previously participating the truths upon which these general attestations are founded, it is impossible to arrive at that state of disposition of mind necessary to make those Epitaphs thoroughly felt which have an especial recommendation. With the same view, I will venture to say a few words upon another characteristic of these Compositions almost equally striking; namely, the homeliness of some of the inscriptions, the strangeness of the illustrative images, the grotesque spelling, with the equivocal meaning often struck out by it, and the quaint jingle of the rhymes. These have often excited regret in serious minds, and provoked the unwilling to good-humoured laughter. Yet, for my own part, without affecting any superior sanctity, I must say that I have been better satisfied with myself, when in these evidences I have seen a proof how deeply the piety of the rude Forefathers of the hamlet[23] is seated in their natures, I mean how habitual and constitutional it is, and how awful the feeling which they attach to the situation of their departed Friends – a proof of this rather than of their ignorance or of a deadness in their faculties to a sense of the ridiculous. And that this deduction may be just, is rendered probable by the frequent occurrence of passages, according to our present notion, full as ludicrous, in the Writings of the most wise and learned men of former ages, Divines or Poets, who in the earnestness of their souls have applied metaphors and illustrations, taken either from holy writ or from the usages of their own Country, in entire confidence that the sacredness of the theme they were discussing would sanctify the meanest object connected with it; or rather without ever conceiving it was possible that a ludicrous thought could spring up in any mind engaged in such meditations. And certainly, these odd and fantastic combinations are not confined to Epitaphs of the Peasantry, or of the lower orders of Society, but are perhaps still more commonly produced among the higher, in a degree equally or more striking. For instance, what shall we say to this upon Sir George Vane, the noted Secretary of State [24] to King Charles 1st?

> His Honour wonne i'th'field lies here in dust,
> His Honour got by grace shall never rust,
> The former fades, the latter shall fade never
> For why? He was Sr George once but St George ever. [25]

The date is 1679. When we reflect that the Father of this Personage must have had his taste formed in the punning Court of James 1st and that the Epitaph was composed at a time when our literature was stuffed with quaint or out-of-the-way thoughts, it will seem not unlikely that the Author prided himself upon what he might call a clever hit: I mean that his better affections were less occupied with the several associations belonging to the two ideas than his vanity delighted with that act of ingenuity by which they had been combined. But the first couplet consists of a just thought naturally expressed: and I should rather conclude the whole to be a work of honest simplicity; and that the sense of worldly dignity associated with the title, in a degree habitual to our Ancestors but which at this time we can but feebly sympathize with, and the imaginative feeling involved, viz, the saintly and chivalrous Name of the Champion of England, were unaffectedly linked together: and that both were united and consolidated in the Author's mind, and in the minds of his contemporaries whom no doubt he had pleased, by a devout contemplation of a happy immortality, the reward of the just.

At all events, leaving this particular case undecided, the general propriety of these notices cannot be doubted; and I gladly avail myself of this opportunity to place in a clear view the power and majesty of impassioned faith, whatever be its object: to shew how it subjugates the lighter motions of the mind, and sweeps away super-ficial difference in things. And this I have done, not to lower the witling and the worldling in their own esteem, but with a wish to bring the ingenuous into still closer communion with those primary sensations of the human heart, which are the vital springs of sublime and pathetic composition, in this and in every other kind. And, as from these primary sensations such composition speaks, so, unless correspondent ones listen promptly and submissively in the inner cell of the mind to whom it is addressed, the voice cannot be heard; its highest powers are wasted.

These suggestions may be further useful to establish a criterion of sincerity, by which a Writer may be judged; and this is of high import. For, when a Man is treating an interesting subject, or one which he ought not to treat at all unless he be interested, no faults have such a killing power as those which prove that he is not in earnest, that he is acting a part, has leisure for affectation, and feels that without it he could do nothing. This is one of the most odious of faults; because it shocks the moral sense: and is worse in a sepulchral inscription, precisely in the same degree as that mode of composition calls for sincerity more urgently than any other. And indeed, where the internal evidence proves that the Writer was moved, in other words where this charm of sincerity lurks in the language of a Tombstone and secretly pervades it, there are no errors in style or manner for which it will not be, in some degree, a recompense; but without habits of reflection a test of this inward simplicity cannot be come at: and, as I have said, I am now writing with a hope to assist the well-disposed to attain it.

Let us take an instance where no one can be at a loss. The following Lines are said to have been written by the illustrious Marquis of Montrose with the point of his Sword, upon being informed of the death of his Master Charles 1st.

> Great, good, and just, could I but rate
> My griefs, and thy so rigid fate;
> I'd weep the world to such a strain,
> As it should deluge once again.
> But since thy loud-tongued blood demands supplies,
> More from Briareus hands than Argus eyes,
> I'll sing thy Obsequies with Trumpets sounds,
> And write thy Epitaph with blood and wounds.[26]

These funereal verses would certainly be wholly out of their place upon a tombstone; but who can doubt that the Writer was transported to the height of the occasion? — that he was moved as it became an heroic Soldier, holding those Principles and opinions, to be moved? His soul labours; — the most tremendous event in the history of the Planet, namely, the Deluge, is brought before his imagination by the physical image of tears, — a connection awful from its very remoteness and from the slender bond that unites the ideas: — it passes into the region of Fable likewise; for all modes of existence that forward his purpose are to be pressed into the service. The whole is instinct with spirit,[27] and every word has its separate life; like the Chariot of the Messiah, and the wheels of that Chariot, as they appeared to the imagination of Milton aided by that of the Prophet Ezekiel.[28] It had power to move of itself but was conveyed by Cherubs.

> — with stars their bodies all
> And wings were set with eyes, with eyes the wheels
> Of Beryl, and careering fires between.[29]

Compare with the above Verses of Montrose the following Epitaph upon Sir Philip Sidney, which was formerly placed over his Grave in St Paul's Church.

> England, Netherland, the Heavens, and the Arts,
> The Soldiers, and the World, have made six parts
> Of noble Sidney: for who will suppose
> That a small heap of Stones can Sidney enclose?
>
> England hath his Body, for she it fed,
> Netherland his Blood, in her defence shed:
> The Heavens have his Soul, the Arts have his Fame,
> The Soldiers the grief, the World his good Name.[30]

There were many points in which the case of Sidney resembled that of Charles 1st: He was a Sovereign but of a nobler kind – a Sovereign in the hearts of Men: and after his premature death he was truly, as he hath been styled, 'the world-mourned Sidney'.[31] So fondly did the admiration of his Contemporaries settle upon him, that the sudden removal of a Man so good, great, and thoroughly accomplished, wrought upon many even to repining, and to the questioning the dispensations of Providence. Yet he, whom Spenser[32] and all the Men of Genius of his Age had tenderly bemoaned, is thus commemorated upon his Tombstone; and to add to the indignity, the memorial is nothing more than the second-hand Coat of a French Commander! It is a servile translation from a French Epitaph, which, says Weever, 'was by some English Wit happily imitated and ingeniously applied to the honour of our worthy Chieftain'.[33] Yet Weever, in a foregoing Paragraph thus expresses himself upon the same Subject; giving without his own knowledge, in my opinion, an example of the manner in which such an Epitaph ought to have been composed. – 'But here I cannot pass over in silence Sir Philip Sidney the elder brother, being (to use Camden's words) the glorious star of this family, a lively pattern of virtue, and the lovely joy of all the learned sort; who fighting valiantly with the enemy before Zutphen in Gelderland, dyed manfully. This is that Sidney, whom, as God's

347

will was, he should therefore be born into the world even to shew unto our age a sample of ancient virtues: so his good pleasure was, before any man looked for it, to call for him again, and take him out of the world, as being more worthy of heaven than earth. Thus we may see perfect virtue suddenly vanisheth out of sight, and the best men continue not long.'[34]

There can be no need to analyse this simple effusion of the moment in order to contrast it with the laboured composition before given: the difference will flash upon the Reader at once. But I may say, it is not likely that such a frigid composition as the former would have ever been applied to a Man whose death had so stirred up the hearts of his Contemporaries, if it had not been felt that something different from that nature which each Man carried in his own breast was in this case requisite; and that a certain *straining* of mind was inseparable from the Subject. Accordingly, an Epitaph is adopted in which the Writer had turned from the genuine affections and their self-forgetting inspirations, to the end that his Understanding, or the faculty designated by the word *head* as opposed to *heart*, might curiously construct a fabric to be wondered at. Hyperbole in the language of Montrose is a mean instrument made mighty because wielded by an afflicted Soul, and strangeness is here the order of Nature. Montrose stretched after remote things but was at the same time propelled towards them; the French Writer goes deliberately in search of them; no wonder then if what he brings home does not prove worth the carriage!

Let us return to an instance of common life. I quote it with reluctance, not so much for its absurdity as that the expression in one place will strike at first sight as little less than impious; and it is indeed, though unintentionally so, most irreverent. But I know no other example that will so forcibly illustrate the important truth I wish to establish. The following Epitaph is to be found in a Church-yard in Westmorland which the present Writer has reason to think of with interest as it contains the remains of some of his Ancestors and Kindred. The date is 1673.

Under this Stone, Reader, inter'd doth lye,
    Beauty and virtue's true epitomy.
At her appearance the noone-son
    Blush'd and shrunk in 'cause quite outdon.
In her concenter'd did all graces dwell:
    God pluck'd my rose that he might take a smel.
I'll say no more: But weeping wish I may
    Soone with thy dear chaste ashes com to lay.
                  Sic efflevit Maritus [35]

Can any thing go beyond this in extravagance? Yet, if the fundamental thoughts be translated into a natural style, they will be found reasonable and affecting – 'The Woman who lies here interred, was in my eyes a perfect image of beauty and virtue; she was to me a brighter object than the Sun in heaven: God took her, who was my delight, from this earth to bring her nearer to himself. Nothing further is worthy to be said than that weeping I wish soon to lie by thy dear chaste ashes – Thus did the Husband pour out his tears.'

These verses are preceeded by a brief account of the Lady, in Latin prose; in which the little that is said is the uncorrupted language of affection. But, without this introductory communication, I should myself have had no doubt, after recovering from the first shock of surprize and disapprobation, that this man, notwithstanding his extravagant expressions, was a sincere mourner; and that his heart, during the very act of composition, was moved. These fantastic images, though they stain the writing, stained not his soul. – They did not even touch it; but hung like globules of rain suspended above a green leaf, along which they may roll and leave no trace that they have passed over it. This simple-hearted Man must have been betrayed by a common notion that what was natural in prose would be out of place in verse; – that it is not the Muse which puts on the Garb but the Garb which makes the Muse. And, having adopted this notion at a time when vicious writings of this kind accorded with the public taste, it is probable that, in the excess of his modesty, the blankness of his inexperience, and the intensity of his affection, he thought that the further he wandered from nature in his language the more would he honour his departed Consort, who now appeared to him to have surpassed humanity in the excellence of her endowments. The quality of his fault and its very excess are both in favour of this conclusion.

Let us contrast this Epitaph with one taken from a celebrated Writer [36] of the last Century.

'*To the memory of* LUCY LYTTLETON, *Daughter &c who departed this life &c aged 29. Having employed the short time assigned to her here in the uniform practice of religion and virtue.*

> Made to engage all hearts, and charm all eyes;
> Though meek, magnanimous; though witty, wise;
> Polite, as all her life in courts had been;
> Yet good, as she the world had never seen;
> The noble fire of an exalted mind,
> With gentle female tenderness combined.
> Her speech was the melodious voice of love,
> Her song the warbling of the vernal grove;
> Her eloquence was sweeter than her song,
> Soft as her heart, and as her reason strong;
> Her form each beauty of the mind express'd,
> Her mind was Virtue by the Graces drest.'

The prose part of this inscription has the appearance of being intended for a Tomb-stone; but there is nothing in the verse that would suggest such a thought. The composition is in the style of those laboured portraits in words which we sometimes see placed at the bottom of a print, to fill up lines of expression which the bungling Artist had left imperfect. We know from other evidence that Lord Lyttleton dearly loved his wife: he has indeed composed a monody to her memory [37] which proves this, and that she was an amiable Woman; neither of which facts could have been gathered from these inscriptive Verses. This Epitaph would derive little advantage from being translated into another style as the former was; for there is no under current, no skeleton or stamina, of thought and feeling. The

Reader will perceive at once that nothing in the heart of the Writer had determined either the choice, the order, or the expression, of the ideas – that there is no interchange of action from within and from without [38] – that the connections are mechanical and arbitrary, and the lowest kind of these – Heart and Eyes – petty alliterations, as meek and magnanimous, witty and wise, combined with oppositions in thoughts where there is no necessary or natural opposition. These defects run through the whole; the only tolerable verse is,

'Her speech was the melodious voice of love.'

Observe, the question is not which of these Epitaphs is better or worse; but which faults are of a worse *kind*. In the former case we have a Mourner whose soul is occupied by grief and urged forward by his admiration. He deems in his simplicity that no hyperbole can transcend the perfections of her whom he has lost: for the version which I have given fairly demonstrates that, in spite of his outrageous expressions, the under current of his thoughts was natural and pure. We have therefore in him the example of a mind misled during the act of composition by false taste – to the highest possible degree; and, in that of Lord Lyttleton, we have one of a feeling heart, not merely misled, but wholly laid asleep by the same power. Lord Lyttleton could not have written in this way upon such a subject, if he had not been seduced by the example of Pope, whose sparkling and tuneful manner had bewitched the men of letters his Contemporaries, and corrupted the judgment of the Nation through all ranks of society.

The course which we have taken having brought us to the name of this distinguished Writer, I will in this place give a few observations upon his Epitaphs, the largest collection we have in our language, from the pen of any Writer of eminence. As the Epitaphs of Pope, and also those of Chiabrera,[39] which occasioned this disquisition, are in metre, it may be proper here to enquire how far the notion of a perfect Epitaph, as given in a former Paper, may be modified by the choice of metre for the vehicle in preference to prose.[40] If our opinions be just, it is manifest that the basis must remain the same in either case; and that the difference can only lie in the superstructure;

and it is equally plain, that a judicious Man will be less disposed in this case than in any other to avail himself of the liberty given by metre to adopt phrases of fancy, or to enter into the more remote regions of illustrative imagery. For the occasion of writing an Epitaph is matter of fact in its intensity, and forbids more authoritatively than any other species of composition all modes of fiction, except those which the very strength of passion has created; which have been acknowledged by the human heart, and have become so familiar that they are converted into substantial realities. When I come to the Epitaphs of Chiabrera, I shall perhaps give instances in which I think he has not written under the impression of this truth: where the poetic imagery does not elevate, deepen, or refine the human passion, which it ought always to do or not to act at all, but excludes it. In a far greater degree are Pope's Epitaphs debased by faults into which he could not I think have fallen if he had written in prose as a plain Man, and not as a metrical Wit. I will transcribe from Pope's Epitaphs the one upon Mrs Corbet (who died of a Cancer); Dr Johnson having extolled it highly and pronounced it the best of the collection.[41]

> Here rests a Woman, good without pretence,
> Blest with plain reason and with sober sense;
> No conquest she but o'er herself desir'd;
> No arts essayed, but not to be admir'd.
> Passion and pride were to her soul unknown,
> Convinc'd that virtue only is our own.
> So unaffected, so compos'd a mind,
> So firm, yet soft, so strong, yet so refin'd.
> Heaven as it's purest gold by tortures tried
> The Saint sustain'd it, but the Woman died.

This *may* be the best of Pope's Epitaphs; but if the standard which we have fixed be a just one it cannot be approved of. First, it must be observed, that in the Epitaphs of this Writer the true impulse is wanting, and that his motions must of necessity be feeble. For he has no other aim than to give a favourable *Portrait* of the Character of the Deceased. Now mark the process by which this is performed. Nothing is represented implicitly, that is, with its accompaniment of circumstances, or conveyed by its effects. The Author forgets that it is a living creature that must interest us and not an intellectual Existence, which a mere character is. Insensible to this distinction the brain of the Writer is set at work to report as flatteringly as he may of the mind of his subject; the good qualities are separately abstracted (can it be otherwise than coldly and unfeelingly?) and put together again as coldly and unfeelingly. The Epitaph now before us owes what exemption it may have from these defects in its general plan to the excruciating disease of which the Lady died; but it too is liable to the same censure; and is, like the rest, further objectionable in this; namely, that the thoughts have their nature changed and moulded by the vicious [42] expression in which they are entangled, to an excess rendering them wholly unfit for the place which they occupy.

> 'Here rest[s] a Woman good without pretence
> Blest with plain reason'

— from which, *sober sense* is not sufficiently distinguishable. This verse and a half, and the one, *so unaffected, so composed a mind*, are characteristic, and the expression is true to nature; but they are, if I may take the liberty of saying it, the only parts of the Epitaph which have this merit. Minute criticism is in its nature irksome; and, as commonly practised in books and conversation, is both irksome and injurious. Yet every mind must occasionally be exercised in this discipline, else it cannot learn the art of bringing words rigorously to the test of thoughts; and these again to a comparison with things, their archetypes; contemplated first in themselves, and secondly in relation to each other; in all which processes the mind must be skilful, otherwise it will be perpetually imposed upon. In the next couplet the word, *conquest*, is applied in a manner that would have been displeasing even from its triteness in a copy of complimentary Verses to a fashionable Beauty; but to talk of making conquests in an Epitaph is not to be endured. *No arts essayed, but not to be admired* — are words expressing that she had recourse to artifices to conceal her amiable and admirable qualities; and the context implies that there was a merit in this; which surely no sane mind would allow. But the meaning of the Author, simply and honestly given, was nothing more than that she shunned admiration, probably with a more apprehensive modesty than was common; and more than this would have been inconsistent with the praise bestowed upon her – that she had an unaffected mind. This couplet is further objectionable, because the sense of love and peaceful admiration, which such a character naturally inspires, is disturbed by an oblique and ill-timed stroke of satire. She is not praised so much as others are blamed – and is degraded by the Author in thus being made a covert or stalking-horse for gratifying a propensity the most abhorrent from her own nature. – '*Passion and pride were to her soul unknown*' – It cannot be meant that she had no Passions, but that they were moderate and kept in subordination to her reason; but the thought is not here expressed; nor is it clear that a conviction in the understanding that *virtue only is our own*, though it might suppress her pride, would be itself competent to govern or abate many other affections and passions to which our frail nature is, and ought, in various degrees, to be subject. In fact, the Author appear[s] to have had no precise notion of his own meaning. If she was '*good without pretence*' it seems unnecessary to say that she was not proud. Dr Johnson, making an exception of the verse, *Convinced that virtue only is our own*, praises this Epitaph for 'containing nothing taken from common places'. [43] Now in fact, as may be deduced from the principles of this discourse, it is not only no fault but a primary requisite in an Epitaph that it shall contain thoughts and feelings which are in their substance common-place, and even trite. It is grounded upon the universal intellectual property of man; – sensations which all men have felt and feel in some degree daily and hourly; – truths whose very interest and importance have caused them to be unattended to, as things which could take care of themselves. But it is required that these truths should be instinctively ejaculated, or should rise irresistibly from circumstances; in a word that they should be uttered in such connection as shall make it felt that they are not adopted – not spoken by rote, but perceived in their whole compass with the freshness and clearness of an original intuition. The Writer must introduce the truth with such accompaniment as shall imply that he has mounted to the sources of things – penetrated the dark cavern from which the River that murmurs in every one's ear has flowed from generation to generation. The line *'Virtue only is our own'* – is objectionable, not from the commonplaceness of the Truth, but from the vapid manner in which it is conveyed. A similar sentiment is expressed with appropriate dignity in an Epitaph by Chiabrera, where he makes the Archbishop of Urbino say of himself, that he was

> – 'smitten by the great Ones of the world,
> But did not fall; for Virtue braves all shocks,
> Upon herself resting immoveably.' [44]

*'So firm yet soft, so strong yet so refined'* – these intellectual operations (while they can be conceived of as operations of intellect at all, for in fact one half of the process is mechanical, words doing their own work, and one half of the line manufacturing the rest) remind me of the motions of a Posture-Master, or of a Man balancing a Sword upon his finger, which must be kept from falling at all hazard[s]. *'The Saint sustained it but the Woman died'* – Let us look steadily at this antithesis – the *Saint*, that is her soul strengthened by Religion supported the anguish of her disease with patience and resignation; – but the *Woma[n]*, that is her *body*, (for if any thing else be meant by the word, woman, it con[tra]dicts the former part of the proposition and the passage is nonsense) was overcome. Why was not this simply expressed; without playing with the Reader's fancy to the delusion and dishonour of his Understanding, by a trifling epigr[am]matic point? But alas! ages must pass away before men will have their eyes open to the beauty and majesty of Truth, and will be taught to venerate Poetry no further than as She is a Handmaid pure as her Mistress – the noblest Handmaid in her train!

### ESSAY UPON EPITAPHS, III

I vindicate the rights and dignity of Nature; and, as long as I condemn nothing without assigning reasons not lightly given, I cannot suffer any Individual, however highly and deservedly honoured by my Countrymen, to stand in my way. If my notions are right, the Epitaphs of Pope cannot well be too severely condemned: for not only are they almost wholly destitute of those universal feelings and simple movements of mind which we have called for as indispensible, but they are little better than a tissue of false thoughts, languid and vague expression, unmeaning antithesis, and laborious attempts at discrimination. Pope's mind had been employed chiefly in observation upon the vices and follies of men. Now, vice and folly are in contradiction with the moral principle which can never be extinguished in the mind: and, therefore, wanting this controul, are irregular, capricious, and inconsistant with themselves. If a man has once said, (see FRIEND No. 6) [45] 'Evil be thou my Good!' [46] and has acted accordingly, however strenuous may have been his adherence to this principle, it will be well known by those who have had an opportunity of observing him narrowly that there have been perpetual obliquities in his course; evil passions thwarting each other in various ways; and, now and then, revivals of his better nature, which check him for a short time or lead him to remeasure his steps: – not to speak of the various necessities of counterfeiting virtue which the furtherance of his schemes will impose upon him, and the division which will be consequently introduced into his nature.

It is reasonable, then, that Cicero,[47] when holding up Catiline to detestation; and, (without going to such an extreme case) that Dryden and Pope,[48] when they are describing Characters like Buckingham, Shaftsbury, Wharton, and the Duchess of Marlborough, should represent qualities and actions at war with each other and with themselves: and that the page should be suitably crowded with antithetical expressions. But all this argues an obtuse moral sensibility and a consequent want of knowledge, if applied where virtue ought to be described in the language of affectionate admiration. In the mind of the truly great and good every thing that is of importance is at peace with itself; all is stillness, sweetness, and stable grandeur. Accordingly the contemplation of virtue is attended with repose. A lovely quality, if its loveliness be clearly perceived, fastens the mind with absolute sovereignty upon itself; permitting or inciting it to pass, by smooth gradation or gentle transition, to some other kindred quality. Thus a perfect image of meekness, (I refer to an instance before given) when looked at by a tender mind in its happiest mood, might easily lead on to the thought of magnanimity: for assuredly there is nothing incongruous in those virtues. But the mind would not then be separated from the Person who is the object of its thoughts: it would still be confined to that Person, or to others of the same general character; this is, would be kept within the circle of qualities which range themselves quietly by each other's sides. Whereas, when meekness and magnanimity are represented antithetically, the mind is not only carried from the main object, but is compelled to turn to a subject in which the quality exists divided from some other as noble, its natural ally: – a painful feeling! that checks the course of love, and repels the sweet thoughts that might be settling round the Person whom it was the Author's wish to endear to us; but for whom, after this interruption, we no longer care. If then a Man, whose duty it is to praise departed excellence not without some sense of regret or sadness, to do this or to be silent, should upon all occasions exhibit that mode of connecting thoughts which is only natural while we are delineating vice under certain relations, we may be assured that the nobler sympathies are not alive in him; that he has no clear insight into the internal constitution of virtue; nor has himself been soothed, cheared, harmonized, by those outward effects which follow every where her goings, – declaring the presence of the invisible deity. And though it be true that the most admirable of Men must fall far short of perfection, and that the majority of those whose worth is commemorated upon their Tomb-stones must have been Persons in whom good and evil were intermixed in various proportions, and stood in various degrees of opposition to each other, yet the reader will remember what has been said before upon that medium of love, sorrow, and admiration through which a departed friend is viewed: how it softens down or removes these harshnesses and contradictions; which, moreover, must be supposed never to have been grievous: for there can be no true love but between the good; and no Epitaph ought to be written upon a bad Man, except for a warning.

The purpose of the remarks given in the last Essay was chiefly to assist the reader in separating truth and sincerity from falsehood and affectation; presuming that if the unction of a devout heart be wanting every thing else is of no avail. It was shewn that a current of just thought and feeling may flow under a surface of illustrative imagery so impure as to produce an effect the opposite of that which was intended. Yet, though this fault may be carried to an intolerable *degree*, the reader will have gathered that in our estimation it is not *in kind* the most offensive and injurious. We have contrasted it in its excess with instances where the genuine current or vein was wholly wanting; where the thoughts and feelings had no vital union; but were artificially connected, or formally accumulated, in a manner that would imply discontinuity and feebleness of mind upon any occasion; but still more reprehensible here! I will proceed to give milder examples, not of this last kind but of the former; namely of failure from various causes where the groundwork is good.

> Take, holy earth! all that my soul holds dear:
> Take that best gift which Heaven so lately gave:
> To Bristol's fount I bore with trembling care,
> Her faded form. She bow'd to taste the wave –
> And died. Does youth, does beauty read the line?
> Does sympathetic fear their breasts alarm?
> Speak, dead Maria! breathe a strain divine:
> Even from the grave thou shalt have power to charm.
> Bid them be chaste, be innocent, like thee:
> Bid them in duty's sphere as meekly move:
> And if so fair, from vanity as free,
> As firm in friendship, and as fond in love;
> Tell them, tho tis an awful thing to die,
> ('Twas e'en to thee) yet, the dread path once trod,

Heaven lifts its everlasting portals high,
And bids 'the pure in heart behold their God.'[49]

This Epitaph has much of what we have demanded: but it is debased in some instances by weakness of expression, in others by false prettiness. '*She bow'd to taste the wave and died.*' The plain truth was, she drank the Bristol waters which failed to restore her, and her death soon followed; but the expression involves a multitude of petty occupations for the fancy – '*She bowed*' – was there any truth in this? – '*to taste the wave,*' the water of a mineral spring which must have been drunk out of a Goblet. Strange application of the word *Wave*! '*and died.*' This would have been a just expression if the water had killed her; but, as it is, the tender thought involved in the disappointment of a hope however faint is left unexpressed; and a shock of surprize is given, entertaining perhaps to a light fancy, but to a steady mind unsatisfactory – because false. '*Speak! dead Maria breathe a strain divine!*' This verse flows nobly from the heart and the imagination; but perhaps it is not one of those impassioned thoughts which should be fixed in language upon a sepulchral stone. It is in its nature too poignant and transitory. A Husband meditating by his Wife's grave would throw off such a feeling, and would give voice to it; and it would be in its place in a Monody to her Memory but, if I am not mistaken, ought to have been suppressed here, or uttered after a different manner. The implied impersonation of the Deceased (according to the tenor of what has before been said) ought to have been more general and shadowy. '*And if so fair, from vanity as free – As firm in friendship and as fond in love – Tell them,*' these are two sweet verses, but the long suspension of the sense excites the expectation of a thought less common than the concluding one; and is an instance of a failure in doing what is most needful and most difficult in an Epitaph to do; namely, to give to universally received truths a pathos and spirit which shall re-admit them into the soul like revelations of the moment.

I have said that this excellence is difficult to attain; and why? is it because nature is weak? – no! Where the soul has been thoroughly stricken, (and Heaven knows, the course of life has placed all men, at some time or other, in that condition) there is never a want of *positive* strength; but because the adversary of nature, (call that adversary Art or by what name you will) is *comparatively* strong. The far-searching influence of the power, which, for want of a better name, we will denominate, Taste, is in nothing more evinced than in the changeful character and complexion of that species of composition which we have been reviewing. Upon a call so urgent, it might be expected that the affections, the memory, and the imagination would be *constrained* to speak their genuine language. Yet if the few specimens which have been given in the course of this enquiry do not demonstrate the fact, the Reader need only look into any collection of Epitaphs to be convinced that the faults predominant in the literature of every age will be as strongly reflected in the sepulchral inscriptions as any where; nay perhaps more so, from the anxiety of the Author to do justice to the occasion: and especially if the composition be in verse; for then it comes more avowedly in the shape of a work of art; and, of course, is more likely to be coloured by the works of art holden in most esteem at the time. In a bulky Volume of Poetry entitled, ELEGANT EXTRACTS [50] in Verse, which must be known to most of my Readers, as it is circulated every where and in fact constitutes at this day the poetical library of our Schools, I find a number of Epitaphs, in verse, of the last century; and there is scarcely one which is not thoroughly tainted by the artifices which have overrun our writings in metre since the days of Dryden and Pope. Energy, stillness, grandeur, tenderness, those feelings which are the pure emanations of nature, those thoughts which have the infinitude of truth, and those expressions which are not what the garb is to the body [51] but what the body is to the soul, themselves a constituent part and power or function in the thought – all these are abandoned for their opposites, – as if our Countrymen, through successive generations, had lost the sense of solemnity and pensiveness (not to speak of deeper emotions) and resorted to the Tombs of their Forefathers and Contemporaries only to be tickled and surprized. Would we not recoil from such gratifications, in such a place, if the general literature of the Country had not co-operated with other causes insidiously to weaken our sensibilities and deprave our judgements? Doubtless, there are shocks of event and circumstance, public and private, by which for all minds the truths of Nature will be elicited; but sorrow for that Individual or people to whom these special interferences are necessary, to bring them into communion with the inner spirit of things! for such intercourse must be profitless in proportion as it is unfrequent, irregular, and transient. Words are too awful an instrument for good and evil to be trifled with: they hold above all other external powers a dominion over thoughts. If words be not (recurring to a metaphor before used) an incarnation of the thought but only a clothing for it, then surely will they prove an ill gift; such a one as those poisoned vestments, read of in the stories of superstitious times, which had power to consume and to alienate from his right mind the victim who put them on. Language, if it do not uphold, and feed, and leave in quiet, like the power of gravitation or the air we breathe, is a counter-spirit, unremittingly and noiselessly at work to derange, to subvert, to lay waste, to vitiate, and to dissolve. From a deep conviction then that the excellence of writing, whether in prose or verse, consists in a conjunction of Reason and Passion, a conjunction which must be of necessity benign; and that it might be deduced from what has been said that the taste, intellectual Power, and morals of a Country are inseparably linked in mutual dependence, I have dwelt thus long upon this argument. And the occasion justifies me: for how could the tyranny of bad taste be brought home to the mind more aptly than by shewing in what degree the feelings of nature yield to it when we are rendering to our friends this solemn testimony of our love? more forcibly than by giving proof that thoughts cannot, even upon this impulse, assume an outward life without a transmutation and a fall?

> 'Epitaph on Miss Drummond in the Church of
> Brodsworth, Yorkshire
> Mason [52]

\*

Here sleeps what once was beauty, once was grace;
Grace, that with tenderness and sense combin'd
To form that harmony of soul and face,
Where beauty shines the mirror of the mind.
Such was the maid, that in the morn of youth,
In virgin innocence, in nature's pride,
Blest with each art, that owes its charms to truth,
Sunk in her Father's fond embrace, and died.
He weeps: O venerate the holy tear!
Faith lends her aid to ease affliction's load;
The parent mourns his Child upon the bier,
The christian yields an angel to his God.'

The following is a translation from the Latin, communicated to a
Lady in her Childhood and by her preserved in memory. I regret
that I have not seen the original.

She is gone – my beloved Daughter Eliza is gone,
Fair, chearful, benign, my child is gone.
Thee long to be regretted a Father mourns,
Regretted – but thanks to the most perfect God! not lost
For a happier age approaches
When again my child I shall behold
And live with thee for ever.

Mathew Dobson to his dear, engaging, happy Eliza

Who in the 18th year of her Age
Passed peaceably into heaven.[53]

The former of these Epitaphs is very far from being the worst of its
kind, and on that account I have placed the two in contrast. Unquestionably, as the Father in the latter speaks in his own Person, the
situation is much more pathetic; but, making due allowance for this
advantage, who does not here feel a superior truth and sanctity, which
is not dependent upon this circumstance, but merely the result of the
expression and the connection of the thoughts? I am not so fortunate
as to have any knowledge of the Author of this affecting Composi-

tion, but I much fear, if he had called in the assistance of English verse the better to convey his thoughts, such sacrifices would, from various influences, have been made *even by him*, that, though he might have excited admiration in thousands, he would have truly moved no one. The latter part of the following by Gray is almost the only instance, among the metrical Epitaphs in our language of the last Century, which I remember, of affecting thoughts rising naturally and keeping themselves pure from vicious[54] diction.

Epitaph on Mrs Clark.

\*

> Lo! where the silent marble weeps,
> A friend, a wife, a mother, sleeps;
> A heart, within whose sacred cell
> The peaceful virtues lov'd to dwell.
> Affection warm, and love sincere,
> And soft humanity were there.
> In agony, in death resigned,
> She felt the wound she left behind.
> Her infant image, here below,
> Sits smiling on a father's woe:
> Whom what awaits, while yet he strays
> Along the lonely vale of days?
> A pang to secret sorrow dear;
> A sigh, an unavailing tear,
> Till time shall every grief remove,
> With life, with memory, and with love.

I have been speaking of faults which are aggravated by temptations thrown in the way of modern Writers when they compose in metre. The first six lines of this Epitaph are vague and languid, more so than I think would have been possible had it been written in prose. Yet Gray, who was so happy in the remaining part, especially the last four lines, has grievously failed *in prose*, upon a subject which it might have been expected would have bound him indissolubly to the propriety of Nature and comprehensive reason. I allude to the conclusion

clusion of the Epitaph upon his Mother, where he says, 'she was the careful tender Mother of many Children, one of whom alone had the misfortune to survive her.' [55] This is a searching thought, but wholly out of place. Had it been said of an ideot, of a palsied child, or of an adult from any cause dependent upon his Mother to a degree of helplessness which nothing but maternal tenderness and watchfulness could answer, that he had the misfortune to survive his Mother, the thought would have been just. The same might also have been wrung from any Man (thinking of himself) when his soul was smitten with compunction or remorse, through the consciousness of a misdeed, from which he might have been preserved (as he hopes or believes) by his Mother's prudence, by her anxious care if longer continued or by the reverential fear of offending or distressing her. But even then (unless accompanied with a detail of extraordinary circumstances) if transferred to her monument, it would have been mis-placed, as being too peculiar; and for reasons which have been before alledged, namely, as too transitory and poignant. But in an ordinary case, for a Man permanently and conspicuously to record that this was his fixed feeling; what is it but to run counter to the course of nature, which has made it matter of expectation and congratulation that Parents should die before their Children? what is it, if searched to the bottom, but lurking and sickly selfishness? Does not the regret include a wish that the Mother should have survived all her offspring, have witnessed that bitter desolation, where the order of things is disturbed and inverted? And finally does it not withdraw the attention of the Reader from the Subject to the Author of the Memorial, as one to be commiserated for his strangely unhappy condition, or to be condemned for the morbid constitution of his feelings, or for his deficiency in judgment? A fault of the same kind, though less in degree, is found in the Epitap[h] of Pope upon Harcourt; of whom it is said that 'he never gave his father grief but when he died.' [56] I need not point out how many situations there are in which such an expression of feeling would be natural and becoming; but in a permanent Inscription things only should be admitted that have an enduring place in the mind: and a nice selection is required even among these. The

Duke of Ormond said of his Son Ossory, 'that he preferred his dead Son to any living Son in Christendom,'[57] – a thought which (to adopt an expression used before) has the infinitude of truth! But, though in this there is no momentary illusion, nothing fugitive, it would still have been unbecoming, had it been placed in open view over the Son's grave; inasmuch as such expression of it would have had an ostentatious air, and would have implied a disparagement of others. The sublimity of the sentiment consists in its being the secret possession of the Father.

Having been engaged so long in the ungracious office of sitting in judgement where I have found so much more to censure than to approve, though wherever it was in my power, I have placed good by the side of evil, that the Reader might intuitively receive the truths which I wished to communicate, I now turn back with pleasure to Chiabrera; of whose productions in this department the Reader of THE FRIEND may be enabled to form a judgment who has attentively perused the few specimens only which have been given.[58] 'An Epitaph' says Weever 'is a superscription (either in verse or prose) or an astrict[59] pithie Diagram, writ, carved, or engraven, upon the tomb, grave, or sepulchre of the defunct, briefly declaring (*and that with a kind of commiseration*) the name, the age, the deserts, the dignities, the state, *the praises both of body and minde*, the good and bad fortunes in the life a[nd] the manner and time of the death of the person therin interred.'[60] This account of an Epitaph, which as far as it goes is just, was no doubt taken by Weever from the Monuments of our own Country, and it shews that in his conception an Epitaph was not to be an abstract character of the deceased but an epitomized biography blended with description by which an impression of the character was to be conveyed. Bring forward the one incidental expression, a kind of commiseration, unite with it a concern on the part of the dead for the well-being of the living made known by exhortation and admonition, and let this commiseration and concern pervade and brood over the whole so that what was peculiar to the individual shall still be subordinate to a sense of what he had in common with the species – our notion of a perfect Epitaph would then be realized, and it pleases me to say that this is the very model upon which those of Chiabrera are for the most part framed. Observe how exquisitely this is exemplified in the one beginning 'Pause courteous Stranger! Baldi supplicates' given in THE FRIEND some weeks ago.[61] The Subject of the Epitaph is introduced in-treating, not directly in his own Person but through the mouth of the Author, that according to the religious belief of his Country a Prayer for his soul might be preferred to the Redeemer of the World. Placed in counterpoize with this right which he has in common with all the dead, his individual earthly accomplishments appear light to his funereal Biographer, as they did to the person of whom he speaks when alive, nor could Chiabrera have ventured to touch upon them but under the sanction of this previous acknowledgement. He then goes on to say how various and profound was his learning and how deep a hold it took upon his affections, but that he weaned himself from these things as vanities and was devoted in later life exclusively to the divine truths of the Gospel as the only knowledge in which he could find perfect rest. Here we are thrown back upon the intro-ductory supplication and made to feel its especial propriety in this case: his life was long and every part of it bore appropriate fruits; Urbino his birth-place might be proud of him, and the Passenger who was entreated to pray for his soul has a wish breathed for his welfare. – This composition is a perfect whole; there is nothing arbi-trary or mechanical, but it is an organized body of which the members are bound together by a common life and are all justly proportioned. If I had not gone so much into detail, I should have given further instances of Chiabrera's Epitaphs, but I must content myself with saying that if he had abstained from the introduction of heathen mythology of which he is lavish – an inexcusable fault for an Inhabitant of a Christian country, yet admitting of some palliation in an Italian who treads classic soil and has before his eyes the ruins of the temples which were dedicated to those ficticious beings as objects of worship by the majestic People, his Ancestors – had omitted also some uncharacteristic particulars and had not on some occasions forgotten that truth is the soul of passion, he would have left his readers little to regret. I do not mean to say that higher and nobler thoughts may not be found in sepulchral Inscriptions than his contain, but he understood his work; the principles upon which he composed are just. The Reader of 'THE FRIEND' has had proofs of this; one shall be given of his mixed manner, exemplifying some of the points in which he has erred.

> O Lelius, beauteous flower of gentleness,
> The fair Aglaia's friend above all friends,
> O darling of the fascinating Loves,
> By what dire envy moved did Death uproot
> Thy days ere yet full blown, and what ill chance
> Hath robbed Savona of her noblest grace?
> She weeps for thee, and shall for ever weep,
> And if the fountain of her tears should fail,
> She would implore Sebeto to supply
> Her need; Sebeto sympathizing stream,
> Who on his margin saw thee close thine eyes
> On the chaste bosom of thy Lady dear.
> Ah what do riches, what does youth avail?
> Dust are our hopes; I weeping did inscribe
> In bitterness thy Monument, and pray
> Of every gentle Spirit bitterly
> To read the record with as copious tears.[62]

This Epitaph is not without some tender thoughts, but a comparison of it with the one upon the youthful Pozzobonelli[63] (see FRIEND No. 20) will more clearly shew that Chiabrera has here neglected to ascertain whether the passions expressed were in kind and degree a dispensation of reason or at least commodities issued under her license and authority.

The Epitaphs of Chiabrera are twenty nine in number, all of them save two upon Men probably little known at this day in their own Country and scarcely at all beyond the limits of it, and the reader is generally made acquainted with the moral and intellectual excellence which distinguished them by a brief history of the course of their

lives or a selection of events and circumstances, and thus they are
individualized; but in the two other instances – namely, those of
Tasso and Raphael – he enters into no particulars, but contents
himself with four lines expressing one sentiment, upon the principle
laid down in the former part of this discourse where the Subject of
an Epitaph is a Man of prime note.

> Torquato Tasso rests within this Tomb;
> This Figure, weeping from her inmost heart,
> Is Poesy: from such impassioned grief
> Let every one conclude what this Man was.[64]

The Epitaph which Chiabrera composed for himself has also an
appropriate brevity and is distinguished for its grandeur, the sentiment being the same as that which the Reader has before seen so
happily enlarged upon.

> [FRIEND, while living I sought consolation from Mount Parnassus.
> You, more prudent, should seek it on Mount Calvary.
> > trans. – ed.][65]

As I am brought back to Men of first rate distinction and public
Benefactors, I cannot resist the pleasure of transcribing the metrical
part of an Epitaph which formerly was inscribed in the Church of St
Paul's to that Bishop of London who prevailed with William the
Conqueror to secure to the inhabitants of the City all the liberties
and privileges which they had enjoyed in the time of Edward the
Confessor.

> These marble Monuments to thee thy Citizens assigne,
> Rewards (O Father) farre unfit to those deserts of thine,
> Thee unto them a faithful friend, thy London people found,
> And to this towne of no small weight a stay both sure and sound.
> Their liberties restorde to them, by means of thee have beene,
> Their publicke weale by meanes of thee, large gifts have felt and seene,
> Thy riches, stocke, and beauty brave, one hour hath them supprest,
> Yet these thy virtues, and good deeds with us for ever rest.[66]

Thus have I attempted to determine what a sepulchral Inscription ought to be, and taken at the same time a survey of what Epitaphs are good and bad, and have shewn to what deficiencies in sensibility and to what errors in taste and judgement most commonly are to be ascribed. — It was my intention to have given a few specimens from those of the Ancients but I have already I fear taken up too much of the Reader's time. I have not animadverted upon such — alas! far too numerous — as are reprehensible from the want of moral rectitude in those who have composed them or given it to be understood that they should be so composed: boastful and haughty panegyrics, ludicrously contradicting the solid remembrance of those who knew the deceased, shocking the common sense of mankind by their extravagance and affronting the very altar with their impious falsehood. These I leave to general scorn, not however without a general recommendation that they who have offended or may be disposed to offend in this manner would take into serious thought the heinousness of their transgression.

Upon reviewing what has been written, I think it better here to add a few favourable specimens such as are ordinarily found in our Country Church-Yards at this day. If those primary sensations upon which I have dwelt so much be not stifled in the heart of the Reader, they will be read with pleasure; otherwise neither these nor more exalted strains can by him be truly interpreted.

### Aged 87 and 83

> Not more with silver hairs than virtue crown'd
> The good old Pair take up this spot of ground:
> Tread in their steps and you will surely find
> Their Rest above, below their peace of mind.

*

> At the Last day I'm sure I shall appear
> To meet with Jesus Christ my Saviour dear,
> Where I do hope to live with him in bliss;
> Oh, what a joy in my last hour was this!

*

Aged 3 Month[s]

What Christ said once he said to all:
Come unto me, ye Children small;
None shall do you any wrong,
For to my kingdom you belong.

\*

Aged 10 Weeks

The Babe was sucking at the breast
When God did call him to his rest.[67]

\*

In an obscure corner of a Country Church-yard I once [es]pied, half-overgrown with Hemlock and Nettles, a very small Stone laid upon the ground, bearing nothing more than the name of the Deceased with the date of birth and death, importing that it was an Infant which had been born one day and died the following. I know not how far the Reader may be in sympathy with me, but more awful thoughts of rights conferred, of hopes awakened, of remembrances stealing away or vanishing were imparted to my mind by that Inscription there before my eyes than by any other that it has ever been my lot to meet with upon a Tomb-stone.

The most numerous class of sepulchral Inscriptions do indeed record nothing else but the name of the buried Person, but that he was born upon one day and died upon another. Addison in the Spectator making this observation says, 'that he cannot look upon those registers of existence whether of brass or marble but as a kind of satire upon the departed persons who had left no other memorial of them than that they were born and that they died.'[68] In certain moods this is a natural reflection, yet not perhaps the most salutary which the appearance might give birth to. As in these registers the name is mostly associated with others of the same family, this is a prolonged companionship, however shadowy; even a Tomb like this is a shrine to which the fancies of a scattered family may repair in pilgrimage; the thoughts of the individuals, without any communication with each other, must oftentimes meet here. – Such a frail memorial then is not without its tendency to keep families together; it feeds also local attachment, which is the tap-root of the tree of Patriotism.

I know not how I can withdraw more satisfactorily from this long disquisition than by offering to the Reader as a farewell memorial the following Verses, suggested to me by a concise Epitaph which I met with some time ago in one of the most retired vales among the Mountains of Westmoreland. There is nothing in the detail of the Poem which is not either founded upon the Epitaph or gathered from enquiries concerning the Deceased made in the neighbour-hood.

[Here Wordsworth quoted from *The Excursion*, VII, 395–481.]

# Preface to Poems (1815)

~~~~~~~~~~~~~~

[*Probably composed January (certainly by 18 February) 1815. First published 1815. The text printed below is taken from* Poetical Works (*1850*), *V*, 233–50.]

*This preface is primarily an attempt to set forth and defend the arrangement of his poems in this, his first collected edition, but the preface also contains much of Wordsworth's creative theory, his examination of imagination and fancy.*

The powers requisite for the production of poetry are: first, those of Observation and Description, – *i.e.,* the ability to observe with accuracy things as they are in themselves, and with fidelity to describe them, unmodified by any passion or feeling existing in the mind of the describer; whether the things depicted be actually present to the senses, or have a place only in the memory. This power, though indispensable to a Poet, is one which he employs only in submission to necessity, and never for a continuance of time: as its exercise supposes all the higher qualities of the mind to be passive, and in a state of subjection to external objects, much in the same way as a translator or engraver ought to be to his original. 2ndly, Sensibility, – which, the more exquisite it is, the wider will be the range of a poet's perceptions; and the more will he be incited to observe objects, both as they exist in themselves and as re-acted upon by his own mind. (The distinction between poetic and human sensibility has been marked in the character of the Poet delineated in the original preface.) 3dly, Reflection, – which makes the Poet acquainted with the value of actions, images, thoughts, and feelings; and assists the sensibility in perceiving their connection with each other. 4thly, Imagination and Fancy, – to modify, to create, and to associate. 5thly, Invention, – by which characters are composed out of materials supplied by observation; whether of the Poet's own heart and mind, or of external life and nature; and such incidents and situations produced as are most impressive to the imagination, and most fitted to do justice to the characters, sentiments, and passions, which the Poet undertakes to illustrate. And, lastly, Judgment, – to decide how and where, and in what degree, each of these faculties ought to be exerted; so that the less shall not be sacrificed to the greater; nor the greater, slighting the less, arrogate, to its own injury, more than its due. By judgment, also, is determined what are the laws and appropriate graces of every species of composition.[1]

The materials of Poetry, by these powers collected and produced, are cast, by means of various moulds, into divers forms. The moulds may be enumerated, and the forms specified, in the following order. 1st, The Narrative, – including the Epopoeia, the Historic Poem, the Tale, the Romance, the Mock-heroic, and, if the spirit of Homer will tolerate such neighbourhood, that dear production of our days, the metrical Novel.[2] Of this Class, the distinguishing mark is, that the Narrator, however liberally his speaking agents be introduced, is himself the source from which every thing primarily flows. Epic Poets, in order that their mode of composition may accord with the elevation of their subject, represent themselves as *singing* from the inspiration of the Muse, 'Arma virumque *cano*';[3] but this is a fiction, in modern times, of slight value: the Iliad or the Paradise Lost would gain little in our estimation by being chanted. The other poets who belong to this class are commonly content to *tell* their tale; – so that of the whole it may be affirmed that they neither require nor reject the accompaniment of music.

2ndly, The Dramatic, – consisting of Tragedy, Historic Drama,

Comedy, and Masque, in which the Poet does not appear at all in his own person, and where the whole action is carried on by speech and dialogue of the agents; music being admitted only incidentally and rarely. The Opera may be placed here, inasmuch as it proceeds by dialogue; though depending, to the degree that it does, upon music, it has a strong claim to be ranked with the lyrical. The characteristic[4] and impassioned Epistle, of which Ovid and Pope have given examples, considered as a species of monodrama, may, without impropriety, be placed in this class.

3rdly, The Lyrical, – containing the Hymn, the Ode, the Elegy, the Song, and the Ballad; in all which, for the production of their *full* effect, an accompaniment of music is indispensable.

4thly, The Idyllium, – descriptive chiefly either of the processes and appearances of external nature, as the Seasons of Thomson; or of characters, manners, and sentiments, as are Shenstone's Schoolmistress, The Cotter's Saturday Night of Burns, The Twa Dogs of the same Author; or of these in conjunction with the appearances of Nature, as most of the pieces of Theocritus, the Allegro and Penseroso of Milton, Beattie's Minstrel, Goldsmith's Deserted Village. The Epitaph, the Inscription, the Sonnet, most of the epistles of poets writing in their own persons, and all loco–descriptive poetry,[5] belong to this class.

5thly, Didactic, – the principal object of which is direct instruction; as the Poem of Lucretius,[6] the Georgics of Virgil, The Fleece of Dyer, Mason's English Garden,[7] &c.

And, lastly, philosophical Satire, like that of Horace and Juvenal; personal and occasional Satire rarely comprehending sufficient of the general in the individual to be dignified with the name of poetry.

Out of the three last has been constructed a composite order, of which Young's Night Thoughts, and Cowper's Task, are excellent examples.

It is deducible from the above, that poems, apparently miscellaneous, may with propriety be arranged either with reference to the powers of mind *predominant* in the production of them; or to the mould in which they are cast; or, lastly, to the subjects to which they relate. From each of these considerations, the following Poems have been divided into classes; which, that the work may more obviously correspond with the course of human life, and for the sake of exhibiting in it the three requisites of a legitimate whole, a beginning, a middle, and an end,[8] have been also arranged, as far as it was possible, according to an order of time, commencing with Childhood, and terminating with Old Age, Death, and Immortality. My guiding wish was, that the small pieces of which these volumes consist, thus discriminated, might be regarded under a two-fold view; as composing an entire work within themselves, and as adjuncts to the philosophical Poem, 'The Recluse'.[9] This arrangement has long presented itself habitually to my own mind. Nevertheless, I should have preferred to scatter the contents of these volumes at random, if I had been persuaded that, by the plan adopted, any thing material would be taken from the natural effect of the pieces, individually, on the mind of the unreflecting Reader. I trust there is a sufficient variety in each class to prevent this; while, for him who reads with reflection, the arrangement will serve as a commentary unostentatiously directing his attention to my purposes, both particular and general. But, as I wish to guard against the possibility of misleading by this classification, it is proper first to remind the Reader, that certain poems are placed according to the powers of mind, in the Author's conception, predominant in the production of them; *predominant*, which implies the exertion of other faculties in less degree. Where there is more imagination than fancy in a poem, it is placed under the head of imagination, and *vice versâ*. Both the above classes might without impropriety have been enlarged from that consisting of 'Poems founded on the Affections'; as might this latter from those, and from the class 'proceeding from Sentiment and Reflection'. The most striking characteristics of each piece, mutual illustration, variety, and proportion, have governed me throughout.

None of the other Classes, except those of Fancy and Imagination, require any particular notice. But a remark of general application may be made. All Poets, except the dramatic, have been in the practice of feigning that their works were composed to the music of the harp or lyre: with what degree of affectation this has been done in modern times, I leave to the judicious to determine. For my own part, I have not been disposed to violate probability so far, or to make such a large demand upon the Reader's charity. Some of these pieces are essentially lyrical; and, therefore, cannot have their due force without a supposed musical accompaniment; but, in much the greatest part, as a substitute for the classic lyre or romantic harp, I require nothing more than an animated or impassioned recitation, adapted to the subject. Poems, however humble in their kind, if they be good in that kind, cannot read themselves; the law of long syllable and short must not be so inflexible, – the letter of metre must not be so impassive to the spirit of versification, – as to deprive the Reader of all voluntary power to modulate, in subordination to the sense, the music of the poem; – in the same manner as his mind is left at liberty, and even summoned, to act upon its thoughts and images. But, though the accompaniment of a musical instrument be frequently dispensed with, the true Poet does not therefore abandon his privilege distinct from that of the mere Proseman;

> 'He murmurs near the running brooks
> A music sweeter than their own.'[10]

Let us come now to the consideration of the words Fancy and Imagination, as employed in the classification of the following Poems. 'A man,' says an intelligent author, 'has imagination in proportion as he can distinctly copy in idea the impressions of sense: it is the faculty which *images* within the mind the phenomena of sensation. A man has fancy in proportion as he can call up, connect, or associate, at pleasure, those internal images ($\varphi\alpha\nu\tau\acute{\alpha}\zeta\epsilon\iota\nu$ is to cause to appear) so as to complete ideal representations of absent objects. Imagination is the power of depicting, and fancy of evoking and combining. The imagination is formed by patient observation; the fancy by a voluntary activity in shifting the scenery of the mind. The more accurate the imagination, the more safely may a painter, or a poet, undertake a delineation, or a description, without the presence of the objects to be characterised. The more versatile the fancy, the more original and striking will be the decorations produced.' – *British Synonyms discriminated, by W. Taylor.*[11]

Is not this as if a man should undertake to supply an account of a building, and be so intent upon what he had discovered of the foundation, as to conclude his task without once looking up at the superstructure? Here, as in other instances throughout the volume, the judicious Author's mind is enthralled by Etymology; he takes up the original word as his guide and escort, and too often does not perceive how soon he becomes its prisoner, without liberty to tread in any path but that to which it confines him. It is not easy to find out how imagination, thus explained, differs from distinct remembrance of images; or fancy from quick and vivid recollection of them: each is nothing more than a mode of memory.[12] If the two words bear the above meaning, and no other, what term is left to designate that faculty of which the Poet is 'all compact'; he whose eye glances from earth to heaven, whose spiritual attributes body forth what his pen is prompt in turning to shape;[13] or what is left to characterise Fancy, as insinuating herself into the heart of objects with creative activity? – Imagination, in the sense of the word as giving title to a class of the following Poems, has no reference to images that are merely a faithful copy, existing in the mind, of absent external objects; but is a word of higher import, denoting operations of the mind upon those objects, and processes of creation or of composition, governed by certain fixed laws. I proceed to illustrate my meaning by instances.[14] A parrot *hangs* from the wires of his cage by his beak or by his claws; or a monkey from the bough of a tree by his paws or his tail. Each creature does so literally and actually. In the first Eclogue of Virgil, the shepherd, thinking of the time when he is to take leave of his farm, thus addresses his goats: –

> 'Non ego vos posthac viridi projectus in antro
> Dumosa *pendere* procul de rupe videbo.'[15]

> —'half way down
> *Hangs* one who gathers samphire,'[16]

is the well-known expression of Shakspeare, delineating an ordinary image upon the cliffs of Dover. In these two instances is a slight exertion of the faculty which I denominate imagination, in the use of one word: neither the goats nor the samphire-gatherer do literally hang, as does the parrot or the monkey; but, presenting to the senses something of such an appearance, the mind in its activity, for its own gratification, contemplates them as hanging.

> 'As when far off at sea a fleet descried
> *Hangs* in the clouds, by equinoctial winds
> Close sailing from Bengala, or the isles
> Of Ternate or Tidore, whence merchants bring
> Their spicy drugs; they on the trading flood
> Through the wide Ethiopian to the Cape
> Ply, stemming nightly toward the Pole: so seemed
> Far off the flying Fiend.'[17]

Here is the full strength of the imagination involved in the word *hangs*, and exerted upon the whole image: First, the fleet, an aggregate of many ships, is represented as one mighty person, whose track, we know and feel, is upon the waters; but, taking advantage of its appearance to the senses, the Poet dares to represent it as *hanging in the clouds*, both for the gratification of the mind in contemplating the image itself, and in reference to the motion and appearance of the sublime object[18] to which it is compared.

From impressions of sight we will pass to those of sound; which, as they must necessarily be of a less definite character, shall be selected from these volumes:

> 'Over his own sweet voice the Stock-dove *broods*;'[19]

of the same bird,

> 'His voice was *buried* among trees,
> Yet to be come at by the breeze;'[20]

> 'O, Cuckoo! shall I call thee *Bird*,
> Or but a wandering *Voice?*'[21]

The stock-dove is said to *coo*,[22] a sound well imitating the note of the bird; but, by the intervention of the metaphor *broods*, the affections are called in by the imagination to assist in marking the manner in which the bird reiterates and prolongs her soft note, as if herself delighting to listen to it, and participating of a still and quiet satisfaction, like that which may be supposed inseparable from the continuous process of incubation. 'His voice was buried among trees,' a metaphor expressing the love of *seclusion* by which this Bird is marked; and characterising its note as not partaking of the shrill and the piercing, and therefore more easily deadened by the intervening shade; yet a note so peculiar and withal so pleasing, that the breeze, gifted with that love of the sound which the Poet feels, penetrates the shades in which it is entombed, and conveys it to the ear of the listener.

> 'Shall I call thee Bird,
> Or but a wandering Voice?'

This concise interrogation characterises the seeming ubiquity of the voice of the cuckoo, and dispossesses the creature almost of a corporeal existence; the Imagination being tempted to this exertion of her power by a consciousness in the memory that the cuckoo is almost perpetually heard throughout the season of spring, but seldom becomes an object of sight.

Thus far of images independent of each other, and immediately endowed by the mind with properties that do not inhere in them, upon an incitement from properties and qualities the existence of which is inherent and obvious. These processes of imagination are carried on either by conferring additional properties upon an object, or abstracting from it some of those which it actually possesses, and thus enabling it to re-act upon the mind which hath performed the process, like a new existence.

I pass from the Imagination acting upon an individual image to a consideration of the same faculty employed upon images in a conjunction by which they modify each other. The Reader has already had a fine instance before him in the passage quoted from Virgil, where the apparently perilous situation of the goat, hanging upon the shaggy precipice, is contrasted with that of the shepherd contemplating it from the seclusion of the cavern in which he lies stretched at ease and in security. Take these images separately, and how unaffecting the picture compared with that produced by their being thus connected with, and opposed to, each other!

> 'As a huge stone is sometimes seen to lie
> Couched on the bald top of an eminence,
> Wonder to all who do the same espy
> By what means it could thither come, and whence,
> So that it seems a thing endued with sense,
> Like a sea-beast crawled forth, which on a shelf
> Of rock or sand reposeth, there to sun himself.
>
> Such seemed this Man; not all alive or dead
> Nor all asleep, in his extreme old age.
>   ★   ★   ★   ★   ★
> Motionless as a cloud the old Man stood,
> That heareth not the loud winds when they call,
> And moveth altogether if it move at all.' 23

In these images, the conferring, the abstracting, and the modifying powers of the Imagination, immediately and mediately acting, are all brought into conjunction. The stone is endowed with something of the power of life to approximate it to the sea-beast; and the sea-beast stripped of some of its vital qualities to assimilate it to the stone; which intermediate image is thus treated for the purpose of bringing the original image, that of the stone, to a nearer resemblance to the figure and condition of the aged Man; who is divested of so much of the indications of life and motion as to bring him to the point where the two objects unite and coalesce in just comparison. After what has been said, the image of the cloud need not be commented upon.

Thus far of an endowing or modifying power: but the Imagination also shapes and *creates*; and how? By innumerable processes; and in none does it more delight than in that of consolidating numbers into unity, and dissolving and separating unity into number, — alternations proceeding from, and governed by, a sublime consciousness of the soul in her own mighty and almost divine powers. Recur to the passage already cited from Milton. When the compact Fleet, as one

Person, has been introduced 'Sailing from Bengala,' 'They,' *i.e.* the 'merchants,' representing the fleet resolved into a multitude of ships, 'ply' their voyage towards the extremities of the earth: 'So,' (referring to the word 'As' in the commencement) 'seemed the flying Fiend;' the image of his Person acting to recombine the multitude of ships into one body, – the point from which the comparison set out. 'So seemed,' and to whom seemed? To the heavenly Muse who dictates the poem, to the eye of the Poet's mind, and to that of the Reader, present at one moment in the wide Ethiopian, and the next in the solitudes, then first broken in upon, of the infernal regions!

'Modo me Thebis, modo ponit Athenis.' [24]

Hear again this mighty Poet, – speaking of the Messiah going forth to expel from heaven the rebellious angels,

'Attended by ten thousand thousand Saints
He onward came: far off his coming shone,' – [25]

the retinue of Saints, and the Person of the Messiah himself, lost almost and merged in the splendour of that indefinite abstraction 'His coming'!

As I do not mean here to treat this subject further than to throw some light upon the present Volumes, and especially upon one division of them, I shall spare myself and the Reader the trouble of considering the Imagination as it deals with thoughts and sentiments, as it regulates the composition of characters, and determines the course of actions: I will not consider it (more than I have already done by implication) as that power which, in the language of one of my most esteemed Friends, 'draws all things to one; which makes things animate or inanimate, beings with their attributes, subjects with their accessaries, take one colour and serve to one effect.' [26] The grand store-houses of enthusiastic and meditative Imagination, of poetical, as contradistinguished from human and dramatic Imagination, [27] are the prophetic and lyrical parts of the Holy Scriptures, and the works of Milton; to which I cannot forbear to add those of Spenser. I select these writers in preference to those of ancient Greece and Rome, because the anthropomorphitism of the Pagan religion subjected the minds of the greatest poets in those countries too much to the bondage of definite form; from which the Hebrews were preserved by their abhorrence of idolatry. This abhorrence was almost as strong in our great epic Poet,[28] both from circumstances of his life, and from the constitution of his mind. However imbued the surface might be with classical literature, he was a Hebrew in soul; and all things tended in him towards the sublime. Spenser, of a gentler nature, maintained his freedom by aid of his allegorical spirit, at one time inciting him to create persons out of abstractions; and, at another, by a superior effort of genius, to give the universality and permanence of abstractions to his human beings, by means of attributes and emblems that belong to the highest moral truths and the purest sensations, – of which his character of Una[29] is a glorious example. Of the human and dramatic Imagination the works of Shakspeare are an inexhaustible source.

> 'I tax not you, ye Elements, with unkindness,
> I never gave you kingdoms, call'd you Daughters!'[30]

And if, bearing in mind the many Poets distinguished by this prime quality, whose names I omit to mention; yet justified by recollection of the insults which the ignorant, the incapable, and the presumptuous, have heaped upon these and my other writings, I may be permitted to anticipate the judgment of posterity upon myself, I shall declare (censurable, I grant, if the notoriety of the fact above stated does not justify me) that I have given in these unfavourable times, evidence of exertions of this faculty upon its worthiest objects, the external universe, the moral and religious sentiments of Man, his natural affections, and his acquired passions; which have the same ennobling tendency as the productions of men, in this kind, worthy to be holden in undying remembrance.

To the mode in which Fancy has already been characterised as the power of evoking and combining, or, as my friend Mr Coleridge has styled it, 'the aggregative and associative power,'[31] my objection is only that the definition is too general. To aggregate and to associate, to evoke and to combine, belong as well to the Imagination as to the Fancy; but either the materials evoked and combined are different; or they are brought together under a different law, and for a different purpose. Fancy does not require that the materials which she makes use of should be susceptible of change in their constitution, from her touch; and, where they admit of modification, it is enough for her purpose if it be slight, limited, and evanescent. Directly the reverse of these, are the desires and demands of the Imagination. She recoils from every thing but the plastic, the pliant, and the indefinite. She leaves it to Fancy to describe Queen Mab as coming,

> 'In shape no bigger than an agate-stone
> On the fore-finger of an alderman.' [32]

Having to speak of stature, she [33] does not tell you that her gigantic Angel was as tall as Pompey's Pillar; much less that he was twelve cubits, or twelve hundred cubits high; or that his dimensions equalled those of Teneriffe or Atlas; – because these, and if they were a million times as high it would be the same, are bounded: The expression is, 'His stature reached the sky!' [34] the illimitable firmament! – When the Imagination frames a comparison, if it does not strike on the first presentation, a sense of the truth of the likeness, from the moment that it is perceived, grows – and continues to grow – upon the mind; the resemblance depending less upon outline of form and feature, than upon expression and effect; less upon casual and outstanding, than upon inherent and internal, properties: moreover, the images invariably modify each other. – The law under which the processes of Fancy are carried on is as capricious as the accidents of things, and the effects are surprising, playful, ludicrous, amusing, tender, or pathetic, as the objects happen to be appositely produced or fortunately combined. Fancy depends upon the rapidity and profusion with which she scatters her thoughts and images; trusting that their number, and the felicity with which they are linked together, will make amends for the want of individual value: or she prides herself upon the curious subtilty and the successful elaboration with which she can detect their lurking affinities. If she can win you over to her purpose, and impart to you her feelings, she cares not how unstable or transitory may be her influence, knowing that it will not be out of her power to resume it upon an apt occasion. But the Imagination is conscious of an indestructible dominion; – the Soul may fall away from it, not being able to sustain its grandeur; but, if once felt and acknowledged, by no act of any other faculty of the mind can it be relaxed, impaired, or diminished. – Fancy is given to quicken and to beguile the temporal part of our nature, Imagination to incite and to support the eternal. – Yet is it not the less true that Fancy, as she is an active, is also, under her own laws and in her own spirit, a creative faculty. In what manner Fancy ambitiously aims at a rivalship with Imagination, and Imagination stoops to work with the materials of Fancy, might be illustrated from the compositions of all eloquent writers, whether in prose or verse; and chiefly from those of our own Country. Scarcely a page of the impassioned parts of Bishop Taylor's Works [35] can be opened that shall not afford examples. – Referring the Reader to those inestimable volumes, I will content myself with placing a conceit (ascribed to Lord Chesterfield) in contrast with a passage from the Paradise Lost: –

> 'The dews of the evening most carefully shun,
> They are the tears of the sky for the loss of the sun.' [36]

After the transgression of Adam, Milton, with other appearances of sympathising Nature, thus marks the immediate consequence,

> 'Sky lowered, and, muttering thunder, some sad drops
> Wept at completion of the mortal sin.' [37]

The associating link is the same in each instance: Dew and rain, not distinguishable from the liquid substance of tears, are employed as indications of sorrow. A flash of surprise is the effect in the former case; a flash of surprise, and nothing more; for the nature of things does not sustain the combination. In the latter, the effects from the act, of which there is this immediate consequence and visible sign, are so momentous, that the mind acknowledges the justice and reasonableness of the sympathy in nature so manifested; and the sky weeps drops of water as if with human eyes, as 'Earth had before trembled from her entrails, and Nature given a second groan.'[38]

Finally, I will refer to Cotton's 'Ode upon Winter', an admirable composition, though stained with some peculiarities of the age in which he lived, for a general illustration of the characteristics of Fancy. The middle part of this ode contains a most lively description of the entrance of Winter, with his retinue, as 'A palsied king,' and yet a military monarch, – advancing for conquest with his army; the several bodies of which, and their arms and equipments, are described with a rapidity of detail, and a profusion of *fanciful* comparisons, which indicate on the part of the poet extreme activity of intellect, and a correspondent hurry of delightful feeling.[39] He[40] retires from the foe into his fortress, where

> – 'a magazine
> Of sovereign juice is cellared in;
> Liquor that will the siege maintain
> Should Phoebus ne'er return again.'[41]

Though myself a water-drinker, I cannot resist the pleasure of transcribing what follows, as an instance still more happy of Fancy employed in the treatment of feeling than, in its preceding passages, the Poem supplies of her management of forms.

> ''Tis that, that gives the poet rage,
> And thaws the gelly'd blood of age;
> Matures the young, restores the old,
> And makes the fainting coward bold.
>
> It lays the careful head to rest,
> Calms palpitations in the breast,
> Renders our lives' misfortune sweet;

*    *    *    *    *    *    *    *[42]

> Then let the chill Sirocco blow,
> And gird us round with hills of snow,
> Or else go whistle to the shore,
> And make the hollow mountains roar,

Whilst we together jovial sit
Careless, and crowned with mirth and wit,
Where, though bleak winds confine us home
Our fancies round the world shall roam.

We'll think of all the Friends we know,
And drink to all worth drinking to;
When having drunk all thine and mine,
We rather shall want healths than wine.

But where Friends fail us, we'll supply
Our friendships with our charity;
Men that remote in sorrows live,
Shall by our lusty brimmers thrive.

We'll drink the wanting into wealth,
And those that languish into health,
The afflicted into joy; th' opprest
Into security and rest.

The worthy in disgrace shall find
Favour return again more kind,
And in restraint who stifled lie,
Shall taste the air of liberty.

The brave shall triumph in success,
The lover shall have mistresses,
Poor unregarded Virtue, praise,
And the neglected Poet, bays.

Thus shall our healths do others good,
Whilst we ourselves do all we would;
For, freed from envy and from care,
What would we be but what we are?'[43]

When I sate down to write this Preface, it was my intention to
have made it more comprehensive; but, thinking that I ought rather
to apologise for detaining the Reader so long, I will here conclude.

# Essay, Supplementary to the Preface

~w~ ~w~ ~w~

[Probably composed January (certainly by 18 February) 1815, although it may contain work performed between 3 October and 18 December 1800. First published 1815. The text printed below is taken from Poetical Works (1850), V, 196–230.]

This defence of his own genius was occasioned by the unfavourable reception of his works after the earlier success of Lyrical Ballads. The unnamed recipient of much of Wordsworth's abuse was Francis Jeffrey, editor of the Edinburgh Review, which had consistently attacked Wordsworth's productions since its inception in 1802. In the process of defence and attack, Wordsworth presents a revaluation of English poetry from Shakespeare to his own time.

With [1] the young of both sexes, Poetry is, like love, a passion; but, for much the greater part of those who have been proud of its power over their minds, a necessity soon arises of breaking the pleasing bondage; or it relaxes of itself; – the thoughts being occupied in domestic cares, or the time engrossed by business. Poetry then becomes only an occasional recreation; while to those whose existence passes away in a course of fashionable pleasure, it is a species of luxurious amusement. In middle and declining age, a scattered number of serious persons resort to poetry, as to religion, for a protection against the pressure of trivial employments, and as a consolation

387

for the afflictions of life. And, lastly, there are many, who, having been enamoured of this art in their youth, have found leisure, after youth was spent, to cultivate general literature; in which poetry has continued to be comprehended *as a study*.

Into the above classes the Readers of poetry may be divided; Critics abound in them all; but from the last only can opinions be collected of absolute value, and worthy to be depended upon, as prophetic of the destiny of a new work. The young, who in nothing can escape delusion, are especially subject to it in their intercourse with Poetry. The cause, not so obvious as the fact is unquestionable, is the same as that from which erroneous judgments in this art, in the minds of men of all ages, chiefly proceed; but upon Youth it operates with peculiar force. The appropriate business of poetry, (which, nevertheless, if genuine, is as permanent as pure science,) her appropriate employment, her privilege and her *duty*, is to treat of things not as they *are*, but as they *appear*; not as they exist in themselves, but as they *seem* to exist to the *senses*, and to the *passions*. What a world of delusion does this acknowledged obligation prepare for the inexperienced! what temptations to go astray are here held forth for them whose thoughts have been little disciplined by the understanding, [2] and whose feelings revolt from the sway of reason! – When a juvenile Reader is in the height of his rapture with some vicious passage, should experience throw in doubts, or common-sense suggest suspicions, a lurking consciousness that the realities of the Muse are but shows, and that her liveliest excitements are raised by transient shocks of conflicting feeling and successive assemblages of contradictory thoughts – is ever at hand to justify extravagance, and to sanction absurdity. But, it may be asked, as these illusions are unavoidable, and, no doubt, eminently useful to the mind as a process, what good can be gained by making observations, the tendency of which is to diminish the confidence of youth in its feelings, and thus to abridge its innocent and even profitable pleasures? The reproach implied in the question could not be warded off, if Youth were incapable of being delighted with what is truly excellent; or, if these errors always terminated of themselves in due season. But, with the majority, though their force be abated, they continue through life. Moreover, the fire of youth is too vivacious an element to be extinguished or damped by a philosophical remark; and, while there is no danger that what has been said will be injurious or painful to the ardent and the confident, it may prove beneficial to those who, being enthusiastic, are, at the same time, modest and ingenuous. The intimation may unite with their own misgivings to regulate their sensibility, and to bring in, sooner than it would otherwise have arrived, a more discreet and sound judgment.

If it should excite wonder that men of ability, in later life, whose understandings have been rendered acute by practice in affairs, should be so easily and so far imposed upon when they happen to take up a new work in verse, this appears to be the cause; — that, having discontinued their attention to poetry, whatever progress may have been made in other departments of knowledge, they have not, as to this art, advanced in true discernment beyond the age of youth. If, then, a new poem fall in their way, whose attractions are of that kind which would have enraptured them during the heat of youth, the judgment not being improved to a degree that they shall be disgusted, they are dazzled; and prize and cherish the faults for having had power to make the present time vanish before them, and to throw the mind back, as by enchantment, into the happiest season of life. As they read, powers seem to be revived, passions are regenerated, and pleasures restored. The Book was probably taken up after an escape from the burden of business, and with a wish to forget the world, and all its vexations and anxieties. Having obtained this wish, and so much more, it is natural that they should make report as they have felt.

If Men of mature age, through want of practice, be thus easily beguiled into admiration of absurdities, extravagances, and misplaced ornaments, thinking it proper that their understandings should enjoy a holiday, while they are unbending their minds with verse, it may be expected that such Readers will resemble their former selves also in strength of prejudice, and an inaptitude to be moved by the unostentatious beauties of a pure style. In the higher poetry, an enlightened Critic chiefly looks for a reflection of the wisdom of the heart and the grandeur of the imagination. Wherever these appear, simplicity accompanies them; Magnificence herself, when legitimate, depending upon a simplicity of her own, to regulate her ornaments. But it is a well-known property of human nature, that our estimates are ever governed by comparisons, of which we are conscious with various degrees of distinctness. Is it not, then, inevitable (confining these observations to the effects of style merely) that an eye, accustomed to the glaring hues of diction by which such Readers are caught and excited, will for the most part be rather repelled than attracted by an original Work, the colouring of which is disposed according to a pure and refined scheme of harmony? It is in the fine arts as in the affairs of life, no man can *serve* (i.e. obey with zeal and fidelity) two Masters.[3]

As Poetry is most just to its own divine origin when it administers the comforts and breathes the spirit of religion, they who have learned to perceive this truth, and who betake themselves to reading verse for sacred purposes, must be preserved from numerous illusions to which the two Classes of Readers, whom we have been considering, are liable. But, as the mind grows serious from the weight of life, the range of its passions is contracted accordingly; and its sympathies become so exclusive, that many species of high excellence wholly escape, or but languidly excite, its notice. Besides, men who read from religious or moral inclinations, even when the subject is of that kind which they approve, are beset with misconceptions and mistakes peculiar to themselves. Attaching so much importance to the truths which interest them, they are prone to over-rate the Authors by whom those truths are expressed and enforced. They come prepared to impart so much passion to the Poet's language, that they remain unconscious how little, in fact, they receive from it. And, on the other hand, religious faith is to him who holds it so momentous a thing, and error appears to be attended with such tremendous consequences, that, if opinions touching upon religion occur which the Reader condemns, he not only cannot sympathise with them, however animated the expression, but there is, for the most part, an end put to all satisfaction and enjoyment.[4] Love, if it before existed, is converted into dislike; and the heart of the Reader is set against the Author and his book. – To these excesses, they, who from their professions ought to be the most guarded against them, are perhaps the most liable; I mean those sects whose religion, being from the calculating understanding, is cold and formal.[5] For when Christianity, the religion of humility, is founded upon the proudest faculty of our nature, what can be expected but contradictions? Accordingly, believers of this cast are at one time contemptuous; at another, being troubled, as they are and must be, with inward misgivings, they are jealous and suspicious; – and at all seasons, they are under temptation to supply by the heat with which they defend their tenets, the animation which is wanting to the constitution of the religion itself.

Faith was given to man that his affections, detached from the treasures of time, might be inclined to settle upon those of eternity; – the elevation of his nature, which this habit produces on earth, being to him a presumptive evidence of a future state of existence; and giving him a title to partake of its holiness. The religious man values what he sees chiefly as an 'imperfect shadowing forth'[6] of what he is incapable of seeing. The concerns of religion refer to indefinite objects, and are too weighty for the mind to support them without relieving itself by resting a great part of the burden upon words and symbols. The commerce between Man and his Maker cannot be carried on but by a process where much is represented in little, and the Infinite Being accommodates himself to a finite capacity. In all this may be perceived the affinity between religion and poetry; between religion – making up the deficiencies of reason by faith; and poetry – passionate for the instruction of reason;[7] between religion – whose element is infinitude, and whose ultimate trust is the supreme of things, submitting herself to circumscription, and reconciled to substitutions; and poetry – ethereal and transcendent, yet incapable to sustain her existence without sensuous incarnation. In this community of nature may be perceived also the lurking incitements of kindred error; – so that we shall find that no poetry has been more subject to distortion, than that species, the argument and scope of which is religious; and no lovers of the art have gone farther astray than the pious and the devout.

Whither then shall we turn for that union of qualifications which must necessarily exist before the decisions of a critic can be of absolute value? For a mind at once poetical and philosophical; for a critic whose affections are as free and kindly as the spirit of society, and whose understanding is severe as that of dispassionate government? Where are we to look for that initiatory composure of mind which no selfishness can disturb? For a natural sensibility that has been tutored into correctness without losing anything of its quickness; and for active faculties, capable of answering the demands which an Author of original imagination shall make upon them, associated with a judgment that cannot be duped into admiration by aught that is unworthy of it? – among those and those only, who, never having suffered their youthful love of poetry to remit much of its force, have applied to the consideration of the laws of this art the best power of their understandings. At the same time it must be observed – that, as this Class comprehends the only judgments which are trust-worthy, so does it include the most erroneous and perverse. For to be mistaught is worse than to be untaught; and no perverseness equals that which is supported by system, no errors are so difficult to root out as those which the understanding has pledged its credit to uphold. In this Class are contained censors, who, if they be pleased with what is good, are pleased with it only by imperfect glimpses, and upon false principles; who, should they generalise rightly, to a certain point, are sure to suffer for it in the end; who, if they stumble upon a sound rule, are fettered by misapplying it, or by straining it too far; being incapable of perceiving when it ought to yield to one of higher order. In it are found critics too petulant to be passive to a genuine poet, and too feeble to grapple with him; men, who take upon them to report of the course which *he* holds whom they are utterly unable to accompany, – confounded if he turn quick upon the wing, dismayed if he soar steadily 'into the region;' [8] – men of palsied imaginations and indurated hearts; in whose minds all healthy action is languid, who therefore feed as the many direct them, or, with the many, are greedy after vicious provocatives; – judges, whose censure is auspicious, and whose praise ominous! In this class meet together the two extremes of best and worst.

The observations presented in the foregoing series are of too ungracious a nature to have been made without reluctance; and, were it only on this account, I would invite the reader to try them by the test of comprehensive experience. If the number of judges who can be confidently relied upon be in reality so small, it ought to follow that partial notice only, or neglect, perhaps long continued, or attention wholly inadequate to their merits – must have been the fate of most works in the higher departments of poetry; and that, on the other hand, numerous productions have blazed into popularity, and have passed away, leaving scarcely a trace behind them: it will be further found, that when Authors shall have at length raised themselves into general admiration and maintained their ground, errors and prejudices have prevailed concerning their genius and their works, which the few who are conscious of those errors and prejudices would deplore; if they were not recompensed by perceiving that there are select Spirits for whom it is ordained that their fame shall be in the world an existence like that of Virtue, which owes its being to the struggles it makes, and its vigour to the enemies whom it provokes; – a vivacious quality, ever doomed to meet with opposition, and still triumphing over it; and, from the nature of its dominion, incapable of being brought to the sad conclusion of Alexander, when he wept that there were no more worlds for him to conquer.[9]

Let us take a hasty retrospect of the poetical literature of this Country for the greater part of the last two centuries, and see if the facts support these inferences.

Who is there that now reads the 'Creation' of Dubartas?[10] Yet all Europe once resounded with his praise; he was caressed by kings; and, when his Poem was translated into our language, the Faery Queen faded before it. The name of Spenser, whose genius is of a higher order than even that of Ariosto, is at this day scarcely known beyond the limits of the British Isles. And if the value of his works is to be estimated from the attention now paid to them by his countrymen, compared with that which they bestow on those of some other writers, it must be pronounced small indeed.

> 'The laurel, meed of mighty conquerors
> And poets *sage*' —[11]

are his own words; but his wisdom has, in this particular, been his worst enemy: while its opposite, whether in the shape of folly or madness, has been *their* best friend. But he was a great power, and bears a high name: the laurel has been awarded to him.

A dramatic Author, if he write for the stage, must adapt himself to the taste of the audience, or they will not endure him; accordingly the mighty genius of Shakspeare was listened to. The people were delighted: but I am not sufficiently versed in stage antiquities to determine whether they did not flock as eagerly to the representation of many pieces of contemporary Authors, wholly undeserving to appear upon the same boards. Had there been a formal contest for superiority among dramatic writers, that Shakspeare, like his predecessors Sophocles and Euripedes, would have often been subject to the mortification of seeing the prize adjudged to sorry competitors, becomes too probable, when we reflect that the admirers of Settle and Shadwell[12] were, in a later age, as numerous, and reckoned as respectable in point of talent, as those of Dryden. At all events, that Shakspeare stooped to accommodate himself to the People, is sufficiently apparent; and one of the most striking proofs of his almost omnipotent genius, is, that he could turn to such glorious purpose those materials which the prepossessions of the age compelled him to make use of. Yet even this marvellous skill appears not to have been enough to prevent his rivals from having some advantage over him in public estimation; else how can we account for passages and scenes that exist in his works, unless upon a supposition that some of the grossest of them, a fact which in my own mind I have no doubt of, were foisted in by the Players, for the gratification of the many?

But that his Works, whatever might be their reception upon the stage, made but little impression upon the ruling Intellects of

the time, may be inferred from the fact that Lord Bacon, in his multifarious writings, nowhere either quotes or alludes to him.[13] His
dramatic excellence enabled him to resume possession of the stage
after the Restoration; but Dryden tells us that in his time two of the
plays of Beaumont and Fletcher were acted for one of Shakspeare's.[14]
And so faint and limited was the perception of the poetic beauties of
his dramas in the time of Pope, that, in his Edition of the Plays, with
a view of rendering to the general reader a necessary service, he
printed between inverted commas those passages which he thought
most worthy of notice.[15]

At this day, the French Critics have abated nothing of their
aversion to this darling of our Nation: 'the English, with their bouffon
de Shakspeare,' is as familiar an expression among them as in the
time of Voltaire.[16] Baron Grimm [17] is the only French writer who
seems to have perceived his infinite superiority to the first names of
the French Theatre; an advantage which the Parisian Critic owed to
his German blood and German education. The most enlightened
Italians, though well acquainted with our language, are wholly incompetent to measure the proportions of Shakspeare. The Germans
only, of foreign nations, are approaching towards a knowledge and
feeling of what he is. In some respects they have acquired a superiority over the fellow-countrymen of the Poet: for among us it is a
current, I might say, an established opinion, that Shakspeare is justly
praised when he is pronounced to be 'a wild irregular genius, in
whom great faults are compensated by great beauties.'[18] How long
may it be before this misconception passes away, and it becomes
universally acknowledged that the judgment of Shakspeare in the
selection of his materials, and in the manner in which he has made
them, heterogeneous as they often are, constitute a unity of their
own, and contribute all to one great end, is not less admirable than
his imagination, his invention, and his intuitive knowledge of human
Nature?

There is extant a small Volume of miscellaneous poems in which
Shakspeare expresses his own feelings in his own person.[19] It is not
difficult to conceive that the Editor, George Steevens,[20] should have

been insensible to the beauties of one portion of that Volume, the Sonnets; though in no part of the writings of this Poet is found, in an equal compass, a greater number of exquisite feelings felicitously expressed. But, from regard to the Critic's own credit, he would not have ventured to talk of an [21] act of parliament not being strong enough to compel the perusal of those little pieces, if he had not known that the people of England were ignorant of the treasures contained in them: and if he had not, moreover, shared the too common propensity of human nature to exult over a supposed fall into the mire of a genius whom he had been compelled to regard with admiration, as an inmate of the celestial regions – 'there sitting where he durst not soar.' [22]

Nine years [23] before the death of Shakspeare, Milton was born; and early in life he published several small poems, which, though on their first appearance they were praised by a few of the judicious, were afterwards neglected to that degree, that Pope in his youth could borrow [24] from them without risk of its being known. Whether these poems are at this day justly appreciated, I will not undertake to decide: nor would it imply a severe reflection upon the mass of readers to suppose the contrary; seeing that a man of the acknowledged genius of Voss, [25] the German poet, could suffer their spirit to evaporate; and could change their character, as is done in the translation made by him of the most popular of those pieces. At all events, it is certain that these Poems of Milton are now much read, and loudly praised; yet were they little heard of till more than 150 years after their publication; and of the Sonnets, Dr Johnson, as appears from Boswell's Life of him, [26] was in the habit of thinking and speaking as contemptuously as Steevens wrote upon those of Shakspeare.

About the time when the Pindaric odes of Cowley [27] and his imitators, and the productions of that class of curious thinkers whom Dr Johnson has strangely styled metaphysical Poets, [28] were beginning to lose something of that extravagant admiration which they had excited, the Paradise Lost made its appearance. 'Fit audience find though few,' [29] was the petition addressed by the Poet to his inspiring

Muse. I have said elsewhere [30] that he gained more than he asked; this I believe to be true; but Dr Johnson has fallen into a gross mistake when he attempts to prove, by the sale of the work, that Milton's Countrymen were '*just* to it' [31] upon its first appearance. Thirteen hundred Copies were sold in two years; an uncommon example, he asserts, of the prevalence of genius in opposition to so much recent enmity as Miton's public conduct had excited. But, be it remembered that, if Milton's political and religious opinions, and the manner in which he announced them, had raised him many enemies, they had procured him numerous friends; who, as all personal danger was passed away at the time of publication, would be eager to procure the master-work of a man whom they revered, and whom they would be proud of praising. Take, from the number of purchasers, persons of this class, and also those who wished to possess the Poem as a religious work, and but few I fear would be left who sought for it on account of its poetical merits. The demand did not immediately increase; 'for,' says Dr Johnson, 'many more readers' (he means persons in the habit of reading poetry) 'than were supplied at first the Nation did not afford.' [32] How careless must a writer be who can make this assertion in the face of so many existing title-pages to belie it! Turning to my own shelves, I find the folio of Cowley, seventh edition, 1681. A book near it is Flatman's [33] Poems, fourth edition, 1686; Waller, [34] fifth edition, same date. The Poems of Norris of Bemerton [35] not long after went, I believe, through nine editions. What further demand there might be for these works I do not know; but I well remember, that, twenty-five years ago, the booksellers' stalls in London swarmed with the folios of Cowley. This is not mentioned in disparagement of that able writer and amiable man; but merely to show – that, if Milton's work were not more read, it was not because readers did not exist at the time. The early editions of the Paradise Lost were printed in a shape which allowed them to be sold at a low price, yet only three thousand copies of the Work were sold in eleven years; and the Nation, says Dr Johnson, had been satisfied from 1623 to 1664, that is, forty-one years, with only two editions [36] of the Works of Shakspeare; which probably did not together make one-thousand Copies; facts adduced by the critic to prove the 'paucity of Readers.' [37] – There were readers in multitudes; but their money went for other purposes, as their admiration was fixed elsewhere. We are authorised, then, to affirm, that the reception of the Paradise Lost, and the slow progress of its fame, are proofs as striking as can be desired that the positions which I am attempting to establish are not erroneous. [38] – How amusing to shape to one's self such a critique as a Wit of Charles's days, or a Lord of the Miscellanies or trading Journalist of King William's time, would have brought forth, if he had set his faculties industriously to work upon this Poem, everywhere impregnated with *original* excellence.

So strange indeed are the obliquities of admiration, that they whose opinions are much influenced by authority will often be tempted to think that there are no fixed principles [39] in human nature for this art to rest upon. I have been honoured by being permitted to peruse in MS. a tract composed between the period of the Revolution and the close of that century. It is the Work of an English Peer [40] of high accomplishments, its object to form the character and direct the studies of his son. Perhaps nowhere does a more beautiful treatise of the kind exist. The good sense and wisdom of the thoughts, the delicacy of the feelings, and the charm of the style, are, throughout, equally conspicuous. Yet the Author, selecting among the Poets of his own country those whom he deems most worthy of his son's perusal, particularises only Lord Rochester, Sir John Denham, and Cowley. Writing about the same time, Shaftesbury, an author at present unjustly depreciated, describes the English Muses as only yet lisping in their cradles. [41]

The arts by which Pope, soon afterwards, contrived to procure to himself a more general and a higher reputation than perhaps any English Poet ever attained during his life-time, are known to the judicious. And as well known is it to them, that the undue exertion of those arts is the cause why Pope has for some time held a rank in literature, to which, if he had not been seduced by an over-love of immediate popularity, and had confided more in his native genius, he never could have descended. He bewitched the nation by his melody, and dazzled it by his polished style, and was himself blinded by his own success. Having wandered from humanity in his Eclogues with boyish inexperience, the praise, which these compositions obtained, tempted him into a belief that Nature was not to be trusted, at least in pastoral Poetry. To prove this by example, he put his friend Gay upon writing those Eclogues [42] which their author intended to be burlesque. The instigator of the work, and his admirers, could perceive in them nothing but what was ridiculous. Nevertheless, though these Poems contain some detestable passages, the effect, as Dr Johnson well observes, 'of reality and truth became conspicuous even when the intention was to show them grovelling and degraded.' [43] The Pastorals, ludicrous to such as prided themselves upon their refinement, in spite of those disgusting passages, 'became popular, and were read with delight, as just representations of rural manners and occupations.' [44]

Something less than sixty years after the publication of the Paradise Lost appeared Thomson's Winter; which was speedily followed by his other Seasons. [45] It is a work of inspiration; much of it is written from himself, and nobly from himself. How was it received? 'It was no sooner read,' says one of his contemporary biographers, 'than universally admired: those only excepted who had not been used to feel, or to look for anything in poetry, beyond a *point* of satirical or epigrammatic wit, a smart *antithesis* richly trimmed with rhyme, or the softness of an *elegiac* complaint. To such his manly classical spirit could not readily commend itself; till, after a more attentive perusal, they had got the better of their prejudices, and either acquired or affected a truer taste. A few others stood aloof, merely because they had long before fixed the articles of their poetical creed, and resigned themselves to an absolute despair of ever seeing any thing new and original. These were somewhat mortified to find their notions disturbed by the appearance of a poet, who seemed to owe nothing but to nature and his own genius. But, in a short time, the applause became unanimous; every one wondering how so many pictures, and pictures so familiar, should have moved them but faintly to what they felt in his descriptions. His digressions too, the overflowings of a tender benevolent heart, charmed the reader no less; leaving him in doubt, whether he should more admire the Poet or love the Man.'[46]

This case appears to bear strongly against us: — but we must distinguish between wonder and legitimate admiration. The subject of the work is the changes produced in the appearances of nature by the revolution of the year: and, by undertaking to write in verse, Thomson pledged himself to treat his subject as became a Poet. Now it is remarkable that, excepting the nocturnal Reverie of Lady Winchilsea,[47] and a passage or two in the Windsor Forest of Pope, the poetry of the period intervening between the publication of the Paradise Lost and the Seasons does not contain a single new image of external nature; and scarcely presents a familiar one from which it can be inferred that the eye of the Poet had been steadily fixed upon his object, much less that his feelings had urged him to work upon it in the spirit of genuine imagination. To what a low state knowledge of the most obvious and important phenomena had sunk, is evident from the style in which Dryden has executed a description of Night in one of his Tragedies, and Pope his translation of the celebrated moonlight scene in the Iliad.[48] A blind man, in the habit of attending accurately to descriptions casually dropped from the lips of those around him, might easily depict these appearances with more truth. Dryden's lines are vague, bombastic, and senseless;[49] those of Pope, though he had Homer to guide him, are throughout false and contradictory. The verses of Dryden, once highly celebrated, are forgotten; those of Pope still retain their hold upon public estimation, — nay, there is not a passage of descriptive poetry, which at this day finds so many and such ardent admirers. Strange to think of an enthusiast, as may have been the case with thousands, reciting those verses under the cope of a moonlight sky, without having his raptures in the least disturbed by a suspicion of their absurdity! — If these two distinguished writers could habitually think that the visible universe was of so little consequence to a poet, that it was scarcely necessary for him to cast his eyes upon it, we may be assured that those passages of the elder poets which faithfully and poetically describe the phenomena of nature, were not at that time holden in much estimation, and that there was little accurate attention paid to those appearances.

Wonder is the natural product of Ignorance; and as the soil was *in such good condition* at the time of the publication of the Seasons, the crop was doubtless abundant. Neither individuals nor nations become corrupt all at once, nor are they enlightened in a moment. Thomson was an inspired poet, but he could not work miracles; in cases where the art of seeing had in some degree been learned, the teacher would further the proficiency of his pupils, but he could do little *more*; though so far does vanity assist men in acts of self-deception, that many would often fancy they recognised a likeness when they knew nothing of the original. Having shown that much of what his biographer deemed genuine admiration must in fact have been blind wonderment – how is the rest to be accounted for? – Thomson was fortunate in the very title of his poem, which seemed to bring it home to the prepared sympathies of every one: in the next place, notwithstanding his high powers, he writes a vicious [50] style; and his false ornaments are exactly of that kind which would be most likely to strike the undiscerning. He likewise abounds with sentimental common-places, that, from the manner in which they were brought forward, bore an imposing air of novelty. In any well-used copy of the Seasons the book generally opens of itself with the rhapsody on love, or with one of the stories [51] (perhaps Damon and Musidora); these also are prominent in our collections of Extracts, and are the parts of his Work, which, after all, were probably most efficient in first recommending the author to general notice. Pope, repaying praises which he had received, and wishing to extol him to the highest, only styles him 'an elegant and philosophical Poet; [52] nor are we able to collect any unquestionable proofs that the true characteristics of Thomson's genius as an imaginative poet [53] were perceived, till the elder Warton, almost forty years after the publication of the Seasons, pointed them out by a note [54] in his Essay on the Life and Writings of Pope. In the Castle of Indolence (of which Gray speaks so coldly) [55] these characteristics were almost as conspicuously displayed, and in verse more harmonious, and diction more pure. Yet that fine poem was neglected on its appearance, and is at this day the delight only of a few!

When Thomson died, Collins breathed forth his regrets in an Elegiac Poem,[56] in which he pronounces a poetical curse upon *him* who should regard with insensibility the place where the Poet's remains were deposited. The Poems of the mourner himself have now passed through innumerable editions, and are universally known; but if, when Collins died, the same kind of imprecation had been pronounced by a surviving admirer, small is the number whom it would not have comprehended. The notice which his poems attained during his lifetime was so small, and of course the sale so insignificant, that not long before his death he deemed it right to repay to the bookseller the sum which he had advanced for them, and threw the edition into the fire.

Next in importance to the Seasons of Thomson, though at considerable distance from that work in order of time, come the Reliques of Ancient English Poetry;[57] collected, new-modelled, and in many instances (if such a contradiction in terms may be used) composed by the Editor, Dr Percy. This work did not steal silently into the world, as is evident from the number of legendary tales, that appeared not long after its publication; and had been modelled, as the authors persuaded themselves, after the old Ballad. The Compilation was however ill-suited to the then existing taste of city society; and Dr Johnson, 'mid the little senate to which he gave laws,[58] was not sparing in his exertions[59] to make it an object of contempt. The critic triumphed, the legendary imitators were deservedly disregarded, and, as undeservedly, their ill-imitated models sank, in this country, into temporary neglect; while Bürger, and other able writers of Germany,[60] were translating, or imitating these Reliques, and composing, with the aid of inspiration thence derived, poems which are the delight of the German nation. Dr Percy was so abashed by the ridicule flung upon his labours from the ignorance and insensibility of the persons with whom he lived, that, though while he was writing under a mask he had not wanted resolution to follow his genius into the regions of true simplicity and genuine pathos (as is evinced by the exquisite ballad of Sir Cauline and by many other pieces), yet when he appeared in his own person and character as a poetical writer, he adopted, as in the tale of the Hermit of Warkworth,[61] a diction scarcely in any one of its features distinguishable from the vague, the glossy, and unfeeling language of his day. I mention this remarkable fact[62] with regret, esteeming the genius of Dr Percy in this kind of writing superior to that of any other man by whom in modern times it has been cultivated. That even Bürger (to whom Klopstock gave, in my hearing,[63] a commendation which he denied to Goethe and Schiller, pronouncing him to be a genuine poet, and one of the few among the Germans whose works would last) had not the fine sensibility of Percy, might be shown from many passages, in which he has deserted his original only to go astray. For example,

> Now daye was gone, and night was come,
> And all were fast asleepe,
> All save the Lady Emeline,
> Who sate in her bowre to weepe:
> And soone she heard her true Love's voice
> Low whispering at the walle,
> Awake, awake, my dear Ladye,
> 'Tis I thy true-love call.[64]

Which is thus tricked out and dilated:

> Als nun die Nacht Gebirg' und Thal
> Vermummt in Rabenschatten,
> Und Hochburgs Lampen überall
> Schon ausgeflimmert hatten,
> Und alles tief entschlafen war;
> Doch nur das Fräulein immerdar,
> Voll Fieberangst, noch wachte,
> Und seinen Ritter dachte:
> Da horch! Ein süsser Liebeston
> Kam leis' empor geflogen.

'Ho, Trudchen, ho! Da bin ich schon!
Risch auf! Dich angezogen!'[65]

But from humble ballads we must ascend to heroics.

All hail, Macpherson! hail to thee, Sire of Ossian![66] The Phantom
was begotten by the snug embrace of an impudent Highlander upon
a cloud of tradition – it travelled southward, where it was greeted
with acclamation, and the thin Consistence took its course through
Europe, upon the breath of popular applause. The Editor of the
'Reliques'[67] had indirectly preferred a claim to the praise of invention, by not concealing that his supplementary labours were
considerable! how selfish his conduct, contrasted with that of the
disinterested Gael, who, like Lear,[68] gives his kingdom away, and is
content to become a pensioner upon his own issue for a beggarly
pittance! – Open this far-famed Book! – I have done so at random,
and the beginning of the 'Epic Poem Temora,'[69] in eight Books,
presents itself. 'The blue waves of Ullin roll in light. The green hills
are covered with day. Trees shake their dusky heads in the breeze.
Grey torrents pour their noisy streams. Two green hills with aged
oaks surround a narrow plain. The blue course of a stream is there.
On its banks stood Cairbar of Atha. His spear supports the king; the
red eyes of his fear are sad. Cormac rises on his soul with all his
ghastly wounds.' Precious memorandums from the pocket-book of
the blind Ossian!

If it be unbecoming, as I acknowledge that for the most part it is,
to speak disrespectfully of Works that have enjoyed for a length of
time a widely-spread reputation, without at the same time producing
irrefragable proofs of their unworthiness, let me be forgiven upon
this occasion. – Having had the good fortune to be born and reared
in a mountainous country, from my very childhood I have felt the
falsehood that pervades the volumes imposed upon the world under
the name of Ossian. From what I saw with my own eyes, I knew that
the imagery was spurious. In nature every thing is distinct, yet
nothing defined into absolute independent singleness. In Macpherson's work, it is exactly the reverse; every thing (that is not

stolen) is in this manner defined, insulated, dislocated, deadened, – yet nothing distinct. It will always be so when words are substituted for things. To say that the characters never could exist, that the manners are impossible, and that a dream has more substance than the whole state of society, as there depicted, is doing nothing more than pronouncing a censure which Macpherson defied; when, with the steeps of Morven before his eyes, he could talk so familiarly of his Car-borne heroes;[70] – of Morven, which, if one may judge from its appearance at the distance of a few miles,[71] contains scarcely an acre of ground sufficiently accommodating for a sledge to be trailed along its surface. – Mr Malcolm Laing has ably shown[72] that the diction of this pretended translation is a motley assemblage from all quarters; but he is so fond of making out parallel passages as to call poor Macpherson to account for his '*ands*' and his '*buts*'! and he has weakened his argument by conducting it as if he thought that every striking resemblance was a *conscious* plagiarism. It is enough that the coincidences are too remarkable for its being probable or possible that they could arise in different minds without communication between them. Now as the Translators of the Bible, and Shakspeare, Milton, and Pope, could not be indebted to Macpherson, it follows that he must have owed his fine feathers to them; unless we are prepared gravely to assert, with Madame de Staël,[73] that many of the characteristic beauties of our most celebrated English Poets are derived from the ancient Fingallian; in which case the modern translator would have been but giving back to Ossian his own. – It is consistent that Lucien Buonaparte, who could censure Milton for having surrounded Satan in the infernal regions with courtly and regal splendour, should pronounce the modern Ossian to be the glory of Scotland;[74] – a country that has produced a Dunbar, a Buchanan, a Thomson, and a Burns![75] These opinions are of ill omen for the Epic ambition of him who has given them to the world.

Yet, much as those pretended treasures of antiquity have been admired, they have been wholly uninfluential upon the literature of the Country. No succeeding writer appears to have caught from them a ray of inspiration; no author, in the least distinguished, has ventured formally to imitate them – except the boy, Chatterton,[76] on their first appearance. He had perceived, from the successful trials which he himself had made in literary forgery, how few critics were able to distinguish between a real ancient medal and a counterfeit of modern manufacture; and he set himself to the work of filling a magazine with *Saxon Poems*, – counterparts of those of Ossian, as like his as one of his misty stars is to another. This incapability to amalgamate with the literature of the Island, is, in my estimation, a decisive proof that the book is essentially unnatural; nor should I require any other to demonstrate it to be a forgery, audacious as worthless. – Contrast, in this respect, the effect of Macpherson's publication with the Reliques of Percy, so unassuming, so modest in their pretensions! – I have already stated how much Germany is indebted to this latter work; and for our own country, its poetry has been absolutely redeemed by it. I do not think that there is an able writer in verse of the present day who would not be proud to acknowledge his obligations to the Reliques; I know that it is so with my friends; and, for myself, I am happy in this occasion to make a public avowal of my own.

Dr Johnson, more fortunate in his contempt of the labours of Macpherson than those of his modest friend, was solicited not long after to furnish Prefaces biographical and critical for the works of some of the most eminent English Poets.[77] The booksellers took upon themselves to make the collection; they referred probably to the most popular miscellanies, and, unquestionably, to their books of accounts; and decided upon the claim of authors to be admitted into a body of the most eminent, from the familiarity of their names with the readers of that day, and by the profits, which, from the sale of his works, each had brought and was bringing to the Trade. The Editor was allowed a limited exercise of discretion, and the Authors whom he recommended[78] are scarcely to be mentioned without a smile. We open the volume of Prefatory Lives, and to our astonishment the *first* name we find is that of Cowley! – What is become of the morning-star of English Poetry?[79] Where is the bright Elizabethan constellation? Or, if names be more acceptable than images, where is the ever-to-be-honoured Chaucer? where is Spenser? where Sidney? and, lastly, where he, whose rights as a poet, contradistinguished from those which he is universally allowed to possess as a dramatist, we have vindicated, – where Shakspeare? – These, and a multitude of others not unworthy to be placed near them, their contemporaries and successors, we have *not*. But in their stead, we have (could better be expected when precedence was to be settled by an abstract of reputation at any given period made, as in this case before us?) Roscommon, and Stepney, and Phillips, and Walsh, and Smith, and Duke, and King, and Spratt – Halifax, Granville, Sheffield, Congreve, Broome,[80] and other reputed Magnates – metrical writers utterly worthless and useless, except for occasions like the present, when their productions are referred to as evidence what a small quantity of brain is necessary to procure a considerable stock of admiration, provided the aspirant will accommodate himself to the likings and fashions of his day.

As I do not mean to bring down this retrospect to our own times, it may with propriety be closed at the era of this distinguished event. From the literature of other ages and countries, proofs equally cogent might have been adduced, that the opinions announced in the former part of this Essay are founded upon truth. It was not an agreeable office, nor a prudent undertaking, to declare them; but their importance seemed to render it a duty. It may still be asked, where lies the particular relation of what has been said to these Volumes? – The question will be easily answered by the discerning Reader who is old enough to remember the taste that prevailed when some of these poems were first published, seventeen years ago; who has also observed to what degree the poetry of this Island has since that period been coloured by them; and who is further aware of the unremitting hostility with which, upon some principle or other, they have each and all been opposed.[81] A sketch of my own notion of the constitution of Fame has been given; and, as far as concerns myself, I have cause to be satisfied. The love, the admiration, the indifference, the slight, the aversion, and even the contempt, with which these

Poems have been received, knowing, as I do, the source within my own mind, from which they have proceeded, and the labour and pains, which, when labour and pains appeared needful, have been bestowed upon them, must all, if I think consistently, be received as pledges and tokens, bearing the same general impression, though widely different in value; – they are all proofs that for the present time I have not laboured in vain; and afford assurances, more or less authentic, that the products of my industry will endure.

If there be one conclusion more forcibly pressed upon us than another by the review which has been given of the fortunes and fate of poetical Works, it is this, – that every author, as far as he is great and at the same time *original*, has had the task of *creating* the taste by which he is to be enjoyed: so has it been, so will it continue to be. This remark was long since made to me by the philosophical Friend [82] for the separation of whose poems from my own I have previously expressed my regret. [83] The predecessors of an original Genius of a high order will have smoothed the way for all that he has in common with them; – and much he will have in common; but, for what is peculiarly his own, he will be called upon to clear and often to shape his own road: – he will be in the condition of Hannibal among the Alps. [84]

And where lies the real difficulty of creating that taste by which a truly original poet is to be relished? Is it in breaking the bonds of custom, in overcoming the prejudices of false refinement, and displacing the aversions of inexperience? Or, if he labour for an object which here and elsewhere I have proposed to myself, does it consist in divesting the reader of the pride that induces him to dwell upon those points wherein men differ from each other, to the exclusion of those in which all men are alike, or the same; and in making him ashamed of the vanity that renders him insensible of the appropriate excellence which civil arrangements, less unjust than might appear, and Nature illimitable in her bounty, have conferred on men who may stand below him in the scale of society? Finally, does it lie in establishing that dominion over the spirits of readers by which they are to be humbled and humanised, in order that they may be purified and exalted?

If these ends are to be attained by the mere communication of *knowledge*, it does *not* lie here. — TASTE, I would remind the reader, like IMAGINATION, is a word which has been forced to extend its services far beyond the point to which philosophy would have confined them. It is a metaphor, taken from a *passive* sense of the human body, and transferred to things which are in their essence *not* passive, — to intellectual *acts* and *operations*. The word, Imagination, has been over-strained, from impulses honourable to mankind, to meet the demands of the faculty which is perhaps the noblest of our nature. In the instance of Taste, the process has been reversed; and from the prevalence of dispositions at once injurious and discreditable, being no other than that selfishness which is the child of apathy, — which, as Nations decline in productive and creative power, makes them value themselves upon a presumed refinement of judging. Poverty of language is the primary cause of the use which we make of the word, Imagination; but the word, Taste, has been stretched to the sense which it bears in modern Europe by habits of self-conceit, inducing that inversion in the order of things whereby a passive faculty is made paramount among the faculties conversant with the fine arts. Proportion and congruity, the requisite knowledge being supposed, are subjects upon which taste may be trusted; it is competent to this office; — for in its intercourse with these the mind is *passive*, and is affected painfully or pleasurably as by an instinct. But the profound and the exquisite in feeling, the lofty and universal in thought and imagination; or, in ordinary language, the pathetic and the sublime; — are neither of them, accurately speaking, objects of a faculty which could ever without a sinking in the spirit of Nations have been designated by the metaphor — *Taste*. And why? Because without the exertion of a co-operating *power* in the mind of the Reader, there can be no adequate sympathy with either of these emotions: without this auxiliary impulse, elevated or profound passion cannot exist.

Passion, it must be observed, is derived from a word which signifies *suffering*; [85] but the connection which suffering has with effort, with exertion, and *action*, is immediate and inseparable. How strikingly is this property of human nature exhibited by the fact, that, in popular language, to be in a passion, is to be angry! – But,

> 'Anger in hasty *words* or *blows*
> Itself discharges on its foes.'[86]

To be moved, then, by a passion, is to be excited, often to external, and always to internal, effort; whether for the continuance and strengthening of the passion, or for its suppression, accordingly as the course which it takes may be painful or pleasurable. If the latter, the soul must contribute to its support, or it never becomes vivid, – and soon languishes, and dies. And this brings us to the point. If every great poet with whose writings men are familiar, in the highest exercise of his genius, before he can be thoroughly enjoyed, has to call forth and to communicate *power*, this service, in a still greater degree, falls upon an original writer, at his first appearance in the world. – Of genius the only proof is, the act of doing well what is worthy to be done, and what was never done before: Of genius, in the fine arts, the only infallible sign is the widening the sphere of human sensibility, for the delight, honour, and benefit of human nature. Genius is the introduction of a new element into the intellectual universe:[87] or, if that be not allowed, it is the application of powers to objects on which they had not before been exercised, or the employment of them in such a manner as to produce effects hitherto unknown. What is all this but an advance, or a conquest, made by the soul of the poet? Is it to be supposed that the reader can make progress of this kind, like an Indian prince or general – stretched on his palanquin, and borne by his slaves? No; he is invigorated and inspirited by his leader, in order that he may exert himself; for he cannot proceed in quiescence, he cannot be carried like a dead weight. Therefore to create taste is to call forth and bestow power, of which knowledge is the effect; and *there* lies the true difficulty.

As the pathetic participates of an *animal* sensation, it might seem – that, if the springs of this emotion were genuine, all men, possessed of competent knowledge of the facts and circumstances, would be instantaneously affected. And, doubtless, in the works of every true poet will be found passages of that species of excellence, which is proved by effects immediate and universal. But there are emotions of the pathetic that are simple and direct, and others – that are complex and revolutionary; some – to which the heart yields with gentleness; others – against which it struggles with pride; these varieties are infinite as the combinations of circumstance and the constitutions of character. Remember, also, that the medium through which, in poetry, the heart is to be affected, is language; a thing subject to endless fluctuations and arbitrary associations. The genius of the poet melts these down for his purpose; but they retain their shape and quality to him who is not capable of exerting, within his own mind, a corresponding energy. There is also a meditative, as well as a human, pathos; an enthusiastic, as well as an ordinary, sorrow; [88] a sadness that has its seat in the depths of reason, to which the mind cannot sink gently of itself – but to which it must descend by treading the steps of thought. And for the sublime, – if we consider what are the cares that occupy the passing day, and how remote is the practice and the course of life from the sources of sublimity, in the soul of Man, can it be wondered that there is little existing preparation for a poet charged with a new mission to extend its kingdom, and to augment and spread its enjoyments?

Away, then, with the senseless iteration of the word, *popular*, applied to new works in poetry, as if there were no test of excellence in this first of the fine arts but that all men should run after its productions, as if urged by an appetite, or constrained by a spell! – The qualities of writing best fitted for eager reception are either such as startle the world into attention by their audacity and extravagance; [89] or they are chiefly of a superficial kind, lying upon the surfaces of manners; or arising out of a selection and arrangement of incidents, by which the mind is kept upon the stretch of curiosity, and the fancy amused without the trouble of thought. But in everything which is to send the soul into herself, to be admonished of her weakness, or to be made conscious of her power; – wherever life and nature are described as operated upon by the creative or abstracting virtue of the imagination; wherever the instinctive wisdom of antiquity and her heroic passions uniting, in the heart of the poet, with the meditative wisdom of later ages, have produced that accord of sublimated humanity, which is at once a history of the remote past and a prophetic enunciation of the remotest future, *there*, the poet must reconcile himself for a season to few and scattered hearers. – Grand thoughts (and Shakspeare must often have sighed over this truth), as they are most naturally and most fitly conceived in solitude, so can they not be brought forth in the midst of plaudits, without some violation of their sanctity. Go to a silent exhibition of the productions of the sister Art,[90] and be convinced that the qualities which dazzle at first sight, and kindle the admiration of the multitude, are essentially different from those by which permanent influence is secured. Let us not shrink from following up these principles as far as they will carry us, and conclude with observing – that there never has been a period, and perhaps never will be, in which vicious poetry, of some kind or other, has not excited more zealous admiration, and been far more generally read, than good; but this advantage attends the good, that the *individual*, as well as the species, survives from age to age; whereas, of the depraved, though the species be immortal, the individual quickly *perishes*; the object of present admiration vanishes, being supplanted by some other as easily produced; which, though no better, brings with it at least the irritation of novelty, – with adaptation, more or less skilful, to the changing humours of the majority of those who are most at leisure to regard poetical works when they first solicit their attention.

Is it the result of the whole, that, in the opinion of the Writer, the judgment of the People is not to be respected? The thought is most injurious; and, could the charge be brought against him, he would repel it with indignation. The People have already been justified, and their eulogium pronounced by implication, when it was said, above – that, of *good* poetry, the *individual*, as well as the species, *survives*. And how does it survive but through the People? What preserves it but their intellect and their wisdom?

' – Past and future, are the wings
On whose support, harmoniously conjoined,
Moves the great Spirit of human knowledge –'
                                    *M.S.* [91]

The voice that issues from this Spirit, is that Vox Populi [92] which the
Deity inspires. Foolish must he be who can mistake for this a local
acclamation, or a transitory outcry – transitory though it be for
years, local though from a Nation. Still more lamentable is his error
who can believe that there is any thing of divine infallibility in the
clamour of that small though loud portion of the community, ever
governed by factitious influence, which, under the name of the
PUBLIC, passes itself, upon the unthinking, for the PEOPLE. [93]
Towards the Public, the Writer hopes that he feels as much deference
as it is entitled to: but to the People, philosophically characterised,
and to the embodied spirit of their knowledge, so far as it exists and
moves, at the present, faithfully supported by its two wings, the past
and the future, his devout respect, his reverence, is due. He offers it
willingly and readily; and, this done, takes leave of his Readers, by
assuring them – that, if he were not persuaded that the contents of
these Volumes, and the Work [94] to which they are subsidiary, evince
something of the 'Vision and the Faculty divine;' [95] and that, both in
words and things, they will operate in their degree, to extend the
domain of sensibility for the delight, the honour, and the benefit of
human nature, notwithstanding the many happy hours which he has
employed in their composition, and the manifold comforts and enjoyments they have procured to him, he would not, if a wish could
do it, save them from immediate destruction; – from becoming at
this moment, to the world, as a thing that had never been.

# A Letter to a Friend of Robert Burns

~~·~~·~~

[*Probably composed between early December 1815 and early February 1816. First published 1816. The full title reads: 'A Letter to a Friend of Robert Burns: Occasioned by an Intended Republication of the Account of the Life of Burns, by Dr Currie; and of the Selection Made by Him from His Letters.'*]

*This letter was apparently written at the request of Gilbert Burns (1760–1827), younger brother of the poet. Despite a contrary comment within the letter itself, it was Wordsworth's idea to publish it, and it was published at his own expense. James Gray (d. 1830) was a master at the High School at Edinburgh and an acquaintance of Wordsworth.*

TO

## JAMES GRAY, ESQ.

EDINBURGH

DEAR SIR,

I have carefully perused the Review of the Life of your friend Robert Burns,[1] which you kindly transmitted to me; the author has rendered a substantial service to the poet's memory; and the annexed letters are all important to the subject. After having expressed this opinion, I shall not trouble you by commenting upon the publication;

but will confine myself to the request of Mr Gilbert Burns, that I would furnish him with my notions upon the best mode of conducting the defence of his brother's injured reputation; a favourable opportunity being now afforded him to convey his sentiments to the world, along with a republication of Dr Currie's book,[2] which he is about to superintend. From the respect which I have long felt for the character of the person who has thus honoured me, and from the gratitude which, as a lover of poetry, I owe to the genius of his departed relative, I should most gladly comply with this wish; if I could hope that any suggestions of mine would be of service to the cause. But, really, I feel it a thing of much delicacy, to give advice upon this occasion, as it appears to me, mainly, not a question of opinion, or of taste, but a matter of conscience. Mr Gilbert Burns must know, if any man living does, what his brother was; and no one will deny that he, who possesses this knowledge, is a man of unimpeachable veracity. He has already spoken to the world[3] in contradiction of the injurious assertions that have been made, and has told why he forbore to do this on their first appearance. If it be deemed adviseable to reprint Dr Currie's narrative, without striking out such passages as the author, if he were now alive, would probably be happy to efface, let there be notes attached to the most obnoxious of them, in which the misrepresentations may be corrected, and the exaggerations exposed. I recommend this course, if Dr Currie's Life is to be republished, as it now stands, in connexion with the poems and letters, and especially if prefixed to them; but, in my judgment, it would be best to copy the example which Mason has given in his second edition of Gray's works.[4] There, inverting the order which had been properly adopted, when the Life and Letters were new matter, the poems are placed first; and the rest takes its place as subsidiary to them. If this were done in the intended edition of Burns's works, I should strenuously recommend, that a concise life of the poet be prefixed, from the pen of Gilbert Burns, who has already given public proof[5] how well qualified he is for the undertaking. I know no better model as to proportion, and the degree of detail required, nor, indeed, as to the general execution, than the life of Milton by Fenton,[6] prefixed to many editions of the Paradise Lost. But a more copious narrative would be expected from a brother; and some allowance ought to be made, in this and other respects, for an expectation so natural.

In this prefatory memoir, when the author has prepared himself by reflecting, that fraternal partiality may have rendered him, in some points, not so trust-worthy as others less favoured by opportunity, it will be incumbent upon him to proceed candidly and openly, as far as such a procedure will tend to restore to his brother that portion of public estimation, of which he appears to have been unjustly deprived. Nay, when we recal to mind the black things which have been written of this great man, and the frightful ones that have been insinuated against him; and, as far as the public knew, till lately, without complaint, remonstrance, or disavowal, from his nearest relatives; I am not sure that it would not be best, at this day, explicitly to declare to what degree Robert Burns had given way to pernicious habits, and, as nearly as may be, to fix the point to which his moral character had been degraded. It is a disgraceful feature of the times that this measure should be necessary; most painful to think that a *brother* should have such an office to perform. But, if Gilbert Burns be conscious that the subject will bear to be so treated, he has no choice; the duty has been imposed upon him by the errors into which the former biographer has fallen, in respect to the very principles upon which his work ought to have been conducted.

I well remember the acute sorrow with which, by my own fire-side, I first perused Dr Currie's Narrative, and some of the letters, particularly of those composed in the latter part of the poet's life. If my pity for Burns was extreme, this pity did not preclude a strong indignation, of which he was not the object. If, said I, it were in the power of a biographer to relate the truth, the *whole* truth, and nothing *but* the truth,[7] the friends and surviving kindred of the deceased, for the sake of general benefit to mankind, might endure that such heart-rending communication should be made to the world. But in no case is this possible; and, in the present, the opportunities of directly acquiring other than superficial knowledge have been most scanty;

for the writer has barely seen the person who is the subject of his tale; nor did his avocations allow him to take the pains necessary for ascertaining what portion of the information conveyed to him was authentic. So much for facts and actions; and to what purpose relate them even were they true, if the narrative cannot be heard without extreme pain; unless they are placed in such a light, and brought forward in such order, that they shall explain their own laws, and leave the reader in as little uncertainty as the mysteries of our nature will allow, respecting the spirit from which they derived their existence, and which governed the agent? But hear on this pathetic and awful subject, the poet himself, pleading for those who have transgressed!

> 'One point must still be greatly dark,
>   The moving *why* they do it,
> And just as lamely can ye mark
>   How far, perhaps, they rue it.
>
> Who made the heart, 'tis *he* alone
>   Decidedly can try us;
> He knows each chord – its various tone,
>   Each spring, its various bias.
>
> Then at the balance let's be mute,
>   We never can adjust it;
> What's done we partly may compute,
>   But know not what's *resisted*.' [8]

How happened it that the recollection of this affecting passage did not check so amiable a man as Dr Currie, while he was revealing to the world the infirmities of its author? He must have known enough of human nature to be assured that men would be eager to sit in judgment, and pronounce *decidedly* upon the guilt or innocence of Burns by his testimony; nay, that there were multitudes whose main interest in the allegations would be derived from the incitements which they found therein to undertake this presumptuous office. And where lies the collateral benefit, or what ultimate advantage can be expected, to counteract the injury that the many are thus tempted to do to their own minds; and to compensate the sorrow which must be fixed in the hearts of the considerate few, by language that proclaims so much, and provokes conjectures as unfavourable as imagination can furnish? Here, said I, being moved beyond what it would become me to express, here is a revolting account of a man of exquisite genius, and confessedly of many high moral qualities, sunk into the lowest depths of vice and misery! But the painful story, notwithstanding its minuteness, is incomplete, – in essentials it is deficient; so that the most attentive and sagacious reader cannot explain how a mind, so well established by knowledge, fell – and continued to fall, without power to prevent or retard its own ruin.

Would a bosom friend of the author, his counsellor and confessor, have told such things, if true, as this book contains? and who, but one possessed of the intimate knowledge which none but a bosom friend can acquire, could have been justified in making these avowals? Such a one, himself a pure spirit, having accompanied, as it were, upon wings, the pilgrim along the sorrowful road which he trod on foot; such a one, neither hurried down by its slippery descents, nor entangled among its thorns, nor perplexed by its windings, nor discomfited by its founderous passages – for the instruction of others – might have delineated, almost as in a map, the way which the afflicted pilgrim had pursued till the sad close of his diversified journey. In this manner the venerable spirit of Isaac Walton was qualified to have retraced the unsteady course of a highly-gifted man, who, in this lamentable point, and in versatility of genius, bore no unobvious resemblance to the Scottish bard; I mean his friend COTTON – whom, notwithstanding all that the sage must have disapproved in his life, he honoured with the title of son.[9] Nothing like this, however, has the biographer of Burns accomplished; and, with his means of information, copious as in some respects they were, it would have been absurd to attempt it. The only motive, therefore, which could authorize the writing and publishing matter so distressing to read – is wanting!

Nor is Dr Currie's performance censurable from these considerations alone; for information, which would have been of absolute worth if in his capacity of biographer and editor he had known when to stop short, is rendered unsatisfactory and inefficacious through the absence of this reserve, and from being coupled with statements of improbable and irreconcileable facts. We have the author's letters discharged upon us in showers; but how few readers will take the trouble of comparing those letters with each other, and with the other documents of the publication, in order to come at a genuine knowledge of the writer's character! – The life of Johnson by Boswell had broken through many pre-existing delicacies, and afforded the British public an opportunity of acquiring experience, which before it had happily wanted; nevertheless, at the time when the ill-selected medley of Burns's correspondence first appeared, little progress had been made (nor is it likely that, by the mass of mankind, much ever will be made) in determining what portion of these confidential communications escapes the pen in courteous, yet often innocent, compliance – to gratify the several tastes of correspondents; and as little towards distinguishing opinions and sentiments uttered for the momentary amusement of the writer's own fancy, from those which his judgment deliberately approves, and his heart faith-fully cherishes. But the subject of this book was a man of extraordin-ary genius; whose birth, education, and employments had placed and kept him in a situation far below that in which the writers and readers of expensive volumes are usually found. Critics upon works of fiction have laid it down as a rule that remoteness of place, in fixing the choice of a subject, and in prescribing the mode of treating it, is equal in effect to distance of time; – restraints may be thrown off accordingly. Judge then of the delusions which artificial distinc-tions impose, when to a man like Doctor Currie, writing with views so honourable, the *social condition* of the individual of whom he was treating, could seem to place him at such a distance from the exalted reader, that ceremony might be discarded with him, and his memory sacrificed, as it were, almost without compunction. The poet was laid where these injuries could not reach him; but he had a parent, I understand, an admirable woman, still surviving; a brother like Gilbert Burns! – a widow estimable for her virtues; and children, at that time infants, with the world before them, which they must face to obtain a maintenance; who remembered their father probably with the tenderest affection; – and whose opening minds, as their years advanced, would become conscious of so many reasons for admiring him. – Ill-fated child of nature, too frequently thine own enemy, – unhappy favourite of genius, too often misguided, – this is indeed to be 'crushed beneath the furrow's weight!'[10]

Why, sir, do I write to you at this length, when all that I had to express in direct answer to the request, which occasioned this letter, lay in such narrow compass? – Because having entered upon the subject, I am unable to quit it! – Your feelings, I trust, go along with mine; and, rising from this individual case to a general view of the subject, you will probably agree with me in opinion that biography, though differing in some essentials from works of fiction, is never-theless, like them, an *art*, – an art, the laws of which are determined by the imperfections of our nature, and the constitution of society. Truth is not here, as in the sciences, and in natural philosophy, to be sought without scruple, and promulgated for its own sake, upon the mere chance of its being serviceable; but only for obviously justifying purposes, moral or intellectual.

Silence is a privilege of the grave, a right of the departed: let him, therefore, who infringes that right, by speaking publicly of, for, or against, those who cannot speak for themselves, take heed that he opens not his mouth without a sufficient sanction. De mortuis nil nisi bonum,[11] is a rule in which these sentiments have been pushed to an extreme that proves how deeply humanity is interested in main-taining them. And it was wise to announce the precept thus absol-utely; both because there exist in that same nature, by which it has been dictated, so many temptations to disregard it, – and because there are powers and influences, within and without us, that will prevent its being literally fulfilled – to the suppression of profitable truth. Penalties of law, conventions of manners, and personal fear, protect the reputation of the living; and something of this protection is extended to the recently dead, – who survive, to a certain degree, in their kindred and friends. Few are so insensible as not to feel this, and not to be actuated by the feeling. But only to philosophy enlightened by the affections does it belong justly to estimate the claims of the deceased on the one hand, and of the present age and future generations, on the other; and to strike a balance between them. – Such philosophy runs a risk of becoming extinct among us, if the coarse intrusions into the recesses, the gross breaches upon the sanctities, of domestic life, to which we have lately been more and more accustomed, are to be regarded as indications of a vigorous state of public feeling – favourable to the maintenance of the liberties of our country. – Intelligent lovers of freedom are from necessity bold and hardy lovers of truth; but, according to the measure in which their love is intelligent, is it attended with a finer discrimination, and a more sensitive delicacy. The wise and good (and all others being lovers of licence rather than of liberty [12] are in fact slaves) respect, as one of the noblest characteristics of Englishmen, that jealousy of familiar approach, which, while it contributes to the maintenance of private dignity, is one of the most efficacious guardians of rational public freedom.

The general obligation upon which I have insisted, is especially binding upon those who undertake the biography of *authors*. Assuredly, there is no cause why the lives of that class of men should be pried into with the same diligent curiosity, and laid open with the same disregard of reserve, which may sometimes be expedient in composing the history of men who have borne an active part in the world. Such thorough knowledge of the good and bad qualities of these latter, as can only be obtained by a scrutiny of their private lives, conduces to explain not only their own public conduct, but that of those with whom they have acted. Nothing of this applies to authors, considered merely as authors. Our business is with their books, – to understand and to enjoy them. And, of poets more especially, it is true – that, if their works be good, they contain within themselves all that is necessary to their being comprehended and relished. It should seem that the ancients thought in this manner; for of the eminent Greek and Roman poets, few and scanty memorials were, I believe, ever prepared; and fewer still are preserved. It is delightful to read what, in the happy exercise of his own genius, Horace [13] chooses to communicate of himself and his friends; but I confess I am not so much a lover of knowledge, independent of its quality, as to make it likely that it would much rejoice me, were I to hear that records of the Sabine poet and his contemporaries, composed upon the Boswellian plan, had been unearthed among the ruins of Herculaneum. You will interpret what I am writing, *liberally*. With respect to the light which such a discovery might throw upon Roman manners, there would be reasons to desire it: but I should dread to disfigure the beautiful ideal of the memories of those illustrious persons with incongruous features, and to sully the imaginative purity of their classical works with gross and trivial recollections. The least weighty objection to heterogeneous details, is that they are mainly superfluous, and therefore an incumbrance.

But you will perhaps accuse me of refining too much; and it is, I own, comparatively of little importance, while we are engaged in reading the Iliad, the Eneid, the tragedies of Othello and King Lear, whether the authors of these poems were good or bad men; whether they lived happily or miserably. Should a thought of the kind cross our minds, there would be no doubt, if irresistible external evidence did not decide the question unfavourably, that men of such transcendent genius were both good and happy: and if, unfortunately, it had been on record that they were otherwise, sympathy with the fate of their fictitious personages would banish the unwelcome truth whenever it obtruded itself, so that it would but slightly disturb our pleasure. Far otherwise is it with that class of poets, the principal charm of whose writings depends upon the familiar knowledge which they convey of the personal feelings of their authors. This is eminently the case with the effusions of Burns; – in the small quantity of narrative that he has given, he himself bears no inconsiderable part, and he has produced no drama. Neither the subjects of his poems, nor his manner of handling them, allow us long to forget their author. On the basis of his human character he has reared a poetic one, which with more or less distinctness presents itself to view in almost every part of his earlier, and, in my estimation, his most valuable verses. This poetic fabric, dug out of the quarry of genuine humanity, is airy and spiritual: – and though the materials, in some parts, are coarse, and the disposition is often fantastic and irregular, yet the whole is agreeable and strikingly attractive. Plague, then, upon your remorseless hunters after matter of fact (who, after all, rank among the blindest of human beings) when they would convince you that the foundations of this admirable edifice are hollow; and that its frame is unsound! Granting that all which has been raked up to the prejudice of Burns were literally true; and that it added, which it does not, to our better understanding of human nature and human life (for that genius is not incompatible with vice, and that vice leads to misery – the more acute from the sensibilities which are the elements of genius – we needed not those communications to inform us) how poor would have been the compensation for the deduction made, by this extrinsic knowledge, from the intrinsic efficacy of his poetry – to please, and to instruct! [14]

In illustration of this sentiment, permit me to remind you that it is the privilege of poetic genius to catch, under certain restrictions of which perhaps at the time of its being exerted it is but dimly conscious, a spirit of pleasure wherever it can be found, – in the walks of nature, and in the business of men. – The poet, trusting to primary instincts, luxuriates among the felicities of love and wine, and is enraptured while he describes the fairer aspects of war: nor does he shrink from the company of the passion of love though immoderate – from convivial pleasure though intemperate – nor from the presence of war though savage, and recognized as the hand-maid of desolation. Frequently and admirably has Burns given way to these impulses of nature; both with reference to himself and in describing the condition of others. Who, but some impenetrable dunce or narrow-minded puritan in works of art, ever read without delight the picture which he has drawn of the convivial exaltation of the rustic adventurer, Tam o' Shanter? [15] The poet fears not to tell the reader in the outset that his hero was a desperate and sottish drunkard, whose excesses were frequent as his opportunities. This reprobate sits down to his cups, while the storm is roaring, and heaven and earth are in confusion; – the night is driven on by song and tumultuous noise – laughter and jest thicken as the beverage improves upon the palate – conjugal fidelity archly bends to the service of general benevolence – selfishness is not absent, but wearing the mask of social cordiality – and, while these various elements of humanity are blended into one proud and happy composition of elated spirits, the anger of the tempest without doors only heightens and sets off the enjoyment within. – I pity him who cannot perceive that, in all this, though there was no moral purpose, there is a moral effect.

> 'Kings may be blest, but Tam was glorious,
> 'O'er a' the *ills* of life victorious.' [16]

What a lesson do these words convey of charitable indulgence for the vicious habits of the principal actor in this scene, and of those who resemble him! – Men who to the rigidly virtuous are objects almost of loathing, and whom therefore they cannot serve! The poet, penetrating the unsightly and disgusting surfaces of things, has unveiled with exquisite skill the finer ties of imagination and feeling, that often bind these beings to practices productive of so much unhappiness to themselves, and to those whom it is their duty to cherish; – and, as far as he puts the reader into possession of this intelligent sympathy, he qualifies him for exercising a salutary influence over the minds of those who are thus deplorably enslaved.

Not less successfully does Burns avail himself of his own character and situation in society, to construct out of them a poetic self, – introduced as a dramatic personage – for the purpose of inspiriting his incidents, diversifying his pictures, recommending his opinions, and giving point to his sentiments. His brother can set me right if I am mistaken when I express a belief that, at the time when he wrote his story of 'Death and Dr Hornbook', [17] he had very rarely been intoxicated, or perhaps even much exhilarated by liquor. Yet how happily does he lead his reader into that track of sensations! and with what lively humour does he describe the disorder of his senses and the confusion of his understanding, put to test by a deliberate attempt to count the horns of the moon!

'But whether she had three or four
He could na' tell.' [18]

Behold a sudden apparition that disperses this disorder, and in a moment chills him into possession of himself! Coming upon no more important mission than the grisly phantom was charged with, what mode of introduction could have been more efficient or appropriate?

But, in those early poems, through the veil of assumed habits and pretended qualities, enough of the real man appears to shew that he was conscious of sufficient cause to dread his own passions, and to bewail his errors! We have rejected as false sometimes in the letter, and of necessity as false in the spirit, many of the testimonies that others have borne against him: — but, by his own hand — in words the import of which cannot be mistaken — it has been recorded that the order of his life but faintly corresponded with the clearness of his views. It is probable that he would have proved a still greater poet if, by strength of reason, he could have controlled the propensities which his sensibility engendered; but he would have been a poet of a different class: and certain it is, had that desirable restraint been early established, many peculiar beauties which enrich his verses could never have existed, and many accessary influences, which contribute greatly to their effect, would have been wanting. For instance, the momentous truth of the passage already quoted, 'One point must still be greatly dark,' &c. [19] could not possibly have been conveyed with such pathetic force by any poet that ever lived, speaking in his own voice; unless it were felt that, like Burns, he was a man who preached from the text of his own errors; and whose wisdom, beautiful as a flower that might have risen from seed sown from above, was in fact a scion from the root of personal suffering. Whom did the poet intend should be thought of as occupying that grave over which, after modestly setting forth the moral discernment and warm affections of its 'poor inhabitant,' it is supposed to be inscribed that

'— Thoughtless follies laid him low,
'And stained his name.' [20]

Who but himself, — himself anticipating the too probable termination of his own course? Here is a sincere and solemn avowal – a public declaration *from his own will* – a confession at once devout, poetical, and human – a history in the shape of a prophecy! What more was required of the biographer than to have put his seal to the writing, testifying that the foreboding had been realized, and that the record was authentic? – Lastingly is it to be regretted in respect to this memorable being, that inconsiderate intrusion has not left us at liberty to enjoy his mirth, or his love; his wisdom or his wit; without an admixture of useless, irksome, and painful details, that take from his poems so much of that right – which, with all his carelessness, and frequent breaches of self-respect, he was not negligent to maintain for them – the right of imparting solid instruction through the medium of unalloyed pleasure.

You will have noticed that my observations have hitherto been confined to Dr Currie's book: if, by fraternal piety, the poison can be sucked out of this wound, those inflicted by meaner hands may be safely left to heal of themselves. Of the other writers who have given their names, only one lays claim to even a slight acquaintance with the author, whose moral character they take upon them publicly to anatomize. The Edinburgh reviewer – and him I single out because the author of the vindication of Burns has treated his offences with comparative indulgence, to which he has no claim, and which, from whatever cause it might arise, has interfered with the dispensation of justice – the Edinburgh reviewer thus writes:[21] 'The *leading vice* in Burns's character, and the *cardinal deformity*, indeed, of ALL his productions, was his contempt, or affectation of contempt, for prudence, decency, and regularity, and his admiration of thoughtlessness, oddity, and vehement sensibility: his belief, in short, in the dispensing power of genius and social feeling in all matters of morality and common sense;' adding, that these vices and erroneous notions 'have communicated to a great part of his productions a character of immorality at once contemptible and hateful.'[22] We are afterwards told, that he is *perpetually* making a parade of his thoughtlessness, inflammability, and imprudence; and, in the next paragraph, that he is *perpetually* doing something else; i.e. 'boasting of his own independence.'[23] – Marvellous address in the commission of faults! not less than Caesar shewed in the management of business; who, it is said, could dictate to three secretaries upon three several affairs, at one and the same moment![24] But, to be serious. When a man, self-elected into the office of a public judge of the literature and life of his contemporaries, can have the audacity to go these lengths in framing a summary of the contents of volumes that are scattered over every quarter of the globe, and extant in almost every cottage of Scotland, to give the lie to his labours; we must not wonder if, in the plenitude of his concern for the interests of abstract morality, the infatuated slanderer should have found no obstacle to prevent him from insinuating that the poet, whose writings are to this degree stained and disfigured, was 'one of the sons of fancy and of song, who spend in vain superfluities the money that belongs of right to the pale industrious tradesman and his famishing infants; and who rave about friendship and philosophy in a tavern, while their wives' hearts,' &c. &c.[25]

It is notorious that this persevering Aristarch,[26] as often as a work of original genius comes before him, avails himself of that opportunity to re-proclaim to the world the narrow range of his own comprehension. The happy self-complacency, the unsuspecting vainglory, and the cordial *bonhommie*, with which this part of his duty is performed, do not leave him free to complain of being hardly dealt with if any one should declare the truth, by pronouncing much of the foregoing attack upon the intellectual and moral character of Burns, to be the trespass (for reasons that will shortly appear, it cannot be called the venial trespass) of a mind obtuse, superficial, and inept. What portion of malignity such a mind is susceptible of, the judicious admirers of the poet, and the discerning friends of the man, will not trouble themselves to enquire; but they will wish that this evil principle had possessed more sway than they are at liberty to assign to it; the offender's condition would not then have been so hopeless. For malignity *selects* its diet; but where is to be found the nourishment from which vanity will revolt? Malignity may be appeased by triumphs real or supposed, and will then sleep, or yield its place to a repentance producing dispositions of good will, and desires to make amends for past injury; but vanity is restless, reckless, intractable, unappeasable, insatiable. Fortunate is it for the world when this spirit incites only to actions that meet with an adequate punishment in derision; such, as in a scheme of poetical justice, would be aptly requited by assigning to the agents, when they quit this lower world, a station in that not uncomfortable limbo – the Paradise of Fools![27] But, assuredly, we shall have here another proof that ridicule is not the test of truth, if it prevent us from perceiving, that *depravity* has no ally more active, more inveterate, nor, from the difficulty of divining to what kind and degree of extravagance it may prompt, more pernicious than self-conceit. Where this alliance is too obvious to be disputed, the culprit ought not to be allowed the benefit of contempt – as a shelter from detestation; much less should he be permitted to plead, in excuse for his transgressions, that especial malevolence had little or no part in them. It is not recorded, that the ancient, who set fire to the temple of Diana, had a particular dislike to the goddess of chastity, or held idolatry in abhorrence: he was a fool, an egregious fool, but not the less, on that account, a most odious monster.[28] The tyrant who is described as having rattled his chariot along a bridge of brass over the heads of his subjects,[29] was, no doubt, inwardly laughed at; but what if this mock Jupiter, not satisfied with an empty noise of his own making, had amused himself with throwing fire-brands upon the house-tops, as a substitute for lightning; and, from his elevation, had hurled stones upon the heads of his people, to shew that he was a master of the destructive bolt, as well as of the harmless voice of the thunder! – The lovers of all that is honourable to humanity have recently had occasion to rejoice over the downfull of an intoxicated despot,[30] whose vagaries furnish more solid materials by which the philosopher will exemplify how strict is the connection between the ludicrously, and the terribly fantastic. We know, also, that Robespierre[31] was one of the vainest men that the most vain country upon earth has produced; – and from this passion, and from that cowardice which naturally connects itself with it, flowed the horrors of his administration. It is a descent, which I fear you will scarcely pardon, to compare these redoubtable enemies of mankind with the anonymous conductor of a perishable publication. But the moving spirit is the same in them all; and, as far as difference of circumstances, and disparity of powers, will allow, manifests itself in the same way; by professions of reverence for truth, and concern for duty — carried to the giddiest heights of ostentation, while practice seems to have no other reliance than on the omnipotence of falshood.

The transition from a vindication of Robert Burns to these hints for a picture of the intellectual deformity of one who has grossly outraged his memory, is too natural to require an apology: but I feel, sir, that I stand in need of indulgence for having detained you so long. Let me beg that you would impart to any judicious friends of the poet as much of the contents of these pages as you think will be serviceable to the cause; but do not give publicity to any *portion* of them, unless it be thought probable that an open circulation of the whole may be useful.[32] The subject is delicate, and some of the opinions are of a kind, which, if torn away from the trunk that supports them, will be apt to wither, and, in that state, to contract poisonous qualities; like the branches of the yew, which, while united by a living spirit to their native tree, are neither noxious, nor without beauty; but, being dissevered and cast upon the ground, become deadly to the cattle that incautiously feed upon them.

To Mr Gilbert Burns, especially, let my sentiments be conveyed, with my sincere respects, and best wishes for the success of his praise-worthy enterprize. And if, through modest apprehension, he should doubt of his own ability to do justice to his brother's memory, let him take encouragement from the assurance that the most odious part of the charges owed its credit to the silence of those who were deemed best entitled to speak; and who, it was thought, would not have been mute, had they believed that they could speak beneficially. Moreover, it may be relied on as a general truth, which will not escape his recollection, that tasks of this kind are not so arduous as, to those who are tenderly concerned in their issue, they may at first appear to be; for, if the many be hasty to condemn, there is a reaction of generosity which stimulates them – when forcibly summoned – to redress the wrong; and, for the sensible part of mankind, *they* are neither dull to understand, nor slow to make allowance for, the aberrations of men, whose intellectual powers do honour to their species.

> I am, dear Sir,
> respectfully yours,
> WILLIAM WORDSWORTH

*Rydal Mount, January, 1816.*

# Appendix A

❦~❦~❦

# A GUIDE THROUGH THE DISTRICT OF THE LAKES

*Contents*

## DIRECTIONS AND INFORMATION FOR THE TOURIST

Windermere. – Ambleside. – Coniston. – Ulpha Kirk. – Road from Ambleside to Keswick. – Grasmere. – The Vale of Keswick. – Buttermere and Crummock. – Loweswater. – Wastdale. – Ullswater, with its tributary Streams. – Haweswater, &c.

[The following four sections are printed in the text above.]

## DESCRIPTION OF THE SCENERY OF THE LAKES

### Section First
### View of the Country as Formed by Nature

Vales diverging from a common Centre. – Effect of Light and Shadow as dependent upon the Position of the Vales. – Mountains, – their Substance, – Surfaces, – and Colours. – Winter Colouring. – The Vales, – Lakes, – Islands, – Tarns, – Woods, – Rivers, – Climate, – Night.

# Directions and Information for the Tourist

~x~~x~~x~

In preparing this Manual, it was the Author's principal wish to furnish a Guide or Companion for the *Minds* of Persons of taste, and feeling for Landscape, who might be inclined to explore the District of the Lakes with that degree of attention to which its beauty may fairly lay claim. For the more sure attainment, however, of this primary object, he will begin by undertaking the humble and tedious task of supplying the Tourist with directions how to approach the several scenes in their best, or most convenient, order. But first, supposing the approach to be made from the south, and through Yorkshire, there are certain interesting spots which may be confidently recommended to his notice, if time can be spared before entering upon the Lake District; and the route may be changed in returning.

There are three approaches to the Lakes through Yorkshire; the least adviseable is the great north road by Catterick and Greta Bridge, and onwards to Penrith. The Traveller, however, taking this route, might halt at Greta Bridge, and be well recompenced if he can afford to give an hour or two to the banks of the Greta, and of the Tees, at Rokeby. Barnard Castle also, about two miles up the Tees, is a striking object, and the main North Road might be rejoined at Bowes. Every one has heard of the great fall of the Tees above Middleham, interesting for its grandeur, as the avenue of rocks that leads to it, is to the geologist. But this place lies so far out of the way as scarcely to be within the compass of our notice. It might, however,

433

be visited by a Traveller on foot, or on horseback, who could rejoin the main road upon Stanemoor.

The second road leads through a more interesting tract of country, beginning at Ripon, from which place see Fountain's Abbey, and thence by Hackfall, and Masham, to Jervaux Abbey, and up the vale of Wensley; turning aside before Askrigg is reached, to see Aysgarthforce, upon the Ure; and again, near Hawes, to Hardraw Scar, of which, with its waterfall, Turner has a fine drawing. Thence over the fells to Sedbergh, and Kendal.

The third approach from Yorkshire is through Leeds. Four miles beyond that town are the ruins of Kirkstall Abbey, should that road to Skipton be chosen; but the other by Otley may be made much more interesting by turning off at Addington to Bolton Bridge, for the sake of visiting the Abbey and grounds. It would be well, however, for a party previously to secure beds, if wanted, at the inn, as there is but one, and it is much resorted to in summer.

The Traveller on foot, or horseback, would do well to follow the banks of the Wharf upwards, to Burnsall, and thence cross over the hills to Gordale — a noble scene, beautifully described in Gray's Tour, and with which no one can be disappointed. Thence to Malham, where there is a respectable village inn, and so on, by Malham Cove, to Settle.

Travellers in carriages must go from Bolton Bridge to Skipton, where they rejoin the main road; and should they be inclined to visit Gordale, a tolerable road turns off beyond Skipton. Beyond Settle, under Giggleswick Scar, the road passes an ebbing and flowing well, worthy the notice of the Naturalist. Four miles to the right of Ingleton is Weathercote Cave, a fine object, but whoever diverges for this must return to Ingleton. Near Kirkby Lonsdale observe the view from the bridge over the Lune, and descend to the channel of the river, and by no means omit looking at the Vale of Lune from the Church-yard.

The journey towards the lake country through Lancashire, is, with the exception of the Vale of the Ribble, at Preston, uninteresting; till you come near Lancaster, and obtain a view of the fells and mountains of Lancashire and Westmorland; with Lancaster Castle, and the

Tower of the Church seeming to make part of the Castle, in the foreground.

They who wish to see the celebrated ruins of Furness Abbey, and are not afraid of crossing the Sands, may go from Lancaster to Ulverston; from which place take the direct road to Dalton; but by all means return through Urswick, for the sake of the view from the top of the hill, before descending into the grounds of Conishead Priory. From this quarter the Lakes would be advantageously approached by Coniston; thence to Hawkshead, and by the Ferry over Windermere, to Bowness: a much better introduction than by going direct from Coniston to Ambleside, which ought not to be done, as that would greatly take off from the effect of Windermere.

Let us now go back to Lancaster. The direct road thence to Kendal is 22 miles, but by making a circuit of eight miles, the Vale of the Lune to Kirkby Lonsdale will be included. The whole tract is pleasing; there is one view mentioned by Gray and Mason especially so. In West's Guide it is thus pointed out: — 'About a quarter of a mile beyond the third mile-stone, where the road makes a turn to the right, there is a gate on the left which leads into a field where the station meant, will be found.' Thus far for those who approach the Lakes from the South.

Travellers from the North would do well to go from Carlisle by Wigton, and proceed along the Lake of Bassenthwaite to Keswick; or, if convenience should take them first to Penrith, it would still be better to cross the country to Keswick, and begin with that vale, rather than with Ulswater. It is worth while to mention, in this place, that the banks of the river Eden, about Corby, are well worthy of notice, both on account of their natural beauty, and the viaducts which have recently been carried over the bed of the river, and over a neighbouring ravine. In the Church of Wetheral, close by, is a fine piece of monumental sculpture by Nollekens. The scenes of Nunnery, upon the Eden, or rather that part of them which is upon Croglin, a mountain stream there falling into Eden, are, in their way, unrivalled. But the nearest road thither, from Corby, is so bad, that no one can be advised to take it in a carriage. Nunnery may be reached from Corby by making a circuit and crossing the Eden at

Armathwaite bridge. A portion of this road, however, is bad enough.

As much the greatest number of Lake Tourists begin by passing from Kendal to Bowness, upon Windermere, our notices shall commence with that Lake. Bowness is situated upon its eastern side, and at equal distance from each extremity of the Lake of

## WINDERMERE

The lower part of this Lake is rarely visited, but has many interesting points of view, especially at Storrs Hall and at Fell-foot, where the Coniston Mountains peer nobly over the western barrier, which elsewhere, along the whole Lake, is comparatively tame. To one also who has ascended the hill from Graythwaite on the western side, the Promontory called Rawlinson's Nab, Storrs Hall, and the Troutbeck Mountains, about sun-set, make a splendid landscape. The view from the Pleasure-house of the Station near the Ferry has suffered much from Larch plantations; this mischief, however, is gradually disappearing, and the Larches, under the management of the proprietor, Mr Curwen, are giving way to the native wood. Windermere ought to be seen both from its shores and from its surface. None of the other Lakes unfold so many fresh beauties to him who sails upon them. This is owing to its greater size, to the islands, and to its having *two* vales at the head, with their accompanying mountains of nearly equal dignity. Nor can the grandeur of these two terminations be seen at once from any point, except from the bosom of the Lake. The Islands may be explored at any time of the day; but one bright unruffled evening, must, if possible, be set apart for the splendour, the stillness, and solemnity of a three hour's voyage upon the higher division of the Lake, not omitting, towards the end of the excursion, to quit the expanse of water, and peep into the close and calm River at the head; which, in its quiet character, at such a time, appears rather like an overflow of the peaceful Lake itself, than to have any more immediate connection with the rough mountains whence it has descended, or the turbulent torrents by which it is supplied. Many persons content themselves with what they see of Windermere during their progress in a boat from Bowness to the head of the Lake, walking thence to Ambleside. But the whole road from Bowness is rich in diversity of pleasing or grand scenery; there is scarcely a field on the road side, which, if entered, would not give to the landscape some additional charm. Low-wood Inn, a mile from the head of Windermere, is a most pleasant halting-place; no inn in the whole district is so agreeably situated for water views and excursions; and the fields above it, and the lane that leads to Troutbeck, present beautiful views towards each extremity of the Lake. From this place, and from

## AMBLESIDE

Rides may be taken in numerous directions, and the interesting walks are inexhaustible;[1] a few out of the main road may be particularized; – the lane that leads from Ambleside to Skelgill; the ride, or walk by Rothay Bridge, and up the stream under Loughrigg Fell, continued on the western side of Rydal Lake, and along the fell to the foot of Grasmere Lake, and thence round by the church of Grasmere; or, turning round Loughrigg Fell by Loughrigg Tarn and the River Brathay, back to Ambleside. From Ambleside is another charming excursion by Clappersgate, where cross the Brathay, and proceed with the river on the right to the hamlet of Skelwithfold; when the houses are passed, turn, before you descend the hill, through a gate on the right, and from a rocky point is a fine view of the Brathay River, Langdale Pikes, &c.; then proceed ro Colwithforce, and up Little Langdale to Blea Tarn. The scene in which this small piece of water lies, suggested to the Author the following description, (given in his Poem of the Excursion) supposing the spectator to look down upon it, not from the road, but from one of its elevated sides.

'Behold!
Beneath our feet, a little lowly Vale,
A lowly Vale, and yet uplifted high
Among the mountains; even as if the spot
Had been  from eldest time by wish of theirs,
So placed, to be shut out from all the world!

437

Urn-like it was in shape, deep as an Urn;
With rocks encompassed, save that to the South
Was one small opening, where a heath-clad ridge
Supplied a boundary less abrupt and close;
A quiet treeless nook,[2] with two green fields,
A liquid pool that glittered in the sun,
And one bare Dwelling; one Abode, no more!
It seemed the home of poverty and toil,
Though not of want: the little fields, made green
By husbandry of many thrifty years,
Paid cheerful tribute to the moorland House.
– There crows the Cock, single in his domain:
The small birds find in spring no thicket there
To shroud them; only from the neighbouring Vales
The Cuckoo, straggling up to the hill tops,
Shouteth faint tidings of some gladder place.'

From this little Vale return towards Ambleside by Great Langdale,
stopping, if there be time, to see Dungeon-ghyll waterfall.
   The Lake of

# CONISTON

May be conveniently visited from Ambleside, but is seen to most
advantage by entering the country over the Sands from Lancaster.
The Stranger, from the moment he sets his foot on those Sands,
seems to leave the turmoil and traffic of the world behind him; and,
crossing the majestic plain whence the sea has retired, he beholds,
rising apparently from its base, the cluster of mountains among
which he is going to wander, and towards whose recesses, by the
Vale of Coniston, he is gradually and peacefully led. From the Inn at
the head of Coniston Lake, a leisurely Traveller might have much
pleasure in looking into Yewdale and Tilberthwaite, returning to his
Inn from the head of Yewdale by a mountain track which has the
farm of Tarn Hows, a little on the right: by this road is seen much
the best view of Coniston Lake from the south. At the head of

Coniston Water there is an agreeable Inn, from which an enterprising Tourist might go to the Vale of the Duddon, over Walna Scar, down to Seathwaite, Newfield, and to the rocks where the river issues from a narrow pass into the broad Vale. The stream is very interesting for the space of a mile above this point, and below, by Ulpha Kirk, till it enters the Sands, where it is overlooked by the solitary Mountain Black Comb, the summit of which, as that experienced surveyor, Colonel Mudge, declared, commands a more extensive view than any point in Britain. Ireland he saw more than once, but not when the sun was above the horizon.

> 'Close by the Sea, lone sentinel,
>   Black-Comb his forward station keeps;
> He breaks the sea's tumultuous swell, —
>   And ponders o'er the level deeps.
>
> He listens to the bugle horn,
>   Where Eskdale's lovely valley bends;
> Eyes Walney's early fields of corn;
>   Sea-birds to Holker's woods he sends.
>
> Beneath his feet the sunk ship rests,
>   In Duddon Sands, its masts all bare:
>
>       *       *       *       *       *'

*The Minstrels of Windermere*, by Chas. Farish, B.D.

The Tourist may either return to the Inn at Coniston by Broughton, or, by turning to the left before he comes to that town, or, which would be much better, he may cross from

## ULPHA KIRK

Over Birker moor, to Birker-force, at the head of the finest ravine in the county; and thence up the Vale of the Esk, by Hardknot and Wrynose, back to Ambleside. Near the road, in ascending from

Eskdale, are conspicuous remains of a Roman fortress. Details of the Duddon and Donnerdale are given in the Author's series of Sonnets upon the Duddon and in the accompanying Notes. In addition to its two Vales at its head, Windermere communicates with two lateral Vallies; that of Troutbeck, distinguished by the mountains at its head – by picturesque remains of cottage architecture; and, towards the lower part, by bold foregrounds formed by the steep and winding banks of the river. This Vale, as before mentioned, may be most conveniently seen from Low Wood. The other lateral Valley, that of Hawkshead, is visited to most advantage, and most conveniently, from Bowness; crossing the Lake by the Ferry – then pass the two villages of Sawrey, and on quitting the latter, you have a fine view of the Lake of Esthwaite, and the cone of one of the Langdale Pikes in the distance.

Before you leave Ambleside give three minutes to looking at a passage of the brook which runs through the town; it is to be seen from a garden on the right bank of the stream, a few steps above the bridge – the garden at present is rented by Mrs Airey. – Stockgill-force, upon the same stream, will have been mentioned to you as one of the sights of the neighbourhood. And by a Tourist halting a few days in Ambleside, the *Nook* also might be visited; a spot where there is a bridge over Scandale-beck, which makes a pretty subject for the pencil. Lastly, for residents of a week or so at Ambleside, there are delightful rambles over every part of Loughrigg Fell and among the enclosures on its sides; particularly about Loughrigg Tarn, and on its eastern side about Fox How and the properties adjoining to the northwards.

## ROAD FROM AMBLESIDE TO KESWICK

The Waterfalls of Rydal are pointed out to every one. But it ought to be observed here, that Rydal-mere is no where seen to advantage from the *main road*. Fine views of it may be had from Rydal Park; but these grounds, as well as those of Rydal Mount and Ivy Cottage, from which also it is viewed to advantage, are private. A foot road passing behind Rydal Mount and under Nab Scar to Grasmere, is very favourable to views of the Lake and the Vale, looking back towards Ambleside. The horse road also, along the western side of the Lake, under Loughrigg fell, as before mentioned, does justice to the beauties of this small mere, of which the Traveller who keeps the high road is not at all aware.

## GRASMERE

There are two small Inns in the Vale of Grasmere, one near the Church, from which it may be conveniently explored in every direction, and a mountain walk taken up Easedale to Easedale Tarn, one of the finest tarns in the country, thence to Stickle Tarn, and to the top of Langdale Pikes. See also the Vale of Grasmere from Butterlip How. A boat is kept by the innkeeper, and this circular Vale, in the solemnity of a fine evening, will make, from the bosom of the Lake, an impression that will be scarcely ever effaced.

The direct road from Grasmere to Keswick does not (as has been observed of Rydal Mere) shew to advantage Thirlmere, or Wythburn Lake, with its surrounding mountains. By a Traveller proceeding at leisure, a deviation ought to be made from the main road, when he has advanced a little beyond the sixth mile-stone short of Keswick, from which point there is a noble view of the Vale of Legberthwaite, with Blencathra (commonly called Saddle-back) in front. Having previously enquired, at the Inn near Wythburn Chapel, the best way from this mile-stone to the bridge that divides the Lake, he must cross it, and proceed with the Lake on the right, to the hamlet a little beyond its termination, and rejoin the main road upon Shoulthwaite Moss, about four miles from Keswick; or, if on foot, the Tourist may follow the stream that issues from Thirlmere down the romantic Vale of St John's, and so (enquiring the way at some cottage) to Keswick, by a circuit of little more than a mile. A more interesting tract of country is scarcely any where to be seen, than the road between Ambleside and Keswick, with the deviations that have been pointed out. Helvellyn may be conveniently ascended from the Inn at Wythburn.

## THE VALE OF KESWICK

This Vale stretches, without winding, nearly North and South, from the head of Derwent Water to the foot of Bassenthwaite Lake. It communicates with Borrowdale on the South; with the river Greta, and Thirlmere, on the East, with which the Traveller has become acquainted on his way from Ambleside; and with the Vale of Newlands on the West – which last Vale he may pass through, in going to, or returning from, Buttermere. The best views of Keswick Lake are from Crow Park; Frier's Crag; the Stable-field, close by; the Vicarage, and from various points in taking the circuit of the Lake. More distant views, and perhaps full as interesting, are from the side of Latrigg, from Ormathwaite, and Applethwaite; and thence along the road at the foot of Skiddaw towards Bassenthwaite, for about a quarter of a mile. There are fine bird's eye views from Castle-hill; from Ashness, on the road to Watenlath, and by following the Watenlath stream downwards to the Cataract of Lodore. This Lake also, if the weather be fine, ought to be circumnavigated. There are good views along the western side of Bassenthwaite Lake, and from Armathwaite at its foot; but the eastern side from the high road has little to recommend it. The Traveller from Carlisle, approaching by way of Ireby, has, from the old road on the top of Bassenthwaite-hawse, much the most striking view of the Plain and Lake Bassenthwaite, flanked by Skiddaw, and terminated by Wallowcrag on the south-east of Derwent Lake; the same point commands an extensive view of Solway Frith and the Scotch Mountains. They who take the circuit of Derwent Lake, may at the same time include BORROWDALE, going as far as Bowderstone, or Rosthwaite. Borrowdale is also conveniently seen on the way to Wastdale over Styhead; or, to Buttermere, by Seatoller and Honister Crag; or, going over the Stake, through Langdale, to Ambleside. Buttermere may be visited by a shorter way through Newlands, but though the descent upon the Vale of Buttermere, by this approach, is very striking, as it also is to one entering by the head of the Vale, under Honister Crag, yet, after all, the best entrance from Keswick is from the lower part of the Vale, having gone over Whinlater to Scale Hill, where there is a roomy Inn, with very good accommodation. The Mountains of the Vale of

## BUTTERMERE AND CRUMMMOCK

Are no where so impressive as from the bosom of Crummock Water. Scale-force, near it, is a fine chasm, with a lofty, though but slender, fall of water.

From Scale Hill a pleasant walk may be taken to an eminence in Mr Marshall's woods, and another by crossing the bridge at the foot of the hill, upon which the Inn stands, and turning to the right, after the opposite hill has been ascended a little way, then follow the road for half a mile or so that leads towards Lorton, looking back upon Crummock Water, &c., between the openings of the fences. Turn back and make your way to

## LOWESWATER

But this small Lake is only approached to advantage from the other end; therefore any Traveller going by this road to Wastdale, must look back upon it. This road to Wastdale, after passing the village of Lamplugh Cross, presents suddenly a fine view of the Lake of Ennerdale, with its Mountains; and, six or seven miles beyond, leads down upon Calder Abbey. Little of this ruin is left, but that little is well worthy of notice. At Calder Bridge are two comfortable Inns, and, a few miles beyond, accommodations may be had at the Strands, at the foot of Wastdale. Into

## WASTDALE

Are three horse-roads, viz. over the Stye from Borrowdale; a short cut from Eskdale by Burnmoor Tarn, which road descends upon the head of the Lake; and the principal entrance from the open country by the Strands at its foot. This last is much the best approach. Wastdale is well worth the notice of the Traveller who is not afraid of fatigue; no part of the country is more distinguished by sublimity. Wastwater may also be visited from Ambleside; by going up Langdale, over Hardknot and Wrynose – down Eskdale and by Irton Hall to the Strands; but this road can only be taken on foot, or on horseback, or in a cart.

We will conclude with

## ULLSWATER

As being, perhaps, upon the whole, the happiest combination of beauty and grandeur, which any of the Lakes affords. It lies not more than ten miles from Ambleside, and the Pass of Kirkstone and the descent from it are very impressive; but, notwithstanding, this Vale, like the others, loses much of its effect by being entered from the head: so that it is better to go from Keswick through Matterdale, and descend upon Gowbarrow Park; you are thus brought at once upon a magnificent view of the two higher reaches of the Lake. Araforce thunders down the Ghyll on the left, at a small distance from the road. If Ullswater be approached from Penrith, a mile and a half brings you to the winding vale of Eamont, and the prospects increase in interest till you reach Patterdale; but the first four miles along Ullswater by this road are comparatively tame; and in order to see the lower part of the Lake to advantage, it is necessary to go round by Pooley Bridge, and to ride at least three miles along the Westmorland side of the water, towards Martindale. The views, especially if you ascend from the road into the fields, are magnificent; yet this is only mentioned that the transient Visitant may know what exists; for it would be inconvenient to go in search of them. They who take this course of three or four miles *on foot*, should have a boat in readiness at the end of the walk, to carry them across to the Cumberland side of the Lake, near Old Church, thence to pursue the road upwards to Patterdale. The Church-yard Yew-tree still survives at Old Church, but there are no remains of a Place of Worship, a New Chapel having been erected in a more central situation, which Chapel was consecrated by the then Bishop of Carlisle, when on his way to crown Queen Elizabeth, he being the only Prelate who would undertake the office. It may be here mentioned that Bassenthwaite Chapel yet stands in a bay as sequestered as the Site of Old Church; such situations having been chosen in disturbed times to elude marauders.

The Trunk, or Body of the Vale of Ullswater need not be further noticed, as its beauties show themselves: but the curious Traveller may wish to know something of its tributary Streams.

At Dalemain, about three miles from Penrith, a Stream is crossed called the Dacre, or Dacor, which name it bore as early as the time of the Venerable Bede. This stream does not enter the Lake, but joins the Eamont a mile below. It rises in the moorish Country about Penruddock, flows down a soft sequestered Valley, passing by the ancient mansions of Hutton John and Dacre Castle. The former is pleasantly situated, though of a character somewhat gloomy and monastic, and from some of the fields near Dalemain, Dacre Castle, backed by the jagged summit of Saddle-back, with the Valley and Stream in front, forms a grand picture. There is no other stream that conducts to any glen or valley worthy of being mentioned, till we reach that which leads up to Ara-force, and thence into Matterdale, before spoken of. Matterdale, though a wild and interesting spot, has no peculiar features that would make it worth the Stranger's while to go in search of them; but, in Gowbarrow Park, the lover of Nature might linger for hours. Here is a powerful Brook, which dashes among rocks through a deep glen, hung on every side with a rich and happy intermixture of native wood; here are beds of luxuriant fern, aged hawthorns, and hollies decked with honeysuckles; and fallow-deer glancing and bounding over the lawns and through the thickets. These are the attractions of the retired views, or constitute a foreground for ever-varying pictures of the majestic Lake, forced to take a winding course by bold promontories, and environed by mountains of sublime form, towering above each other. At the outlet of Gowbarrow Park, we reach a third stream, which flows through a little recess called Glencoin, where lurks a single house, yet visible from the road. Let the Artist or leisurely Traveller turn aside to it, for the buildings and objects around them are romantic and picturesque. Having passed under the steeps of Styebarrow Crag, and the remains of its native woods, at Glenridding Bridge, a fourth Stream is crossed.

The opening on the side of Ullswater Vale, down which this Stream flows, is adorned with fertile fields, cottages, and natural groves, that agreeably unite with the transverse views of the Lake; and the Stream, if followed up after the enclosures are left behind, will lead along bold water-breaks and waterfalls to a silent Tarn in the recesses of Helvellyn. This desolate spot was formerly haunted by eagles, that built in the precipice which forms its western barrier. These birds used to wheel and hover round the head of the solitary angler. It also derives a melancholy interest from the fate of a young man, a stranger, who perished some years ago, by falling down the rocks in his attempt to cross over to Grasmere. His remains were discovered by means of a faithful dog that had lingered here for the space of three months, self-supported, and probably retaining to the last an attachment to the skeleton of its master. But to return to the road in the main Vale of Ullswater. – At the head of the Lake (being now in Patterdale) we cross a fifth Stream, Grisdale Beck: this would conduct through a woody steep, where may be seen some unusually large ancient hollies, up to the level area of the Valley of Grisdale; hence there is a path for foot-travellers, and along which a horse may be led, to Grasmere. A sublime combination of mountain forms appears in front while ascending the bed of this valley, and the impression increases till the path leads almost immediately under the projecting masses of Helvellyn. Having retraced the banks of the Stream to Patterdale, and pursued the road up the main Dale, the next considerable stream would, if ascended in the same manner, conduct to Deep-dale, the character of which Valley may be conjectured from its name. It is terminated by a cove, a craggy and gloomy abyss, with precipitous sides; a faithful receptacle of the snows that are driven into it, by the west wind, from the summit of Fairfield. Lastly, having gone along the western side of Brotherswater and passed Hartsop Hall, a Stream soon after issues from a cove richly decorated with native wood. This spot is, I believe, never explored by Travellers; but, from these sylvan and rocky recesses, whoever looks back on the gleaming surface of Brotherswater, or forward to the precipitous sides and lofty ridges of Dove Crag, &c., will be equally pleased with the beauty, the grandeur, and the wildness of the scenery.

Seven Glens or Vallies have been noticed, which branch off from the Cumberland side of the Vale. The opposite side has only two Streams of any importance, one of which would lead up from the point where it crosses the Kirkstone-road, near the foot of Brotherswater, to the decaying hamlet of Hartsop, remarkable for its cottage architecture, and thence to Hayswater, much frequented by anglers. The other, coming down Martindale, enters Ullswater at Sandwyke, opposite to Gowbarrow Park. No persons but such as come to Patterdale, merely to pass through it, should fail to walk as far as Blowick, the only enclosed land which on this side borders the higher part of the Lake. The axe has here indiscriminately levelled a rich wood of birches and oaks, that divided this favoured spot into a hundred pictures. It has yet its land-locked bays, and rocky promontories; but those beautiful woods are gone, which *perfected* its seclusion; and scenes, that might formerly have been compared to an inexhaustible volume, are now spread before the eye in a single sheet, —magnificent indeed, but seemingly perused in a moment! From Blowick a narrow track conducts along the craggy side of Place-fell, richly adorned with juniper, and sprinkled over with birches, to the village of Sandwyke, a few straggling houses, that with the small estates attached to them, occupy an opening opposite to Lyulph's Tower and Gowbarrow Park. In Martindale,[3] the road loses sight of

447

the Lake, and leads over a steep hill, bringing you again into view of Ullswater. Its lowest reach, four miles in length, is before you; and the view terminated by the long ridge of Cross Fell in the distance. Immediately under the eye is a deep-indented bay, with a plot of fertile land, traversed by a small brook, and rendered cheerful by two or three substantial houses of a more ornamented and showy appearance than is usual in those wild spots.

From Pooley Bridge, at the foot of the Lake, Haweswater may be conveniently visited. Haweswater is a lesser Ullswater, with this advantage, that it remains undefiled by the intrusion of bad taste.

Lowther Castle is about four miles from Pooley Bridge, and, if during this Tour the Stranger has complained, as he will have had reason to do, of a want of majestic trees, he may be abundantly recompensed for his loss in the far-spreading woods which surround that mansion. Visitants, for the most part, see little of the beauty of these magnificent grounds, being content with the view from the Terrace; but the whole course of the Lowther, from Askham to the bridge under Brougham Hall, presents almost at every step some new feature of river, woodland, and rocky landscape. A portion of this tract has, from its beauty, acquired the name of the Elysian Fields; – but the course of the stream can only be followed by the pedestrian.

NOTE. – *Vide* pp. 440–1. – About 200 yards beyond the last house on the Keswick side of Rydal village the road is cut through a low wooded rock, called Thrang Crag. The top of it, which is only a few steps on the south side, affords the best view of the Vale which is to be had by a Traveller who confines himself to the public road.

# Excursions

~~ * ~~ * ~~ * ~~

TO

## THE TOP OF SCAWFELL AND ON THE BANKS
## OF ULLSWATER

It was my intention, several years ago, to describe a regular tour
through this country, taking the different scenes in the most favourable order; but after some progress had been made in the work it
was abandoned from a conviction, that, if well executed, it would
lessen the pleasure of the Traveller by anticipation, and, if the contrary, it would mislead him. The Reader may not, however, be
displeased with the following extract from a letter to a Friend, giving
an account of a visit to a summit of one of the highest of these
mountains; of which I am reminded by the observations of Mr West,
and by reviewing what has been said of this district in comparison
with the Alps.

Having left Rosthwaite in Borrowdale, on a bright morning in
the first week of October, we ascended from Seathwaite to the top
of the ridge, called Ash-course, and thence beheld three distinct
views; – on one side, the continuous Vale of Borrowdale, Keswick,
and Bassenthwaite, – with Skiddaw, Helvellyn, Saddle-back, and
numerous other mountains, – and, in the distance, the Solway Frith
and the Mountains of Scotland; – on the other side, and below us,
the Langdale Pikes – their own vale below *them*; – Windermere, –
and, far beyond Windermere, Ingleborough in Yorkshire. But how
shall I speak of the deliciousness of the third prospect! At this time,

449

*that* was most favoured by sunshine and shade. The green Vale of Esk – deep and green, with its glittering serpent stream, lay below us; and, on we looked to the Mountains near the Sea, – Black Comb pre–eminent, – and, still beyond, to the Sea itself, in dazzling brightness. Turning round we saw the Mountains of Wastdale in tumult; to our right, Great Gavel, the loftiest, a distinct, and *huge* form, though the middle of the mountain was, to our eyes, as its base.

We had attained the object of this journey; but our ambition now mounted higher. We saw the summit of Scaw-fell, apparently very near to us; and we shaped our course towards it; but, discovering that it could not be reached without first making a considerable descent, we resolved, instead, to aim at another point of the same mountain, called the *Pikes*, which I have since found has been esti-mated as higher than the summit bearing the name of Scawfell Head, where the Stone Man is built.

The sun had never once been overshadowed by a cloud during the whole of our progress from the centre of Borrowdale. On the summit of the Pike, which we gained after much toil, though without diffi-culty, there was not a breath of air to stir even the papers containing our refreshment, as they lay spread out upon a rock. The stillness seemed to be not of this world: – we paused, and kept silence to listen; and no sound could be heard: the Scawfell Cataracts were voiceless to us; and there was not an insect to hum in the air. The vales which we had seen from Ash-course lay yet in view; and, side by side with Eskdale, we now saw the sister Vale of Donnerdale terminated by the Duddon Sands. But the majesty of the mountains below, and close to us, is not to be conceived. We now beheld the whole mass of Great Gavel from its base, – the Den of Wastdale at our feet – a gulph immeasurable: Grasmire and the other mountains of Crummock – Ennerdale and its mountains; and the Sea beyond! We sat down to our repast, and gladly would we have tempered our beverage (for there was no spring or well near us) with such a supply of delicious water as we might have procured, had we been on the rival summit of Great Gavel; for on its highest point is a small triangular receptacle in the native rock, which, the shepherds say, is never dry. There we might have slaked our thirst plenteously with a pure and celestial liquid, for the cup or basin, it appears, has no other feeder than the dews of heaven, the showers, the vapours, the hoar frost, and the spotless snow.

While we were gazing around, 'Look,' I exclaimed, 'at yon ship upon the glittering sea!' 'Is it a ship?' replied our shepherd-guide. 'It can be nothing else,' interposed my companion; 'I cannot be mistaken, I am so accustomed to the appearance of ships at sea.' The Guide dropped the argument; but, before a minute was gone, he quietly said, 'Now look at your ship; it is changed into a horse.' So indeed it was, — a horse with a gallant neck and head. We laughed heartily; and, I hope, when again inclined to be positive, I may remember the ship and the horse upon the glittering sea; and the calm confidence, yet submissiveness, of our wise Man of the Mountains, who certainly had more knowledge of clouds than we, whatever might be our knowledge of ships.

I know not how long we might have remained on the summit of the Pike, without a thought of moving, had not our Guide warned us that we must not linger; for a storm was coming. We looked in vain to espy the signs of it. Mountains, vales, and sea were touched with the clear light of the sun. 'It is there,' said he, pointing to the sea beyond Whitehaven, and there we perceived a light vapour unnoticeable but by a shepherd accustomed to watch all mountain bodings. We gazed around again, and yet again, unwilling to lose the remembrance of what lay before us in that lofty solitude; and then prepared to depart. Meanwhile the air changed to cold, and we saw that tiny vapours swelled into mighty masses of cloud which came boiling over the mountains. Great Gavel, Helvellyn, and Skiddaw, were wrapped in storm; yet Langdale, and the mountains in that quarter, remained all bright in sunshine. Soon the storm reached us; we sheltered under a crag; and almost as rapidly as it had come it passed away, and left us free to observe the struggles of gloom and sunshine in other quarters. Langdale now had its share, and the Pikes of Langdale were decorated by two splendid rainbows. Skiddaw also had his own rainbows. Before we again reached Ash-course every cloud had vanished from every summit.

I ought to have mentioned that round the top of Scawfell-PIKE not a blade of grass is to be seen. Cushions or tufts of moss, parched and brown, appear between the huge blocks and stones that lie in heaps on all sides to a great distance, like skeletons or bones of the earth not needed at the creation, and there left to be covered with never-dying lichens, which the clouds and dews nourish; and adorn with colours of vivid and exquisite beauty. Flowers, the most brilliant feathers, and even gems, scarcely surpass in colouring some of those masses of stone, which no human eye beholds, except the shepherd or traveller be led thither by curiosity: and how seldom must this happen! For the other eminence is the one visited by the adventurous stranger; and the shepherd has no inducement to ascend the PIKE in quest of his sheep; no food being *there* to tempt them.

We certainly were singularly favoured in the weather; for when we were seated on the summit, our conductor, turning his eyes thoughtfully round, said, 'I do not know that in my whole life, I was ever, at any season of the year, so high upon the mountains on so *calm* a day.' (It was the 7th of October.) Afterwards we had a spectacle of the grandeur of earth and heaven commingled; yet without terror. We knew that the storm would pass away; — for so our prophetic Guide had assured us.

Before we reached Seathwaite in Borrowdale, a few stars had appeared, and we pursued our way down the Vale, to Rosthwaite, by moonlight.

Scawfell and Helvellyn being the two Mountains of this region which will best repay the fatigue of ascending them, the following Verses may be here introduced with propriety. They are from the Author's Miscellaneous Poems.

[Here Wordsworth quotes 'To –, on her first ascent to the summit of Helvellyn'.]

Having said so much of *points of view* to which few are likely to ascend, I am induced to subjoin an account of a short excursion through more accessible parts of the country, made at a *time* when it is seldom seen but by the inhabitants. As the journal was written for one acquainted with the general features of the country, only those effects and appearances are dwelt upon, which are produced by the changeableness of the atmosphere, or belong to the season when the excursion was made.

A.D. 1805. – On the 7th of November, on a damp and gloomy morning, we left Grasmere Vale, intending to pass a few days on the Banks of Ullswater. A mild and dry autumn had been unusually favourable to the preservation and beauty of foliage; and, far advanced as the season was, the trees on the larger Island of Rydal-mere retained a splendour which did not need the heightening of sunshine. We noticed, as we passed, that the line of the grey rocky shore of that island, shaggy with variegated bushes and shrubs, and spotted and striped with purplish brown heath, indistinguishably blending with its image reflected in the still water, produced a curious resemblance, both in form and colour, to a richly-coated caterpillar, as it might appear through a magnifying glass of extraordinary power. The mists gathered as we went along; but, when we reached the top of Kirkstone, we were glad we had not been discouraged by the apprehension of bad weather. Though not able to see a hundred yards before us, we were more than contented. At such a time, and in such a place, every scattered stone the size of one's head becomes a companion. Near the top of the Pass is the remnant of an old wall, which (magnified, though obscured, by the vapour) might have been taken for a fragment of some monument of ancient grandeur, – yet that same pile of stones we had never before even observed. This situation, it must be allowed, is not favourable to gaiety; but a pleasing hurry of spirits accompanies the surprise occasioned by objects transformed, dilated, or distorted, as they are when seen through such a medium. Many of the fragments of rock on the top and slopes of Kirkstone, and of similar places, are fantastic enough in themselves; but the full effect of such impressions can only be had in a state of weather when they are not likely to be *sought* for. It was not till we had descended considerably that the fields of Hartshope were seen, like a lake tinged by the reflection of sunny clouds: I mistook them for Brothers-water, but, soon after, we saw that Lake gleaming faintly with a steelly brightness, – then, as we continued to descend, appeared the brown oaks, and the birches of lively yellow – and the cottages – and the lowly Hall of Hartshope, with its long roof and ancient chimneys. During great part of our way to Patterdale, we had rain, or rather drizzling vapour; for there was never a drop upon our hair or clothes larger than the smallest pearls upon a lady's ring.

The following morning, incessant rain till 11 o'clock, when the sky began to clear, and we walked along the eastern shore of Ullswater towards the farm of Blowick. The wind blew strong, and drove the clouds forward, on the side of the mountain above our heads; – two storm-stiffened black yew-trees fixed our notice, seen through, or under the edge of, the flying mists, – four or five goats were bounding among the rocks; – the sheep moved about more quietly, or cowered beneath their sheltering places. This is the only part of the country where goats are now found;[4] but this morning, before we had seen these, I was reminded of that picturesque animal by two rams of mountain breed, both with Ammonian horns, and with beards majestic as that which Michael Angelo has given to his statue of Moses. – But to return; when our path had brought us to the part of the naked common which overlooks the woods and bush-besprinkled fields of Blowick, the lake, clouds, and mists were all in motion to the sound of sweeping winds; – the church and cottages of Patterdale scarcely visible, or seen only by fits between the shifting vapours. To the northward the scene was less visionary; – Place Fell steady and bold; – the whole lake driving onward like a great river – waves dancing round the small islands. The house at Blowick was the boundary of our walk; and we returned, lamenting to see a decaying and uncomfortable dwelling in a place where sublimity and beauty seemed to contend with each other. But these regrets were dispelled by a glance on the woods that clothe the opposite steeps of the lake. How exquisite was the mixture of sober and splendid hues! The general colouring of the trees was brown – rather that of ripe hazel nuts; but towards the water, there were yet beds of green, and in the highest parts of the wood, was abundance of yellow foliage, which, gleaming through a vapoury lustre, reminded us of masses of clouds, as you see them gathered together in the west, and touched with the golden light of the setting sun.

After dinner we walked up the Vale: I had never had an idea of its extent and width in passing along the public road on the other side. We followed the path that leads from house to house; two or three times it took us through some of those copses or groves that cover the little hillocks in the middle of the vale, making an intricate and pleasing intermixture of lawn and wood. Our fancies could not resist the temptation; and we fixed upon a spot for a cottage, which we began to build: and finished as easily as castles are raised in the air. – Visited the same spot in the evening. I shall say nothing of the moonlight aspect of the situation which had charmed us so much in the afternoon; but I wish you had been with us when, in returning to our friend's house, we espied his lady's large white dog, lying in the moonshine upon the round knoll under the old yew-tree in the garden, a romantic image – the dark tree and its dark shadow – and the elegant creature, as fair as a spirit! The torrents murmured softly: the mountains down which they were falling did not, to my sight, furnish a back-ground for this Ossianic picture; but I had a consciousness of the depth of the seclusion, and that mountains were embracing us on all sides; 'I saw not, but I *felt* that they were there.'

Friday, November 9th. – Rain, as yesterday, till 10 o'clock, when we took a boat to row down the lake. The day improved, – clouds and sunny gleams on the mountains. In the large bay under Place Fell, three fishermen were dragging a net, – a picturesque group beneath the high and bare crags! A raven was seen aloft; not hovering like the kite, for that is not the habit of the bird; but passing on with a straightforward perseverance, and timing the motion of its wings to its own croaking. The waters were agitated; and the iron tone of the raven's voice, which strikes upon the ear at all times as the more dolorous from its regularity, was in fine keeping with the wild scene before our eyes. This carnivorous fowl is a great enemy to the lambs of these solitudes; I recollect frequently seeing, when a boy, bunches of unfledged ravens suspended from the churchyard gates of H——, for which a reward of *so* much a head was given to the adventurous destroyer. – The fishermen drew their net ashore, and hundreds of fish were leaping in their prison. They were all of the kind called skellies, a sort of fresh-water herring, shoals of which may sometimes be seen dimpling or rippling the surface of the lake in calm weather. This species is not found, I believe, in any other of these lakes; nor, as far as I know, is the chevin, that *spiritless* fish, (though I am loth to call it so, for it was a prime favourite with Isaac Walton,) which must frequent Ullswater, as I have seen a large shoal passing into the lake from the river Eamont. *Here* are no pike, and the char are smaller than those of the other lakes, and of inferior quality; but the grey trout attains a very large size, sometimes weighing above twenty pounds. This lordly creature seems to know that 'retiredness is a piece of majesty'; for it is scarcely ever caught, or even seen, except when it quits the depths of the lake in the spawning season, and runs up into the streams, where it is too often destroyed in disregard of the law of the land and of nature.

Quitted the boat in the bay of Sandwycke, and pursued our way towards Martindale along a pleasant path – at first through a coppice, bordering the lake, then through green fields – and came to the village, (if village it may be called, for the houses are few, and separated from each other,) a sequestered spot, shut out from the view of the lake. Crossed the one-arched bridge, below the chapel, with its 'bare ring of mossy wall,' and single yew-tree. At the last house in the dale we were greeted by the master, who was sitting at his door, with a flock of sheep collected around him, for the purpose of smearing them with tar (according to the custom of the season) for protection against the winter's cold. He invited us to enter, and view a room built by Mr Hasell for the accommodation of his friends at the annual chase of red deer in his forests at the head of these dales. The room is fitted up in the sportsman's style, with a cupboard for bottles and glasses, with strong chairs, and a dining-table: and ornamented with the horns of the stags caught at these hunts for a succession of years – the length of the last race each had run being recorded under his spreading antlers. The good woman treated us with oaten cake, new and crisp; and after this welcome refreshment and rest, we proceeded on our return to Patterdale by a short cut over the mountains. On leaving the fields of Sandwycke, while ascending by a gentle slope along the valley of Martindale, we had occasion to observe that in thinly-peopled glens of this character the general want of wood gives a peculiar interest to the scattered cottages embowered in sycamore. Towards its head, this valley splits into two parts; and in one of these (that to the left) there is no house, nor any building to be seen but a cattle-shed on the side of a hill, which is sprinkled over with trees, evidently the remains of an extensive forest. Near the entrance of the other division stands the house where we were entertained, and beyond the enclosures of that farm there are no other. A few old trees remain, relics of the forest, a little stream hastens, though with serpentine windings, through the uncultivated hollow, where many cattle were pasturing. The cattle of this country are generally white, or light-coloured; but these were dark brown, or black, which heightened the resemblance this scene bears to many parts of the Highlands of Scotland. – While we paused to rest upon the hillside, though well contented with the quiet every-day sounds – the lowing of cattle, bleating of sheep, and the very gentle murmuring of the valley stream, we could not but think what a grand effect the music of the bugle-horn would have among these mountains. It is still heard once every year, at the chase I have spoken of; a day of festivity for the inhabitants of this district except the poor deer, the most ancient of them all. Our ascent even to the top was very easy; when it was accomplished we had exceedingly fine views, some of the lofty Fells being resplendent with sunshine, and others partly shrouded by clouds. Ullswater, bordered by black steeps, was of dazzling brightness; the plain beyond Penrith smooth and bright, or rather gleamy, as the sea or sea sands. Looked down into Boardale, which, like Stybarrow, has been named from the wild swine that formerly abounded here; but it has now no sylvan covert, being smooth and bare, a long, narrow, deep, cradle-shaped glen, lying so sheltered that one would be pleased to see it planted by human hands, there being a sufficiency of soil; and the trees would be sheltered almost like shrubs in a greenhouse. – After having walked some way along the top of the hill, came in view of Glenriddin and the mountains at the head of Grisdale. – Before we began to descend, turned aside to a small ruin, called at this day the chapel, where it is said the inhabitants of Martindale and Patterdale were accustomed to assemble for worship. There are now no traces from which you could infer for what use the building had been erected; the loose stones and the few which yet continue piled up resemble those which lie elsewhere on the mountain; but the shape of the building having been oblong, its remains differ from those of a common sheep-fold; and it has stood east and west. Scarcely did the Druids, when they fled to these fastnesses, perform their rites in any situation more exposed to disturbance from the elements. One cannot pass by without being reminded that the rustic psalmody must have had the accompaniment of many a wildly-whistling blast; and what dismal storms must have often drowned the voice of the preacher! As we descend, Patterdale opens upon the eye in grand simplicity, screened by mountains, and proceeding from two heads, Deepdale and Hartshope, where lies the little lake of Brotherswater, named in old maps Broaderwater, and probably rightly so; for Bassenthwaite-mere at this day, is familiarly called Broadwater; but the change in the appellation of this small lake or pool (if it be a corruption) may have been assisted by some melancholy accident similar to what happened about twenty years ago, when two brothers were drowned there, having gone out to take their holiday pleasure upon the ice on a new-year's day.

A rough and precipitous peat track brought us down to our friend's house. – Another fine moonlight night; but a thick fog rising from the neighbouring river, enveloped the rocky and wood-crested knoll on which our fancy-cottage had been erected; and, under the damp cast upon my feelings, I consoled myself with moralising on the folly of hasty decisions in matters of importance, and the necessity of having at least one year's knowledge of a place before you realise airy suggestions in solid stone.

Saturday, November 10th. At the breakfast-table tidings reached us of the death of Lord Nelson, and of the victory at Trafalgar. Sequestered as we were from the sympathy of a crowd, we were shocked to hear that the bells had been ringing joyously at Penrith to celebrate the triumph. In the rebellion of the year 1745, people fled with their valuables from the open country to Patterdale, as a place of refuge secure from the incursions of strangers. At that time, news such as we had heard might have been long in penetrating so far into the recesses of the mountains; but now, as you know, the approach is easy, and the communication, in summer time, almost hourly: nor is this strange, for travellers after pleasure are become not less active, and more numerous than those who formerly left their homes for purposes of gain. The priest on the banks of the remotest stream of Lapland will talk familiarly of Buonaparte's last conquests, and discuss the progress of the French revolution, having acquired much of his information from adventurers impelled by curiosity alone.

The morning was clear and cheerful after a night of sharp frost. At 10 o'clock we took our way on foot towards Pooley Bridge, on the same side of the lake we had coasted in a boat the day before. – Looked backwards to the south from our favourite station above Blowick. The dazzling sunbeams striking upon the church and village, while the earth was steaming with exhalations not traceable in other quarters, rendered their forms even more indistinct than the partial and flitting veil of unillumined vapour had done two days before. The grass on which we trod, and the trees in every thicket were dripping with melted hoar-frost. We observed the lemon-coloured leaves of the birches, as the breeze turned them to the sun, sparkle, or rather *flash*, like diamonds, and the leafless purple twigs were tipped with globes of shining crystal.

The day continued delightful, and unclouded to the end. I will not describe the country which we slowly travelled through, nor relate our adventures: and will only add, that on the afternoon of the 13th we returned along the banks of Ullswater by the usual road. The lake lay in deep repose after the agitations of a wet and stormy morning. The trees in Gowbarrow park were in that state when what is gained by the disclosure of their bark and branches compensates, almost, for the loss of foliage, exhibiting the variety which characterises the point of time between autumn and winter. The hawthorns were leafless; their round heads covered with rich red berries, and adorned with arches of green brambles, and eglantines hung with glossy hips; and the grey trunks of some of the ancient oaks, which in the summer season might have been regarded only for their venerable majesty, now attracted notice by a pretty embellishment of green mosses and fern intermixed with russet leaves retained by those slender outstarting twigs which the veteran tree would not have tolerated in his strength. The smooth silver branches of the ashes were bare; most of the alders as green as the Devonshire cottage-myrtle that weathers the snows of Christmas. – Will you accept it as some apology for my having dwelt so long on the woodland ornaments of these scenes – that artists speak of the trees on the banks of Ullswater, and especially along the bays of Stybarrow crags, as having a peculiar character of picturesque intricacy in their stems and branches, which their rocky stations and the mountain winds have combined to give them.

At the end of Gowbarrow park a large herd of deer were either moving slowly or standing still among the fern. I was sorry when a chance-companion, who had joined us by the way, startled them with a whistle, disturbing an image of grave simplicity and thoughtful enjoyment; for I could have fancied that those natives of this wild and beautiful region were partaking with us a sensation of the solemnity of the closing day. The sun had been set some time; and we could perceive that the light was fading away from the coves of Helvellyn, but the lake, under a luminous sky, was more brilliant than before.

After tea at Patterdale, set out again: – a fine evening; the seven stars close to the mountain-top; all the stars seemed brighter than usual. The steeps were reflected in Brotherswater, and, above the lake, appeared like enormous black perpendicular walls. The Kirkstone torrents had been swoln by the rains, and now filled the mountain pass with their roaring, which added greatly to the solemnity of our walk. Behind us, when we had climbed to a great height, we saw one light, very distinct, in the vale, like a large red star — a solitary one in the gloomy region. The cheerfulness of the scene was in the sky above us.

Reached home a little before midnight. The following verses (from the Author's Miscellaneous Poems,) after what has just been read may be acceptable to the reader, by way of conclusion to this little Volume. ★

[Here Wordsworth quoted 'Ode: The Pass of Kirkstone'.]

### THE PUBLISHERS,
### WITH PERMISSION OF THE AUTHOR,
### HAVE ADDED THE FOLLOWING
### ITINERARY OF THE LAKES,
### FOR THE USE OF TOURISTS.

| Stages | Miles |
|---|---|
| Lancaster to Kendal, by Kirkby Lonsdale, . . . . | 30 |
| Lancaster to Kendal, by Burton, . . . . . . | 22 |
| Lancaster to Kendal, by Milnthorpe, . . . . | 21 |
| Lancaster to Ulverston, over Sands, . . . . | 21 |
| Lancaster to Ulverston, by Levens Bridge, . . . | $35\frac{1}{2}$ |
| Ulverston to Hawkshead, by Coniston Water Head, . . | 19 |
| Ulverston to Bowness, by Newby Bridge, . . . | 17 |
| Hawkshead to Ambleside, . . . . . . | 5 |
| Hawkshead to Bowness, . . . . . . . | 6 |
| Kendal to Ambleside, . . . . . . | 14 |
| Kendal to Ambleside, by Bowness, . . . . | 15 |
| From and back to Ambleside, round the two Langdales, . | 18 |
| Ambleside to Ullswater, . . . . . . | 10 |
| Ambleside to Keswick, . . . . . . | $16\frac{1}{4}$ |
| Keswick to Borrowdale, and round the Lake, . . . | 12 |
| Keswick to Borrowdale and Buttermere, . . . | 23 |
| Keswick to Wastdale and Calder Bridge, . . . | 27 |
| Calder Bridge to Buttermere and Keswick, . . . | 29 |

Inns and Public Houses, when not mentioned, are marked thus.★

## LANCASTER to KENDAL, by KIRKBY LONSDALE, 30 m.

| Miles. | | Miles. | Miles. | | Miles. |
|---|---|---|---|---|---|
| 5 | Caton . . . | 5 | 2 | Tunstall . . . | 13 |
| 2 | Claughton . . | 7 | 2 | Burrow . . . | 15 |
| 2 | Hornby★ . . . | 9 | 2 | Kirkby Lonsdale . | 17 |
| 2 | Melling . . . | 11 | 13 | Kendal . . . | 30 |

INNS. – *Lancaster*, King's Arms, Commercial Inn, Royal Oak.
INNS. – *Kirkby Lonsdale*, Rose and Crown, Green Dragon.

## LANCASTER to KENDAL, by BURTON, 21¾ m.

| | | | | | |
|---|---|---|---|---|---|
| 10¾ | Burton . . . | 10¾ | ½ | End Moor★ . . | 16 |
| 4¾ | Crooklands★ . . | 15½ | 5¾ | Kendal . . . | 21¾ |

INNS.—*Kendal*, King's Arms, Commercial Inn. – *Burton*, Royal Oak, King's Arms.

## LANCASTER to KENDAL, by MILNTHORPE, 21¼ m.

| | | | | | |
|---|---|---|---|---|---|
| 2¾ | Slyne★ . . . | 2¾ | 4 | Hale★ . . . | 12 |
| 1¼ | Bolton-le-Sands★ . | 4 | ½ | Beethom★ . . | 12½ |
| 2 | Carnforth★ . . | 6 | 1¼ | Milnthorpe . . | 13¾ |
| 2 | Junction of the Milnthorpe and Burton roads | 8 | 1¼ | Heversham★ . . | 15 |
| | | | 1½ | Levens-bridge . . | 16½ |
| | | | 4¾ | Kendal . . . | 21¼ |

INN. – *Milnthorpe*, Cross Keys.

## LANCASTER to ULVERSTON, over Sands, 21 m.

| | | | | | |
|---|---|---|---|---|---|
| $3\frac{1}{2}$ | Hest Bank★ | . . $3\frac{1}{2}$ | $1\frac{1}{4}$ | Flookburgh★ | . . 15 |
| $\frac{1}{4}$ | Lancaster Sands | . $3\frac{3}{4}$ | $\frac{3}{4}$ | Cark | . . $15\frac{3}{4}$ |
| 9 | Kent's Bank | . . $12\frac{3}{4}$ | $\frac{1}{4}$ | Leven Sands | . . 16 |
| 1 | Lower Allithwaite | . $13\frac{3}{4}$ | 5 | Ulverston | . . 21 |

INNS. – *Ulverston*, Sun Inn, Bradyll's Arms.

## LANCASTER to ULVERSTON, by LEVENS BRIDGE, $35\frac{1}{2}$ m.

| | | | | | |
|---|---|---|---|---|---|
| 12 | Hale★ | . . 12 | 3 | Lindal★ | . . 23 |
| $\frac{1}{2}$ | Beethom★ | . . $12\frac{1}{2}$ | 2 | Newton★. | . . 25 |
| $1\frac{1}{4}$ | Milnthorpe | . . $13\frac{3}{4}$ | 2 | Newby Bridge★ | . $27\frac{1}{2}$ |
| $1\frac{1}{4}$ | Heversham★ | . . 15 | 2 | Low Wood | . . $29\frac{1}{2}$ |
| $1\frac{1}{2}$ | Levens-bridge | . . $16\frac{1}{2}$ | 3 | Greenodd | . . $32\frac{1}{2}$ |
| 4 | Witherslack★ | . . $20\frac{1}{2}$ | 3 | Ulverston | . . $35\frac{1}{2}$ |

## ULVERSTON to HAWKSHEAD, by CONISTON WATER-HEAD, 19 m.

| | | | | | |
|---|---|---|---|---|---|
| 6 | Lowick-bridge | . . 6 | 8 | Coniston Water-Head★ | 16 |
| 2 | Nibthwaite | . . 8 | 3 | Hawkshead | . . 19 |

INN. – *Hawkshead*, Red Lion.

## ULVERSTON to BOWNESS, by NEWBY-BRIDGE, 16 m.

| | | | | | |
|---|---|---|---|---|---|
| 3 | Green Odd | . . 3 | 2 | Newby-bridge | . . 8 |
| 3 | Low Wood | . . 6 | 8 | Bowness | . . 16 |

INNS. – *Bowness*, White Lion, Crown Inn.

## HAWKSHEAD to AMBLESIDE, 5 m.

## HAWKSHEAD to BOWNESS, 5½ m.

| | | | | | | |
|---|---|---|---|---|---|---|
| 2 | Sawrey . . . | 2 | 1½ | Bowness . . . | 5¼ |
| 2 | Windermere-ferry★ | 4 | | | |

## KENDAL to AMBLESIDE, 13½ m.

| | | | | | | |
|---|---|---|---|---|---|---|
| 5 | Staveley★. . . | 5 | 1½ | Troutbeck-bridge★ . | 10 |
| 1½ | Ings Chapel . . | 6½ | 2 | Low Wood Inn . | 12 |
| 2 | Orrest-head . . | 8½ | 1½ | Ambleside . . | 13½ |

INNS. – *Ambleside*, Salutation Hotel, Commercial Inn.

## KENDAL to AMBLESIDE, by BOWNESS, 15 m.

| | | | | | | |
|---|---|---|---|---|---|---|
| 4 | Crook★ . . . | 4 | 2½ | Troutbeck-bridge . | 11¼ |
| 2 | Gilpin Bridge★. . | 6 | 2 | Low Wood Inn . | 13½ |
| 3 | Bowness . . . | 9 | 1½ | Ambleside . . | 15 |

## A CIRCUIT from and back to AMBLESIDE, by LITTLE and GREAT LANGDALE, 18 m.

| | | | | | |
|---|---|---|---|---|---|
| 3 | Skelwith-bridge★ . | 3 | 2 | Langdale Chapel Stile★ 13 |
| 2 | Colwith Cascade . | 5 | 5 | By High Close and |
| 3 | Blea Tarn . . | 8 | | Rydal to Ambleside 18 |
| 3 | Dungeon Ghyll . | 11 | | |

## AMBLESIDE to ULLSWATER, 10 m.

| | | | | | |
|---|---|---|---|---|---|
| 4 | Top of Kirkstone . | 4 | 3 | Inn at Patterdale . 10 |
| 3 | Kirkstone Foot . | 7 | | |

## AMBLESIDE to KESWICK, 16¼ m.

| | | | | | | |
|---|---|---|---|---|---|---|
| 1½ | Rydal | . | . | . | 1½ | 4 Smalthwaite-bridge . 12¼ |
| 3½ | Swan, Grasmere★ | . | 5 | | | 3 Castlerigg . . 15¼ |
| 2 | Dunmail Raise. | . | 7 | | | 1 Keswick . . . 16¼ |
| 1¼ | Nag's Head, | | | | | |
| | Wythburn | . | . | 8¼ | | |

---

## EXCURSIONS FROM KESWICK.

INNS. – *Keswick*, Royal Oak, Queen's Head.
## To BORROWDALE, and ROUND THE LAKE, 12 m.

| | | | | | | |
|---|---|---|---|---|---|---|
| 2 | Barrow-house | . | . | 2 | | 1 Return to Grange . 6 |
| 1 | Lowdore | . | . | 3 | | 4½ Portinscale . . 10½ |
| 1 | Grange | . | . | 4 | | 1½ Keswick . . . 12 |
| 1 | Bowder Stone | . | . | 5 | | |

---

## To BORROWDALE and BUTTERMERE.

| | | | | | |
|---|---|---|---|---|---|
| 5 | Bowder Stone | . | . | 5 | 4 Gatesgarth . . 12 |
| 1 | Rosthwaite | . | . | 6 | 2 Buttermere★ . . 14 |
| 2 | Seatoller | . | . | 8 | 9 Keswick, by Newlands 23 |

---

## TWO DAYS' EXCURSION TO WASTDALE, ENNERDALE, and LOWES-WATER.

### FIRST DAY.

| | | | | | |
|---|---|---|---|---|---|
| 6 | Rosthwaite | . | . | 6 | 6 Strands,★ Nether |
| 2 | Seatoller | . | . | 8 | Wastdale . . 20 |
| 1 | Seathwaite | . | . | 9 | 4 Gosforth★ . . 24 |
| 3 | Sty-head | . | . | 12 | 3 Calder Bridge★ . 27 |
| 2 | Wastdale-head | . | . | 14 | |

---

| | | | | | | |
|---|---|---|---|---|---|---|
| 7 | Ennerdale Bridge | . | 7 | 2 | Scale-hill★ . . | 16 |
| 3 | Lamplugh Cross★ | . | 10 | 4 | Buttermere★ . . | 20 |
| 4 | Lowes Water . | . | 14 | 9 | Keswick . . . | 29 |

## KESWICK ROUND BASSENTHWAITE WATER.

| | | | | | | |
|---|---|---|---|---|---|---|
| 8 | Peel Wyke★ . | . | 8 | 3 | Bassenthwaite Sand- | |
| 1 | Ouse Bridge . | . | 9 | | bed . . . | 13 |
| 1 | Castle Inn . | . | 10 | 5 | Keswick . . . | 18 |

## KESWICK to PATTERDALE, and by POOLEY BRIDGE to PENRITH.

| | | | | | | |
|---|---|---|---|---|---|---|
| 10 | Springfield★ . | . | 10 | 10 | Pooley Bridge★ through | |
| 7 | Gowbarrow Park | . | 17 | | Gowbarrow Park . | 32 |
| 5 | Patterdale★ . | . | 22 | 6 | Penrith . . . | 38 |

INNS. – *Penrith*, Crown Inn, The George.

## KESWICK to POOLEY BRIDGE and PENRITH.

| | | | | | | |
|---|---|---|---|---|---|---|
| 12 | Penruddock★ . | . | 12 | 3 | Pooley Bridge . . | 18 |
| 3 | Dacre★ . | . | 15 | 6 | Penrith . . . | 24 |

## KESWICK to PENRITH, 17½ m.

| | | | | | | |
|---|---|---|---|---|---|---|
| 4 | Threlkeld★ . | . | 4 | 3½ | Stainton★ . . . | 15 |
| 7½ | Penruddock . | . | 11½ | 2½ | Penrith . . . | 17½ |

## WHITEHAVEN to KESWICK, 27 m.

| | | | | | | | |
|---|---|---|---|---|---|---|---|
| 2 | Moresby . | . | . | 2 | 5 | Cockermouth . | . 14 |
| 2 | Distington | . | . | 4 | 2½ | Embleton | . 16½ |
| 2 | Winscales. | . | . | 6 | 6½ | Thornthwaite . | . 23 |
| 3 | Little Clifton | . | . | 9 | 4 | Keswick . | . . 27 |

INNS. – *Whitehaven*, Black Lion, Golden Lion, the Globe.
INNS. – *Cockermouth*, The Globe, The Sun.

---

## WORKINGTON to KESWICK, 21 m.

The road joins that from Whitehaven to Keswick 4 miles from Workington.

INNS. – *Workington*, Green Dragon, New Crown, King's Arms.

---

## EXCURSION from PENRITH to HAWESWATER.

| | | | | | |
|---|---|---|---|---|---|
| 5 | Lowther, or Askham★ | 5 | 5 | Over Moor Dovack to | |
| 7 | By Bampton★ to Hawes | | | Pooley . | . . 21 |
| | Water . | . . 12 | 6 | By Dalemain to | |
| 4 | Return by Butterswick | 16 | | Penrith | . . 27 |

---

## CARLISLE to PENRITH, 18 m.

| | | | | | | | |
|---|---|---|---|---|---|---|---|
| 2½ | Carlton★ . | . | . | 2½ | 2 | Plumpton★ | . . 13 |
| 7 | Low Hesket★ | . | . | 9½ | 5 | Penrith . | . . 18 |
| 1½ | High Hesket★ | . | . | 11 | | | |

INNS. – *Carlisle*, The Bush, Coffee House, King's Arms.

---

## PENRITH to KENDAL, 26 m.

| | | | | | | | |
|---|---|---|---|---|---|---|---|
| 1 | Eamont Bridge★ | . | . | 1 | 6¾ | Hawse Foot★ . | . 17 |
| 1½ | Clifton★ . | . | . | 2½ | 4 | Plough Inn★ . | . 21 |
| 2 | Hackthorpe★ | . | . | 4½ | 2½ | Skelsmergh Stocks★ . | 23½ |
| 5¾ | Shap | . | . | 10¼ | 2½ | Kendal . | . . 26 |

INNS. – *Shap*, Greyhound, King's Arms.

# Selected Further Reading

~~~~~~~~~~~~~~~

The authoritative modern edition of Wordsworth's prose is W. J. B. Owen and J. W. Smyser, *The Prose Works of William Wordsworth*, 3 vols., Oxford: Clarendon Press, 1974. Unlike previous editions, this contains no letters or notes of Wordsworth nor does it contain the reported conversations included in Alexander Grosart's edition (1876). The Owen and Smyser edition otherwise contains all the prose written by Wordsworth, no matter how brief and fragmentary, along with brief general introductions, textual introductions, variants, extensive annotation, and an index.

There has been no large-scale study of Wordsworth's prose; several shorter studies are nevertheless useful: David R. Sanderson, 'Wordsworth's World, 1809: A Stylistic Study of the Cintra Pamphlet', *The Wordsworth Circle*, 1 (1970), 104–113, a study with wider implications than the title suggests; John R. Nabholz, '*My Reader, My Fellow-labourer': A Study of English Romantic Prose*, Columbia, Mo: University of Missouri Press, 1986, Chapter III.

Of the individual categories of Wordsworth's prose, his literary criticism has received most attention. Two full-length studies were published in 1969: W. J. B. Owen, *Wordsworth as Critic*, Toronto: University of Toronto Press, with chapters on larger issues and on individual works; and James A. W. Heffernan, *Wordsworth's Theory of Poetry: The Transforming Imagination*, Ithaca, NY: Cornell University Press, a study of Wordsworth's creative theory. For a view of

Wordsworth's theory as it fits into the central tradition, see John O. Hayden, *Polestar of the Ancients*, Newark, NJ: University of Delaware Press and London: Associated University Presses, 1979, Chapter 8. The *Essays on Epitaphs* have received individual attention in D. D. Devlin, *Wordsworth and the Poetry of Epitaphs*, Totowa, NJ: Barnes and Noble Books, 1981.

Wordsworth's political prose has never been studied separately, but the *Convention of Cintra* pamphlet received extensive attention in G. K. Thomas, *Wordsworth's Dirge and Promise*, Lincoln, Nebraska: University of Nebraska Press, 1971.

Several other of Wordsworth's prose works have been the focus of useful short studies: The Preface to *The Borderers* by Ernest de Selincourt in *Oxford Lectures on Poetry*, Oxford, 1934; *Description of the Scenery of the Lakes* by W. M. Merchant in his introduction to his edition of *A Guide through the District of the Lakes*, Bloomington, Ind: Indiana University Press, 1952; *The Essay on Morals* by Geoffrey Little in *Review of English Literature*, 2 (1961), 9–20.

# Notes

[William Wordsworth is abbreviated to 'W.']

## Autobiographical Memoranda

1 *April 7th, 1770*: For more specific, and sometimes corrected, dates, see Mark Reed, *Wordsworth: The Chronology of the Early Years*, Cambridge, Mass. (1967) and *Wordsworth: The Chronology of the Middle Years*, Cambridge, Mass. (1975).

2 *Col. Beaumont*: Thomas Wentworth Beaumont (1792–1848).

3 *Miss Hamilton*: Not identified.

4 *Shaw*: Joseph Shaw (1756?–1825?), usher at various grammar schools.

5 *a long poem*: 'The Vale of Esthwaite', the conclusion of which was printed in 1815 as 'Extract of the Conclusion of a Poem'.

6 *Dr Cookson*: William Cookson (1754–1820), fellow of St John's College until 1788. John Chevallier, Master of St John's, died in March, 1789.

7 *Isola*: Agostino Isola (1713–97), teacher of Italian and Spanish at Cambridge University, was reappointed to his position in 1768 by Thomas Gray, Professor of Modern History.

8 *Vision of Mirza*: Written by Joseph Addison, *Spectator*, No. 159.

9 *Robert Jones*: (1769–1835), a fellow student at St John's College, to whom W. dedicated *Descriptive Sketches*, the record of their continental tour.

10 *one volume*: *Lyrical Ballads* (1798).

11 *Mr Chester*: John Chester of Nether Stowey, a neighbour of Coleridge.

12 *Klopstock the poet*: W. kept a brief record of these conversations. See W. J. B. Owen and Jane Worthington Smyser, *The Prose Works of William Wordsworth*, Oxford (1974), I, 91–5.

13 *The Hutchinsons*: Henry Hutchinson (1769–1839), Thomas Hutchinson

471

(1773–1849), Sara Hutchinson (1775–1835), George Hutchinson (1778–1864), Joanna Hutchinson (1780–1843), and Mary Hutchinson (1787–1859), who became W.'s wife in 1802.

14 *small cottage at Town-end, Grasmere*: Dove Cottage.

15 *two younger . . . died*: W. made a mistake here: only Catherine of the younger two children died in 1812; the other child who died in 1812 was Thomas, the third oldest child. William, the youngest, lived till 1883.

### Description of the Scenery of the Lakes

1 *Langdale*: 'Anciently spelt Langden, and so called by the old inhabitants to this day – *dean*, from which the latter part of the word is derived, being in many parts of England a name for a valley.' [W.]

2 *Memorandum-book of a friend*: Samuel Taylor Coleridge, *The Notebooks*, ed. Kathleen Coburn, New York: Pantheon Books (1957), I, 1812, entry dated 5 January 1804.

3 *The visible . . . lake*: *The Prelude*, V, 409–13.

4 *The haunt . . . clang*: *Paradise Lost*, XI, 835: 'The haunt of Seals and Orcs, and sea-mews' clang'.

5 *lusus naturae*: A prank of nature.

6 *fas habeas . . . natantes*: 'See that admirable Idyllium, the Catillus and Salia, of Landor.' [W.] Walter Savage Landor, *Idyllia Heroica Decem, Librum Phaeleuciorum Unum*, Pisa (1820), p. 66. 'You should visit the fields of Tivoli and the lake of Albunea with its floating foliage and lands.' To the last three Latin words, Landor added a note (translated here from Latin): 'In this very deep lake there *float* small islands with, as it were, groves on them.'

7 *vivi lacus*: Living lakes; Virgil, *Georgics*, II, 469.

8 *Carver . . . one*: Jonathan Carver, *Travels Through the Interior Parts of North-America* (1778), pp. 132–3. Carver, however, was writing about Lake Superior.

9 *There . . . blast*: W.'s 'Fidelity', lines 25–31.

10 *low water*: 'In fact there is not an instance of a harbour on the Cumberland side of the Solway frith that is not dry at low water; that of Ravenglass, at the mouth of the Esk, as a natural harbour is much the best. The Sea appears to have been retiring slowly for ages from this coast. From Whitehaven to St Bees extends a track of level ground, about five miles in length, which formerly must have been under salt water, so as to have

been made an island of the high ground that stretches between it and the Sea.' [W.]

11 *Scotch firs*: 'This species of fir is in character much superior to the American which has usurped its place: where the fir is planted for ornament, let it be by all means of the aboriginal species, which can only be procured from the Scotch nurseries.' [W.]

12 *Sylvan*: 'A squirrel (so I have heard the old people of Wytheburn say) might have gone from their chapel to Keswick without alighting on the ground.' [W.]

13 *Skiey influences*: *Measure for Measure*, III, i, 9.

14 *grateful*: Agreeable.

15 *Buchanan . . . habitations*: George Buchanan (1506–82), 'Calendae Maiae', 17–28.

16 *Milton . . . itself*: *Paradise Lost*, IV, 606–607.

17 *spot . . . Rasselas*: Samuel Johnson's philosophical novel *Rasselas* (1759) begins in a valley enclosed by mountains.

18 *Now sunk . . . night*: 'Dr Brown, the author of this fragment, was from his infancy brought up in Cumberland, and should have remembered that the practice of folding sheep by night is unknown among these mountains, and that the image of the Shepherd upon the watch is out of its place, and belongs only to countries, with a warmer climate, that are subject to ravages from beasts of prey. It is pleasing to notice a dawn of imaginative feeling in these verses. Tickel[l], a man of no common genius, chose, for the subject of a Poem, Kensington Gardens, in preference to the Banks of the Derwent, within a mile or two of which he was born. But this was in the reign of Queen Anne, or George the first. Progress must have been made in the interval; though the traces of it, except in the works of Thomson and Dyer, are not very obvious.' [W.] W. here quotes the whole poetic fragment by Dr John Brown (1715–66). Others mentioned in the note are Thomas Tickell (1686–1740), author of *Kensington Gardens*, James Thomson (1700–48), author of *The Seasons*, and John Dyer (1700?–58), author of *Grongar Hill*.

19 *When . . . beasts*: Thomas West, *The Antiquities of Furness* (1774), p. xlvii. *Bellum inter omnia*: War among all (possibly a translation of Thomas Hobbes' 'Warre of every one against every one' [ *Leviathan*, I, xiv]).

20 *Druids*: 'It is not improbable that these circles were once numerous, and that many of them may yet endure in a perfect state, under no very deep covering of soil. A friend of the Author, while making a trench in a level

piece of ground, not far from the banks of the Emont, but in no connection with that river, met with some stones which seemed to him formally arranged; this excited his curiosity, and proceeding, he uncovered a perfect circle of stones, from two to three or four feet high, with a *sanctum sanctorum*, – the whole a complete place of Druidical worship of small dimensions, having the same sort of relation to Stonehenge, Long Meg and her Daughters near the river Eden, and Karl Lofts near Shap (if this last be not Danish), that a rural chapel bears to a stately church, or to one of our noble cathedrals. This interesting little monument having passed, with the field in which it was found, into other hands, has been destroyed. It is much to be regretted, that the striking relic of antiquity at Shap has been in a great measure destroyed also.

The DAUGHTERS of LONG MEG are placed not in an oblong, as the STONES of SHAP, but in a perfect circle, eighty yards in diameter, and seventy-two in number, and from above three yards high, to less than so many feet: a little way out of the circle stands LONG MEG herself – a single stone eighteen feet high.

When the Author first saw this monument, he came upon it by surprise, therefore might over-rate its importance as an object; but he must say, that though it is not to be compared with Stonehenge, he has not seen any other remains of those dark ages, which can pretend to rival it in singularity and dignity of appearance.' [W.]

This note was added in 1822, but a long passage (omitted here) was deleted in 1823. The 'friend of the author' mentioned in the note was Thomas Wilkinson. The present note is followed by W.'s sonnet 'The Monument Commonly called Long Meg and Her Daughters, near the River Eden', first published in this note but omitted here.

21 *When . . . Furness*: West, pp. xlv and xxiii. *Quillet*: a small plot of land.
22 *Robinson Crusoe*: Daniel Defoe, *Robinson Crusoe* (1719). During his first years on the island, as described in the novel, Crusoe built several enclosures.
23 *union of the two crowns*: The Act of Union (1707) combined England and Scotland under one crown.
24 *Sir Launcelot . . . wars*: Joseph Nicolson and Richard Burn, *The History and Antiquities of the Counties of Westmorland and Cumberland* (1777), I, 498.
25 *Cluster'd . . . between*: Home at Grasmere, 122–5.
26 *Specimens remain*: 'Written some time ago. The injury done since, is more than could have been calculated upon.

*Singula de nobis anni praedantur euntes.* This is in the course of things; but why should the genius that directed the ancient architecture of these vales have deserted them? For the bridges, churches, mansions, cottages, and their richly fringed and flat-roofed outhouses, venerable as the grange of some old abbey, have been substituted structures, in which baldness only seems to have been studied, or plans of the most vulgar utility. But some improvement may be looked for in future; the gentry *recently* have copied the old models, and successful instances might be pointed out, if I could take the liberty.' [W.]

This note was added in 1823. *Singula de nobis anni praedantur euntes* – Horace, *Epistles*, II, ii, 55: 'One by one the passing years rob from us.'

27 *school-house adjoining*: 'In some places scholars were formerly taught in the church, and at others the school-house was a sort of ante-chapel to the place of worship, being under the same roof; an arrangement which was abandoned as irreverent. It continues, however, to this day in Borrowdale. In the parish register of that chapelry is a notice, that a youth who had quitted the valley, and died in one of the towns on the coast of Cumberland, had requested that his body should be brought and interred at the foot of the pillar by which he had been accustomed to sit while a school-boy. One cannot but regret that parish registers so seldom contain any thing but bare names; in a few of this country, especially in that of Loweswater, I have found interesting notices of unusual natural occurrences – characters of the deceased, and particulars of their lives. There is no good reason why such memorials should not be frequent; these short and simple annals would in future ages become precious.' [W.]

*Short and simple annals*: Thomas Gray, 'Elegy in a Country Churchyard', 32.

28 religio loci: Places of worship.

29 *his neighbour*: 'One of the most pleasing characteristics of manners in secluded and thinly-peopled districts, is a sense of the degree in which human happiness and comfort are dependent on the contingency of neighbourhood. This is implied by a rhyming adage common here, '*Friends are far, when neighbours are nar*' (near). This mutual helpfulness is not confined to out-of-doors work; but is ready upon all occasions. Formerly, if a person became sick, especially the mistress of a family, it was usual for those of the neighbours who were more particularly connected with the party by amicable offices, to visit the house, carrying a present; this practice, which is by no means obsolete, is called *owning* the

family, and is regarded as a pledge of a disposition to be otherwise serviceable in a time of disability and distress.' [W.]

30 *Dr Brown . . . Enthusiast*: Dr John Brown, *A Description of the Lake at Keswick (and the Adjacent Country) in Cumberland: Communicated in a Letter to a Friend, by a Late Popular Writer*, Kendal (1771).

31 *Not a single . . . attire*: Thomas West, *A Guide to the Lakes*, 5th ed. (1793), p. 213.

32 *plantations*: 'These are disappearing fast, under the management of the present Proprietor, and native wood is resuming its place.' [W.]

33 *Into that forest . . . delight*: Fairie Queene, III, v, stanzas 39–40.

34 *not obvious . . . retired*: Paradise Lost, VIII, 504.

35 *Child . . . age*: 'Address to Kilchurn Castle, upon Loch Awe', lines 1–3.

36 *If you would . . . choice*: Unidentified source.

37 *Mr Gilpin . . . landscape-painting*: William Gilpin, *Observations on the River Wye* (1782), pp. 53–6. William Lock (or Locke) of Norbury (1732–1810).

38 *pointed out*: 'A proper colouring of houses is now becoming general. It is best that the colouring material should be mixed with the rough-cast, and not laid on as a *wash* afterwards.' [W.]

39 *Many . . . remain*: 'Sonnet Composed at — Castle' ('Degenerate Douglas'), 8–14.

40 *August*: West, *Guide*, p. 8.

41 *yean*: To give birth.

42 *humbler excitement*: 'The only instances to which the foregoing observations do not apply, are Derwent-water and Lowes-water. Derwent is distinguished from all the other Lakes by being *surrounded* with sublimity: the fantastic mountains of Borrowdale to the south, the solitary majesty of Skiddaw to the north, the bold steeps of Wallow-crag and Lodore to the east, and to the west the clustering mountains of New-lands. Lowes-water is tame at the head, but towards its outlet has a magnificent assemblage of mountains. Yet as far as respects the formation of such receptacles, the general observation holds good: neither Derwent nor Lowes-water derive any supplies from the streams of those mountains that dignify the landscape towards the outlets.' [W.]

43 *Qui bene distinguit bene docet*: He who distinguishes well explains well. Unidentified source.

44 *While . . . melodies*: 'The Pass of Kirkstone', 39–40.

45 *Masters . . . the Italian Alps*: Of the six painters mentioned, Titian (1489–

1576), Nicholas Poussin (1594–1665), Gaspar Poussin [Dughet] (1615–75), Claude Lorrain [Gelée] (1600–82), Pellegrino Tibaldi (1527–96), and Bernardino Luini (c. 1475–1532), only Lorraine and Luini seem to have spent much time in the Alps. As for the English experiments (in the sentence that follows), W. probably has at least J. M. W. Turner in mind.

46 *in general*: 'The greatest variety of trees is found in the Valais.' [W.]

47 *said in poetry*: 'Lucretius has charmingly described a scene of this kind.

"Inque dies magis in montem succedere sylvas
Cogebant, infraque locum concedere cultis:
Prata, lacus, rivos, segetes, vinetaque laeta
Collibus et campis ut haberent, atque olearum
*Caerula* distinguens inter *plaga* currere posset
Per tumulos, et convalleis, camposque profusa:
Ut nunc esse vides vario distincta lepore
Omnia, quae pomis intersita dulcibus ornant,
Arbustisque tenent felicibus obsita circum."'

[W.]

*De Rerum Natura*, V, 1370–8:

Day by day they made the forests climb
higher up the mountains and yield the place
below to their tilth, that they might have meadows,
pools, and streams, crops and luxuriant vineyards
on hill and plain, and that a grey-green belt of
olives might run between to mark the boundaries
stretching forth over hills and dales and plains:
even as now you see the whole place mapped
out with charming variety, laid out and intersected
with sweet fruit-trees and set about with fertile
plantations of trees.

trans. W. H. D. Rouse

48 *the winds*: 'It is remarkable that Como (as is probably the case with other Italian Lakes) is more troubled by storms in summer than in winter. Hence the propriety of the following verses.

"Lari! margine ubique confragoso
Nulli coelicolum negas sacellum
Picto periete saxeoque tecto;
Hinc miracula multa navitarum
Audis, nec placido refellis ore,
Sed nova usque paras, Noto vel Euro
*Aestivas* quatientibus cavernas,
Vel surgentis ab Adduae cubili
Caeco grandinis imbre provoluto."'

Landor.
[W.]

Walter Savage Landor, 'Ad Larium' ['To Lake Como'] in *Idyllia Heroica*, Pisa (1820), p. 161 (lines 9–17):

Lake Como! Everywhere on your jagged shoreline
You welcome the shrines of all the gods
With painted wall and stony roof;
Hence you hear the many marvels undergone by sailors
Nor disprove them with a calm surface,
But continually furnish new ones, either when the South or East
Wind
Shake the *summery* grottoes,
Or when a blinding storm of hail
Has rolled forth from the bed of the rising Addua.

(italics added by W.)
trans. ed.

49 *two comprehensive tours . . . Alps:* in 1790 and 1820.
50 *September morning*: Actually on 17 November 1799, while W. was guiding Coleridge on his first visit to the Lakes. See *The Notebooks of Samuel Taylor Coleridge*, ed. Kathleen Coburn, New York, Pantheon Books (1957), I, 553, for Coleridge's account.
51 *West's Guide*: p. 5.

### Kendal and Windermere Railway

1 *Tourists*: Those who travel about for recreation. Apparently W. is implying that a railway is too fast and direct for touring.

2 *In this district ... benefit*: *The Correspondence of Henry Crabb Robinson with the Wordsworth Circle*, ed. Edith J. Morley, Oxford (1927), p. 586: 'The great probability is that over the majority the letters will have no effect – Except perhaps the beginning of the first letter – which in truth does briefly suggest precisely the reasons to which persons of their office are especially accessible – indeed I cannot persuade myself that the meanest and lowest of all considerations, (that of the *Dividend*) will not be alone quite sufficient to secure the lake district from the threatened invasion.'

3 scenery ... *understood*: In the *Biographia Literaria* (eds. J. Engell and W. J. Bate, Princeton, NJ and London, Princeton University Press and Routledge and Kegan Paul [1983], II, 103), Samuel Taylor Coleridge criticizes the use of the word *scene* as applied vaguely by W. to a locale without pointing up the theatrical metaphor.

4 *Ray, the naturalist* : John Ray's *Observations Topographical, Moral, and Physiological; Made in a Journey Through Part of the Low-Countries, Germany, Italy, and France*, London (1673), contains passages on Switzerland.

5 *when they ... horror*: Bishop Gilbert Burnet, *Travels Through France, Italy, Germany, and Switzerland*, London (1750), p. 96.

6 *delight or praise*: *The Diary of John Evelyn*, ed. E. S. de Beer, Oxford (1955), II, 506–15.

7 *his language*: Thomas Burnet, *Telluris Theoria Sacra*, London (1681), I, 89–91.

8 *a Latin Ode*: Thomas Gray's 'O Tu, severi Religio loci'.

9 *Dante*: Thomas West, *Guide to the Lakes*, 5th ed., Kendal (1793), p. 206; Dante, *Inferno*, III, 51.

10 *Mr Curwen*: Henry Curwen (1783–1861) was the father-in-law of W.'s son, John.

11 *the picturesque*: James Currie, *The Works of Robert Burns; With an Account of His Life*, Liverpool (1800), I, 170–1.

12 *unfortunate*: Currie, I, 175–6.

13 *his plough*: 'To a Mountain Daisy'.

14 *the symbol dear*: 'Answer to Verses Addressed to the Poet by the Guidwife of Wauchope-House', 23–4.

15 *O, Nature ... charms*: Robert Burns ('the Ayrshire ploughman'), 'To William Simpson', 73–4.

16 *Essays, in the Morning Post*: 18 December 1844, p. 5. The author has not been identified.

17 *Turn we . . . disarm*: 'The Traveller', 165–76.

18 *the Retreat . . . of the Ten Thousand*: See Xenophon, *Anabasis*.

19 *Vane . . . a king*: Samuel Johnson, *The Vanity of Human Wishes*, 321–2.

20 *by bread alone*: Matthew 4:4.

21 *a gallant officer*: Sir Thomas S. Pasley (1804–84), a friend of the Words-worths and later an admiral.

22 *Professor Wilson*: John Wilson (1785–1854), Professor of Moral Philos-ophy at the University of Edinburgh, was an early admirer of W. (see W.'s response to his fan letter in this edition) and lived near Bowness.

23 *No flaring . . . peace*: West, p. 213.

24 *Quanto . . . Herba*: Juvenal, *Satires*, III, 18–20:

> How much more present would be
> The deity of the fount if it were rimmed by a green border of
> Grass . . .

25 *Brook . . . without end*: 'The Simplon Pass', first published in 1845; also part of *The Prelude* (1850), VI, 621–40. Mark Reed, in *Wordsworth: The Chronology of the Early Years*, Cambridge, Mass. (1967), p. 31, dates the composition as 'perhaps composed 1799, probably 1804'.

26 *the same Pass*: W. first crossed the Simplon Pass, as recorded in the above passage, in 1790 and crossed it again in 1820.

27 *the following lines . . . earlier*: 'Steamboats, [Viaducts,] and Railways' was first published in 1835 and composed probably in the summer of 1833.

### Preface to The Borderers

1 *benevolence*: Possibly an instance of the influence of William Godwin. See his *Enquiry Concerning Political Justice*, ed. F. E. L. Priestley, Toronto (1946), I, 433: 'Benevolent intention is essential to virtue.'

2 *Rousseau had observed*: Jean-Jacques Rousseau, *Emile* (*Oeuvres Complètes*, Paris, Editions du Seuil [1971], III, 46).

3 *the Orlando of Ariosto*: Ariosto, *Orlando Furioso*, xxiii, 131–5.

4 *the Cardenio of Cervantes*: In Cervantes, *Don Quixote*, Book III, chapters IX–X, Cardenio is represented as mad, but he does not lay waste groves.

5 *chusing*: An acceptable spelling of *choosing* in the 1790s, written so DCMS 27, although *chasing* might have been intended.

6 *the milk of human reason*: Cf. *Macbeth*, I, v, 18: 'the milk of human kindness'.

7  *an empiric*: Possibly an empirical relativist (but no such meaning is given in the Oxford English Dictionary).

8  *struggle* [          ]: A blank occurs in the manuscripts, preceded by 'so'. I have dropped 'so' in order to avoid impeding the existing sense of the passage.

9  *Of which Iago speaks*: Othello, II, i, 308–309: 'the thought . . . / Doth like a poisonous mineral gnaw my inwards . . .'

10 *I am asked*: Words written into the manuscript, probably by Ernest de Selincourt, to fill a blank.

11 *superstition*: Unfounded belief (for, as W. goes on to explain, not being aware of the constant application of moral sentiments 'to vicious purposes', we shudder when we find such application clearly set forth in literature. This unfounded belief also makes us attractive targets for unscrupulous men and is thus 'one great source of our [mankind's] vices').

12 *Pope*: Moral Essays, I, 35–8.


### [Essay on Morals]

1  *books . . . Mr Paley's*: The books in question are probably William Godwin's *Enquiry Concerning Political Justice* (1793) and William Paley's *Principles of Moral and Political Philosophy* (1785).


### Reply to Mathetes

1  *illustrated*: Adorned.

2  *a Traveller*: 'Vide Ashe's Travels in America' – [W.] Thomas Ashe, *Travels, in America, Performed in 1806* . . ., 3 vols. (1806), I, 318–22.

3  *a mount upon a mount*: Paradise Lost, V, 757–8.

4  *Giants in those days*: Genesis 6:4: 'There were giants in the earth in those days.'

5  *Ancient and Modern*: The dispute between the Ancients and the Moderns concerned the superiority of classical writers to moderns. It arose in the seventeenth century and was satirized in Jonathan Swift's *The Battle of the Books* (1704).

6  *the comparison*: The first instalment of W.'s *Reply* ended here.

7  *shot orient beams*: Cf. *Paradise Lost*, VI, 12–15. John Wycliffe (d. 1384) was a medieval religious reformer, who rebelled against the Church.

8 *fable of Prodicus*: Xenophon, *Memorabilia*, II, i, 21–33. W. adapts the fable freely.

9 *doubtless . . . think*: *The Friend*, No. 6 (21 September 1809), p. 87.

10 *take place of*: Take precedence over.

11 *We may . . . for ever*: This sentence is not in *The Friend*, but only in a letter to the printer requesting this addition.

12 *overlooks*: Surveys.

13 *a passage*: In *The Friend*, No. 4 (7 September 1809), p. 62 n, two passages from Milton's *Areopagitica* are cited. In the remainder of the sentence, W. quotes verbatim (although in different order of phrasing) from the first and last sentence of the first quotation.

14 *that living Teacher*: 'Mathetes' had specified W. by name.

15 *the following words*: 'Ode to Duty', last stanza (lines 57–64), italics added here by W.

16 In the manuscript, there are two inverted 'W's, not two 'M's. But in the periodical version of 1809, the reply is signed 'M.M.', and in the first collected version in *The Friend* of 1818, it is signed 'W.W.'.

### Memoir of the Rev. Robert Walker

1 *he has been described*: In one of the letters omitted above.

2 *Shenstone's schoolmistress*: William Shenstone, *The Schoolmistress* (1742), 45.

3 *never sent empty away*: Cf. Luke I:53: 'He hath filled the hungry with good things; and the rich he hath sent empty away.'

4 *Church-stock*: 'Mr Walker's charity being of that kind which "seeketh not her own", he would rather forgo his rights than distrain for due, which the parties liable refused, as a point of conscience to pay.' – [W.]

5 *O . . . heaven*: *Henry VIII*, III, ii, 384–5.

### A Letter to the Bishop of Llandaff

1 *a sublime allegory*: Joseph Addison, 'The First Vision of Mirzah', *Spectator*, No. 159.

2 *proof . . . without asperity*: *An Apology for Christianity, in a Series of Letters, Addressed to Edward Gibbon* (1779).

3 *Appendix to a sermon*: Richard Watson, *A Sermon Preached before the Stewards of the Westminster Dispensary . . . with an Appendix* (1793).

4 *effect . . . community*: Cf. Watson, *A Sermon*, appendix, first paragraph (p. 17): 'If [the sermon] shall have any effect in calming the perturbation which has been lately excited . . . in the minds of the lower classes of the community . . .'

5 *royal martyr*: The French executed Louis XVI on 21 January 1793.

6 *A bishop*: 'M. Gregoire' – [W.] Henri Gregoire (1750–1831), Bishop of Blois.

7 *Tyran . . . ouvrage*: 'Tyrant, behold your work!' *Archives Parlementaires*, Première Série, LIII, 426.

8 *extinguished David*: See *Athalie*, Scene second

> 'Il faut que sur le trône un roi soit élevé
> Qui *se souvienne un jour* qu'au rang de ses ancêtres
> Dieu l'a fait remonter par la main de ses prêtres,
> L'a tiré par leur main de l'oubli du tombeau,
> Et de David éteint rellume le flambeau.

'The conclusion of the same speech applies so strongly to the present period that I cannot forbear trancribing it.

> 'Daigne daigne, mon Dieu, sur Mathan et sur elle
> Répandre *cet esprit d'imprudence et d'erreur*,
> *De la chute des rois funeste avant-coureur.*'
>
> > [italics added by W.]
> > [W.]

*Athalie*, I, ii, 113–17, 127–9:

> A king must be raised to the throne
> Who *remembers a day* that God made
> Him reascend to the rank of his ancestors
> By the hand of his priests and rescued him
> By their hand from the oblivion of the grave,
> And reillumed the torch of extinguished David.
>
> Deign, deign, my God, on Mathan and on her
> To shed *that spirit of imprudence and error*,
> *The fatal forerunner of the fall of kings.*
>
> > trans. ed.

9 *hero of the necklace* : 'Prince de Rohan' is written on the manuscript across

from this name. Prince de Rohan was a Cardinal-Bishop involved in a court scandal with Marie Antoinette.

10 *Mr Burke . . . moralist*: Edmund Burke, *Reflections on the French Revolution* [1790], London, Everyman ed., (1910) p. 73.

11 *iron . . . enter into it*: Psalms, 105:18, 'whose feet they hurt in the stocks: the iron entered into his soul' (*Book of Common Prayer*).

12 Jean-Jacques Rousseau, *Du Contrat social*, Book I, Chapter 2: 'Every man born in slavery is born as a slave: nothing is more certain: slaves lose everything in their chains, even the desire to escape from them; they love their slavery as Ulysses' companions loved their brutishness.' – trans. ed.

13 *set fire . . . Priestley*: On 14 July 1791 a mob burned the house of the well-known Radical, Joseph Priestley (1733–1804). There was some question at the time whether the mob had been deliberately incited.

14 *Père Gérard*: Michel Gérard (1737–1815), deputy from Rennes.

15 *laws . . . general will*: Cf. *Droits de L'Homme et du Citoyen*, Article 6: 'La loi est l'expression de la volonté générale.'

16 *Government . . . evil*: Cf. Thomas Paine, *Common Sense* Section I (second paragraph): 'Government, even in its best state, is but a necessary evil.'

17 *Tarpeian rock*: A rock at the corner of the Capitoline Hill, from which criminals sentenced to death were hurled.

18 necessary *splendour*: Unidentified source.

19 *maxims of . . . Walpole*: Sir Robert Walpole (1676–1745) was a British statesman who held some cynical political maxims, such as, 'Every man has his price.'

20 *enemy . . . shaft*: Demosthenes (383–322 BC), the Athenian orator, delivered a set of speeches against Philip of Macedon (c.382–336 BC) that were entitled *Phillipics*.

21 *the hermit Peter*: The French priest of Amiens who helped to raise the Crusade of the Paupers in 1096.

22 *Maury . . . Mirabeau*: Jean-Siffrein Maury (1746–1817) and Jacques-Antoine-Marie de Cazalès (1758–1805) were outspoken opponents of some of the effects of the French Revolution, while Marie-Joseph, Marquis de Lafayette (1757–1834) and Count Honoré de Mirabeau (1749–91) were both leaders of the Revolution, later thought to have intrigued with the Court.

### [*Letter to Charles James Fox (1801)*]

1 *Pectus . . . desunt*: Quintilian, *Institutio Oratoria*, X, vii, 15: 'For it is feeling and imagination that make us eloquent. Therefore, words come even to the ignorant, if only they are moved by some strong emotion.' trans. ed. This Latin quotation serves as motto on the half-title of *Lyrical Ballads* (1802, 1805).

2 *thus addressing you*: A brief conventional ending has been omitted here.

### From *The Convention of Cintra*

1 *Ruler*: Napoleon.

2 *Treaty of Amiens*: 17 March 1802. Switzerland was subjugated in 1798.

3 *evil communications*: I Corinthians 15:33.

4 *the rising of . . . the Pyrenean peninsula*: Beginning 2 May 1808 in Madrid.

5 *this corruptible . . . immortality*: I Corinthians 15:53.

6 *embraced each other*: Britain and Spain signed a peace treaty 14 January 1809.

7 *victory of Vimiera*: On 21 August 1808, Wellesley defeated the French under Junot.

8 *Thermopylae and Marathon*: 480 BC and 490 BC, respectively.

9 *present disaster*: Early in 1809, the British army under Sir John Moore suffered several reversals.

10 *in opinion*: From this point to the end of this long paragraph all the material was claimed by Coleridge to have been written almost totally by himself – see Coleridge's letter to Thomas Poole (3 February 1809).

11 *bodies . . . unites again*: See *Paradise Lost*, VI, 328–53.

12 *an Abdiel . . . a Leonidas*: Abdiel was one of the seraphim 'than whom none with more zeal adored / The Diety' (*Paradise Lost*, V, 805–806); Leonidas was the heroic leader of the Greek force which perished delaying the Persian advance at Thermopylae in 480 BC.

13 *dishonour*: W. added here (as 'Appendix B') the following comment: 'It is not necessary to add, that one of these fears was removed by the actual landing of ten thousand men, under Sir J. Moore, pending the negocia-tion: and yet no change in the terms took place in consequence. This was an important consequence; and, of itself, determined two of the members of the Board of Inquiry to disapprove of the convention: such an accession

entitling Sir H. Dalrymple (and, of course, making it his duty) to insist
on more favorable terms. But the argument is complete without it.'

14 *weakness*: W. considered this last sentence potentially libellous (*Letters: the
Middle Years*, II, 341).

15 *bold, bad men*: Spenser's *Faerie Queene*, I, i, 37; Shakespeare's *Henry VIII*,
II, ii, 43. In both sources 'men' is 'man'. Cataline (108?–62 BC) was a
Roman conspirator; Cesare Borgia (1475–1507) was the model for Ma-
chiavelli's *The Prince*.

16 *Phocion, Epaminondas, and Philopoemen*: Three honest patriots treated in
Plutrach's *Lives*.

17 *honest dealing*: See Faulke Greville, *The Life of the Renowned Sir Philip
Sidney* (1652), in *Works*, ed. Grosart (1870), IV, 38: Sidney restored
'amongst us the ancient majestie of noble and true dealing . . .'

18 *Lord Peterborough*: Charles Mordaunt, third Earl of Peterborough (1658–
1735), joint-commander in 1705 of a British expeditionary force to Spain,
where he captured Barcelona.

19 *deeply interested*: In Appendix C, W. added:

> I was unwilling to interrupt the reader upon a slight occasion; but I
> cannot refrain from adding here a word or two by way of comment. – I
> have said at page [189], speaking of Junot's army, that the British were to
> encounter the same men, &c. Sir Arthur Wellesley, before the Board of
> Inquiry, disallowed this supposition; affirming that Junot's army had not
> then reached Spain, nor could be there for some time. Grant this: was it
> not stipulated that a messenger should be sent off, immediately after the
> conclusion of the treaty, to Buonaparte – apprising him of its terms, and
> when he might expect his troops; and would not this enable him to hurry
> forward forces to the Spanish frontiers, and to bring them into action –
> knowing that these troops of Junot's would be ready to support him?
> What did it matter whether the British were again to measure swords
> with these identical men; whether these men were even to appear again
> upon Spanish ground? It was enough, that, if these did not, others would
> – who could not have been brought to that service, but that these had
> been released and were doing elsewhere some other service for their
> master; enough that every thing was provided by the British to land
> them as near the Spanish frontier (and as speedily) as they could
> desire.

20 'Those rare cases are of course excepted, in which the superiority on the

one side is not only fairly to be presumed but positive – and so prominently obtrusive, that to *propose* terms is to *inflict* terms.' – [W.]

21 *ignoble ease and darling sloth*: Cf. *Paradise Lost*, II, 227: 'ignoble ease, and peaceful sloth'.

22 *submit or yield*: *Paradise Lost*, I, 108.

23 *an example, at Baylen*: When the Spaniards defeated Dupont's army at Baylen on 13 July 1808, the French were taken prisoner, as Junot and his army had not been by the British in Portugal.

24 *necessary*: W. copied much of this sentence verbatim from a report in the *Courier*, 21 November 1808. The end of the next sentence but one was taken verbatim from the same report.

25 *Radice . . . tendit*: Virgil, *Georgics*, II, 292.

26 *one of those generals*: Bernardin Freire de Andrade (b. 1759), Portuguese general.

27 *Morocco*: In Appendix D, W. added:

This attempt, the reader will recollect, is not new to our country; – it was accomplished, at one aera of our history, in that memorable act of an English Parliament, which made it unlawful for any man to ask his neighbour to join him in a petition for redress of grievances; and which thus denied the people 'the benefit of tears and prayers to their own infamous deputies!' For the deplorable state of England and Scotland at that time – see the annals of Charles the Second, and his successor. – We must not forget however that to this state of things, as the cause of those measures which the nation afterwards resorted to, we are originally indebted for the blessing of the Bill of Rights.

28 *head and front*: *Othello*, I, iii, 80.

29 *crude consistence*: *Paradise Lost*, II, 941.

30 *by the petrific . . . look*: *Paradise Lost*, X, 294–7.

31 *under the cover . . . framed it*: This sentence was rewritten by Thomas De Quincey at W.'s request, to avoid libel.

32 *ought to . . . draw light*: Cf. *Paradise Lost*, VII, 364–5: 'Hither as to their Fountain other Stars / Repairing, in their golden Urns draw Light.'

33 *Alfred . . . Milton*: King Alfred (849–901), who delivered England from the Scandinavians; Sir Philip Sidney (1554–86), poet and soldier; Algernon Sidney (1622–82), Republican statesman; John Milton (1608–74), poet and Republican.

34 *we have weighed . . . wanting*: Cf. Daniel 5:27: 'Thou art weighed in the balances, and art found wanting.'

35 *his minister*: M. Crelet, Minister of the Interior.

36 *the Demon*: Quoted by Coleridge in *The Friend*, No. 7 (28 September 1809), p. 111, apparently as having been said by Sir Philip Sidney, but the source is unknown.

37 *I see . . . are*: Samuel Taylor Coleridge, 'Dejection: An Ode', 38.

38 *inspired . . . taught*: Cf. John Dryden, *Absalom and Achitophel*, 883: 'Indued by nature and by learning taught'.

39 regni novitas: Virgil, *Aeneid*, I, 563: 'the newness of rule'.

40 *the Sword . . . surrendered*: The sword of Francis I, King of France, surrendered at the battle of Pavia (1525) to Emperor Charles V of Spain, was given to Napoleon in April 1808.

41 *life of Man sustained*: Matthew 4:4.

42 *of those nobler . . . of his country*: Added by De Quincey.

43 *Llewellin . . . Wallace*: Llywelyn the Great (d. 1240) was a Welsh prince who resisted the English; William Wallace (1272?–1305) was a similar Scottish patriot.

44 *feudal tenures . . . inquisition*: In December 1808, Napoleon abolished feudal rights and the Inquisition.

45 *saluted him*: In Appendix E, W. added:

I allude here more especially to an address presented to Buonaparte (October 27th, 1808) by the deputies of the new departments of the kingdom of Italy; from which address, as given in the English journals, the following passages are extracted: –

'In the necessity, in which you are to overthrow – to destroy – to disperse your enemies as the wind dissipates the dust, you are not an exterminating angel; but you are the being that extends his thoughts – that measures the face of the earth – to re-establish universal happiness upon better and surer bases.'

        ★     ★     ★

'We are the interpreters of a million of souls at the extremity of your kingdom of Italy.' – 'Deign, *Sovereign Master of all Things*, to hear (as we doubt not you will)' &c.

The answer begins thus: –

'I *applaud* the sentiments you express in the name of my people of Musora, Metauro, and Tronto.'

46 *Per me . . . gente*: Dante, *Inferno*, III, 1–3 [engraved over the gates of Hell]:

> Through me one goes into the sorrowful city,
> Through me one goes to eternal pain,
> Through me one goes among the lost people.
>
> trans. ed.

47 *Système de la Nature*: An atheistical treatise written by Paul Heinrich Dietrich, Baron D'Holbach (1723–89). Etienne Bonnot de Condillac (1715–1780) was another French encyclopaedist.

48 *may be done*: In Appendix F, W. added:

This principle, involved in so many of his actions, Buonaparte has of late explicitly avowed: the instances are numerous: it will be sufficient, in this place, to allege one – furnished by his answer to the address cited in the last note: –

'I am particularly attached to your Archbishop of Urbino: that prelate, animated with the true faith, repelled with indignation the advice – and braved the menaces – of those who wished to confound the affairs of Heaven, which never change, with the affairs of this world, which are modified according to circumstances of *force* and policy.'

49 *trunk . . . clay*: Cf. Daniel 2:32–3: 'This image's head was of fine gold, his breast and his arms of silver, his belly and his thighs of brass, / His legs of iron, his feet part of iron and part of clay.'

50 *Magna parvis obscurantur*: After Lord Peterborough's capture of Barcelona (see note 18), which came under a total eclipse, he ordered captured brass cannon melted down and recast with an image of the sun eclipsed and the Latin motto ('the great is obscured by the small'). Marlborough, mentioned below, was John Churchill, first Duke of Marlborough (1650–1722), an English general successful in the War of the Spanish Succession.

51 *A little more . . . destroyed*: Plutarch, *Pyrrhus*, XXI.

52 *Numantia and Saguntum*: Both Spanish towns that withstood long sieges, the first by the Romans in 134–133 BC (Appian, *Iber*, 84–98), the other by the Carthaginians in 219 BC (Livy, XXI, vi–xv).

53 *'Cromwell . . . obedience'*: Quoted and paraphrased from *Memoires of the Reigne of King Charles I*, London (1701), pp. 252–3.

54 *commander-in-chief*: Charles Richard Vaughan, *Narrative of the Siege of Zaragoza*, 4th ed. London, (1809). pp. 27–8.

55 *God's work*: Sir Philip Sidney (1554–86), letter to Sir Francis Walsingham (24 March 1586).

56 *Be ye . . . perfect*: Matthew 5:48.

57 *bright consummate flower*: *Paradise Lost*, V, 481.

58 *Kosciusko*: Tadeusz Kościuzsko (1746–1817), Polish patriot.

59 *Palafox*: José de Palafox y Melzi (1780–1847), Spanish commander during the sieges of Saragossa, was released in 1813. Toussaint L'Ouverture (1743–1803) was an Haitian revolutionary who died in a French prison.

60 *Haec . . . expleti nihil*: Petrarch, *De Vita Solitaria*, I:

> I should say these things and whatever indignation and grief over our present situation dictated, unless I believed our minds had become numb and our affairs were over. Without a doubt, we who were accustomed to show the straight way to others, now (and this is the nearest thing to destruction) are dragged across rough terrain, the blind led by the blind, and are turned around by example of others, not knowing what we want. To complete the point I began with, all this evil – whether our own or whether the common lot of all people – is caused by IGNOR-ANCE OF THE GOAL. Unreflective men do not know what they do: therefore whatever they do in the future, as soon as they have begun, turns to disgust . . . Hence this bustle without end; next, discord midway; and, before the end, DOOMED BEGINNINGS, and nothing accomplished.
>
> > [Capitals added by W. in his quotation from the Latin]
> > trans. ed.

61 *Valiant . . . affairs*: John Milton, *History of Britain*, ed. G. P. Krapp, in *Works*, ed. F. A. Patterson, New York (1932), X, 325.

## Postscript (1835), Part I

1 *the present volume*: *Yarrow Revisited and Other Poems*.

2 *some . . . poems*: In a manuscript of *Postscript*, W. refers specifically to two poems, 'The Warning' and 'Humanity'.

3 *entitled . . . by law*: W., in a letter to Joshua Watson (16 June 1835), mentioned the inclusion in the *Postscript* of his 'little Paragraph upon the *right* of the poor to public support' (*Letters: Later Years*, VI, 62), but the particular paragraph has not been identified.

4 *'remedial measures'*: Title given the last section of the *Report from His*

Majesty's Commissioners *for* Inquiring *into the* Administration *and* Practical Operation *of the Poor Laws*, London (1834), p. 227.

5 in loco parentis: In the position of a parent.

6 *Did I . . . being*: Paradise Lost, X, 743–7.

7 *prodigal son*: Luke 15:11–32.

8 *Northern Indian . . . alive*: In Samuel Hearne, *A Journey from Prince of Wales's Fort in Hudson Bay, to the Northern Ocean*, London (1795), there are reports throughout of Indians starving from want of game.

9 *Homeless . . . food*: 'Guilt and Sorrow', 368–9.

10 *a pair*: Sarah Pashley and her husband. This case was reported in *The Times*, 10 January 1835. Information in *The Times* five days later, however, suggests that the case may have been fraudulent.

11 *refuge . . . heat*: Isaiah 25:4.

12 *beforehand with the world*: To have more than sufficient to meet present demands.

13 *one innocent man should suffer*: Sir William Blackstone, *Commentaries on the Laws of England*, Book IV, Chapter 27 (under 'Presumptive Evidence').

14 *Slave Trade and Slavery*: Abolished in 1807 and 1833 respectively.


[*The Sublime and the Beautiful*]

1 *the stature with which it appears to reach the sky*: Cf. Paradise Lost, IV, 988: 'His stature reacht the Skie.'

2 *the head and the front*: Othello, I, iii, 80.

3 *takes place of*: Takes precedence over.

4 *Who would . . . Eternity*: Paradise Lost, II, 146–8.

5 *the fall of the Rhine at Chafhausen*: In Coleridge's *Shakespearean Criticism* (ed. T. M. Raysor, 2nd ed., London and New York [1960], I, 224) occurs the following comment of 1813: 'The sense of sublimity arises, not from the sight of an outward object, but from the reflection upon it; not from the impression, but from the idea. Few have seen a celebrated waterfall without feeling something of disappointment: it is only subsequently, by reflection, that the idea of the waterfall comes full into the mind, and brings with it a train of sublime associations.' W. was disappointed when he saw the fall in 1790 (*Letters: Early Years*, I, 35).

6 *ludicrous as it . . .*: A passage is omitted here, thought to be a quarto sheet filled on both sides.

7 *influences*: Probably an error for *inferences*.

8 *that a tree . . . lifeless*: W. may have drawn some of his wording from an account of this anecdote given in Dorothy Wordsworth's *Journals*, ed. Ernest de Selincourt, New York (1941), I, 402.

9 *pikes of Langdale . . . sublime*: Probably a reference to William Gilpin, *Observation Relative to Picturesque Beauty* (1786), I, 144–5, where he found fault with the Langdale Pikes.


*Advertisement to* Lyrical Ballads

1 *Reynolds . . . composition*: Sir Joshua Reynolds, *Discourses on Art*, ed. R. R. Wark, San Marino, Calif., Huntington Library (1959), pp. 219–20.

2 *authenticated fact*: The 'authentication' can be found in Erasmus Darwin's *Zoonomia* (1794–6), II, 359.

3 *The Rime of the Ancyent Marinere*: One of five poems contributed by Samuel Taylor Coleridge to the anonymous *Lyrical Ballads* (1798).

4 *a friend*: Thought to have been William Hazlitt, who argued about metaphysics with W. at Nether Stowey, where Hazlitt visited Coleridge in 1798.


*Preface to* Lyrical Ballads *and Appendix*

1 *Appendix . . . Edition*: The title and first paragraph first appeared in 1845.

2 *Preface . . . 'Lyrical Ballads'*: This title first appeared in 1815. The expanded Preface to the third edition of *Lyrical Ballads* (1802) is the text essential to the version printed here.

3 *Note . . . contents*: The parenthetical material was added in 1845.

4 *The result . . . please*: For a description of the reception of *Lyrical Ballads*, see John O. Hayden, *The Romantic Reviewers 1802–1824*, Chicago and London (1969), pp. 78–91.

5 *they have advised me*: According to W. in 1838 and 1845, Samuel Taylor Coleridge was the friend who got him to write the Preface (*Letters: Later Years*, VI, 508–509, W. to William Rowan Hamilton, 4 January 1838; *Letters: The Later Years*, Oxford [1939], III, 1248–9, W. to Edward Moxon, 10 April 1845).

6 *Catullus . . . Claudian*: Catullus, lyric poet (c. 84–c.54 BC); Terence, comic playwright (195 or 185–159 BC) and Lucretius, philosophical poet (c. 99–c. 55 BC) – poets of the Golden Age. Statius, epic poet, (c. AD 40 – c. 96) and Claudian, political poet, (third century AD) – poets of the Silver Age.

7 *Shakespeare ... Pope*: William Shakespeare (1564–1616), Francis Beaumont (1584–1616), and John Fletcher (1579–1625) – the Elizabethan age; John Donne (1573?–1631), Abraham Cowley (1618–67) – the Jacobean period; John Dryden (1631–1700) and Alexander Pope (1688–1744) – the Augustan period.

8 *their own creation*: 'It is worth while here to observe, that the affecting parts of Chaucer are almost always expressed in language pure and universally intelligible even to this day.' – [W.]

9 *we shall describe ... purified*: The first instance in the history of literary theory in which the morality of literature is clearly said to work indirectly, not directly by precept or example.

10 *national events*: Especially events in the war with France.

11 *rapid communication*: The improved roads and the recently developed system of mail-coaches, as well as improved and expanded shipping, were making the delay in the communication of news a matter of days or even hours rather than of weeks.

12 *German Tragedies*: Especially the work of August Friedrich von Kotzebue (1761–1819).

13 *when prose is well written*: W. may have derived his ideas about the general use of the same diction in poetry and in prose from an anonymous article by William Enfield, 'Is Verse Essential to Poetry?' (*Monthly Magazine*, II [1796], 455), but the idea is so consonant with W.'s overall views on diction that the proposal of such influence is unnecessary. There are no verbal echoes.

14 *Gray ... Metrical composition*: See Thomas Gray, *Correspondence*, ed. P. Toynbee and L. Whibley, Oxford (1971), I, 192 (Gray to West, 8 April 1742): 'The language of the age is never the language of poetry ...'

15 *In vain ... in vain*: 'Sonnet on the Death of Richard West' (1742).

16 *Poetry*: 'I here use the word "Poetry" (though against my own judgment) as opposed to the word Prose, and synonymous with metrical composition. But much confusion has been introduced into criticism by this contradistinction of Poetry and Prose, instead of the more philosophical one of Poetry and Matter of Fact, or Science. The only strict antithesis to Prose is Metre; nor is this, in truth, a *strict* antithesis, because lines and passages of metre so naturally occur in writing prose, that it would be scarcely possible to avoid them, even were it desirable.' – [W.] A similar statement about the division of writing into *poetry* and *philosophy* occurs in the article in the *Monthly Magazine*, II (1796), 456.

17 *tears such as Angels weep*: *Paradise Lost*, I, 620.

18 *comprehensive soul*: Cf. John Dryden, *Essay of Dramatic Poesy* (in *Essays of John Dryden*, ed. W. P. Ker, Oxford (1900), I, 79: Shakespeare 'had the . . . most comprehensive soul'.

19 *disposition . . . present*: W. was possibly influenced here by Quintilian, *Institutio Oratoria*, VI, ii, 29: '. . . we call such things visions whereby absent things are presented to our imagination so vividly that we seem to have them actually before our eyes. Whoever can imagine things so well will wield most power over the emotions.' – trans. ed.

20 *language . . . in himself*: W. used Quintilian, *Institutio Oratoria*, X, vii, 15 as a motto on the half-title of *Lyrical Ballads* (1802, 1805): 'For it is feeling and imagination that make us eloquent. Therefore, words come even to the ignorant, if only they are moved by some strong emotion.' – trans. ed.

21 *his feelings . . . with theirs*: That a poet should feel the emotions of his characters can be traced back to Aristotle's *Poetics* (the opening of Chapter 17).

22 *Aristotle . . . operative*: Aristotle, *Poetics*, Chapter 9: '. . . Poetry is something more philosophical and more worthy of serious attention than history; for while poetry is concerned with universal truths, history treats of particular facts.' – trans. T. S. Dorsch.

23 *that he looks before and after*: *Hamlet*, IV, iv, 37: 'looking before and after'.

24 *poems are extant*: That is, traditional ballads.

25 *Clarissa Harlowe, or the Gamester*: Samuel Richardson, *Clarissa Harlowe* (1748); Edward Moore, *The Gamester*(1753).

26 *I put . . . his hand*: Samuel Johnson, *Poems*, ed. D. N. Smith and E. L. McAdam, Oxford (1941), p. 158.

27 *These pretty Babes . . . Town*: A traditional ballad, collected in Thomas Percy, *Reliques of Ancient English Poetry* (1765), under the title 'The Children in the Wood'. The passage quoted deals with two infants just abandoned in a forest.

28 *best models of composition*: Sir Joshua Reynolds, *Discourses on Art*, ed. R. R. Wark, San Marino, Calif., Huntington Library (1959), pp. 219–20.

29 *if my purpose . . . relations*: Much of this sentence is repeated verbally from the opening of the third paragraph of the Preface above.

30 *Appendix*: The Appendix, which is meant to comment further on the phrase 'by what is usually called POETIC DICTION' (p. 294), was first added in 1802.

31 *earliest poets . . . figurative*: W. was possibly influenced here again by the *Monthly Magazine*, II (1796), 454, but the idea of the early writers being more natural is hardly new; it is, for example, a principal argument in the Battle of the Books in the late seventeenth century. See John Dryden's *An Essay of Dramatic Poesy* (*Essays of John Dryden*, ed. W. P. Ker, I, 38).

32 *Pope's 'Messiah' . . . chap. xiii*: Alexander Pope, *Messiah* (1712); Matthew Prior, 'Charity: A Paraphrase on the Thirteenth Chapter of the First Epistle to the Corinthians' (1703).

33 *Turn . . . ambush'd foe*: Samuel Johnson, 'The Ant' (first published 1766).

34 *Proverbs, chap. vi*: Verses 6–11.

35 *Religion . . . to see*: William Cowper, 'Verses Supposed to be Written by Alexander Selkirk' (first published 1782), 25–40.

36 *the epithet 'church-going'*: In a manuscript version of stanza XXIV of *Guilt and Sorrow*, W. used the expression 'the church-inviting bells'.

37 *vicious*: Corrupt.

38 *the same language*: In a manuscript version (W. Hale White, *Description of the Wordsworth and Coleridge Manuscripts in the Possession of Mr T. Norton Longman*, London [1897], pp. 49–50) appears the following passage placed at this point in the text but deleted:

The Reader, I hope, will believe that it is with great reluctance I have presumed, in this note, to censure so freely the writings of other Poets and that I should not have done this, could I otherwise have made my meaning intelligible. The passages which I have condemned I have condemned upon principle, and I have given my reasons, else I should have been inexcusable. Without an appeal to laws and principles there can be no criticism. What passes under that name is, for the most part, little more than a string of random and extempore judgements, a mode of writing more cheap than any other and utterly worthless. When I contrast these summary decisions with the pains and anxieties of original composition, especially in verse, I am frequently reminded of a passage of Drayton on this subject which, no doubt, he wrote with deep feeling:

Detracting what laboriously we do
Only by that which he but idly saith.

**[Letter to John Wilson (1802)]**

1 *grateful*: Agreeable.

2 *some . . . shepherds*: Possibly a reference to Samuel Johnson; see his Life of Milton or his Life of Pope (*Lives of the English Poets*, ed. G. B. Hill, Oxford [1905], I, 163–4; III, 224).

3 *The [Mad] Mother*: After 1805 known as 'Her Eyes are Wild'.

4 *Adam Smith . . . gentleman*: European Magazine, XX (August 1791), 135: 'It is the duty of a poet to write like a gentleman. I dislike that homely style which some think fit to call the language of nature and simplicity, and so forth.' 'The Ballad of Clym of the Clough' is cited as an example.

5 *my Friend's Poem*: Samuel Taylor Coleridge's 'The Nightingale', especially lines 14–15: 'A melancholy bird? Oh! idle thought! / In Nature there is nothing melancholy.'

6 *and even . . . for me*: William Cowper, The Task, I, 205–206 (italics added by W.)

7 *unsightly and unsmooth*: Cf. Cowper, The Task, I, 526–30:

> The common, overgrown with fern, and rough
> With prickly gorse, that, shapeless and deform'd,
> And dang'rous to the touch, has yet its bloom,
> And decks itself with ornaments of gold,
>     Yields no unpleasing ramble . . .

8 *their life is hidden with God*: Unidentified source, but cf. Colossians 3:3: 'For ye are dead, and your life is hid with Christ in God.'

9 *whether in cunning . . . not a few*: 'The Idiot Boy,' 378 and 65.

## [Letter to Lady Beaumont (1807)]

1 *my Poems*: Poems in Two Volumes, published 8 May 1807.

2 *Mr Pitt or Mr Fox*: William Pitt, the Younger (1759–1806), leader of the Tories; Charles James Fox (1749–1806), the Whig opponent of Pitt.

3 *Mr Paul . . . Election*: James Paull (1770–1808) and Sir Francis Burdett (1770–1844) were both Radicals. Paull was the Reform candidate at the recent Westminster election and was supported by Burdett. They eventually quarrelled and fought a duel; Paull then withdrew and Burdett was elected.

4 *the Borough of Honiton*: The seat of Thomas, Lord Cochrane, which he gave up to run against Burdett in the Westminster election.

5 *love and admiration*: Cf. The Excursion, IV, 763: 'We live by Admiration, Hope, and Love . . .'

6 *Mr Rogers*: Samuel Rogers (1763–1855), a minor poet of the period and later to become more closely acquainted with the Wordsworths. The quotation below ascribed to Rogers may have been reported to W. by Lady Beaumont from London – his letter is addressed to her London residence.

7 *Mrs Fermor*: Frances Fermor (1754–1824), Lady Beaumont's sister.

8 *the other*: 'O Mountain Stream!'

9 *Now glowed . . . mantle threw*: Paradise Lost, IV, 604–609.

10 *the Sonnet*:

> With Ships the sea was sprinkled far and nigh,
> Like stars in heaven, and joyously it showed;
> Some lying fast at anchor in the road,
> Some veering up and down, one knew not why.
> A goodly Vessel did I then espy
> Come like a Giant from a haven broad;
> And lustily along the Bay she strode,
> Her tackling rich, and of apparel high.
> This Ship was nought to me, nor I to her,
> Yet I pursued her with a Lover's look;
> This Ship to all the rest did I prefer:
> When will she turn, and whither? She will brook
> No tarrying; where she comes the winds must stir:
> On went She, and due north her journey took.

11 *Daffodils . . . snowdrops*: 'I Wandered Lonely as a Cloud' and 'Who Fancied What a Pretty Sight'.

12 *sonnet upon Sleep*: 'To Sleep' ('A Flock of Sheep'), 13: 'Come, blessed barrier between day and day . . .'

13 *Coleridge . . . relished*: Cf. *Essay Supplementary*, p. 408, where the remark was later made in almost the same words.

### Essays upon Epitaphs

1 *I'm careless . . . will save*: William Camden, *Remains of a Greater Work Concerning Britain* (1605), quoted in John Weever, *Ancient Funerall Monuments Within the United Monarchie of Great Britaine* (1631), p. 23.

2 *proceeded . . . sepulchres*: Weever, p. 9, who is again silently quoting Camden.

3 *the mind . . . this assurance*: For other of W.'s comments on feelings of immortality, see the notes to the 'Ode. Intimations of Immortality', in *Poetical Works*, ed. E. de Selincourt, Oxford, Clarendon Press (1947), IV, 463–4.

4 *Simonides*: The story is also told by W. in a sonnet, 'I Find it Written of SIMONIDES'. W. could have found the story either in Valerius Maximus I, viii ('De Miraculis') or Cicero's *De Divinatione*, I.

5 *another ancient Philosopher* : Unidentified.

6 *undermined . . . fed it*: unidentified source.

7 *Then in some rural . . . of God*: John Edwards (1751–1832), *All Saints' Church, Derby: A Poem*, Derby (1805), pp. 40–1.

8 *to the fact . . . at all*: Samuel Johnson, *Lives of the English Poets*, ed. G. B. Hill, Oxford, Clarendon Press (1905), III, 264. The phrase 'have no character at all' is used in Pope's *Moral Essays*, II, 2.

9 *equalises . . . low*: 'Epitaphs translated from Chiabrera' ('There never breathed a man'), 24. The ultimate source is probably Isaiah 2:12 – 'For the day of the Lord of hosts shall be upon every one that is proud and lofty, and upon every one that is lifted up; and he shall be brought low.'

10 *Yet even . . . to die*: Thomas Gray, 'Elegy Written in a Country Church-yard', 77–84.

11 *brief Chronicles*: *Hamlet*, II, ii, 524.

12 *where are . . . buried*: Charles Lamb, *Rosamund Gray* (1798), Chapter XI.

13 *It is such . . . gratitude*: Cf. this sentence to *The Excursion*, VI, 634–45:

> And, in the centre of a world whose soil
> Is rank with all unkindness, compassed round
> With such memorials, I have sometimes felt,
> It was no momentary happiness
> To have *one* Enclosure where the voice that speaks
> In envy or detraction is not heard;
> Which malice may not enter; where the traces
> Of evil inclinations are unknown;
> Where love and pity tenderly unite
> With resignation; and no jarring tone
> Intrudes, the peaceful concert to disturb
> Of amity and gratitude.

14 *monsters of the deep*: *King Lear*, IV, ii, 50.

15 *which Clarence saw in his dream*: *Richard III*, I, iv, 24–33.

16 *Statistical account of Scotland*: Sir John Sinclair, *A Statistical Account of Scotland, drawn up from the Communications of the Ministers of the Different Parishes*, Edinburgh (1791–9), V, 550; XII, 137; XIII, 632, XIX, 120, 176–7.

17 *Ach . . . viele*: Coleridge, the 'friend' who provided the quotation, gives a slightly different version of the last line of this epitaph in a letter to Thomas Poole (19 May 1799), where he locates the churchyard as 'at Catlenberg' and identifies the deceased as 'Johann Reimbold of Catlenburg'. It is also quoted in his notebook (*The Notebooks of Samuel Taylor Coleridge*, ed. Kathleen Coburn, New York, Pantheon Books [1957–62], I, 418), where the editor identifies the epitaph as 'an adaptation of a poem by Matthias Claudius Bei dem Grabe meines Vaters'.

18 *inherent* [          ]: In the manuscript 'inherent' is written over an erasure and a mark following covers more erasure with a caret underneath and an 'X' in the margin.

19 *Farwel . . . redemption*: Quoted in Weever, p. 545.

20 *When the bells . . . abyde*: Quoted in Weever, p. 392, where it is identified as from St Leonard's in Foster Lane. Also quoted in Camden, p. 384.

21 *Palmers . . . heaven*: Quoted in Weever, pp. 331–2.

22 *Hic, inscriptum*: Quoted in Weever, p. 556.

23 *rude Forefathers of the hamlet*: Thomas Gray, 'Elegy Written in a Country Churchyard', 16.

24 *Secretary of State*: Sir George Vane (1618–79) was actually the son of the noted Secretary of State to King Charles, Sir Henry Vane (1589–1655).

25 *His Honour . . . ever*: Quoted in William Hutchinson, *The History and Antiquities of the County Palatine of Durham*, Carlisle (1794), III, 168, where the location of the epitaph is given as the parish church of Long Newton. 'Fade' in line 3 reads 'faile' in the original.

26 *Great . . . wounds*: Quoted in William Winstanley, *England's Worthies*, London (1684), pp. 532–3. James Graham, first Marquis of Montrose (1612–1650).

27 *instinct with spirit*: Paradise Lost, VI, 752. See also *The Excursion*, VII, 509.

28 *the Prophet Ezekiel*: Ezekiel 1:16–18.

29 *with stars . . . between*: Paradise Lost, VI, 754–6.

30 *England . . . Name*: Quoted in Weever, p. 321.

31 *'the world-mourned Sidney'*: Joshua Sylvester, *Dubartas his Second Weeke: Babylon. The Second Part of the Second Day of the II Weeke*, 664.

32 *Spenser*: Edmund Spenser, *Astrophel* (1591).

33 *was ... Chieftan*: Weever, p. 320.

34 *But here ... not long*: Weever, p. 320, quoting William Camden, *Britannia*, trans. Philemon Holland, London (1637), p. 329.

35 *Under ... Maritus*: Joseph Nicolson and Richard Burn, *The History and Antiquities of the Counties of Westmoreland and Cumberland*, London (1777), I, 405. The Latin sentence at the end is translated by W. at the end of the paragraph.

36 *a celebrated writer*: George, Lord Lyttelton (1709–73). *Poetical Works* (1801), p. 104.

37 *a monody to her memory*: 'To the Memory of a Lady lately deceased. A Monody' (1747).

38 *interchange of action from within and from without*: See *The Prelude* (1805), XII, 376–7.

39 *Chiabrera*: Gabriello Chiabrera (1552–1638), a number of whose epitaphs were translated by W. in 1809–10.

40 *in preference to prose*: In his *Curious Epitaphs*, 2nd ed., London (1899), pp. 144–5, William Andrews prints a prose epitaph he claims W. wrote for his brother-in-law: 'In memory of HENRY HUTCHINSON, born at Penrith, Cumberland, 14th June 1769. At an early age he entered upon a Seafaring life in the course of which, being of a thoughtful mind, he attained great skill, and knowledge of his Profession, and endured in all climates severe hardships with exemplary courage and fortitude. The latter part of his life, was passed with a beloved Sister upon this Island. He died at Douglas the 23rd of May 1839, much lamented by his Kindred and Friends who have erected this stone to testify their sense of his mild virtues and humble piety.'

41 *the collection*: See Samuel Johnson, *Lives of the English Poets*, ed. G. B. Hill, Oxford (1905), III, 262.

42 *vicious*: Corrupt.

43 *containing ... places*: Johnson, III, 262.

44 *smitten ... immoveably*: W.'s translation. See 'O Thou Who Movest Onward with a Mind', 10–12.

45 *FRIEND No. 6*: 21 September 1809, p. 85.

46 *Evil ... Good*: *Paradise Lost*, IV, 110.

47 *Cicero*: Marcus Tullius Cicero (106–65 BC), a great Roman orator, delivered a series of orations against Cataline in 63 BC.

48 *Dryden and Pope*: John Dryden, *Absalom and Achitophel*: (Shaftesbury) 150–99, (Buckingham) lines 544–68; Alexander Pope, *Moral Essays*:

(Wharton) Epistle I, 174–209, (the Duchess of Marlborough) Epistle II, 115–50.

49 *Take . . . God*: William Mason, 'Epitaph on Mrs Mason, in the Cathedral at Bristol' (1767).

50 *ELEGANT EXTRACTS*: *Elegant Extracts; or, useful and entertaining Pieces of Poetry, Selected for the Improvement of Young Persons* ed. Vicesimus Knox (c. 1770).

51 *the garb is to the body*: Cf. Alexander Pope, *Essay on Criticism*, II, 118: 'Expression is the dress of thought.'

52 *Epitaph . . . Mason*: William Mason (1724–97).

53 *She is gone . . . heaven*: The original Latin epitaph has never been traced.

54 *vicious*: Corrupt.

55 *survive her*: Thomas Gray, *Works*, ed. Edmund Gosse, New York (1885), IV, 339.

56 *when he died*: Alexander Pope, 'Epitaph On the Honble. Simon Harcourt', 4.

57 *Christendom*: Sir Walter Scott, ed., *Works of John Dryden*, Rev. George Saintsbury, Edinburgh (1884), IX, 298.

58 *have been given*: W.'s translations of Chiabrera appeared in *The Friend*, No. 19 (28 December 1809), pp. 289–90; No. 20 (4 January 1810), pp. 319–20; No. 25 (22 February 1810), pp. 401–402.

59 *astrict*: Concise.

60 *therein interred*: Weever, p. 8 (italics added by W.).

61 *Some weeks ago*: *The Friend*, No. 20 (4 January 1810), p. 320.

62 *O Lelius . . . tears*: W.'s translation of Epitaph XXIV ('O Lelio, o fior gentil di gentilezza'), on Lelio Pavese.

63 *Pozzobonelli*: Epitaph IX ('Not without heavy Grief'), on Monsignor Abbate Francesco Pozzobonello.

64 *Torquato . . . was*: W.'s translation of Epitaph XXIII on Tasso ('Torquato Tasso e qui sepolto').

65 *FRIEND . . . ed*: At this point, a space was left in the manuscript in which W. most probably planned to include a translation of Chiabrera's epitaph on himself:

> AMICO Io vivendo cercava il conforto per lo
>  Monte Parnaso.
>  Tu, meglio consigliato, fa di cercarlo sul
>  Monte Calvario.

66  *These marble . . . ever rest*: Quoted in Weever, pp. 361–2, who claims that the epitaph was written for 'William a Norman, who enjoyed this Bishopricke' and that it was translated by John Stow (1525?–1605).

67  *Aged 87 . . . rest*: These four epitaphs appear in *The Notebooks of Samuel Taylor Coleridge*: the first and last, II, 2982; the second and third, I, 1267. Details about the locations of the epitaphs are given, as well as some other information. Especially significant are the ages of those about whom the epitaphs are written: the second was twenty-two years old, the third, *two years and* three months.

68  *they died*: Spectator, No. 26 (*Spectator*, ed. D. F. Bond, Oxford, Clarendon Press [1965], I, 109).

## Preface to Poems (*1815*)

1  *composition*: 'As sensibility to harmony of numbers, and the power of producing it, are invariably attendants upon the faculties above specified, nothing has been said upon those requisites.' [W.]

2  *metrical novel*: That is, the verse romance, such as Sir Walter Scott's *Lady of the Lake* (1810) and *Marmion* (1808) or Lord Byron's Eastern Tales.

3  *Arma virumque cano*: 'I *sing* of arms and of the man' (italics added by W.) – the first line of Virgil's *Aeneid*.

4  *characteristic*: Typical.

5  *loco-descriptive poetry*: Poetry that describes one locale, such as W.'s *An Evening Walk*.

6  *The Poem of Lucretius*: De Rerum Natura (first century B C).

7  *The Fleece . . . English Garden*: John Dyer, *The Fleece* (1757); William Mason, *The English Garden* (1772–81).

8  *three requisites . . . end*: Aristotle, *Poetics*, the beginning of Chapter VII.

9  '*The Recluse*': W. set forth his overall plan for *The Recluse* in his short Preface to *The Excursion*. *The Recluse* was to consist of three parts, of which *The Excursion* was the only one completed, although *The Prelude* was seen as preparation and has the same relation to *The Recluse* 'as the antechapel has to the body of a gothic church'. As for the 'small pieces' mentioned in the text: 'Continuing this allusion . . . , his minor pieces, which have been long before the Public, when they shall be properly arranged, will be found by the attentive reader to have such connection with the main Work as may give them claim to be likened to the little cells, oratories, and sepulchral recesses, ordinarily included in those edifices.'

10 *He murmurs . . . own*: W.'s 'A Poet's Epitaph', 39–40.

11 *W. Taylor*: William Taylor (of Norwich), *English Synonyms Discriminated*, London (1813), p. 242.

12 *a mode of memory*: Cf. Coleridge's definition of fancy in the *Biographia Literaria*, Chapter XIII (ed. J. Engel and W. J. Bate, London and Princeton, N.J. [1983], I, 305): 'The Fancy is indeed no other than a mode of Memory emancipated from the order of time and space . . .'

13 *all compact . . . to shape*: *Midsummer Night's Dream*, V, i, 8–9, 12–17.

14 *illustrate . . . by instances*: W.'s illustrations based on the verb *hang* are almost certainly taken from an essay 'Poetry Distinguished from Other Writing', (in *The Works of Oliver Goldsmith*, ed. Peter Cunningham, New York and London [1908], VII 347–8), attributed to Oliver Goldsmith (1730?–74) but possibly written by Tobias Smollett (1721–71) – see C. F. Tupper, 'Essays Erroneously Attributed to Goldsmith,' *PMLA* 39 (1924), 325–42.

15 *Non ego . . . videbo*: Virgil, *Eclogue* I, 75–76 (italics added by W.): 'stretched out in a green grotto, I shall not hereafter watch you *hanging* from a bushy crag'.

16 *half way . . . samphire*: *King Lear*, IV, vi, 14–15 (italics added by W.).

17 *As when . . . Fiend*: *Paradise Lost*, II, 636–43 (italics added by W.).

18 *object*: 1815–27; objects, 1832–50.

19 *Over . . .* broods 'Resolution and Independence', 5 (italics added by W.).

20 *the voice . . . breeze*: 'O Nightingale', 13–14 (italics added by W.).

21 *O, Cuckoo . . .* Voice: 'To the Cuckoo', 3–4 (italics added by W.).

22 *said to* coo: 'O Nightingale', 15.

23 *As a huge . . . at all*: 'Resolution and Independence', 57–65, 75–7.

24 *Modo . . . Athenis*: Horace, *Epistles* II, i, 213: '[the poet] sometimes sets me down at Thebes, sometimes at Athens.'

25 *Attended . . . shone*: *Paradise Lost*, VI, 767–8.

26 *one effect*: 'Charles Lamb upon the genius of Hogarth.' [W.] 'On the Genius and Character of Hogarth', *The Works of Charles and Mary Lamb*, ed. E. V. Lucas, New York and London (1903), I, 73.

27 *poetical . . . dramatic imagination*: A contradistinction derived from John Dennis (*Critical Works*, ed. E. N. Hooker, Baltimore [1939–43], I, 338); see *Letters: The Middle Years*, III, 88.

28 *our great epic Poet*: John Milton (1608–74).

29 *Una*: A character in Edmund Spenser's *The Faerie Queene*, Book I.

30 *I tax . . . Daughters*: *King Lear* III, ii, 16–17. Coleridge provides a gloss of

W.'s meaning here (*Shakespearean Criticism*, ed. T. M. Raysor, 2nd ed., London and New York [1960], I, 188): 'Still mounting, we find undoubted proof in [Shakespeare's] mind of imagination, or the power by which one image or feeling is made to modify many others and by a sort of *fusion to force many into one* – that which after shewed itself in such might and energy in *Lear*, where the deep anguish of a father spreads the feeling of ingratitude and cruelty over the very elements of heaven.'

31 *associative power*: Samuel Taylor Coleridge and Robert Southey, *Omniana, or Horae Otiosores*, London (1812), II, 13. A more familiar source is Coleridge's *Biographia Literaria*, I, 293.

32 *In shape ... alderman*: *Romeo and Juliet*, I, iv, 55–6.

33 *she*: The Imagination.

34 *reached the sky*: *Paradise Lost*, IV, 985–8: 'On th' other side Satan alarmed/ Collecting all his might dilated stood, / Like Teneriffe or Atlas unremoved:/His stature reached the sky ...'

35 *Bishop Taylor's Works*: Bishop Jeremy Taylor (1613–67). Coleridge shared W.'s high estimate of Taylor; see *Coleridge on the Seventeenth Century*, ed. R. F. Brinkley, Durham, N.C., Duke University Press (1955), pp. 258–63.

36 *The dews ... sun*: 'Advice to a Lady in Autumn', 25–6, *The Life of the Late Earl of Chesterfield: Or, The Man of the World*, London (1774), II, 249.

37 *Sky ... sin*: *Paradise Lost*, IX, 1002–1003.

38 *second groan*: *Paradise Lost*, IX, 1000–1001. In a paragraph omitted after 1836, W. continued the discussion of the 'communion and interchange of instruments and functions between the two powers'. Owen and Smyser (*Prose Works*, III, 51) observe that the example from *Paradise Lost* is one in which the 'Imagination stoops to work with the materials of Fancy.'

39 *the middle ... feeling*: Charles Cotton, 'Ode upon Winter', stanzas XXIV–XXVIII.

40 *He*: 1815–20; *Winter*: 1827–50. In the poem it is the poet who retires into his fortress from the foe (Winter) (stanza XXXVIII): 'Fly, fly; the foe advances fast; / Into our fortress, let us haste ...'

41 *a magazine ...again*: stanza XXXIX.

42 *'Tis that ... sweet*: W. omitted a line from stanza XLI: 'And Venus frolic in the sheet'.

43 *'Tis that ... are*: stanzas XL–XLIX.

*Essay, Supplementary to the Preface*

1 *With*: The following first paragraph appeared only in the 1815 edition:

By this time, I trust that the judicious Reader, who has now first become acquainted with these poems, is persuaded that a very senseless outcry has been raised against them and their Author. – Casually, and very rarely only, do I see any periodical publication, except a daily newspaper; but I am not wholly unacquainted with the spirit in which my most active and persevering Adversaries have maintained their hostility; nor with the impudent falsehoods and base artifices to which they have had recourse. These, as implying a consciousness on their parts that attacks honestly and fairly conducted would be unavailing, could not but have been regarded by me with triumph; had they been accompanied with such display of talents and information as might give weight to the opinions of the Writers, whether favourable or unfavourable. But the ignorance of those who have chosen to stand forth as my enemies, as far as I am acquainted with their enmity, has unfortunately been still more gross than their disingenuousness, and their incompetence more flagrant than their malice. The effect in the eyes of the discerning is indeed ludicrous; yet, contemptible as such men are, in return for the forced compliment paid me by their long-continued notice (which, as I have appeared so rarely before the public, no one can say has been solicited) I entreat them to spare themselves. The lash, which they are aiming at my productions, does, in fact, only fall on phantoms of their own brain; which, I grant, I am innocently instrumental in raising. – By what fatality the orb of my genius (for genius none of them seem to deny me) acts upon these men like the moon upon a certain description of patients, it would be irksome to inquire; nor would it consist with the respect which I owe myself to take further notice of opponents whom I internally despise.

2 *understanding*: 'Judging powers'. See Owen and Smyser, II, 98 (lines 25–7) and III, 85.

3 *no man can serve . . . two Masters*: Matthew 6:24.

4 *religious faith . . . enjoyment*: W. had recently encountered such a reaction to *The Excursion*; see *Letters: The Middle Years*, III, 188.

5 *those sects . . . cold and formal*: Especially the Unitarians; see *Letters: The Middle Years*, III, 189.

6 *imperfect shadowing forth*: Unidentified source.

7 *instruction of reason*: Cf. John Dennis (*Critical Works*, ed. E. N. Hooker,

Baltimore [1939–43], I, 337): ' . . . Poetry by the force of the Passion, instructs and reforms the Reason . . .'

8 *into the region*: Unidentified source.

9 *there were . . . to conquer*: Cf. Robert Burton, *Anatomy of Melancholy*, ed. Holbrook Jackson, London and New York (1932), I, 60: 'Alexander was sorry because there were no more worlds for him to conquer . . .'

10 *Creation of Dubartas*: Guillaume de Saluste, Seigneur du Bartas, *Semaine* (1578). This work described the week of the Creation and was translated in various parts by Joshua Sylvester beginning in 1592.

11 *The laurel . . . sage*: *The Faerie Queene*, I, i, 9.

12 *Settle and Shadwell*: Elkanah Settle (1648–1724). Thomas Shadwell (1642?–92). The final clause of the sentence should probably read: 'the admirers of Settle and Shadwell were, in a later age, as numerous, and *the works of Settle and Shadwell were* reckoned as respectable in point of talent, as those of Dryden.'

13 *alludes to him*: 'The Learned Hakewill (a third edition of whose book bears the date 1635), writing to refute the error "touching Nature's perpetual and universal decay", cites triumphantly the names of Ariosto, Tasso, Bartas, and Spenser, as instances that poetic genius had not degenerated; but he makes no mention of Shakespeare.' [W.] George Hakewill, *An Apologie or Declaration of the Power and Providence of God in the Government of the World*, Oxford (1635), I, 290. What W. misses, however, is that Hakewill is comparing epic poets with Virgil.

14 *Dryden tells us . . . Shakespeare's*: John Dryden, *Essay of Dramatic Poesy*, in *Essays of John Dryden*, ed. W. P. Ker, Oxford (1900), I, 81.

15 *inverted commas . . . notice*: *The Works of Shakespeare*, ed. Alexander Pope (1747), I, xiv.

16 *time of Voltaire*: For a similar remark by Voltaire himself, see *Dictionaire philosophique* under 'Art dramatique' (*Oeuvres Complètes*, Paris (1878), XVII, 402).

17 *Baron Grimm*: Friedrich Melchior, Baron von Grimm, *Correspondence littéraire* [1753–73] ed. M. Tourneux, Paris (1877–82), XI, 215, 298–9.

18 *great beauties*: Unidentified source.

19 *small volume . . . in his own person*: Shakespeare's sonnets, first published in 1609, were edited by George Steevens in 1766.

20 *George Steevens*: George Steevens (1736–1800) in his edition of Shakespeare (*The Plays of William Shakespeare*, London [1793], I, vii–viii), rejected his sonnets as inferior.

21 *talk of an:* 'This flippant insensibility was publicly reprehended by Mr Coleridge in a course of Lectures upon Poetry given by him at the Royal Institution. For the various merits of thought and language in Shakespeare's Sonnets, see Numbers 27, 29, 30, 32, 33, 54, 64, 66, 68, 73, 76, 86, 91, 92, 93, 97, 98, 105, 107, 108, 109, 111, 113, 114, 116, 117, 129, and many others.' [W.]

22 *durst not soar:* Paradise Lost, IV, 829.

23 *Nine years:* Actually, approximately seven and a half years.

24 *Pope . . . could borrow:* W. probably was influenced here by Thomas Warton (Preface to his edition of John Milton, *Poems upon Several Occasions*, London [1785], vii–ix).

25 *Voss:* Johann Heinrich Voss (1751–1826). His translations of 'L'Allegro' and 'Il Penseroso' appear in *Gedichte von Johann Heinrich Voss*, Hamburg (1785), II, 269–92.

26 *Boswell's Life of him:* See entry for 13 June 1784. Johnson, however, was much more critical of Milton's sonnets in his life of Milton.

27 *the time . . . Cowley:* Abraham Cowley, *Pindarique Odes* (1668).

28 *styled metaphysical Poets:* Samuel Johnson, Life of Cowley (*Lives of the English Poets*, ed. G. B. Hill [1905], I, 18–19).

29 *though few:* Paradise Lost, VII, 31. *Paradise Lost* was first published in 1667.

30 *I have said elsewhere:* See the 'Prospectus' to *The Recluse*, 24 (in Preface to *The Excursion*).

31 *just to it:* Lives of the Poets, I, 143. Johnson actually wrote: 'The sale . . . will justify the publick.'

32 *did not afford:* Lives of the Poets, I, 144.

33 *Flatman:* Thomas Flatman (1637–88). The fourth was the last edition.

34 *Waller:* Edmund Waller (1606–87). The tenth edition was published in 1772.

35 *Bemerton:* John Norris (1657–1711). The ninth and last edition of *A Collection of Miscellanies: consisting of poems, essays, etc.* was published in 1730.

36 *two editions:* There were three editions of Shakespeare's works between 1623 and 1664.

37 *paucity of Readers:* Lives of the Poets, I, 143.

38 *not erroneous:* 'Hughes is express upon this subject: in his dedication of Spenser's Works to Lord Somers, he writes thus. "It was your Lordship's encouraging a beautiful edition of Paradise Lost that first brought that incomparable Poem to be generally known and esteemed."' [W.] John Hughes, ed., *The Works of Mr Edmund Spenser*, London (1715), I, v.

39 *no fixed principles*: 'This opinion seems actually to have been entertained by Adam Smith, the worst critic, David Hume not excepted, that Scotland, a soil to which this sort of weed seems natural, has produced.' [W.]

40 *an English Peer*: Never positively identified.

41 *describes . . . in their cradles*: Anthony Ashley Cooper, Third Earl of Shaftesbury, *Characteristics of Men, Manners, Opinions, Time* (1711), 'Advice to an Author', Part II, Section I.

42 *Eclogues*: John Gay, *The Shepherd's Week in Six Pastorals*, London (1714).

43 *grovelling and degraded*: *Lives of the Poets*, II, 269.

44 *occupations*: *Lives of the Poets*, II, 269.

45 *Thomson's Winter . . . Seasons*: James Thomson, *Winter* (1726), *Summer* (1727), *Spring* (1728), *Autumn* (1730).

46 *love the Man*: Patrick Murdoch, ed. *The Works of James Thomson*, London (1762), I, vii.

47 *nocturnal . . . Lady Winchilsea*: Anne Finch, Countess of Winchilsea, 'A Nocturnal Reverie', in *Miscellany Poems, on Several Occasions*, London (1713), pp. 291–3.

48 *the Iliad*: VIII, 687–98:

> As when the Moon, refulgent Lamp of Night!
> O'er Heav'ns clear Azure spreads her sacred Light,
> When not a Breath disturbs the deep Serene;
> And not a Cloud o'ercasts the solemn Scene;
> Around her throne the vivid Planets roll,
> And Stars unnumber'd gild the glowing Pole,
> O'er the dark Trees a yellower Verdure shed,
> And tip with Silver ev'ry Mountain's Head;
> Then shine the Vales, the Rocks in Prospect rise,
> A Flood of Glory bursts from all the Skies:
> The conscious Swains, rejoicing in the Sight,
> Eye the blue Vault, and bless the useful Light.

In a footnote in his *Biographia Literaria* (ed. J. Engell and W. J. Bate, London and Princeton, N.J. Princeton University Press [1983], I, 40) Coleridge mentions his criticism of the passage in a lecture.

49 *senseless*:

> 'CORTES *alone in a night-gown.*
> All things are hush'd as Natures self lay dead;
> The mountains seem to nod their drowsy head.
> The little Birds in dreams their songs repeat,
> And sleeping Flowers beneath the Night-dew sweat:
> Even Lust and Envy sleep; yet Love denies
> Rest to my soul, and slumber to my eyes.
> DRYDEN'S *Indian Emperor*' [II,ii,1–6] [W.]

50 *vicious*: Corrupt.

51 *rhapsody . . . stories*: *The Seasons*: *Spring* 963–1112; *Summer* 1269–1370.

52 *philosophical Poet*: Alexander Pope, 'Testimonies of Authors Concerning our Poet and his Works', prefixed to *The Dunciad* (*The Poems of Alexander Pope*, ed. John Butt, New Haven [1963], p. 335): 'his elegant and philosophical poem of the Seasons.'

53 *imaginative poet*: 'Since these observations upon Thomson were written, I have perused the second edition of his Seasons, and find that even *that* does not contain the most striking passages which Warton points out for admiration; these, with other improvements, throughout the whole work, must have been added at a later period.' [W.] The passages in question are *Summer*, 936, 977–9, 1048–9.

54 *a note*: Joseph Wharton, *Essay on the Genius and Writings of Pope,* in *Eighteenth-Century Critical Essays*, ed. Scott Elledge, Ithaca, NY (1961), II, 730–3.

55 *Gray speaks so coldly*: Thomas Gray, *Correspondence*, ed. P. Toynbee and L. Whibley, Oxford (1971), I, 307 (Gray to Warton, 5 June 1748): ' . . . The Castle of Indolence [has] some good stanzas.' James Thomson, *Castle of Indolence* (1748).

56 *Elegiac Poem*: William Collins, *Ode Occasion'd by the Death of Mr Thomson* (1749), stanza VII. W. wrote a similar elegy for Collins, 'Remembrance of Collins' (1800).

57 *Reliques of Ancient English Poetry*: First published in 1765.

58 *little senate . . . laws*: Alexander Pope, *Epistle to Dr Arbuthnot*, 209.

59 *Dr Johnson . . . exertions*: James Boswell, *Life of Johnson*, ed. G. B. Hill, rev. by L. F. Powell, Oxford (1934), II, 212.

60 *writers of Germany*: Especially Gottfried August Burger (1747–94), Johann

Gottfried von Herder (1744–1803), and Friedrich Heinrich Bothe (1770–1855).

61 *Warkworth*: The Hermit of Warkworth. A Northumberland Ballad (1771).

62 *remarkable fact*: 'Shenstone, in his Schoolmistress, gives a still more re-markable instance of this timidity. On its first appearance, (See D'Israeli's 2d Series of the Curiosities of Literature) the Poem was accompanied with an absurd prose commentary, showing, as indeed some incongruous expressions in the text imply, that the whole was intended for burlesque. In subsequent editions, the commentary was dropped, and the People have since continued to read in seriousness, doing for the Author what he had not courage openly to venture upon for himself.' [W.] William Shenstone, *The School-Mistress* (1742), 'Index'. Isaac D'Israeli, *Curiosities of Literature*, 2nd series (1793).

63 *Klopstock . . . in my hearing*: Owen and Smyser, *Prose Works of Wordsworth*, I, 98.

64 *Now daye . . . call*: 'The Child of Elle', stanzas XIV–XV, from Bishop Percy, *Reliques of Ancient English Poetry*.

65 *Als nun . . . angezogen*: Die Entfuhrung, oder Ritter Karl von Eichenhorst und Fräulein Gertrude von Hochburg (1777), 88–100:

> When now the night in raven-black shadows
> Enwraps mountains and valleys,
> And the lamps of Hochburg everywhere
> Had already stopped glimmering,
> And all things were sound asleep;
> When, nevertheless, only the maiden
> Full of feverish fear, still watched
> And thought of her knight:
> Hark, there! A sweet sound of love
> Came floating gently aloft
> 'Ho, Trudy, ho! Here am I!
> Rise quickly! Get dressed!'
>
> trans. ed.

66 *all hail . . . Sire of Ossian!*: Cf. *Macbeth*, I, iii, 48: 'All hail, Macbeth, hail to thee, Thane of Glamis.' James Macpherson (1736–96) was a Scottish poet who purportedly translated (into English) poems by a blind Gaelic bard, Ossian, but who was determined by 1797 to have written them himself.

67 *The Editor of the 'Reliques'*: Bishop Thomas Percy (1729–1811).

68 *like Lear*: *King Lear*, I, i, 37–41.

69 *'Epic Poem Temora'*: The second of the Ossianic poems (1763). The passage is taken from near the beginning.

70 *Car-borne heroes*: 'Car-borne' is an epithet used in the Ossianic poems.

71 *appearance . . . of a few miles*: See *Journals of Dorothy Wordsworth*, ed. E. de Selincourt, New York (1941), I, 318.

72 *Mr Malcolm Laing . . . shown*: 'Dissertation on the Supposed Authenticity of Ossian's Poems', in *The History of Scotland* (1804), IV, 409–502.

73 *with Madame de Stael*: *Treatise on Ancient and Modern Literature*, London (1803), I, 273–87. The 'Literature of the North', including English literature, is said to derive ultimately from Ossian.

74 *Lucien Buonaparte . . . Scotland*: *Charlemagne: ou L'Eglise délivrée*, London (1814), I, 376, 379.

75 *a Dunbar . . . a Burns*: William Dunbar (1460?–1530?); George Buchanan (1506–82); James Thomson (1700–48); Robert Burns (1759–96).

76 *Chatterton*: Thomas Chatterton (1752–70), who imitated Ossianic prose in the *Town and Country Magazine*, I (March 1769), 144–6. W. calls him 'the marvellous Boy' in 'Resolution and Independence', 43.

77 *Dr Johnson . . . Poets*: *Lives of the Most Eminent English Poets* (1779–81).

78 *Authors . . . recommended*: Sir Richard Blackmore (*c.* 1655–1729); Isaac Watts (1674–1748); John Pomfret (1667–1702); Thomas Yalden (1670–1736).

79 *the morning-star of English Poetry*: Geoffrey Chaucer (1340?–1400), first called such by Elizabeth Cooper in *The Muses Library; or a Series of English Poetry* (1737), p. 23.

80 *Roscommon . . . Broom*: Wentworth Dillon, Earl of Roscommon (*c.* 1633–85); George Stepney (1663–1707); John Phillip (1631–1706); William Walsh (1663–1708); Edmund Smith (1672–1710); Richard Duke (*c.* 1659–1710); William King (1663–1712); Thomas Sprat (1635–1713); Charles Montague, Earl of Halifax (1661–1715); George Granville (1667–1735); John Sheffield (1648–1721); William Congreve (1670–1729); William Broome (1689–1745). All these seventeenth-century poets are said to have been chosen by the booksellers to protect copyrights of their works.

81 *each and all been opposed*: W.'s publications up to 1815 had hardly been the target of 'unremitting hostility', although *The Poems in Two Volumes* (1807) had been attacked by most critics. See John O. Hayden, *The Romantic Reviewers 1802–24*, Chicago (1969), pp. 78–91.

82 *philosophical Friend*: Samuel Taylor Coleridge. See also *Letters: The Middle Years*, II, 150 (W. to Lady Beaumont, 21 May 1807 [see the text above, p. 321]), where the remark was made previously in almost the exact words.

83 *separation . . . regret*: This comment should have been omitted after deletion of the penultimate paragraph of the *Preface of 1815*, in which W. had mentioned dropping Coleridge's poems.

84 *Hannibal among the Alps*: Livy, Chapter XXI.

85 *Passion . . .* suffering: Latin: *patior* (verb), to suffer – from which the word *passion* derives.

86 *Anger . . . foes*: Edmund Waller, 'Of Love', 1–2 (italics added by W.).

87 *Genius . . . universe*: Such a definition had been made before by Alexander Gerard, *Essay on Genius*, London (1774), pp. 8–9.

88 *enthusiastic . . . sorrow*: This distinction between the two kinds of passion, which is at the centre of the argument of this paragraph, is from John Dennis, *The Advancement and Reformation of Modern Poetry* (1710), Chapter V (*Critical Works of John Dennis*, ed. E. N. Hooker, Baltimore [1939], I, 215–16).

89 *The qualities . . . extravagance*: Probably an allusion to Byron's Eastern Tales, just then appearing.

90 *sister Art*: painting.

91 *Past . . . knowledge*: Later appeared in *The Prelude*, VI, 448–50.

92 *Vox Populi*: Voice of the people, from the expression 'vox populi, vox dei' (the voice of the people [is] the voice of God), which W. is alluding to as he continues: 'that Vox Populi which the Deity inspires'. This voice of the people W. immediately distinguishes from the voice of the public.

93 *PUBLIC . . . PEOPLE*: Cf. *Letters: The Middle Years*, II, 194 (W. to Sir George Beaumont, February 1808): 'The *People* would love the Poem of Peter Bell, but the *Public* (a very different Being) will never love it.'

94 *the Work*: The Recluse.

95 *Vision . . . divine*: The Excursion, I, 79.

### A Letter to a Friend of Burns

1 *Robert Burns*: 'A Review of the Life of Robert Burns, and of various criticisms on his character and writings, by Alexander Peterkin, 1814 [1815].' [W.]

2 *Dr Currie's Book*: Dr James Currie, *The Works of Robert Burns; with an*

*Account of His Life*, 1800 (8th ed. published 1820 with additional biography and notes by Gilbert Burns).

3 *spoken to the world*: In a letter appended to Alexander Peterkin, *A Review of the Life of Robert Burns* (1815), pp. lxxx–lxxxii.

4 *Gray's works*: *The Poems of Mr Gray. To Which Are Added Memoirs of His Life and Writings*, ed. William Mason, 4 vols, York (1778) [not designated as 2nd ed., but no other exists].

5 *public proof*: In plentiful extracts of a letter printed in Currie, I, 57–77.

6 *Life of Milton by Fenton*: The short life of Milton by Elijah Fenton (1683–1730) was contained in many editions of *Paradise Lost* from 1725 on.

7 *the truth . . . the truth*: Part of the oath administered to witnesses in a British court of law.

8 *One . . . resisted*: 'Address to the Unco Guid', 53–64.

9 *his friend COTTON . . . son*: Izaac Walton (1593–1683) called himself the 'father' of Charles Cotton (1630–1687) at the end of his 'Epistle to Cotton', printed at the end of editions of the two-part *Compleat Angler* published in 1678.

10 *crushed . . . weight*: 'To a Mountain Daisy', line 53.

11 *De mortuis . . . bonum*: '[Speak] nothing but good of the dead.' A Latin translation of a Greek saying attributed to one of the 'Seven Sages' of Greece (650–600 BC), specifically either Diogenes Laertius or Chilon of Sparta.

12 *The wise . . . liberty*: Cf. Milton's 'Sonnet XII', 11–12: 'License they mean when they cry liberty;/For who loves that, must first be wise and good.'

13 *Horace*: The Roman poet Horace (65–8 BC) was called the Sabine poet. Herculaneum was an excavation site in Italy begun in 1738.

14 *to instruct*: One of the few appearances in W.'s works of the Horatian formula (*Ars Poetica*, 333).

15 *O'Shanter*: 'Tam O'Shanter' (1791).

16 *Kings . . . victorious*: 'Tam O'Shanter', 57–8.

17 *Dr Hornbook*: 'Death and Doctor Hornbook' (1785).

18 *But tell*: 'Death and Doctor Hornbook', 23–4.

19 *dark, &c*: See note 8.

20 *Thoughtless . . . name*: 'A Bard's Epitaph', 19, 23–4.

21 *thus writes*: 'From Mr Peterkin's pamphlet, who vouches for the accuracy of his citations; omitting, however, to apologize for their length.' [W.] pp. xxxii–xxxiii (most is repeated on p. lxii).

22 *hateful*: *Edinburgh Review*, XIII (1809), 253.

23 *independence*: XIII (1809), 254.

24 *Caesar . . . same moment*: Plutarch, *Lives*, Caesar, XVII, 4.

25 *hearts, &c &c*: XIII (1809), 253–4.

26 *Aristarch*: 'A friend, who chances to be present while the author is cor-
recting the proof sheet, observes that Aristarchus is libelled by this application of his name, and advises that "Zoilus" should be substituted.
The question lies between spite and presumption; and it is not easy to
decide upon a case where the claims of each party are so strong: but the
name of Aristarch, who, simple man! would allow no verse to pass for
Homer's which he did not approve of, is retained, for reasons that will be
deemed cogent.' [W.] Both Aristarch (*c.* 217–215 to 145–143 BC) and
Zoilus (fourth century BC) were types of severe critics, but Zoilus was
reputedly more bitter.

27 *limbo – the Paradise of Fools*: Milton's version of the Roman Catholic
limbo: see *Paradise Lost*, III, 4, 95–6.

28 *the ancient . . . monster*: Strabo, *Geography*, XIV, 22.

29 *the tyrant . . . subjects*: Virgil, *Aeneid*, VI, 585–91.

30 *downfall . . . despot*: Napoleon was defeated at Waterloo, 18 June 1815.

31 *Robespierre*: Maximilien Robespierre (1758–94), bloodthirsty leader of
the Jacobins in the French Revolution.

32 *may be useful*: 'It was deemed that it would be so, and the letter is
published accordingly.' [W.]

## Appendix A

1 *inexhaustible*: 'Mr Green's Guide to the Lakes, in two vols., contains a
complete Magazine of minute and accurate information of this kind,
with the names of mountains, streams, &c.' [W.]

2 *treeless nook*: 'No longer strictly applicable, on account of recent plantations.' [W.]

3 *Martindale*: 'See Page 456.' [W.]

4 *now found*: 'AD 1805. These also have disappeared.' [W.]